RIBBONS OF ASPHALT

GEOFF SAWYER

Ribbons of Asphalt

Publisher: Linda Holderness

Cover Artist: Tatiana Vila

First printed: January 2023

ISBN: 9798371894861

This book is dedicated to all aspiring racers

GLOSSARY

Aero package/aero wings: Aerodynamic fixtures on the front and rear of the car that help increase down-force for traction and stability.

Air pressure: The amount of air, measured in pounds per cubic inch, in a tire.

Brake horsepower (sometimes referred to as "pure" horsepower): The amount of power generated by a motor without taking into consideration any of the auxiliary components that may slow down the actual speed of the motor, measured within the engine's output shaft.

BRM (British Racing Motors): A particular Formula One car.

Bump Day: After general qualifying is set for the Indianapolis 500, this avails a driver to make a qualifying run in hopes of obtaining a better lap time than the lowest qualifier, replacing him/her and allowing the driver into the 33-driver field.

Chicane: A shallow S-turn designed to reduce the speed of traffic.

Carb Day: A full day (Friday), before the Indianapolis 500, that is used by drivers and teams to finalize race strategies, test the car's strength and speed, and make sure every piece of equipment is working properly and all personnel are ready for the long race.

DNF: Did Not Finish.

Double apexing: Making two different turns in the same corner.

Downforce levels: Measured in PSI (Pounds per Square Inch). The downward force created by wind over a car's chassis and aero wings, allowing important grip to the racing surface.

Drop Off: Time difference.

FIM: Federation of International Motorcycling. Sanctioning body for world motorcycle racing.

GCU: Gearbox Control Unit.

Groove (or line): The path around the track where cars run the fastest and handle the best.

Hans Device: A safety feature that controls the movement of one's head and neck in the event of a crash.

IMS: Indianapolis Motor Speedway.

IMSA Series: International Motor Sports Association Series.

IRL: Indy Racing League.

Karting (Go-Kart): A small, open-wheel race car, typically with a frame but very little body work, used for entry-level racing.

Kink: A short curve in a straight section of racetrack, not severe enough to be a corner.

Lap. Lapped: One time around the track. Being passed by another car so that car becomes one lap ahead of a particular driver.

Lap time: The precisely measured time it takes for a car to make one lap.

Marbles: Excessive rubber buildup above the groove of the track, the result of normal tire wear throughout a race or practice session.

Moto GP: International championship motorcycle road racing.

"Pinching him out of the groove": Forcing another driver to run a line other than optimal.

Pit-in, pit-out: Entering or exiting the pits.

Pole day (at Indy): The day drivers qualify, trying to get the #1 starting position.

Qualifying set-up: How a car is adjusted to obtain the most capable speed, in order to start a race in the highest position possible.

Race-trim: The optimal setup of a car for a race – tires, suspension, and aerodynamics.

Ride Height: The distance from the bottom of the chassis to the ground when a car is at speed. Indycar standard = 2 inches off the ground on both sides of the car, for all race tracks

RPMs: Revolutions Per Minute.

S's: A series of right and left turns.

Tach/Tachometer: A device that measures the speed at which the engine is turning.

Toe: The alignment of the front and rear tires. Toe-in = tires pointing inward. Toe-out = tires pointing outward.

Tow: A vacuum draft of air behind a car at speed that a trailing car can use to be pulled, or "towed," along, thereby not needing to use as much horsepower as the lead car.

Tech/Tech Inspection: A mandatory inspection by race- sanctioned officials of the car and its components, making sure that all technical engineering and mechanical specs were followed according to the sport's racing rules and regulations.

Took A Look: Driver making sure that no other car or optical is in their path, usually while planning to pass another car or cars on the race track.

CHAPTER 1

In the wee hours of the morning on the last Sunday of May, a young girl lay curled up into a slight fetal position, blankets tucked in warmly around her. With steady breathing, her dream is powerful and vivid. *A Formula One car growls and explodes to life then winds up through the gears and around a twisty race track. The tarmac ribbon is bold against the lush green grass all around, and the colorful banners and advertising boards are prominently displayed. The striking red Ferrari screams in front of a pack by a wide margin and an announcer starts speaking excitedly in French. The dream cuts oddly to many forms of racing. Boat, bicycle, bobsled, and all manner of different motor-sports. A rock band is playing just above the start/finish line and the crowd is cheering in a spiking roar.*

Suddenly sitting up, wide awake, the young girl's breathing came quick and shallow as she remembered what she thought she'd just been through. Shaking her head, it seemed impossible that not a bit of the dream was real. It had to be that she was smelling racing fuel vapors and hearing all the racetrack sounds. In actuality, the aroma of breakfast had reached her and she was hearing her family awake and making noise. Her dad had turned on the radio and was trying to find a particular station. Just then it hit her. … "Indy!" she exclaimed aloud, clawing her way out of bed. She burst through her bedroom door, raced into the living room and made a swift beeline to her father, wrapping her arms around him tightly. He looked down smiling. "Mornin' Tiger," he said, nodding his approval as he stroked the top of her small head gently with a warm giant hand. "I was wondering how long it was gonna take you to get out here," he said with a quick laugh. "We still have a little while. Go see if your mom needs help setting the table, will you? I won't let you miss a thing. I promise." The excited girl darted into the kitchen and didn't have to even ask, her mom immediately putting silverware onto the counter for her while getting five blue-and-white plates down from the cabinet above. Working as fast as she could for the next number of minutes, Sondra was finally ready to rejoin her father when her mother spoke. "Thank you, Sondra. Now go and get dressed. We eat in about ten minutes." Before the girl could get cleanly out of the room, her mom's instructive voice again reached her ears. "Put on the dress we talked about last night and I don't want any arguing about it."

Once in her Sunday-best clothes, Sondra stood on the threshold between the living room and the dining room. Her mom was almost a blur in getting a big breakfast on the table and making sure the whole family was seated quickly. Her dad was noticeably perturbed at all the talking and commotion and turned up the living room radio loud enough to be heard clearly from the dining room. Sondra felt completely out of place in the frilly dress her mom had insisted she wear this morning but sat down quietly a few feet from her dad on the living room couch, listening intently to the broadcast of the Indianapolis 500 for every trackside sound and announcement. Exasperated, Maureen (mom) called everyone to the table for the third time. "Before the food gets cold and breakfast is spoiled" she scolded her family. Both father and daughter frowned, looked to each other, toward the radio, back at each other, then reluctantly moved to the table. Kal (dad) put up his hands and warned the family that he wouldn't tolerate any disturbances. "I'm trying to listen to this. If you kids can't sit still and eat quietly, you can go to your rooms." There were a few instances of spilled milk and other minor interruptions, resulting in annoyed stares from the dad, and mom's displeasure at going to all this family Sunday breakfast trouble only to have it hampered by this radio race thing she had to endure each May.

Much to the family's disgust, Sondra and her dad wolfed down their food and hurried back into the living room nearest the radio. During the commercials, Sondra was careful to ask only short pertinent questions. This pleased her father, who answered authoritatively. For over two hours they clenched fists, held breaths, gasped upon hearing of wrecks, experienced disappointments over blown engines, cheered about passes and then for the car and driver screaming across the start/finish line as the announcer called the win. Both got up and walked around during the last commercial break, returning in front of the living room radio to hear the many interviews and finally the Indianapolis Motor Speedway's Radio Network signoff. As if on cue, Maureen entered the room, insisting that her husband start the minor repairs to the clothes washer plumbing he'd been promising to do for over two weeks. Most of the time Sondra was at her father's side, holding flashlights, hanging onto nuts and bolts and handing him tools as he worked on the family cars or made the many home repairs and improvements. She loved his concentration and determination that he could fix anything, and especially that he was always teaching her about tools and repair techniques. Since this was a one-man job in a tight space, Sondra's help would not be needed on this day and she fled to her room, where all the visions, sounds and excitement of the race she'd just heard seemed to consume her. The 12-year old practically dove into a T-shirt and jeans, slipped outside and in minutes was whipping around the nearby elementary school's blacktop on an old clunker of a bicycle, pretending she was in a shiny race car going 200 miles per hour.

CHAPTER 2

A series of rainstorms kept Sondra mostly indoors and focused on schoolwork. She hated math but was always surprised and sometimes downright shocked at the high marks she received in this subject and others, adapting to new concepts with ease and enthusiasm. Her retention of facts and figures and the gift of a photographic memory were always non-conscious factors for how well she did at school. Sondra was a middle child, shy, quiet and acutely observant of people and her surroundings. She kept a surprisingly low profile at school, surprising because she was intelligent, had a sharp and dry sense of humor and was attractive despite her stubbornness for tomboyish attire. She never had an interest in joining after-school team sports but was a fierce and admired competitor in gym class. This combination would help to make any kid popular, but she mostly kept to herself. Her competitive spirit showed up in her school work as well as her personal determination to beat her fellow classmates from point A to point B when walking or running. Riding her bicycle, she always wanted to be the fastest, and when the bell rang at the end of her last seventh grade class, she not only raced to beat her own time getting home but was highly driven to pass everyone she could on the roads leading away from the campus. It was an enormous adrenaline rush when she could beat cars past the middle of an intersection after waiting at a stoplight. If traffic was backed up on a stretch of roadway, she'd experience a powerful sense of pride as she breezed past.

One very stormy Wednesday afternoon she had raced the weather home. Her bicycle was an old garage-sale boy's bike and not a particularly handsome one at that. All the same, she coveted her machine as one might a restored vintage Ferrari. With her father's assistance, she had learned every aspect of the mechanics and physics of it and systematically changed every spoke, gear and bearing in order for it to run as smoothly and quickly as possible. Upon arriving home just as the first raindrops started coming down like slow large pellets, Sondra locked and covered the bike in the backyard rack her dad had welded together years ago. Once inside she shrugged out of her jacket and backpack and let them fall at her heels as she opened the refrigerator door to survey her snack options. Sondra was almost sorry not to have any homework on this day, and though she was content to be indoors, warm and dry, the dreary gray wet scene outside her bedroom window draped a blanket of melancholy over her. The preteen, having seen nothing particularly exciting to snack on in the kitchen, had gone straight to her bedroom and knelt down with her arms folded on top of the window sill. While studying the outdoor activity, she imagined how it would feel to drive in the rain. Any time Sondra had the chance to ride in the front seat of the family's two cars, she intently but coyly studied the actions of the driver, whether it was her mom or dad. She highly anticipated the day she would possess her own driver's license.

Sondra's older brother, Dave, was twenty-two months her senior and had interests that were increasingly becoming more focused on girls, baseball, TV and his many friends. He never seemed to care about tools, cars or any kind of motor sports and had a new steady girlfriend whom Sondra couldn't stand. This was a very close and warm family and she had always had a great relationship with Dave. Ever since he'd discovered girls, however, he just wasn't around quite as much. Sondra's younger brother Haley, by fourteen months, was always up for riding bikes, digging dirt forts in the backyard and creating elaborate dirt towns with roads upon which they drove their many Tonka trucks and cars. She was quickly growing out of that stage in her life and was starting to feel intense restlessness for something with a real motor.

"Whatcha lookin' at?" asked Dave, entering Sondra's bedroom and seeing his sister staring out the window as if there was something of great interest. Sondra shrugged and turned her head toward her brother. He'd changed from his school clothes and was now wearing tan corduroy pants and a yellow and green Oakland A's T-shirt, given to him just over a week ago by his girlfriend, Beth.

"People are such idiots when it rains," she announced. "Bad drivers and ill-prepared pedestrians."

"Yeah, I know," agreed Dave with a nod. "Saw a guy on my way home today in a convertible VW Bug."

"Was it light blue and rusty?" Sondra asked. "That's our around-the-block neighbor who always gives out candy from other countries at Halloween."

"Yeah," confirmed Dave. "Loved those little licorice things last year. So the folks forgot to lock the basement door" he announced in a non sequitur. "Want to watch some TV before they get home?"

Sondra followed her brother happily. Kal and Maureen were fairly strict when it came to what their children watched on television. They not only disapproved of most programming but wanted their children's after-school activities to include homework, chores, as well as both creative and physical activities. Sitting in front of the boob tube was highly discouraged and the door to the basement/family room was often locked.

In the middle of summer vacation Sondra often spent several hours at Graceada Park. It was a pleasant one-mile walk from home and she usually tried to find different routes to and from this vast playground. She loved the swings, especially the rush of wind in her face and hair and the intense feel of speed as she raced toward the ground and again back up in the air. Sondra also got a strange kick out of lying flat and rolling down the backside embankment of the amphitheater. The grass was soft and cool and had an aroma that for some reason she couldn't seem to put into words how or why this made her happy. One day on the way to the park Sondra came upon a garage sale. She meandered from table to table then stopped dead in her tracks when she spotted a 50cc scooter. It was filthy, red and smelled of old dirty oil and gasoline. Her insides began doing flip-flops as she immediately saw herself fixing it up and zipping along the dirt canal banks. There was a piece of stained cardboard leaning against the front wheel with a price written in black magic marker. She stood there for quite some time, taking it all in and trying to remember just how much money she had in her savings account. A slightly grizzly-looking man in his late fifties was far from enthusiastic about her questions and interest in purchasing the thing. This however did not stop her from running excitedly as fast as she could all the way home. When she burst through the back door into the kitchen, completely out of breath and looking as if she'd just been chased by wild dogs, her mother, in mid-chop, parsley heaped on a cutting board in front of her, had a look of concern that the girl was all too familiar with, especially because it so easily could turn to one of extreme displeasure. In Sondra's mind the scooter wasn't a non-running old piece of junk but a motorcycle that represented speed and freedom. She was so excited about it that she broke kid rule #1: NEVER mention even the slightest interest in anything with wheels and a motor to your mother, especially if it only has TWO wheels.

Maureen didn't let her daughter get started, refusing any acknowledgment of the girl's great new find. Her orders were firm yet not angry. "Go wash your face, comb your hair and change out of that ugly old shirt. You dress so unladylike. And come back in here when you're presentable. I want you to help me get dinner ready." Sondra did as her mother asked, feeling the weight of such a crushing blow but decided to bide her time and carefully appeal to her dad's enthusiasm when it came to all things motorized. Her opportunity came roughly three hours later. Kal listened with patience as his daughter presented her case for purchasing the scooter. He nodded sympathetically but pointed out a number of factors she hadn't fully thought through about taking on such a project. "Besides" he added.

"There's no way in hell we'd get something like that past your mother. There's an old lawn mower engine buried somewhere in the garage loft. If you tidy up in there and find the thing, you might like taking it apart, cleaning it up and getting it running. I'll help if you need it." Sondra flashed a smile that always melted his heart. He gave her a quick kiss on the forehead and made a pointing gesture. "Grab the other end of the pool cover, will ya?" he encouraged. "Wind's picking up and there's already enough leaves and crap in there."

Sondra's 13th birthday was a tad atypical. For the summer she'd taken on several lawn and gardening jobs around the neighborhood until school started in the fall. On this day she had close to six hours of work ahead of her. Haley was away at summer camp and Dave was on a week-long camping trip with friends. Maureen made her daughter a special birthday breakfast of waffles and a chocolate milkshake. Kal was in a hurry to get to his job at an industrial machine shop and was not at all impressed with his wife's indulgence of giving Sondra a milkshake for breakfast but said nothing and didn't outwardly react to it. Getting up from the table he pulled a small card from his shirt pocket, handing it to his daughter. "Don't open that 'til you finish work today. Bye, sweetie." He patted her head, gave his wife a kiss and was out the door before Sondra could swallow and say goodbye.

After breakfast and some cleanup, Sondra and her mother left the house at the same time. Maureen had taken a job as a medical transcriptionist two weeks prior and often enthused to her kids about being part of the workforce. For the most part, Sondra breezed through her jobs. Mrs. Duncan was irritating as usual, kibitzing and watching over every last detail of the mowing, watering and weeding of her small yards. In the end, however, she gave Sondra five dollars extra for being "such a good little worker-bee." *Eww,* thought Sondra. She hated that expression. Her next job was at cranky old-man Treller's house two blocks away, and he was in fine form, spewing out his distrust at the lawn mower shop and claiming they had ruined it. Sondra quickly regapped the spark plug and made a slight adjustment to the carburetor. All that time spent with the old loft mower engine had been paying off in spades. Mr. Treller was indeed impressed with the little Sierre neighbor girl that morning. During the next few months he proceeded at every opportunity to inform his neighbors of her astonishing mechanical prowess, even embellishing a bit on her overall landscaping skills.

Sondra's last job of the day didn't include gardening or lawn care at all. Mr. and Mrs. Scheck were fat, lazy and well-off financially. They used and abused Sondra's innocence and eagerness to do a good job without paying her nearly enough for what she actually did for them. She cleaned up after a gross and sometimes frightening dog. She resealed cracks in their driveway and then dug four deep holes in very dry solid earth, where a contractor was going to install support posts for a new deck. When Sondra got back home she peeled a portion of pool cover away and jumped in, clothes and all. After changing into dry clothing, she discovered her mom had made her a birthday lunch. The new teen smiled and laughed out loud as she pulled the large bag out of the refrigerator. Her mom had taped to it a special birthday wish she'd written on a piece of Snoopy note paper. The house was eerily quiet, and as Sondra pulled each item from the bag it seemed to her as if she was making an insane amount of noise. Finishing her meal she wrote a response to her mother on the back of the small piece of note paper. "Thanks for a great birthday lunch and the car coin purse. I love you, Mom."

Sitting on her bed, Sondra took stock of her room. She noticed her prized book collection and was pleased with herself for keeping a nice tidy room. She studied the pictures and posters on her walls – images of her family on various vacations and outings, posters of cars and motorcycles. One of the enlarged paper images was a copy of a famous poster featuring a past scene from a Formula One race at Laguna Seca Raceway in Monterey, California. She'd never seen a car race at this venue but had gone there with her dad several times to watch motorcycle road-racing, a sport they both found incredibly exciting. Sondra fell back on the bed staring up at the ceiling, wondering why this particular light fixture was chosen for her room. She then sprung up remembering the card her dad had given her that morning. Her hands were on the verge of shaking with excitement as she tore the envelope open and read aloud in a whisper. “Sondra, I think you’ll enjoy this. It’s not new. I’ll tell you all about it when I get home. Look for a box with an orange lid in the hall closet under the heavy coats. Happy birthday. Love, Dad.” She felt like a cartoon character as she rifled through the closet on her hands and knees, throwing various coats and hats out and behind her. When she discovered the box she hugged and kissed it. She almost didn’t care what was inside because she knew that if it was something her dad wanted her to have, it had to be great. After carrying her treasure box to her room, she set it gently on her bed, smiling down at it, then went sheepishly back out to the hallway. With her right foot, Sondra raked all the tossed-out items back inside the closet and firmly shut the door. Hurrying back to her room she pulled the lid off the old cardboard box and peered inside, puzzled at the contents. What IS this? she pondered. It looked like a bunch of plastic pieces and wires. She gingerly started taking each item out of the box and then discovered a ‘60s era race car. Her eyes grew wide and sudden chills went through her when she realized this was a slot-car racing set. The birthday girl then put everything back in the box and carried it down to the newly refurbished basement/family room, where she knew there’d be plenty of room for a great race track. She was so absorbed in setting it up and figuring out how to make everything work that time stood still for her.

Kal and Maureen arrived home only minutes apart, but their daughter was so engrossed with her great present that she hadn’t noticed. Sondra practically jumped out of her skin when her father came hurrying down the stairs with a grin. When she caught her breath and regained her composure, she flew into his powerful arms. Maureen breezed down with a tray of juice and cubed watermelon and arranged napkins and small plates as her husband switched the wires on the slot-car set’s transformer. Maureen then watched as father and daughter knelt shoulder to shoulder, racing each other with ear-to-ear smiles. Happy tears welled up in her eyes as she drank in the sights and sounds of pure joy. Over a month prior she and Kal had come across this toy collection at a garage sale several blocks to the north.

She had tried in vain to talk her husband out of purchasing this bunch of junk to give to Sondra for her thirteenth birthday.

"Kal, I find it adorable that she's your little buddy" Maureen had said to him. "But you have two other little buddies, Dave and Haley. Sondra's gonna be a teenage girl."

"I know that" said Kal with a shrug of his right shoulder. "But she likes what she likes, no matter how many little dresses you put her in."

"Fine" said Maureen, rolling her eyes. "But I'm getting her that gemstone necklace and earring set we looked at last week" she announced defiantly.

On a warm September day, six days before school was to begin, Maureen took her three children to the DMV with the intention of Dave obtaining his learner's permit. Kal was on an out-of-town job but had called to wish his son good luck just before they'd left. Just for kicks, Sondra took the written test. She had paid close attention to her dad and Dave as they spent numerous sessions after dinner discussing every aspect of the Motor Vehicle Handbook. She knew every question and answer, and unbeknownst to the family her dad had taken her out to a vast parking lot on several occasions and taught her to drive. At the beginning of the first lesson she had a tough time going from a standing stop to first gear, but after patience and practice it was as if she'd been driving for years. Kal took her to lunch afterwards and bragged about his young driving superstar daughter to anyone who would care to listen. Dave had taken driver's ed and driver training in high school. He missed three questions on the written test but ended up with a temporary permit. Sondra got 100 percent but was pulled out of the processing line by her mother. "You're too young for this yet, sweetheart" Maureen lightly scolded. "And this is Dave's day." Sondra stuffed the test into her pocket and Maureen bent down, gently putting her hands on her daughter's shoulders. "Don't be in such a hurry to grow up" she told Sondra. "That'll happen soon enough."

Kal arrived back home early the next morning with tales of how he and a couple of other guys had saved the company's ass. Dave chose his moment and produced his new driving document. A very proud father spontaneously announced a celebration dinner later at a favorite family steak-house. Sondra allowed her brother to bask in the driving glory as Dave drove perfectly, taking them all to the restaurant. At the dining table Sondra made sure she was seated next to her father. In between the salad and entrée she slipped him her folded-up test. Kal wasn't quite sure what she was handing him so he excused himself and headed off toward the restrooms. When out of sight, he took a few minutes to enjoy what his daughter had given him. Sitting back down at the table, he messed up the top of the girl's hair with his hand. "Dad!" complained Sondra, trying to contain a large proud grin. That night, about twenty minutes after Sondra's head touched her pillow, Maureen slipped quietly into her daughter's room and brushed a kiss on the girl's left cheek. "You little scamp," she whispered. "So you took the test and got a hundred percent, did you?" Sondra's smile exploded and she deftly pulled her triumphant masterpiece from under the white fluffy pillow.

"When I take the test for real in a couple of years I'll probably get a thousand percent," bragged the girl. Maureen chuckled and rained multiple kisses on her daughter's head. "Sweet dreams, angel."

In the dark, snuggled into her warm bed feeling safe and happy, Sondra thought about the test and her parents' reactions. Kal and Maureen each viewed what Sondra had done at the DMV in much different ways. The proud dad saw it as testament to his daughter's love of all things mechanical, motorized and wheeled. He knew that driving meant more to Sondra than just freedom and transportation, as Dave mostly thought of it. Maureen on the other hand was equally proud of her daughter and loved the fact that Sondra had done well on the driving test but was more focused on Sondra's comprehension and general academic prowess than prospects of future license procurement and car driving ability. When Maureen was in the third grade, her teacher would take approximately thirty minutes toward the end of each class to read from the book *Little House on the Prairie*, by Laura Ingalls Wilder. The story and the act of reading struck a chord with Maureen. She'd done well in school and had dreams of becoming a doctor. Her medical school ambitions wavered over the years but not her passion for reading and knowledge. With each of her three children, she made sure to schedule storytimes, although it was Sondra who seemed to glean the most out of the experience. Maureen took a dim view of her daughter engaging in the numerous less-than-feminine activities, especially the girl's penchant for playing in dirt or mud and her fascination with all things mechanical. She did however treasure every moment she was able to share her passion with Sondra, the knowledge and love of a vast literary world.

CHAPTER 3

After the holidays the Sierre family were invited by their good neighbors and friends the Jenners to a weekend at their cabin near Lake Tahoe. Jack and Kathy lived around the block and their properties met at the left-corner fence with the Sierres' backyard. Owing to the fencing and the trees, the only parts of the Jenner's property visible to the Sierres were the steep-pitch red clay Spanish roof tiles of the Jenners' two-story, three-bedroom home. Jack and Kathy were a few years older than Kal and Maureen. They had no kids of their own, choosing to focus on their careers once discovering that Kathy was medically unable to bear children. When the Sierres had first moved to the neighborhood, Kal took a chainsaw to the much overgrown vegetation in the backyard. The Jenners were thrilled as this opened up a view of the westerly skies that had been long obstructed. The massive pruning eliminated overhanging tree and bush branches that dropped leaves and debris into their pool. An immediate friendship was formed and as time passed the Jenners and the Sierres became family. Jack and Kathy insisted on babysitting the Sierre kids when needed, and they were all frequent guests in each other's homes. The second New Year's Eve the Sierres spent in their new home, they invited the Jenners over for the long celebratory night. Just past midnight, after the kids were tucked into bed, Kal and Maureen asked Jack and Kathy to be their children's god-parents. The couple's response was emotional and enthusiastically happy.

For the entire week prior to the Tahoe vacation at the Jenners' cabin, the Sierre household was energized by conversation of cold-weather clothing options as well as talk of skiing, snow-boarding and sledding. Both Kal and Maureen made sure to create a fun way for the kids to learn about the climate, geography and the history of the area. On the appointed day, the car ride to the Jenner's cabin was long and at times seemed tedious but it was mostly a happy and excited one. It took some time to search the small meandering streets but they all seemed to spot the address numbers at the same time. Sondra especially noticed Mr. and Mrs. Jenner's brand new SUV in the driveway. The cabin was much larger on the inside than it appeared from the street. The thick dark-wood front door led into a narrow hallway with many hooks for jackets, and there was a series of wooden boot boxes along the floor. The hall opened into a large room that was warm and cheery, smelling of wood and smoke, evidence of a large fire roaring and snapping in the rustic stone fireplace. There was also the aroma of something cooking away in the kitchen. Kathy took up the role as tour guide as Jack and Kal headed back out the front door to bring in luggage. Sondra was torn. She was curious about the cabin but hated the idea that she might miss out on the chance that her dad and Mr. Jenner would discuss and explore the engine of that large powerful glossy silver newly purchased vehicle in the driveway. She lagged behind for a few seconds but then committed to the vacation-home tour.

After a lunch of chicken lasagna and salad, with store-bought oatmeal-raisin cookies for dessert, the Jenners left to meet some friends in town and the Sierre family could no longer contain their hyper-enthusiasm to explore every option of the snow-covered heaven. Maureen wanted the family to learn to ski together. This was serious business at first, but after about thirty minutes it was obvious that it wasn't quite as easy as it looked on TV. That's when the clowning around began to creep into the lesson. Sondra and her brothers took turns stepping on each other's skis, eventually unclipping from them all together and tossing snowballs in the air, trying to catch them without destroying the light fluffy spheres.

The Jenner's three-bedroom two-story cabin was devoid of television by choice but this entertainment entity was miraculously never missed. A living room picnic in front of the roaring fire was chosen for this evening's meal. Hotdogs were cooked on long sticks and a kettle of popcorn soon erupted into popping goodness. Kathy made a roasted green bean with bacon-bits dish and Maureen created a winter-mix salad. After ice cream and oatmeal-raisin cookies, the kids put on their flannel pajamas and returned to the living room for the final stages of the day. Maureen was filled with an overflowing sense of peace and contentment, smiling to herself as she glanced around the pleasant room. On one end of a powder-blue sofa were Jack and Kathy, with Haley between them, making happy sounds as they perused a toy catalog. Haley's birthday was a month away and the Jenners were coyly trying to find out what he might like for a present this year. On the other end of the couch were father and son, discussing at length the details of a book of *Aircraft Through The Ages* Dave had checked out from the school library. Kal had learned to fly while in the Army. During the five years the Sierre family lived on five acres of farmland, before moving to town, he'd owned a 1946 single-engine J-3 Cub. He had reluctantly sold the plane in order to put a more substantial down payment on their dream-home. Airplanes and flying were a common topic in the Sierre household and Dave had recently revealed his acute interest in planes and that he might like to join the Air-Force in the future. Maureen hadn't been thrilled with this development but said nothing to discourage her son's current ambitions, owing to the fact that Dave's career interests had always changed about every six months.

Maureen and Sondra sat next to the fireplace on a blue lounger that was one of the most comfortable chairs Maureen had ever known. She breathed deeply and temporarily closed her eyes, holding Sondra in her arms with the girl snuggled warmly in her lap. She'd given her daughter some shampoo and conditioner with a honeysuckle fragrance for her tenth birthday and Sondra had since insisted on using nothing else. After planting three kisses above Sondra's ear, Maureen smiled to herself at the girl's focus. She was reading a book that she'd brought with her, *The Mouse And The Motorcycle.*

The next day was just as full of fun and excitement as the previous. Kal and Maureen decided to stick to the ski lessons as the kids dashed off to new adventures. Dave discovered that he was instantly good at snowboarding and soon made new friends. Haley and Sondra spent almost four solid hours trekking their disks up a hill and then swishing down an icy mountain as fast and fun as ever possible. After her 27th run, Sondra slowed to a stop at the bottom of the hill and noticed a snowmobile sitting alone about 200 yards away. Without thinking she ran to it and threw her leg over, grabbing the handle bars. She sat there for a moment, taking it all in and imagining the possibilities. "Comfortable there, kiddo?" came a man's voice from behind, bordering on harshness. Sondra whipped her head around and jumped off in one swift and controlled motion, apologizing. The man stepping toward her was tall with very short hair and Sondra guessed him to be in his mid-20s. He was arm in arm with an equally tall and extremely beautiful blond woman who smiled sweetly as Sondra explained that she thought snowmobiles were really cool and had only seen them in pictures or on TV, not in real life. The young man laughed, and as he and the blond both got on the snow-going marvel, he again spoke to Sondra. "Yeah, they are cool. We're heading to a lodge on the other side of the lake for a few days. If you're around Tuesday afternoon maybe we'll give you a little ride." She thanked him, knowing full-well that the next morning she'd be in the car and on her way home. The blond woman looked over her shoulder at Sondra and waved goodbye as the young man started the motor. He gunned it and kicked up a large cloud of snow as they sped away. As Sondra leaned down to pick up her disk, she muttered under her breath, "showoff." She figured he was just trying to impress the girl. Heading up the hill again she cataloged the sound of the two-stroke 500cc engine in her brain and wondered what it would be like to race snowmobiles.

Sondra soon learned of the big kids' hill from overhearing Haley and a boy his age talking about how high it was and how much speed could be attained. She ran, tripping several times, up and over the ridge separating the two disk and sled runs. This new one was indeed significantly steeper and faster. As she panted up the hill, noticing her breath blowing out and around her, she got an unbelievable rush and a chill went through every part of her being. This was dangerous, reckless, bordering on incredibly stupid. Still, there was no way she was backing out of this. She didn't put much stock in the fact that there weren't the throngs of disk riders going down this new hill as the one she'd been enjoying. Sondra waited until there weren't many of the older kids around in case they'd try to stop her. After a quick study of the slope and planning her route, she dropped onto the disk and was instantly going faster than she'd ever been on her own, completely out of control and gaining speed. She didn't think, only reacted, instinctively shifting her body. An intense feeling of ultimate power exploded inside her and with that came maximum concentration. She flashed by three others going down as if they were sitting still and tucked her body in tighter to gain more speed. She didn't notice that everyone who'd caught sight of her stopped talking or moving and watched this blur flash down the hill. In a matter of seconds Sondra was halfway to the bottom and very close to where she'd figured would be her perfect line. She quickly came to her peak speed nearing the bottom. When the end of the slick ice was reached, she instantly began plowing through hard-packed slush with foot holes all over, which pounded at her furiously. She stretched out and relaxed her body, then put her gloved hands down slowly on the bumpy ice and quickly gained control. It gave her another thrill to steer a little to the right and stop three feet from a metal fence made of thick brown tubing.

After turning around to take a triumphant look at what she was determined to always think of as Sondra Speed Mountain, she stood up, noticing a crowd of people cheering and rushing toward her. When it was discovered that the downhill racer was only thirteen, she received many congratulations and hearty pats on the back. She took a bow and headed over to the other run to collect Haley. She didn't have to go far. Her little brother was standing about a hundred yards away with his mouth open, staring in disbelief and in awe of his older sister. They walked back to the cabin side by side not saying a word, with Haley occasionally glancing at a continuously smiling Sondra.

Since this was the Sierres' last night on their winter vacation, the Jenners insisted they be their guests for dinner at a very nice restaurant overlooking the lake. Maureen had figured there would be at least one occasion where the family would be nicely dressed and had carefully planned and packed specific clothes for each of her children. She began to pull items from a suitcase, the one that Kal had moaned about being finally the one too many, and laid out three outfits neatly on the bed. Maureen wanted Sondra to wear a turquoise-blue dress, similar to the one she was planning on wearing this evening, but her little tomboy launched into her usual complaints and arguments over clothing. Since this was a happy vacation, Maureen elected to let go the issue of appropriate feminine attire. When Sondra bounced into the living room with her hair brushed and pulled back neatly, wearing black jeans that were pretty new, Maureen smiled with pride. She made a fuss over how the new long flowing purple top looked on her daughter, the one Sondra had originally complained about being too girlie. Maureen was also elated to see that Sondra was wearing the colorful beaded necklace she'd given her daughter for her birthday. This was one of two sets of jewelry, necklace and earrings, that had originally come in a special black-velvet box. One set was inexpensive costume jewelry made from plastic, while the other was made of real gemstones. The gemstone set Maureen had kept hidden and secret, planning to give them to her daughter in the future. The cost of this purchase had triggered a number of arguments with Kal over the absurdity of buying a child expensive jewelry but Maureen won out in the end, stating that this was important to her and that she now would have something of significance to give Sondra on her Sweet Sixteen birthday.

When Maureen produced a tube of lipstick, Sondra began to move away but was caught by the upper arm and turned back around.

"We're going to a very fancy place, Sweetheart" said the mom. "And a little of this won't kill you just this once." Sondra gave in, remembering the events of her victorious sledding afternoon. She was content to have that amazing world out there and have her indoor world be a little glamorous, if her mom insisted.

The restaurant was elegant yet featured rustic high-country fixtures, was dimly lit in most places and had an air of excitement. The main room held a sizable crowd, and Sondra, Dave and Haley all made comments about how special it was to have reservations. They felt like royalty. The Sierre family rarely ate out at fancy restaurants. Since Maureen had taught herself to become a very good cook, she and Kal were of the same mind that their hard-earned dollars had far more practical uses.

As the group was escorted to a large table, Haley quickly grabbed the seat next to his father but then jumped up and ushered his sister into that spot. Sondra gave him a quick hug and kissed him on the cheek before they came to rest on high-backed wooden chairs. She was dying to tell her dad all about her day and was profoundly baffled why Haley hadn't spilled the beans, especially to mom. Once the menus were passed around and everyone had settled in, Jack offered a touching toast. The adults had long, fluted glasses of sparkling wine while the children had thick, clear wine goblets of water with small slivers of lemon. Sondra just couldn't stand it anymore. As everyone pored over their menus, she whispered excitedly into her dad's right ear an abbreviated account of her major accomplishment of the day and that feeling of freedom and power. Her father didn't seem to immediately react. Instead Kal turned to face his daughter and looked directly into her eyes. His smile came slow and deliberate, as did his offer of a sample of the adult beverage. Sondra took a victorious sip, made a slight face at the taste and smiled triumphantly. Maureen was seated directly across from her husband. When Kal glanced up at her, she had a slight disapproving frown and narrowed eyes. Kal shook his head and gave her a smile conveying to his wife that all was well.

Back at the cabin and after the children had gone to bed, Jack, Kathy, Maureen and Kal sat near the glowing fire in the living room with glasses of a special Cabernet Sauvignon the Jenners had brought. "The kids looked so nice tonight" said Kathy. "And such well-behaved little dears." Maureen smiled to herself with pride at hearing this. She'd instructed her children beforehand, especially Sondra, to mind their table manners.

"Sondra was quite the picture of a pretty and poised young lady" added Kathy.

"She's gonna be quite a little heartbreaker" said Jack, nodding his head.

"Oh bite your tongue" said Kal with a coughing laugh. "I plan on getting an arsenal of baseball bats and shotguns. No nefarious little punk is getting anywhere near my daughter."

"Oh, Kal" laughed Maureen, lightly swatting her husband on the arm.

"Not sure we're gonna have to worry about that for quite some time" she added. "Sondra's usually far more interested in cars and all things mechanical and greasy than boys. It's like pulling teeth to get her to even wear a dress or acknowledge that she's a girl."

"Oh I don't know" argued Kathy. "Give it another year. Maybe two. I bet she'll blossom into a very beautiful smart and strong young woman before you know it."

"I guess I'm really not that worried" said Kal. "All three kids have pretty good heads on their shoulders. Haley's really matured just in the last six months, and Dave's thinking more about his future than just baseball and girls."

"Well I wish you wouldn't encourage that military stuff" said Maureen. "Hearing him talk about wanting to go into the Air Force scares the hell out of me."

"Scared the hell out of my parents when I joined the Marines," offered Jack. "Different times though now and I don't see that Dave's really the gung-ho military type. He's becoming quite a respectable young man."

"Yeah" agreed Kal. "He wants to fly those high-tech military jets but I think he truly loves aviation in general. Maybe he'll be an airline captain one day."

The light snow during the night had turned to a heavy cold and oppressive rain by morning. At 5:56 a.m., Kal opened his eyes feeling instantly wide awake. He was mentally prepared for the drive home and jumped out of bed with high energy, fumbling around and knocking various things over in the dim light. Irritated at this, he flicked on the overhead light, waking Maureen out of a deep sleep. With her eyes in squint-mode, she watched Kal get dressed. He then put several items into his suitcase and closed the lid, putting the brown Samsonite case next to the black canvas bag containing his snow and cold-weather gear. "Hey" groaned Maureen. Kal offered his wife a hand out of bed but she refused then dove further under the warm covers. "Fine" he laughed as he took the suitcase and bag out of the room and softly closed the door behind him.

Emerging from the hall, Kal slowed and smiled to see his daughter fully dressed and rekindling the embers in the massive fireplace. The Jenners had set a coffee pot on timer for 6 a.m. and he and Sondra both looked toward the kitchen counter when the unit started making noises. "Haley's being quite the parent this morning" announced Sondra. "It's downright adorable. He woke Dave and me twenty minutes ago. They should be out here and ready to go any minute." Kal knelt down in front of the erupting fire and put an arm around his daughter. They watched smoke turn into flame and he spoke in a low heartfelt voice.

"We talked about you a little last night, your brothers too. Your mom and I are really proud of you and how you're growing up."

"Dad?" said Sondra, not really meaning this to be a question. "I feel like something changed inside me yesterday on the hill. I want to drive."

There was a bit of a pause. "And I want to race cars."

Kal took a slow deep breath, never letting his arm slacken around his daughter's shoulder. Maureen shuffled in just as the Jenners drifted out of their room and into the warmth of the living room. Kal kissed his daughter sweetly above her left ear and whispered, "Okay."

The heavy rain had stopped. Jack and Kal immediately struck up a conversation about the weather and road conditions as Sondra settled on a barstool at the kitchen counter, watching her mom and Kathy make a dazzling display of coffee, hot chocolate and donuts magically appear. Dave and Haley jumped up on the stools next to Sondra. The three kids all put their elbows loudly on the counter top, oddly at the same time, all three grinning.

The long weekend had been a whirlwind of non-stop fun and adventure. Hugs and tears were shared as the Sierres and the Jenners said their good-byes. After a few minutes on the main highway, the Sierre family settled down with their individual silent thoughts and memories. The rain slowed to a mist for the next thirty minutes and then began to get increasingly heavier. Soon it began to hail and the occupants of the sleek, light-blue station wagon all started talking and commenting on this fact at once. Conversation and the hail soon died down to a dull roar and they all shared aloud a favorite moment from their weekend. Maureen put her hand on Kal's shoulder and smiled back at her kids, exclaiming, "What a great trip this has been."

A few seconds prior, in the far lane of the four-lane highway and traveling in the opposite direction, a Volkswagen Jetta sped around a large tractor-trailer rig that was hauling boxes of candles. The dark blue car spun in front of the truck on glare ice and slid off the road against the guard railing for about fifty feet until it stopped. The truck driver panicked, yanked the wheel to the left to avoid the vehicle and stomped on the brakes. The trailer picked up enormous speed as it whipped around the cab, jumping the median strip and into the oncoming lane. No one had time to see this coming or even react to it. The edge of the strong metal trailer bumper pierced forcefully through the passenger door of the Sierres' station wagon, collapsing the entire vehicle into a twisted V shape. The right front tire blew and the car flipped and spun with catastrophic violence, four complete revolutions, scraping for seconds on its roof, turning over and skidding to rest in a shallow ditch. The tractor-trailer rig hit the same ditch a short distance behind the car and instantly crushed the cab, fire springing out almost ten feet in every direction.

A couple in a brand new white Mercedes luxury sedan had stopped along the designated shoulder for snow-chain removing or installing. Frank Brandon had taken off the chains and was putting the jack away in its compartment in the trunk when he heard the awful sound of crushing metal and the frantic slides and horrific, sickening loud thuds. His wife, Sheila, watched the whole ugly scene play out in front of her from the front passenger seat. Frank and Sheila had met at law school, obtaining jobs at different firms. After being married for six years, they formed their own small but successful practice in Reno, where they also had recently purchased a very high-priced new home. The couple was headed to Sacramento to take a deposition and then were planning to enjoy San Francisco for a few days.

Sheila dialed 911, instantly springing out of the car, frantically talking to the dispatch operator. She sloshed in the snow at the side of the road, hanging onto the car to keep from slipping, hurrying around to her husband. Since Frank had been driving, he had a much better idea of exactly where they were on the interstate, so Sheila handed him the cell phone. The couple then grabbed two heavy jackets and a large picnic blanket from the trunk and hurried to the station wagon, both headed to different sides. Sheila had been through CPR training a few years back and quickly determined that the front passenger and the young side passenger were not alive. Frank reached into the driver's broken window and exclaimed excitedly, "Driver's alive." Frank then moved to the side of the vehicle and Sheila quickly joined him. What they witnessed was such an unbelievably gruesome vision of Dave that Sheila slumped to her knees in tears and Frank turned away with dry heaves.

Groans and voices from the dark blue Jetta could be heard, then came the distant sound of multiple emergency sirens. Frank opened his eyes. He was clutching the heavy blanket and immediately draped it over the driver's side of the station wagon to keep out the wet sleet and cold wind. Sheila sat hard in the snowbank a few feet from the shredded and torn family vehicle while her husband went first to the tractor-trailer rig, determining that the fiery cab was unapproachable. He then trudged over to the sedan where three dazed but unhurt young men were moving around and attempting to open the car doors. Frank did a quick assessment, seeing no blood or need for immediate attention. After asking the driver if anyone was seriously hurt, thinking the lackadaisical response odd, he turned his attention back to the station wagon. He came to sit next to his wife in absolute disbelief, watching the paramedics in action. One by one the bodies of the Sierre family were taken out and put onto stretchers of the two ambulances that had just pulled up to the scene. Kal Sierre groaned and swallowed noisily as he tried with all his might to find out about his precious family. He collapsed into a rescuer's arms and took his last breath just as they were pulling him out through the window. Sheila clutched her husband tightly as they both looked down, tears blurring their vision.

Amongst all the sad commotion, paramedic Sally Milnor called out, "Got a live one. Young female, not conscious. Weak pulse and low breath sounds." Sondra had been sitting in the middle between Dave and Haley and was pinched into a tiny space surrounded and ultimately protected by the vehicle's roof, flooring and the back of the front seat. A Jaws-of-Life device had to be used to extract her small limp body from the sharp and mangled wreckage. At the exact moment the wheels of the stretcher touched the inside of the paramedic van, a portable life-support system was administered.

The Brandons were ushered into a warm Highway Patrol car and asked to recount any and all details of the accident. It took almost 30 minutes for this process, but in that time they were able to calm down and regain their composure. They also found out a few bits of information from the chatter on the car's police radio. The dark blue vehicle that had started this mess held three young men in their late teens. The underage driver and two passengers were unharmed in the accident and were all found to have three times the legal blood-alcohol limit. They apparently had been kicked out of a ski lodge for rowdy behavior and the driver's parents had reported the vehicle stolen the night before. Frank and Sheila Brandon signed witness forms and gave the patrolman a business card with their contact information. "Our law practice deals mostly with small business claims," Sheila told officer Jared. "But if there's anything else we can do, even testify for the prosecution in the case against the drunk driver, get in touch with us any time." The highway patrol officer thanked them and several minutes later Paul Jered watched the Brandons gingerly pull away from the scene. Remaining in the car, Paul poured a cup of hot coffee from his thermos, thinking about his young family and knowing it was going to be a long cold day.

Sondra's condition worsened slightly on the mile and a half drive to the nearest Medivac field, where she would be airlifted to a Valley hospital. As the craft began to rise and move away, the paramedic crew gathered together inside their large van. Even though they'd all seen their share of major traumas, this one had an oddly profound effect on the three-man, one-woman crew.

"Damn. A whole innocent family," Mick said in a low deliberate voice. He had trained in the Coast Guard in Florida five years back and had witnessed a number of tragic family incidents.

Sally's voice was cracking when she spoke in an almost whisper: "That poor little girl. She's so fragile and now she's all alone."

"Yeah" said Steven, a six-year emergency response veteran. "She's pretty bad off but I just have this feeling she's a fighter."

The confined space turned otherworldly sad and quiet, and when Dereck, the oldest member of the group, who would be retiring within a year, began to speak, it was like receiving an intense quick shock. Since graduating high school, Dereck had served 15 years as a medic in the Army. He never talked about any of his past experiences and was usually a quiet and seemingly unfeeling soldier, but on this day he had something of significance to offer. "I've seen more ugly things than anyone should have to see," he began. "It doesn't matter if it's war in another country or if it's an accident across the street. It always comes down to a huge damn reality that life is precious and our most important treasure."

At the same time Sondra was admitted to the hospital, a search was conducted for next of kin or any living relatives. It took three days before the Jenners were located and notified. Jack and Kathy were forced to suffer through another two maddening days of paperwork and phone calls to go through channels in order for them to legally be permitted to see their godchild. For a full month and eight days, the Jenners endured intense worry and heartache as Sondra lay motionless in the ICU. During the first gut-wrenching two weeks, Jack and Kathy came to the hospital and spent every minute permitted. They then alternated days due to work schedules. One Saturday evening just ten minutes from the time the Jenners were told that visiting hours were over and they'd have to leave, Sondra's right eye twitched slightly open. Monitor alarms went off and soon a team of doctors and nurses surrounded the girl. Jack and Kathy were ushered into a small waiting area, not really a room, more an alcove. It was nearby but for them it was like being on the other side of the planet. When a doctor finally swished in, they shot up, reaching out for each other's hands and holding their breath. "Mr. and Mrs. Jenner" began the medical professional, "Sondra's stable. It's common for comatose patients to have an adverse reaction when they begin to show signs of alertness. Now, there's no guarantee when or if she'll become fully conscious and I don't want to get your hopes up too high. Her injuries are quite extensive. For now though she's resting comfortably and in no danger." The Jenners were completely worn out and took the doctor's advice to go home and get some rest.

"Oh, Jack," cried Kathy after entering their relatively newly remodeled kitchen, the one in which the Sierre family had spent numerous happy times. "This just can't be happening."

"I know," said Jack as they sat at the round shiny white-oak table. "But Sondra's gonna be okay, I just know it, and tonight we saw that glimmer of hope we've been counting on." Jack watched his wife use a pale blue dinner napkin to catch her tears. "We need to talk about some stuff," he added.

Kathy sniffled and eyed her husband: "You look so tired," she noted. "You okay?"

"Yeah," he said trying to reassure her. "I guess I am pretty tired. So, uh, I got that teaching job at UCLA. It comes with a house in Santa Monica and I was able to find a rehabilitation hospital nearby for Sondra. When she's stable enough for the trip, we'll take her there."

Kathy stood and walked toward the counter where the coffee-maker sat. Before she made the motions to start the brewing process, she turned to face her husband. "You took the job?" she asked in astonishment. "You just took the job without talking to me about it? I'm a tenured high school teacher. I can't just up and leave, and Sondra isn't even awake yet. I just …" She stood staring at him, tears rolling down her face.

"I didn't accept," argued Jack. "Give me some credit. I know how important your teaching career is to you and we're dealing with a really tough situation. Why the hell are you making coffee at ten-thirty at night? It's late and we need to go to bed."

Kathy defiantly filled the carafe and set it down hard on the counter, again turning to face her husband. He got up and held her tenderly. "Take the position," she whispered, crying into his chest. "I don't want to live here anymore. Not with all this."

They pulled apart and stared at each other for a few seconds. "A fresh start will do us a world of good," she continued. "I'll take a sabbatical to be Sondra's physical therapy coach. It's gonna be tough but …"

Jack loved his take-charge wife and he nodded. "We'll get the family's house packed up and put in storage," he stated. "And the sale from the home will help Sondra in the future. We got a letter forwarded to us from a law firm in Reno, Brandon and Brandon. I'll call them tomorrow."

"And we need to get in touch with all Kal and Maureen's friends and any relatives," added Kathy. "There was that one that played the bagpipes. Leo something."

"I don't think he was a relative" said Jack. "And I can't really recall Kal or Maureen ever saying if they had any family in the states. A second cousin or something of Maureen's in England, maybe."

With each following day there came to be more and more hope. In two weeks time, Sondra was eating solid food and beginning to make faint unintelligible vocal sounds. She was also regaining some movement in small daily increments. On a chilly but clear morning in April, Kathy pestered the desk nurse for the entire eighteen minutes she was early for visiting hours. From then on, Kathy referred to her as Nurse Ratched to her husband and to their supportive friends. Moments after entering Sondra's room, Kathy heard Sondra's voice for the first time since the accident. It was a pained, high-pitched, labored squeaky tone but glorious music to Kathy. She wished her husband were there to witness this, but in addition to his job as a political science professor at the nearby junior college he was taking care of the many details securing the Sierres' estate and setting up the move to Santa Monica.

Sondra woke with Kathy gently stroking the girl's head. Sondra then began asking the questions she'd been struggling to ask from the day she'd become cognizant. "Where is everyone? Where's Mom and Dad? Where's Dave and Haley? I wanna see 'em." Kathy leaned forward and gave Sondra a long kiss on the forehead. "Oh sweetie, they're gone," she told the girl. "You were in a really bad car accident. They didn't make it, Honey. I am so sorry. I was told your dad gave everything he had but it was just too much." Tears flowed in rivers down Sondra's cheeks and suddenly the monitoring system's alarms for her vital signs began to sound. Kathy was permitted to stay and held Sondra's hand tightly. A second nurse darted into the room as the one on the opposite side of the bed from her began to inject a clear liquid from a syringe into one of several clear plastic liquid-filled bags hanging above the bed, which led to the now quiet patient. Both nurses assured Kathy that Sondra's system was still very fragile and that she was given something to help her rest. A feeding tube had to be put back in place, and for the next nine days Sondra rarely awoke. Her physical setback took an enormous emotional toll on the Jenners but it also gave them time to set future plans in place and get the Sierre family estate in order.

When Sondra was finally released from the hospital, she stayed at the Jenners' home for close to a month, eventually getting strong and healthy enough for the move to Southern California. Since the house was not quite ready and Sondra still required around-the-clock aid, the Jenners rented a short-term apartment for themselves and set the girl up in a room at a rehabilitation facility Jack had researched some weeks prior. It was basically a local and state-run hospital that cared for the elderly as well as disabled patients requiring long-term care. With the passage of days and weeks, Sondra's speech patterns were almost completely back to normal and it seemed to the Jenners as if she were making good strides with the new physical therapist. Sondra hated the medical professional, secretly adopting Kathy's nickname for a previous nurse, Nurse Ratched. Nurse Malinda often hurled cliché after cliché at Sondra, having the girl do nothing she couldn't already think to do herself. Sondra began to bitterly resent the fact she'd been taken so far away from the home she'd known and loved and was acutely aware that visitation from the Jenners had slightly decreased. The girl had basically been in survivor mode since the accident. She needed positive thoughts and actions all around her and treasured every second the Jenners visited. "I'm gonna be working and have my own place soon," the young teen told Jack and Kathy one early evening. "I'll have you over for a dinner party and we can celebrate your new jobs and my independence." The couple didn't have the heart to laugh at such a silly statement from the young and fragile girl.

CHAPTER 4

Just under a month before Sondra was set to be released and begin her new life with the Jenners, she was informed by Nurse Ratched that Jack had suffered a massive heart attack while lecturing and had died en-route to the hospital. Kathy had collapsed upon hearing the news and was taken to a different hospital, across town. Sondra shook her head in disbelief at the news. It didn't seem real or possible. She was now truly alone and felt completely done with where and how she was living. With a powerful sense of urgency she put the few possessions she had into a bag with the hospital's logo on it and waited until there were no nurses or doctors present. None of the items were from her childhood or family. They were basically meaningless trinkets the Jenners had brought her from time to time to cheer her up but they were hers and she wanted them with her.

Sondra began her escape. Numerous times she had seen where nurses and doctors obtained new scrubs. She grabbed three sets and stuffed them into her bag, then headed down the stairs. It bothered her that she felt like a felon on the run, but she quickly decided to think of this as escaping from a POW camp. She was on her own now and had no one but herself on which to rely. At the bottom stair landing, she put on one of the green tops. It was two sizes too big.

She waited for a few seconds and listened, then jumped into the scrub pants, also too big but she manipulated the drawstring tight and rolled up the pant-legs. After putting on the oversized booties, she pulled on the cap and opened the door to the main lobby. It was empty and she could see the double doors to freedom just ahead. Sondra stepped just outside the staircase door and composed herself as if she were a medical technician with a purpose. She walked past the Admit Desk with her head slightly lowered, a determined and very focused look on her face. The cool of the morning hit her hard as did the energy this all had taken, but within a few seconds she continued on, feeling a powerful sense of freedom. She was later found and picked up by police in the early evening. Sondra had walked over three miles from that awful hospital only to collapse under a large tree in a park overlooking the ocean. Fatigue and pain from her injuries had overtaken her. As she leaned up against the trunk of a palm tree, she told herself that this would be only a temporary resting place. Several hours later a homeless man, who normally would take advantage of and steal from vulnerable people, saw this sweet frail little girl dressed in a medical uniform. He was drunk as usual and stumbled into the street, managing to get a cab to pull over and stop. When a very reluctant taxi driver halted the white sedan he listened to the tattered homeless man's slurred speech, with him pointing to the girl. The cabby called 911 and in broken English tried to explain the situation. The dispatch operator then relayed information to a nearby patrol unit. "There's a woman in an altered state causing a disturbance."

Sondra was awakened from her sound sleep by two male police officers. Without discussion she was turned over face-down and placed in handcuffs. When she struggled and tried to explain her situation she was forcibly dragged to a squad car. The young teen was then taken to a detention center and shoved roughly into a holding cell. The 9x12 cell was cold, dirty and had a stench that was strange and unexplainable to all who had had the misfortune to be held there. Sondra slumped against the wall a few feet from the heavy locked door. Shivering cold, she folded her head in her bruised and sore arms and eventually cried herself to a very weary sleep.

The entire police communication was picked up by John Farnsal, half asleep in a well-worn, semi-comfortable chair listening to a police scanner. He had a dusty, sparsely decorated run-down office and was the modern-day image of a 1950s gumshoe or private-eye, playing that angle quite well in his dress, mannerisms and how he conducted his life. His ground floor front office was in an old hotel. Small businesses occupied the first story and the top three were cheap apartments. His own cramped single apartment was in the back corner of the building on the second floor. John Henry Farnsal was a defense attorney and an avid homeless rights activist. He eked out a living defending the undefendable and tried to help as many as he could get off the street and into some kind of mainstream of society. That phrase had long since lost all real meaning for him, although several of his clients had pulled themselves up and acquired jobs, and a few were even renting apartments in the building. The owner of the Misty Ocean Inn and Apartments was a 52-year-old widow. She had a soft spot for what John was doing for the community and they'd occasionally dined and spent time together. She was a stickler with the rent to all other tenants and always raised the rates each year, but not to John. In the seven years he'd rented the office and apartment, she never made mention of changing their original rental agreement. He was not oblivious to this fact and from time to time would shower Leanna Blevins with little gifts or a nice meal out, whenever he had the spare cash.

There was something annoyingly wrong about the radio communication John was hearing from officer to officer and to the police dispatcher. It didn't sound as though the "subject" fit any of the typical criteria for a "drunk and disorderly" arrest, especially the description of her being in hospital scrubs. Raw instinct took over as he scrambled to his feet, pulling on his long dark-tan coat, and made an attempt to straighten up his desk. After gliding on a faded dark-brown fedora and exiting the door, he first drove to a nearby grocery store, purchasing several simple items. He practically threw the large paper bag – he always insisted on paper, not plastic – into the messy small back seat of his '68 VW Beetle and roared off to save his new damsel in distress. John was a well-liked regular figure at the police substation and knew how to finesse the system to create favorable outcomes. After paperwork and formalities, he was permitted to see his new potential client. What he walked in on was disturbing and sad to the core. Sondra was lying on her side in handcuffs and leg irons. She was completely visible through thick, paneled, wire-embedded glass windows. Her face was red. She was crying and screaming, flailing wildly on the faded pinkish, dirty-looking floor. "What the hell are you monsters doing?" John asked in a low voice. His next voice came loud and angry. "Open this damn door and give me cuff keys."

Once inside the cell he sat down immediately and in a calm soft voice told Sondra his name and that everything was going to be all right. Her eyes were shut, a pool of tears on the floor beneath her cheek. Even though she was thrashing around he deftly unlocked and removed the cuffs from her wrists, then made quick success with the leg restraints. She flashed up and away with shocking speed and strength, her back hitting the filthy dim-white painted brick cell wall with a boom that made John's stomach sink. He cringed, stood up and took a step forward, thinking that the figure before him looked like a caged wild animal. Her face was scrunched up, her eyes narrowed and her long dark-brown hair was wild. Her wrists were red from the where the handcuffs had been and her fists began tightening. John wondered if she was going to pounce on him like a tiger in a vicious attack. Through clenched teeth she spoke in a guttural low tone: "Stay the hell away from me, asshole." The 58-year-old man immediately dropped to his knees and then sat with his legs folded. "Sondra, I promise on everything you hold sacred, I won't touch you or hurt you. I'm here to get you out of this insane hell. I'm a lawyer and you have rights. I'll make them pay for what they've done to you." He got on his knees again and gathered up the handcuffs and barbaric leg restraints. Without his eyes ever leaving Sondra's, he flung the evil devices against the thick front window. They made a horrifically loud sound that reverberated with ear-crunching intensity. He turned to everyone who was watching. "You disgusting jack-booted thugs," he yelled. He then sat back down into his previous position and again softly addressed Sondra. "Please trust me, even if it's just a tiny bit. Sit and talk with me. I can get you out of this nightmare. I need you to relax. I'm here to help. I promise you I can make things better. I'm not a weirdo. I'm not mean and I'm not a jerk. All my friends think I'm a good guy and I have a lot of friends. Don't let these ignorant bullies win. Sit with me and show 'em how well you and I can communicate."

Sondra's expression and stance remained unchanged. Again through tightly clenched teeth, she growled in quick sentences. "I don't need a lawyer. I didn't do anything wrong." John took a deep breath that he immediately regretted, because it smelled so awful in that room.

"Okay" he said to appease her. "But some people at St. Julian's are concerned that you ran away. You're now at a police station, locked in a disgusting room with pathetic dregs of humanity staring at you. So yeah, you need a lawyer right now. Sit down, kiddo. Let's jump through a few hoops and I'll get you to a safe place tonight. You can have a tomorrow that won't be awful and it won't have to be here."

What the man said made some sense to Sondra and her jaw slackened. She unclenched her fists a little and walked toward him, sitting in a similar position. She intentionally sat close enough for their knees to touch. It was an unconscious trust exercise. Sondra spoke in a very unstable voice. "I miss my …" She collapsed forward, doubling onto herself and sobbing loudly with tears coming out in sheets. John reached over and gathered her up as if she were a child of four or five who had fallen and scraped a knee. "Everything's gonna be okay," he tried to reassure her. "I promise." He picked the girl up and turned toward the door, was amazed at how little she weighed. It hit him hard that this was all happening to someone so young. John set Sondra down on a chair in a small but much nicer room used mainly for obtaining detailed subject interrogation and/or witness statements.

During the time it took for two EMT personnel to arrive and make a medical assessment, John was able to extract a number of details from Sondra about how she had come to be in this situation. He was a man of many resources and was able to have the girl released into his custody. Once at his car he gingerly set the skinny and shaking Sondra onto the passenger seat and secured the safety harness. John then noticed a number of other bruises the bullies had given her. So many issues were at play here. He knew she didn't know or fully trust him. She was physically weak and tired and all the recent events had to be completely overwhelming for her. When he got into the driver's seat he offered her his jacket as a wrap. She hesitated. She didn't want anyone's anything. He wasn't her dad and it wasn't something from her family. He wore a cologne similar to that of Mr. Jenner, however, so she finally gave in and welcomed being enveloped in the jacket's warmth and comforting aroma. John then reached behind the seat and fumbled to get hold of the bag of food. Sondra's eyes and face showed instant fear. She strained against the seat belt and leaned into the car door. He caught sight of this as he pulled the bag noisily over the seat. "It's okay" he assured her. "I have food for you." He set the bag in her lap. Her hands came out from under the coat and she peered inside, grabbing a blueberry muffin and fighting with the plastic wrapping for a couple of seconds. It burst open and she savagely stuffed it into her mouth. Sondra chewed and swallowed with such voraciousness it was almost frightening to witness. John started to reach into the bag and Sondra grunted angrily, her eyes getting that rage he'd seen just a short time ago. He pulled back and placed his hands firmly on his legs. "No, no" he apologized, shaking his head. "I was just gonna get something for you to drink. Everything in this bag is yours. All yours." She studied his face, then nodded quickly and stabbed her left hand inside the bag, coming up with a miniature container of milk. This was a major and welcomed comfort. These classic small cartons of milk were a part of her many pleasant kindergarten memories. Sondra bit down on the muffin to hold it in place while she tore open the flap on the carton, using both hands. She pulled the doughy Shangri-La away and drank the milk, swallowing noisily, then resumed her furious eating. When she'd finished she let out an enormous sigh. She was now full, even though she could see and feel there were many more items in the bag.

Weariness was now coming over Sondra like a fast-moving storm.

It seemed odd to her that she had been painfully hungry when she'd sat down against the tree in the park earlier that day and how so little food could now be so much. "What next?" she half asked, half demanded. John turned the key in the ignition and she perked up at the sound of the engine, especially since she could tell right away it needed a tune-up.

"A safe place to sleep" he told her. "Mrs. Blevins' comfy couch for tonight." Sondra clutched the bag containing her belongings and repositioned her knees to more securely hold in place the bag John had given her, finding it hard to keep her eyes from closing. The sounds of the rise and fall of the engine's rpm and the gear changes as they sped off into the night were soothing. She drifted off to sleep and remained in deep slumber as John drove to the apartment building. He then carried her, still clutching the bags, into his office and laid her down softly on a gray vinyl couch at the side of the room. He adjusted the coat to surround her securely, grabbed the cordless phone from his desk and started dialing Leanna's number as he gingerly closed the door behind him and stepped into the dark-wood musky hallway.

Just as soon as the call came in, Leanna Blevins was up and out the door, flying down the stairs toward John as he explained in brief detail. They stood face to face and continued to talk on their phones to one another for a few seconds, each then realizing the nuttiness of their behavior. Putting the phones to their sides, Leanna seemed to take charge of the situation. "John, I really think the best thing to do is to bring the little angel to my apartment. When she wakes up your office might seem like a scary place. My couch is far more comfortable and I have nice warm blankets and a good pillow." He nodded approvingly and kissed her on the cheek. "She's been through such a lot today. Poor kid," he told Leanna, thinking how appropriate it was that she refer to Sondra as "little angel." John and Leanna tucked the girl in on the plush powder-blue couch as if they were parents bringing home their newborn baby for the first time. Sondra woke with a start, a defiant fight or flight response at the ready. She tried her best to retreat but there was nowhere to go and she had very little physical strength. Her eyes, however, once again showed that fierceness that John had first seen in the holding cell.

"You're okay," he assured her.

"I wanna go home" said Sondra in a desperate squeaky voice.

"Where's home?" asked John.

Sondra shook her head. "There is no home. Gone."

"What happened, sweetheart?" asked Leanna. "Tell me and maybe I can help."

Tears came out in sheets as Sondra fixated on the fact that this woman wasn't going to be able to help get back what she'd lost. No one could bring back her family and the life she'd been having. The young teen cried for several minutes but then related a brief and bitter version of recent events. Through the telling she became even more bitter and angry than she'd been since the accident. "I need to go see Mrs. Jenner" concluded the girl.

John patted Sondra on the knee. "You get some rest tonight" he told her. "I'll take you there tomorrow." Sondra desperately didn't want to wait a minute more to see Mrs. Jenner. She tried her best to make this point clear to the strangers before her but couldn't seem to move her arms and legs. After fighting with intense weariness, she closed her eyes and fell immediately asleep.

John and Leanna took Sondra to breakfast at a small coffee shop located at one end of a nearby bowling alley. Though Santa Monica was host to many special morning eateries, this was John's favorite place to dine. He'd taken Leanna there for lunch when they'd first met, telling her about his deep appreciation for something so wholesome and so traditionally American. It pleased John on this morning to see Sondra gobbling her food, two eggs, two slices of bacon, a piece of sourdough toast and a glass of milk. The couple sat on either side of the girl and watched the display with amusement and some concern. Handing Sondra a second napkin, John spoke between bites of his three-egg, sausage and hash-browns breakfast. "So I made a number of calls this morning," he informed the girl. "You have some paperwork to fill out and a woman to meet with at St. Jillian's, then we'll go over to St. John's Health Center. That's the hospital where Mrs. Jenner is. She's on a seventy-two hour hold so I can't guarantee that you'll actually get to see her today." Sondra chewed with bitterness and stared at her plate, not understanding what a seventy-two hour hold meant. Neither John nor Leanna wanted to tell the girl that Kathy had taken an overdose of sleeping pills, trying to end her life because of all the unbearable emotional pain stemming from first the Sierre tragedy and then losing her husband. Two nights prior, a neighbor had spotted Kathy through an open door lying on the kitchen floor of the apartment and had called for help.

"I'm going to see her first" growled a demanding Sondra. "Before that other crap hospital."

"All right," said John, half agreeing with her. He wasn't sure if this was the best idea. He'd been told that Mrs. Jenner was in a state of extreme mental anguish and that she was under close watch and heavy sedation. He was concerned that by witnessing this it would do the child more harm than good. At the hospital, where access to Mrs. Jenner was denied, Sondra became irate and belligerent to the point that security was rushed in, but John and Leanna defused the situation and herded the girl outside.

At the rehabilitation hospital there were several doctors, nurses and social workers waiting for young Miss Sierre. Sondra again became irate when a plan was revealed that she be taken to a Child Protective Services center across town. John wrapped his strong arms around the girl and did his best to calm her. The processing procedure for all this was to take some time, but John and Leanna were permitted to remain with the girl through it all.

In a cluttered office Sondra's future was discussed. A short pudgy man with a bad comb-over informed her, in no uncertain terms, that she was going to the Child Protective Services facility that night. Sondra snapped, feeling this was an unjust jail sentence. She pounded her fists on the desktop and loudly growled every foul word she'd ever learned. Two security officers appeared and John had his hands full defusing an intensely volatile situation. John and Leanna reluctantly drove Sondra to her new temporary home at CPS, vowing to do anything and everything they could for her. The next day John made a number of phone calls on her behalf and was surprised when he was permitted to see Kathy Jenner that afternoon. The chat was far more coherent than he'd expected and he convinced her to sign over her power of attorney privileges to him. Now acting as Sondra's legal counsel, John was able to get in touch with Frank and Sheila Brandon. Wrongful death lawsuits were filed, estate planning and handling procedures and paperwork were put into place, and John was not only granted regular visitation privileges at CPS, which Sondra's caseworker tried to block, but he along with Leanna was able to take Sondra to many meals and outings around town. One outing was to see Sondra's godmother. Kathy was a shell of her former self and with the medication she was on barely recognized Sondra. On the way out of the mental health hospital unit Sondra shook her head. "Gone" she lamented. "Everyone's gone now. It's just me." John and Leanna expected a flood of emotion out of the girl but Sondra was calm and stoic. They took her to lunch at Ye Ole Fish & Chips restaurant. During the meal Sondra informed the couple that there was a gym within the CPS building and that she was getting stronger by the day. "It's a hideous weird place," she announced of the overall CPS facility. "Lotta kids. Too many. A few are decent though and there are school classes. Not great but at least it counts like a real school."

CHAPTER 5

Though Sondra was usually grateful and sweet around John and Leanna she'd developed a bit of a dubious reputation at CPS. She was solemnly bitter, often verbally combative with authority figures and got into many fights with other girls. The altercations were almost always with those bigger and taller than she and Sondra was usually on the losing end. John and Leanna were asked to help with "Miss Sierre's attitude problem," and one afternoon they collected her for lunch, taking her to a fish and chips restaurant for clam chowder on this cool but sunny April 29th. They sat at a long, low, bar-style table looking out at the length of the pier, with the beach and ocean beyond. The couple actually had some horrific news for Sondra but decided that this would wait until they'd finished their meal. After their order had been placed, a muscular man with short blond-brown hair brought them each a plate of sourdough bread and butter. With Sondra sandwiched between John and Leanna, they first engaged in conversation about the weather and the volleyball games that were often played on the other side of the pier. When their chowder arrived, Leanna chose this moment to inform Sondra of a particular recent development. "So we have some happy news for you," she told the girl. John leaned in with his elbows on the table, watching Sondra wipe her mouth with the sleeve of her right arm. “Leanna and I are getting married,” he told her. “Yay!” smiled Sondra. “I mean it’s about time, you crazy kids,” she chirped. Leanna hugged the girl and John leaned back, smiling.

After a lunch that seemed more like a celebration, with talk of wedding plans, the three took a walk farther down the pier. Reaching the farthest end, they leaned against the blue railing and looked out to sea. “Sondra” said John in a tentative voice. “I’m afraid I have some really bad news.” Sondra shrugged her shoulders. She was still basking in the warmth of the couple’s joyous wedding announcement and couldn’t imagine anything worse than she’d already been through. “Your godmom didn’t get better. She’s gone. She died late last night.” Sondra stood frozen and stunned, gripping the railing with her right hand. She stared at John for further answers but he had no intention of giving her the gruesome details, that Kathy had sunk further and further into depression and despair. She had stolen medication meant for another patient, and late into the night she’d taken these plus those of hers she’d been secretly hoarding, producing a lethal dose.

Sondra stepped a few feet away and pounded her fists as hard as she could on the metal tubing. “No!” she wailed. She began screaming, swearing and crying, making an alarming scene. John tried to contain the girl in his arms, but she flailed about hysterically. The injuries from the Tahoe accident had Sondra in constant major pain and she still only had a small fractional amount of strength that she’d once had. Raw emotion now immediately depleted her energy and she collapsed into John, with Leanna wrapping her arms around the girl as well. “I’m so sorry, Angel” said Leanna, trying to reassure the girl. “We’re gonna do everything we can for you,” added John. “Come on, lets go back to our building and talk,” said Leanna.

Once inside Leanna’s familiar apartment, Sondra cried herself into a very weary slumber, and roughly three hours later caseworker Judith Tredou and two police officers came knocking on the door. Sondra was taken, literally kicking and screaming, back to CPS. The next afternoon she was taken to a foster family home in Burbank. She hated the idea that John and Leanna were left out of the decision-making process and now were farther away. Sondra also found out that Mrs. Tredou and CPS initially tried to keep John and Leanna from knowing the address and phone number of the group home. Legal privileges prevailed, however, and John promised Sondra that he and Leanna would stay in touch on a regular basis. The kind attorney also continued to work on Sondra's behalf in matters of estate planning and other legal affairs.

Mr. and Mrs. Collins, the homeowners and caregivers of the group home, were sweet and went out of their way to make sure Sondra was welcomed, comfortable and quickly settled. Bill and Judy were a retired couple whose two children were grown and had successful careers, evidenced by photos throughout the house. The caregiving couple had a nice large four-bedroom Craftsman-style home. Seven years prior, through a local community outreach program, they had taken on a second career as caregivers to kids in need of shelter and guidance. There were three other teen girls living in the house, each of varying ages and races. When Sondra was introduced to her new foster family, the kids tried their best to engage their new sister with kindness and conversation. Sondra was relatively polite but had a tsunami of anger that was always just beneath the surface. During her first week she was noticeably sullen and shut off. She tried her best to keep to herself, which was not easy in a household that was a noisy bustling universe of domestic chores, meals, schoolwork as well as games and TV. Eventually Sondra appeared to be taking her new surroundings in stride and was offered enrollment as a freshman at the relatively nearby high school, though there was much concern over her size, age and personal situation. Sondra quickly rediscovered her passion for knowledge, but entering a new school with kids she didn't know and doing this two months into the semester was an uphill daunting task. She rose to the challenge delving into academia with full force, and though she wasn't cognizant of it, the hours of intense studying were her way of avoiding the horrific thoughts of her family being gone and that her life had been severely and permanently changed forever. This truth did rear its ugly head from time to time. Sondra's foster sisters occasionally tried to pry into her past, but she began honing her skills of deflection. At school she'd come across a number of inquisitive kids. When vocal deflection didn't work and she felt attacked and cornered, Sondra would invariably precipitate in physical altercations, just as she had at CPS, resulting in blood and bruises as well as three warnings from teachers and a school counselor, then one detention. The school's principal finally insisted on a meeting with the Collinses about the girl's behavior and possible future punishments. In hopes of deescalating Sondra's anger issues, she was permitted to speak with John and Leanna once and sometimes twice a week. This seemed to help somewhat, and she began to spend as many hours at the public library as she could without raising too much suspicion. Her 14th birthday went by mostly unnoticed, for which she was grateful, and when classes let out for the summer break she not only enrolled in summer school but obtained a job as a hand-dryer at a nearby car wash. Her insatiable love of cars and attention to detail brought her some positive feedback at her new job, along with some very nice customer tips.

Bill Collins had health issues that began to worsen and was advised by his doctors to make drastic changes in his lifestyle. He and Judy reluctantly decided to forgo presiding over the group home. They would sell the house and move to an assisted living facility in San Diego, near their daughter's home. Sondra's constant anxieties over her future were now heightened and two weeks later Judith Tredou once again became a regular fixture/annoyance in her life. Sondra was taken back to CCS and Judith saw to it that no phone privileges were allowed. Several weeks later Judith drove Sondra three hours north of LA to a small section of town just outside Bakersfield. Sondra experienced the drive to her new home as an eternity in hell, with Judith's voice and never-ending spiel getting on her every last nerve. It was hot that late morning and the slop offered for breakfast seemed particularly inedible. That, combined with the ups and downs, twists and turns of the Grapevine mountainous pass reminded her how miserable she'd felt that night in Santa Monica when Mr. Farnsal had rescued her from the jail holding cell. Her mouth watered and physically ached when she thought of that blueberry muffin John had purchased for her on that harsh night over a year ago.

After a seeming lifetime, Judith pulled into to a dusty gravel driveway. The house was a triple-wide mobile-home with an add-on large single car garage. When Judith put the car in park, Sondra exclaimed, "You gotta be kidding." She didn't actually mean to say that out loud. Judith scolded the girl. "You mind your manners, missy. These are good folks and happy to take you in." Sondra said nothing as she pushed the heavy car door open. The front door of the house swung in slowly and out came what Sondra saw as a wannabe Vegas showgirl a few years past her prime. Ms. Brenda Johnson had platinum blond hair and bright clothes that were too tight in some places and not near tight enough in others. It was only through Judith's dubious and manipulative dealings that Brenda and her fiancé had been awarded foster parent status. The fact of the matter was that the fiancé in question wasn't actually betrothed to Brenda nor had he officially signed off on fostering a child. Brenda and Judith had known each other for years and had become the best of friends during the four years they were on the cheerleading squad in high school. Brenda had become pregnant her senior year and had a son, Pete, just three months short of graduating. The boy's father skipped town and only was in contact with Brenda and their son when authorities caught up with him. Brenda's next boyfriend was a violent alcoholic. She had purposely tricked him into getting her pregnant with daughter Tracy in hopes that he'd settle down. He didn't, and in just under a year she became pregnant a third time, with Jennifer. Before the baby was born, Billy skipped town and was in and out of prison. Brenda then met a Marine sergeant, producing her youngest son, Josh. She was sure a military man was going to give them all a proper life but he had the same personality traits as the other men. While on a three-day leave, he and three other men were driving to Las Vegas, while drinking heavily. The driver of the car lost control and smashed into a telephone pole. Frank was in the front passenger seat and was not wearing a seatbelt. On impact he went through the windshield and was killed. While working as a checker at a large chain grocery store,

Brenda had met her current boyfriend, grateful that this man was kind, stable and completely unlike the other men in her life. While she and Judith were having lunch one afternoon, Judith suggested that Brenda take in a foster child. Brenda saw dollar signs at this prospect and did her best to avoid talking to her boyfriend about it, lest he disapprove.

It was obvious to Sondra that Ms. Johnson and Mrs. Tredou were good friends by the eruption of high pitched squeals and greetings after arriving at the Bakersfield home. The two women talked for several minutes, completely ignoring Sondra, then with a strange non-sequitur Brenda made a mid-sentence announcement. "And here we have our newest member. Such a tiny little thing. Gonna have to get some meat on those bones before winter." The two friends laughed loudly and Sondra followed them inside. The living room was dimly lit and smelled of past cigarette smoke and old spilled Kool-Aid. Judith and Brenda sat facing each other at two ends of a faded green couch. Sondra remained standing but Judith, in mid-sentence to Brenda, pointed to a lounge chair. "Don't be rude, hon, take a seat" she ordered. Sondra immediately sat at the edge of the chair, clutching the straps of her two backpacks tightly and bristling that the woman had just called her hon.

Two teenage girls burst through the front door, the strength of their perfume and hair product causing Sondra to lightly and momentarily cough. They were only a year or two older but dressed to try to give the impression they were in their early twenties. "Tracy, Jennifer!" announced Brenda. "This is Sondra. She'll be your new foster sister." The two girls gave Sondra a quick look of disdain. "Hi" said Jennifer. "Hey" breathed Tracy. The girls then turned to Judith and their mother with an opened magazine. As the four engaged in a loud discussion of clothing and what the popular Gina Marsh was wearing at school that day, Sondra felt more alone than she'd ever imagined possible. This was such a contrast to how excited and happy the girls at the Collins House had seemed when they greeted her. Just as quickly as Tracy and Jennifer had entered and consumed the room they vanished into a bedroom. As Judith and Brenda were standing up and saying their goodbyes the girls came bursting back out, hair done differently, makeup overdone, and wearing very skimpy tops and skirts. Sondra thought they looked like idiots. She would have thought them to look like sluts or whores but she'd lived such a sweet protected life until recently that idiots seemed more the appropriate term.

Sondra and Brenda were now alone in the house. Brenda motioned to her. "Come on hon, I'll show you around and where you're gonna sleep." The home tour didn't last long and gave Sondra an uneasy feeling. She was used to the clean staleness of CPS and this home seemed to her that it was covered in layers of filth.

In the room where the two girls had come in and out earlier, Brenda pointed to a small army-style cot with a few blankets folded on its top. "You'll sleep here and you can put your stuff in there" she said, pointing to a mid-sized lidded cardboard box in the space between the cot and the wall. "Maybe we can try and find you a little dresser at a garage sale that'll fit there. They have 'em all over 'round here." As they left the room Brenda looked back over her shoulder. "Those bags glued to your hands, girl? Go ahead and put 'em on the bed." Sondra desperately wanted to keep everything that was hers right with her but reluctantly set the two backpacks on the cot. Upon coming to the doorway of one very messy room Brenda announced that this was the boys' room. "Pete's my oldest, seventeen, and Josh is fourteen." At the end of the hall was a closed door. Brenda shot a forefinger at Sondra with such intensity it had her careening against the opposite hallway wall. Brenda didn't notice and continued the tour. "This is mine and Doug's room," she announced to Sondra. "It's off limits to all the kids. I mean it," she said in warning, her finger making dagger movements as she spoke. "You understand?" Sondra nodded her head. "Kay then" said Brenda. A whistling buzz came from another room, a wall-mounted Tweetie Bird telephone in the kitchen that Brenda hurried to answer. When Sondra appeared a few seconds later, the woman shot her a look that made her feel as though she was the most hated and unwelcome person on the planet. Brenda folded around the corner into the living room for privacy and Sondra rushed to retrieve her backpacks. She then waited to make sure the coast was clear so she could quietly slip through the kitchen and out the back doorway. The backyard looked more like a large dog kennel, with a low chain-link fence all around. The scarce Bermuda grass was littered with soda and beer bottles, fast food trash, a deflated basketball, several rusty bicycles with missing wheels and she counted three dirty shirts.

As Sondra drifted her head around a little more toward the garage, her insides suddenly jumped. There, leaning up against the wall, were two dirt-bikes. She raced over to them. One was a Honda 250 and the other a Yamaha 250. They were both covered with mud and dirt and the Yamaha had a flat rear tire. She set her backpacks on the surprisingly clean concrete slab, the entrance to a flimsy-looking garage back door. She grabbed hold of the Honda's handle bars pulling the motorcycle toward her. The feel of the weight and balance and the pull of the brake lever gave her goose bumps. She was excited and hopeful as she thought to herself, *maybe living here isn't going to completely suck after all. Maybe the two boys won't be as awful as the girls and their mom.* Sondra didn't have long to wait until that dream was harshly dashed. "Hey!" came an angry voice a distance behind her. "Get the hell away from there." Sondra gently leaned the Honda back against the wall and gathered up her backpacks as Pete, a black-haired intense mass, came through the metal gate just off the alley. Normally Sondra would apologize and start to make conversation but clearly these people were animals. She took several steps away from the bike and from the tall boy's path, then turned and held her ground, facing him expressionless. "So you the new girl?" He thought he was entitled to know. Sondra stared at him, starting to tremble. "Nice manners," she retorted, racing past him and out the gate to the alley. Running as fast as she could for about four and a half minutes, hunger and exhaustion fell on her like the toppling of a condemned building. Sondra sank to her knees and grabbed onto a telephone pole, becoming violently ill. She knelt there spitting and crying briefly but stood up wiping her mouth and eyes, then began walking with purpose so as not to draw attention to herself. She continued in a daze until the back of a small grocery market caught her eye. Laboring around to the front she set her backpacks down just inside the door, after feeling the evil eye of the nearest clerk. She wanted to get all the things that John Farnsal had picked out for her that night roughly a year ago. When the cashier started tossing her treasures into a plastic bag she waved her hands and shook her head. "Paper only" she instructed. She'd learned this from John Farnsal and needed that feel and sound of a paper bag full of goodies in her arms. On the way out she slipped her backpacks on her left shoulder and headed down the street clutching the bag, making a mental note to explore more of her surroundings and find out what other stores and places of interest would be safe havens from that awful household.

After making her purchases, Sondra she spotted a dirt path off to the left, heading toward a nice long patch of lush green grass with a little creek in the distance and soon came across a small area she deemed to be the perfect getaway spot. Settling down comfortably, Sondra took a long swig of milk and a bite of apple then breathed in deeply, slowly exhaling. She stayed in her secluded haven for the rest of the afternoon, repacking both backpacks, transferring the food from the paper sack to the top of the smaller pack, careful not to crush the packets of cheese and crackers or the several health bars she'd bought. She carefully ripped the brown paper bag into several wide strips to use as note-paper and put all but one into a side pocket of the larger knapsack. Sondra then took out a pen and started making a list of needed items. She was going to have to rely on herself as if she was on a long backpacking trip. The first thing she put on the list, however, was to call John and Leanna.

It was just after 6:30 p.m. when Sondra reluctantly returned to the house. The driveway was car-less, meaning that perhaps Brenda had a job to go to or would at least be out for a while. Sondra hesitated in opening the front door, afraid of encountering that monster she'd met in the backyard earlier, who she figured to be Pete. She entered the residence and made a straight-line dash for the bedroom, putting her bags down inside the cardboard box, and sat down on the cot for a few seconds, unhappy with its lack of softness or comfort. Since she'd noticed at least someone different sitting on the living room couch and watching TV as she'd made her way to the bedroom, she went back out in hopes of a better exchange from someone at this house. "Hi, I'm Sondra," she offered with her hand extended. The way the boy was positioned and the glare from the TV, she had a millisecond vision of Haley but bit down on her tongue when reality hit. The person on the couch could never be mistaken for her sweet little brother. " 'Sup?" Josh uttered, slowly extending his hand. Sondra stared at him in disbelief. Instead of a regular handshake, he did a hip-hop slapping thing. "You're Josh, right?" she asked. He didn't respond. "Where is everyone?" she inquired. The blond-headed boy never moved nor took his eyes off the TV and his answer was short. "Dunno." Sondra stood there for a moment feeling absolutely amazed. These people are nuts she thought to herself, convinced of her decision to call John and Leanna as soon as possible. She slipped quietly away and went into the bedroom. Drained, she unfolded the one blanket to make at least a softer mattress for the cot, then covered herself with her own sweatshirts as blankets and curled up, eventually falling asleep.

Sondra woke a few minutes before six the next morning. As quietly as possible so as not to wake up her two roommates, she carefully folded her sweatshirts over her arm, gathered up her two backpacks and slipped out of the room. The living room wreaked of stale cigarette smoke and cheap wine. She went outside and sat on the front porch, folding her clothes and putting them into her larger pack. From the smaller one she took out a small bottle of water and a nutrition bar. This was breakfast in Bakersfield. Finishing her meal she sat for a few minutes enjoying the rising sun on her face, then began walking in a westerly direction. Spotting a pay phone she called John Farnsal's office number, leaving a long detailed message of anguish and how much she missed him and Leanna. She then continued her walk of discovery.

In the Saturday morning light, Sondra's little sectional view of town had its certain charm. She passed the market she'd been to the day before and spotted a number of other businesses farther down the street. Off to the right was a tall fire station building, which she instinctively headed toward. Almost halfway there she walked by the large open industrial metal doorway of an auto repair shop. Her eyes were focused ahead but her nose caught a whiff of gas, grease and cleaning solvent. She stopped, eyes now straining against the sun to get a peek inside. A booming but friendly voice came from within. “Lookin’ for somethin’ or someone, honey?” Sondra took several steps closer so that the top of the building shaded the brightness of the sun. “No” she responded. “I just like cars and garages.” She heard a deep-throated wheezing laugh as a large man appeared. He was wearing stained coveralls with rips and holes and had a very visible pot belly. A gray greasy baseball cap sat slightly askew on his balding head and he had about a three-day growth of dirty beard. He studied her, wondering what a young girl carrying two backpacks was doing walking around alone with an interest in cars and garages. “So ya like cars, huh?” inquired the garage man. “I’m going to be a race car driver” stated Sondra. The man convulsed into laughter but when he saw the look of hurt on the kid’s face he stifled the laugh and introduced himself. “Well I’m Bobby. Bobby Shnider. I’d shake your hand but as you can see it’s pretty dirty.” He held his right hand out as unnecessary proof. Sondra gave a friendly wave of her hand.

“I’m Sondra. Sondra Sierre” she announced.

“Well, well,” said Bobby. “Hi Sondra. You’re a whole lot smaller than I was expectin’. I heard tell of a girl that was gonna be comin’ to town. Nice to meet you. Come on in and I’ll give you the nickel tour of the shop.”

“You were expecting me?” Sondra inquired. She moved forward and followed Bobby into the garage. He led her directly to a white Ford F-150 pickup that was about to go up on the hoist.

“So, Sondra Sierre. When’d ya get into town?”

“Yesterday” she said in a sad voice.

“Brenda’s mentioned you several times” informed Bobby. “You haven’t met Doug yet, have you?” Sondra shook her head. She’d heard the name several times associated with Brenda and the foster family. “Well I’ve known him for quite a few years now,” said Bobby. “He has his own towing service so he has to be away maybe a day or a couple of days a week. That's one hard-working S.O.B., and he's a hell of a good guy."

Bobby began wiping his hands on a dirty red rag as he watched the girl turn her head, looking all around the inside of the somewhat disorderly garage. He smiled to himself as he looked at Sondra, now fully noticing that she clung on to the two backpacks as if someone were trying to steal them from her. He made a gesture with his hands and commenced with a more detailed tour of the shop. "So here's the office" he told Sondra. Bobby was about to head toward the massive tool panel just outside the cluttered room when Sondra exclaimed, "Whoa. Is your secretary on vacation or something? This place is a mess. And who rang up this sales slip? Someone added it up wrong. You're about to lose eighteen dollars and seventy-two cents."

"How old are you, Sondra?" asked Bobby. "Fourteen," she asserted. The phone rang and Bobby was quick to answer it. Sondra waved goodbye and whispered, "Thanks, Bobby. Nice to meet you."

A new boost of self confidence and hope came over Sondra as she continued her search for good things in a seemingly bad place. She felt good about her new potential friend and ally, Bobby, not to mention a potentially safe place to hang out when necessary. More importantly was her hope that this guy Doug could help her with attaining some kind of tolerable home-life. By that evening Sondra had managed to have a very pleasant and extremely productive day. She had taken notes on where to find many items and services that would be needed in the future, finding a discount store that had some of the same items as the neighborhood market but at much lower prices. Arriving back at the house at 4:37 p.m. she found utter chaos. The inhabitants were engaged in serious arguing, but as she headed toward the bedroom it all came to an odd stop.

"Where the hell you been?" demanded Brenda.

"Just familiarizing myself with the town," Sondra defended.

"You took off early without tellin' anyone where you was goin' or what you was plannin' to do," scolded the woman. "And what's this about you tryin' to take Pete's motorcycle?"

Sondra felt betrayed and attacked but the confidence she'd gained at the auto repair shop propelled her to stand up for herself. "First of all" she began. "It's were going, and were planning to do. Not was. Secondly, I don't take things that don't belong to me. I was just checking it out. Besides, that thing isn't going anywhere with a flat rear tire, a frayed spark-plug wire and dried mud caked all over the air cleaner." Pete was well aware of the flat tire but he had no idea why the engine wouldn't start. He didn't say it but he was impressed at the girl's quick diagnosis as well as her having the guts to stand up to his mother.

Sondra didn't wait for a response or for permission to leave the room. Instead she went to the bedroom and slammed the door behind her. Just as she was noticing that her cot was missing, the door was violently slung open and Brenda rushed in and slapped her squarely on the right cheek. Sondra had never before been hit like this by an adult in anger. The pain welled up with every succeeding second where Brenda's ring had struck her and there was quickly becoming a darkening red mark. She was stunned and unable to move or fully comprehend the situation. Brenda stood watching the girl, almost daring her to make a move. Sondra's hands clung tighter to the straps of her two backpacks and Brenda's next voice was filled with ugliness and contempt. "What the hell's in those damn bags anyway?" When she lunged toward the girl and the bags, Sondra snapped. She dropped the smaller pack on the floor and swung the other one with such speed and force that it hit the woman heavily on the right shoulder, knocking her down instantly. Before Brenda had time to think or react, Sondra was on her knees, her face next to Brenda's. She growled angrily through clenched teeth.

"Don't you ever touch me again. If you don't want me here, just say the word and Tredou can take me back to CPS. I'd rather be there anyway. I've been nothing but nice to everyone here. I don't deserve to be treated like this. Not from you, not from anyone."

Sondra retrieved her belongings and stood briefly in a fight stance. She saw Tracy, Jennifer and Josh standing in the doorway and for a second thought of asking, Who's next? Instead she ran past them and found herself inside the garage. After hearing a series of loud voices and then the kitchen/garage door being deliberately locked, she slumped against an old brown Studebaker truck that was being restored. She remained in the same position for quite some time, then carefully opened the passenger door and climbed inside. She pulled out several sweatshirts as blankets and a pillow, curled up on the seat and cried herself to sleep.

Sondra woke the next morning with a start. The garage door swung open noisily and in flashed the bright sun. She crawled down as far under the dashboard as possible and tried to cover herself completely with her clothing. She made every attempt to make herself invisible but Doug Trent knew his pride and joy all too well. He'd been gone for just less than a week, ferrying a disabled mini-bus from just north of Merced to Vancouver, Canada. Whenever Doug returned home from a job he always came in through the garage, checking on his tools and his truck. On this morning he spotted the unusual lump of clothing and immediately thought that one of Brenda's kids was trying to hide a dog or cat in there, knowing that their mother had a strange aversion to any and all pets. The truck owner opened the passenger door and yanked away a handful of material. A frightened and shivering little girl stared back at him. "Hey there" said the man. "I'm Doug. What's your name?" Sondra said nothing but made a fist visible, her eyes fiery-fierce and intensely studying the large figure before her. Doug took a long breath and closed his eyes for a second. "Whoa" he voiced. "The kids didn't scare you into this, did they?" Sondra didn't speak. She couldn't. The man left the door open and went to close the large garage door, giving Sondra time to quickly stuff her sweatshirts into the larger pack and crawl up onto the seat. When Doug reappeared he was carrying a large sports bag, slightly similar to the one her dad had often carried. The man didn't say anything further but held out his right hand, callused and strong-looking. Sondra slipped the two backpacks over her left shoulder and grabbed hold of Doug's powerful hand. She wasn't sure why but she didn't feel afraid or threatened by him as he lifted her easily out and down, setting her slightly unsteady feet on the dusty concrete. “You hungry?” Doug asked. Sondra looked up at him, noticing his face in the light. She nodded her head and he gestured toward the garage’s back door. “I know a great place for breakfast. Ever ride in a diesel tow truck before?” She shook her head. “No” she offered in an unstable voice. “Well my little friend” offered Doug with a warm smile. “If you like pickups in a garage, you’ll probably like this beast.” Sondra returned the man’s smile and Doug suddenly felt as if he’d just won the lottery. He lifted his new diminutive friend into the tall tow-truck cab and started the engine, quite pleased with his passenger’s excited gasp. “Wow” she marveled as he stabbed the throttle, watching the girl’s eyes become wide as she studied the gauges on the dashboard.

Doug Trent was a man with a deep and caring heart, a factor for how he’d chosen the tow-truck profession. He was strong on intelligence and usually had good intuition. He did have one main weakness, however. Throughout his entire dating life he’d chosen women and relationships that were not exactly good for him. He’d been an only child with older parents who had passed away before he turned 23. Unconsciously he was always trying to put together a family and his last several relationships had been with single moms. He’d met Brenda two years prior while passing through Bakersfield on his way to pick up a crashed Ford Escort near the town of Taft. He’d driven from Fresno, where he’d been living, and stopped at a Ralph’s grocery store to purchase snacks and beverages for his long day. An outgoing and energetic seemingly fun-loving blond woman was the check-out clerk and they flirted shamelessly throughout the entire transaction. He found himself going back to that store and her checkout line as often as possible and soon they began dating. In the beginning, Brenda’s oldest boy Pete was quite standoffish but the other kids took to him right away. Without really thinking things through, he jumped into the relationship with Brenda with both feet and in less than a month of dating moved in with her and her four children. Doug loved being a parent and having a family to come home to, but after a year the novelty had worn off and the reality of a drastically changing situation was sliding in on him like a slow-moving avalanche. The children's personalities and behaviors began to rapidly change with the passage of time, especially the two eldest. There soon began instances of smoking, drinking and sneaking out at night. This became an odd norm and nothing Doug could say or do would change their attitudes and behaviors. In addition, Brenda's personality and behavior changed as well. When they'd first begun dating, she did her best to hide the fact that she smoked and was a regular heavy drinker. With familiarity and time there came a lack of pretense. The more Doug voiced his displeasure regarding her vices the more Brenda's robust defiance of her behavior emerged. Before he'd gone on this last towing job, he'd told her that they needed to have a good long talk, thinking he'd made himself perfectly clear that entering into a foster-care situation at this time was not a good idea. His trust and respect for Brenda had been slowly waning, which seemed to make her more desperate and unpredictable. He came to regret not being more forceful about putting the brakes on the foster-care idea when Brenda's friend Judith had first come up with the plan.

Sondra was impressed by how well Doug was known and obviously liked at Flappin' Jack's Finer Diner. The place was noisy and packed but Doug had a gift of gab and they were soon seated at a warm and cozy corner booth. Sondra loved the hustle and bustle as well as the amazing mix of aromas. She had to force away memories, however, of all her family breakfasts. She developed a determined focus on asking Doug about Bobby and his garage. He gave her only vague answers because he wanted her to eat a good breakfast and also have a serious conversation about why she was sleeping in the garage rather than in the house.

"Hey-ya, Doug" greeted waitress Ruth heartily. "How ya doin' and who's your new little friend here?"

"Mornin', Ruth" responded Doug. "I'd like you to meet Miss Sondra Sierre. She's going to be living with us. I think we may be hungry so bring us the works, will ya?"

"Sure thing. Coffee?" asked Ruth.

"For me" he answered. "But my friend here and I will start with some orange juice, and we might end up havin' a touch of the hard stuff ... milk."

"Well, I dunno," said Ruth, picking up on the man's dry sense of humor. "I just might have to see some IDs." She smiled and patted the table before disappearing into the crowd.

When the two small glasses of orange juice arrived, Doug let his new companion take several long sips before he put his elbows on the table and leaned in toward her. "So, you like car seats instead of comfortable beds?" he inquired. She shrugged her shoulders and looked down. "Sondra" he prodded gently. She looked back up at him with narrowed eyes and gritted her teeth. Doug then asked a second question. "What's with the red mark on your cheek?" Sondra swallowed down the last of her juice and set the glass firmly on the table upside down, just as she'd once seen someone do with his empty whisky shot-glass in a TV Western. She gave Doug a hard look. "Thanks for breakfast" she said flatly, moving her legs into position to exit the booth. Before she could get two feet from the table Doug swiftly picked her up and set her in the seat next to him. "What's really goin' on, kiddo?" Tears began rolling and Sondra convulsed with heavy sobs. "I want to go home" she cried. "I miss my house. I miss everything. They're gone. All gone." Doug did his best to soothe the girl as her crying became more intense, catching the attention of other patrons. "I didn't do anything wrong" she sobbed. "They hate me. And she hit me." "Who hit you?" Doug wanted to know. Sondra sniffled loudly before answering. "Brenda" she said firmly and deliberately. She used the woman's first name instead of Ms. Johnson because she was quite sure that horrible person didn't deserve her respect or any honor that she was taught by her parents to give to her elders.

"Damn it" breathed Doug. "I'm so sorry" he told Sondra. "I promise I'll fix things and make everything right, okay?" He held her head into his shoulder and again reassured her that things from this moment on were going to be better. Ruth arrived, setting two large plates of food on the table. Taking a swift view of the situation, she knelt down and put a hand on Sondra's delicate shoulder. "Hey, sweetie" she said in a concerned voice. "Cheer up, hon. You got friends here." She kissed the top of Sondra's head. "Thanks, Ruth" Doug said in appreciation. "Can you wrap all this to go, please? I think we'll head over to Bobby's shop." Doug had a hunch that Sondra had made a connection with Bobby just by her earlier inquiries and thought it might be a way to get her to eat and open up a little more. Ruth soon came back with two white plastic bags filled with Styrofoam containers of food. Doug handed her a twenty dollar bill, telling her to keep the change. She protested a little but stuffed the bill in her pocket, then pulled the glass dome off a plate of donuts and put the pastry treats into the bag, telling Doug to share them with Bobby and the guys at the shop.

Back inside the safety of the tow truck's cab and still parked in the diner's parking lot, Sondra spilled her guts. She found herself telling Doug every detail of the last two years of her life, not believing all this was coming out of her mouth. She couldn't seem to help it, though the horrific tale erupted with more power and anger than with pain. Sondra didn't speak of the Tahoe accident, cry or fall apart, even when she mentioned John and Leanna. She went on to detail all the exchanges that had happened since her arrival in Bakersfield, with Doug sitting there dumbfounded and shaking his head. "Man" he exclaimed when Sondra stopped talking. "Unbelievably awful. I'm so sorry. That's a hell of a lotta crap to have to deal with." She believed him but shot him a fierce look that had him shifting in his seat. Doug felt a sudden sense of urgency to right the wrongs and figure out the best course of action. He drove in anger at the situation and soon pulled into an alley, parking the tow rig in a large grass and dirt lot beside B.A.S.S., Bobby's Auto Service Shop.

Bobby Shnider knew the sound of Doug's big truck and came out from the large back rollup door to greet his friend. He was animated and pleased to see Doug carry Sondra down from the giant cab.

"Dougy-boy" greeted Bobby. "How the hell are you, man?"

"Damn good, you old goat" responded Doug. "I see the place is still standin'."

"Yep" nodded Bobby. "Still got three good legs." This was a verbal routine that had taken place many times between the two great friends.

"We bring questionable food but unquestionably good company," Doug told Bobby, holding out the bags of food with one hand and putting his other on top of Sondra's head. "Well that's the only thing that can be tolerated around here" returned the garage owner. Sondra briefly closed her eyes and smiled, feeling the most relieved she'd felt in quite some time. "Hi Bobby" she greeted. "Ruth the waitress gave us donuts for everyone." Doug and Bobby laughed and they headed into the cozy, always disorderly office. The two men talked non-stop, all the while opening the food containers and pushing them toward their famished little friend. It wasn't so much that Sondra was starved or malnourished. It was simply that she now felt completely safe for the first time since her last normal meal at the Collins' House. Her appetite was enormous and pleasantly encouraged. When Sondra felt full she held out the extra plastic forks to Doug and Bobby, telling them that there was still plenty of food. Bobby favored the donuts even though his wife had made him a good breakfast just two hours prior, but Doug was indeed hungry and polished off the rest of the morning meal, relating to Sondra that he liked hash browns just as much as she. "So you want to race cars do ya, Sondra?" asked Bobby in a complete non sequitur. Doug looked over at the girl, not sure if this was a silly joke or if it was a heartfelt ambition of hers. It became obvious seconds later when she looked at both men with such seriousness and intense conviction giving Doug and Bobby a quick chill. Sondra then made a determined claim. "I am a race car driver. I just don't have a car yet." Doug patted the girl lightly on the back and stood, pointing to a picture on the wall. "Know who this is?" Her answer came quick. "Mario Andretti" she asserted. "Nineteen Sixty Seven. Daytona Five Hundred." Doug was amazed at how a seemingly frightened and sensitive child could become so instantly powerful and authoritative. If this could happen with a question and a photo, who knew what strengths she possessed.

Bobby and Doug soon entered into long-winded tales of historic races and drivers, then of recent events in their lives. When they noted that Sondra had fallen asleep curled up in a tight ball at one end of an old faded yellow vinyl couch the two men exited the office, shut the door carefully and walked into the approximate center of the garage.

"Well this really throws a wrench into the works" said Doug, shaking his head. "Looks like Brenda went ahead with the foster-care thing, even after I told her no."

"That friend of hers, Judith's handiwork," offered Bobby. "Got Brenda all charged up about extra income and food stamps that are made available for foster parents." Doug again shook his head. "That's disgusting" he growled. "To work the system like that. I hate it that Brenda's not the woman I thought she was. You know, this whole trip to Canada and back, I was really contemplating an exit strategy. I pretty much had it all worked out in my head. Things with Brenda and the kids have been bad for a while and getting worse, but with this? I'm now basically trapped. Can't just walk away."

"No" agreed Bobby. "That's not your style" he added. "So whatcha gonna do?"

"What can I do?" said Doug. "I mean she's here, frightened and innocent little Sondra. Not like I can just send her away."

Doug told Bobby the tale Sondra had related to him about her life since the Tahoe accident. When he ended the story he gave his temples a quick massage with his thumb and forefinger. "That poor kid" added Doug. "She's been through too much hell. No way can I just let her slip through the cracks. It's weird. Being around her for even a few minutes you want to scoop her up in your arms and protect her."

"Yeah" agreed Bobby. Doug picked up a dirty solvent-laden gray shop rag nearest him and threw it down on the bench in frustration. "I really tried to make a difference with Brenda and the kids" he told his friend. "I completely failed." "That's not true" offered Bobby. Doug shrugged his shoulder and took a deep breath. "Well I'll never just give up on them but I think the perfect-family ship has sailed. I really think I'm basically done with Brenda." Doug looked down at his watch. "She'll be at work 'til three-thirty" he continued. "And there shouldn't be anyone at the house right now. Hopefully the kids are at school, not god-knows where else. I'm gonna pack a bunch of my stuff. Mind if I store some things here?" Bobby gestured that there was plenty of room for his items. "You're welcome to stay with Diane and me," he offered Doug. "Sondra, too" he added.

"That's incredibly kind" smiled Doug. "But I can't just move out like that. Gonna take some careful doing now that Sondra's in the picture. Man, this is quite a tangled mess I've gotten myself into" he added, blowing a long breath through his lips. "Can you look after the kid here while I go to the house and then have a chat with Brenda?" asked Doug. Bobby nodded. "Be prepared" he warned his friend, "might get ugly."

Doug collected a number of his most cherished items from the house and drove to the grocery store where Brenda worked. He parked in a side lot waiting for Brenda to come out for her usual shift-break, honking the horn when he spotted her following a coworker exiting a door with no handles. Brenda soon climbed into the passenger seat of Doug's truck and was already talking a mile a minute about her day.

"I swear, it was the funniest thing. The entire shelf came crashing down. Eggs oozing out everywhere and Randy trying to catch 'em. Slipped and fell on his ass. I 'bout died laughing." Doug exhaled a loud breath through his nose and shook his head. He didn't find this quite as amusing as she. "Yeah" he said with no emotion. "Sounds like a real mess." "You okay?" asked Brenda. Doug stared at her, chewing slowly on a stick of peppermint gum. "No" he responded. "I'm not okay. We're not okay. You and Judith hatched this little foster-care scheme and I told you not to do it but you went ahead and did it anyway. I work damn hard for you and this family and I sure as hell wasn't expecting to come home to find some frightened little girl hiding in my old Studebaker. What the hell's wrong with you? You hit her and locked her out of the house?" Brenda tried to defend herself, claiming that Sondra was the initial aggressor but Doug didn't want to hear it. He'd had enough. "No," he said forcefully. "There's no excuse for hitting that little girl. You were drunk, weren't you?" Brenda's over-exaggerated denial was enough to convince him that this was the case. He'd seen this before, all too many times.

"Stop" he yelled. "I've had enough of this. I told you time and time again the smoking and drinking crap has to stop. I'm done. You lie to me and tell me you're quitting and that everything's gonna be fine. Well it's not fine. I've done everything I could to be good to you and the kids but I've had enough. You and I are through. I'm moving out." Brenda became irate and threatened him with palimony and told him she was under the impression they had a verbal agreement to foster the girl. She argued that he now had a legal obligation to continue with it. Doug knew this was absurd but he also knew that she and Judith Tredou would do their best to make his life a living hell. He watched Brenda climb down from the cab and slam the truck's door shut, hurrying back to work. He pounded the steering wheel in anger and frustration with his fist before making his way to the house to do a more thorough job on a permanent move-out process.

Before leaving the home Doug had known for past number of years, he straightened the disheveled living room and began washing dishes and cleaning the kitchen. He soon heard the front door open and close. "What are you doing home from school?" he asked Tracy. "I don't feel good" cried the girl, making her way into her room. Doug followed and watched Tracy collapse onto her light green and pink bedspread. He rushed over and felt her forehead, surprised that she wasn't lying, faking or simply hung over. "You're burning up," he stated. She groaned and grabbed and her midsection.

"You in pain?" asked Doug. The girl nodded and cried louder. "It hurts. My tummy hurts."

"All right" he said. "We're gonna get you all better." He scooped her up and took her to the nearest hospital's emergency room. After the girl was admitted for acute appendicitis with immediate surgery scheduled, he called Brenda. She arrived 23 minutes later in a panicked state and, as always, Doug was of great comfort.

"You still love us" she sobbed into his shoulder.

Doug took a deep breath. "There's a big part of me that'll always love you and the kids," he told her in a soft voice.

"I'll change," cried the woman. "We'll all change."

"Shh," soothed Doug. "Let's just focus on Tracy getting better right now."

Doug's move-out plan had now been altered by Tracy's medical emergency and subsequent recovery. Brenda went back to doing a better job at hiding her smoking and drinking but it didn't fool Doug for a moment. He saw this as a clock-reset and a chance to better formulate solid future plans.

With Doug, Brenda and her kids rallying around the recovering Tracy, Sondra felt shut-out and alone. She was bitter and angry that they were making such a fuss over Tracy's simple medical procedure, though she kept this to herself. What the hell is wrong with these idiots, she thought to herself. I almost died three times and I'm still in a ton of damn pain, but nobody cares. By the end of that first hard week however, there came a fairly normal domestic routine. Unbeknownst to Sondra, Doug had found the opportunity to scold and warn each of Brenda's kids to be kind and accepting of their new foster sister, though Sondra could definitely feel underlying resentment from Brenda and Tracy. A single bed and a dresser were found for Sondra and the following week she was enrolled as a sophomore at the nearby high school where Pete was a senior and Tracy a junior. Sondra found it disappointing and then downright annoying that neither Pete nor Tracy ever offered her a ride. It was only an eighteen-minute walk to the campus and as in the past she delved headlong into schoolwork, relieved that it distracted nicely from her now-life.

After a number of phone conversations with John and Leanna, Sondra asked them to call Doug about setting up a face-to-face meeting. Doug welcomed the concept and looked forward to meeting the Farnsals but knew Brenda, Judith, CPS and the like would never approve of this. He purposely neglected to inform Brenda about the meeting, instead telling her on the appointed day that he was taking the kid along with him on an all-day towing job. On the southbound journey to Santa Monica, Doug and Sondra carried on light conversation about Doug's job until encountering unusually heavy traffic coming into the San Fernando Valley. Doug then switched off the truck's radio and began a more serious talk. "So I'm hearing from your school that you've been getting into a lot of fights," he prompted. Fellow students had quickly come to see a very closed-off serious person in Sondra. This combined with a number of unkind words Tracy had said about her resulted in taunting and teasing. Sondra shrugged and looked out the side window as they traveled at 42 miles per hour, watching the freeway brick wall patterns as they rolled past. "What do you care?" she muttered. Sondra had never before been rude or flippant with Doug and her sudden attitude alarmed him. He wondered if the girl was thinking that John Farnsal was going to help her make a living situation change. She was, and she'd been thinking about some sort of escape from her perceived hell for weeks. "I care a lot, Sondra," said Doug. She turned to face him. "Sorry," she half meant. He flashed a smile at her before continuing their captive chat. "Well I also hear you're gettin' good grades, so at least your teachers are impressed with that, not your little world-wide boxings matches."

"I guess I've always liked school" admitted Sondra, ignoring Doug's comment on her dubious behavior. "The learning part," she added. "When I was in the fifth grade there was talk of moving me up a grade. I didn't get to do that, but they gave me an advanced curriculum and I got all A's."

"Did you have a lot of friends at that school?" asked Doug.

"Yeah, I guess" said Sondra. "I mean the grade school I went to was walking distance from our house."

She swallowed hard and made a tight fist before continuing, hating that her previous life was gone. "A lot of the kids that went to that school lived in the neighborhood so it was easy to make friends because we had that in common," she found herself telling Doug. "My best friend, Gina, lived around the block on this huge corner lot. She and I almost always played on the jungle gym at recess and we sat next to each other in class." Sondra went back to looking out the side window. "She and her family moved to Seattle that last summer," she said in a low voice. "I'm sorry," said Doug. Sondra shrugged and bit down on her tongue.

John and Leanna were overjoyed to see Sondra and she them. While Leanna showed Sondra the wedding photo album and detailed the happy event, John took Doug down to his office for serious conversation. Doug told of basically being Shanghaied into the foster situation but that he definitely was a fully committed and dedicated foster dad for Sondra. "Yeah, well" said John. "I'm well aware of Judith Tredou," he offered Doug. "That woman is quite a piece of work. What she did in fast-tracking Sondra through and around the system is possibly criminal but at the very least so far out of the realm of CPS procedures it's not even funny. I'm really glad to meet you and that you came today. Sondra's left several messages. So damn heartbreaking but my hands with the foster situation are tied legally. Can't really do anything about it but scream and yell and write letters in hopes that someone will review her case."

"Thanks" said Doug. "But I'm really sure I can make this work and give Sondra a good life. She's not happy though, far from it. I'm sure she came here today thinking you'll rescue her."

"Wish I could but that just can't ever happen," John told Doug.

He poured two glasses of iced tea and the men entered into an important topic. "She's been asking about becoming an emancipated minor," said Doug. "Is that possible? Could this in some way help her?" John gave it serious thought. "She turns fifteen in a number of months, so yeah, that's a possibility," he told Doug. "Not sure I really recommend it. I honestly think that girl is in serious need of structure and stability, some semblance of home-life." Doug nodded, feeling the full weight of Sondra's life and future happiness and successes on his shoulders. A powerful need hit him hard to make necessary changes and it was somewhat comforting when John bought him up to speed with all he had done on Sondra's behalf, and he'd done a lot. He entrusted Doug with detailed information and paperwork on all the girl's current financial holdings as well as the law suits filed and the Sierre family's estate situation. "Until Sondra turns eighteen or if she does become an emancipated minor," he offered Doug, "I'd keep this all on the back-burner. Strictly to yourself," he added quickly. "She needs to keep moving forward with her life, not be dragged backwards by all this." Sondra's time with John and Leanna was concluded with a clam chowder and sourdough bread meal at The Boathouse Cafe on the Santa Monica Pier. She was glad to share this with Doug, but when it came time to head back to Bakersfield, she made a scene, pleading for John and Leanna to let her stay. In the end, however, she and Doug began their journey back to what Sondra had begun to refer to as the evil house.

"You're being awfully quiet" stated Doug as he transitioned onto the northbound I-5 freeway. "I know you wanted to stay but we'll make this work, I promise. You keep your grades up and stop getting into fights and things'll change for the better sooner than you think."

"Kay" whispered Sondra. She was sure there was no change for the better in her near future and kept her eyes locked on the roadway ahead.

Chapter 6

Sondra's life became a series of ups and downs, though she thought them all down. She childishly and secretly began thinking of her new home as the evil house. There were a few bright moments here and there. Bobby Shnider hired Sondra to work in the B.A.S.S. office a few hours a week after school. She loved it. This was her sanctuary and during periods where business was slow it allowed her to engage in homework and in-depth study. Sondra's favorite moment so far however was on her fifteenth birthday when she and Doug went to see John and Leanna. John had promised to take her to the DMV for her learner's permit during the brief time before she'd gone to the Collins' House. On this late-July day, John, Leanna and Doug enjoyed the girl's hyper-enthusiasm in obtaining the coveted document. She held it up in triumph and announced proudly that she'd gotten 100 percent on the written test, bitterly remembering this same triumph years ago with her family.

While taking a break from required reading for her history class, Sondra discovered a 125cc Suzuki dirt bike in the corner of the auto shop. It was covered with thick dust and debris and mostly hidden from view by boxes, long since written off as worthless junk. In the days that followed, she began systematically ordering new parts for it and used her alone-time in the garage to clean and work on her new friend. Her father had ridden motorcycles and she'd been his passenger for quite a few miles. She knew by heart the aspects of riding and didn't really need anyone to teach her to ride but asked for a few pointers from Bobby, mostly wanting his approval. He was downright surprised as he watched her first ride. In no time at all it seemed as though she'd been riding for years. After work a few days later Sondra had been out on the bike for roughly an hour. She came rushing through the wide back entrance of the garage and skidded to a halt, dismounting with dramatic flair. "So what's this?" asked Doug. He and Bobby had been talking for roughly fifteen minutes, watching for her arrival. "I'm gone for almost a week and you're building motorcycles, terrorizing the neighborhood and running the shop?" he said with a broad smile. Doug pulled an envelope from his jacket pocket, holding it even with his head. "And you made the honor role at school. Straight A's. You're quite the little powerhouse," he smiled, tapping Sondra on the right shoulder with his fist. She beamed, speechless. "Helluva kid," Bobby roared loudly, clapping once. Doug handed the envelope to Sondra and pulled out two small pieces of paper from the same jacket pocket, fanning them out in front of her. "You and I are going to the big sprint-car races next weekend. Both days." Her eyes got wider with each word as he continued. "We have pit passes to boot." "Wow" was all she could manage, her smile straining every muscle in her face. "You earned this, Sondra" said Doug, his voice soft and serious. "You weren't exactly dealt a good hand here but you didn't let that bury you. I'm sure you'll find this hard to believe, but even Brenda and her kids have been saying good things about you lately." Her smile disappeared and she looked down at the ground. When she glanced back, however, she flashed him that smile he was growing so fond of and he resisted the urge to pick her up as if she were his own biological daughter. Doug's build and features were astonishingly similar to Sondra's father's, though this didn't consciously register to her. The men each had a football player's type of broad shoulders and muscular upper body that narrowed significantly at the waist. Both men had smooth but strong faces and sported deep healthy tans. Doug's temperament was also quite similar to Kal's and this was a factor in how Sondra had become instantly comfortable around him. The two main differences were the eyes and hair. Kal had the same hazel-green eye coloring as his daughter and his hair was thick soft and black. Doug had sky-blue eyes and neatly styled short light-brown hair.

The anticipated weekend with Doug at the sprint-car races was even better than Sondra had hoped and Doug reveled in the fact that he'd brought someone to the event as excited and enthusiastic as he. On a Saturday afternoon that Sondra deemed perfect, they walked all around the dusty facility, scouting out a favorite spot to see the main Sunday race. They watched practice sessions and heat races and after a long yet action-packed day Doug and Sondra started their trek back to the parking lot, a huge sea of vehicles on dusty dried grass with orange cones and small yellow ropes cordoning off particular numbered areas. They talked non-stop about what they'd witnessed that day, each reciting car numbers and the names of various drivers of interest they figured would place well or win in the next day's main event. Doug and Sondra were amongst a large crowd of fellow race fans all headed to the same parking area, and at one point the throngs of humanity bottled up and were temporarily stopped. Doug chose this opportunity to inform her of the evening's events. "Oh" he began. "We're having a family dinner tonight. No big deal but Brenda's had this planned for a little while and it's important to her, okay?" Sondra executed a small grunt, staring straight ahead at an obese man nervously tapping a faded red baseball cap on his plump right thigh. Doug continued. "It's at Rossario's. You know, the Italian place on Ness Avenue." He knew Sondra wasn't going to like this but he was trying to keep the peace with Brenda just a little while longer before making his permanent break from her. His apartment hunting had taken on a more frequent and urgent status lately and he'd also been in touch with John Farnsal, who'd put him in touch with a lawyer who specialized in tricky custody cases.

As they approached Doug's bright yellow Toyota Tacoma pickup, he grabbed hold of Sondra's left wrist and put a wad of keys into her hand. "Lets give that learner's permit a little workout, shall we?" he offered. Sondra's smile exploded as he gave her two pats on the top of her head. Before putting the key in the ignition she glanced down at the gear shift knob, noticing the shift sequence pattern. She knew it by heart but was being deliberately thorough. Doug helped her move the seat forward and she adjusted the rear-view mirror. Sondra brought the V-6 motor to life and noisily released the parking brake, just as she'd watched and heard her mom and dad do so many cherished times in her young life. She stomped down on the clutch, shifting into reverse then gunned the engine, turning her head to look in all directions. When traffic was clear she spun the rear tires, producing a small cloud of dust and dried grass. The truck backed up spinning quickly into the corridor leading out of the parking lot but the stop that followed was precise. Doug was impressed yet shot Sondra a sideways glance of disapproval. She shrugged her shoulders and flashed a devilish grin. "All right little Miss A.J. Foyte," he scolded, trying not to smile. "Lets just get home without being such a damn showoff."

After dinner at the Italian restaurant, where Sondra finally felt included as a family member, Tracy and Jennifer insisted on riding back to the house with Doug and their mother. This gave Sondra a sudden jolt of anxiety as it meant being forced to ride home with Pete and Josh. She'd ridden with Pete twice before and found him to be a lousy reckless driver. She chose the seat behind Pete and tightened her seat belt carefully, soon noticing that they were making a detour as he pulled the dual cab rusted white Chevy pickup onto streets that she didn't recognize. He parked in front of a rundown two-bedroom home, where one of his friends was having a noisy party. "Come on in for a minute" he insisted. Sondra followed them inside but stayed less than seven minutes. She slipped back out the front door unnoticed. On the long walk back to the evil house she began angrily muttering to herself and kicking at the ground every once in a while. There came overwhelming feelings of resentment for her now-hard life and having been dragged to this hillbilly hellhole.

Sunday morning just couldn't come quick enough for Sondra. She was up before daylight and Doug was soon ready to roll as well. They stopped at a McDonald's for an Egg McMuffin halfway to the race track, both so excited they could hardly eat. The air was cool and still and the sun was just rising as Sondra, again at the wheel, eased the pickup onto the highway, swift and smooth in fourth gear. An hour later they entered the long, roughly paved entrance to Tumbleweed Speedway, a multipurpose facility on 150 acres. Most of it was for various dirt and all-terrain vehicles for people to enjoy as they pleased. There was a motocross track and a quarter-mile dirt oval, where Doug and Sondra had watched the many midget sprint exhibition and qualifying races the day prior. The main event was on the one-mile dirt oval track, where they'd watched the larger sprint-car race that had excited Sondra to no end.

During the day they watched two midget races and one sprint car event, then came a 40-minute lunch break. Doug grabbed Sondra's hand and started off to where, the day before, he'd made a mental note of a spot that might make a perfect place for an afternoon meal. It was off the beaten-path, under one of a scarce number of trees in the area, and overlooked the motocross course. Sondra was just about to suggest they go back so she could buy lunch from one of the concession booths but Doug stealthily produced a sub sandwich along with two small bottles of water and a bag of potato chips. Sondra let out a slight squeal as he handed his little race buddy her half of the sub.

There were a number of riders practicing on the motocross track. The bursts from the relatively small engines wafted up the hill to them and Sondra thought this to be better than any kind of music at this moment in time. "Want a cookie?" asked Doug after they'd polished off their subs. Sondra wiped her mouth with the back of her hand and crumpled the empty sandwich wrapper into a ball, handing it to Doug. "Sure" she cheered. Doug placed the wrapper along with his in a plastic bag meant for trash, but instead of the promised cookie he handed her the present he'd been dying to give her. Her eyes became wide as she looked at what Doug had put into her hands. She unfolded the handkerchief and spotted the sunglasses. "Wow" she exclaimed, her smile making the sun seem dim. She immediately put on the eye wear and took better note of the monogrammed handkerchief embroidered in golden thread. Holding it to her chest with both hands she fell into Doug's shoulder. The white cloth item had her first and last name embroidered in yellow on the top-left corner and underneath was a rendition of a Formula One race car. Doug could tell the girl was moved by this and was hit by a sudden realization that, even though he'd only known Sondra a short time, this truly felt the closest thing to having a real daughter. He loved Brenda's kids and knew they loved him but there was always a kind of disconnect. They used him and were constantly testing him. It was as if he always had to work hard to be in their good graces. Sondra on the other hand was a guarded, tough, angry kid but once trust had been established it was never questioned. The trust and respect had grown with each day and the connection deepened.

"You're an amazing human being, Sondra," Doug told her. "The world is what you make it. It may have shown you some awful cruelty but the strength of who you are at the core is what counts."

"Thanks for all this," she said, her voice brimming with emotion. She deftly wiped away tears with her fingers from under the sunglasses as Doug put his arm around her. Sondra briefly closed her eyes and took a deep breath, remembering how it felt to have her father's arm around her.

After the main sprint-car Sunday event, Doug slipped their program into Sondra's backpack and suggested they spend some time in the pits. The drivers and crew members of each race participant couldn't have been nicer and more welcoming to their fans. One car owner even helped Sondra into the midget car that had placed eighth. Doug soon caught on to the generosity and kind behavior the teams and drivers were showing them. It was Sondra. He was used to thinking of her as this tiny little frightened creature he'd first encountered curled up under the dash of his Studebaker, and then an often angry tomboy. She now had a strength and radiance that far exceeded these images. He leaned against a metal light post and looked on as the #36 car owner and driver, Mike Jones, attentively showed Sondra the inner workings of his race car, having her sit in the driver's seat. As he helped her out of the vehicle, Doug suddenly saw Sondra in a completely different light. She was a cute kid. Smart, funny and full of youthful exuberance. Sondra had snapped her cap to one of the belt loops on her jeans. Her long dark hair glistened in the late afternoon sun, blowing softly around her neck and back in the light breeze. She also kept alternating her new beloved sunglasses from the top of her head to their proper position.

Towards the end of pit-row a man and a woman were presiding over the Snap-on tool booth under a large white temporary canopy. Sondra was more interested in the booth that came just before it, selling race gear from three large cardboard boxes. Doug however became instantly mesmerized by the striking Snap-on business woman, dressed sharply in a dark blue pantsuit with the company's name and logo silk-screened prominently. He studied her for a few minutes as she interacted with browsing fans and customers. Sondra had spotted some racing gloves that might fit her and came back to pull on his hand. He glanced back at the Snap-on goddess as Sondra guided him toward her found treasure. After insisting on purchasing the gloves for Sondra, Doug enjoyed her squealing delight and the heartfelt hug she gave him. The girl was indeed ecstatic, guessing that by this action Doug intended to support her quest to race. She pulled away still smiling, examining the gloves, struck with a happy memory flashback of her 13th birthday of that glorious day with her dad and the slot car racing set. "Gloves down, the rest to go," she told Doug, trying to suppress major emotion. He took one of the driving implements from her and gently swatted her left cheek.

"Miss Sierre, I challenge you to a duel," he said in a very bad French accent imitation. "Shall it be pistols at dawn?" She giggled and watched him begin to walk away, then ran after him and swatted his arm with the glove's mate.

"Monsieur, I accept your challenge, but I prefer rifles at noon." He briefly put his arm around her shoulder and handed her back the other glove. Sondra took hold of them in her left hand and looked up at him, bringing her sunglasses toward the tip of her nose with her right index finger.

"Nutty girl," he laughed.

Doug guided them to the Snap-on booth, and after looking over and discussing a number of items Sondra shifted her focus a few feet away. "Well it looks to me that you two are having the most fun here today" said the Snap-on representative Doug had been coyly watching the past number of minutes. He glanced over at Sondra but was far more interested in the woman before him than any dazzling display of shiny tools or accessories.

"I have a set of these" he said with a smile, picking up an open-end wrench.

"All solid American-made, high-quality tools" said the saleswoman with a smile. "Your daughter's adorable," she added, more interested in the man and the girl than a discussion on the product for sale.

"Thanks," smiled Doug, not sure whether or not to get into the fact that Sondra was not his biological daughter. He didn't. "She got all A's at school so this was basically a reward," he told her.

"Aw, sweet," said the woman, looking closely to see if there was a wedding band on the handsome man's finger. There wasn't.

"I'm Doug," he smiled, extending his hand. "I have a towing service and quite a few of my tools are Snap-on."

"I'm Karen" said the woman, enjoying his grip. "So your daughter's mom couldn't make it today?" she asked, hoping to extract information.

Doug shook his head. "I'm her foster dad," he explained. "Her parents were killed in an accident several years ago."

"Oh how sad," said Karen. "And is there a foster mom?" she asked.

"Well, kind of. Things are over and changing. It's complicated," he said, looking over at Sondra and a small group of men being given a sales pitch by Karen's business partner for the day. Doug smiled and changed the subject. "Well if you're out and about at other sprint-car events maybe we'll see you again" he said in hopes.

Karen smiled and nodded. "If you need a line on more tools for your towing service, let me know," she said, handing him one of her business cards.

Sondra came hurrying over with some paperwork in her hand. "That guy told me that Snap-on has really good driver sponsorship program," she told him, tugging on his hand to continue their exploration of other concession tents. "We do," said Karen, calling after them and feeling a bit cheated. Doug felt this way as well. He waved goodbye at the classic beauty and his eyes remained a few more seconds on the woman as she began to assist other fans and potential customers.

Doug would have let Sondra drive home but as they got to the dust covered vehicle she grabbed the tailgate and let out a tired sigh. He helped her into the truck's cab and fastened the seat belt for her as she shut her eyes and yawned. They drove about 30 minutes in silence, each recalling in their minds all the sights and sounds of the day and feeling the effects of being in the sun for a prolonged period of time. Doug eventually pulled off the highway and entered a fast-food drive-through. He ordered a large coffee and tapped the sleepy Sondra on her shoulder with the back of his hand to inquire if she wanted anything.

"Small coffee, cream and four sugars" she answered, deftly handing him a five dollar bill. He hesitated in taking it but he could see how important it was for her to buy him the coffee. They sipped their steaming beverages as the miles rolled on and soon began to get back their energy. There was talk of driving technique, about engine and chassis design, and Doug recounted exciting tales of races he'd seen in person and on TV. He made Sondra feel so comfortable and at ease that she broached the subject of actually obtaining a race car and beginning a racing career. They discussed it in a practical manner as well as enthusiastically, and both agreed it was in fact doable. There was a long stretch of highway with no cars around and Doug took a second to glance over at his passenger. "I want you to finish school, Sondra," he told her. "It's important, okay?" Sondra agreed and divulged her secret, that she'd been studying for her GED and was planning on taking the high school equivalency test just after school started in September. He nodded, not too surprised.

"What about college?" he inquired.

"Well," she pondered out loud. "Junior college classes are most likely just as easy as what I'm doing now and I'm sure I can afford the time and money to get at least my AA degree. You think I can do both school and racing, don't you?"

"Yeah, kiddo," he nodded. "I'm convinced you can do pretty much anything, and do it a thousand times better than most. You keep your end up in the education department and I'll do whatever I can to help you get a start in racing. Let's talk to Bobby about a car. We're having dinner with him and his wife Diane and they want you to stay there tonight. That sound okay with you?"

The girl's vigorous nodding was all the answer Doug needed. Sondra was in fact elated beyond belief at this development, especially since they weren't ending such a perfect day by going straight to the evil house.

Sondra liked Bobby's wife, Diane, from the first moment. She had kind eyes and neatly styled short graying hair. "Oh it's so good to have you two here and your timing couldn't be more perfect," Diane told her expected visitors. "Come on in and head on out to the back patio. Bobby's getting the barbecue ready for the steaks."

This was the happiest dinner Sondra had experienced in quite some time, a real family dinner with nice polite conversation. The day before, at the restaurant with her foster family, was the only time they'd all eaten together. Sondra had seen Brenda and her kids snack at home and suspected they ate their meals at fast food restaurants with the various friends they spoke of on occasion. Even on holidays, Sondra found herself eating mostly alone.

Doug and Sondra arrived back at the evil house just past 9:30 p.m. and found the front door wide open. They soon found the kitchen glass sliding door leading onto the back patio to be in the same state as well. None of Brenda's kids were home but Brenda and several of her grocery store coworkers were seated outside on white plastic chairs, drinking beer and smoking cigarettes. Sondra was repulsed by the scene and went straight to the girls' bedroom where she unfolded her sleeping bag out onto her bed's mattress. She'd purchased the bag through a mail-order catalog that had come to the auto-shop. Sondra had never been a germaphobe, but Tracy, Jennifer and their friends came to carelessly use Sondra's bed as a makeshift couch. Beverages got spilled on a regular basis and dirty clothes and other objects found their way on top of her bed as well during frequent impromptu small parties. Just being in that constantly unkempt room was hard enough for Sondra but the first time she'd discovered evidence of her bed being used as party furniture was an anxiety-inducing gross nightmare for her. She had no intention of sleeping in filth and the sleeping bag, which could be rolled up and put away, seemed the best solution.

Sondra brushed her teeth and got ready for bed, listening to the spiking party sounds in the backyard. As she crawled inside her down-filled bag she could hear Doug and Brenda arguing in the hallway, and soon there was the unmistakable sound of the diesel engine of Doug's tow-truck as it came to life, then faded into the relative silence of the night as it rolled away. Sondra felt instantly sick to her stomach, as if she'd been kicked or punched. There also came that all-too familiar panicky feeling of being left behind, which was always lurking under the surface. Bitterness and sadness seemed to almost suffocate her and she cried herself to eventual slumber.

Doug had been disappointed but not surprised to find Brenda and a party atmosphere when he'd arrived home with Sondra that night. He politely greeted the house guests and tried not to make a scene when he spoke with Brenda alone, but her inebriated speech and behavior began to infuriate him and he let her know his displeasure on no uncertain terms. When she tried to argue and get him to come join the party, he informed her that he would be spending the night at Bobby and Diane's. He felt guilty about leaving Sondra there at the house, but the great day he'd had with her along with its unfortunate end had convinced him to double his efforts to get away from Brenda and file for sole custody of Sondra. The next day, while Sondra was at school, Doug went back to the house just after 12 p.m. when he figured Brenda would be awake and sober.

"This isn't working," he told her. "It really hasn't been working for a while now. We keep having the same conversation and it gets us nowhere. You and I need to move on."

Brenda gave him her patented hurt and please-don't-leave-me face but this time it had no effect on him. In fact this fueled his conviction that he needed to have this hard conversation. "I care a hell of a lot about you and the kids and have no intention of leaving you high and dry," he told her. "I'll be staying with Bobby and Diane for a few days, then getting an apartment."

At first Brenda's tears were genuine, but she was a master manipulator and Doug knew it. Her whining, pleading and sobbing this time didn't have quite the effect on him that it had previously and he had no intention of getting sucked back into this messy routine. He stood, kissed the top of her head and walked out the door. He knew Brenda would pull all sorts of shenanigans but was prepared and ready to move on with his life. The biggest concern for him however was Sondra.

Sondra was a bit cold to Doug when he met her at school after her last class. She bitterly resented him for leaving her at the evil house the night before and hated the thought that he might leave permanently. She hesitated in getting into the passenger seat of his Tacoma but relaxed just a little when Doug turned on the radio and drove without speaking for a number of minutes. He entered a Taco Bell drive-through, and a short time later they ate their meal seated side by side at a wooden picnic table in a small nearby park. Doug listened and watched out of the corner of his eye as Sondra crunched down on the end of a taco, then chewed in anger.

"The last thing I ever want to do is bring more pain and uncertainty to your life," he told her. "Life is messy sometimes, even in the best of circumstances." He thought he could actually feel anger welling up in the girl. "Things have ended with me and Brenda," he continued.

"Brenda and me," said Sondra correcting his grammar, growling through clenched teeth. She wiped her mouth with the cuff of her sweatshirt sleeve and gave him a fierce look. "I guess this little exercise in futility is finally done," she said, making a fist on the rough wooden surface. "So much for another damn foster so-called family," she added bitterly. She then threw the taco on the table and stood. "I'm not going back to CPS," she growled. "I'm done with this crap. I filed for emancipation and I don't need any of you idiots."

Before Sondra could get away Doug touched her arm and she halted, looking back at him with explosive demanding eyes. "Sondra," he said in a strong but soft voice. She bit down on her tongue and stared at him, daring him to continue. Doug gestured for her to sit back down but knew it was a long-shot. "In the grand scheme of things," he began, "you and I haven't really known each other all that long but you're smart and intuitive. You know me well enough. I promised you I'd make things better and I'm a man of my word, and you know that. Just because a few things are changing doesn't mean that everything's going to a bad place. I'm on your side, kiddo. Always." Sondra wanted to run away but stood frozen.

"You're not gonna make me eat all these tacos by myself, are you?" Doug prompted with a hint of a smile. She sat back down and folded her elbows on the table as he patted her back. "I'm always gonna be here for you," he reassured her. "The emancipation thing is a lot more complicated than you may think, but if that gets you to a better place I'm all for it. I talked to John Farnsal several times about this and I'm working on legal issues."

The taco meal and talk with Doug seemed to eventually relieve a considerable amount of anger and anxiety for Sondra, especially when Doug informed her of his temporary living situation with Bobby and Diane. He noted a definite change in her attitude when he spoke of looking at several apartments, one in particular that he might soon rent. Sondra returned to a bitter demeanor however when Doug dropped her back off at the evil house, trying to again reassure her that this was temporary and that she needed to make the best of it. She entered the house through the garage/kitchen door and found Brenda sitting on the sofa in the living room drinking cheap Chardonnay and crying, a cigarette smoldering in an ashtray on the coffee table. Sondra sat softly at the opposite end. "I s'pose you know about me'n Doug?" said Brenda. Sondra resisted the temptation to correct her grammar. She wondered why so many people were so sloppy and careless in this area. Her mother had been a stickler for proper grammar and pronunciation.

"I'm sorry" said Sondra. "That must be awful to have a relationship end." The woman sniffed loudly and looked at the girl.

"Well you're just a kid now but you'll find out soon enough," said Brenda. Sondra thought this was a horrible thing to say but she held her silence.

"S'pose you're goin' with him, huh?" wondered Brenda.

"Nothing's been decided one way or the other," said Sondra. "But you know I wasn't really supposed to be here in the first place." The front door swung open and in walked Tracy and her friend Jill. Sondra made a quiet exit to the bedroom to do her homework.

Sondra made a determined effort to maintain a low profile at school, trying to cease being goaded into arguments or fights. She studied for the GED, planning on taking it as soon as possible. At work Sondra streamlined the auto-shop office to be far more efficient and embarked on a vigorous physical fitness routine, which included riding the Suzuki. On a slow Wednesday afternoon, 3:56 p.m., Sondra was at her desk in the B.A.S.S. office studying for a history test when a woman in a white and blue flowery dental-assistant uniform top and bright white pants entered the room.

"Hi" greeted the woman. "I'm Sara Wilken. I'm sorry I'm so early but I have an appointment at five-thirty and I was hoping maybe someone could get to it sooner rather than later."

Sondra glanced down at the schedule and nodded. "You're the white Volkswagen Jetta, in for an oil and filter change. Let me find Jim and see what we can do."

As Sondra walked through the garage looking for the shop's lead mechanic, she recognized a young woman talking on a cell phone and standing near the front entrance. Kari Wilken, a popular figure at school, was an attractive blond with a rather dubious reputation. She was known in particular circles as Wild Kari. The high school junior had a penchant for getting into all sorts of trouble, though nothing serious. She smoked, she drank and she snuck into bars and

R-rated films. Kari wore provocative clothing, was quite popular with the boys and ran with other tough-girls and burnouts known for their occasional bullying ways. Sondra had heard many tales of Kari's exploits but had so far never interacted with her. She'd once or twice wondered why their particular clique didn't include her foster sister Tracy and her friends.

"Heard you worked here," said Kari, ending her call and walking toward Sondra.

"It's a job," shrugged Sondra. "Got a problem with that?"

Kari coughed a quick laugh, not expecting a sharp comeback. "Just askin'" she told Sondra. "No need to go all ghetto on me."

Sondra narrowed her eyes and shrugged her right shoulder before continuing her search for Jim. She found him under a hoist, grease gun in hand, working on a black Chevy Blazer. "Hey, Jim" Sondra called out. "Can you let Mrs. Wilken's oil and filter change skip to the front of the line? Blazer's not really due 'til tomorrow mid-morning anyway."

Jim looked over at her, annoyed and wiping his hands on a grease-streaked red shop rag. "Right" he said with a reluctant nod. "You bring in the other lift and bring me the filter and oil."

"On the lift, Jim" corrected Sondra with a laugh. "You put the car on the other lift," she explained. Jim had lived in California for six years, moving his family from a town just outside of Mexico City. His English was improving but still left much to be desired.

As the mechanical work was under way Sondra offered Mrs. Wilken and Kari each a seat in the office, along with a beverage. Sara poured herself a cup of coffee and Sondra brought Kari a Coke from the vending machine just outside the office.

"Heard you kicked Laurel Brenaman's ass," said Kari to Sondra. Sara scolded her daughter for her language and Sondra shrugged.

"She pushed me off the sidewalk and into the mud," Sondra said bitterly through gritted teeth. "So I pushed her into a bush. Not really an ass kicking but she got the message."

"Can't you girls ever play nice at that school?" asked Sara. She'd heard many tales of Sondra's high school troubles since coming to town. Sara had gone to that very high school years ago and had been in the same class as Brenda. They weren't friends but knew one another, and when Doug appeared on the scene he'd befriended her and her daughters, coming to their automotive and home-repair rescue on more than one occasion.

Kari chewed her gum loudly as she eyed the Sierre girl, expecting some kind of angry response from her mother's question. She was disappointed when none materialized. "There are magazines on that table there" Sondra told the customers. "I'll go check with Jim on the progress and be back." While Jim completed his tasks, Sondra joined in the car care, cleaning the front windshield, the side windows, the mirrors and polishing the tires with Armor-All. She then returned to her desk and prepared the bill.

"Car's ready, Mrs. Wilken."

"Thank you, Sondra," said the woman. "So you and Kari know each other from school?" she asked, trying to extract more information than her daughter had been willing to divulge.

"Not really," said Sondra with a shrug of her right shoulder.

"Oh that's too bad," said Sara. "I've known Brenda for years. My girls used to play with Brenda's kids when they were little."

Sondra looked over at Kari, instantly hating her for being associated with her so-called foster siblings. "Yeah" acknowledged Sondra, trying not to sound angry. "Bobby told me. Sorry you missed him today. So everything looks good here," she added, deliberately directing the conversation to the matters at hand. "Your wiper fluid was a little low so we topped that off, no charge." When the transaction was complete, Sondra walked them out to their waiting vehicle. "See ya 'round, tough girl" said Kari. Sondra gave a partial wave and watched Kari ease onto the front passenger seat, marveling that she'd never before been referred to as tough. She smiled to herself as she walked back to her office, pleased with the tough-girl moniker.

On a hot humid afternoon Sondra walked from school to the B.A.S.S. garage feeling pretty good about herself. She'd managed to do well on a math quiz, a history test and had made it through the entire day with no altercations or ugly interactions with any of her fellow students. Entering the garage, she spotted Doug and Bobby looking in the engine compartment of a forest-green Range Rover. Doug had been working out of town for the last two days and she forgot herself completely, dropping her backpack and running to him, wrapping her arms around the man tightly. "Hey there, kiddo," laughed Doug. Sondra let go and stepped a few feet away, feeling embarrassed for her emotional outburst. He gestured with his head toward the back rollup door. "Got somethin' that might interest you," he told her.

Several weeks prior during the steak dinner at Bobby and Diane's, Doug had talked to Bobby about Sondra's quest to race while Diane and Sondra chatted in the kitchen. The two men had discussed finding a sprint car for Sondra and helping her get into racing.

Sondra stood speechless, gazing at what was on top of the trailer behind Doug's Toyota Tacoma. She hurried toward it and soon Doug scooped her up and set her onto the borrowed trailer's bed, then jumped up beside her. Sondra's mouth dropped open and her eyes darted all around. When she didn't speak or move, Doug again picked her up and set her in the seat of her new used sprint-car. This was a 900-pound midget racer that utilized a 4-cylinder, 400-horsepower engine at the rear and featured steel-tube construction with small aluminum front and side panels. This type of USAC-sanctioned vehicle was generally known as a starter-level racer, as opposed to the professional 900 horsepower winged sprint-cars. As soon as Sondra's hands grabbed the wheel she came alive, squealing and wriggling all around, with a smile that strained the muscles in her face. Doug came around to the other side and Bobby jumped up on the trailer where Doug had been. "Needs some work," said Doug. "But you're keeping up your end of the bargain with the good grades and at least trying to maintain a good attitude. We'll get 'er fixed up and go racing."

"Where'd you find the thing?" asked Bobby. "Back of a car dealership in Fresno," said Doug. "Big, long story. Tell you over dinner tonight."

During the evening meal with Diane and Bobby, Doug revealed the details of the race vehicle he'd acquired. "I took a crashed Honda

Civic to a dealership in Fresno. Got to talking with the owner, Dan Stoltz. He liked my tow rig and offered me a job, working exclusively for the dealership and their customers. Good benefits, a retirement package and far more stable income than I have now. And get this. The guy owns an interest in a quarter-mile dirt track. It's a lot closer from here than Tumbleweed and they have races going on almost every weekend."

"Wow!" marveled Sondra.

"Wow indeed," chuckled Doug. "Turns out ol' Dan Stoltz has plans to own a pro sprint-car team in the future. Maybe a year or two."

The dealership owner had been unreceptive to Doug's idea of perhaps utilizing Sondra as the driver for his team but Doug kept this little tidbit to himself. "Anyway," he continued, "he's had this old chassis and motor sitting around in one of his warehouses and gave me a really good deal on it."

Sondra carefully completed the purchase of a race suit and pro-level gear, not just the minimum requirements for the series she was about to enter. Bobby and Jim encouraged her to learn as much as she could about rebuilding and maintaining cars and she began to spend several hours each day working alongside them. They showed her basic auto electronics and she picked up on many aspects of proper set-ups for transmissions and suspensions. As parts trickled in for her sprint-car she spent many late nights by herself on her knees, figuring out how to set things up for as much speed and strength necessary to win races. She was determined. To her this was no garage toy. The more time she spent with it the more it became like a living breathing being, with a voice and a soul.

Though Sondra had forged several relationships with her foster family, there was always a bit of a feeling of dread anytime she would enter the evil house after being at school or work. On this particular Wednesday, she stepped into the living room and couldn't help but notice Pete and a girlfriend engaged in playful wrestling on the couch. They stopped immediately, Pete looking annoyed.

"Hey Pete," greeted Sondra. "Your mom around?"

"She's out. What do you want?" Pete demanded in a close-to-angry voice.

"Just to say hi and to get my mail and messages" answered Sondra. She slipped quickly into the kitchen to see if any written messages were for her in the box near the phone. There were none so she returned to the living room and opened the desk drawer that Brenda had on numerous occasions retrieved mail for her.

"What the hell do ya think you're doing?" yelled Pete. "That's my mom's personal business."

Sondra's eyes and hands went through the papers with lightening speed, and just as Pete was getting off the couch and coming toward her she spun around holding up a long white envelope. "This is mine," she growled. "It's addressed to me." She was white-hot angry but tried to speak in as calm a voice as possible. "Please tell your mother to give me my mail as soon as she gets it."

She flashed around Pete and slammed the front door behind her, running as fast as she could back to the shop. With shaking hands, Sondra unlocked the side door to the B.A.S.S. garage. As it slammed and locked behind her, she was thankful that Jim was gone and the shop was closed for the day. She went to her office, shutting and locking the door, then tossed the letter on the desk and sat down hard in her chair.

Sondra closed her eyes and focused on her breathing, but when her attention went back to the letter moments later, she became anything but calm. The envelope had previously been opened. There was evidence that an attempt had been made to hide this fact but the seal had definitely been compromised. She pulled out five neatly folded pages and began reading. The top sheet was from John Farnsal, dated just under a month prior, and when she came to the last word on the last page she slammed her right fist hard onto the desk. She wasn't angry or upset at John but was infuriated with Brenda for keeping this from her. Along with his heartfelt personal letter to Sondra was a document stating that Sondra J Sierre was being granted a hearing for her emancipated minor status. There were two other important documents included as well. These were estate planning statements, with financial disclosures. "Damn that bitch" Sondra growled under her breath about Brenda. She got up and went out into the shop, walking around, trying to regain her composure. Staring at the label on a box containing oil filters, her rage suddenly consumed her. She was bursting with a thousand emotions and hurried over to the Suzuki and pushed the bike through the side door. Seconds later she was speeding down the alley in a cloud of smoke, dust and angry noise, arriving at the dunes where she'd ridden many times before, raw emotion pushing her and the motorcycle to absolute limits. Almost forty feet in the air, she took the bike out of gear and breathed out slowly. The landing was hard but stable and she rode slowly back to the garage, scolding herself for going out like that without her helmet.

Cleaning up the dirt-going motorcycle was therapy, especially when she checked to make sure the fluid levels were at the right places. She dropped some change in the soda machine and picked out a Pepsi. Long hard angry swallows resulted in some of the sugary liquid dribbling down her chin but she didn't care. Sondra swatted at the largest of the droplets just below her chin and went back to the desk, composing a letter to John and Leanna in which she described in detail her current life and that she missed them terribly. Sondra then returned to the house and stealthily retrieved her belongings. On her way back to the garage she went into Dusty's Market and purchased a pack of gum, a small bottle of cranberry juice and a package of mini chocolate donuts. She recognized the clerk as being a boy from school and he looked down at her items with what Sondra thought to be an expression of questioning disapproval. She put her folded elbows onto the counter and stared back at him, daring him to say a word about her choices. Back in the safety of the garage, she ran her hand over the handlebars of the Suzuki then walked over to her sprint-car, kissing the metal tubing of the roll-cage. She went to her office tossing the bag of purchased items onto her desk, no longer feeling at all hungry. Sondra sat down on the office couch, painful tears finding her, feeling that she'd been kicked in the stomach. "I miss you, Mommy and Daddy," she said in convulsing sobs. "Dave and Haley," she cried out, slamming her right fist against the back of the sofa. "Why did you guys all leave me here?" she screamed.

"Why?" Sondra cried in hysterics for several minutes, thrashing at the couch cushions with her fists. An hour and fifty-two minutes later she was in a curled and twisted position, deep in weary slumber. She woke with a start from a loud sound of an air compressor's electric motor kicking on then reluctantly went home, feeling sorry for herself that no-one even noticed her late arrival.

CHAPTER 7

Doug's new job kept him busy. Sondra noticed his absence but pushed to her subconscious just how much she missed him when he wasn't around. She began working later and later in the garage and contrived an idea of bringing her sleeping bag and camping out in the office at night. Sleeping in the garage office instead of the evil house seemed like the best idea and she was glad that no one openly questioned her or put a stop to the practice. Sondra only went to the house when she was sure Brenda would not be there to perhaps scold her and put an end to her new sleeping arrangement. Her last home visit had not been so lucky. Brenda's car was nowhere to be seen when Sondra had approached the property, but the woman emerged from the bedroom while Sondra was collecting her mail. Brenda started an odd unprompted dialog. "If you'd dress more like a girl and wore a little make-up once in a while, you might get your own boyfriend and stop hanging around with mine." Sondra thought this a weird statement but wasn't about to argue the fact that Doug was no longer Brenda's boyfriend. Brenda's words and meaning didn't fully sink in until hours later when Sondra was enacting her usual nighttime routine of making sure all the B.A.S.S. doors were locked and the alarm set. As she was getting ready for bed it hit her. Eww, that's sick she thought of Brenda's earlier words. The very idea of her being even remotely interested in that way to anyone, let alone Doug, was beyond comprehension.

During hectic days at the garage Sondra would run to the little corner market and pick up a prepackaged sandwich and eat quickly. In the weeks that followed her first days of working at B.A.S.S. she'd gone through all of the other sandwich choices and then always picked chicken-salad. It read "Chicken Salad" on the label but in a blind taste test you'd really have to go to great lengths to tell whether it was chicken or fish. On a pleasantly warm afternoon, Doug stuck his head into the B.A.S.S. office. "That looks disgusting," claimed Doug of Sondra's meal choice as he entered the room. "It is" said Sondra, raising the unopened plastic packaging. "Gets the job done though. Want the other half?" Doug sat down on the only part of the desk that didn't have inches or mountains of paper work on it. "You tryin' to poison me and take the family fortune?" he joked. Sondra leaned back in her chair, smirking. "Yeah," she said in a drawn-out voice. "I'm diabolical that way." She then leaned forward and changed the subject. "Bobby says he's happy with the sprint car engine rebuild. I'm glad he and Jim let me help, and I learned a ton, too. He said we might start it up today. I'm so glad you're here." Her eyes sparkled as she stood. "Yeah," said Doug. "Bobby called me last night. I wouldn't miss this for the world, kiddo." She grabbed hold of his shirt sleeve and dragged him to the refurbished sprint-car with the newly installed engine.

Bobby, Jim and Doug stood and watched as Sondra took a few seconds to get comfortable, making sure everything appeared to be in perfect condition. With deliberate motions she pushed down on the clutch with her left foot and pushed up with her right index finger on the ignition toggle-switch. The four-cylinder engine popped to life and she gunned it five times then mashed down steadily on the accelerator until getting the needle on the tachometer gauge to stay where she wanted it. After almost a full minute she let the engine come back to idle, her concentration turning deadly serious. When Sondra and the car didn't move, Bobby shot a bewildered and concerned look to Doug, who shook his head slowly, reassuring his friend that all was right and normal. Doug knew exactly what Sondra was doing. She was listening and studying the hundreds of moving engine parts. She needed to know what was right and normal so she could have total confidence in pushing all that spinning and moving metal to its extremes. He got chills when he noticed the absolute fierce concentration in her eyes. Sondra gunned the engine a few more times, and in another exaggerated motion put the car in gear and sputtered slowly toward the open back door and out into the alley. The engine screamed to life, catching the men off guard, and the rear tires spun on the compacted dirt roadway for a few seconds, sending a rooster-tail of dust and small rocks eight feet into the air. She then blasted away, doing exactly what she'd done with the dirt bike months ago. Every second she was in motion her brain recorded the sounds, feel and visual of what she and the car were experiencing. Sondra knew there was only time enough to make three all-out runs before neighbors would complain and used her time to the fullest. When satisfied with the results of her first test-hop, she cut the motor and rolled majestically into the shop. Before she had time to jump out, Doug leaned over and patted the top of her head firmly as Bobby looked over the engine, making sure there were no oil leaks or overly heated parts. "I'm gonna win this weekend," announced Sondra. "I have solid equipment and I want this more than anyone else." Doug enjoyed her confidence but Bobby coughed a laugh and threw a grease-stained rag at her. Sondra narrowed her eyes as she looked up at the man. She had been deadly serious and her intense stare drilled into him. "Okay" said Bobby, nodding his head. "No jokes. We're behind you a thousand percent." Sondra flashed her boss a smile, climbed out and picked up the rag to throw back at him. "I'll give you a thousand percent right here," she taunted, shaking her fist. Bobby snatched up a more oily rag and started toward her as she ran squealing. "Damn kids," announced Doug with a smile and a shake of his head.

Doug took Sondra to an early dinner across town. "So I have some pretty important stuff to talk with you about," he told the girl as they were perusing their menus.

"Me, too," she said, slightly annoyed at his incorrect sentence structure. "I'm ready for our first race weekend. I know this sounds insane but I'm not doing this just for fun and games. If the motor's strong and nothing breaks, I'm going for the win. I don't know how to explain it exactly but this is me. Even with just a few minutes in the alley, I ..." Sondra swallowed hard and made a fist before continuing. "This is what I'm supposed to be doing." On the surface, Doug thought this sounded like a silly teenager saying silly things but there was something about Sondra that defied conventional wisdom. "I have every confidence in you, kiddo," he told the girl. "But here's the thing. You filed for emancipation and it's touched off a hell of a firestorm with Brenda, Judith Tredou, CPS, and some others. I know you're not gonna want to hear this, and I'm sorry, but I need you to stop sleeping in the garage office until the deal is done. After that, Bobby and Diane have friends who have an apartment over their garage you can rent until other arrangements are in place."

Sondra didn't like the idea of having to go back to the evil house, even if it was just temporary, and wondered about the other arrangements he'd mentioned. Watching Sondra clench her fists and make a face prompted Doug to say more. "I'm workin' on a lot of things with you in mind," he told her. "John Farnsal's been a big help and he put me on to a shark of a custody lawyer."

"That has to be costing you a fortune you don't have," guessed Sondra out loud. Doug shook his head. "Don't you worry about any of the details. I got this covered, and like I've told you before, you're not falling through the cracks. Not on my watch. You deserve a good home and the best possible life. I got a line on a condo in Fresno that's not too far from Fresno State. With your good grades I'm sure you'll be able to get in there when the time comes. The condo's in a nice safe well-maintained area. The units all have really small back patios but the one I looked at has a nice big kitchen and there's a separate dining area, with two bedrooms. One of 'em's gonna be yours." Sondra's eyes went from her menu to Doug's, but before she could respond their waiter came to the table. Doug ordered the red snapper meal and Sondra chose a pasta dish with shrimp. "So Fresno?" said Sondra, watching Doug butter a piece of bread. He nodded. "Dan Stoltz, the guy who owns the dealership and hired me. …" he began.

"The guy that's part owner of the track we're going to next weekend?" inquired Sondra.

"Yeah" said Doug. "He got me on to this real estate lady and she was a wealth of information on the area and the schools. There's a nearby gym and several grocery stores. Even a movie theater in a shopping mall not too far away."

"What if this doesn't work out?" asked Sondra. "I mean with the custody thing. You're putting a ton of effort and money into this. Into me. How do you know they're not gonna just send me back to CPS or let Brenda have custody? I mean how do you know I'm really even worth all this?"

"Stop that," ordered Doug. "Don't ever question your worth." He was about to launch into what he hoped would be a profound speech but their food arrived, breaking the moment. Sondra stabbed a sauce-covered shrimp with her fork and looked up at her dining companion. "So, um," she uttered in a questioning, pleading tone. Doug took a deep breath before speaking. "I'm gonna make this work, Sondra," he told her authoritatively. "I can't bring back your parents and brothers but I've come to love the hell out of you, kiddo, and I'll move heaven and earth for you. Now finish your lunch and stop worrying. Lets concentrate on how we're gonna prepare for next weekend."

Sondra was having what she considered a just okay day at school. On her walk to her next class she was surrounded by four older girls. "Hey, tough-girl," greeted Kari Wilken. "What class you got next?"

"Have," corrected Sondra. "What class do you have next." Kari punched Sondra on the upper arm. Not too hard but it did hurt a little. "Didn't know you were such a nerd," laughed the blond. "Yeah, well," responded Sondra, flashing the girl a rude finger gesture. "Smart is the new tough. Deal with it." The girls laughed. "She's funny," said Gina Marsh. Feeling accepted, not threatened, Sondra answered Kari's earlier question. "Science," she told the small group. "I have Mr. Vindell's science."

"Oh I had him last year," said Kari. "Now he's a nerd." Sondra had never been a judgmental person but Kari and the others were being decent to her so she agreed. “Yeah,” she told the group. “And he wears that same pocket protector and planetarium tie almost every day.” This short interaction didn’t necessarily ensure Sondra a place within the clique but for the rest of the day she rode high in the knowledge that, for the first time since coming to this school, she was accepted and welcomed as is. Later that afternoon Bobby stuck his head in the auto-shop office.

“We’re pretty slow today, Sondra. Let’s knock off a little early.”

“Kay” she responded. “I’ll finish my homework and then change the oil and filter on the Suzuki.” Before Sondra had the chance to get to the mechanical work, she had a visitor to the office. “Oh, hey, Kari,” said Sondra, surprised to see the young woman. Kari swished through the office door chewing gum and looking all around. “So my mom’s taking my sister to her Brownie meeting,” she announced. “I’m basically on my own for dinner. Wanna come with? I’m going to Grif’s Grill. You ever go there?” Sondra shook her head. She was hungry and this furthered her earlier feeling of fitting in with someone near her own age.

Grif’s Grill was popular with the local high school teens and being seen there with the popular Wild Kari would prove beneficial to Sondra. Kari Wilken was a talker, for which Sondra was grateful. She barely got a word in edgewise but when Kari asked Sondra questions about her life and family, she skillfully sidestepped the inquiries, always turning the conversation back to Kari and her life. That night at the evil house Tracy and Jennifer had somehow gotten wind of their foster sister’s extra-curricular excursion with Kari Wilken and were not nearly as cold or rude. They engaged Sondra in a little light-hearted conversation, then left her alone to read and go to bed early.

Saturday afternoon’s first foray into midget sprint-car racing for Sondra was a series of qualifying heats. Starting in the 17th position on the grid wasn’t ideal, but just before the event got underway Doug planted three heavy pats of his hand on the top of Sondra’s helmet and gave her what he hoped was sage advice. “Lotta cars and not a lotta laps. Go to school and pass people, and don’t forget to enjoy this.”

The young first-time racer ended up with an eighth place finish. For weeks Sondra had convinced herself that she would win, and win easily. Finishing her heat race in anything other than the top spot would have been a devastating blow had it not been for her team's excited reaction. They had pulled off a top-ten finish in a car they'd spent considerable time and effort putting together, and she was now awarded the opportunity to advance to the Main. Sondra may not have been willing to acknowledge her own accomplishments in her first-ever race but what she subconsciously gained in experience was far more than anyone could know or predict. She'd inadvertently found strengths and weaknesses that she would be using from that moment forward.

In car #18 Sondra immediately found holes in the traffic ahead as soon as the green flag waved on this her first-ever championship points-paying midget sprint-car race. She slotted into fifth place in the running order, catching a glimpse of Doug out of the corner of her eye. He was holding up a white board with P 5 written in grease pen. The new race driver gained confidence from this and relaxed her body, finding her way. In four laps she gained another spot and found that edge she'd been reading and hearing about her whole life. Sliding out of Turn 3, Sondra had driven hard to the outside of the car in front of her. The right-rear tire brushed the hay bales, sending a small cloud of debris into the air. With speed and momentum down the straight she trained her focus to the three cars in the lead pack. She darted down ferociously to the inside of the track, overtaking the #4 car then followed the leaders for the next two laps. A feeling of absolute power came to her, just as it had years ago on the Tahoe sled hill. She went by the second-place car like he was standing still coming out of Turn 2. The momentum from this shot her right to the outside of the lead car. They stayed two-wide for almost a half a lap until Sondra noticed that Doug was no longer holding up the pit-board. He was jumping up and down, waving excitedly. This was all she needed to propel her machine three car lengths in front of her opponent. Six laps later she took the checkered flag in first place feeling proud of the win but sad that the race was over so quickly.

Jubilation from her team in the winner's circle seemed a tad over the top for such a small dirt-track win, but to Doug, Bobby and Jim this was a triumphant beginning. It certainly warranted a little over-the-top celebration, and it was Doug who sprayed Sondra with a well-shaken bottle of 7-Up. He then handed it to her so she could enact the traditional victory spray. Sondra childishly envisioned herself a Formula One driver on the top step of the podium with an oversized bottle of champagne. One of the owners and promoters of the racetrack stood about twenty feet away and watched the exuberance with interest. The man was indeed a race enthusiast but didn't attend many events at this track and rarely gave any of the driving participants much notice. His new employee, Doug, had talked him into coming down and he couldn't help but notice something special about the small winning race team. Doug hadn't mentioned Sondra's name to the man or that she was the driver of the #18. Daniel A Stoltz was a mostly bald hefty man in his mid-fifties. He had operated a successful car dealership in Fresno for over 20 years and had purchased an interest in the small speedway several years back. The man had a stubborn sexist streak and was more than just a little surprised to see a skinny girl with long dark hair in his Winner's Circle. He wormed his way into the celebratory fun to offer his congratulations but ignored the driver, refusing to acknowledge her accomplishments or make an attempt to shake her hand. Sondra instantly detested the man as he slathered on praise and compliments to Bobby, Jim and Doug, but never to her. She went from being annoyed to fuming-mad when watching him hand Bobby a business card and suggest they obtain an older male driver for future success. Doug watched Sondra's face during all this and ushered her away and out of earshot.

"Sondra," he began. "You're gonna have to get used that kind of attitude. I'm sorry but that's just the way this business is. You can't take it so personally. He's really not such a slime-ball once you get to know him, and you're gonna have to get to know him. He's my boss and part owner of this track. Today you became a race winner and Mr. Stoltz saw that. Everyone did. He just basically gave us his stamp of approval and promised future support. We're in, kiddo, and we'll get on a regular schedule here." He smiled and grabbed Sondra by both shoulders, giving her a gentle shake. "You won, Sondra. You won," he enthused. She let Doug's words echo in her head and took a deep breath, then turned her back to him, falling backwards. Doug put his arms around her briefly, kissed the top of her winner's cap and pushed her away. "Nutty girl," he told her in a low voice. She turned to face him with a larger-than-life smile as an impeccably dressed woman in a dark blue business suit entered the fray. "Impressive, and quite fun to watch," said Karen McCormick with an extended hand. She and Sondra shook hands. "Oh, hi," said Sondra. "You're the Snap-on lady from the Tumbleweed Speedway booth."

"That's cute," laughed Karen of how the girl had remembered her. "You make me sound like a cartoon character" added Karen. "I'm actually the Regional Sales rep for Snap-on. You keep up that kind of driving and we're going to need to talk sponsorship."

Sondra beamed as Doug wrapped his left arm around his young race car driver and extended his right hand to greet the woman. "Well this is a pleasant surprise" said Doug. "From our little phone-tag exchange I thought you were more San Jose-area based."

"Oh, I cover quite a bit of territory," Karen informed Doug. "In fact, I have a meeting in Visalia tomorrow morning. Should be done by lunchtime, though." Doug tried to hide a triumphant grin. The woman was giving him quite an opening. Sondra was oblivious and began to resize her cap, but Doug proceeded. "Hmm," he voiced, pondering the possible availability of the young lady's mid-day meal schedule. "I just happen to know of a really nice place for lunch in Visalia" he informed her. "Little Greek restaurant. The family who runs it is a little loud and crazy but the food is not to be missed."

"Really," said Karen in an exaggerated tone.

"Oh yeah," enthused Doug. Karen glanced over at Sondra. In this moment the girl seemed more like four or five years old instead of a teenager and she smiled watching Sondra lean against Doug. "Well," said Karen, looking directly into the man's eyes. "I'm not one to miss out on good things," she informed him, hoping he would catch the bigger meaning. "I'll call you when I'm through with my meeting," she added.

"Looking forward to it," said Doug, maintaining his grin. "Bye, champ," said Karen to Sondra.

After a team celebration at a barbecue restaurant, Doug and Sondra went to the B.A.S.S. garage, pulling inside and unhitching the trailer. Doug thought it cute that the kid patted the race car's metal tubing as if she were saying goodbye to a dear friend. At the evil house all the lights were on and there were six cars in front. Music could be heard as Doug double-parked. He looked at his watch and shook his head. "Damn kids are having a party while Brenda's at work. Your choice," he offered. "Garage office or Bobby and Diane's living room couch."

Alone in the garage later that night, Sondra sat on the right front tire of her sprint-car, glad that she'd talked Doug into bringing it down off the trailer. She got up and walked all around her mechanical partner and kissed its nose. After crawling into her sleeping bag on top of the office couch Sondra looked up at the Mario Andretti photo hanging on the wall, childishly wondering if she was now closer to someday meeting him and perhaps being on his IndyCar team.

CHAPTER 8

Racing and dealing with running the garage office plus studying were a constant for Sondra. Saturdays and Sundays at the track she never stopped learning important lessons. During the second heat in her third Sunday race she was on old tires and the ambient air temperature was 104 degrees. Sondra had fought hard for the win in the first heat and had unknowingly abused the rear tires. The race team had stuck to a very detailed limited budget and were forced to use that same rubber for the main. Eight laps in, she spun viciously and without warning coming out of Turn 2. She'd never spun unintentionally before, and as her world was streaking by, she froze. With unbelievable luck, the car's circular journey slowed and she came to face roughly in a forward direction. It was almost as if she'd gone to sleep and woken from a dream to find that she'd automatically taken the car out of gear and was gunning the engine. Sondra instantly found her composure and control, slammed the gear shift knob forward and stabbed the throttle. Knowing her car's absolute slide characteristics was now a major advantage. She began to think further ahead, now having the car in a slide pretty much the entire way around the track, the engine close to redline, becoming just as much a mechanical part as the car itself. Sondra had lost six spots due to the spin but the leader was still in sight. Many laps later with just five to go, she power-glided handily in front of the #21 winning by mere inches. Eighteen minutes after her triumph she was handed a cell phone by a dark-haired woman in a purple jogging suit. "This is Sondra," greeted the race winner. "Dan Stoltz here, honey." Sondra cringed at being called honey but kept listening. "Hear you been tearin' it up every weekend. Keep that up and you won't have to worry about tires again. You guys are doin' all right but I think you could use some more sponsor support. I'll talk to Bobby tomorrow. You take care now, honey." Sondra hated how Mr. Stoltz always seemed to talk to her in a backhanded condescending tone but had a smile on her face as she handed back the phone to the woman and went looking for Doug, Bobby and Jim.

For Sondra, racing was a world she loved. It consumed and sustained her, and inside her sprint-car she felt in total control of her life. School however was an entirely different matter. Tracy had recently spread several new and particularly vicious rumors about Sondra. These created quite a stir and there came some ugly reactions toward her from a number of students. The first lie was that Sondra was a little geek that works and dresses like a guy, and has to sleep in a garage because she's out of control and can't be trusted to be in the house. The second rumor was that she had tried to steal Tracy and Jennifer's mom's boyfriend. Sondra did her best to shrug off all this high school pettiness because the rumors were both completely absurd, especially the latter. She also figured that most would realize this and that everything would blow over quickly. She resisted the temptation to go on an out-of-control rage when taunted by several students the first days of the rumors, even when her books were kicked out of her hands. Her breaking point came two days later. Sondra was severely scolded and warned by campus security about being where she was at that particular time of day, for eating lunch in a small park adjacent to the high school. At first she tried to reason with them but the exchange became more unpleasant by the minute. "Freak little wannabe thug cops," she told the two campus security officers, her voice low and throaty as she stormed away grumbling to herself. Her voice then became louder as soon as she figured the man and woman were out of ear shot. "I hate this damn place," she announced to no one in particular. "I hate my life." Sondra had eaten about three quarter's of a peanut butter sandwich when the campus security had come upon her. After the demand to move was executed, she'd stood and angrily threw the lunch item back in the paper bag. The campus guards had followed her for about two hundred yards until she took off running, heading straight to her locker. Before she got within 15 feet of the dull orange metal units, a group of three girls rushed over to her, taunting and lashing out with their hands. The action had caught Sondra off guard and her left foot caught on an uneven portion of concrete. She fell to the ground, crushing the rest of her lunch. As the girls disappeared after erupting into cruel laughter, Sondra lay on the cold concrete for a few seconds, the hallway now clear and silent. She got up slowly and deliberately and examined the stained sack containing the smashed uneaten sandwich and half an orange. With her right fist she pounded once on the nearest locker with all of her might, not caring about how much it hurt her hand. She then went quickly to her own locker, pulling out three books and two notepads, stuffing them into her backpack. She pulled the thin metal door a few inches from being closed then slammed it open as hard as she could. After running to the administration office, she used all her force to pull open the heavy building door, creating a loud bang and a dramatic swoosh of air. Surprise and shock came to the many who were inside but Sondra ignored them and went straight into Principal Merson's office without knocking. She slammed the door shut behind her and threw the stained brown paper lunch sack onto his desk.

Principal Stanley Merson was on the phone and froze at the sudden chaos caused by the young angry student. "Lets talk," growled Sondra through clenched teeth as she mashed down on the small plastic buttons of the desk phone system with three fingers of her left hand, cutting off his connection. She launched into a tirade without letting him immediately respond. The man sat stunned and motionless, with a blank expression as Sondra described the last very upsetting four days of school. She then demanded to be able to take the equivalency test that day. "Whew" sighed the principal, shaking his head. "I didn't catch your name, young lady." Sondra studied the man's face for a few seconds, trying to figure out if the anger thing was working for her or if she should apologize and appear to be nice and calm. "Sondra Sierre," she told him through gritted teeth, not able to curb her anger. Stanley sat back and positioned his computer's keyboard toward him. He pulled up her records while playing with his neatly trimmed, graying dark brown beard.

"Have a seat, honey," he ordered as he perused paragraphs of her unique situation.

"Don't call me honey, you son of a bitch," Sondra growled, making a fist with her right hand. "You either didn't hear me or you don't care," she furthered. "I have every right to take that test and I'll take it with or without you."

Stanley Merson was not a meek individual. He'd been class president of his high school, a leader in several college groups and a sergeant in the army in Afghanistan serving as a special ops tactical enforcement officer for two years. This was his seventh year as a high school principal and he'd seen his fair share of troubled teens. "I apologize for calling you honey" he said, intending to defuse Sondra's hard attitude. "And I'm sorry for what you've had to go through, today and in your life. Truly sorry. I'm not the one who did all these mean or bad things to you so have a little respect. Normally I'd try and dissuade a young person such as yourself from leaving high school. You're an angry girl and you seem to get into an awful lot of fights but your grades are top-notch. Do you have any plans for further education?" Sondra sat softly on one of the chairs in front of the principal's heavily used pine desk. "I apologize for calling you a son of a bitch," she began. "After I get my GED I plan on getting my AA degree," she told the man. "I always wanted to go to college but I don't know. I'll have to see how that fits into my racing career."

Stanley was curious about the girl's mention of a racing career but was short on time. "There's a fee to take the test," he informed her. "And you can take it Friday at four-thirty here on campus. I see that

Brenda Johnson and Doug Trent are your legal guardians. Your foster mother and father."

"Brenda's no mother of mine," said Sondra bitterly. "And I've petitioned the court to become an emancipated minor."

"I see," he said with a questioning look. "Well, come to my office after school on Friday. We'll go over the details of the test and get you set up to take it if you're ready. But," he warned, leaning forward and putting his elbows on the edge of his work station. "Don't come in with that attitude. You're going to have to be a much bigger person out in the real world. And take your bag off my desk."

Sondra grabbed the sack as if it were about to fly away, feeling larger than life. She walked through the double doors of the building savoring her triumph and the fresh air.

Neither Doug nor Brenda was exactly thrilled about the events of Sondra's day. Doug wasn't happy that Sondra was quick to lose her temper and had misgivings about her wanting to bypass the rest of her time in high school. He'd hoped the experiences, both good and bad, would produce meaningful and important growth within her. On the other hand he was extremely proud of her for standing up for herself. He liked and approved her plan to continue further education and respected her pursuit of making her career dreams come true. The girl had a stable and sustainable job and was taking action to better her life. Brenda, on the other hand, had quite a fit after her phone call from Principal Merson, where he explained the particulars of Sondra taking the equivalency test. Brenda then made a screaming angry phone call to Doug, accusing him of putting her up to it. She saw Sondra as an out-of-control teenager who needed strong discipline, not "coddling or special privileges." Brenda also became instantly fearful that her foster parent status and subsequent monies would soon be ending.

Daniel Stoltz and a handful of his friends came to see Sondra's last race of the season. He had successfully arranged for the small racing facility to be renamed Stoltz Alley. He, along with Doug and Sondra's small race team, took note of the girl's demeanor on this day. There was an eerie calmness in her voice and in her actions but as always a fiery volcano raged just beneath the surface. In the first heat Sondra struggled with quite a bit of understeer but, being such a quick learner, she was able to compensate for the handling issues by changing her line and driving style. With five laps to go she darted to the lead, defending and fighting off three other drivers for the checkered flag. She took this victory just 0.496 seconds ahead of the 2nd Place car, with her right fist pumping in the air. In heat #2 Sondra led from flag to flag, claiming pole position for the start of the main.

"How ya feelin', Ace?" asked Doug while Bobby and Jim concentrated on setting up the car for the final event. There was a different group of cars taking to the track for their Last Chance Qualifier race and Sondra shrugged, her eyes going from the on-track action to glancing down at Doug's shiny but slightly dusty fake alligator cowboy boots. "Okay, I guess," she said with another shrug. "Hard to think my race season's gonna be over so quick. The Snap-on lady's here," she added, not wanting to dwell on any sadness.

"You mean, Karen?" corrected Doug with a quick laugh.

Sondra flashed a smile and shrugged her right shoulder. "She waved to me earlier," she told Doug, glancing over to watch Bobby and Jim as they made last-minute adjustments, rechecking some of the components on her car. "Dan Stoltz is around somewhere, too," informed Doug, putting an arm around Sondra. "You have a really good car," he continued. "But win or lose you're the Regional champion. Seen the trophy?" Sondra nodded but held her silence. She bit down on her tongue as her brain flashed on the painful thought that her family would never be able to share in something she treasured most in life. Racing.

The 45-lap midget sprint-car race was Sondra's from the drop of the green flag. It was just no contest. Her car was powerful as was her confidence. The anger, the fear and the vulnerability she often felt from losing so much of her past normal life slipped away and in its place a magically strong sense of new-normal materialized. It was a blend of pride mixed with ego that lifts and propels one to greatness, without pushing aside the pride, ego and greatness of others. At the start of the race Sondra had launched to the middle of the track, then dove in hard to the first turn, setting herself up for a lightning pace and a line more akin to pavement tracks than short dirt ovals. In under two seconds she was five car lengths ahead of the pack. She darted to the outside on the straight to set up a classic sprint-car line, allowing the drift in the corners to be her breaks. Even with the seven caution periods for car spin-outs and entanglements she never stopped improving the distance between her and the 2nd Place car. When her #18 crossed the start/finish line with the checkered flag waving dramatically, Sondra spun the car two revolutions. The crowd-pleasing donuts sprayed a rooster-tail of dust and dirt and she waved to the fans while driving majestically along the outside line on her cooldown lap. Her dominant win and post-race victory stunt made her a very popular Sunday afternoon hero. There was a seemingly endless string of camera flashes, cheers, hugs and pats to her back and shoulders. Two tall women dressed in white bikinis with red and black checkered sashes slipped an oversized wreath over her head and pretended to kiss her cheeks for the official victory photo. Dan Stoltz and his new track manager Jeremy Cranes melodramatically presented her with a trophy that looked as if it might weigh more than she did. After a while Sondra began to think the celebration was going on way too long for something so small-town. A fellow competitor, one who'd raced her without mercy all these many weeks, hugged her tightly. Jerry Brooks whispered in her ear. "You have it, my friend. Keep doing what you're doing and I'll be watching you on TV, winning the big championships. Just don't ever forget your roots." She turned to say thanks just as he turned to give her a kiss on the cheek and their lips met. Sondra had never kissed a boy before and pulled away, shocked. He smiled, patted her shoulder and disappeared into the crowd.

Doug and Sondra drove home in his Tacoma, pulling the trailer with their winning race car. Pop-County music played on the radio and Sondra was lost in silent thought. Doug reached over and grabbed Sondra just above her left knee. It startled her and she let out an involuntary giggle. Her dad had been prone to do this and Sondra tried to think whether or not she'd ever told Doug of this. "Pretty amazing that in the last race of the season the car was so perfect," she said, desperately trying to keep precious memories of her father from clobbering her. "I mean changing right-side tire pressures made a huge difference with the understeer I'd been fighting. Oh, and that weird throttle-linkage issue went away almost immediately after the start."

Doug didn't necessarily want to talk shop. He was more concerned about the girl than the car. She'd been distant, silent and moody most of the day. "In most ways this has been exactly how I pictured racing," continued Sondra.

"Yeah?" asked Doug, intending to prompt further explanation.

Sondra shrugged. "Well I mean it's so much more intense and physical than you'd think from just watching," she said. "It's weird. From that very first race I felt alive again. I never thought I'd ever have that and now every time I'm in the car I get that back. That part of me that was taken away by that hideous drunken monster." Sondra pounded her right fist on her leg and burst into tears, hating that her emotions were suddenly getting the better of her. Doug put a gentle hand on the girl's shoulder. "I want the hell away from Brenda and her kids," Sondra growled through clenched teeth. "I'm workin' on it, kiddo," Doug promised her. "I really am," he added. "Don't give up hope. I'm waiting to hear from Mr. Shalen, the lawyer. He's supposed to let me know when we can get the custody hearing in front of a judge. You're gonna need some nicer clothes for court. Diane'll help you with that."

"My friend Kari keeps saying I need new clothes" said Sondra. Doug wasn't quite sure what to make of Sondra's friendship with Kari Wilken. He'd known the Wilkens for years now. Kari's father, Gary, was a mostly nonexistent deadbeat dad but Sara was a mom he held in high regard. The woman worked two jobs and was active in both her daughters' education. On several occasions Sara had let him know of her concerns about Kari's behavior possibly getting out of control, and Doug certainly didn't want any of Kari's bad influence to rub off on Sondra. He worried that Sondra's pain and anger would lead her to drugs and alcohol. So far he saw no evidence of this but did have his concerns.

After backing into the B.A.S.S. garage, Doug unhitched the trailer. “It kills me to have to ask you to go back to the house tonight,” he told Sondra, “but we need to keep up a good front just a little while longer.” Sondra was mentally and physically exhausted. She’d put everything she had into her final race of the year. Standing side by side, staring at the race car, Sondra once again let her pent-up emotions get the better of her and she wrapped her arms tightly around Doug. “Don’t leave me,” she squeaked, beginning to cry.

“Shh,” he soothed. “It’s gonna be okay, Sondra. You gotta hang in there for me just a little while longer.” She pulled away and wiped her eyes with her fingers. “Kay” she whispered, forcing herself to be strong. With Doug’s arm firmly around her the two leaned against the welding table in silence for several minutes. All to soon for Sondra, Doug left to get a good night’s sleep before an early and busy following day. Sadly alone after experiencing such triumph, she remained propped up against the scraped, burnt and dirty table, listening to Doug’s pickup drive away.

Before heading to the evil house Sondra walked out into the alley and enjoyed the quiet evening. The air smelled oddly sweet and felt good on her skin. It had a thickness but the usual choking dusty smog was not so prevalent. She looked up at the sky, noticing that there were only few stars visible. Back inside the garage she closed and locked the large metal back rollup door and leaned against its warmth surveying the shop, her eyes coming to rest on her mechanical race friend majestically poised on top of the trailer. She walked to the YWCA to shower and change into her normal street clothes and do a little race-suit cleanup. Though the facilities and the women she often encountered at the YWCA were questionable she preferred this to showering and changing at the evil house.

With wet hair from her long hot shower slowly drying in the night air, Sondra walked in the direction of the mobile home. A shiny black Nissan pickup drove by with two horn blasts. She waved, recognizing the vehicle. Billy Conrad was one of the part-time clerks at the corner grocery store, working at Dusty’s Market three days a week after school and on some weekends. Twice Sondra had noticed he'd brought his pickup in for service at the B.A.S.S. garage and she'd given him advice on a particular brand of motor oil. Sondra watched the truck pull to a stop and reverse with two more blasts of the horn.

"You win?" asked Billy, stopping just two feet from her. Sondra smiled and raised her arms, pumping her fists victoriously.

"Trophy as big as me," she told him.

"Cool, Sondra," he smiled. "A bunch of us are hangin' at Grif's tonight. You in?"

She began to shake her head but quickly switched to a nod, realizing how much she was starved for food and company. She was also in no particular hurry to return to the house that she never considered a home. "Yeah," she answered. "I'm in. Thanks."

Grif's Grill was a true California timeless classic eatery. Burgers, fries, sodas and chocolate or vanilla milkshakes, just off Highway 99. The other classic ingredient was the constant popularity with the local teenagers. Sondra didn't frequent Grif's because there were a number of other establishments offering similar fair that were cleaner and closer to the B.A.S.S. garage. On three occasions however she and Doug had found it a quick and easy place to pick up lunch or dinner on the way home from a race, and she'd been there twice with Kari Wilken.

There was a deluge of cars and people as Billy and Sondra got near the burger joint. Billy parked in a friend's driveway off the alley and around the corner. He was fairly popular at school, especially because he could get free or marked-down items from Dusty's Market. Young Conrad was a fair-haired boy with a medium build and a freckled face. His love of baseball was well-known and he often sported the jerseys, caps or pins supporting his favorite team, the Arizona Diamondbacks. Oddly enough he did not play on the high school baseball team. He'd heard all the gossip and rumors surrounding Sondra but never took stock in any of them, knowing her before the rumors had begun. He also strongly disliked Tracy and her friends. They'd been verbally unkind to him on more than one occasion, making fun of his freckles and his fervor for an out of state sports team.

Billy and Sondra were well received as they walked up to the main entrance. At first no one recognized Sondra. Soon however a number of male patrons did take notice of her. With her mind completely on racing that morning before leaving the house, she'd mindlessly stuffed different clothes into her backpack. Several items were Kari's influence. On this night Sondra wore new black jeans and black low-top boots that were far more feminine than she would have picked out for herself. Kari had insisted she buy them one afternoon when all Sondra wanted was socks from a nearby department store. Besides the boots, she wore a light blue high-sleeve T-shirt with ruffled edges. When she bent in any direction a little bit of her bare midriff would show. This had been a gift from Rachel at the Collins House. Sondra had only worn it a few times that summer to make Rachel happy but deemed it too girlie to wear on a regular basis. Her long dark hair was still wet from the shower and she hadn't fully combed or brushed it, so she had a very alluring wild look. What she didn't realize was that her wet hair had soaked through the fabric in the front, giving her a slight wet T-shirt contest appearance. She didn't notice the guys ogling her chest or hear the girls commenting to each other about the new brazen chick. To her the dampness felt soothing since even at 8:20 p.m. it was still quite warm. It had been 106 degrees that afternoon.

Sondra had never been comfortable with popularity but winning so many races and her job as office manager for the garage had forced her to deal with that issue. She'd learned to have confidence in handling all types of different personalities and on this night felt a kind of magic in the air as seemingly everyone wanted to be near her and be in a conversation with her. In attendance at the restaurant were a number of people who had been at the race that day and some had attended a few previous races. Soon the place was buzzing with the fact that race-girl was there. Sondra's popularity grew even more when it was discovered that she had a vast knowledge of cars and engines. She was amazed that she never once had to buy anything to eat or drink. She was constantly and generously offered many items. Sondra was mostly surrounded by boys but a number of girls wanted to know about her clothes and the intriguing medallion she had on a metallic chain around her neck. Doug had given this to her the day she'd won her first race. Sondra treasured it just as she'd treasured the embroidered handkerchief and sunglasses he'd given her during the Tumbleweed sprint-car weekend. On this evening at Grif's, the young women who surrounded her also commented on her tight and toned figure and asked if she worked out in a nearby gym. Sondra hadn't a gym routine but told them she had a fitness regimen all the same.

While in the women's restroom washing her hands, Tracy and her best friend Heather entered the light-green stuffy room. Tracy looked Sondra up and down, then spat out a derogatory comment in a snotty tone. "Nice shirt. Going pole dancing later?" Sondra gave her back the same up and down look and smiled before giving her a sarcastic return. "You're one to talk." Heather suddenly figured out with whom they were having this exchange. "Oh my gawd," she exclaimed. "You're that little garage freak." With lightning speed and power Sondra twisted Heather around and bent her over the sink, grabbing the back of her hair and forcing her to look into the mirror. "That's the freak" growled Sondra. She let go and Heather slumped to the floor. On her way out, Sondra deliberately pounded her shoulder into Tracy's, knocking her off balance and onto the counter. Sondra then kicked the door open and walked out with a large wicked grin. She stood for a moment waiting for the restroom door to shut behind her before returning to the main dining area. In a quiet voice that came from deep within her throat she announced to herself, "Full circle." She was popular. She had been told numerous times that night that she was pretty, and now she was the one who was victorious in a petty high school duel. It was all the sweeter knowing that she was done with high school. She tossed her hair, emulating women in TV commercials, then caught several people eyeing her. With a slight smile she turned to the left, walked through the kitchen door and out to the alley.

Sondra hailed a taxi to take her back to the B.A.S.S. garage where she collected her backpacks and reluctantly headed home. After a fitful night's sleep, worrying about her future and a possible confrontation with Tracy, Sondra left the evil house at 4:27 a.m., hurrying to the B.A.S.S. garage. Jim found Sondra fast asleep in her race car when he came in at exactly 7:30 a.m. He chuckled to himself but didn't wake her. Twelve minutes later Bobby woke the girl with a roaring laugh. He shook the vehicle's steel tubing and her world faded from peaceful to annoying as Jim noisily tugged on the chain to open the back door. He soon came to stand next to Bobby as they watched Sondra, now fully awake, extricate herself from the vehicle. "She's probably gonna eat, sleep and live in that car from now on," roared Bobby in hysterics. The jokes never let up, even when the office phone rang a few minutes later. Sondra hurried to answer it, closing the office door behind her. It was Doug. "Asleep at the wheel, huh, Tiger?" She could hear Bobby and Jim continue with the silliness, figuring that Bobby had tipped Doug off about her morning nap. "You three are a regular comedy team," she told him in a scratchy morning voice. "I hear the Tonight Show's looking for new writers. So are you gonna come by?"

"Sorry, kiddo," said Doug, hating to disappoint her. "Long day today and tomorrow. I'll call you tonight though. We have some legal stuff to go over."

"Kay" said Sondra on the verge of tears. She didn't know why but she suddenly missed him terribly. "You drive safe," she added.

"Were you really sleeping in your car?" he asked, trying to lighten her mood.

"Oh gee," she said rolling her eyes. "There's the other line. Gotta go."

"Well, tell Laurel and Hardy there to behave," he said, laughing. She giggled as the call ended, trying to figure out if Bobby was more a Laurel than a Hardy.

At 3:49 p.m. Kari Wilken came by the garage. She'd heard all about Sondra's outing at Grif's Grill the night before and was eager for more details from Sondra herself. Kari entered the garage through the front rollup door and found the owner and his office manager chatting next to a parked forklift cradling a large metal drum of solvent.

"Hi Bobby. Hey girl," Kari said in greeting. Sondra gave a slight wave of her hand as Bobby began to speak.

"Hi Kari. Talked to your mom earlier. Diane's makin' cupcakes for your sister's class as we speak. She'll bring 'em to the school herself at seven tomorrow morning."

"Thanks," nodded Kari.

"Diane's a lifesaver," she told Bobby. "Brianna screwed up and forgot to tell mom that she was supposed to bring stuff for the bake sale. Sprung it on her at the last minute and mom was so pissed."

"Well Diane's happy to step in" said Bobby, climbing on board the forklift. "We're pretty much done for the day," he announced. "Why don't you go ahead and clock out, Sondra. See ya bright and early tomorrow."

"Whatcha doin' for dinner?" Kari then asked Sondra. She didn't give Sondra time to answer. "My mom's like the queen of the slow-cooker these days. She's wanted to have you over to our house for dinner for like ever. I'll give her a quick call to let her know we're on our way." Sondra smiled as Kari chatted briefly with her mom. Something so simple as going to a friend's house for dinner was a bit of normalcy she had thought she'd lost forever.

The modest but clean and tidy 2-bedroom mobile home sported many keepsakes and knickknacks on shelves, and unlike the evil house, the TV and couch were not the focal point of the living room. Kari led Sondra straight to the kitchen where Sara was putting the finishing touches on dinner and trying to get her 13-year-old daughter Brianna to finish setting the table. "Oh good" Sara greeted Sondra and Kari. "You're just in time. We're having southwestern chicken chili with homemade tortillas that one of my coworkers brought in to the office today. Hope that's all right with you, Sondra." "Yeah" enthused the girl. "Smells amazing." After dinner, Sondra and Kari took small bowls of mint chocolate chip ice cream and sat in decorative semi-comfortable wicker chairs on the back porch. The Wilken's backyard was the same size and layout as Brenda's but the spotless yard was encircled by a redwood fence and the gardens were well maintained. "Thanks for this" said Sondra to Kari as they savored the tasty coolness.

Discussion emerged about the particulars of Sondra's Grif's Grill experience the night before, but Kari was actually far more interested in getting to know Sondra and about her circumstances. Sondra was extremely guarded at first but did loosen up the longer they talked. She even provided her friend with a few anecdotes of her brother Dave, thinking that he would have loved the beautiful blond Kari. Conversation between the two continued to flow and remained fairly light, with Kari doing most of the talking. She spoke of the three different boys she was currently dating and wondered out loud why such a pretty girl like Sondra wasn't seeing anyone. Sondra managed to sidestep this issue, sighing that work, school and racing had demanded the bulk of her time. Kari later offered her friend a ride home but Sondra politely declined, stating that it wasn't too far and she wanted the alone-time before having to deal with whatever situation she might encounter at the evil house. As she strolled along the sidewalk she thought about the dinner and conversations she'd enjoyed that evening. She was glad to find that Kari had a far greater depth to her than the wild school image, and that her mom was a real mom, like hers had been. She'd also found Kari's sister Brianna to be sweet and funny. The dinner table atmosphere had felt comfortable and familiar, with Sondra wondering bitterly why Brenda and her kids couldn't have been more like this.

Chapter 9

Now that the racing season was over and Sondra wouldn't have high school to contend with, her life was far more relaxed. She'd taken and passed the Equivalency test but the three-week wait for her high school diploma produced stomach-churning anxiety. When the document finally arrived in the mail, Brenda's reaction was a pleasant surprise. She was in the midst of one of her rare sober and lucid moments. Brenda was genuine, caring and the most mom-like Sondra had ever seen from her. "Now that's more like it, Sondra" cheered Brenda of the diploma. "I'm proud of you. Ya put the fists away and buckled down, and now you really have something to show for it. You can do just fine in life with that, despite what so many people say, but I know you wanted to at least go to junior college."

"Yeah," said Sondra. "Principal Merson and the guidance counselor, Mrs. Waldnepler, helped me set up some stuff. There's a Learning Annex across town and they have classes for getting your AA degree, and they help you with scholarships, college and everything."

"Well maybe you've been doing some growing up here after all," said Brenda, taking undo credit. "You're even dressing better and keeping your hair combed and tidy. Maybe there's hope for you yet to become a young lady."

The day finally came for Doug and Sondra to go to court on emancipation and custody issues. The proceedings went nothing like Sondra had predicted or imagined. She pictured big courtroom drama, going in as if she were the lawyer, arguing with the judge, laying out hard evidence to a jury, citing precedents in past cases and utilizing ingenious tactics. The reality was quite different. Sondra saw the inside of the courtroom only long enough to state her name, her age and that it was her wish to proceed with what was set before the judge. She was happy that John Farnsal was there on this day and surprised that neither Brenda nor Judith Tredou was present. Sitting on hardwood benches in the stuffy wood-paneled hallway of the courthouse, Sondra fidgeted and held her stomach as if it were about to erupt. "Positive thoughts" encouraged Doug, seated next to her. John Farnsal came to join them roughly twenty minutes later. "Well I'm glad I got to do my character-witnessing in person," he said. "Michael Shalen's a sharp attorney and I got what I think is a good read on the judge. This same type of procedure will go on in a few days with the same judge, with Brenda and her attorneys," he added. "But I'd say upper percentile that things will go as planned. Wish I could spend more time with you, Sondra, but I gotta be heading back to LA." He stood and bent down to give Sondra a gentle kiss on the top of her neatly combed hair but before he could walk away she stood and wrapped her arms around him in a tight embrace.

With the emotional roller coaster of the mid-morning and afternoon, Doug suggested lunch at a small deli. While waiting for their sandwiches, they discussed a wide variety of issues and topics, avoiding any talk of legal proceedings. Nearing the end of their meal Sondra became more serious. "Hey, Doug?" she said. "Brenda's not exactly my favorite person in the world but you do know I appreciate the few things she's actually done for me, right? I mean I'm not doing this emancipation thing to be mean."

"You don't have to make excuses for her, Sondra" Doug told her. "I know what a bitch Brenda's been to you. She's not gonna take this well, and I've been warned that custody fights can get very ugly, but we'll get through it. You stay focused. Get your AA degree and keep doing what you're doing."

Eight torturous days went by until Doug and Sondra were given confirmation of the judge's decision. Sondra was granted Limited Emancipation. This meant she was free to make her own important living and life decisions, financial and otherwise, but under the supervision of Mr. Doug Edward Trent, who was awarded sole custody and pre-approved to proceed with the adoption process. Doug went to see Brenda on an early blustery October afternoon. She stood momentarily motionless and stared at him coldly after answering the front door. "I was hoping we could talk" he said, holding out a small vase of flowers. She turned and went to sit down on the couch. Doug gently closed the door behind him and set the vase on the coffee table, sitting on the opposite side of the old elongated piece of furniture. "I didn't do this to hurt you" he told Brenda. "Neither did Sondra."

"I'm not hurt," Brenda lied. "And that little tomboy's pretty screwed up. Good luck dealing with all that."

"Well there may be some truth in that," he said. "Thanks. I basically came by to make sure you and the kids are okay and to let you know that I'm moving to Fresno. Sondra's gonna rent the Zellers' little apartment for a few months, then she'll move in with me. She has her job and she's enrolled in college-prep courses at that Learning Annex."

Tears began to roll down Brenda's cheeks as she nodded. "Was it really so terrible with me?" she sobbed.

"No" he tried to reassure her. "And I'm really grateful for all the good times I got to have with you and the kids. I hear Pete and Alyssa moved in together." Doug pulled an envelope from his pocket and set it on the table. "Here's a little house-warming present. The greeting card's a little cheesy but there's a fifty dollar gift card for the grocery store."

"That's sweet," said Brenda. "You always cared about my kids."

"Always will," he told her. "By the way, tell Pete to bring his truck by the auto shop. He needs a new fan belt and Sondra'll put it in for free." Doug put his hand inside his shirt pocket and came up with a pair of dolphin earrings. "I promised Tracy I'd get these for her. And tell Jennifer and Josh I'll take them shoe shopping soon, and if you're still planning on getting a new sofa, I'd be happy to help you out with that." Brenda nodded, looking down at the well-worn cushion between her and her ex-boyfriend.

"I should get going," said Doug, beginning to stand. "Found a new home for the Studebaker so now you'll have your garage back."

Brenda didn't care about the garage or the vehicle but she nodded and stood, giving him a desperate hug. Driving away from the house that had been his home and his life, Doug got an uncomfortable sensation that he'd just bought his way out. He went over in his head how hard he'd worked and how many sacrifices he'd made for this family, but when he thought of Sondra he felt a surge of confidence that he was doing the right thing.

CHAPTER 10

On a cold morning, October 28, Mr. and Mrs. Zeller entered into a month-to-month rental agreement with Sondra for their above-the-garage apartment. Diane and Bobby had known Bill and Susan Zeller for years. Their son Andrew was the same age as the Zellers' youngest son and the two boys had been best friends throughout their childhood. The Zellers had built the unit for Shane because they hadn't wanted their baby to move far away as their other two children had done while attending college. The apartment was a small single but much nicer than Sondra had hoped for or imagined when the landlords had described it to her over the phone. The walls were white and there was newish tan berber carpeting. Susan had Sondra sign the rental agreement before giving her the keys and a quick tour. The kitchen area contained a mini refrigerator and a mini gas stove. As a house-warming gesture, Bobby gave Sondra the Andretti picture from the garage office and Diane gave her a small potted ficus tree.

Sondra and Doug had previously talked about her future in racing and of a particular organization which operated a Formula Ford driving school and race team. She called and did eventually hear back from Gavins Racing. The man she talked with on the phone was extremely polite and friendly, inviting her to tour the facility. On the appointed day, she and Doug drove to Willow Springs Raceway. The Director of Operations, Steven Barnes, encouraged Sondra to sit in one of their Formula Ford cars. She felt completely at home in the cockpit. Steven started talking a bit more seriously. "So Sondra, you look pretty good in there, but here's the thing. We like to see a little more experience than you have for our students and race team. It's impressive that you won so many races and the Midget championship but that's pretty amateur-level dirt-track driving and you drove only half the season." Sondra gave a reluctant nod and mentioned the opportunity that was on the table for her to drive for Dan Stoltz. "I'd be driving in a pro-level sprint-car next season," she asserted. "I'm gonna win a lot of races for them, and the championship, but I'd rather be driving for you. Give me a chance. I won't make a fool out of you." As soon as that sentence had escaped her lips she regretted it. She made a quick eye-dart over to Doug, whose own eyes were closed and his head was turning. She was thinking, *Oh no. I can't believe I just used a line from a movie*. Sondra looked up at Steven. Luckily the *Days of Thunder* reference had gone over his head and she was sure Tom Cruise would be choking on a sandwich if he knew she'd just said that in real life.

The movie reference did eventually register to Steven, and days later, as promised, he made a follow-up call to her. His voice was cold and stern. "This is not a Hollywood movie, Sondra," he told her. "But here's the thing. You've got a good image, a good story and I dig your tenacity. We'll be watching you. Come through on your sprint-car claims. You can't simply jump from a handful of backwoods victories in the dirt to starting at Indy. You're young but you don't strike me as a naive kid, either. Impress me and I'll let you test. Lose races and the championship for Stoltz and you can go back to playing Xbox games on the couch." Sondra took a brief second to let all this sink in, her anger welling up quickly. "Mr. Barnes," she began. "You're wasting my time. Sorry about the movie line but I'm damn sure about my claims. I'd seriously reconsider not testing me immediately. Sure, I can drive for Stoltz, and by the way, I will win a lot of races and the championship. This crap is like shooting fish in a barrel for me. You wanna pass on me, fine. I'll find someone else who won't."

Sondra continued, trying not to sound as furious as she felt: "I'll make you a thousand-dollar promise, and I'll put it in writing and send it off to you tomorrow. I'm going to end up on the starting grid at Indy in a couple of years. The question is ... do you want to be a part of that or not? If I don't hear from you by Mr. Stoltz's signing deadline then I hope you do follow through and watch my success." Without waiting for a response, she hit the red button on her cell phone and threw the device onto her unfurled sleeping bag.

The following Sunday, Doug and Sondra had breakfast together at Flappin' Jack's Finer Diner. Waitress Ruth was happy to see them seated at her station and asked myriad questions about how things were going for each of them. During the meal Sondra told Doug about the disappointing outcome with Gavins Racing. "So I decided to give Steven Barnes another call yesterday to make my case," she began. "He was short and flippant and told me that I'm way too childishly eager. He suggested I try a few years in karting before I start wasting people's time." Doug watched the girl angrily stab at a piece of sausage with her fork. "So you'll drive for Dan Stoltz's new sprint car team," he suggested. "Now calm down and finish your breakfast, then you can show me your new home." Sondra smiled at that, her mood changing on a dime.

Doug surprised Sondra with two house-warming presents. A microwave oven and a chair with brass-plated metal tubing. The blue chair cushions folded out to make a comfortable mattress. Though the carpeting and Sondra's sleeping bag offered some cushion, she was ecstatic about her new bed/chair. "I'm riding the Suzuki a lot more," she told Doug as they talked in the still mostly empty apartment. "I mean I ride it to school through the alleys and back-streets and I take it to the dunes for a hard workout ride whenever I can. Usually it's an hour a day. I'm gonna get some free-weights so I can work out, too. I've been streamlining and doing a little remodeling in the B.A.S.S. office to be more efficient so in the future I can devote more time for school, riding, and racing. Bobby and Jim have been giving me a little more hands-on shop work and I'm teaching Bobby the new computer system. It's kinda funny when he comes rushing out, begging me to fix or take over some office catastrophe." Doug laughed and nodded, knowing Bobby's aversion to all things computery. "What about school?" he queried, looking down at a stack of text books neatly placed against the wall under the large window that looked out onto the residential street. "Not too shabby," Sondra said with a smile and a nod. "It's three nights a week. Monday through Wednesday, six to nine. The Learning Annex is actually a pretty cool place. The classrooms are fairly new, and so far everyone's been really nice to me. I mean I'm by far the youngest one in all three classes but that's okay, I'm not there for social hour. A few of us formed a study group," she added. Doug nodded, thinking about what Judge Manthom had told him of Sondra's proper socialization. "You still hang out with Kari?" he asked. "Well I'm way busier now" she said. "But yeah, we still talk on the phone and eat together fairly regularly."

Doug looked out the window for a few seconds and turned back with a serious face. "I'm really proud of you, Sondra," he said in a low soft voice. "You're not letting the worst of circumstances take you down and I'm so thankful you never turned to bad things." He took a deep, sad breath. "Don't ever smoke, drink or use drugs, Sondra. It's not cool and it'll run your life backwards and down in ugly ways. You're gonna have such a great life. I'm very sure of that." Sondra wasn't quite sure what to make of this little speech. "My parents once had a talk with Dave and me about drinking and smoking after we found a crushed carton of cigarettes by the swings at this park we used to go to often," she imparted. She made a fist and pounded the carpet beside her. "For the rest of my life." she spoke angrily through gritted teeth, "I have to live with what a drunk little bastard did. He took everything from me." She pounded both fists on the floor several times and burst into uncontrolled tears. Doug held her tight for a few seconds, but Sondra was learning to control and suppress her emotions. She pulled away sniffling went into the small kitchen. When she returned it was as if the outburst had never happened. Doug let out a long loud breath as the girl sat back down next to him. "You don't have to worry about any of that stuff with me," she told him of their earlier words. Doug pondered Sondra's words and actions for a few seconds before speaking. "Alcohol sure changed Brenda," he said with a sad nod. "Such a shame you never knew the woman I first met. Over time the heavy drinking and partying with her drunken girlfriends just took an ugly toll. And now her kids are getting so out of control." Sondra moved closer so that their shoulders touched as they leaned against the wall, staring at the opposite blank white surface. "I had to bail Pete and his idiot friend out of jail last night," Doug continued. "They were in a neighbor's garage smoking a joint. They're gonna have to go to court and pay a whopping fine. When I dropped them off at home, Brenda and I were discussing the kids and Tracy came home messed up on god only knows what. The shocking thing is that Brenda didn't seem wildly upset about any of this." Doug took another loud breath and shook his head. Sondra had never before known him to talk so openly about anything bad. He always seemed to be focused on how she was doing, or fun and exciting future events. "I'm so sorry you have to deal with all this," she told him. "You're the most amazing person I know. You and my dad would have been best friends, I'm sure of it." Doug felt honored by Sondra's words. He knew how determined she always was to never let that impossible-to-heal scar of losing her dad and family out in the open. "You're a most amazing person as well, Sondra," he told her, briefly leaning into her shoulder. "I called Dan Stoltz," said Sondra, changing the subject. "Said he's willing to give me a shot in his sprint-car and he'd have a contract ready for me to sign next week."

"That's great," cheered Doug. Unbeknownst to Sondra, he'd already set this in motion, having numerous talks with the man about her many strengths and what a major asset she'd be for the race team. "I'll firm up a date and drive you," he said, smiling over at the girl. "You know, there's special circumstances the DMV allows for emancipated minors to get their license a little early." Sondra nodded vigorously. "I know," she said. "I was gonna talk to you about that."

"We'll make that happen soon" he promised her. "You need appropriate transportation," he added. "And the dirt bike's not quite gonna cut it. You can use my Tacoma 'til you find your own wheels."

He turned his attention to the stack of books. "I'm really happy to see you're doing the college degree thing" he said. "I want you to pursue that as much as you can. You have a natural affinity for academics as well as your driving talent." He looked down at his watch. "I gotta go. Long drive to Fresno. I'm looking forward to when you move in there so I don't have all this commuting. You're gonna like the place and the area." After Doug's departure, Sondra felt the emptiness of room as if it were squeezing the life out of her.

For Sondra, the morning drive to Fresno with Doug felt like more of a job interview than a contract signing to become the driver of a race team. Doug dropped her off at the dealership, telling her he'd be back in about three hours and Sondra enjoyed the many photos hanging on the walls of the showroom. As she was studying a particular corner display Dan Stoltz lumbered out and stood beside her. She pointed to an old picture of a young man at a racetrack she didn't recognize. "Is that you?" she asked. He coughed a laugh. "Yeah" he confirmed. "I was once young, thin and had hair. I drove in some minor stock car races and was a tire-changer for a few teams. After three years of bumming around the circuit, I decided I hated the Gypsy nomad life and being poor. I've been in auto sales ever since." The adjoining corner wall was covered with shelves containing various high school sports trophies, many military photographs and framed medals and certificates. "So you were in the Army?" inquired Sondra. Dan touched an enlarged picture of a man in uniform standing by a helicopter and spoke in a low soft tone. "Yeah. I flew recon missions the tail-end of Nam. This here picture's actually my son, Travis. My father was a transport pilot in World War II. Trav idolized him. I did too, I guess. Dad had a million stories. Travis's mother divorced me because she thought I pushed him into going into the military. He and his crew were shot down in the first six weeks of Desert Storm. He's an American hero. Too bad nobody gets to tell him that." Sondra could actually feel pain and loss radiating from him. She said nothing but lightly touched his arm. She could have easily spoken of her situation and just how much she could relate to him about his loss. She didn't. She couldn't. She didn't want him to think of her as emotionally fragile.

After what Sondra considered a surprisingly comfortable conversation with the man she'd previously detested, they entered into a six-month contract for her to drive his #82 professional sprint car for the next race season. Doug returned to the dealership just as he had said and took Sondra to his new Fresno condo instead of driving her straight back to the Bakersfield apartment. He enjoyed her favorable response, with her telling him that she wished she could just move in right then and there. "That'll come soon enough," he promised her. Sondra gave Doug the details of her day as they sat down in the den, which doubled as the entertainment room and office. On a massive audio/video system they watched a video of vintage auto racing and talked of ordering pizza for dinner. Doug had just asked Sondra what toppings she favored when the doorbell gave off its sing-song ring. Sondra was seated on a new black imitation-leather couch and didn't have a straight view of the doorway, but she could hear Doug and a woman exchanging pleasantries. "Hi Doug," greeted Karen McCormick. "Well this is a pleasant surprise," cheered Doug. "Sorry I didn't call first," she told him. "But I was in the area and thought I'd take a chance." Karen wasn't just in the area and this was no chance meeting. The two had been talking by phone on a fairly regular basis and they'd gone to lunch once and had been on two dinner dates. She liked him. She really liked him. She thought him a man of high caliber and his devotion to Sondra touched her deeply.

"Well you couldn't have timed it better" Doug told Karen. "Sondra just signed a full-support contract to drive a pro sprint-car for Dan Stoltz and we're just about to order pizza to celebrate. Come on in." Doug led Karen to the den. "Hi champ," she greeted Sondra warmly, handing Doug her thin light-blue jacket. "So great to see you again," she added. Sondra stood, intending to shake hands but Karen was a hugger. "So you've gone pro," said Karen as they released each other. "That's exciting."

"Yeah," said Sondra, smiling and nodding. "The cars are a definite step up in horsepower and they have the aero wings. Mr. Stoltz said that in a few weeks they'll have the car ready so I can do some testing.

I can't wait to put that nine-hundred horsepower V-Eight machine through its paces."

The large supreme pizza was enjoyed in the living room, with the three sitting around the coffee table. Karen asked Sondra many questions about the classes she was taking at school and her future academic plans. Over bowls of chocolate ice cream, Karen mentioned a TV food show she'd seen about a restaurant in San Francisco that offered an eating challenge called The Kitchen Sink. "That sounds insane," said Doug. "Yeah," agreed Sondra. "I mean think of the colossal freezy-brain headache, not to mention how sick of ice cream you'd probably be for quite some time after eating that much, maybe even the rest of your life."

"We used to make our own ice cream when I was growing up," said Karen. "And I've always loved cooking. Maybe next time I'll make you my famous Chicken Cacciatore Ala Karen."

"Well as long as it's famous," quipped Sondra with a quick laugh. "I mean we only eat famous food,s" she continued with a smile. "You know, like Famous Amos cookies, Famous Star hamburgers."

"Yeah," added Doug with a chuckle. "You got your vegans, your vegetarians, your gluten-free and the lactose-intolerant crowds, but Sondra and I adhere to a very strict dietary constraint. Famous-only."

"Oh you two," laughed Karen, shaking her head. She beamed, feeling completely at home and that she so easily fit in with them. When it came time for Karen to leave, Doug volunteered to walk her to her car. "Thank you for such a lovely evening" she told him. "Your Sondra is everything you said she is and more. Such a dear. Absolutely atrocious table manners though, but don't worry, I'll help you with that." Doug smiled, pondering Karen's offer to help. Reaching Karen's silver E-class Mercedes sedan, she unlocked the door and turned back toward him. They shared a tender kiss, and moments later Doug watched the tail-lights disappear. He liked her. He really liked her.

"Well?" asked Doug as he and Sondra began the kitchen cleanup. "Well she doesn't smoke and she isn't a wino," said Sondra. "And she's smart and has a decent sense of humor." She placed a third plate in the dishwasher rack and moved a foot away, leaning against the counter.

"You're not gonna suddenly move in with her though, are you?" she asked. "No, Sondra" said Doug, shaking his head as he rinsed the clear glass mugs that had held cranberry juice. "We're taking things slow, and if things work out she'll have to fit into our lives, not the other way around."

"But you're hoping she will?" asked Sondra. "Fit into our lives?" Doug wiped his hands on a dishtowel and looked squarely at the girl. He spoke in a soft but strong voice. "You're my number one priority, Sondra. Your safety, your comfort and your happiness comes first. I like Karen a lot but your life's been unstable enough. I'll never allow anyone in our lives that you're not comfortable with."

"Kay" whispered the girl. She went back to dish-doing tasks. "I like her a lot" she admitted, handing Doug a succession of bowls and silverware to rinse. "So I guess maybe this means I'll have to stop calling her the Snap-on Lady."

"You nutty girl," he laughed. Sondra leaned against the counter and watched Doug push the button to start the dishwasher.

"Can I stay here tonight?" she asked. "I mean it's getting late and that would be an insane four-hour round trip for you."

"Yeah" he told her. "Good time as any to give your room and new bed a test spin. I didn't have time to get anything like a comforter but the blankets, sheets and pillows are new."

"Are the pillows hypoallergenic and the sheets Egyptian cotton, with a thread-count at least above eight-hundred?" she joked. "Oh sure," laughed Doug with a roll of his eyes. They weren't but he loved Sondra's sense of humor. "Nothing but the best for my kid," he told her. "Your tiara arrives on Tuesday, you nutty girl." He enjoyed her giggle as they returned to the den to watch the remainder of the vintage auto racing video.

The next morning Sondra breathed deeply, enjoying the aroma of the new furniture and the smell of bacon beginning to come from the kitchen. "I love my room" she announced as she came to stand next to Doug. "Thank you for not painting it pink."

"Oh rats," said Doug, snapping his finger. "Now I'm gonna have to take all those cans of pink paint back." She swatted at his arm and looked on as he began to prepare scrambled eggs. "One of my culinary specialties," he announced. "Learned this technique from my dad," he told her. "You see, most people crack the eggs into a bowl and whisk the hell out of 'em before pouring them into the skillet. With that you get the traditional one-color-yellow fluffiness, but if you crack the eggs directly into the pan, break the yokes and stir 'em around like this with the spatula, they turn out just as fluffy. And see? Now you have a mixture of white and yellow. It's the craftsman's technique. Tastes better, too. Trust me." Sondra smiled at Doug's words but then briefly bit down on her tongue, remembering her dad's limited culinary skills.

"When I was nine, my mom got the flu really bad" she related, both afraid and determined to produce this childhood anecdote. "So dad did all the cooking for three days. I mean he brought home a bucket of chicken for dinner on the second night, and my god-parents brought over a ton of food that we had for the rest of the week, but that first day we had scrambled eggs for breakfast. For school lunches he made Dave and me peanut butter sandwiches. Straight peanut butter on bread. Nothing else. Well he did put an orange in our bags, off our tree. The thing was huge, with oranges as big as soccer balls." Doug smiled at the girl's penchant for exaggeration and was happy that Sondra was talking about her family, which she rarely did. "Anyway," continued Sondra, "on that first night he made fried egg sandwiches for dinner. It had pickles, tomatoes, tons of stuff. When he told us what he was making I thought he said Friday sandwiches, and Dave and I always called 'em that from then on. They were so great but it seemed weird. I mean mom always made dinner seem so elaborate and special. To be eating a breakfast or lunch thing for dinner seemed so strange." Sondra bit down on her tongue, tears instantly streaming down her face, but before Doug could say or do anything of comfort, little Miss Tough-as-Nails deftly wiped the moisture away with the cuff of her sweatshirt sleeve and took the plate of bacon to the kitchen table and sat down. Doug soon set a plate of scrambled eggs in front of the girl, bending down to kiss the top of her head. "Sorry, Sondra," he whispered. "So unfair for you to have to be without your amazing family, but thank you for sharing that with me."

Chapter 11

Sondra's classes at the Learning Annex added a much- appreciated level of busyness to her life. More activities equaled less worrying about her future and less time to dwell on her enormous loss. With school, study group and work, the weeks seemed to blur by for Sondra. When Thanksgiving arrived, she saw this as a hideous unfair interruption. Over the past several years she'd developed a serious dread of the major holidays. Growing up, her family had always made a big deal out of each of them, even the ones that most people tend to take for granted or not give much significance or credence. The Sierres proudly marked Presidents Lincoln's and Washington's birthdays. They celebrated May Day, had a blast with April Fools and took Memorial and Labor days seriously and not just as an excuse to be off work or school. The biggies, Thanksgiving and Christmas, were always extra-magical to them.

Kari Wilken extended an invitation to Sondra to join her family for Thanksgiving, as did the Shniders, but Sondra made crafty excuses. The excuses weren't actually as crafty as she'd thought, but everyone knew how hard these kinds of family holidays were for her. Doug however wasn't about to take no for an answer. He drove down the evening before, picked up his brooding kid and headed back to Fresno. On the ride to the condo, Doug asked Sondra many questions about how her studies were going, and she was interested to know how things were going with the Snap-on lady. Getting close to Fresno, a farming town that over the years had grown into a sizable metropolis, Sondra began a conversation about the holiday after Thanksgiving. For her, December twenty-fourth and twenty-fifth were truly the hardest days of the year to get through. The entire month of December for the Sierres had always been a nonstop epic journey. Just days after Thanksgiving the kids would enact their brand of pressure on Kal until he would put up the five strings of Christmas lights all over the front of the house. This activity always led to a drive around the neighborhood to see if there were other lighting displays. Maureen would have daily projects for her children. Dave, Sondra and Haley would help in the kitchen making dozens of different cookies, and they made numerous decorations for the tree and house. Ever since the accident, Sondra went to great lengths to be distracted so that those Norman Rockwell-type memories wouldn't completely shred her insides.

"So I was thinking," Sondra said to Doug as he was passing a SaveMart tractor-trailer rig, "I don't want to hurt your feelings or abandon you on Christmas but I just, well, I was thinking about asking you if I could borrow the truck and take a road trip, by myself." Doug let out a long loud breath through his nose and checked his rear-view mirror. "Well my first instinct is to say no" he told her. "But you've been working damn hard and I get why you'd want to get away, especially at Christmas."

"Well maybe this way you and the Snap-on lady could have a first Christmas alone together," suggested Sondra. "Possibly," he said. "And it's Karen," he scolded. "Karen told me she always spends Christmas with her folks in Pennsylvania. That's where she is now, but she might go for a change. Worse-case scenario, I have Christmas dinner with Dan Stoltz, his new girlfriend and his younger brother and wife and kids."

"It was just a thought" said Sondra. "I mean if you say no it won't upset me or hurt my feelings."

"Well if your plan is to drive up to Modesto and see your old home," he began, "then my answer is no. I can understand why you'd want to but I'm leaning toward discouraging that. You'd just be inflicting emotional torture on yourself and I don't want that for you. It scares me how almost constantly blind-angry you are, and you just keep it all bottled up, refusing to talk about the accident or really any part of your childhood." Several seconds passed. Doug was hoping Sondra would say something but the girl mostly stared out the side window. "I get it," he continued. "Hard to talk about that. There really aren't words for how awful this has been for you, and you have absolutely every right to be angry. But, Sondra, you also have absolutely every right to heal and be whole." She stared down at her fidgeting hands with a hard angry look. "Sondra," prompted Doug. He glanced over and noted that she'd made a tight fist with her right hand. "We'll make a pilgrimage someday," he promised her. "But not on a holiday and not when your emotions are still so heavily churned up."

Sondra folded her arms, glanced at him and then stared out the front window, noticing a fast-approaching Burger King billboard. "Maybe you're right," she accepted. "But it doesn't make it better. Maybe the road trip was a stupid idea."

"No," said Doug, "not stupid. I think a road trip would do you some good, but I'm thinking it should be to a destination that would lift your spirits and enrich your life. Like maybe the Grand Canyon or something."

"Yeah," smiled Sondra. "I like that. I've always wanted to go there. I mean you see pictures in magazines or scenes of it in movies but I always thought it would be great to go there in person."

At the condo Doug encouraged Sondra to deposit her backpack in her future bedroom. "Oh, wow," she exclaimed, finding that he had covered her bed with a cheery deep yellow, thick bedspread. There were also three new posters of supercars taped to the walls. Sondra bit down on her tongue, feeling happy and cared about but not wanting to appear overly emotional. "You really do want me here," she said, her voice giving her away.

Doug stepped forward and put his hands on her shoulders from behind. "You'd be living here now if the judge hadn't stipulated that you stay where you are and finish the classes you started," he told her. "Less than three months to go, and that'll go by in a flash," he added. "Come on, kiddo. Lets get that barbecue started." Doug led the way through the condo and out onto the petite patio. "I probably should have told you this before," he said as he proceeded to light a mound of charcoal briquets. "We're having chicken instead of turkey. I guess I waited too long to go to the grocery store. Yesterday all I could find were mammoth-sized frozen turkeys and it would have taken two days or more to thaw. Besides, I don't really care for the taste or texture of turkey. I did always like the Thanksgiving tradition of cooking one though. My aunt used to get up at daybreak and get one started in the oven every year, and one year my buddies and I deep-fried a turkey. Last couple of years I used the barbecue. Turned out pretty darn good, if I do say so myself."

Sondra wanted to tell Doug all about her many Thanksgiving experiences but knew she wouldn't be able to get through them without becoming emotional. "Well this is way better than that Thanksgiving at that CPS place," she told Doug, her voice edgy with bitterness. "It was really weird, and it smelled awful in that dining hall. I told 'em I wasn't hungry and I went back to my dorm room but they sent this mean old hag to take me back, and she stood over me while I ate. I made myself throw it up later. Luckily no one heard."

Doug became instantly concerned. It was heartbreaking that Sondra had been through so much adversity in such a short period of time, and he worried about her future ability to cope with the things that would come up in life.

"I won't throw up our Thanksgiving dinner," promised Sondra.

Doug played with the growing fire as he pondered what to say. "I'm gonna do my best to make sure you never have another bad holiday, Sondra," he told her. He intended to say more but his cell phone rang out, and before he could let the girl know he was willing to let the call go to voicemail, Sondra went back inside. Doug took the call, which lasted roughly 20 minutes, and he later found the girl in the kitchen staring at a framed photograph on the wall behind a rectangular table. "This your parents?" she asked. Doug nodded. "The friend I was just talking with knew 'em," he told her. "I was ten when Paul and his family moved in across the street and a few houses down. Wild how we've stayed in touch all these years. He's a really good guy. I'm sure you'll meet him one of these days."

The two ate in front of the TV. Doug had purchased several automotive-themed videos, and as they watched the movie *Tucker* they agreed the mashed potatoes, green beans and chicken meal was not half bad. At one point Doug tried unsuccessfully to get Sondra to talk about her past Thanksgivings but the girl always managed to change the subject. During the movie *Trains, Planes and Automobiles,* Doug smiled to himself as Sondra shifted closer and leaned her head against his shoulder. Soon after she fell asleep in that position and Doug took stock in the fact that his instincts to enact a personal change in life direction seemed to be working out as planned. From the first day he'd encountered Sondra, he was sure he'd be able to help the kid. She needed him, but a more startling realization came to him: He needed her as well. His life choices had been somewhat haphazard and mainly dictated by the women with whom he'd been in relationships and their kids. The year before Sondra had come into his life had been a mostly uninteresting, non-growing zombie-like blur of an existence. The Sierre girl's unique set of circumstances required some out-of-the-box thinking, and it had empowered and energized him to rise to the occasion.

At the conclusion of the movie, Doug was surprised that Sondra didn't wake when he carried her into her room. He removed her shoes and folded the edges of the bedspread all around her, wrapping her up cocoon-style. From the doorway he watched her sleep for a few seconds, feeling like the dad he'd always wanted to be and knowing that his life was on the right path.

Before Sondra left for her journey to the Grand Canyon, she spent two days with Doug in Fresno. He gave her an ultra-soft purple scarf, denying that it was a Christmas present. "It's freezing cold there this time of year," he told her. "And it can snow like you wouldn't believe around the rim."

She loved the scarf and the protective fatherly advice to stay warm and be careful. "Well as long as we're through the looking glass on the Christmas present thing," she told him, "I may have gotten you something, too." She dug in her backpack and pulled out a framed photograph of the two of them at the Tumbleweed Speedway facility, where they'd watched sprint-car races together.

Sondra's drive back to her apartment that evening in Doug's shiny yellow Tacoma was a mixture of sadness and exhilaration. She was excited to be driving and was looking forward to her tri-state adventure to the Grand Canyon but hated to leave Doug alone on Christmas. She felt the physicality of guilt but was determined to follow through with the plan.

Once in Bakersfield she stopped at a familiar gas station to fill the tank then parked the truck inside the B.A.S.S. garage. She checked the oil and fluid levels, the pressure of each tire and cleaned the Toyota's windows. Sondra hated to leave the Tacoma alone for the night but knew she needed a good night's sleep in her own bed. Now, at just before 9 p.m., it was a cold blustery walk to her apartment, and when it started sprinkling she grumbled to herself for not having an umbrella with her. A gold Nissan Maxima pulled over toward the sidewalk.

"Hey Sondra," yelled out a young woman. "Get in outta the rain. I'll give you a ride." It was Kari. Sondra didn't hesitate to get into the car but was a bit taken aback at her friend's nuclear explosion of energy, and she smelled of cloudy perfume, cigarettes and mint gum. Kari asked a string of questions, not always waiting for Sondra to answer.

Inside Sondra's warm and dry apartment Kari launched into an animated one-sided discussion about her uncool mom for not letting her spend Christmas with her dad, who had purchased the used Nissan for her a month prior in Las Vegas. "I can't wait to get my own place. You're so lucky," Kari told Sondra. "You have no idea," she furthered. "Hey I'm going to this big party at Gina Marsh's house. Her parents are out of town for two days and it's supposed to be a rager. Gonna be a band and everything. You should come with."

Sondra declined, stating that she was leaving early the next morning for her Grand Canyon trip. It also became clear to her that her wild friend mostly wanted to use her bathroom and then get something to blend with the remaining contents of a small brown bottle.

Sondra watched Kari hurricane herself through the apartment. The young woman opened the double louvered closet doors and picked through Sondra's clothes. "Holy crap" she exclaimed. "We got some serious wardrobe reconstruction to do here," she announced. "I keep telling you we should do some more clothes shopping together but I had no idea things were this bad." She then launched into more nonstop talk of clothes and boys. Kari then had Sondra get out two glasses and split the whiskey evenly from the bottle she had in the pocket of her long dark green coat. "Just swiped this from my boyfriend's dad's liquor cabinet," she told her. "He had several that are mostly empty so I'm sure he won't miss it." Kari filled the glasses the rest of the way with cranberry juice from Sondra's refrigerator and handed her one of the cocktails. She turned on the radio and the two girls sat on the rug in the middle of the room. The concoction tasted simply awful to Sondra but in the moment she sipped it with a combination of pride and reckless defiance. The conversation flowed, with Sondra eventually getting a bit more chatty with her intense house guest, but then Kari stood and announced that she was heading to the party. Sondra once again tactfully declined, and as Kari was putting one arm through her coat, Sondra grabbed at the car keys. "Eight hours between bottle and throttle," said Sondra, now wrestling the taller girl. Kari thought this all wildly amusing but for Sondra it was deadly serious. She secured the keys, pinning Kari on the tan carpet. When she let go of her wrists and began to sit up, Kari sat up quickly as well and wrapped her arms around Sondra's neck, giving her kiss on the lips. Sondra scrambled to her feet, stunned. "I'm uh. I'm calling you a cab" she announced. As she pushed memorized numbers on her cell phone, Kari stood up, giggling. "Here's twenty bucks," said Sondra. "That'll get you there and home safely." Kari smiled at her for a few seconds, then quoted a TV public service announcement. "Friends don't let friends drive drunk. Thanks for the bucks. I'm good for it, and have a great trip."

Kari was gone in a flash. To Sondra the apartment seemed dim and to close in around her, especially when she turned off the radio. She sat down scanning her surroundings with the same steady motion of a search-light, not stopping on any one particular area. In the now-serenity she could hardly believe that the little impromptu party with Kari had actually happened. Her breathing was shallow as her brain worked overtime trying to figure out what to make of the kiss. Is Kari secretly in love with me? Am I supposed to like girls now instead of boys? Her stomach felt as if it were twisted into jagged knots and she missed her mom something fierce.

Sondra embarked on a four-day, tri-state adventure to and from the Grand Canyon. She thought of visiting John and Leanna first but easily talked herself out this detour. Instead she stuck to her route on Highway 58 to Barstow. After reaching Lake Havasu City, her first destination, Sondra walked across the London Bridge experiencing a surreal feeling before getting a bite to eat and securing a motel room for the night. The next afternoon she arrived at the Grand Canyon National Park, finding a space in the crowded parking lot and hurrying over to the edge. The spectacular array of colors, shapes and vastness took her breath away and she sank to her knees, staying in that position for over ten minutes, thinking that "grand" was clearly the appropriate description. She obtained a room for her duration and picked up an armload of pertinent brochures and papers from the Visitors Center. Each moment Sondra spent at the national park seemed continuously magical, though she made a definite mental note to come back when it was warmer. The people she encountered were all so dear and every sight and sound gave her some profound life perspectives. This was a place on earth that took millions of years to create while the human race has only been around for a fleeting brief moment in time by comparison. She felt small but not in a bad or insignificant way. As she explored the insides of a primitive stone dwelling, she was struck by the thought that her parents and brothers had been taken away from her in a blink of an eye but she had her own Grand Canyon-esque lifespan ahead of her. Sondra didn't want to leave all this splendor. She'd cherished these two days, but with an armful souvenirs she reluctantly headed for home. On the journey, she spent time at the Glen Canyon Dam, passed by Vermillion Cliffs, stopped to explore Indian Cave Dwellings and had a picnic lunch at Zion National Park that nearly gave her frost bite. She would never forget her unbelievably cold mid-day meal at such a beautiful place nor the family of peacocks she observed making their way along as she ate.

After spending the night at a small motel on Christmas Eve, Sondra cried herself bitterly to sleep. She woke early the next morning and drove a somber fourteen hours to the Las Vegas city limits. The beauty and serenity of the past few days were obliterated by the harsh bright lights and heavy frantic traffic. Weariness hit hard as she pulled off the freeway with no particular destination or plan. She drove around almost in circles and finally parked at a grocery store. When the clerk ringing up her bottle of soda noticed her shirt, he asked her if she'd been to the Grand Canyon. She nodded. "Yeah, it was amazing but I've been on the road for like a trillion hours. I'm wiped. You know a good motel around here?" "This is Vegas, baby" he exclaimed. "Just drive down The Strip 'til you see a casino you like. Plenty of great rooms and food in any of 'em, and good deals too." Sondra obtained a room in one of the newer casinos and had a satisfying meal, but when an employee asked to see her ID after she'd later wandered onto the casino floor, he promptly escorted her back to the dining room.

Standing at the large window in her twelfth story suite, she was fascinated by the brilliant picture before her. This was most definitely not the amazing Grand Canyon but the skyline full of multicolored lights and the constant movement down on the street seemed grand in its own way. She remembered reading a book, with the author describing his high-rise New York apartment view and how all the people moving around in a mostly non-conscious state were like ants scurrying along, too busy to notice the beauty and preciousness of life around them.

Sondra got a very early start the next day, experiencing

anxiousness to get home and the excitement over her adventure. This was exactly what she'd needed. The truck had performed flawlessly, and spending so much time behind the wheel was not only fun but gave her a powerful exclamation point on her career choice. She may not have been on a track with a fast race car but driving was everything to her, with all this time she'd spent at over 80 miles per hour giving her a small inkling of track and wind conditions she'd have to contend with when in an Indy car. It wasn't a matter or question of if. Racing at that level was her extremely focused goal. She saw it clearly in her head and felt it deeply within her soul.

When Sondra reached the top step that led into her apartment she spotted an envelope from Kari. Going inside she dropped her two backpacks at her feet, closing the door behind her and leaning against the cold wooden portal. Looking around at her small drab living space she then read the communiqué and dialed Kari's cell number, having to leave her a voice-mail message. "Hey, I'm back. Thanks for the note and the twenty. That's really sweet. I had a great time and I got you something from Vegas. Meet me at the garage tomorrow and we'll have lunch or dinner. Bye for now."

Sondra then called Doug and was surprised that she was forced to leave a message as well. This wasn't the homecoming she'd expected and the aloneness she felt seemed just as wide and deep as the Grand Canyon. She felt like crying but the tears wouldn't come. After a long hot shower, Sondra crawled into her sleeping bag, exhausted. Her cell phone rang out and she hesitated to answer it but was glad she did when she heard Doug's voice asking her how the trip had gone. She was far too weary for any kind of inspired detail but she went to sleep happy knowing that Doug had missed her and would be at the B.A.S.S. garage the next day at 4 p.m.

While Sondra had been on her journey, Kari had come to the startling realization she had crossed the line and perhaps damaged her friendship with Sondra. Though Sondra was always fiercely tight-lipped about her family, it was widely known that alcohol, more specifically a drunk driver, had played a role in how she came to live in Bakersfield. To come to Sondra's apartment and be that irresponsible and reckless was embarrassing to Kari and she worried that it might have destroyed their friendship. She worried a little less, however, when, that very next day she had listened to a voicemail message by Sondra explaining that she'd left Kari's car keys in her desk drawer at the B.A.S.S. garage. When Kari had gone to retrieve them she discovered that no word had been spoken to Bobby about her party behavior and why Sondra was in possession of the ignition tools in the first place.

Kari treated Sondra to lunch at an Italian deli, a celebration of her friend's triumphant return from the Grand Canyon and a way to have a heart to heart talk. "Thanks for not ratting me out to Bobby, or apparently to anyone else" she said. "I really am sorry, Sondra," she added, leaning in and playing with the straw in her soda.

"Tracy used to call me an angry little judgmental freak about all things alcohol," related Sondra after swallowing a bite of her Italian sub sandwich. "I mean I don't want to be some judgmental freak but ..." She chewed and swallowed hard, shaking her head twice. "I lost my whole family. My whole normal life because ..."

"Yeah, I get it," said Kari, beginning to cry. "I'm really sorry if I scared you. I thought about it all the next day. Really woke me up, you know? I've been doing a lot of dumb things lately." Kari reached across the table to hold Sondra's hand. Sondra gave her friend's fingers a squeeze and let go, flashing her a smile. "Buck up, buttercup," she told Kari. "Nothing bad happened, and, here, I brought you something." Sondra handed Kari a white plastic bag containing an imitation gold necklace with a small figurine of Elvis kicking his leg out and strumming his guitar. Kari put it on over her gold tresses, visibly moved and shedding a few more tears.

Sondra's later reunion with Doug was equally significant. They picked up Chinese food and went to her apartment. Doug enjoyed hearing Sondra go into great detail about her trip, including her experience behind the wheel for so many miles. When the story of her triumphant excursion concluded, he took a loud deep breath and leaned against the wall. "I'm so glad for you," he told her. "And I do believe you came back older and wiser." He shifted position and continued. "But if this apartment wasn't such a temporary place for you, I'd be insisting you get some chairs in here.'

Sondra rolled her eyes and flashed a smile. "Almost exactly two months 'til I'm done with classes and then I'm outta here with my AA degree," she said with a nod and a victory fist pump in the air. "Then I can start my real life," she added, taking a deep breath and moving next to Doug, settling her back against the wall. Doug put an arm around the girl and smiled when she inquired about his Christmas with Snap-on lady. "You mean Karen," he corrected before regaling her with the tale. "Well I laid it on pretty thick that I was gonna be alone for Christmas," he began. "She's got the same dry sarcastic wit as you," he added with a quick laugh. "She thought I was being pathetically and blatantly transparent but didn't skip a beat in asking me to have Christmas with her."

"So where does she live?" inquired Sondra.

"She rents a really nice but small two-bedroom cottage-style house in Moraga, and man does she keep it immaculate. She had a lot of holiday decorations but absolutely nothing in the cottage was out of place. I got to meet her parents, sort of."

"Wow," said Sondra.

"Yeah." Doug nodded. "They called not long after I got there. Karen put us on speaker-phone and I swear I could hear the disapproval in their voices. I mean it was obvious they thought I was the reason their only daughter wasn't with them for Christmas, but by the end of the call we were on friendly terms. They seem like pretty interesting and nice folks."

"So you stayed overnight at her house?" inquired Sondra. Doug sneezed a laugh through his nose and eyed the girl. "Uncomfortable living room couch," he told Sondra in a lie. Karen's couch was in fact uncomfortable and when she'd invited him for the overnight stay he was the one to suggest he camp out on her sofa. They'd been dating exclusively however for over three months and had numerous times discussed their closeness and a probable future together. Neither Karen nor Doug had any intention of his sleeping on her couch on Christmas eve. Doug was determined to keep all this from Sondra however. There was no way he would ever intentionally say or do anything that would cause the girl a minute's worry in this area.

"Karen's an amazing cook," announced Doug, intentionally leading them away from any further sleeping arrangement discussion. "We talked about a lot of things, fun things and serious stuff. Actually, you came up in conversation quite a bit. She likes you a lot."

"I'm glad you had a good time" Sondra told Doug. "I mean I guess we could use a good cook in our lives," she joked.

"Hey," he exclaimed, feigning indignation and briefly leaning into Sondra. "I've never poisoned anyone … yet."

Sondra giggled and leaned into him as well. "So has Mr. Stoltz made any progress with the new sprint car and team?" she asked in an obvious non sequitur. Doug nodded. "Car's ready to roll and he's been stockpiling tires and equipment," he told her. "I've been doing quite a bit of research and I talked to Karen about it. How would you feel about me becoming your career manager and getting Snap-on on board as a major sponsor?"

Sondra nodded with an enthusiastic smile. "Good," said Doug. "There's a bunch of other stuff we'll go over in the coming days and weeks, but I think I've done more than just spark the interest of quite a few people, and Karen knows this marketing and publicity stuff backwards and forwards. She's offered future help, if you're interested."

"I'm interested," said Sondra, continuing to smile and nod.

Chapter 12

The month of January was bitter cold and often foggy but Sondra was steadfastly focused on her job and scholastic endeavors. One evening near the end of the month Kari stopped by the apartment and handed Sondra a bag of clothes she'd carefully picked out and wanted her to have. Kari seemed unusually emotional and it was obvious that she'd been crying. As the young woman had done on a number of occasions, Kari insisted on being Sondra's fashion consultant with the clothes she'd brought. The two girls went through the items and outfits, with Kari commenting the entire time on whether it was a hit or a miss. "Well I should get going," said Kari, after straightening the shoulders of the last garment she'd had Sondra model for her. Kari had been there for just over two hours and suddenly threw her arms around Sondra in a tight embrace. "My mom's boyfriend got this great job and big apartment in Stockton," she said, releasing Sondra and struggling with her composure. "We're moving day after tomorrow. I can't believe it. Just like that." Kari proceeded with a profanity-laced rant about this particular predicament and again gave Sondra a tight hug. "I love you and I'll never forget you."

"Well, it's not like you're leaving the planet," said Sondra, stunned and feeling the pangs of anxiety and panic. "You can call me and write to me," she told her friend. "And I'll come visit you. Besides, there's the Stockton Speedway. I'm sure I'll be at that racetrack in the future."

Kari burst into tears, kissed Sondra on the cheek and was gone in a flash. When the door closed, it seemed like the loudest sound Sondra had ever experienced. She and Kari hadn't known each other all that long, but this was yet another crushing blow she had to endure. She stood staring at the back of the door, with its cracking paint, in a stunned trance. Kari leaving her behind seemed so out of the blue and Sondra became aware of that all-too-familiar dreaded physical sensation, as though she'd just been kicked in the stomach.

In the days that followed, Sondra delved even harder into work, classes and dirt bike workouts. Bobby was aware of a change in Sondra almost immediately. He'd known of Sara's pending move for over a month but had said nothing, simply because he was unaware that Kari and Sondra were all that close. Sondra's behavior, while altered, wasn't rude or neglectful of her normal work duties but was cold and cut off emotionally. With this increasing demeanor, Bobby alerted Doug to the developments and Doug did everything he could to alleviate her pain, though the stubborn girl refused to talk about anything but work, school and racing.

By the end of March, the Learning Annex courses Sondra had put so much effort into ended just as unceremoniously as they had begun, even though this meant she'd completed the associate of arts program. Nothing had come up that was an extreme challenge and she saw this as more of an I-told-you-so rather than a joyous academic achievement. Doug, Bobby and Diane insisted, however, that a celebration dinner was warranted, and the evening at the Shniders' was extremely pleasant, as always. After dessert they discussed Sondra's future in Fresno with Doug. Bobby and Diane shed tears as Doug looked on, aware of Sondra's new-found stoic toughness. "We're going to miss you so much, sweetheart," said Diane. "Garage won't be the same without you," added Bobby. Sondra responded by employing a similar line she'd used with Kari. "Well it's not like I'm going to another solar system," she told the couple. "I'll be in touch, and I'll be back for visits."

On the ride with Doug to Fresno, with all her belongings, few as they were, Sondra took a loud deep breath. “That was really nice,” she said of their time with the Shniders. “Sad but nice,” she added. “I talked with John and Leanna yesterday,” she added in a non sequitur. “They’re moving to Florida near Miami to be closer to Leanna’s sister. I guess she has some medical problems. I made double sure they had our address in Fresno.” Doug glanced over at his passenger. The girl’s face registered a determined anger. “Everyone’s leaving everywhere,” said Sondra. “Not to bad places,” countered Doug, trying to ease the girl’s sense of abandonment. “Yeah I guess,” she half agreed. “I mean I wanted to leave Bakersfield before I even got there and I never thought it could actually happen.” “You made it happen, Sondra,” asserted Doug. “You knew in your heart that you wanted better things and you worked your ass off to get ’em. Just like you do every time the green flag drops. Your strength and determination’s gonna get you a whole lot more, with racing, college and life.” Sondra shrugged her shoulders and stared out the side window, watching the world streak by as she pondered Doug’s words.

A week later, Sondra took Doug’s truck back to Bakersfield to tie up loose ends. She felt a sudden and odd sense of sadness. Everywhere she looked was a memory of her life there. She hated having this sense that she was going to miss it but couldn’t shake the feeling. Her first stop was to her apartment, where she met with Susan Zeller to do a final walk-through and give her the keys. After a warm goodbye and well-wishes, Sondra drove over to the B.A.S.S. garage. The office she had painstakingly redone months ago had a completely different feel, though it hadn’t actually changed in appearance. She stopped short just inside what had been her domain. Victoria, a trashy blond with the reddest fingernails Sondra had ever seen, noticed the girl standing in the doorway. “Help you, hon?” Sondra could definitely have gone the rest of her life without ever having to be called hon. She forced a recovery from the hideousness. “I’m looking for Bobby,” she asserted. “Is he around today?” Victoria looked the girl up and down. “You his kid or somethin’?” she asked. “He’s out but he’ll probably be back about three.”

Sondra corrected the woman. "I'm Sondra Sierre. I used to work here."

"Oh, hey" exclaimed Victoria. "There's a bunch of your mail here." After a few minutes of rummaging around she handed Sondra a large handful of paper items. It was mostly catalogs and junk-mail. "Thanks," Sondra told the woman. "I filled out a change of address card quite a while ago," she explained. "But this must have slipped through. Tell Bobby I stopped by and that I'll call him."

Sondra sat in the Toyota and examined the stack, noting a few important mail items, a bank statement and two legal-size envelopes. She opened those first and discovered they were notices of significant sums of money owed to her, and there were dates and dollar figures. The dates were from when she was still living at the evil house. Sondra then perused the bank statement, but try as she might she found no checks or record that her account actually received any money listed within the other documents. She went over everything two more times but nothing added up, and a thought as to why was becoming all too clear. A suspicious Sondra went to her bank to find out answers. She had to get a little loud and angry because the woman at the Customer Service counter kept repeating the few things she'd retained from her training. The only solid bit of information Sondra came away with was that her suspicions were confirmed. No funds from the letters' claims were ever processed through that bank. Sondra withdrew all her money and closed the account. She then drove straight over to confront Brenda. After much knocking she discovered the door to the mobile home was unlocked. The place was filthy and smelled of rotting trash, cigarette smoke and stale alcohol. As she went though the house, she kept calling out the inhabitants' names, to no avail. Every room was stomach-churning-gross to her, and she went to the corner of the living room where Brenda's desk was located. She retrieved an astonishing handful of papers and envelopes with her name on them, which were obviously opened and gone through. She then ran back to the truck. She unclipped her cell phone from her belt loop and called Doug, figuring that she'd get his voice-mail. He answered in a cheery voice but she was far from cheery.

"Hi Doug, it's Sondra." Doug could tell right away that something was not right with her. She continued. "I picked up some of my mail at the shop and it led me to find out that Brenda's stolen a bunch of money from me. I can't believe she would pull this kind of crap. How could she do this to me?" Sondra could hear Doug's loud exhale into the phone and then his voice was strong. "You need to go to the police, sweetie. They'll know what to do. And then I want you to come straight home. We can handle everything from here."

"Kay" she squeaked, trying not to cry. Though Sondra still harbored some hatred of police because of what they'd done to her in Santa Monica, she drove to the station to file a complaint and full report. She was absolutely done with this part of the world. There had been frustration and resentment for being brought there in the first place and now this was the crowning blow. On the drive to Fresno her rage grew, but nearing the neighborhood that was to be her new permanent surroundings she relaxed with the idea that she'd escaped hell.

During the dinner Doug had prepared, he watched Sondra sullenly pick at her fried hamburger patty and microwaved baked potato. "So I think we should make copies of all the stuff you found in Brenda's desk," he suggested. "And everything pertinent, like past bank statements. Tomorrow we'll go through all your records for the past two years."

"I don't care," she growled with a shrug. "It's just blood money anyway. I don't want it. Let that bitch have it all."

"Sondra," Doug said in a scolding whisper.

"What'd you put in the hamburger?" she asked, deliberately changing the subject. "It's really good."

"Thanks," acknowledged Doug, deciding not to pursue further talk of Brenda and the money. They'd discuss it all the next day when Sondra was in a better mood and not so tired. "A few spices" he said in answer to her culinary question. "Garlic powder, onion powder, lemon pepper, and this little steak seasoning packet that came in an outdoor catalog my old friend Wally sent me."

"Wally?" she asked. "Jim Waldeguard," he clarified. "I've known

Wally since I was in high school. My friend Paul and I used to hang with him and two other guys. After graduation, Wally and I went on this epic cross-country road trip on our bikes. I had an old Kawasaki Z1 R that I'd just rebuilt. Stevie and Springer, Steve Flint and Gary Springer, drove along with us in a blue MG. That thing broke down about every seventy miles. We had a running joke that it was basically held together by gum, shoe laces and duct tape." This story perked up Sondra's spirits, as Doug knew it would. She asked a few questions about the motorcycles and his friends, then later watched close to an hour of TV with Doug before going to bed. It took her quite a while to fall asleep that nigh, but she did so knowing she was safe and that she had a person solidly in her life who truly cared about her.

Five days later, a police sergeant contacted Sondra by phone. Brenda and her accomplice/boyfriend had been caught. The sergeant wasn't exactly forthcoming with information but gave Sondra the phone number of the detective who'd be handling the case. He also gave her the phone number of a law firm and the names of two attorneys that kept coming up in the many documents somehow connected. Since the process of resolution would take time, Doug encouraged Sondra to spend her energy and focus elsewhere.

Just weeks before the sprint-car season was to begin, there came a day of testing and practice in the new yellow and blue #82 Stoltz Special. The shakedown took place at Stoltz Alley, the familiar quarter-mile track that had been the stage of Sondra's recent racing success. Dan Stoltz made a point of coming down to witness the action and formally introduce the four-man pit crew members. It didn't take long for both Sondra and Doug to secretly form the opinion that these four men were a strange band of misfits. They weren't mean or unpleasant to Sondra, but their indifference was palpable. The men were expecting to crew for a strong talented male rising-star driver, and their first impression of Sondra was far from that. All they saw was a skinny tomboy who looked twelve years old. As with Steven Barnes from Gavins Racing, they had no confidence in her abilities. By the end of their time on track, Sondra had proved she could more than handle the 700-pound vehicle with its

900-horsepower V-8 motor.

On the drive home, Doug noticed a new energy emanating from Sondra. She talked excitedly about the new car and how much she was looking forward to their first race of the season. Once home she changed into her workout attire and informed Doug she was headed to the nearby gym. "Be home by six," he instructed. "Karen's coming over to make us one of her famous dinners."

"Wow," said Sondra. "A new race car and dinner from Snap-on lady all in one day." You nutty girl" laughed Doug.

Minutes after Sondra's departure, Doug received a phone call. He was expecting it to be from Karen informing him of her whereabouts, but instead an unfamiliar male voice greeted him. "Yes, I'm looking for Mr. Doug Trent," said the man. Upon Doug's confirmation, the man again spoke. "My name's Frank Brandon. My wife Sheila and I are the ones who first came upon the Sierre family accident several years ago. I understand you're now Sondra's legal guardian."

"I am" said a suspicious Doug. "I'm in the process of legally adopting her," he added. "Is that what this is about?"

"No" said the man. "I'm sorry to just call you like this but we've been trying to reach you. We're in the area and we were hoping to meet with you in person. My wife and I are lawyers and we've been in contact with law enforcement over a recent development. It's too complicated to get into over the phone, but do you have some time possibly today?:

"Um, well I guess," said Doug. "You're here in Fresno?"

Frank gave his current location, which was not far, and Doug gave the man directions.

Doug paced the living room and kitchen pondering whether or not this impromptu meeting with the Brandons was a good idea. On one hand, he was curious to meet them and possibly gain more information and understanding of what had happened to Sondra and her family. He also wondered how or if this was tied to the current situation with Brenda. When the door chime rang out, he was relieved to see Karen. He kissed her and ushered her inside. "Sondra's at the gym," he told her, taking one of the bags of grocery items she'd brought. He then led her into the kitchen and went into the recent developments. Karen leaned against the counter, listening in silence, taking it all in. "I was sure this whole Brenda mess would have been cleaned up by now," Doug told Karen with a shake of his head. "But it just keeps dragging on. The Brandons, the lawyers I told you about, they're on their way over supposedly with late-breaking information that can't wait."

"Well I guess it's a good thing that Sondra's not here," said Karen. Doug nodded.

Frank and Sheila Brandon turned out to be a wealth of information. They filled Doug and Karen in on important informational gaps. Sondra's mannerisms and the things she would say and do over these past few years now made a bit more sense to Doug. Karen became visibly shaken when the couple described the horrific accident, and even Doug had tears racing down his cheeks when Frank told of Kal Sierre's last words and that Doug actually looked a bit like him. A dizzying amount of information was exchanged. Sheila then told of their frequent contact with John and Leanna Farnsal. She produced a copy of a letter written to John by Brenda, containing strongly written warnings from her for them to "leave Sondra alone and butt out of our lives." Falsely stated in Brenda's letter were words to the effect that Sondra didn't want anything further to do with the Farnsals, and she insisted John send her any and all legal and financial documents. John never complied with any of Brenda's demands. "Well, unfortunately Brenda was never any kind of mom or parent to Sondra," said Doug bitterly, stunned by all this. "She turned out to be pretty self-serving and manipulative," he added. "I never saw that when I first knew her. The foster-care deal was made behind my back with her friend Judith Tredou from CPS when I was out of town. Even so, I've tried to do everything I can for Sondra. Always tried to keep her on the right track. That kid means everything to me. She's a strong, amazing, intelligent young lady." Doug put his arm around Karen. "We both love her more than anything on this planet."

Sheila gave detailed content of a letter that Leanna Farnsal had written to her and her husband. In it Leanna described how puzzled and hurt they were, since their relationship with Sondra, although short-lived, had been an extremely loving one. She went on to reminisce about Sondra and how much fun it was to take her on walks and trips to the Santa Monica Pier and to various eateries. At this point Frank again spoke. "Mr. Farnsal's a very thorough and tenacious man, as you may or may not know already, especially when it comes to Sondra." He then proceeded to divulge more information than Doug had been privy to regarding the Jenners and their tragic and sad end of life story, and how this had dramatically compounded poor little Sondra's situation. With hesitation and care, Frank and Sheila described any and all events, everything they knew leading up to Sondra being placed with the Bakersfield foster family. Frank then went into the details about Brenda's current situation and the arrest. Doug sat stunned to hear the tale about the woman he thought he'd known and had once loved.

Not long after Brenda and Doug had split, according to Frank, Brenda took up with her old crowd. The tragedy of it was that her old crowd had attracted a worse one. Within this group, Brenda met an exciting and dangerous biker-type man who eventually introduced her to crystal meth. At first, Brenda had kept Sondra's correspondence and checks out of spite and residual resentment for the ungrateful girl moving out and petitioning the court to become an emancipated minor. She'd actually planned on giving them to her eventually, but with the new guy and the growing expensive drug habit, together they came up with the idea to use that money for themselves. They'd been getting away with it for months until an insanely high Brenda tried to cash another of Sondra's checks, which was blatantly forged. The boyfriend was sitting on his Harley in front of a Southern New Mexico Credit Union when the police were notified by an alert teller, who'd been shown Brenda's picture and description by her supervisor just two days prior. They were taken without much incident into custody. After their motel room was searched they found drugs, guns and quite a stash of Sondra's stolen documents.

Doug and Karen shook their heads at this bizarre tale. "I can't believe this," said Karen. "This is like something out of a movie."

Doug stood and walked over to the unlit gas fireplace, then returned to his seat. "What about Brenda's kids?" he asked. "Do you know how they are? Where they are? I mean the two youngest, Jennifer and Josh, were such sweet kids, and Tracy was a dear with a lot of potential. And Pete … Well he was always a handful but I loved all of them." The two attorneys couldn't legally discuss details but did divulge that Pete was currently incarcerated for drug possession and attempted auto theft, and the other kids were with friends and relatives.

"Sondra's gonna be home soon," said Doug. "Aside from the legal matters at hand, she's in a really great place in her life. I can't thank you enough for being here and telling us so much and now wanting to help her again. That kid's been through too much. I get that you want to see her, see if she turned out okay, but she hangs on by just a thread a lot of the time."

"We didn't come here to upset her, or you," said Frank. "This will take about three months to get cleared up. If you don't want Sondra to be involved in any of the process, she'll lose the over nine thousand dollars that Brenda and her boyfriend spent."

"She won't care about the money," said Doug, with a shake of his head. "I can assure you of that, but I'll let her know the options in due time." He then softened and spoke of Sondra, regaling the Brandons with many funny and heartwarming anecdotes. It was quite a shock to them all when the front door suddenly burst open.

"I'm home!" exclaimed a cheery Sondra. "They have a new gift shop at our gym. I bought this cool sweater for only ten bucks and it gave me a brilliant idea for a …" Still smiling, although somewhat diminished, she noticed the eyes of four adults locked upon her. "Hi," she greeted the visitors.

Doug got up and stood behind Sondra. Frank and Sheila were speechless. They couldn't get over what they were seeing. At the accident site they had witnessed a tiny crumpled and bleeding little girl, barely hanging on to life. Now before them was this strong radiant young woman who looked like a model. After her gym workout, she'd showered and changed into stylish black jeans and a light blue top under the new deep purple fleece sweater she'd just purchased. Her long dark brown straight hair cascaded over her shoulders and back, with a top portion of it tied with a short white silk ribbon.

"Frank, Sheila," announced Doug. "I'd like you to meet our Sondra. And Sondra, these are the Brandons."

"Oh yeah," said the girl, recognizing the name and holding out her hand. "You're the lawyers that are helping us. Thank you so much. John Farnsal mentioned you. I mean he's a lawyer as well and he's done a ton of great stuff for me. It's nice to finally meet you."

The couple were still mostly speechless but managed a polite greeting. They exchanged more pleasantries, impressed that Sondra was so far along in her schooling and that she was planning on attending college shortly.

"So how'd you get involved in my case?" asked Sondra.

"Well," said Sheila. "We've kinda been involved from the beginning, sweetheart." Sondra swallowed hard, looking instantly white as a ghost. She grabbed hold of Doug's hand and moved into him. "You were there," she said in a low tortured voice, somehow knowing this instinctively. The Brandons gave a sad nod. Sondra pulled away from Doug and stepped closer to the couple. "Tell me," she pleaded. "I have to know. What, what did you see? What did you hear?"

"Sondra," said Doug in restraint as he moved forward. He put his hand on the girl's shoulder and shook his head at the couple, nonverbally warning them not to repeat the gruesome story they'd told earlier. Sondra pulled away from Doug in a sudden angry violent motion, glaring at Frank and Sheila. Frank wasn't sure he should say anything and he tried to convey this, but Sondra stood her ground and demanded to know.

"You were there," said Sondra through gritted teeth. "And you've come all this way. You're here now and I have the right to know. My family," she added in a growl.

"Oh honey" said a tearful Sheila. "I don't want to put those images in your head."

"Words and images can't hurt me," insisted Sondra. "I have

these nightmares," she said, looking at the couple. Frank and Sheila suddenly again saw the little girl they'd come across years ago as Sondra continued. "These horrible nightmares about car crashes or ..."

"We've had nightmares as well," said Frank. "All we saw and heard was a loud frightening crash. One car caused it but a big-rig's trailer did the damage. We were on the side of the highway and I was removing our snow chains. Sheila called for help immediately and paramedics got there right away. In no time at all you were taken to a place where you could be air-lifted to a hospital."

"But?" Sondra asked. "What about?. .."

"Your family didn't suffer, sweetheart" assured Sheila. "It was all so instant. The truck driver didn't make it but the three boys in the car were mostly unharmed. The driver and the other two are paying a very high price for that day, I'm sure."

"Not near high enough," growled Sondra.

"We really should be going," said Frank to Doug. "We didn't come here to upset you, and I'm sorry if we did," he told Sondra. He again addressed Doug. "All the documents you'll need going forward are in the packet we brought you. If we can help you with anything, anything at all, please don't hesitate to call."

"And Sondra," added Sheila. "We're so sorry for your enormous loss but we're so glad to see that you're well."

Frank and Sheila Brandon left that evening relieved and happy in the knowledge that the little girl they'd seen taken away on life-support years ago had overcome such medical trauma and was now thriving. From their conversation with Doug and Karen, they saw clearly that Sondra had two loving and fiercely protective people looking out for her. They hated the idea that the exchange they'd just had with the girl would upset her in any way but hoped that knowing some truths would give her much needed closure.

"I should get going, too," said Karen after the couple had left, feeling that her presence might not be appropriate at this time. "No" insisted Sondra, her voice strong and forceful. "You're a part of us now," she told Karen. She wrapped her arms around the woman in a tight embrace. Doug smiled. Not that this was a joyous occasion, but that the two people he cared most about clearly cared about each other. "You're staying here tonight" added Sondra after releasing her. "And you're not sleeping on the couch" she said, looking over at Doug. "You love each other and I'm not four. Now then. Dinner. We're going to that steak place that Stoltz likes so much."

Doug and Karen loved Sondra for her resilience and energy but the fact that the girl was so quick to just emotionally sweep recent events under the proverbial carpet, just as one might turn on or off a light switch, was a concern. Karen was a bit disappointed that she didn't get to cook the meal she'd planned but felt honored and grateful that Sondra and Doug had insisted she be part of their evening. That night she did sleep on the couch as did Sondra. After coming home from the restaurant Karen, Doug and Sondra watched a TV movie. Just over halfway through, Doug covered the sleeping Karen and Sondra with a thick blanket and went to bed with a deep smile.

CHAPTER 13

It took time, but eventually Sondra's legal and financial items were sent to her. She didn't read any of the letters or documents but took out checks and asked Doug to let her know if there was any important information. She wasn't at all interested in pursuing Brenda for the money she'd taken and spent, just as Doug had predicted. Sondra knew the legal system would deal with that witch, and she didn't want to see or think about the woman ever again. She needed to be completely done with that particular part of her life. Perhaps one day she'd look back on this chapter and appreciate the good, but right now she wanted her focus to be on the present and a hopeful future. Sondra put determined time and effort into preparing both mentally and physically for her first professional race season. She researched sprint-car history, with its past and current drivers, the machinery utilized and the upcoming race schedule. Dan Stoltz put Sondra in contact with a man he thought could give her advice on everything from race tactics to the business side of the sport. The phone calls with Darren Brown were few and far between but he answered her many questions without seeming chauvinistic or that she was somehow wasting his time. The season opener took place at a one-mile oval dirt track in San Jose, California. AMA motorcycle races at the San Jose

Mile had been an annual event that Sondra and her father had read and talked about many times. Each year when the event would roll around Kal and Sondra would discuss attending, but "one of these days" had never manifested and now could never happen.

After practice laps, Sondra told her new engine tuner that she was down on horsepower from what she'd remembered during the test run weeks prior. She also wanted the suspension adjusted to free up the car in order to make it turn easier. Between not really getting what she wanted in the tuning of her car plus incredibly aggressive drivers, it was a wonder she finished the race at all let alone placed in the top ten, allowing her to advance to another round. She'd started that first qualifying race 17th. During the event she struggled with the car's handling, then steadily managed to improve her position. Sondra was shocked at having her competitors deliberately try to wreck her or push her out of the way, far more aggressively and deliberately than her previous racing experiences. In her next heat she started 10th and fell almost immediately to 18th place, beginning to lose more ground. She got pushed from behind coming out of Turn 4 but this worked to her advantage. When she recovered, her car was positioned just right. Pushing down on the accelerator, she fired through a hole between three cars, then had clean race track to start making up time. She spotted the lead pack but turned her focus on the car just ahead of her. The track surface was slick but in some places jarring. She didn't have the horsepower to overtake anyone on the straights but very few in that field seemed to have the instincts and skill in the corners that she possessed on this night. She let the car drift to the ragged edge, then was lightning-quick to accelerate off the turns. She took the checkered flag with a miraculous one-and-a-half-car-length lead. The fans had been amazed by the progress of this unknown driver and team, and even Doug was astonished at the finish, but to Sondra this didn't feel like a victory. The team was high-fiving themselves as she unbuckled and jumped out of the car. Her pit crew was shocked by her attitude. "The only reason I just won is because I can win driving a barn door," she barked at them. "I told you exactly what I needed and you didn't even bother to try." Lead Mechanic Chad Emmers caught up with

Sondra as she walked quickly toward Doug. Chad was 38, divorced with two young boys and had jet black hair with streaks of gray. His sun-tanned face looked slightly leathery from years of outdoor activity. He handed Sondra a small bottle of water. "Hey, man, you gotta chill," he told her. "It's our first race of the season and you just won a qualifying race and now we're going on to the main. Forget the circumstances. It's all good."

Sondra knew Chad was trying to be nice and calm her down, but his words just further enraged her. Growling through clenched teeth, she turned quickly in response. "I'm here to win races, not drive around in a circle with equipment that's like a glorified riding lawn mower." He took immediate offense but didn't have a leg to stand on with any kind of argument. Truth be told, he and the other guys had basically decided that they weren't going to take orders from some little girl. Sondra stood waiting for Chad to say something. An apology. Instead, his offer sounded like an excuse. "Well, like I said, this is just our first race of the season. You just won and things'll get better from here."

She wasn't feeling any less angry but she knew she had to let this go. There was another race to run and many more to follow in the next six months. "If this is going to work," she imparted, "you have to start trusting me, and you guys are gonna have to step up and be a team I can count on. I plan on winning tonight and tomorrow night. I hope you're gonna want that too." Sondra did win the main race. It was far from perfect or pretty, however. There were many crashes throughout the field during the event but luck was on her side at the end. She was in 3rd Place with seven laps to go when the leaders came together and spun into the guard rail. The last laps were run under Caution but Sondra was declared the winner.

Doug drove Sondra home later that night, with her in a somber mood at first. "You impressed a lot of people," he said.

"I don't care," she said, staring straight ahead.

"Yes you do," Doug countered, grabbing her briefly just above her left knee. "You did good and you proved to Stoltz that you're the real deal. Now lighten the hell up, will you? You hungry?"

Sondra looked over at him, shrugged her right shoulder but flashed a smile. They went to a fast food restaurant for hamburgers and sat in a corner booth. "Sorry for being so intense," she apologized. Doug shook his head. "No need to ever apologize for being passionate about what you do," he told her. "But the takeaway is that you won tonight. Build off the positive not the negative." He handed Sondra a napkin after watching her wipe her mouth with the back of her hand. "Karen and her supervisor from Snap-on were there tonight," he continued. "You basically made her look good in front of her boss. She texted me that she hit him up for a better future sponsorship deal." Sondra sat back and took a deep breath. She smiled as she reached for another French fry. "She's not half bad, for a Snap-on lady, and you kinda rock as a manager," she said.

"Yeah, well," he said with a bit of a smirk, "you're not half bad yourself, for a nutty girl." He then leaned in and spoke in a more serious tone. "I have to admit, I was a little nervous about how things would go tonight. These guys are older, with a lot more experience. Whole different ball game than before."

"I was built for this racing stuff," said Sondra, her voice full of conviction. "I mean when the handling got worse and track conditions got ugly something inside me just came alive."

It was close to midnight when Doug and Sondra arrived at the condo. Dan Stoltz had left a voicemail first giving Sondra a chewing out for not being more of a team player but then congratulating her on the overall win.

The next day, in the pre-noon Saturday haze, Sondra again sat in the passenger seat and loved every second of the drive back to San Jose with Doug. Her mood had lightened considerably from the previous night. She'd accepted her triumph and was excited about the next challenge. Walking to her assigned pit area, Sondra wasn't too surprised to see Dan Stoltz shuffle toward them. She hid behind Doug. "Save me, save me," she joked, figuring she was about to get yelled at or receive a stern lecture. Dan smiled as he watched Doug reach around and try to pull Sondra out from behind. "Howdy, Doug," he greeted. "Seen my driver around anywhere?" he joked.

Stoltz didn't wait for an answer and continued. "No? Well I guess I'll have to put Eddie in." Eddie was one of the three guys on her pit crew from the previous night, and upon hearing his name Sondra shot out from behind. "Don't you dare," she exclaimed. "I'm right here." Her smile was radiant as she stepped forward with her outstretched hand.

Sondra had a powerful handshake that had caught more than a few people off guard in the past. When she was nine she had made a wager with her father that if she got straight A's on her next report card she'd get the tan rawhide cowboy boots she'd been wanting for months. After shaking on the deal, he schooled her on the proper and respectable execution of this particular ritual. "No limp dishrag handshakes," he told his daughter. "You want people to know you really mean it." Sondra's mom was sitting in her favorite living room chair and was reading an article on horticulture. She lowered the newspaper and shook her head. "Oh that's great, Kal," said Maureen in a sarcastic tone. "I thought we were raising a daughter. I had no idea we were raising an old trucker. What's next, spitting lessons?" Without thinking it through, Sondra quickly added, "Oh I'm already good at that." Her words tapered off, realizing she probably shouldn't have revealed this bit of information. Neither parent was pleased or amused. The first time Dan Stoltz had shaken hands with Sondra he commented on her unladylike greeting. "Now, honey," he'd said. "Lets see you spit and grab your crotch like the big boys." She had cringed upon hearing something so gross and she'd bitten down on her tongue as she pictured her dad coming to her defense. Over time Dan had come to have a considerable amount of respect for her and now appreciated the solid gesture.

"Got about thirty minutes before your driver's meeting," Stoltz told Sondra. "Come on over and meet the two new guys on your pit crew." She was relieved that the lame ducks from before were history. Dan introduced them. "Sondra, this is Gil. He's your new tire and chassis guy, and over here's Andy, your gas man and general mechanic. And you already know Mr. Emmers," he said pointing to Chad, who was kneeling over her car's engine.

"Nice to meet you, Gil," greeted Sondra. She noted his surprise at her handshake and turned to the other young man, guessing him to be maybe twenty or twenty-one.

"Hi Andy," greeted Sondra. The young man didn't immediately grasp her hand because he was overtly staring at her chest.

"Hey," he said in a barely audible voice. Sondra positioned her left arm as if she were about to recite the pledge of allegiance then again reached out with her right hand. The boy reached out and as they shook hands his face turned many shades of red. Sondra was in her racing suit but as usual before and after a race it was unzipped with the top half and sleeves hanging down at her hips. Her tie-dyed T-shirt was purple and turquoise. Leanna and John Farnsal had bought it for her one Saturday while they walked up and down the Venice Beach Boardwalk looking at all the shops and people. Not only had it shrunk slightly over the years from washing but she was 13 at the time. Today she was a 15 1/2 year-old young woman and the shirt fit snugly. She wasn't thinking of making a wild or provocative fashion statement when putting it on that morning, only wanting to be able to write to John and Leanna that she'd worn it the weekend of her season-opener. Andy hurried over to a tall rollaway tool cabinet and pretended to be busy. Dan Stoltz was oblivious to the boy's rudeness but Doug had taken notice and envisioned smashing the little creep's face in with his fist. He liked thinking of himself as a fiercely protective father.

During the evenings's first heat race, Sondra didn't get a clean start and was bumped, jostled and bullied in and out of positions. The #82 fell immediately from the 2nd grid-start position to 5th and was drifting steadily back before she was able to settle down and sharpen her focus. It took most of the race but she picked her way through the lead cars one by one, and with just over two laps to go it was Sondra who did the bumping to gain the lead. She didn't mean to be this aggressive but the left-side tires caught a rut for a fraction of a second and forced her into the #34. It wasn't a hard hit and they raced each other neck and neck, with Sondra taking the checkered flag inches in the lead. This was a critical race for her. She'd made strong statements and had laid down the law the night before. Her car and team owner may have been initially displeased with her attitude, but Stoltz had put major effort into making positive changes for her and the future success of his race team. Earlier that day Dan had gone to breakfast with some of his old buddies.

"I've known Chad for quite a while now" he'd told them. "He seems to think the Sierre kid's the real deal. When I asked him what the hell went on last night and why the kid was so pissed, he didn't hand me some BS line or excuse. He gave me the god's honest truth. That's why he's still in and the other two dopes are out. I'm giving the girl everything she needs. She'll basically have enough rope to hang herself and shut her the hell up, or she'll make me some money. Either way, I win."

Sondra sat on the grid for the evening's main race in the Pole Position with the engine idling. She eyed the gauges on the instrument panel: fuel pressure, oil temperature and tachometer. She was also aware of her shaking car but it wasn't a concern because she'd always heard that no racing engine runs that smooth at idle. She re-tightened her safety harness and settled into the seat, pressing the medallion that Doug had given her against her chest. It lay just beneath her race suit and she'd come to think of it as a good-luck charm. When the green flag dropped Sondra launched forward with a perfect start. She developed an involuntary smile. The 900-horsepower naturally aspirated V-8 engine came on loud and strong. Sondra had to fight hard. These guys wanted the win as much as she and they weren't about to back off and give up anything. She allowed herself to run in 3rd for many laps, dealing with a bit of understeer in the wake of the cars ahead. Sondra tried to relax as best she could, intentionally saving her equipment and studying the two lead cars. The #09 just ahead was second because of brute horsepower in the straights. After seven laps she slid past him coming out of Turn 2. It only took three laps to catch the leader. Sondra had a pretty decent car but gained the lead with twelve laps to go owing to her instinctive ability to read the car, her competitor's cars and the race track better than anyone in the field. Dirt racing surfaces change slightly, sometimes dramatically, and at lightning speed. Sondra's instincts and reaction times matched and anticipated all of this. When the checkered flag waved she had a four-second lead.

For the first time since he was a young man, Dan Stoltz had stood for an entire race. He nodded slightly, watching Sondra's post-race antics of making donuts. He listened to the announcer call out her finishing lap time and speed and heard his name mentioned as the car owner. He was pleased that his investment had paid off. His little driver really had come through and she'd backed up her claims and convictions. From that night forward, a fan base started to develop. The first autograph Sondra signed was for a father and son. While writing her name in their program she had a quick flashback of a time many years ago when she and her dad had gone into the pits after a motorcycle road race and were lucky enough to get an autograph from their hero. Now, as she watched the little boy and his dad walk away, commenting on how great that was, she realized that she'd just had a childhood memory that didn't immediately reduce her to tears or raging anger at losing her family. Even so, the relief was enormous when Doug appeared next to her.

Close to the halfway point back to the condo, Doug pulled into a Denny's parking lot. Although it was just after 10 p.m. they were both hungry. On race days, Sondra would eat a good breakfast, no lunch, and then a light meal after the event. She hated the idea of eating late but this system worked for her. Besides, she wasn't going straight to bed afterwards anyway because they still had a long drive ahead of them. The pictures on the menu looked quite appetizing and Doug announced his culinary choice.

"I think I'll have this steak and eggs breakfast thing."

Sondra coughed a laugh, and without immediately looking up from the large laminated display of food commented on his decision. "Breakfast for dinner. Only in America." She looked up and started to giggle. "Do you want fries with that?" she asked. "Or maybe French toast? What about pancakes?"

Doug smiled and shook his head slowly. He held out his menu, pointing to the meal in question. When Sondra saw that it came with a choice of waffles, French toast or pancakes, she doubled over sideways in the booth laughing. He threw a piece of ice at her and snorted a laugh himself. "All right little Miss Julia Child," he joked sarcastically. "Let's hear your brilliant culinary selection."

She sat up and appeared to be calming down. "Not telling," she breathed, trying hard not to let more laughter escape. He snatched the menu from her, tapped her on the head with it and set it on top of his at the end of the light brown Formica table. "You don't have to tell me," he announced. "I already know."

"Na uh," she returned, still having a hard time talking without laughing.

When their waitress arrived minutes later, she smiled at what she assumed was a fun father/daughter outing. "Hi, I'm Melanie," she announced. "What can I get you tonight?"

Sondra pointed at Doug and giggled. "He'll have breakfast for dinner."

Melanie couldn't help but smile as she watched this sweet girl in complete hysterics, holding her stomach as she vibrated in her seat.

"Don't mind her" said Doug. "She had dinner for breakfast." All three had a good laugh at that. Doug picked up his menu and pointed to what he wanted. Sondra's laughing increased slightly when, barely able to speak clearly, she repeated his choice. "Steak and pancakes," she giggled. She was now laughing so hard that tears started streaming down her face. She didn't know why she found this so funny. Maybe it was the late hour. Maybe it was that she'd put a hundred percent into her racing effort and this was a big release. Maybe it was because she was in the presence of her favorite person and felt safe and whole. She buried her head in her arms on the table, trying hard to stop laughing. Doug did in fact know what Sondra wanted and relayed that to Melanie. "She'll have a Patty Melt, medium well, not too much fries and a small salad with blue cheese dressing. Oh, and she'll have milk instead of the soda." When the food arrived, the two hungry diners continued to joke around while enjoying their meal. As Melanie took orders and brought food to other patron, she'd steal glances over at Doug and Sondra, noticing others smiling and looking over in their direction occasionally as well.

When clearing plates and slipping the bill toward Doug, she had tears in her eyes and her voice wavered with emotion as she spoke. "You and your daughter totally made my night. Thanks. I hope you'll come back real soon." Sondra's eyes darted to Doug's. She smiled at the daughter reference and sank comfortably into the dull pink vinyl seat. Doug avoided looking across the table at her as he pulled out his wallet and settled their bill.

CHAPTER 14

The next weekend's race was at a quarter-mile track in Stockton. Sondra's friend Kari hadn't stayed in touch with her as she'd promised. The girl's cell number no longer worked and when Sondra called Directory Assistance there was not a Wilken listing. Compounding this disappointment was the fact that Doug had told her he wasn't going to be able to attend this weekend's event due to work. She took his Tacoma with his blessing however.

Over the next number of weeks Sondra went through tremendous ups and downs, and everything in between. By the middle of September there were only three races remaining, and ironically she was only three points out of the championship lead going into the next venue. She won the first Friday night heat but finished 4th in the next. She led all but four laps in the main, finishing 2nd behind famed driver Alan Cobb. On Saturday it was basically reversed. Sondra got a 3rd in heat #1 and was victorious in heat #2. She went on to win the main event by micro-inches. The championship Points Leader Vincent Wells had crashed in the second heat, and in the main he'd finished 15th. This now put Sondra firmly in the number two spot behind two-time champion Jimmy Geraldo. After the long drive to Fresno on the second to last race of the year in Arizona, where

Sondra had placed sixth in her heat but went on to win the main, she and her miscreant entourage, as she secretly and affectionately named her teammates, arrived home. Doug invited the men inside, though Sondra would have preferred to be dropped off so she could take a long hot shower and luxuriate in the peace and quiet of being home. Gil, Andy and Chad assembled themselves around the kitchen table and regaled Doug with tales of their travels throughout the western states. Included were numerous anecdotes of Sondra's behavior and attitude ranging from suborn and feisty to fun and energetic. Sondra was both pleased and annoyed at these, especially Doug's smiling and nodding reaction.

"Oh my god," said Sondra after the men had departed. "Funny how I didn't like or trust any of 'em in the beginning. And now we're like family." She blew out a long breath. "This wasn't easy. Sorry for all the calls but thank you for paying for 'em."

Doug reached over and held Sondra's hand for a few seconds. "Sorry I didn't get to be with you," he told her. "You were definitely there in spirit, Dad," she assured him. Doug was quite taken aback that Sondra had just called him dad. He wondered if this was due to weariness or if she now truly thought of him as her dad. He hoped for the latter. "I mean you did some amazing management stuff by remote control," she continued. "We picked up sponsors and you kept track of tons of detail for us. Stoltz even eventually quit being so mother hen-ish. I mean, in the beginning he micromanaged us to death. I hate to think this is coming to an end. Even though the guys sometimes annoyed the crap out of me, I'm gonna miss the hell out of them, but I want to move on. I mean I know I can't just jump to IndyCar from here. …"

"Yeah," agreed Doug. "Don't worry, we'll get you into a Formula Ford or an Indy Lights car if we have to build 'em ourselves," he assured her.

Sondra's season finale at the San Jose dirt track quickly turned into the kind of duels and challenges that promoters dream of, with fans on their feet and cheering just as loud as the field of cars. The speedway's lights seemed brighter and the air more alive. Sondra immediately slid back to fifth, summoning patience, then sat back and let the car and track come to her. Just after the halfway point, she was firmly in the lead. In the closing laps she was challenged hard by two other drivers. The three lead cars swapped positions continuously. Sondra loved this. She was in control and having fun. With two laps to go she slid to second, then shot around the leader coming out of Turn 4, taking the white flag. As the checkered flag was forcefully waved she streaked past and had an odd sense of *deja vu.* She was glad to have won the race but the season was over all too soon. She did a few high-powered donuts without actually realizing she was doing them. When she came to a complete stop and silenced the motor, the entire venue became a loud universe of mayhem. It was dizzying to have so many people yell, scream and cheer for her. As Chad, Andy and Gil hugged her and patted her on the back and shoulders, she desperately looked around for Doug. The excited jubilation did eventually settle down, but the victory celebration continued. Sondra was presented with two trophies. one for winning the race, the other for the championship. She was doused in champagne, water, soda, and one guy dumped the small remains of a snow-cone on her Snap-on-capped head. Several microphones were thrust before her and there were demands for her to speak. She was a tad tentative and overwhelmed at first but gracious in her appreciation for her sponsors, the promoters and the fans. She thanked each member of her pit crew as well as the car/team owner. Finding the strength to hold both heavy trophies above her head, she announced one more heartfelt sense of gratitude. "I want to say a special thank you to someone who lifted me out of darkness and encouraged me to grow and believe in myself. This is especially for you, Doug. My awesome dad."

Daniel A. Stoltz hosted a celebration dinner in a banquet room at The Stravagansa, a hotel named for the famous mispronunciation of the word extravaganza from Ricky Ricardo in the *I Love Lucy* TV series. After a lavish meal and some speeches, there was music from a pop jazz band. In attendance of the evenings celebration were a number of Dan's friends, car dealership colleagues and as many racing dignitaries that he could find. Darren Brown, who'd coached Sondra via phone before the season began, found the young racer standing by herself watching the band's guitarist. "Good job today," he told her. "That was some smart driving."

"Thanks," said Sondra. "Sorry I didn't figure out who you were when we talked earlier in the year. My goal and focus is getting to IndyCar in the future, near future."

Darren, a race strategist, was a prominent figure in IndyCar. He pointed to her and shook his head, remembering some of the televised sprint-car races he'd seen that year as well as the two he'd attended. "You're an angry hothead," he told her. "That only works some of the time. I got my eye on you." He patted her shoulder and walked away, leaving her with a smile and a feeling of anxiousness about her future.

Sondra was noticeably quiet during the drive home. After just under an hour of travel, Doug turned off the radio. "You okay?" he inquired. Sondra shrugged and gave a nod. Doug patted the girl's knee and glanced over at her. "I'm okay with telling Karen to back off about the belated birthday dinner she volunteered to make you." Sondra had been on the road during the week she turned 16 and Karen had been at the condo when Doug wished her "Happy Birthday" over the phone. "No" said Sondra quickly. "Don't do that. I don't know why but I feel comfortable around her and we had a couple of nice little talks tonight."

"Talked to some guys from Blue Sea Racing," said Doug, changing the subject. "They're entering a car in the Formula Ford North American Division for next season and are currently scouting for the right driver. Their biggest interest has been running a Nascar team out of Tennessee but they also run a racing school in Sonoma. They use a couple of different cars for the school, including the F-Ford, and want to explore their junior division competition options. Sounds like an overall pretty-together operation. I had a good talk with Greg Wilente, one of the owners. He said he might consider letting you test in one of their cars."

"Hmm," voiced Sondra, folding her arms. "I don't mean to be a pessimist but isn't this like Gavins Racing all over again?"

"I don't think so," countered Doug. "Wilente saw you drive three times this year and they've had students come from dirt racing who did really well on pavement because of that. I'll call him and we'll get you in one of their cars." Sondra beamed, grateful that she had Doug in her life.

CHAPTER 15

Karen was early on the prearranged day she was to cook the belated birthday dinner for Sondra as promised. The advanced time of her arrival at the Fresno condominium was by design. She knew Doug would be working until at least 4 p.m. and this would award her the chance for one-on-one time with Sondra. Doug had warned her the previous day of recent slight changes he'd noticed in the girl. Now that Sondra no longer had school, a job or racing to occupy her time, she'd turned into a more typical young teen. Sondra watched what Doug considered to be inane TV, and on a number of occasions listened to very loud music in her room. She also dressed differently. With the warm pre-fall weather, Sondra's new normal attire consisted of T-shirts and black gym shorts. She did go to the gym, applying her usual hard-work ethic, and her bedroom was always kept neat and tidy, but mostly stayed indoors with her nose in a book.

"Wow, you're here early," exclaimed Sondra as she greeted Karen at the front door. "Dad won't be home 'til about six," she added, offering to carry one of the two heavy-looking paper bags of groceries Karen had brought. Karen smiled at the greeting and that Sondra had referred to Doug as dad. She was also pleased to see that the girl was dressed in a high-sleeve navy-blue T-shirt, tan jeans and white fuzzy socks. "Well, while the mouse is away ..." joked Karen, following Sondra into the kitchen. "So what have you been up to?"

"Oh, not much" shrugged the girl as she pulled items from one of the large paper sacks and set them on the counter. "I mean it's weird to have so much free time. I'm sure most people would kill for that but I hate it. I can't wait to get back into a race car."

"What about college?" asked Karen. "Well, yeah," said Sondra. "Getting my BA is a goal I set for myself, but it's weird. I don't know if it's really something I want or if its something I'm supposed to want. I mean going to college, at least junior college, was always a given when I was growing up. Doug's really pushing for me to go further academically, but it's like I've been taken on this hideous bus ride and I finally got off. Now I get to choose where and how I go."

"Sure," nodded Karen. "But as they say, with great freedom comes great responsibility."

"Hmm," voiced Sondra. "A bit of a cliché but I get it."

"So did you like going to Penn State?" Sondra asked.

"Loved college," said Karen as she searched a drawer left of the sink for a large spoon. "I did a lot of growing as a person there. And I have some very dear and lifelong friendships that came from those four years."

"Well I wouldn't be going for that long," said Sondra. "Just the two that'll get me the degree."

"What exactly are you planning on making?" she asked with a curious look after the contents of both bags had been emptied. Karen smiled and stepped next to the girl, surveying their bounty. "Well, what you see here are choices," she told the girl. Karen had brought items for three possible main courses, and after encouraging Sondra to pick which protein, Karen set the package of pork chops on a plate. "So is this gonna be one of your famous specialties?" asked Sondra.

"Oh, you," smiled Karen, giving the girl a quick heartfelt hug.

At 5:48 p.m. Doug slipped quietly through the front door and could hear Sondra and Karen talking in the kitchen. They were seated at the table with a mass of papers in front of them. A college course catalog lay open, notepaper strewn here and there, with the formal

Cal State Fresno application all filled out and on display. "Welcome home, stranger," said Karen as Doug stepped into the room. Sondra watched the two kiss, feeling a sense of *deja vu*. This basic scene had played out many times between her parents when she was growing up and it now filled her with a mix of contented joy and gut-wrenching anxiety. She was excited and hopeful about her future but was always being clobbered by reminders of her past.

After dinner and watching a Hepburn and Bogart movie, *The African Queen,* which Karen had brought, Sondra went to bed, leaving Doug and Karen to sit and talk in the den.

"Thanks again for an amazing dinner and for helping Sondra with the college stuff," said Doug, casually putting an arm around his girlfriend. "Every time I've brought up the college thing lately she just rolls her eyes and becomes angry-dismissive. I want the best for that kid, and I really want to encourage her to use any of these important building-blocks-of-life sorts of things that she can. But I'm always worried about pushing her too hard. Now knowing what she's gone through, I just want to protect her and keep her safe."

"Well, I hate to play devil's advocate here, Doug," said Karen. "But racing cars isn't exactly safe."

"I know," he agreed. "It is a worry, but it's also something that really makes her come alive, and she's good at it. Damn good. I don't want my fears to get in the way of her happiness or what may be her true calling in life."

"She told me all about the F-Ford possibility," said Karen. "And I do mean all about it."

Doug chuckled with a knowing nod. "Yeah, she can go into long-winded detail when she talks about cars or racing," admitted Doug.

"That girl has obviously done an enormous amount of research," said Karen, with a nod of her head. "She knows the history of the cars and the series. She knows the names and stats of famous drivers that got their start there, and she went on and on about the mechanical detail and on which race tracks they run, especially here in the states."

"Well I may be a little guilty of encouraging that" admitted Doug. "Actually, I haven't told Sondra this, but Dan Stoltz has had some pretty significant offers to buy his sprint-car and team. Even though Sondra's now got her sights set on open-wheel road racing, I think it would crush her if she knew the Stoltz Special Racing team was sold and that she wasn't named as the driver for the new owners."

Karen shifted in her seat to face her boyfriend. "There's a lot going on with that girl," she said in a serious tone as she studied Doug's strong, smooth, handsome face. "Both good and bad," she added. "I'm so glad I got to spend time with her today because now I can see all the things you've been telling me. She's fun and sweet but you're right, just under the surface she's so angry. Really angry. I'm sure she thinks she masks it really well, but it just comes out in some of the little things she says. And have you noticed that she often starts her sentences with 'I mean'? That's one of those little vocal ticks that may or may not have significance."

"Yeah," said Doug with a nod. "I have noticed because it seems like it's become more and more pronounced in the past year. I think I do that sometimes," admitted Doug. "And her friend Kari used to say that as well once in a while, as I recall. Sondra won't admit it, but I know she was pretty devastated when Kari moved away." Doug glanced down at the coffee table noticing a fitness magazine Sondra was reading. "Sondra just recently started calling me dad more often as well," he continued. "So maybe the I mean thing is my fault. Maybe it's like a subconscious thing to be like me. Flattering to think that but it scares me, too," he added, conscious not to start this last sentence with I mean. "I don't know," he shrugged, enjoying Karen's soft-blue eyes and how her chestnut-brown hair curled and fell on her delicate yet strong shoulders.

"I hate to sit here and be an armchair psychologist," said Karen. "But, well you're a parent, Doug. That's part of what parents do." She leaned in and the two shared an energy-charged kiss. "That girl has a good head on her shoulders," she whispered. "And you're a great dad. I love you both."

Doug cupped the woman's cheeks in his hands and kissed her tenderly. "I'm glad," he whispered. "I love you, too."

Nearing the end of October, Sondra had completed her daily

workout at the gym and was a half mile from the condo when her cell phone buzzed in her pocket. "This is Sondra" she greeted.

"Hi Sondra, this is Greg Wilente from Blue Sea Racing. We talked briefly at your San Jose victory party and I had a nice chat with your dad."

"Oh, hi," she said. "I remember. Nice to hear from you."

"I got your message," said Greg. "And the two your dad left. I've been out of town. Sorry I've not been able to get back to you sooner. It's been a couple of crazy weeks."

"That's cool," said Sondra. "I have a lot of calls in to a lot of different people, so I'm glad you caught me." This was an exaggeration but she wanted to give the impression she was a sought-after race car driver.

"Well I can believe that," said the man. "There seems to be a bit of a buzz going on about you, my little friend. The racing community can sometimes be very tight-knit. I've been doing a bit of checking up on you and I think we should talk."

"Talk's cheap," she insisted. "I'm looking for a Formula Ford ride for next season. I don't mean to come across as an arrogant jerk but I know what my capabilities are and will be, and I definitely know what I want."

Sondra was now a block and 3/4 away from home. She held the phone a few inches away and took a deep breath, then listened for a response thinking that she'd be hearing a hang-up at any second. After anxious seconds she heard some shuffling and a new extremely deep voice.

"Hi there, Sondra. I'm Joe Alders. First of all, I think you should know that you've been on speaker-phone and there's about five guys here. You're right, talk is cheap, so here's what we're willing to do. You go through our racing school in our Formula Mazda cars. You do what we tell you to do and when we tell you to do it. You complete the program and we'll evaluate your performance and then take it from there."

Sondra stood frozen in disbelief, beginning to fume to eruption level. She tried to remain calm. "Well, Joe, and all five of you. Your racing school isn't cheap and it sounds like a waste of my time, but I'll tell you what I'm willing to do. You let me run five laps in one of your F-Ford cars and I'll pick up the tab for fuel and track-time."

She heard Greg's voice next and it was much stronger than before. "That's pretty damn arrogant talk from a sixteen-year-old kid with no road-racing experience," he told Sondra. "And by the way, I doubt you can afford the fuel and track time."

"I can afford it," she quickly responded. "Do we have a deal?"

Sondra heard a few chuckles and snorts but Greg continued. "Bring your checkbook and if you damage the car you pay for that too."

"Fine," agreed Sondra. "Do we have a deal?"

The phone again went quiet and a long pause ensued while Greg picked up the receiver, no longer on speaker phone. "Yeah, we have a deal but you're gonna need to bring your dad or an adult with you."

"I'm an emancipated minor," asserted Sondra. "I don't need Doug or anyone else to go with me, but he's my manager as well as my adoptive dad. He'll be there. What day and time?"

Greg was about to inquire about the emancipated minor issue but figured he'd find out about that soon enough. "Why don't you come by next Tuesday morning, ten-thirty. Do you know where Sonoma Raceway is?"

She wanted to ask a thousand questions, jump up and down and thank him but she didn't want to destroy the integrity of the conversation. "Yeah," she answered flatly. "I watched motorcycle road races there a number of years ago. We'll be there." She hung up the phone grinning ear to ear and began to run as fast as she could home, wishing Doug hadn't had to work that day. She was eager to give him the great news.

Sondra and Doug left at 6:30 a.m. the following Tuesday morning. About twenty minutes into the drive Doug couldn't wait any longer and grabbed two periodicals from the side door pocket, handing them to his favorite passenger. "This is me!" exclaimed Sondra as she perused the thin magazine. It was a fairly small-circulation periodical and this week's edition featured an article and a color photograph of Sondra and her Stoltz Special race team at the San Jose Mile. There were two smaller black and white pictures and a nice little write-up on Sondra herself as well as Dan Stoltz. The second magazine, in mini-newspaper form, was a bimonthly that featured a number of different auto racing events and news stories. There, too, were a picture and article about Sondra Sierre. Doug glanced over several times and enjoyed her smile as she took in the article and then held the magazines to her chest. "Thought you might like that," he said. "Maybe you should start a scrapbook."

"That's a great idea," she nodded. "I already have enough stuff to fill at least one."

Sondra had been doing more than a little research on the Formula Ford series and its cars. She was excited about her opportunity to drive one, so much that she couldn't help but recite things she knew about the vehicles and history of the series and what she'd recently uncovered. "I found a few new websites," she told her now-dad. "They all basically say the same, that the cars weigh less than a thousand pounds and develop a hundred and fifty horsepower. I've read where there's been a bunch of engine controversy over the years but now there's a sixteen-hundred cc Duratec motor that's used all over the world. It's a sixteen-valve design, only one point six liters, with dual overhead cams and it's capable of a hundred and forty miles an hour. The suspension is a lot like Indy cars or Formula One but there aren't aero wings. I love that David Coulthard, Jenson Button and so many other greats got their start in this series. If they can start this way and become Formula One drivers, so can I."

Doug wasn't about to rain on her parade by pointing out that there'd been only one obscure female in Formula One many years ago, and even in this modern day and age there existed some ugly chauvinistic resistance in Europe for allowing women drivers to get to this ultimate level of auto racing. He supported her unconditionally, however, and knew she believed in herself that much. She didn't care if she was a girl or a boy. All she cared about was winning races and championships on the highest levels possible.

Doug pulled onto the Sonoma Raceway property earlier than expected, amazed at how Sondra could go from light and silly to intense seriousness, as if she had a switch for that. When they approached the prearranged meeting spot, walking down pit lane to where the #12 car and Blue Sea Racing team had assembled, Sondra was all business. Her race suit was zipped up and her long shiny dark hair was tucked tightly behind her head in order to play down any of her feminine features. She boldly introduced herself to three men she assumed to be pit crew members. They seemed nice enough and she walked all around the glossy bright blue race car with black pin-striping. Greg Wilente and Joe Alders drove up in a blue golf cart the same color as the race car and spoke sharply, reaching out a hand. "Hi there, I'm Joe Alders. You must be Doug." The two men shook hands and exchanged pleasantries. When Sondra asked their lead mechanic and engineer, Vince Melenza, a string of questions, Joe shot her a look. *Was she making this crap up or did she actually know what she was talking about?* Joe thought to himself. Greg Wilente stepped forward. He remembered Doug from the San Jose banquet and greeted him warmly. "Hi Doug, nice to see you again." He then hollered over to Sondra. "Hey, kiddo. Why don't you come on over. We'll take care of some business and then Vince and Sam here will go over some basics with you."

Twenty-four minutes later Sondra was sitting in the car. Now, with the engine running, there came last-minute instructions from Sam Fenton. With everyone gathered behind the pit wall, Sondra took off as if she'd been driving that car for years and had simply come into the pits for fuel and tires during a race. She'd been told to take it easy, to slowly get the feel of the car and track but deliberately spun the rear tires, producing a small amount of thin white smoke. She did this for several reasons. Sondra was sure that she'd only get in a lap or two before getting orders to come back in and park it, so this was a way of immediately getting some heat in the tires for grip on the asphalt as soon as possible. She didn't have the luxury of a few warm-up laps as she would have at the start of a race or in a normal practice session. The second reason for screaming out onto the race track like this was pure and simple. She was sixteen and in a lightweight race car with a half tank of fuel and an empty track. So in this moment in time she could be considered a brash kid by the race team owners.

From his position on pit lane, Sam Fenton barked out orders over the radio to Sondra. "Watch your speed. pit lane limit is Thirty-five." As soon as Sondra exited pit lane and started to drift firmly onto the racing surface, she knocked off the pyrotechnics without responding to the man's disapproval of her pit-exit. She steadily went through the gears, accelerating in the first left-hand kink going up the hill. When she was out of the line of sight from the little group in the pits, however, she back-shifted, getting the rpms up and producing more horsepower. The four-cylinder motor made a noticeably dramatic change in pitch, almost an octave higher. Greg and Joe gave each other annoyed and slightly concerned looks. Going through the esses of Turns 8 and 9, Sondra developed an involuntary smile. With every vibration, sound and sensation she was gobbling up an enormous amount of extremely usable information and confidence. She knew that the next time by this section of track she'd alter her line in order to be considerably smoother and much faster. She found being on the track to be much different than what she had in the past imagined from her viewing points leaning up against the spectator fence years ago with her father. Sondra, even from quite a young age, had studied racing as if the tiniest of detailed information was going to be on a test. This was that test, though that fact was now obscured by the sights, sounds and feel of what she was experiencing in the car. She went into Turn 11 with an overabundance of speed but was hard on the brakes early enough. This was a slow, tight, right-hand hairpin, and her acceleration out was explosive, to say the least. When she flashed by the start/finish line and headed back up the hill, Vince Melenza started a stopwatch. Vince had been with Blue Sea Racing for five years, was gifted mechanically and had had a rewarding career.

Sondra knew better than to drive this hard. It wasn't her car and she hadn't yet been offered the ride. She simply couldn't help it and was constantly being amazed. The harder she drove, the more the car seemed to stick to the ground. It was far more agile and stable than she'd imagined. Sondra did find that it took considerably more muscle strength to turn, but in most ways it didn't matter that she was in a car unlike anything she'd ever been in before or on a paved racetrack for the first time. The fact of the matter was that she gained knowledge and experience at lightening speed and was just naturally talented. This kind of racing felt right to her. Though Sondra was loving every second of the experience, she lost the smile and her level of concentration was absolute. The #12 car screamed past the start/finish line for the second time and Vince hit a button on the stop-watch. "Damn," Melenza exclaimed. He held the device out for Greg and Joe to view. "That would have given her a solid top-three finish in last year's F-Ford race here, man." Standing next to Vince was one of the pit crew members, and he immediately chimed in with his opinion. "Yeah, and she's on old tires in a car that wasn't even set up for her." Greg glanced over at Doug, who was proudly displaying an I-told-you-so grin as the group of men watched and listened to the young driver continue to work her magic. By lap four, Sondra had a sizable audience but was far too focused to notice. She did however notice her car. She was done playing and testing limits and was now aware of just how badly the thing was handling, although it did please her somewhat that her abilities were stronger than the car's. The tires were fading fast and fourth gear was not tall enough. There also was a growing understeer problem. These annoyances didn't reflect in her lap times however. She was actually using them to her advantage in different parts of the track, and her lap times steadily came down. After completing a fifth lap, she heard what she dreaded. Her ears filled up with Greg's sharp over-the-radio voice. "All right, Sondra. That's enough. Come on in. Pit this lap. Pit this lap." "Pit this lap," she repeated.

Greg Wilente invited Sondra to the Blue Sea Racing headquarters, one of the prefab buildings near the main raceway ticket entrance. Once inside his office, Greg gestured at a chair in front of his desk. "Sit down and let's have a chat, shall we?" Sondra crossed her arms. The room was freezing and the noise from the powerful air conditioner was beginning to give her a headache. Greg went around and sat in a comfortable-looking chair, leaned in toward Sondra and put his elbows on the glass table top of his desk. “So,” he began. “You have some fun out there?” Sondra spoke flatly. “I didn’t come here to have fun. I gave you five solid and really fast laps.” He responded with a bit of harshness in his voice. “You were told to take it easy and you went out like some hot-headed teenager on a Saturday night. Then you waited ’til you knew we couldn’t see you and drove around like a maniac. I take it you never worked with a real crew chief before.” He pointed to a large photo of himself on the wall to his right with a pit crew, kneeling in front of a famous NASCAR vehicle. “When someone tells you what to do in their race car, you do it. You’re damn lucky you didn’t wreck and hurt yourself.” She wasn’t buying that he was all that upset or angry with her performance or her behavior in the car. With a soft smile and sparkling eyes, she produced her checkbook, pen poised for action. “I don’t crash cars,” she told Greg simply. “What do I owe you, and keep in mind that I didn’t wreck or harm your car in any way.” Greg sat back and studied her for a few seconds before speaking in an almost tired-sounding voice. “Put the checkbook away, kiddo. You don’t owe a thing.” He really didn’t want to say anything that would encourage a puffed-up ego but was impressed by her and her driving. He was determined not to let her know this, however. If she already thought she was hot stuff, she might get to be too difficult to deal with in the future or would perhaps take dangerous and unnecessary risks on the racetrack. Greg had learned years ago that racing is a bit more of a team sport than most people realize and was convinced that Sondra had way more to learn about that and driving on paved tracks than she obviously thought she knew.

“Tell me something,” said Greg. “Where do you see yourself in six months, and in six years?” Sondra answered without hesitation. “I’ll win a lot of races and the championship for you or for someone else who’ll believe in me. In six years I’ll have won races and championships for IndyCar and I’ll be working on wins and championships in Formula One.” Greg laughed heartily, not acknowledging the seriousness in her statement. “Sounds like my six-year-old with pipe-dreams of being a fireman or an astronaut.”

Sondra rose, stepping toward the photos on the wall to her left. She spoke with a soft intensity, trying not to sound as angry as she had instantly become from his last words. "I had to grow up damn quick. Trust me, I'm no child with a pipe dream. Maybe your kid'll be a fireman or an astronaut or maybe not. I've known exactly what I was supposed to do with my life ever since I can remember." She turned toward him, a fierceness now in her eyes. "What you just saw today wasn't a fluke. You gave me a piece of crap car on purpose and you know it. I didn't complain, I didn't spin, and I didn't crash." She stepped toward him, leaning over with her hands on the desk. Once again she spoke in a soft yet firm voice. "You have no idea what I learned in just five laps. Try, just try to imagine what I can do with track-time and experience." She sat back down in such a delicate way it was hard for Greg to put that action and what he'd just heard from her together. He took a deep breath and exhaled forcefully. "I know a little about your family situation, Sondra, and I'm sorry," he told her. "What a horrible thing to have to go through." He eyed the girl as she stared down at a brass airplane paperweight on his desk. "Well," he added, "there's a lot of details to work out but we'll get you in a car again soon." Sondra wanted to jump up and down and scream for joy but instead she smiled serenely and looked directly at him. He completely melted but wasn't about to let her know or see it.

Roughly an hour into their journey back home they stopped for lunch at a chain family restaurant. "This scampi thing looks pretty good," said Doug as he and Sondra perused their menus. "With the rice and steamed vegetables," he added. "And it comes with soup or salad."

"Mmm," voiced Sondra, exploring her own menu. "A very healthy choice. Is that what you're gonna have?"

"No," he voiced, uncertain. "What exactly is scampi, anyway?" he pondered. "Stupid name for seafood if you ask me. Ah, here we are. New York strip steak, and it even comes with the steamed vegetables so it's very healthy." Sondra giggled at his sarcastic wit but the meal actually sounded pretty good, until she saw on her own menu that it came with sautéed mushrooms, and Sondra hated sautéed mushrooms. She despised them just as vigorously as she did avocado. Doug forced out the juice from a lemon wedge in his water glass with a fork and glanced up at Sondra. "You okay?" he asked. Sondra had an expression that seemed both angry and thoughtful.

"Yeah, I guess," she said with a shrug of her right shoulder. He watched the girl use her fingers to pick out an ice cube from her water glass. "Sondra," he said softly with a furrowed brow. She was oblivious to the scolding of her table manners but spoke up feeling prompted.

"I've been there before," she said in a voice laced with emotion. "Sonoma Raceway," she clarified. "The name's changed since then but my dad and I walked all around that track and in the garage area, like a thousand times." A chill went though Doug. Sondra so rarely spoke of her past. "I took a picture looking down the track from the top of Turn Two at the start of an AMA motorcycle race," continued the girl. "A rider fell mid-pack and slid up pretty close to us. He got back on the bike and ended up finishing eighth place. When we got the slide film back a week later, we discovered that I'd snapped the picture at the exact moment the rider was starting to lose the back end, with dozens of riders all around him."

"Wow," said Doug, amazed at the tale and that Sondra could remain so calm and collected through a memory of her father.

"I know that track," reiterated the girl. "I mean, yeah, I've never actually been on it until this morning but I used to study the track from the outside and the motorcycles that raced on it." She swallowed hard and loud remembering one particularly warm afternoon that she and her father spent waiting for the next race to begin, reveling in the procurement of icy half gallon milk-carton containers of Coca-Cola.

"I know that racetrack inside and out," said Sondra, now making a fist. "We used to talk about it and my dad once read an article to me from Cycle World about it. It's an eleven-story elevation gain from the pits, and the two hairpin turns at both ends are nowhere near the same. The look of the facility has changed over the years, with a lot of really nice improvements, but the track's basically the same." She took a sloppy gulp of water and set the clear plastic glass down hard enough that liquid splashed onto the table. "Should have been with us today" she whispered through clenched teeth.

"Is that why you drove the way you did?" asked Doug. "Thinking about your dad?"

Sondra bit down on her tongue. Her breathing through her nose was jagged and pronounced. "That's how I drive," she asserted, sounding instantly angry. "I drive fast and I push things to the limit. That's what gets results."

Before Doug could say anything further, their waiter came by with a basket of rolls and a small plate of individually foil-wrapped pats of butter. Doug watched Sondra tear a roll apart and insert butter between the two halves and squeeze it as if the roll had made her mad. His cell phone was sitting on the table next to his fork and he glanced down, noticing that Karen had sent him a text. "I sent Karen two pictures and a message this morning," he informed Sondra as he read the message from K McCormick. "She says you look good in the car and she can't wait for you to tell her all about it." Sondra flashed a smile but tossed the roll onto the small white plate before her.

"I'm not hungry," she announced, her voice edgy, bordering on anger. "I'll just wait for you outside." The girl was gone before Doug could respond. He left money on the table and went after her. Back in the truck, Doug and Sondra drove roughly 30 minutes in silence, save the radio. "Need some gas," he announced as he exited the freeway. When the task was complete Doug drove across the street and down the block, turning into a McDonald's drive-through. "I'm gonna get some coffee," he explained.

"I guess I could go for a Coke," said Sondra as she fished her wallet out of her backpack. They came to a stop behind a dusty black Honda Accord with a small dent in the back bumper. "We didn't go to fast-food very often but my mom always got a Filet-O-Fish when we went to McDonald's," volunteered Sondra. Doug looked over at the girl. A single tear was trying to meander its way down from her left eye and she quickly wiped it away with a swipe of her right forefinger. "What about your dad?" Doug asked.

"Big Mac," said Sondra.

"Well why don't you get a Filet-O-Fish in honor of your mom and

I'll get a Big Mac in honor of your dad?"

"Yeah," said Sondra. "And lets get some fries for Dave and Haley."

Two days after Sondra's test in the F-Ford at Sonoma Raceway, Doug received a call from Greg Wilente. "So Blue Sea Racing has narrowed things down considerably, mostly thanks to Sondra raising the bar like she did here the other day," he told Doug after greetings and a bit of small-talk. "We're lookin' at two other guys as well but no matter what happens Sondra should feel really good about how she did. We started with fifty-eight kids and quickly went down from there. A week ago it was twelve. So like I told you, we'll do some more testing at Willow Springs and see how things shake out. If Sondra drives anything like she did the other day she'll be my top pick."

"Good," said Doug. "She won't disappoint you. She's a fast driver and a really fast learner. She's smart as a whip, too."

"Yeah, and with her life story and everything," Greg inserted, "she's a marketing and publicist's dream. But here's the thing. We're a little concerned about her size and her stamina, and based off what I saw and my conversation with her I'd say she has a bit of a temper. It's been my experience that angry hot-headed teenagers don't usually last too long or go too far in this sport."

"Well don't mistake intense determination for teenage angst," argued Doug. "Sondra has a good head on her shoulders, I can promise you that, and she's tough as nails. The kid's had to deal with a lot in her young life but if I wasn't absolutely sure she could handle it I wouldn't let her near a race car. All we want is a fair shot."

"That I can guarantee," said Greg. "But be prepared," he added. "We're gonna put her through her paces at Willow in two weeks."

When Doug later told Sondra of Wilente's call he purposely watered down the exchange. "You beat out over fifty guys," he said as they searched a department store for a particular rice cooker that Karen had suggested. "And you're gonna get a bunch of seat-time in that same car when we go to Willow Springs."

Karen began to be a more frequent visitor to the Fresno condominium, staying overnight most times. She paid close attention to Sondra's moods and attitudes concerning this, but the three together seemed so natural. When there were multiple days that Karen wasn't able to be there, Sondra would tell Doug that she missed her. On a cool late October afternoon Sondra met with a college academic advisor. Her good mood was elevated all the more when she later arrived home to find Karen and Doug sautéing onions, garlic and tomatoes for Karen's famous spaghetti and meatballs. "Hey, kiddo," chirped Karen as Sondra breezed into the room with a thin folder.

"Wow that smells good," said the girl. "You must be psychic or something," she told Karen, "because I was planning on calling you." She held up the folder and continued. "I got the classes we talked about and as luck would have it I snuck in under the wire. Classes for the winter semester start next Monday."

"Oh I'm so happy, sweetheart," cheered Karen.

"That's great," said Doug. "I'm proud of you."

"Thanks," said Sondra. "But the greatest thing is that the semester ends just before racing season begins. Gonna be perfect." Karen liked the girl's confidence that she was going to be picked to drive for Blue Sea Racing but didn't think starting college and then taking time off to race cars was perfect. She kept this to herself however. "Hmm" voiced Sondra, twirling childlike and pondering her future. "A genius on the track as well as off," she quipped.

"You nutty girl," chuckled Doug.

Karen continued with her culinary tasks but Doug directed Sondra's attention to a stack of mail on the kitchen counter. There were bills and junk mail but the eye-catcher was a large thick padded envelope with the girl's past full legal name on the label. Miss Sondra Jean Sierre. Sondra guessed at the contents. Both John Farnsal and Doug had told her some time back that due to her becoming an emancipated minor and turning sixteen she'd be receiving some legal documents and important papers from a law office the Jenners had entrusted.

"Family stuff," Sondra surmised out loud. "I'm afraid to open it." Karen halted her actions and turned to face Sondra and Doug. Sondra picked up the padded item off the table but soon set it on the kitchen counter as if it were a live grenade.

"This may sound silly but it makes it too real. That they're really gone forever."

Doug set a gentle hand on the girl's shoulder as Karen walked over, intending to only stand close for emotional support. It surprised her when Sondra suddenly wrapped her arms around her in a tight embrace. "I'm so sorry, baby," whispered Karen. She bent down to kiss the top of Sondra's head as the girl convulsed in tears. However, Little-Miss-Tough-As-Nails abruptly pulled away and picked up the envelope. She ripped open the sturdy flap and dumped the contents onto the counter. It was mostly paperwork but there was a black rectangular box underneath. Without hesitation she opened the lid revealing a dazzling gemstone necklace.

"Beautiful," said Karen. Sondra stared at it for several seconds, not taking it out of it's velvet-lined case. She swallowed hard and her hands were visibly trembling as she lightly touched the box. "My folks, mostly my mom," she began in an unsteady voice, "gave me one just like this. Plastic beads but really pretty, and so smooth. I was wearing it the day ..." Sondra ground her teeth, breathing out angrily through her nose. "Paramedics or doctors must have ripped it off me and thrown it away. Bastards."

"Those bastards saved your life," said Doug in a low soft voice.

"And we're so glad they did," added Karen.

"They didn't save enough," growled Sondra bitterly. "Going to my room for a bit," she stated, disappearing quickly.

Doug knocked on Sondra's bedroom door and entered the room. It had been forty-two minutes since she'd left the kitchen and he found the girl sitting on the edge of her bed doubled over with her arms resting on her knees, staring down at her sock-covered feet. "Karen must think I'm some nutty emotional loon," said Sondra as she sat up straight.

"She doesn't think that," assured Doug, sitting next to the girl and putting a solid hand on her back. "She cares about you very, very much."

"I'm glad," said Sondra with a nod and flash of a smile. Doug handed Sondra the jewelry box and she set it on top of her dresser, running her fingers over the beads.

"I smell dinner and I'm hungry" she announced. Doug would have preferred Sondra sit and talk to him about the necklace and what was going on with her but didn't have the heart to push the issue. They returned to the kitchen as Karen was draining the boiling pasta water into the sink. "Sorry for the freak-out" said Sondra.

Karen shook her head and transferred the spaghetti into the dish with the sauce and meat balls. "You never have to apologize for your memories and your feelings" she assured the girl, giving her a quick hug. "Now then" she announced. "Who's hungry, besides me?"

After dinner, including a scoop of chocolate ice cream and homemade peanut-butter cookies that Karen had brought, the three joined forces and made quick work of the kitchen cleanup. They watched an old black and white movie that Karen had also brought, but nearing the end Sondra couldn't manage to keep her eyes open. She thanked Karen for the meal and said her good-nights. Doug and Karen watched the movie to its conclusion, then some of the 10 o'clock news.

"Lets have a look at that envelope of Sondra's," suggested Doug. They soon found themselves at the kitchen table. The packet included a large Ziplock bag containing the original birth certificates of the Sierre family. There were also a significant number of insurance documents, bank statements and a few pages that only had particular meaning to Maureen Sierre. One page, a hand-written note, shook Doug and Karen to the core. It was a letter to Sondra written by Kathy Jenner:

My dearest Sondra, I'm sitting beside you while you lie in a hospital bed. You've been asleep for nineteen long days. Jack and I would do anything in the world to change what has happened. We've done our best to carefully pack your dear family's belongings and put them in storage for you. We've set aside some important paperwork that will hopefully help you in the future. Open your eyes, sweetheart.

Love, J & K Jenner

Karen convulsed into tears upon the reading. She and Doug held each other for some time. “You can’t let Sondra see this, Doug,” sobbed Karen. “Not now. Maybe in the future but not now. She tries so hard to act tough and all grown-up but really that poor little girl is so fragile. She’s just hanging on by a thread.”

“Yeah,” whispered Doug in agreement. “I love you, Karen,” he said in full voice. “I love how much you care about Sondra and me.”

“I do love you and Sondra,” said a still tearful Karen. “With all my heart.”

After a tender kiss, Doug pulled away and dug into the pocket of his jeans. He held out a small shiny metallic object. Karen took the new condo front-door key from his fingers and kissed it before speaking. “This is a big step,” she said to Doug.

“I know a bigger one,” he said in a low voice. Goosebumps raced through Karen as she briefly wondered if he was about to pull a ring from his pocket as well. It was a bit too soon for this but she was prepared for anything. “Sondra has to want this, too,” said Karen of the key’s implication.

“She does,” said Doug. “We’ve talked. I don’t want to rush things,” he added. “I’ve done that before and every time it’s ended in disaster, but with you I don’t want to risk going too slow. This thing with you and me has been right from the start.”

Karen flung her arms around him and a passionate kiss ensued. Doug held Karen’s hands in his, her fingers cradling the key. “No pressure” he whispered. “You’ll move in when the time is right for you.”

On a bright and early Thursday morning, Doug and Sondra found themselves heading toward the Mojave desert, their destination Willow Springs International Raceway in Rosamond, California. As usual, Sondra had done her research. “The six hundred acre place was established in nineteen fifty-two,” she explained to Doug. “It now has eight different racetracks but the main one is called the Big Willow, a nine-turn road course. That’s what I’ll be on today. Oh boy, oh boy, oh boy,” she enthused, excitedly rubbing her hands together. Inside one of the old buildings used as driving school classrooms and/or race team temporary headquarters, Sondra signed the Blue Sea Racing contract, watched two training videos and spend thirty minutes with a computer simulator program. She then was introduced to Mr. Gerard De Alfenio, her new driving instructor. His skin was fair and he had a few wisps of reddish/white hair on his mostly bald head. He spoke with a slight British accent and Sondra thought him to be a thousand years old. He was 68 and a very accomplished driver of Formula 3 and the 24 Hour Le Mans annual event in his hey-day.

Finally, thought Sondra, her chance had come to once again get into the cockpit of the bright blue #12 race car. Gerard was in a similar car in front of her and they were in direct radio communication. She was an attentive and focused student for the first few laps, then became frustrated and impatient at the low speed. To Sondra, Gerard's instructions seemed increasingly harsh and she took his criticisms personally. She began to lag back then launch forward, heavy on the gas entering into corners at the speed she wanted. Sam Fenton spotted the behavior right away and shook his head as he watched the on-track action. "Damn it," he said under his breath. At the end of their thirty minutes of track time Gerard spoke to a pit crew member as he was climbing out of his car. "I have no patience for silly little girls who don't listen."

On the recommendation of one of the pit crew members, Doug took Sondra to a nearby eatery, a quaint Tudor-style house converted into a popular restaurant. Sondra was in an obvious mood and told Doug she wasn't hungry as they were seated. He didn't outwardly react, knowing the girl's temperament and that she would calm down as they ate. Across town, just over a mile away, Sam, Joe and Greg were feverishly snacking on chips and salsa while sipping beer. They had been making jokes and crude comments about a few of the scantily clad waitresses when Sam started a serious conversation. "Hey guys. So I think it was worth a shot to have Gerard come down this morning. He's done some good work with a number of other drivers I've worked with."

Joe was more interested in flirting with a particular waitress but reluctantly began listening to what Sam had to say. "I don't think we're dealing with the average kid here," Sam said of Sondra.

"Yeah," said Joe with a quick laugh. "She's a sixteen-year-old childishly stubborn hothead. I told you this was a bad idea."

That angered Sam and he directed his defense of Sondra at the man. "That's no mere child," he said in Sondra's defense. "It doesn't take a genius to see that we got one of the most instinctive new drivers we've seen in a hell of a long time here." Sam got out his wallet and threw a wad of bills onto the table. "Hundred bucks says what she learned this morning will give us pro-level lap-times when we turn her loose this afternoon." The two men started sniping at one another about how smart, or not, it was to actually hire her, then Greg put a stop to it. "Guys, guys. Lets focus here. She obviously has something or we wouldn't be here having this conversation. I say we let her run ten laps any way she wants. No advice, no instruction. We bring her in and check tire-wear. If she's blistered them, we give her hell and tell her to do exactly what we say. I mean really lean on her. If the tires are okay, we send her back out until our time's up."

The engine of the #12 Formula Ford fired easily and held a steady idle, with Sondra tightly strapped into her car on pit lane. Blue Sea Racing had forty-five minutes of track time. It was split into two segments, with a pit stop in between. Doug gave the top of Sondra's helmet two hard pats for luck, the way he'd done in her first sprint-car season. It didn't hurt but these were good hard knocks, always producing an involuntary quick giggle. This gesture was also like a good-luck hug only more macho and appropriate in these kinds of situations. When Sondra got the okay from crew chief Sam, she screamed out of the pits and onto the track. She went into the 90 degree steeply banked first turn fast and deep, knowing she was on cold tires and had to be cautious because it was a blind corner until nearing the exit. When the back end slid coming out, it wasn't a surprise. She was on the absolute edge of the racing surface and went up through the gears quickly. There was nothing gentle about Sondra's driving and she was breathing hard. She didn't feel mad but was certainly acting it. The slideout of Turn 9, the last corner of her first lap, was a bit more wicked than she'd expected. It was understandable, however, because it was a top-gear 90-degree right-hander that quickly decreased in radius. Just like Turn 1, the exit couldn't be seen until she was right there. Sondra told herself to settle down. After getting through 1 again cleanly, she took a breath in the short-straight as she was shifting down to third gear, getting ready to enter the gentle right-hand Turn 2. The engine made crackling and popping noises on down-shifts but this time there came an oddly loud pop temporarily distracting her. She'd never before heard the motor make this sound and missed her usual braking point. She was forced to drive deeper into the corner and then brake. All of a sudden things just clicked for her. The car felt right and seemed easier to drive. Her photographic memory kicked in everything she'd learned from the morning and things now made total sense. She had basically forced herself to use the exact braking point that Gerard was earlier trying to teach her. An involuntary smile swept across her face. All this couldn't have happened at a better time. Sondra didn't know it, but this was a critical run. If she didn't do well here today, she'd basically be put on the proverbial back-burner. They couldn't just fire her easily but they didn't have to let her race either, which also meant no money would be going to her. It was a very limited contract and in six short months she'd be out. Clearly her future was looking bright and getting brighter by each turn and twist on the racetrack.

There was a small crowd starting to develop. Steven Barnes from Gavins Racing had the track booked for two hours right after Blue Sea Racing's time. He was overseeing the training of five student, and they plus the support crew had wandered over to watch. Doug knew that Steven was scheduled to be there but he'd kept this information from Sondra because he didn't want her to be upset or distracted. Gerard De Alfenio joined the onlookers as well. He had an interest in seeing if anything he had tried to teach the girl had actually gotten through to her. As soon as he'd seen Sondra take the right line and in the right braking zone he almost jumped a foot in the air. He excitedly pointed to her, pumping his arm. "That's my girl," he yelled. "I taught her that." He had an enormous look of relief and pride as he hurried over and patted Sam Fenton heavily on the man's back.

When Sondra flashed by the start/finish line, Sam looked down at the laptop telemetry readings. The technology they had was far from that of IndyCar and was most definitely not even in the same realm as the multimillion dollar military fighter-jet-type technology of Formula One. The limited display, however, was enough. Sondra's fourth lap of 1:18.03 was impressive by anyone's standards there that day. She was feeling home. This was absolutely what she was living for now and wanted to go faster. Her breathing was back to normal. She was taking the car to its limits and her lap-times continued to decrease. Doug had a noticeable smirk when he looked over at Steven Barnes. Their eyes met and Doug nodded to the man. It was his way of telling the jerk that he'd blown it, big time.

Just short of the completion of Lap 14, Sondra spoke to Sam Fenton over the radio. "Vibration in the left-front. I think I have a tire going down and it doesn't feel like a brake issue."

Sam quickly responded. "Hang onto it. You'll pit in two. Keep us informed."

"P two," she responded, hoping the tire would last another two laps. Despite the car's developments and Sondra's concerns, her speed and lap-times improved by two-thousandth's of a second. She hit her marks right on the money while pitting. After getting four tires and full fuel she drag-raced her way back out onto the track. Sam yelled at her. "Watch your speed. Watch your speed on pit-out. If this had been an actual race we would have been penalized for speeding on pit lane. You should know better than that. No more stupid mistakes."

Sondra didn't respond but her performance during the following laps were nothing but impressive. Sam then had a look at the tire wear. He couldn't believe what he was seeing. They were used and worn exactly how they should be, and Sondra was absolutely correct. The left-front tire had picked up a rock or some sort of sharp debris and was soon going to be dead-flat.

At the conclusion of Sondra's practice session she was met in the pits by Gerard. "Good student, good student," he excitedly told her. "I'll teach you more," he promised. Sondra was pretty worn out but she was instantly happy and energized.

"Yeah," she exclaimed. "And did you see how I could brake early and get through Five so fast and then I could drift the front end a little in Six? It totally set me up for Seven, like it wasn't even a corner." The two talked wildly for several minutes and at one point he patted her on the back so hard it almost knocked her to the ground. The triumphant driver saw Doug out the corner of her eye and raced over to him, slightly squealing as she flew into his arms. Ordinarily she'd never do anything so childish, especially in front of these guys, but she was happier than she thought possible. Doug set her down laughing and Sondra immediately went back into a more professional mode. They walked over to where Greg and Joe were standing. Joe was actually pleasant to her for a change. "Keep that up and we'll need to revise your contract." Greg handed her a white plastic bag. "Here," he explained. Sondra looked inside and found three complete team uniform sets. She slipped away unnoticed while the men talked of scheduling more seat time for Sondra and putting together a pit crew for the upcoming season.

As the small group of men continued to talk, Doug looked around suddenly concerned he hadn't seen Sondra in quite some time. To his relief she soon came into view, casually walking toward them. As usual, she had her backpack slung over her shoulder. She was now dressed in the blue and black team uniform, her long hair flowing gently in the light breeze from beneath the Blue Sea Racing baseball cap atop her head. Greg was pleased to see her in the uniform. It had been another one of his little tests to see whether or not she would easily be a team-player. Sondra came up to Doug from behind, dropped the pack and flung her arms around him, resting the right side of her face against his back. She had put everything she had physically into the last hour's run and was worn out. Doug reached back and pulled her around, which amused Joe, Greg, Sam and Gerard. As Steven Barnes' fleet of students took to the track Sondra's strength came back to her and she pointed to the roaring pack. "Bet you a thousand bucks that none of them can come even close to what I just did." Joe laughed sarcastically. "Humble little thing, aren't you?" This produced a group chuckle, with the exception of Sondra and Doug. Sondra folded her arms and with a small closed-mouth smile she shot daggers at Joe with her eyes. Doug reached down, picked up the girl's backpack and started pushing his proud driver toward the parking lot. "We gotta get home before we turn into pumpkins," he told the small group. Greg called out to Sondra. "We'll be in touch with you in a day or two with a practice schedule. It's gonna be intense so be prepared."

Roughly twenty minutes after Doug had pulled onto the north-bound interstate, the sun slanted in the pre-evening sky and the air temperature dropped significantly. He turned on some heat and glanced over at Sondra. She was still, her eyes shut and head down. He smiled to himself and beamed with pride at being a part of her life. Just under thirty minutes later Sondra woke full of energy. "Hey," she exclaimed. Doug glanced over briefly. "I think I get it," said Sondra. "I have some bad habits that I can get away with on the dirt but they really don't work on pavement. I want to work with Gerard again. I hated him this morning. You should have heard how he talked to me. It was like he thought I was four or something. Do you think I pissed him off? I hope not, and I hope Greg can get him to show me some more stuff." Sondra became quiet again, embarrassed by her sudden babbling. Without taking his eyes off the road Doug reached over and bumped her shoulder with his fist. "You did so great today, Tiger, and you know Gerard's dying to teach you more."

Sondra's next venture at Willow Springs Raceway was a forty-minute afternoon practice session that started out as pure follow-the-leader driving. Gerard's usual continuous banter and instruction, which had seemed to Sondra like he was barking out orders, were noticeably nonexistent. Their speed gently increased and soon Gerard began slipping beside Sondra and pinching her to the outside on some spots of the track and to the inside on others. She would flinch and back off. The instructor's actions began to get more frequent and more aggressive. After almost three laps of this Sondra had had enough. The flinching stopped. She held her line and refused to back out of the gas. By Lap 9 Sondra was finding opportunities to force him into tight spots, only he never gave up track position. Crew chief Sam watched all this with a slightly concerned look but Doug and Lead Mechanic Vince Melenza, the first man picked as a permanent pit crew member of the #12 team, cheered Sondra on for each advantage gained. When the two drivers flashed across the Start/Finish line going two-wide on Lap 19 there was no doubt about it, this wasn't a training exercise and it wasn't a show. It was a real race and a growingly more intense one at that. In the next number of circuits their wheels touched on more than one occasion. They made seemingly insane attacks on each other and were running laps that were almost two seconds faster than the Formula Ford race there last June. Gerard pulled a tricky move in Turn 7. Sondra was trying to stay to the left, going into this slight jog in order to set up for Turn 8, but he blocked her line so severely that it forced her to squeeze on brakes or she would have hit him and spun them both out. Just over a half a lap later she had the opportunity to make a move that he'd actually taught her the week prior in Turn 3, the slowest corner of the course. It took him by surprise as she out-broke him and drifted slowly past. They both wanted the same line going into the last turn and their wheels came freakishly close to intertwining.

Doug had been watching so intently he hadn't noticed the growing number of on-lookers and certainly hadn't noticed that Steven Barnes had come up from behind. As the two stood side by side a few feet apart, they watched the blue #12 car exit out of Turn 1. Steven tapped Doug on the arm. "Is that Sondra?" he asked in utter amazement. Doug gave a nod, not taking his eyes off the action. "Damn impressive, man," said Steven. Doug could have easily told him off, that he was such a moron for not believing in her months ago. He was suddenly filled with a sense of pride mixed with over-protectiveness. He didn't even want this idiot to watch his Sondra. After many breathtaking laps, Crew chief Sam called out to the drivers over the radio. "White flag, last lap." Sondra made a drastic and daring move on the outside of Turn 5 after forcing her left front wheel into the dirt at the apex of 4. She and Gerard's tires touched hard enough to produce a small puff of white smoke and Sondra snagged the lead by inches going into 6. Gerard had a slight lead coming into the last few turns but Sondra never gave up. After another insane-looking move she let the car roll gently through the last corner, and with her determination and youthful agility accelerated more quickly on their drag-race to the start/finish line. She'd beaten her instructor by half a car length. Gerard was just as proud and excited as Doug at that moment. This was a big deal, and later Sam put in a call to Greg and Joe about their new driver's performance.

Sondra spent two days the following week at Sonoma Raceway. On what she considered a glorious bright sunny happy Tuesday she was allowed two 50-minute on-track practice sessions, complete with pit stops. Crew chief Sam Fenton and Engineer Vince Melenza were on the radio with her the whole time, encouraging her and acting as driver coaches. Greg Wilente provided Sondra two opportunities to partake in Sonoma Raceway's official driving/racing school, utilizing the Lola Formula 3 car. These were more powerful and advanced than the F-Ford, but it was noticed by more than a few how quickly and seamlessly she was able to adapt. The cars also utilized aero wings to help with downforce and paddle shifters instead of the F-Ford's stick. The school's instructor called Greg after hearing radio transmission from a large number of students complaining about the red #29 car's speed and perceived aggression. In theory, Sondra shouldn't have been this much faster but in this situation it became a case where the student had become the master. Greg and Joe Alders soon appeared on the pit lane to watch the last number of minutes of the school's track time. "Have the Sierre kid come to my office," Greg told the school's instructor. They soon watched Sondra come to a stop on the pit lane and exit the car with her fist punching the air as if she'd just won a significant race. In Greg's office he told Sondra that she was race ready. "We're finalizing the personnel for the pit crew. After the holidays there will be two team practices, one here and one at Willow Springs. In the meantime, stay fit, stay healthy and stay in touch."

On a lazy Sunday afternoon Sondra was in the kitchen putting together chicken sandwiches for Doug and herself. "Just got off the phone with Karen," Doug announced, walking in from the living room. "She's in San Diego all week, on the job at a tool trade-show. She's not going back east for Thanksgiving this year because of work, and besides there's been some pretty bad weather back there lately. I invited her to have Thanksgiving with us."

"Kay," said Sondra with a quick nod.

"Kay?" prompted Doug. "You mean, Kay, like you're really okay with this or Kay, your brain is working overtime on what to do or where to go so you can avoid the holiday all-together?" He watched Sondra bite down on her lower lip, mulling this over in her mind. "Nah," she voiced with a shrug of her right shoulder, trying to sound tough. "It's okay. I mean we'll put the little lady to work in the kitchen while we dudes hang in the den, chompin' cigars and watchin' football," she joked with a straight face.

"You nutty girl," laughed Doug. He put away the jars of mayonnaise and mustard, then briefly put his arm around her before taking their lunch to the table. "So," began Doug, chewing a bite of his sandwich, "Karen and I talked last night about the whole moving-in thing. She wants to make sure that you're good with this. So do I."

"I am," said Sondra as she took the paper towel she was planning on using as a napkin off the table and set it on her right leg. "Are you guys gonna get married?" she inquired.

"I hope so" said Doug with a nod. "Eventually," he added. "When I told my ol' friend Greg about her a month ago, he pointed out that I don't exactly have the best track record with relationships. Karen's different in all the good ways though. We can talk openly and honestly and I know for sure I can trust her."

"Yeah," said Sondra. "She's no Brenda."

"Yeah, and ouch," said Doug with a coughing laugh. "I mean this time I've been careful and cautiously optimistic," he continued. "She and I really fit together so naturally. It's nice to be in a relationship where so many positive things just mesh, but the most important thing to me is that she loves you too."

Doug took a breath while contemplating his next words and he watched Sondra wipe her lips with the back of her sleeve before taking a gulp of milk. "I've even done a little preliminary ring shopping," he announced. Sondra chose to skip over the ring-shopping comment.

"She loves me?" asked the girl, glancing down at the grip she had on her sandwich. Doug nodded, feeling the need to say more. "Even if

I were to ask her to marry me and she were to accept, it'd be at least a year before we'd get married. And like I've told you before, I won't do anything to disrupt the balance of your life."

Sondra shook her head. "I think it might be more disruptive if you don't eventually get married," she told him with a slight trace of anxiety in her voice. "I really like how it is when the three of us are together," she added.

"I do too," said Doug, watching Sondra reach for the glass of milk with her left hand. "So Karen doesn't have some weird or gross old family recipe for Thanksgiving stuffing, does she?" asked Sondra, deliberately changing to a lighter topic. "I mean when I lived at the Collins House, Mrs. Collins put raisins, oysters and a ton of other creepy things in her stuffing. Blecch."

Doug thought this funny and suspected it was a bit of an exaggeration of ingredients. "Well," he told the girl, "I'm not sure she actually has a stuffing recipe, but we'll make sure she doesn't put in anything you deem weird, gross or creepy."

Thanksgiving morning, Sondra returned home from the gym treasuring the aroma of food being prepared. "Smells amazing," she told Karen. "I always loved Thanksgiving mornings when I was growing up." Before Karen had a chance to inquire about childhood holiday memories, Sondra exited the kitchen with a bag of charcoal briquets. Doug was rearranging the patio furniture when Sondra came through the sliding glass door. "Have a good workout?" he asked, pleased that the girl had remembered to obtain more charcoal as he had asked. Sondra shrugged and set the bag on a small wooden rectangular table. "Sort of annoying," she answered. "It was super crowded." She took a loud deep breath. "Just had a total mom flashback," she admitted. "So what time did Karen get here?" Doug opened the new bag of briquets and put a few squares inside the barbecue. "Literally minutes after you left" he told her.

Close to 15 minutes before dinner, Sondra entered the kitchen. "Well I'll be darned," Karen said to Doug. "So the girl actually owns more than T-shirts and jeans." Sondra folded her arms and rolled her eyes. She was dressed in one of the Blue Sea Racing uniform slacks and a plaid long-sleeve top with ruffles at the bottom that Kari Wilken had given her. After sitting down to their great feast, and not ten minutes in, there came a phone call. Normally Doug would have let it go to voice-mail but he'd been expecting to hear from at least one of Brenda's children. He took the roughly 18 minute call in the den and returned to the table, apologizing for the interruption. "Jennifer says hi and happy Thanksgiving," Doug told Sondra. "How is she?" asked a surprised ex-foster-sibling. Doug took several bites and made mm noises before answering. "Well she's four months pregnant and she and her boyfriend are living with his parents in Oxnard."

"Gee, there's a shock" said Sondra sarcastically.

"Be nice" warned Doug.

"Sorry," Sondra apologized.

"What else did she say?" Doug took a deep breath after he chewed and swallowed a bite of mashed potatoes and turkey. "Pete's now up for possible parole in twenty months because of stellar conduct. Apparently he found religion in prison and leads a bible-study group, and he's in regular letter-writing contact with his mother. Apparently he's the only one of Brenda's kids that wants contact with her." *Makes sense,* Sondra thought. She stabbed two green beans with her fork as Doug continued. "Josh is spending his Thanksgiving in Juvenile Hall for underage drinking and vandalizing a park playground. The other kid he was with did the bulk of the damage so Josh'll be out in two weeks. He and Tracy are living with Brenda's sister in Anaheim."

"Sondra, use your napkin not your sleeve, please," scolded Karen. The girl rolled her eyes and complied as if this were a major inconvenience.

"I'm afraid to ask about Tracy," said Sondra. Doug smiled and nodded.

"Well be prepared to be shocked," he told her. "Tracy's completely cleaned up her act. She's doing quite well at junior college and has a part-time job as a waitress at a Fifty's diner. And get this … her new boyfriend's a cop and they attend church together with his family every Sunday."

"Wow," said Sondra, shaking her head. "Good for her," she added with a shrug of her right shoulder. Karen wondered what the shrug was about and wanted to ask about Sondra's views on religion but decided to let this go for another time. An after-dinner walk preceded a piece of pumpkin pie, with freshly made whipped cream. The evening was rounded off by watching a DVD. Sondra chose the 1966 Oscar-winning film *Grand Prix*. The pick amused Karen, but Doug told her he could have won millions in Vegas betting on Sondra's movie selection that night. During the viewing Sondra sat between the two adults, and close to the end of the movie Karen smiled over at Doug. The girl had fallen asleep and was resting her head on her shoulder. Karen mouthed the words, *I love you*.

Doug and Sondra helped Karen move into the Fresno condo on an unusually warm Saturday, December 3. For just over a week, Karen had been transferring small amounts of her belongings, and since the cottage she'd been renting had come mostly furnished it took only one trip with a U-Haul van to move the rest of her possessions. Karen could have easily made the move by herself but Doug thought it important, especially for Sondra, that they embark on this as a family. He was still concerned with Sondra's comfort level when it came to making this major change in her life and including the girl in the moving process seemed appropriate. He was pleased with himself when later he noted that both women were in good moods before, during and after the move. Their take-home Chinese dinner that evening at the Fresno condo was served on a set of Karen's green and white grape-leaf china her parents had given her a year ago for Christmas.

The next day Dan Stoltz invited to go in with him on a classic-car restoration business. Stoltz had been noticing how Doug's towing service had inadvertently and greatly increased both used and new car sales at the dealership, and Doug's eye and knack for finding a number of choice classic cars that had been hidden away, in various states of look and drivability, was uncanny. On a foggy cold Friday morning Sondra went with Doug to pick up a stash of old automotive parts and body pieces from a home in Chowchilla. The man selling the items was moving his family to Minneapolis for a new job. "Two generations of Petersons have been collecting and storing this junk," Ralph told Doug and Sondra upon arrival. "Always had the idea to build a classic car but this is as far as any of us ever got. I'm makin' a fresh start. New job, new town and new hobbies. Gettin' really into RC planes. Anyway, I'm sellin' the lot."

Doug was somewhat disappointed. The classified ad stated items specific to a particular year of make and model car. "Not a lot here that screams classic car," he told Ralph. "This here is a water pump off an Eighties Ford Courier."

"But it's in good working order," countered Ralph. "Everything here is." Doug folded his arms and continued to study the display. "Well I happen to be somebody who knows the value of what you have here," Doug told the man. "No one's gonna pay what you're asking but I think we can come up with a mutually acceptable deal."

As soon as Doug pulled his tow rig southbound on Highway 99, Sondra looked over at his pleased expression. "Now I know why you and Mr. Stoltz are successful," she said. "You made a killing because that guy didn't know what he had."

Doug shook his head. "I didn't rip the guy off," he assured her. "Never cheat anyone, Sondra. I didn't want or need most of that crap but he wasn't gonna sell me just the Mustang tail lights, fenders and other goodies that I did want. I gave him fair market value and we basically helped each other out."

"Are you gonna put 'em on the green sixty-eight that's in the shop?" asked Sondra. Doug glanced over at the girl with a smile and a nod. He loved that Sondra knew the year of the Mustang he and the other restorers were working on, and liked thinking of himself as a good role model for the girl.

The trip back to Fresno went by unusually fast for Sondra. She loved it when Doug would regale her with stories of places he'd been and things he'd done in his life. In this way he was incredibly similar to her father. There were tales about adventures in Alaska, Hawaii, New York and Washington DC, and Doug elaborated on a motorcycle trip across the US he'd taken with his friends years ago.

Sondra liked knowing that in Doug's past he'd had fascinating jobs and owned some really amazing cars and motorcycles. A billboard caught Sondra's eye. It was an advertisement for home loans. The enormous photo was of a fisherman reeling in a modern two-story house, with a caption in neon-green letters: *Let us help you land a whale of an equity loan.* Sondra asked Doug if he'd ever been into fishing. That was all it took. "Oh I used to love fishing as a kid," he told her. "This one buddy of mine from school and I used to go out on a little lake every chance we got for an entire summer. Got sunburned like you wouldn't believe but we had the greatest time." Sondra thought about her dad's fishing rod and reel that had been stored in the garage loft and remembered listening to her brother Dave's tales of fishing with his friend Bill. She concentrated on Doug's voice as he spoke of an ill-fated fishing adventure off the coast of the northern California bay town, Eureka. "Never been seasick or had motion sickness in my life," said Doug. "But ten minutes in that rocking, heaving boat and the stench from that bait, well that absolutely did me in. I think I was seasick for a week." A part of that story soon dovetailed into another tale of deer hunting with a buddy on the Jack London ranch and how they'd met a relative of the famous author.

By the time Doug and Sondra arrived home, the temperature had dropped seven degrees and the damp fog was becoming thicker by the minute. Stepping through the front door of the condo and beginning to walk to her room, Sondra froze. Karen had been busy during their absence. There were candles dancing cheerily and Christmas music was playing softly. Karen had also placed dozens of decorations carefully throughout the condo and had put a beef roast in the slow-cooker. "Ta-da," she announced to Doug and Sondra as she emerged from the den. "I decked a few halls. Oh, and we're invited to spend Christmas with my parents in Pennsylvania." Sondra's eyes were intense as she scanned the Christmas scene. She headed quickly to her room, with Doug and Karen being none the wiser of the girl's sudden internal torturous struggle. Unbeknownst to them, weeks even before Thanksgiving, Sondra had begun to think about what to do and where she might go as a distraction from the whole Christmas ordeal. The previous year's Grand Canyon excursion had turned out so well and she was sure she could come up with something equally as satisfying. She hadn't.

Though Karen and Doug had both noted an elevated level of anxiety in Sondra lately, they couldn't be sure of its origin, whether it was related to her upcoming race season, her college course load, Karen moving in or the upcoming holidays. "Wow," said Doug, looking around the room. "I uh ... I thought we talked about this." They shared a kiss and Doug continued. "Holidays bring up so much pain for Sondra."

"I know, Doug," nodded Karen. "And I didn't do this to be selfish or mean," she reassured him. "The last thing in the world I'd ever want to do is hurt our Sondra but that girl can't go through life avoiding and running away from her past or her present."

Doug briefly closed his eyes and shook his head. "Well I suppose you're right," he said with a shrug. "But, wow, that's a lot to hit her with all at once."

"Best this way," said Karen. "Like ripping off a Band-Aid. You need to trust me on this, okay?" His nod was reluctant as he took in the detail of Karen's handiwork.

"Well this is really nice," he admitted with an approving nod. "But I think there's a couple of towns that might be missing half their Christmas decorations right about now."

Karen laughed and swatted him on the arm. "Yes, well," her voice dripping with sarcasm. "I probably should have told you. I may be wanted in at least five states for being the infamous decoration redistribution queen. A Christmas Pink Panther, if you will."

"Hmm," voiced Doug, dubious but willing to go along with the joke. "Guess we'll have to check and see if there's anything about you on *America's Most Wanted* tonight," he said, continuing the fun. "Oh, you," chuckled Karen, hanging his coat in the hall closet.

Approximately 20 minutes later, Doug found that Karen's parental instinct had been correct. Sondra emerged from her room to join them in the kitchen. The girl had changed clothes. She now sported an old yellow T-shirt with several small holes and rips on the front.

There was also an area on the garment of overspray from a black spray can she'd used on the frame of the 125 cc Suzuki a year ago. Over the T-shirt she wore an unbuttoned faded red flannel shirt that was frayed and looked as though it belonged in a rag drawer. Sondra's jeans were also old and had cuts and holes in them, and she was wearing a pair of black racing shoes that were well-worn. Doug didn't catch the significance of all this but Karen was quick to recognize the girl's rebellion over the invasion of Christmas decorations. It took restraint on her part in not smiling or laughing at the girl's blatant defiance. She was actually proud of Sondra. This was a tolerable response to what the girl most likely perceived as an injustice. "How 'bout a cup of my famous cinnamon-nutmeg hot chocolate?" Karen asked Sondra.

The girl coughed an involuntary laugh. "No thanks," she said. "Famous?" she then asked.

"Everything she makes is famous." Doug whispered to Sondra.

The girl's mood turned on a dime. "Do you have those little mini-marshmallows?" she asked Karen. "I love those little marshmallows."

Doug picked the girl up and set her in her usual kitchen table chair as if she were a three-year-old. "Dad, jeeze," Sondra exclaimed in an involuntary response. "Nutty girl," said Doug, giving her a kiss on the top of her head as Karen brought over a large Santa pitcher with the steaming hot beverage inside.

"Well of course I have the little marshmallows," she said. "No self-respecting maker of hot chocolate would be caught without mini marshmallows."

An hour later Sondra helped Karen set the table for dinner. She then went to her room only to reappear minutes later dressed in much nicer clothes. The three sat at the dining table to enjoy their meal, which included potatoes and green beans. Just as Karen hadn't reacted to Sondra's first wardrobe change, she refused to say anything about the girl's recent change of attire. She did however revel in the "mmm" noises made by both Doug and Sondra. "You know" she said, taking Sondra's napkin off the table and draping it over the girl's leg. "I learned to cook from my mom, my aunt and my grandmothers. My grandmothers aren't too mobile these days but my mom and aunt

Deirdre can practically make five-star chefs drool with envy." Karen then proceeded with a pointed comment. "All that culinary goodness will be happening in Pennsylvania."

Sondra rolled her eyes. "Okay, okay," she said. "You can stop the carpet-bombing. I'll go. I mean it'll probably be like a thousand degrees below zero."

"Oh, I'm sure it'll just be awful" laughed Karen. "The stock market will plunge, the sky will fall and the airline will lose all our luggage."

"Oh, jeeze," voiced Sondra, rolling her eyes.

Later that night as Doug and Karen were getting settled for bed, Doug commented on the day's events, specifically with Sondra. "You're feeling pretty good about yourself, aren't you?" he asked rhetorically.

"Why yes, yes I am," replied Karen with a smirk and a flip of her hair.

"I hope you know what you're in for," said Doug. "Little Miss Tough-As-Nails is far more stubborn and complex than you think. Decorations and a trip back east are nothing," he continued. "I may not scold her about her table manners but I've learned to pick my battles and keep her on the right path."

Karen nodded with a sweet smile. "I know what I'm in for and I know what I'm doing, Doug," she assured him. "You're a great dad and I wouldn't be here if I didn't love you both. Besides, I know first-hand all the stubborn manipulative tricks of a teenage girl. I was one once, you know. Sondra's life circumstances do present a challenge but I'm more than up for it."

Doug leaned over and they shared a tender kiss. He seized his moment, going first to the closet to fish around in his black sport coat pocket. He had planned on popping the question at an opportune time on Christmas eve but this just felt right. He returned to the bed and waited until Karen had finished putting her hair up into a makeshift bun. He then knelt down on his left knee and presented an opened small black velvet box.

"Karen Kathleen McCormick," he announced. "Will you marry me?"

Her smile said it all but Doug was hoping to hear the word "yes." He did hear it seconds later and she elaborated, her voice a bit unstable with happy tears. "Oh yes, of course I'll marry you, Doug. I've waited for you my whole life. I love you and Sondra so much. I can't wait to be your wife and her mom."

Two days before leaving for Pennsylvania it became apparent that Sondra had caught a cold. Karen suspected it was psychosomatic but quickly snapped into caring-mom mode. She fussed over the girl, trying her best to keep her warm, fed and well hydrated. On the big day of travel Sondra had low energy but never complained. Karen's father, George, and his brother-in-law, Karen's Uncle Tony, were the welcoming party at the airport. While Karen and her father sat up front in the olive-green Lincoln, talking almost nonstop, Sondra was sandwiched in the back seat between Tony and Doug. Tony was a smoker and smelled like an old ashtray. He engaged Doug in a bit of friendly but mostly inconsequential chit-chat, and by the time they arrived at the McCormick's abode Sondra had a major headache and felt quite nauseated. While the McCormicks did technically live on a five-acre farm, the area over a period of many years had slowly but continuously developed into something more akin to an anywhere USA rural neighborhood. The McCormicks' white two-story farmhouse was situated almost geographically in the middle of the block, with an enormous but well-maintained lush green lawn in front. It had snowed four days prior and the patches of green and white of the yard were like a giant jigsaw puzzle before the stoic home. There was a white picket fence spanning the front length of the property, with cheery red bows tied every five feet. A large wreath was attached to the gate, which opened onto a narrow straight brick pathway leading to a screened-in porch.

After excited greetings and the bringing in of luggage, Mary took note of Sondra. The girl looked pale, tired and appeared much younger than the age Karen had mentioned.

"I'm so sorry you're not feeling well, sweetheart," said Mary. "Come with me. I have just the thing to perk you up."

George took Doug, with Karen and Tony in tow, on a tour of the house while Mary had Sondra sat in the kitchen's breakfast nook, a light blue wooden booth that could seat four adults comfortably. Sondra appreciated the ginger ale but would have preferred almost anything to a round of inquiry and mindless chitchat from Karen's mother. "Well, you came on the perfect day," said Mary to Sondra as she fussed about the room, not necessarily completing any particular task. "We had our first significant snowstorm of the season last week. I suppose coming from California you find it absolutely freezing here, but actually we've been having above-normal temperatures the past two days."

"Parts of California get plenty cold," Sondra told Mary, wishing she could just go sit in the living room by the fireplace and close her eyes.

"I hear it's been pretty foggy where you live," said Mary.

"Some days can be pretty bad," Sondra informed the woman. "We're in the Central San Joaquin Valley where moist air gets trapped sometimes between the two mountain ranges. It's usually heaviest around this time of year. You get used to it but I miss the sun after a while."

Sondra was relieved when Karen breezed in and kissed the top of her head. "Love the new upstairs bathroom remodel, Mom," said Karen. "The new tile is beautiful."

"Those actually came from a pool installation company," informed Mary. "Apparently a customer changed their mind after they ordered it. We were able to get all that tile for a steal, and your dad's friend Mike Dischelle put it in for us in just two days."

"Oh I remember Mr. Dischelle," said Karen. "Isn't he retired?"

"Yes, but he gave the construction business to his son," divulged Mary. "And Anthony was on a big job out of town that week."

"Oh yeah," remembered Karen of the boy she'd known throughout grade school and high school. Sondra took a nap as Doug and George talked in the living room while Karen and her mother chatted in the kitchen, preparing dinner. Your dad seems quite taken with Doug," she added in a bit of a non sequitur. "I'm sorry Sondra is so sick."

"Well she has had a cold but she's not all that sick," informed

Karen. "I got her number pretty much right from the start. She's milking this for all it's worth. That girl is the dearest and sweetest little thing but wow does she have a stubborn streak."

"Oh, daughter of mine," laughed Mary. "I seem to recall a number of pretty major bouts of your stubbornness."

"What? Me?" asked Karen. "Oh you must be thinking of your other daughter, Shmaren."

"You silly girl," chuckled Mary, stepping closer for a mother-daughter hug. "Wait'll you get to know Sondra and Doug better," whispered the younger of the McCormick women.

Karen went back to her celery chopping and continued to speak of her situation. "I know you and dad disapprove of how fast things are moving with Doug and me, and the whole concept of me raising a teenage girl with a hard past."

"It's not that we disapprove, honey," negated Mary. "It's just that we have some concerns. It seemed like you broke things off with Mark so abruptly and the next thing we know is that you're in love with a single dad and his teenage adopted daughter who races cars. And now you're engaged to be married. We're thrilled but we're concerned."

Karen glanced over at her mother before responding. "Well maybe it does sound crazy, but once you get to know Sondra you'll get it. Racing cars is her calling. Like someone destined to be a doctor or a teacher. Don't get me wrong. I most certainly was a skeptic at first. She's smart and has so much potential. I'm so glad she's going to college but she's just wired differently. It isn't just a whim or a hobby to her and she's so much stronger than she looks. It's almost frightening." Karen halted her vegetable chopping and leaned against the counter, pondering her recent past. "There was definitely something there the first time I saw Doug and Sondra," she continued. "But that first evening I spent having dinner with the two of them, that was it. I just knew. Then I really got to know Doug. He's so different than any guy I've ever met. After that jerk Steve cheated on me I was content to be alone. The Mark thing just sort of happened by accident."

Mary set three large tomatoes in front of her daughter and

went back to peeling potatoes. "I know you and Dad liked Mark," furthered Karen of the last man she'd dated before Doug. "But dating a coworker is tricky, and he was a bit of a dolt. There was just no real chemistry. Not like with Doug. There are so many depths to him. He's not just a tow-truck driver or a car-guy. He's smart and has a great head for business, is a deep thinker and reads a lot. He's a strong person but there's such a sweet gentleness to him. … And he's an amazing father to Sondra."

Karen started to cry. "And that girl loves me and trusts me, Mom. I know I can be a good mother to her. You and dad taught me well."

Mary stepped closer to hold Karen warmly in her arms. "You'll make a great wife and mother," she told her daughter. "I've always thought that."

Sondra liked getting to know the McCormick family as well as some of their neighbors and friends but secretly brooded that none of the holiday foods or traditions were anything like she and her family had enjoyed each year. On the flight to California, Karen and Doug openly discussed wedding plans in front of Sondra for the first time, glad to find that the girl's mood and facial expressions registered agreeable intrigue. "I got quite the talking to from your mom" said Doug to Karen. "Several times, wanting to know my intentions and if we already picked a date and site for the wedding. She did approve of the engagement ring though, so there's that."

Without missing a beat, Karen smiled and nodded. "Ever since I was a little girl I've always wanted to get married in that big old church in town I pointed out to you. We weren't all that regular churchgoers but we'd go every so often, and whenever Aunt Deirdre and Uncle Tony would come to visit from Connecticut. My cousin Emily and I used to run the pews either before or after service. We'd get scolded for it almost every time but a couple of six-year-old girls can get away with quite a lot, especially if they're in adorable little dresses."

Doug laughed and Sondra rolled her eyes at the dress comment. "I'm not wearing some pink frilly dress at the wedding," stated Sondra.

"It won't be pink," said Karen. "But this most definitely will be one occasion that you won't be in old jeans and a T-shirt, you silly goose."

Sondra flashed a devilish grin and Karen continued speaking of their future. "September twenty-third," she announced of the planned wedding date. "A beautiful fall Sunday with all the amazing colors. And you'll like minister Ericson. He's a down-to-earth guy with a real dry sense of humor. We'll come back soon so you can meet him. Mom's already booked the church, by the way."

Doug smiled and kissed his fiancé. "You McCormicks are something else," he told Karen, chuckling and shaking his head.

Sondra leaned forward to get a clear view of Karen. "A week after my last F-Ford race?" she questioned. "Right when I start new college classes?"

"We'll work out all the details," assured Karen. "Don't you worry. So? I'm not scaring either one of you, am I?"

"Daily," joked Doug with a mischievous smirk.

"Oh, you," said Karen, swatting at his shoulder.

Doug then executed a pleased and proud smile. "I already have my best man picked out," he announced. "And I'm thinkin' the kid here should wear a tux and be like a second best man," he added, tapping Sondra's right knee with the back of his hand.

"Hmm" voiced Karen. "Good luck getting that past your mother-in-law to-be, and I'd love to be there when you pitch this to her. Besides, what makes you think I'm not gonna insist that Sondra be one of my bridesmaids?"

Sondra folded her arms and cleared her throat. "I'm sitting right here," she announced in a fake annoyed tone. "What makes you think the kid here doesn't have ideas of her own about what my role should be and what I should wear?"

The happy couple smiled and Doug leaned right so his shoulder touched Sondra's. He then leaned his left shoulder into his betrothed.

CHAPTER 16

Sondra began her first foray into college with cautiously optimistic energy. Her class load was a bit minimalistic in comparison to other starting juniors, partly due to her academic counselor's concern over her age and partly because of her F-Ford practice schedule. However, by March 15 she had risen to the top one percent of her class in Sociology 101, Intro to Business Math and Economics 101. Doug and Karen could not have been prouder. During dinner on the eve before she was to leave for her start to a new race season Sondra complained that a newly hired pit crew member, Brad Marcobson, was "a total full of himself idiot. I mean he brought like a thousand girls to watch pit practice the other day. Thinks he's God's gift to women or something. Such ego. I mean all the guys on the team seem a little chauvinistic."

"Sondra" scolded Karen. "Don't eat with your fingers."

"Oh Mom" complained Sondra. She bit down on her tongue realizing what she'd just said. It had been getting a little less jarring each time she'd let slip calling Doug Dad. Blurting out Mom had come so unexpected and natural to her she scrambled for a new topic of conversation in order to mask her emotions. Immediate happy tears found Karen and she reached over to briefly hold Sondra's hand. "Sam

Fenton has been so encouraging but after our last practice we had kind of a weird chat."

"What do you mean?" asked a suddenly alarmed Doug.

"Nothing creepy" assured Sondra. "It was just his harsh attitude on making sure I knew he was the boss and was expecting me to be a team player. Told me about other times he's been crew chief and how his guys were so loyal and would basically walk through fire for him. I mean that's good but he also kept saying how I'm young and don't have enough experience. Just made me wonder if I'm actually gonna get to really race or if they're are just using me for publicity or to stroke their ego and order me around like I'm a trained money or something."

"It's far to early for pessimism" said Karen. "You were hired to win races and the championship, Sondra" assured Doug. "Sure wish we could go with you" he added. "You learn all you can and by next race season we'll have things set up so we can go racing as a family."

Saying goodbye at the Visalia airport was hard for both Doug and Karen. The entire terminal was captivated by the small family. Karen was talking a mile a minute about how Sondra should take care of herself, eat right and call every day. Doug gave his kid some typical fatherly advice, trying to sound strong and tough. "You call me any time you want to or need, day or night." Though he did his best to hide his feelings it was obvious that he was having a hard time letting her go. As he looked all around, his short jerky motions gave him away. Sondra had come into his world at the perfect time. It was basically through her that his life had now changed so much for the better. He felt like he'd grown as a person and was deeply proud of the encouragement and influence he'd been able to pass on to her. Sondra was once such a timid, frightened and unfocused angry little girl. Now she was a powerful and confident young woman about to strike out on her own and pursue the career of her dreams. From the day Sondra had signed the contract with Blue Sea Racing, Doug had begun to prepare her for road travel and dealing with situations and attitudes of individuals or groups that she might encounter. Though he was sure he'd done his best he couldn't help think that he should just go with her. This was not something possible, or practical even if it were, but he couldn't shake the worry from his mind. He'd worried over this girl from the start.

In the late afternoon Sondra arrived at the prearranged Canadian hotel. During the check-in process she spotted Greg Wilente and Sam Fenton in an adjoining room. They were seated at the bar and engaged in conversation with three women and a very loud-talking man. Sam had been keeping an eye out for the driver of Blue Sea Racing and came rushing over as Sondra accepted her room key and was waiting for the bellhop to pick up her belongings. "Good, you made it" he told her. "Have a good flight?" He didn't give her a chance to answer. "Once you get settled, come on back down and we'll all grab some dinner. Pit crew's already in the dining room. Oh, by the way, don't get too used to the jet-setting and being in fancy hotels. After this we're in cheap motels and a van like a band of Gypsies."

Early the next morning the Blue Sea Racing team met in the lobby, where they only had minutes to wait until their transportation vehicle was brought around by a non-communicative valet employee. The Blue Sea team members were all nervous but jovial in the van as they headed toward the racetrack. They were forced to share a garage with another team but fortunately someone had the good sense to put a temporary barrier between the two and the Blue Sea crew went straight to work readying the car. It was soon discovered that one of the tire sets was one short. Sam left immediately to hunt down someone at Michelin, the official tire supplier for this F-Ford season, as Sondra headed to Driver's Orientation and Licensing School. She found the expansive banquet room to be chilly in temperature as well as atmosphere, encountering sneering stares from many boys. Several young men mistook her for perhaps the sister of a fellow competitor and others seem to dismiss her altogether. A few however greeted her politely and engaged in light, nervous banter. It was a relief when the proceedings got underway. Sondra paid close attention and tried her best not to stand out, although many did take note of her as she was the only female participant among the room full of male F-Ford championship hopefuls. Sondra was also noticed for being the only one of a few who asked important questions, the ones most wanted to ask but didn't for varying reasons. By the end of the introduction to the series, the officials from the Formula Ford sanctioning board gave lectures and warnings of rules, procedures and appropriate conduct as well as stressing safety. Both the written test and all other proceedings came as an interesting and at times fun several hours – three hours, thirty-eight minutes, nineteen seconds, all necessary to obtain the coveted racing license.

During the first thirty minute practice session Sondra found the car an ugly mess to drive. She immediately noticed the lack of top-end horsepower and that she had to fight and use almost all her strength shifting from fourth to fifth gear. There was also bizarre and severe understeer that would come on quite suddenly in Turns 5 and 8, and the right front brake grabbed so dramatically it was down-right dangerous to try and drive fast through certain sectors of the course. She thought of reporting this to Sam over the radio but decided to test herself and see if she could figure a driving style and a line that could compensate for any of these major glitches. Besides, radio transmission was shoddy at best. Two laps later, the right brake dragged so severely going into Turn 4 that the front end drifted dangerously to the verge of putting her into a spin. She stabbed the throttle, sliding the rear of the car in the opposite direction and straightened slightly. She went off in the grass for about eight feet but recovered, calling to Sam that she was coming in. "There's just too many problems to hang onto at any kind of speed" she told her crew chief . He answered back calmly. "All right, Sondra. Come on in and go directly to the garage."

The Blue Sea Racing team tackled an indeterminate oil leak and carburetion issues. The gear stack was changed and several Right-front suspension elements were replaced, including the brake assembly. Sondra had to fiercely defend herself when jumping in on the mechanical work but after citing that she'd worked in a "successful auto shop in Bakersfield for two years" she was allowed to continue mostly unfettered. When the work was completed the entire team was surprised and proud that they'd actually pulled off this small miracle.

With just six minutes remaining in the practice session, Sondra was back in the car. "Okay, so you only have time for two laps" crew chief Sam Fenton announced to Sondra over the radio while she was headed toward Pit Exit. "Lets rock and roll but don't do anything stupid. Go out easy and lets see what we got." Sondra did exactly as she was told, falling into the same line as the car now in front of her going through the first left-hand turn. At the conclusion of the session Sondra and her team were none too happy when they learned they'd be starting on the last row of the qualifying grid. This was because the car had only made minimal required practice laps.

Before the qualifying race, Sam warned his driver of being a hot-shot. He wanted smooth consistent laps. Even so, she climbed to 8th Place in the running order within ten laps and by race's end Blue Sea Racing finished without incident in 3rd. After a short team debriefing back at the garage Sondra was enthralled in watching the IndyCar Series practice. The rest of her team went to find something to eat but food was the last thing on her mind as she studied how the seasoned professional pit crews worked. Even with her limited vantage point she paid close attention to the different lines the drivers took and what gear the cars were in at that particular place on the track. A man in his fifties with short curly hair and a bushy mustache, wearing a Michelin uniform, introduced himself. "Hi, I'm Carl Burham. It's Sondra, right? Not a bad bit of driving you just did."

"Thanks" she returned flatly. "I was talking with your crew chief earlier" continued Carl. "What do you think of the tires?" Sondra never took her eyes off the racetrack but gave an explanation over the almost deafening engine noise. "They'll probably be better on the smaller circuits but here I wish we had a slightly harder compound." She then went into more detail, which he couldn't really hear, but he was impressed. This was actually the consensus of a number of other drivers and crew-chiefs that he'd spoken with that day. He invited Sondra to the luxury suite that was rented by the company so they could talk in more comfortable surroundings. She was reluctant to leave, wanting to stay where she was until IndyCar practice was over, but she suddenly remembered what Doug had told her, not to pass up important career-developing chances. She gracefully accepted Carl's offer and followed him to a large second-story room. The Indy Lights Series would soon be out for their practice session and Sondra was both relieved and happy to now have a bird's-eye view of the track. There were about fifteen men and women in the room and a buffet table was set with a vast array of mostly finger-food. Sondra reveled in her dining luck, glancing at the view of the track out the window. There was a large flat-screen TV showing the on-track action as well and she occasionally glanced at it while being engaged in conversation by several men. Sam showed up and was unusually and most annoyingly overprotective of his young female driver. Sondra had felt special and important being asked to be there, like an equal with the grownups, but Sam's sudden presence brought her back down to being like a teenager in a place she didn't belong. She resented him for it but didn't outwardly show it.

Starting on the inside of Row 2 in the main race the next morning wasn't quite the advantage Sondra had figured. She was boxed in by the first two cars, and if she hadn't backed off going into that first turn to let them by would have been forced up out of the groove, into the marbles and off the track. Sam was pleasantly surprised that this didn't seem to phase her. The young racer ran most of the laps between 9th and 6th Place. Sondra became consumed with bettering her lap times, and with five laps remaining really had no idea nor did she care about where she was in the running-order. It didn't immediately sink in how much she'd gained when Sam next spoke to her over the radio. "Two laps to go at the line, Sondra. You got the lead by two point eight. Nice and easy. Keep doin' what you're doin' and bring it on home."

During the cool-down lap Sondra suddenly became aware of just how much energy she'd expended. Her hands felt as if they were on fire and the muscles in her arms and legs felt as if they were on the verge of exploding through the skin. The Winners Circle and podium for Formula Ford was not at all what Sondra had expected. It was a makeshift area in between the pit lane and the main garages. The top three finishers of this first championship race were ushered into position on top of multi-tiered wooden step-boxes in front of a large Michelin Tires advertising screen, with white and black lettering. This was not the Grand Prix winner's circle that Sondra had dreamed of, and the First, Second and Third Place trophies were handed out hurriedly while photos were being taken. Sondra thought the boys on either side of her were not particularly nice or sportsmen-like, sneering at her with disdain, and they acted as if she'd somehow cheated to get the win. Though Sondra smiled and extended her hand in congratulatory gesture, they avoided the jovial podium camaraderie she'd come to know in her two sprint-car seasons. Short, abrupt interviews were conducted by a man with a handheld digital recording device and a woman snapping photos of the Winners Circle action made a point in shaking each podium winner's hand. When it came to Sondra she enacted a self-introduction.

"Congratulations, Sondra. Well done. My name's Lydia Velstein. We spoke on the phone a few times. I'll be your and Blue Sea Racing's official publicist for the season."

Lydia was an attractive, moderately tall Southern California blond. She was well educated, had a strong voice and was extremely professional in her dress and mannerisms. After an exchange of pleasantries and a few more pictures, Sondra headed to her team's assigned garage. For the Blue Sea Racing team this win couldn't have been a better way to start the season.

Sam Fenton was proud and satisfied with his rookie team. They had worked well together and had put out major effort, especially the previous day. He wasn't quite as interested in where Sondra finished, just as long as she did finish. To him this weekend was a win, from their first day. He smiled, wide with pride, as he watched the young team members give high-fives, heavy pats on the back and hugs of congratulations to each other and their driver. He paid particular attention to Sondra, a fiercely intense kid who was anything but easy-going. She'd listened to him however and then had given an impressive performance. He thought Sondra had a lot to learn but he now had a stronger sense that the girl had potential. Team owners Greg and Joe were also quite pleased with the end result because this was their gamble and investment but hadn't planned on Sondra doing well at all. In fact Joe's only comment to Sam was snarky at best. "Keep a handle on the kid. I'm not paying for a third van to haul her ego around."

The drive to Florida was much longer and far more tedious than Sondra had anticipated, and she never thought she'd get tired of hamburgers. If it wasn't a fast-food burger restaurant, they'd stop at the dirtiest greasiest truck-stop-style diners, where even the rare salad seemed to be dipped in 10W-30. The guys didn't exactly make things pleasant for her either. They became openly crude with their language and discussions about sex and women as well as producing some foul bodily noises and aromas. She was surprised that even Sam was well entrenched with all the going's-on and made an educated guess that this was some sort of test, to see how far they could go until they got a reaction from her. She was determined not to react or give in to any of it and for the most part closed her eyes and feigned sleep or became engrossed in a book she'd picked up before the trip. *The Lunar Men* by Jenny Uglow was the story about five friends in the 1760s who changed the world with their amateur experiments, basically enabling the Industrial Revolution to blossom. Sondra was enchanted with the book and the brilliant men. It struck her how their discoveries of electronics, new ways of extracting metals from the earth and their medical advancements and enlightenments are often and unfortunately taken for granted today.

It was with indescribable relief to Sondra that they arrived at Sebring International Raceway. Without waiting to hear of an immediate plan, she headed quickly to the racetrack Administration Building, spotting Lydia Velstein who recognized her and gestured for Sondra to come closer. "Nice to see you again, Sondra" greeted Lydia. "Say, do you have some time? I'd love to get a better profile going on you. Mr. Wilente didn't exactly give me much to work with, and I'd prefer some updated photos of you and your team."

Under normal circumstances Sondra would have run straight back to her garage and hidden from her but the woman had been so nice and polite from the start, and smelled a hell of a lot better than the Neanderthals she'd been cooped up with for the past number of days. Sondra nodded, looking down at her watch and pulled a piece of paper from her pocket. "I need to find this motel and get something decent to eat" she explained. "I have just over two hours before our first practice."

Lydia craned her neck to get a better view of the itinerary Sondra was holding in her hand. "Wow" she exclaimed. "So you guys are on a tight budget? This motel is two blocks away from the Hyatt, where I'm staying."

"Wow" said Sondra in a sarcastic tone. "We're paying you too much."

Lydia laughed, reconfirming her notion that they'd be good friends. She made a head gesture and in minutes they were in Lydia's white Ford Escort rental car.

After Sondra had checked in at the Travellodge she and Lydia had an exceptionally good lunch and talk at The Seabring, a fairly upscale seafood restaurant near the race facility with lots of natural light and many potted plants. Lydia barraged her with questions as Sondra enjoyed her very fresh-ingredient salad, with the best blue cheese dressing she'd ever had. Sondra mentioned several times how much she loved seafood while devouring her crab cakes, answering most of Lydia's questions gladly, grateful for the advice offered on dealing with being the only girl traveling with a van full of dudes. Sondra became noticeably tense and quiet however when pressed about her family. Unfortunately Greg hadn't warned the publicist enough of Sondra's painful past – actually he was curious about the details himself. The young race car driver swallowed hard after one particular pointed question and took a deep breath before speaking. "I don't want a lot of details and major things about my past to go into some cheesy bio or PR package" she warned the publicist. "Well, you have my word that I won't make you out like some poor little orphan girl but your life's story and career so far are unique and I'm sure inspirational to some"

Lydia told Sondra "my job is to present a positive image of you" she furthered. "And that can't happen unless you're satisfied with what we come up with as well. Greg alluded to something bad that happened to you as a kid, so this right now is strictly off the record. I just really want to get to know you and understand why a teenage girl would risk her life racing cars."

Sondra got a hard angry look and spoke with a slight growl. "I don't have to justify what I choose to do for a living. Not to you, not to anyone." She bit down on her tongue and began to get up from the table. Lydia grabbed her wrist, apologized and motioned with her head for Sondra to sit back down. "It must have been something awful" she said in a soft voice. "I'm really sorry."

Lydia let go and watched Sondra settle back down on her chair and lean forward as she began to speak in short sentences. "We were coming home from a family winter vacation. A drunk driver caused a big crash. I'm the only one in my family who survived. I was thirteen." Sondra's eyes never left Lydia's. She knew that if she looked anywhere else she would completely lose it. Instead it was her publicist who fell to pieces. With tears streaming down Lydia's face her voice became jagged. "Oh how awful. I'm so, so sorry. I can't even imagine." Her right palm caught her forehead and she stared down at her mostly empty plate. After a few seconds she looked up at Sondra's rock-solid calm expression that hinted at concern. Lydia asked a timid question. "How can you even be around cars let alone race in one? How can you go through something so catastrophic and now do what you do? I don't get it. Aren't you afraid of crashing?"

With a slight relaxed smile Sondra reached across, lightly putting her hand on Lydia's upper arm for a brief second. "For me, the two aren't connected" explained Sondra. "I'm a race car driver. I'd be doing this no matter what. Come on. I need to get back to the track." Lydia would have preferred talking about this more but Sondra stood, dropping a wad of bills on the table pulling her new friend up from her chair.

At the same building where the two women had met up earlier, Sondra changed into her race suit and then headed to her pit. Sam was none too happy about his driver's absence and unknown whereabouts. He began to chew her out something fierce but Sondra held up her hand to stop him, feeling a sense of empowerment from her lunch with Lydia. She gave her crew chief's attitude right back to him. "I've been working with Miss Velstein. You know, like I'm supposed to. I'm now checked into my motel, fed, relaxed and we have over twenty minutes before the first practice. How's my car?"

The #12 car's handling was actually fairly livable but Sondra came into her pit after eight laps and announced that fourth gear was too tall. The motor would bog down and she couldn't accelerate from several corners fast enough. Vince argued with her that this was the gearing that all the other teams were running and Sam backed him up on the set-up choice. Sondra felt like this was their way of punishing her for being gone for a few hours. She qualified a dismal 19th for Saturday's race. Sam was convinced that the girl was pouting for not getting her way and that she had qualified in that spot on purpose. This couldn't have been further from the truth and it was glaringly evident during the next day's race. Sondra didn't use the radio, except to acknowledge pit instructions. Just over halfway through the 24-lap event the car's handling started to go away. Instead of complaining or asking for changes she became consumed with the challenge. Due to mistake-free driving and staying out of other drivers' troubles, of which there were many, she finished in an astonishing third Place. She was physically and mentally exhausted but her team, including Sam, had more respect for this performance than her winning the previous weekend. Her fellow competitors however questioned her finish in the form of snide comments about her size, weight, and that she was a she.

Lydia's advice in dealing with her teammates during travel-time was golden. Instead of ignoring, resenting or secretly being disgusted by them, she joined in, even challenging the validity of some of their stories. She could use profanity with the best of them but there were absolute limits. There was a definite line she wouldn't allow to be crossed when it came to defaming women or anyone of differing ethnicity, skin color or people with physical or mental challenges. She went into attack mode when any of the boys would make clichéd comments or grossly unkind or cruel mocking voice imitations. She was also a stickler for correct grammar and historical facts, not something that necessarily earned her points with this particular group.

The next stop on the schedule was a one-day visit to Putnum Park Speedway for Formula Ford Official Testing. Many performance evaluations and written tests on rules and regulations took place during this regimented 12-hour day. In addition, the drivers were informed that media classes were to be a regular and required activity. There were also some intense pit crew competitions and testing which Sondra enjoyed, mostly because the focus was not on her. This intense day also offered the best opportunity thus far for the competitors to mingle and get to know each other a little better. There were a few boys that Sondra had taken an instant disliking to from that first orientation class, and then there were several drivers who had proven to be obnoxious, arrogant and downright unsportsman-like both on and off the racetrack. Fortunately there were about a dozen boys who at least made an effort to become acquainted with her. At the Mid-Ohio road course Sondra shocked many by dominating both days, mostly because she was only one of a few who seemed to have really paid attention to the previous week's lessons. It was also a track she'd been looking forward to being on and she won Saturday's main race decisively with an 8.375 second lead. These two days, Friday and Saturday, showcased Sondra's natural talent and began to attract interest and change negative attitudes about the girl. A number of competitors, including crew members and several F-Ford officials, made efforts to speak with her, relaying positive and encouraging words.

The weather turned foul and cold as the F-Ford teams next made their way to Lakeville, Connecticut for the New England Grand Prix. Blue Sea Racing arrived at Lime Rock Park Thursday mid-morning. It was raining so heavily that all practices had been canceled for that afternoon and the next morning as well. After taking care of motel arrangements there was much discussion about dinner plans, but the guys eventually took the van and went in search of a particular pub they'd learned of from members of several others teams. Sam had done all the driving from a very early hour and was tired. He and Sondra watched the van pull out of the Best Western motel driveway. "So Lydia Velstein told me you two had a good lunch together not long ago" said Sam to Sondra. He saw the girl in a bit of a different light at this moment in time. In her jeans and slightly oversized unbuttoned flannel shirt over a light-yellow T-shirt, with her hair neatly pulled back, she looked like a sweet and innocent nine- or ten year-old girl. He suddenly couldn't see how she could be so commanding and powerful both in and out of a race car. Sondra noticed him staring at her and looked down to see if she'd spilled something on the front of her. "What?" she asked the man. "I'm gonna grab a nap" he said with a laugh. "But lets meet right back here at six and we'll find a good spot for dinner." Sondra nodded. This would give her time to herself and to make a much-needed call to Doug and Karen.

Sondra liked the pizzeria she and Sam had chosen for their evening meal. It was a converted large historic barn and was popular with the locals. While sitting in a wooden booth waiting for their pizza, Sam began a conversation. "I'm glad it worked out this way, that you and I have a chance for a little uninterrupted one on one" he began. "So you don't seem too unhappy about how things are going so far" he prompted.

Sondra nodded once and responded flatly. "You're right, things are coming along."

Sam then prodded a bit more. "Lydia seems impressed by you. She mentioned that you two have had some good chats. Well, she didn't go into details of your conversations but they must have been something?" Sondra laughed lightly. He clearly was trying to find out what they'd talked about. "Careful there, Sam" she warned sarcastically. "You're gonna need a larger boat for that fishing expedition. If you want to know if she likes you, maybe you two can meet up after sixth-period gym class." With that, she threw a crouton at him that had disgracefully fallen from her salad plate. While Sam was interested in Lydia – all the guys were – he was hoping that Sondra would open up a little about her past. He could see clearly that she wasn't going to so he changed the subject. "That was some damn good driving at Sebring, and you showed some awesome patience and seemed to learn a lot at Putnum Park." Sondra folded her arms on the table and leaned in, her eyes drifting to a table of four college-age individuals laughing and joking just behind and to the right of Sam. "I won in Canada and last week at Mid-Ohio" she asserted, her voice hard and direct. "Why would you focus on races where I didn't win?" Her eyes darted to his and it felt as if he'd just been slapped. He took a long pull of his beer, looked around the room then noticed that she hadn't moved and that her eyes were fiery-intense. He took a deep breath before he spoke. "Whether you like it or not, Sondra, you're a rookie driver in your first Formula season and we have a rookie team. I've been around this a lot longer than any of you. I know how much you want to win every race, but you can't. I'm trying to give you tools so that when you don't win, you don't eat yourself alive. I've seen that happen with a lot of drivers. You're young. Damn young. You may have won a string of races and a championship right out of the box in your first year of racing, and I know you won a bunch of races and a pro sprint-car championship."

Sondra interrupted him coldly. "Yeah, I was there. I don't need my résumé read back to me."

"Why are you so mad all of a sudden?" he demanded to know. "Does this have anything to do with your talks with Lydia?"

That question put Sondra over the edge. "Go to hell" she growled through clenched teeth, clenching her fists. "I'm not a child. I'm not that young. I learn damn quick and I've done every single thing you've asked me to do, even when it was dead wrong." She took several heavy breaths, and in as calm a voice as she could muster she informed him that she was going to go wash her hands and face and would be back in a minute.

When Sondra returned to the table, close to 15 minutes later, she noticed it had been cleared and cleaned, with their drinks refilled. She sat down softly and smiled at Sam. He couldn't help but smile back, and a few seconds later their server delivered a large steaming-hot sausage, pepperoni & onion pizza. Sondra thought it the most amazing pizza she'd ever experienced, even marveling at the crust and Sondra despised crust. It was something all three Sierre kids had in common and a fact that displeased their mother. When young Sondra ate her lunch at school she would carefully peel the crust off her sandwiches. She loved the actual sandwich because her mom was so creative, along with trying to provide a nutritious meal, but Sondra considered the crust an abomination and a barrier to the greatness within. Once in the third grade her mom had given her a sandwich made of buttered home-made bread, banana slices, sprinkles of sugar and chocolate chips in her Speed Racer lunch box. Her classmates kidded her about her crust removal and when she disclosed the ingredients was teased without mercy. Sondra had quite a thin skin in those days but with this she could have cared less. She had the best sandwich there and the greatest mom in the world for giving it to her.

Nearing the end of their dining experience Sam inquired calmly about her earlier mood. "So what was all that really about, before?" Sondra wiped off the pizza sauce that was dribbling down her chin with the back of her hand before responding. "Those first few days on the road" she began. "You guys were foul jerks to me, just to see if I would crack. Not cool. And secondly ... I could have won at Sebring. I asked politely for different gearing and I told you exactly what I needed. For whatever moronic reason you and Vince wouldn't listen to me and that cost us the race. I've told you this before … I'm in this to win races and the championship. You see me as a young kid. Yeah, I get that but I need you to stop underestimating my abilities and maturity level. Maybe I don't have years of driving experience but I'm a really quick learner and I'm not a kid. As far as what Lydia and I discussed? Most of that is personal and none of your damn business. My abilities and where I want to go with them aren't a childish pipe-dream, like Greg tried to suggest they are. You should know that by now because you're watching my progress. Doug believes in me and has from the start. It's too bad he and Karen can't be on the road with us because Doug's technically my manager and he's done everything he can to help me, unconditionally. I need you to believe in me too. If you can't do that then we're all wasting each other's time."

Sam took his time to digest everything Sondra had just set forth. "Well your manager Doug isn't here" he countered. "And you're under contract, but you made your point." He then nodded and held out his mug for a toast. As soon as their glasses made the traditional clink he grabbed hers and handed her his. They took a sip, with Sam smiling at Sondra's grimacing face. He was glad she didn't like the taste of beer. "I feel really good about this exchange" he announced. "This conversation won't go beyond the two of us but communication between you and me has to be this open and this honest." She wholeheartedly agreed and their server dropped the bill on the table. Sondra reached for it while asking the man to bring a box for the remaining three slices. Sam took advantage of her distraction and snatched up the bill. "This is a business meal, Sondra" he told her. "Let's let the company pick this up, shall we?" She flashed a smile that set a better and more positive tone with him. As they were waiting for a taxi they both breathed in the cold misty air, and Sam's voice seemed almost dream-like when he spoke. "I sure hope it clears up enough to get in Saturday's race."

In a steady light rain Sondra found the front of the pack within six laps of the qualifying race, finishing 3.925 seconds in the lead. The next day on a rain-slick track but clearing skies she started on pole for the New England Grand Prix. It was hers from the start, though Sam deliberately held her back a little. Sondra hated that he was being so cautious in these opening laps, especially since they'd recently talked about him letting her drive how she felt was best. However, when he informed her of a solid "fifty-six point four" (00.56.477) second lap-time she relaxed and drove with confidence. Sondra had set a smooth and easy pace for the first three laps in order to build heat in her tires and make sure there were no dangerous puddles of water. In the laps to come she didn't technically drive harder but with smoothness and confidence came speed and she basically drove off and left the pack. She began to use her sprint-car experience in being able to drift and slide in certain spots, being mindful not to abuse her tires. This particular tactic and her basic driving style going into the corners set her up perfectly for fast straights. After seeing his driver run a 00.52.340 second lap Sam let her go and kept his radio transmissions to a minimum, save his announcements for when he wanted his driver to pit. When the checkered flag waved, Sondra was eighteen seconds in the lead, ahead of the #20 car of Brice Crandle and with a lap-time of 00.51.004. Sondra crossed the downhill finish line at 142.639 mph and was beyond happy with her team, the car and her performance but was catching a cold and didn't feel like doing any kind of major post-race celebrating.

Sondra rarely got sick. As a child her mom was the greatest of caretakers during those relatively low-number occasions, and after a day in bed her father would come home from work, always managing to cheer her up with stories of his day and other anecdotal offerings. Her Blue Sea Racing team however went on with their lives as if she didn't exist and they weren't the least bit sympathetic. She entered into an unexplained depression the next few days of van travel and was surly, often refusing to eat when they'd stop for meals. Once they arrived in Indianapolis, the sight of the next championship round in just over two week's time, the team went their separate ways to enjoy their mid-season break. Sam and Vince drove Sondra to a prearranged motel. Sam took charge of getting Sondra checked in to her motel room but during the process noted a very sick girl, barely able to carry in her own luggage. He sat her down in a chair in the small lobby and stepped outside to call Greg Wilente with the weekly team progress and the Sondra situation. He and Vince got Sondra to her room figuring that all she needed was a good night's sleep, then headed to the airport for their connecting flights. Greg contacted Doug who felt instantly concerned and made arrangements to fly to Indiana. When Doug arrived, he was shocked to see her so pale and emaciated. The girl had an extremely high temperature and was so sick that she didn't even recognize him. He took her to the hospital where she was admitted and received IV fluids.

Doug had Sondra's briefcase with him. It was basically her office and desk drawer, containing all her important papers. As he sat next to the sleeping girl in a chair that was growing more and more uncomfortable by the minute he took a peek inside and found her digital camera. Sondra opened her eyes slowly and watched Doug as he carefully examined each photograph. She noticed that he was smiling. “Those are for my scrap book” she said in a soft thin squeaky voice. Doug immediately got up and sat down on the bed, brushing the hair away from the girl’s face, relieved that her fever was gone. She again spoke, obviously trying to sound strong. “I was dreaming that I heard your voice. I’m glad it’s not a dream. Is Karen here too?” Doug brushed her cheek gently with his fingertips, shaking his head. “She’s on her way and she’s thinking about you. I talked to her just a little while ago.” Sondra looked down at the IV. Her eyes got wide and she began to panic. She was having a flashback of when she was in the hospital after the Tahoe accident. Doug did his best to calm her down. “Shh” he soothed. “You just need fluids and some rest.” He was about to say more but the doctor breezed into the room. Dr. Delbanks had a rich energetic voice. The man was about Doug’s age with thinning blond short hair and a neatly trimmed full beard. He was all smiles as he looked over his patient’s chart. “Well we’re looking good here” he announced as he began to scribble on a small pad. He handed a piece of paper to Doug. “She’s a little anemic so I want her to take these iron pills. I recommend plenty of fluids and a few days of rest.” He then turned to his patient. “Now you make sure you eat right and take care of yourself from now on. You’re gonna be just fine.”

After finally being released from the hospital Doug took Sondra directly to the hotel that he’d earlier secured. When she next opened her eyes late that next afternoon she first focused on a nicely manicured hand with red-pink fingernails. “Well hello there, sleepy-head” said Karen with a soft smile.

“Mom. You came” said Sondra, struggling to get into a sitting position.

“Of course I came” said Karen. “No way am I gonna sit at home while my precious girl is sick in bed hundreds of miles away. You feeling a little better?” “Kinda hungry” Sondra said with a nod, looking over at Doug sitting in a chair on the opposite side of her bed. While the girl was in the shower Karen marveled to Doug that Sondra had unapologetically called her mom.

Blue Sea Racing didn’t exactly get off to a good start when competition resumed after the summer break. This was a particularly anticipated weekend owing to the fact that they would be running on the road course on the infield of the famous Indianapolis Motor Speedway. The weather was ugly-hot and muggy, and just over halfway through Thursday morning's practice session Sondra watched her oil temperature gauge climb at an alarming rate. She came in to her pit immediately but the damage had already been done. Upon inspection it was discovered that a seal on an oil coolant line had failed. The overheating of the engine oddly effected only one valve on the Number Three cylinder. It had stuck and was warped and badly burned. Vince Melenza insisted that the entire top end of the motor be overhauled, thus ending Sondra's chance to get back in the car until the qualifying race the next day, where she ended up a dismal 8th Place. Though it was unfounded, Sondra blamed herself for the damage to her beloved engine as well as her awful qualifying effort. Sam gave her no comfort or encouragement. He'd done some thinking over the summer break. If Sondra didn't want to be held back or treated like a kid, he was not only going oblige but decided to really pour it on and put her to the test.

Doug and Karen's presence seemed to offset the many pressures Sondra was dealing with, and this couldn't have come at a better time. In the driver's meeting before Saturday's race Sondra was flanked by two of the four boys she'd grown to loathe. Brice Crandle was the driver of the maroon #20 car, and Andrew Placer was the driver of the white-silver #17 car. "That your parents?" asked young Placer of the couple he'd been seeing Sondra with over the past few days. Sondra nodded as she chewed her gum, glancing over at the annoying boy to her right. "My folks haven't been to any of the races so far either" offered Crandle, sitting on the opposite side of her. "That was a hell of a drive at Lime Rock Park" he added. Sondra nodded at his statement, suspicious of why he was suddenly being nice. She was also trying to concentrate on what the track official was saying and didn't want to get into idle chit-chat with either one of these guys, the ones who'd been consistently over-aggressive with her on the race track. "Get your motor issues worked out?" inquired Andrew.

"Guess you'll find out in about thirty minutes" responded Sondra with a shrug.

"Why are you always so pissed off?" asked Brice. Sondra made an obscene finger gesture and stood. The meeting was adjourned and she gave her answer before hurrying back to her garage. "You guys have been jerks to me and you know it, and I've heard about the crappy things you've said about me, being a girl in a man's sport. I have news for you morons. The car or the track don't give a damn who or what I am, but you'll give a damn every time I beat you to the line."

"Ooh, trash talk" taunted Placer. "Bring it on, baby" laughed Crandle. Sondra ground her teeth and made a fist as she turned and headed to her assigned garage stall.

During Saturday's race Sondra was mostly buried in 15th and 16th Place. She steadily began to move up the field due to mechanical attrition and crashes within the upper portion of the 28-car field. Her driving was impeccable and the team had smart efficient pit stops. She really wanted to get this win for Doug and Karen, and after the encounter with her arch enemies in the driver's meeting it felt especially important to her. There were occasions where she fought savagely for on-track position but mostly her driving was smart and precise. Finishing second behind Brice Crandle felt like a crowning blow, and his gloating as he stood over her on the top step of the winner's podium got on her every nerve. Doug and Karen however were quite proud of their daughter-client's effort as were the entire Blue Sea Racing team, Sondra's sponsors and a number of racing dignitaries. She hated to see Doug and Karen head for home but had a newly re-energized enthusiasm to propel her into this second leg of the season.

Sondra got a hard-fought win in Ohio. She'd been looking forward to this, having seen IndyCar races at the Cleveland Road-Course on TV. The track largely incorporated the Cleveland Burke Airport, off the shores of Lake Eerie. At Elkhart Lake, Wisconsin, Sondra had her first hard crash in a race car. The team was struggling with an insanely puzzling understeer problem that would only present itself at certain portions of the racetrack. During Thursday afternoon's practice, and under heavy braking in Turn 4, the car spun without warning and at lightening speed. Sondra was unfortunately the first to go through oil that had just been sprayed onto the racing surface by a car who's motor was letting go. There was no time for thinking. Her quick instincts and equally lightening-fast reactions allowed her only time enough to take the car out of gear and let go of the steering wheel, so as not to snap her wrists if the front end abruptly hit something. It did. The car spun off the track and the wheels caught hard in the wet, muddy grass. The #12 flipped violently and skidded upside down for about ten feet, then flipped two more times landing upright. If she hadn't spun and flipped, the aftermath looked as though she'd just simply pulled over and parked in the dazzling lime-green grass. For those who witnessed the incident it looked as though a giant hand had picked up the car and slammed it down. Sam called to his driver immediately over the radio. "You okay, Sondra? Sondra? Are you okay? Answer me." She was stunned and air had been momentarily squeezed from her lungs. In no time the track's safety team arrived and she was taken to the infield medical center, triaged and forced to endure a number of X-rays and further evaluation. She didn't remember most of the crash but thought all these check-out procedures were excessive. Her first words were not of concern for herself or even what had happened. "My car" she said in a worried voice. "How's my car? Did they get it back to the garage? Are they working on it yet?" When this little anecdote got out it was to follow her for quite some time. After being cleared medically she walked out of the medical center under her own power. She was sore and definitely moved like it, but to the relief of her team and many others she seemed to be fine. Due to a possible concussion it was ordered that she be closely monitored and not allowed to sleep until 1 a.m. A schedule was formed by Sam for the guys to keep watch over her. They were going to have to work through the night anyway in order to get a car that could pass Tech Inspection let alone be competitive the next day. Sondra was amazed that the car was in as good a shape as it appeared. She'd been imagining a mangled mass of metal and fiberglass but most of the damage was suspension related.

The Elkhart Lake facility was driver Brice Crandle's hometown track and he was the favorite for the win, which he obtained handily. Sondra finished Saturday's main event in fourth, far back from the leaders but a comfortable distance from a pack of six cars behind. After the post-race awards ceremony young Crandle made a point to seek out Sondra. "How ya feelin'?" he asked. For reasons she could not fully articulate she let her guard down and answered him with humbling honesty. "Sore and tired. I mean there's not one tiny part of me that doesn't hurt right now." Brice nodded. "I'm really glad you're okay though" he told her. "Not too many, myself included, could have gotten back in the car and then pulled off a top-five finish after what you went through."

"Thanks" she said in earnest. "It was a pretty awesome team effort" she told him. "But I'm glad my folks weren't here to see any of it."

"Mine were" he offered. "First time in a long time they've come to watch me drive" said Brice with a sudden smile. He lost the facial gesture as he continued. "My sister has some video of your crash. Looked awful. Really glad you're okay." He lightly patted her right shoulder and was soon whisked away by several members of his team. Sondra stood pondering what had just happened. She'd hated the boy this whole time. He'd been rude, crude and had raced her hard and sometimes not at all cleanly. He'd just spoken to her in a nice respectful manner and had seemed genuinely concerned for her safety. Sondra felt confused by this, especially since she'd had the opportunity for the first time to get a long good look at his face, and she didn't hate what she saw. She didn't have a habit of observing boys, being far more interested in all things mechanical and her race craft. Within the past few months she'd had many chats with Lydia Velstein who, like Kari Wilken, always noticed the boys. Only recently had Sondra caught herself noticing the look and build of the young men that surrounded her.

Upon Sondra's crash the previous day, Karen and Doug had been immediately informed. Their first instinct had been to catch the next flight to Wisconsin but after phone conversations with Sam Fenton, Vince Melenza, Greg Wilente and Joe Alders they were all on the same page. Making a big fuss about the incident might possibly do harm to the girl's confidence. It was a relief to Doug and Karen when Sondra called home Saturday evening. After greetings and some small-talk, Sondra expanded on her weekend.

"I hate that I didn't finish higher up than fourth" she told her now-parents. "But in Thursday's practice I spun in someone's oil in Four and really messed up the suspension and stuff. The guys had a super-long night putting Humpty-Dumpty's fall back together again." "Well, little Miss Muffet" joked Doug, going off Sondra's nursery rhyme theme and trying to sound as if he and Karen weren't as freaked out by the accident as they were, "how are your curds and whey?"

"A little bruised and sore" she said with a slight laugh. "But no big deal" she added. "I mean I guess I should see this as a lesson learned." Doug asked a few more details of the crash but was purposely positive. Karen was beside herself with worry as she listened, momentarily unable to speak.

Three quarters of the way into a long and tedious van ride to Denver, the water pump on the Chevy van's V-8 abruptly expired. The gang was not particularly in good spirits on this day, and to compound things for Sondra it was her 17th birthday. She'd grown to dread and hate her birthdays in the past four years because it was just too painful a reminder that her parents and brothers were no longer around to help her celebrate the annual event. She had done what she'd thought was a good job at hiding the date of her birth from her Blue Sea teammates, but standing at the side of the road Vince called Sam to let him know of their predicament. Sam was traveling in another vehicle over an hour ahead of his team, and after coming up with a solid plan he included a further remark. "Tell Sondra I'm sorry she has to spend some of her birthday by the side of the road but we'll have some cake or somethin' when we're all together in Denver." Vince then related the message to Sondra, thus revealing her date of birth, and while the gang waited for roadside assistance from the nearest service station Sondra was teased mercilessly about being the birthday girl and that she must have had a dubious reason for trying to hide it from them.

The Denver Grand Prix was the next-to-last race on this year's schedule. Sondra felt no repercussions from the previous week's crash, mentally or physically. The team had been building momentum all season long and after Friday's practice on the Denver International Raceway track Sondra wanted more equal front brakes and complained of the motor running too lean at the highest point. The rev-limiter would kick in and retard the motor, thus keeping her from obtaining the all-important top speed. She soon found out that this technically had more to do with the gear-stack than the carburetor or the electronics, though they did all work in conjunction. Mr. George McClayton, the president of the Formula Ford North American West division, was on hand throughout the weekend. Four front-runners had emerged in this highly competitive field, Sondra among them. These last two races were intentionally chosen to showcase the brightest in talent. Brice Crandle, Andrew Placer and Wendell Grayson had lately been consistently the three that Sondra could now count on to race her extremely hard but never cross the line or do something rookie-stupid as she put it. They were all in contention for the championship due to multiple wins and high finishes.

This DIR (Denver International Raceway) championship round was not easy for any driver or any of the pit crews. The high altitude was a factor and the track's temperature was completely different from one end to the other. Proper carburetion and taking care of one's gearbox was key. In the race Sondra did as she was instructed, maintaining her speed and lap-times. She was solidly in 5th Place at just over the halfway point. With the last pit stop Sam barked out the usual orders for her to reset her fuel and watch her speed on pit-exit. On this day it grated on her every last nerve because it was such a simple and basic rule. She'd known the importance of this since the age of six, and every time Sam said these words to her she had to fight the urge to tell him where to stick it. This time however Sam had a few words of encouragement to add. "Okay, Sondra. It's your race, kid. Go get 'em but don't do anything stupid." Sam was a little shocked when Sondra didn't immediately jump up in speed or begin to drive with the fierce intensity that had always been her style whenever she even remotely thought she could get away with it. Breaking her of this habit had been something he'd tried so hard to accomplish all season long. Abrupt change in speed and aggressiveness was never good for the equipment and was not smart big picture racing. Even up to a month prior, making an aggressive jump was exactly what she would have done but not this time. Sondra had her hands full, in heavy traffic, so it wasn't as if she could sit there and contemplate her maturity level as a driver but she was now displaying maturity and talent beyond her years. In just under two laps Sondra pulled alongside Andrew Placer's new gray and black paint scheme Motorola-sponsored #27 car. She turned tighter inside him, passing him easily and just under a lap later came upon her usual on-track nemesis, Brice Crandle. It took her only a few corners to see that the maroon car was fighting considerable understeer in several sections on the circuit and she out-accelerated him coming out of Turn 9. With her car working pretty well she caught the leader within three laps. Benny Holmes had been a back-marker most of the season but now had Most Improved Driver status. As Sondra stuck closely to the tail of the green and silver car #14, she noticed that he was pretty good on the faster portions of the track but was clearly not comfortable as a leader. With Sondra being so close and making small moves on him in the more technical sections he was becoming more and more nervous and twitchy. On the exit of Turn 6, heading onto a long straight, he missed a shift and Sondra flashed by him on the outside. Now with open race track and five laps to go she drove flawlessly and finished 1.831 seconds ahead of Holmes. Though it was another win for her and Blue Sea Racing she was oddly not all that thrilled about it. The car was a tick off in the horsepower department and she felt like Sam had held her back too long. The only portion of the race she remotely enjoyed were the laps in which she'd moved from 5th to 1st. She didn't have much of a chance to dwell on the negatives however. It was a solid team victory and they were soon headed to a racetrack that to be driving on had her both nervous and wildly excited.

It was just after 2 p.m. when Blue Sea's van and support truck pulled onto the grounds of Laguna Seca Raceway. To Sondra the place looked and felt magical in the Wednesday afternoon sun. Unlike the greenery they'd been used to back east and in the mid-west, the track was an exciting ribbon of gray amongst the differing shades of golden brown rolling hills. An electrifying chill went through her as they drove across the auto bridge and were soon directed down toward their assigned garage area and pit-stall. Just as at the start of the season, Sondra had a number of Formula Ford-specific activities and events scheduled for the afternoon and the following morning. In addition to being the final weekend match, the Indy Lights and IndyCar Series races were the main weekend attractions, similar to the Canadian Grand Prix. This time however there was the addition of the Continental Tire Sports Car Challenge Series running as well. This put heavy limits on track-time for the Formula Fords. In addition, the permanent garages were reserved for the IndyCar Series teams. The other three series were assigned garage spaces under three different tented areas.

By simply making it to this point Sondra and the entire field of F-Ford drivers and their pit-crews were awarded a Certificate Of Completion in the Formula Ford-West Competitive Driving championships. Over the course of the season Sondra had inadvertently cultivated many friendly alliances among her fellow competitors, although there remained a determined number who continued to hold bitter judgment and resentment for her success. Upon the conclusion of the extended driver's meeting, Sondra's attention was caught by a man she'd met at her sprint-car championship banquet in San Jose. In fact he was one of the four men who'd given her a business card and was so encouraging about her racing career. Darren Brown lightly patted Sondra on her left shoulder as he caught up to her, headed toward the pit area. She recognized the man immediately. "Hi Mr. Brown" she chirped. "Nice to see you again."

"Call me Darren" he insisted in an equally happy voice. "I had a feeling I'd find you in another championship battle. I've been following along. You're a definite talent." She and Darren talked a bit more and he handed her a new card. She noted it sported the Patrero-McDonald's IndyCar logo and was happy to stuff it into the packet of information she and her fellow drivers had all received just moments prior. After she and Darren parted company his words of definite talent echoed in her head and she knew right then that she'd better calm down and get a grip on reality before her first scheduled practice session, just over an hour away.

Record-setting attendance was expected and the weekend was packed full of on-track activities and races. As with the Canadian Grand Prix, practice schedules were tight and limited. The Formula Ford field had just 20 minutes to go out and dial in their cars. The sun had not yet burned off the morning coastal fog and there were two places where it was dense enough to be a little dangerous. All drivers were warned about the first few corners as well as going under the auto bridge. There were corner-workers displaying caution flags in these spots, but Sondra's photographic memory kicked in and she built up speed immediately, even though this was her first lap ever on the famous circuit. "Whoa" she exclaimed, her voice crackling through the headphones of Vince Melenza and front-tire changer Ted Bilson. Sondra had started down from the highest point on the course for the first time in her young life. Vince was just about to make an inquiry about her vocal reaction but seconds later her car came into view coming down the hill, under the pedestrian footbridge before entering Turn 10. Her voice was now oddly calm as she explained, "way wrong line at the top of the Corkscrew." The Corkscrew was aptly named. At the highest elevation of the Laguna Seca circuit is a series of severe downhill S-turns, the first being off-camber. It was the most exciting and action-packed spot to watch a race or practice, and it was also the most technical and dangerous section of the track for race car drivers or motorcycle riders. What Sondra had just done at the top of the hill was go into that left-hand corner too tight, too fast. After running over the inside curbing, the left-side tires lifted from the pavement for a few thousandth's of a second. Just as soon as the car settled, the rear end slid to the outside but Sondra's lightning-quick reaction had caught it. She was now on the absolute edge of the racing surface but had a straight-line shot going down the hill. Had she panicked or applied heavy braking her day and most likely her weekend would have ended there, and she might have been severely injured.

Sam Fenton wandered back over from where he'd been talking on his cell phone and took the headset from Bilson. Even with her slight miscalculation in negotiating the entrance to the Corkscrew, Sondra's speed and lap-time had been impressive. As she flashed by and was going through Turns 1 and 2 Sam spoke in his usual crew chief demeanor. "Watch your speed until the fog lifts" he barked. "I don't want your first laps here to be your last. Slow down, find your braking zones and get more familiar with the track." Sondra drove in anger and didn't slow down until she saw the caution flag wave before the entrance going under the auto bridge. She downshifted, then slowly rolled on power, cornering to the left and heading back up the hill. Sam didn't catch the first part of her radio transmission response because of the communication drop from going under the bridge but he was sure it was something he didn't want her to repeat. Four laps later the fog began to quickly dissipate and there were no more caution flags being displayed on the course. At the end of the practice session Sondra was shown quickest by a substantial margin.

During the post-practice team debrief Sondra had constant goosebumps as she asked for a few minor handling and setup changes. Being on the racetrack for the first time hadn't disappointed her. The speed, the elevation gain and the challenge of getting through Turns 1 and 2 efficiently were everything she'd always thought they would and should be. The rest of Sondra's day was split between enduring publicity stints with Lydia Velstein and watching the on-track action of IndyCar, Indy Lights and the sports car series. After a marginally satisfying fast-food meal and entering her motel room, Sondra called Doug and Karen. The couple thought they could hear weariness and anxiety in her voice and they assured her they would be at the track the next morning as soon as the gates open.

Friday morning's practice for Blue Sea Racing ran the gambit from good to "flippin' horrible," according to Sondra. They struggled with a mysterious carburetion problem at the beginning of the session and went on to suffer with intermittent radio transmission issues. Soon after, a brake bias problem manifested resulting in left-rear tire blistering. Most of the 20 minute practice was spent in the pits, but with time running down Sondra went back out and put up four laps that blistered the speed charts, not the tires.

Doug and Karen arrived just over twenty minutes before the gates to the raceway had been opened to the public. However, there were already two very long lines of cars and motorcycles waiting to go through this main ticket check-point. Sondra had made sure her now-parents were mailed tickets for Friday, Saturday and Sunday, with Pit Passes for each day. This also included two VIP grandstand seats for her Formula Ford graduation ceremony, taking place that evening. A second set of VIP passes were for Saturday night's extravagant banquet dinner, held at a five-star restaurant overlooking the ocean on the Monterey peninsula. By the time Doug and Karen arrived at the main bridge, which went over the race track and down to the vast infield, there were a number of cars on the track. It was the final and most important practice for the Formula Ford field. This was a twelve-minute session before their second-to-last championship round coming up in 43 minutes.

Doug loved how visibly excited Karen became upon seeing and hearing the on-track commotion. "It sounds like extremely loud mosquitoes flashing by underneath us" she announced.

"Gotta be the F-Fords" said Doug.

"Our Sondra's somewhere down there" Karen said with a large smile. After parking and making their way in the slow-lifting morning fog they hiked up the steep dusty path to the top of the great Corkscrew, where Doug had years ago witnessed races featuring classic and antique cars, sport cars, and two Champ Car events. Karen herself was no stranger to auto racing. Her parents had owned a hardware store all the time she was growing up and she had worked in the store from time to time. Her father had taken her to countless Go-Kart and sprint-car races, and later some Nascar events. Post college graduation, Karen's steady boyfriend yearned to move to California, but after seven months of living together in San Jose she found that he'd been cheating on her with some of her new girlfriends. She scrambled a bit but landed a good job at Snap-on Tools, where she'd worked her way from secretary to sales, and then to the Regional Sales Representative position she currently held. Office talk and discussion of their product in street cars as well as race cars was a common theme, and now that she had a vested personal interest, with corporate sponsorship she'd instigated for Sondra, she was excited to be where she was, especially with her fiancé.

Doug and Karen leaned against the weathered chain-link fence and watched in amazement as the cars careened over the top of the hill and then went speeding and twisting down out of sight. Karen pulled on the sleeve of Doug's navy-blue windbreaker, jumping up and down in excitement. "There she is" she hollered. "That's Sondra." Just as fast as Karen could get the words out Sondra was down and away in a dramatic hurry. She had asked for two small changes to her car from the previous day's practice and was driving harder than she'd ever driven in her life in order to make sure her car had the best setup possible. Her pit crew watched excitedly as her crew chief grew more nervous by the second. On the way up the hill Sondra had overtaken a much slower car and this had forced her to run a line quite similar to the one she'd run on the first lap of her first day there. She carried so much speed into the corner before the downhill S's that it produced those same results. The fact that she'd made a dangerous choice or that she could have crashed never entered her mind. She was concentrating on getting around the two cars in front of her and her left-side tires again went airborne for a few thousandth's of a second. She flashed past the black and purple car on that impossible outside of Turn 8, with many eyes on her. This set her up for a straight-line shot going down the hill, and when the car was fully stable she whipped past the next car as if he were parked.

Doug couldn't believe this was actually Sondra, that skinny shy child who had looked so frail the last time he'd seen her. He'd watched her drive hard before, on dirt and on pavement, but this wasn't something he'd expected to see.

"I can't believe she just did that" he hollered to Karen over a constant string of screaming four cylinder engines.

"Maybe that's not her." Karen shook her head. "Oh my god!" she exclaimed. Just then a deep and commanding voice came over the loudspeaker, which was almost directly overhead. "Well hello and good morning there, race fans. If you were asleep or otherwise distracted, you r-e-a-l-l-y missed something coming down the hill. It seems that one of the Formula Ford drivers is giving up on cars and is going for a pilot's license. The Blue Sea Racing entry, car number Twelve, got a little airborne at the top of the hill. And look here, it's young Miss Sondra Sierre, the only female in this highly competitive field. Hell hath no fury like a woman trying to win a race. Coming up in less than twenty minutes the IndyCar Series will be on the track for their first mandatory practice of the weekend. Keep an eye out for native Californian and rookie driver, Denny Hearn. No relation to the great Richie Hearn but he's shown some great promise this year. If seventeen-year-old Sondra Sierre can keep her wheels on the ground, maybe we'll see her here in the IndyCar field in a few years." Doug's jaw dropped and he had to fight to hold back tears as Sondra and seven other cars again came flashing by them. There had been so many times he'd listened to her talk about her dreams, goals and plans, and he'd supported and believed in her unconditionally from that very first day. Standing there hand in hand next to his fiancé and seeing Sondra give this her all was overwhelming. He was definitely a proud dad, especially since her name had just been mentioned several times by the announcer and in the same sentence as the IndyCar Series. His eyes glistened in the emerging morning sun and Karen fell into his arms for a joyful kiss. "Lets go down to the pits and surprise her" she then told him.

Sam Fenton was cosmically seething during Sondra's glorified antics. Greg Wilente appeared next to him. "What the hell have you been teaching that kid?" he asked, half joking. Greg produced a wide smile and patted his crew chief heavily on the shoulder. Sam shook his head. "You're the moron who went ahead and hired her" he responded, also half joking. "Can you afford to buy Texas? That's the only state big enough to hold her ego if she wins, you know that, don't you?" Their pit area was now filling up with instant fans and reporters, Lydia Velstein leading the pack. When Sondra pulled to a stop she was breathing hard and was unusually hot and exhausted, even with the relatively short track-time and the ambient air temperature being only 66 degrees.

It took a while for Doug and Karen to get through all the heavy security but when they spotted their girl they both stopped dead in their tracks. Sondra looked so young and relaxed, sitting in a low faded blue beach chair. Her race suit was unzipped to the waist and her long thick dark hair flowed freely out from under the team baseball cap and around her favorite T-shirt, the one with a yellow tiger design. She was crunching on a bright green apple but it bounced sadly to the deteriorating blacktop at the flick of her wrist as soon as she spotted her now-parents. She instantly jumped up, and completely out of character with her behavior for the past six months flew into Doug's powerful arms, hugging him tightly as Karen's arms attempted to reach around them both. This was a pleasing and memorable sight for all who witnessed.

Sondra started from Pole position for Round 16 of the F-Ford championship. This was where all of her life so far came into play and was absolutely everything to her at this moment. She managed a tremendous start and it was her most dominant race, leading from flag to flag. Doug and Karen watched from her #12 pit, and at Lap 17 Doug asked a question to no one in particular. "How the hell's she doing this? I mean, I can still see ..." He didn't know how to finish that sentence or whom to direct a statement or question to because her driving style still had the basic components that he'd always seen, but there was definitely something different. She was unbelievably fast but never seemed frantic or desperate. It took most of the race until it finally came to him. Sondra was no longer driving in anger, fear or to prove that she was valid and worth something. She was purely driving and was a race car driver in the truest sense. She won by 8.472 seconds and was instantly swarmed by her team in the winner's circle. There were many post-race interviews along with sponsor and promotional obligations that kept her busy for the next several hours. She would have much preferred to watch the day's racing action with Doug and Karen but as Lydia pointed out, what she said and did out of the car was equally as important as what she did behind the wheel. Despite the significant career-building aspects of Sondra's afternoon, sitting between Doug and Karen during the graduation ceremony that evening made Sondra feel more secure in her future than she'd thought possible.

During the Saturday morning Formula Ford warmup lap before the 17th and final race of the year, Sondra didn't drive at any great speed. She didn't need to. She was already set to start from the Pole position and was simply feeling out the car and track conditions. With a light and quickly dissipating morning fog, she led the field of cars up over the hill and back around to the starting grid. Now at a complete stop, Sondra readjusted her left-hand grip on the steering wheel and her right-hand grip on the gearshift knob as she sat poised on the front straight, eyeing both the man in the flag stand and the facility's light-system bar that stretched across the track. The Formula Ford Series used the standard European F1 style start, as opposed to the rolling race starts of Indy Lights and IndyCar. One by one red lights illuminated from the track's Start/Finish light system. With her #12 car in first gear and her foot on the clutch, Sondra brought up the rpms. At the same time the lights all went out, there was the traditional green flag wave and Sondra's car launched forward. The start of the race was no stroll through the hills. Brice Crandle was either inches behind or at times side by side. Andrew Placer, Wendell Grayson and Benny Helmes stuck right with the leaders and this pack immediately began to distance themselves from the others. Sondra was the first over the hill, her engine screaming in anger as she threaded her way down through the Corkscrew, leading a snarling and hungry pack to the start/finish line. Crandle caught her going under the auto bridge, and for the next nine and a half laps the lead and each position changed constantly among the first five drivers.

Just before the halfway point, Sondra watched Wendell Grayson get wicked-loose in Turn 8, with Andrew Placer locking up his brakes in order to keep from hitting him. They both recovered quickly and Sondra was able to slice around them easily, coming to the realization that these guys were driving over their heads. She worried that someone was going to get hurt. She'd set the bar awfully high the day before. After half a lap of driving behind Benny Holmes, Sondra watched his car step out under heavy braking at the top of the hill. She cut inside and dove over the crest in front of him, going down through the corkscrew with the same ferocity she'd enacted many times during the weekend. She then charged quickly to the right-rear tire of Brice Crandle's machine with such a head of steam coming down the hill that she slid around him on the outside of Turn 11. At the Start/Finish line Sondra was half a car length ahead of Crandle. From that moment forward it was basically the Brice and Sondra show. The two pulled away from the rest of the field and were constantly challenging each other and blowing past lapped cars. Just as Sondra had feared, there was a huge crash involving five cars in Turn 10. Observing the caution flag in the corner of the accident, then accelerating away, she called to her crew chief . "Hope they're all okay. These guys are just driving too far over their limits. Someone's really gonna get hurt."

"You're the one setting the pace, sweetheart" returned Sam. "Keep your eyes forward and your head focused. Caution's out. Full course caution" he warned. Sondra hated and resented the sweetheart remark as well as his stating the obvious. She closed up on lapped traffic, and when the track went green again she knew how badly Crandle wanted around her. Their cars were pretty evenly matched and for the most part so were their driving abilities. There were two critical exceptions, however. Sondra could read and react to her car and the track's ever-changing conditions at an unfathomable speed, and winning at this time was more important to her than anyone else out there that day. Sierre and Crandle continued to duel but the fun and games were over for Sondra. She let him get by, thinking: *Let him do the work. Let him make holes in lapped traffic and take the brunt of the tire and equipment wear and tear. Let him put up with the pressure of being the leader for a while.* There were still places where she'd overtake him for short periods of time. After all, she hadn't backed off in the least.

With four laps remaining, Sondra finally figured out how to counter Crandle's move going under the bridge and closed in, nose-to-tail, heading up the hill. They came upon a slower car and each split around him. It set her up on that seemingly impossible line that she'd previously gotten away with, but this time it was different. She could have easily backed off and sliced around the slow car farther down the hill and then catch right back up to Brice, but with supercomputer speed went through the geometrical calculations and again made the choice to commit to the top-of-the-hill race tactic. The hillside came alive with a deafening roar as daylight showed briefly under the #12's left-side tires. This time, however, Sondra had done it deliberately and it didn't actually look all that insane. On the outside of Turn 8 she rocketed past Brice Crandle for the lead and started stretching it with each corner. She was a precision-aimed bolt of lightening on her last lap and won by 1.864 seconds, with a top speed on the fastest portion of track of 142.003 mph.

Brice and Sondra drove side by side most of the way around on their cool-down lap, waving at each other and the crowd. After pulling to a stop in the Winner's Circle, Sondra didn't want to get out of her car. Her pit crew ran over to her and their animated motions seemed frightening. She was also immensely sad the race was over and the season itself had come to an end. The weight of the entire year suddenly hit her like a massive tidal wave. She felt like crying, not celebrating, however no tears formed. Arms and hands appeared all around her, unbuckling her safety harness and disconnecting the steering wheel and communication cord. As the members of her team pulled her from the car and passed their champion around for hugs, Sondra began to feel light-headed. When put back down her legs buckled but she regained her composure as a microphone was thrust toward her. "So, Sondra Sierre. You just won this final race in dramatic form, and you're now the Formula Ford North American West Series champion. How's that feel, and what's going through your mind right now?" Sondra pulled off her helmet and her voice was a bit hoarse and weak as she answered. "So great. I mean my Blue

Sea Racing team is really amazing. They've been great all season and they put everything they had into giving me a phenomenal car today. This is just as much their win and championship as it is mine." She mentioned her sponsors, her crew chief and team owners as well as fellow competitors. She praised the fine job that the promoters had done for Formula Ford and sung the praises of the race venue. "I love this race track and I just want to say … the Laguna Seca hill-people so totally rock. I could actually hear you guys several times and it was awesome. Thanks, and thank you Doug and Karen."

The podium ceremony and pictures had a duration much longer than any Sondra had been through, and there was a more robust post-season celebration. Just before Sondra was about to head back to Blue Sea Racing's tented garage stall, Brice Crandle grabbed hold of her arm, then gave her a strong hug. "I had fun racing with you" he told her. "You beat me fair and square and I uh ... I think you're great." He gave her a quick peck on the cheek just as Vince Melenza, who was normally pretty subdued, came over to them.

"Woo" he hollered, picking Sondra up and dragging her off on his shoulder as if she were a sack of potatoes. She lifted her head and waved to her greatest competitor. "See you at the big dinner tonight" she told Brice. The fact that the boy really liked her didn't even enter into her brain.

Doug and Karen took Sondra to her motel for a much needed nap before the championship banquet that night, then headed to the nearby home of Karen's college roommate. It had been several years since Karen had seen or talked with Valerie Hughes but months ago, when making plans for Sondra's Formula Ford finale weekend she'd remembered that Val lived not far from the race track. During a joyous phone conversation she told of her engagement to the greatest guy on earth with an amazing daughter and that they had plans to be in the area. Val immediately insisted that Karen and Doug stay with her for the weekend.

The reunion of Karen and Valerie was fun for Doug, especially hearing some of their memories from the past. When the time came for then to depart for the banquet, Valerie insisted they bring Sondra back with them that night. "I have plenty of room and I'd love to meet your Sondra, and we have so much more catching up to do."

Arriving back at the Wayward Travel Lodge, Karen took one look at the jeans, T-shirt and black blazer that Sondra was wearing. "Oh absolutely not" she told the girl. Karen asked Doug to wait in the car while pushing her little champion back inside the room. "The Sea Lion Inn is a really fancy place" she informed Sondra. "You're not going to your banquet dinner and awards ceremony dressed like that."

"Mom," complained Sondra. Since Karen and Doug had missed Sondra's seventeenth birthday due to the fact that the girl and her race team had been in transit at the time, there were a number of items and activities she and Doug had planned to surprise her with once they were all together. Buying Sondra new clothes was something Karen had wanted to do for months. She loved the idea of a mother-daughter shopping spree, although she wasn't under any delusions that Sondra, the constant tomboy, would be too keen on the concept. Around the time of the girl's birthday Karen had done a little shopping, but after showing the clothing items to Doug he reminded her of Sondra's stubbornness when it came to what she wore.

"I don't know who you thought you were buying that for" Doug told Karen as she held up a long-length silky blue garment. "But trust me, Sondra would never wear a fancy dress like that, not even for you."

For Doug it seemed like two hours had gone by as he waited for Karen and Sondra. It was only 19 minutes, but finally the two women emerged from the motel room and headed toward him. As Karen buckled her seatbelt she noticed Doug's slight curious look as he watched Sondra get settled in the car as well. The girl was fishing around for her seat belt and complaining that it was not a five-point harness like the one she was used to in her race car.

"What?" she asked, looking up to see Doug staring at her.

"Oh nothing" he laughed.

Karen gave a scolding shake of her head. "It took me ten minutes to chase her around the room with lipstick and make-up" she told Doug. "She looks beautiful and I don't want a single word out of either one of you." Sondra rolled her eyes and shrugged as Doug began to pull away with a bit of a smirk.

With the exception of a half sandwich, water, a can of 7-Up and a nutrition bar, Sondra hadn't eaten much since the evening before. Her eating habits had somewhat become fodder for many jokes amongst her lead mechanic and pit crew during the season. Often she was teased for eating like a bird, but there were occasions that she demonstrated a voracious appetite. Crew chief Sam Fenton had once watched the skinny girl practically inhale salad and many slices of pizza. This however was nothing compared to what he and the others were now observing during the elaborate banquet dinner. Sondra attacked her steak, lobster, baked potato and green beans entrée with the ferocity of what might have been requested as a last-ever meal. To the entertainment of the men and women sitting at the table, they listened to the mom lightly admonish her daughter. "Sondra" scolded Karen. "Slow down. There's plenty of food and plenty of time. And use your napkin, not the back of your hand." Throughout the season Sondra's table-manners and eating habits had greatly amused her race family, and Karen's light scolding soon led to jokes that were hurled at and about the young driver. "I once watched her eat pickled beets, right out of a can" said front-tire changer Ted Bilson.

"Oh yeah" remembered Brad Marcobson, Blue Sea's rear-tire changer. "She had red beet juice stains all over her T-shirt. Looked like a bad tie-dye job." Sondra folded her arms and feigned indignation as the comments continued to flow. "Remember that weird little hamburger joint we stopped at on the way to Wisconsin?" asked Josh Tanner, pit-marker holder and general mechanic. "Where we stopped" corrected Sondra of Josh's grammar. Josh continued unfazed. "The place with all those concrete hands sticking out of the wall."

"Ho, man" said Vince Melenza, shaking his head. "Worst fries I ever ate, but the burgers weren't bad. Thick as my fist. Greasy as hell though."

"I'd still like to know how Sondra got ketchup all over the back of her ears" said Mark Princeton, refueler. Raucous laughter went around the table as Sondra put down her fork and folded her arms. "All right you guys" she defended. "I mean I could write a book about all your disgusting eating habits and foul travel manners." Karen leaned in and gave her daughter several soft pats to the shoulder. Discussion then emerged on some of the interesting places they'd encountered during their travels. Crisscrossing the country was a tedious task but the different towns and cities they'd encountered almost always produced interesting people, landmarks and memorable features.

Brice Crandle, with his parents and younger sister in tow, arrived at the table. He put his hand on Sondra's left shoulder. "Congratulations on the championship, Sondra." She was seated between Doug and Karen and both took a serious look at this boy daring to stand so close and touch their girl. Feeling every eye suddenly on him, young Crandle retracted his hand and quickly introduced his family, trying desperately to cover his smitten-ness by congratulating the entire Blue Sea Racing team. After Brice and his entourage disappeared from sight Sondra had to endure an embarrassing round of hazing from almost everyone at the table about her new boyfriend. It was Karen who had kicked it off, leaning her shoulder briefly into Sondra. "He's cute, and clearly into you." Sondra shook her head vigorously. "Na-uh. Gross" she told the group. "No one's into anyone. Besides, he was always trying to run me off the road. And did you see how he kept making that stupid blocking move today, going under the bridge? I got him back though." She enjoyed a sudden sense of pride and happiness amongst her current family. There were a few other comments made by her pit crew about Crandle's driving and how the season had unfolded but soon Vince did his best to put a stop to it. "No, no, no" he groaned, shaking his head. No more shop talk." He turned to Greg Wilente, who'd been oddly quiet this whole time. "See what I've had to put up with for the last six months? I'm begging you, let me lock 'em in a trailer for at least an hour, especially her" Vince added, pointing to Sondra, who was simply beaming.

The awards ceremony itself seemed to drag on a bit for Sondra. The top ten drivers received awards and the championship Runner-up, Brice Crandle, received the second largest monetary award and a substantial driving scholarship. Sondra's name was mentioned and announced quite a number of times. Winning the championship was big enough for her but she was also named Rookie of the Year. In addition, she received a special plaque for Excellence in Sportsmanship and Diplomacy owing to the fact that she'd became most instrumental in working with track, race and F-Ford officials on issues pertaining to safety and career-furthering issues during the many driver's meetings.

Sondra was invited on stage and presented with a championship wreath. A large heavy trophy, possibly weighing as much as she, was then placed next to her and photos were taken while she was presented with two oversized cardboard checks. Sondra was then invited to speak a few words. Not knowing exactly what to say, she went for humor to cover her nervousness. "I'd like to thank members of the academy, the writers, the directors, oh and all the little people who've allowed me to become what I am today… Star of stage, screen and television." The room erupted into laughter and groans as well as various other comments. Sondra's next voice was calm and she spoke from the heart. "Well this is sort of overwhelming" she said, pointing to the tall trophy and the checks. "Sort of wish I was back in my race car right about now." This produced another loud group laugh. "I liked what Mr. McClayton said earlier because it really has been a privilege to be part of this series. The guys from Blue Sea Racing put in long hours and gave me some great equipment." This was a bone of contention with her. Sondra hadn't actually felt as though she'd always been given the best of supplies and equipment. Wilente and Alders ran a tight ship financially and did everything they could to keep costs down. Sondra had also felt from the start she'd been given the ride reluctantly, that they'd really wanted a male driver and were hoping to prove wrong her convictions and predictions she'd win a significant number of races and the championship. "This was such a positive experience" continued Sondra. "The incredible efforts made by the Formula Ford North American West organization gave us the chance to challenge ourselves and each other." Sondra then pointed to several fellow drivers. "Some a little harder than others" she joked. This produced laughter and chuckling from the crowd. "But it was all fun and safe and I think the skill levels for all of us rose because of it. I worked hard for this and I'm proud to be this year's US Formula Ford champion." She hurried off the stage and dashed out of the room, into the open-air corridor. It was an elongated pergola with latticework sides covered with hundreds of large deep-red roses in full bloom, connecting the auditorium to the dining hall. Doug knew exactly what was going on with Sondra and he'd been a little concerned all evening. As she was ending her speech she had looked out among the crowd and had become painfully aware of the many families that were there to support their sons, brothers and or nephews. Though she loved Doug and Karen and was grateful they were there supporting her, the family she'd grown up with was not in this room. Doug quickly appeared next to Sondra, putting a strong hand on her shoulder as Karen immediately joined. Sondra nodded twice, indicating she was okay and was not going to allow herself to fall apart. Before any words of comfort or advice could be uttered from her now-parents, she was pulled away for more photos by Lydia Velstein. A quick succession of photo-ops and interviews preceded a conversation with The Michelin Man, Carl Burham. Darren Brown soon stepped closer to join the conversation. The two men mostly asked questions with one primary objective: to find out if she was serious in pursuing a career in open-wheel racing. Sondra pounced on the opportunity in making it positively clear that this was her objective.

Brice Crandle walked cautiously toward the trio, not wanting to interrupt but determined to hear Sondra speak and to hopefully have the chance to say a farewell to the girl who had intrigued and enthralled him. Sondra told Carl and Darren on no uncertain terms of her plans to be in IndyCar and Formula One. She had a practical plan, step by step, and spoke with conviction. "Well" said Carl, patting Sondra on the shoulder, impressed with the girl. "Good luck to you. I'm sure I'll be seeing you again."

Darren nodded. "You have my card" he reminded her. "Use it" he added before he disappeared from sight.

Brice gave Sondra a light tentative hug. His voice was pensive yet soothing when he spoke. "I'm heading out tonight with my folks and sister. We have a four-hundred and thirty-five acre wheat farm in Wisconsin and I kinda have an important position there in the fall and winter. So what's your plans now?" Sondra shrugged before giving an answer. "I guess I'll continue with school" she told the sharply-dressed young man. "I'm going for my bachelor's degree in business management" she continued. "I'm also now on the hunt for a ride for next season." Brice got a puzzled look. "Bachelor's degree?" he asked. "I thought you were in high school." Sondra shook her head and her smile made him feel week in the knees and his stomach jump up and down. "No" she confessed. "I took the equivalency test early and then got my AA degree."

"Wow, that's amazing" he responded. "So you don't think you're gonna be with the same Formula Ford team next year?" he asked, trying not to sound too inquisitive or desperate.

"It depends what they offer me" she said with another shrug of her right shoulder. "Besides, I think you and I are ready for IndyCar, or at least Indy Lights" she added.

Brice nodded vigorously. "Yeah" he agreed. "I totally think so too. Lets keep in touch." There was so much more time he wanted to spend with her and he had a thousand more questions he wanted to ask, but his parents came into view calling his name and complaining that they'd been looking for him for over fifteen minutes. As he started to follow them he suddenly turned back and gave Sondra a tight embrace. "You're an awesome driver and an awesome person" he whispered. He began to let go but then pulled her toward him and kissed her strongly on the lips. She wasn't sure what to do with that but he had such a goofy smile on his face that her reciprocal smile was involuntary. As Brice began to walk away he kept his eyes glued to her for a few seconds longer. When she waved with her smile remaining in place he felt as if he were flying through the air.

Karen spent Sunday with her friend Valerie Hughes while Doug and Sondra thoroughly enjoyed their day as spectators and race fans at Laguna Seca, fondly remembering their two days at Tumbleweed Speedway. They traipsed all around the facility to watch the Indy Lights, IndyCar and the Continental Tire Sports Car Challenge races from many exciting vantage points of the circuit. They also treasured their VIP status, receiving free food and access to secured areas. It was just after 10 p.m. by the time Doug, Karen and Sondra arrived home. To Sondra, the Fresno condominium had a welcoming warmth and she tingled with a kind of joy she was sure she shouldn't feel. Doug and Karen had taped a "Happy Birthday, Sondra" sign to her dresser mirror and there was a nicely wrapped box sitting on her bed. She tore through the colorful paper and discovered a blue and green flannel shirt. After a long soothing shower, her hair still a bit damp, she entered the den wearing her new shirt and a pair of dark blue cotton pajama bottoms. Doug and Karen were seated on the couch watching a documentary on the history of the Concorde jetliner. They moved apart and patted the cushion, encouraging Sondra to sit between them. Karen was both pleased and amused. "You do know that's not a pajama top?" she asked the girl rhetorically. With a contented and perhaps sheepish grin, Sondra swayed so that her shoulders touched first Karen then Doug. "Nutty girl" chuckled the dad. The three sat in silence until the program ended, then Doug touched the mute button on the remote with his thumb and set it on the coffee table. He took from his pants pocket a set of keys and began pulling the Toyota key off the ring. "The truck's yours, Sondra" he announced, handing the girl the embossed ignition item. "The paperwork's all ready for you to sign and send in to the DMV. We'll negotiate a better deal on insurance as well. You'll need transportation to school and for a lot of other things" he continued. "You've earned this, kiddo" he told the girl, patting her knee. "I'm proud of you."

"We're proud of you" corrected Karen. Sondra had an open-mouthed look of astonishment. "Are, are you sure?" she asked. "Very sure" nodded Doug.

CHAPTER 17

Sondra loved the idea of now being a goal-oriented full-time college student. She had gained a powerful sense of self-confidence from winning the F Ford championship and delved headlong into the semester's first week of academia. After Sondra's third day of classes she reveled in the spaghetti dinner with her now-parents as well as a lively dinner-table discussion of the age-old question, Is man intrinsically good or evil? Sondra's cell phone began to give off a classic bell and hammer ring. The small communication device was sitting on the coffee table and Sondra apologized for the interruption, promising it would go to voice-mail in a few more rings. Doug jumped up, retrieved the phone and handed it to the girl. Sondra took the call and disappeared into her bedroom, returning minutes later to sit at the table with a look of the proverbial cat that had swallowed the proverbial canary. "What?" demanded Doug and Karen in unison after maddening seconds of contrived silence from their girl. With a mischievous smile, Sondra made a deliberate stab at a piece of tomato with her fork, then began chewing slowly. Both Doug and Karen put their silverware down, making loud clanks on the ceramic plates. With folded arms they waited impatiently for the girl to stop being so melodramatic. Barely able to contain herself Sondra spoke excitedly. “Remember Darren Brown? He was at the Formula Ford banquet, and I think you might have met him in San Jose.” Doug and Karen nodded, waiting somewhat impatiently on the edge of an anticipation cliff. “Well that was Darren on the phone” Sondra continued. “He’s the Lead Strategist for the Patrero-McDonald’s number forty-eight Indy car. You know ... Adrian Valderez, the former Formula One driver and three-time IndyCar champion? Well Darren just invited me to test in one of their backup cars, the number eighty-four, at Laguna Seca next Tuesday. This is incredible” she added, slightly jumping up and down in her chair. “And perfect timing, too” she continued. “I can easily switch my Business Math test to next Wednesday.” Doug shared in the excitement of Sondra’s incredible opportunity but Karen, although happy for her daughter’s perceived fortune, was a bit more subdued. She loved how things had been lately and was getting such a thrill out of Sondra’s academic prowess. The thought of her dear girl getting back into a race car was a bit frightening. Karen never let on about her worries and concerns, however. Not to Sondra at least.

When the morning came for Sondra’s chance to drive the Indy car, Karen and Doug were up early to see the girl off as she rolled away in the shiny yellow Tacoma. Work schedules wouldn’t allow Doug or Karen to join Sondra but it was important to them that they show their support. The drive to Monterey by herself allowed Sondra to go over in her head all the things she knew about the race track and everything she’d read or heard about Indy cars. This was a huge jump in horsepower, technology and aerodynamics. Though her performance this day was more important to her than any of her previous racing challenges she was calm and focused. Her life was good and her confidence level was at an all-time high. She made only one stop, in Gilroy for gas and to have a cup of hot chocolate from the thermos Karen had prepared for her. Arriving at the racetrack Sondra was greeted and welcomed by track security, and as soon as she’d parked in the directed space was immediately met by Darren Brown and team manager Craig Pines. Noticing that the two men had cups of coffee in hand, she took her thermos and opened the Toyota’s tailgate, hopping up onto it and gesturing for the two gentlemen to join her. There was no fog that morning but the threat of rain in the afternoon was imminent. As the men sipped their steaming coffee and Sondra her cocoa they began a pleasant conversation, initially chatting about the weather. Unlike Sondra's Formula Ford beginnings, these men made her feel at ease. Darren spoke mostly, although it was Craig who inquired about her age and current status. "Lotta potential here" Craig told Sondra after a bit of information had been exchanged. He'd been amused and impressed that the girl had arrived dressed in her race suit. Darren hopped down, tossing out the remaining drops of liquid from his coffee cup. "You're gonna have less than thirty minutes of track-time today but that'll give you enough to learn the car and then give us four laps any way you want. You won't get the drift like your F Ford car but I have a feeling you're gonna like this." He looked at his watch. "Well it looks about that time to make a little smoke and noise" he added with a grin. Sondra had to keep telling herself to calm down because she was almost giddy with excitement about this once-in-a-lifetime opportunity. She hid her emotions well as she collected her helmet, gloves and Hans device.

Darren and Craig had been impressed by her career progress and past statistics as a driver. They weren't seeing her as just a kid or a young girl on this day. She had a very focused, determined and professional look about her. Once at the team's assigned pit-box she was introduced to the pit crew members and engineers as well as the team owner, Hugo Patrero, a tall stern man who seemed to Sondra a bit skeptical. She was then introduced to esteemed driver Adrian Valderez, who couldn't have been nicer and more encouraging. She knew this was in no way an invitation to join this famed race team. Darren had made this clear a number of times in his recent phone conversations with her. Hugo Patrero, in addition to his two IndyCar teams, owned an Indy Lights car and had an interest in putting together a second Lights team. Sondra had been added to their short-list of drivers to test and see if they might find the right driver for that new car. Patrero and Brown and several others in management for the Hugo Patrero organization were interested in knowing if the

Sierre girl was worth taking a financial and publicity risk for future endeavors. None of this however was fully disclosed to Sondra.

Once strapped in, Sondra paid close attention to the engineers as they went over a number of key items. When the two men backed away, Darren spoke to Sondra over the radio. "So how we doin', Sondra?" Her answer was immediate. "Great. Can I get all this installed in my truck?" After a bit of laughter subsided from the men in the pits Darren gave her specific instructions and the powerful Chevrolet turbo-charged V-6 was brought to life. It had a throaty sound as Sondra made slow revs and checked all the in-car telemetry. She gunned the motor more quickly, then looked up and spoke to Darren. "Okay" she said, watching a man with his hand in the air at her Right-front tire. When he put his arm down Darren again spoke to her. "All right, Sondra. Track's all yours. Watch your pit lane speed and remember you're on cold tires. Ease into things and remember smooth is what we're after, not speed." Sondra didn't mean to leave the pit stall in such haste but with all that horsepower under her it was easy to spin the rear tires before they caught solid traction. Her smile was involuntary as she pushed down with her thumb the rev limiter on the steering wheel she was told to use while on pit lane. Once on the familiar racing surface she went up slowly through the gears, getting used to paddle-shifters instead of a stick. She eased through Turns 1 and 2 steadily accelerating, with a car that felt rock-solid and seemed to beg for more speed. Sondra ran a total of eight laps, managing to impress the men on this race team, at the same time boosting her confidence in her race craft.

After lunch in a room in the raceway's administration building Sondra and Darren walked to the garage where she was formally introduced to the mechanics and engineers who'd prepared the car she'd earlier driven. She received quite a few compliments on her driving and the condition of the car when she'd finished. Walking with Darren back to her beloved Toyota, Sondra thanked him for lunch and the opportunity for the ride. He laughed lightly. "You just spent a bunch of time and gas money, and we got you to work for free" he imparted. "The team's going to Barber Motorsports Park next week for some off-season testing. The tires you just scuffed in and the information you gave our engineers was invaluable. The least we could do is send you home with a little something to eat. So Cal State Fresno, huh? Fax or email me your class schedule so we can work around it. If you're interested, maybe we can use you again." Sondra nodded her head vigorously and smiled. Darren couldn't help but smile back, and as they reached her truck he watched her unlock the door and get situated behind the wheel. She put the key in the ignition and then rolled down the window. Darren set his crossed elbows on the door window frame and spoke in a serious tone. "So what's your deal with Wilente and Blue Sea Racing?"

Sondra shook her head and answered solidly. "As of a week from next Thursday, there is no deal. My contract runs out. The Formula Ford cars are fun to drive but after this, kinda like an amusement-park ride." Darren laughed, snorting through his nose. He enjoyed Sondra's grin but she lost the expression as she expounded more on her former boss and team. "I was underpaid, underestimated and they treated me like a child most of the time. Greg was a royal jerk to me in the beginning. I really don't think he expected me to do as well as I did."

"Well that's a fairly small operation by comparison" said Darren.

"And they put most of their resources into their Nascar organization." Sondra nodded. "When I first started with them" she divulged to Darren, "they told me they had two Formula Three cars in Europe, but no one's mentioned that since. I mean maybe they sold 'em off. I don't know. Their race school at Sonoma uses cars modeled after European F-Three cars."

"Yeah" said Darren. "The FJR-Fifty." Sondra nodded. "They'd have to make a bunch of changes with their F-Ford program, like giving me better equipment and offering me a lot more money for me to sign with them again" she added. "I mean don't get me wrong. I don't really care about the money. It's the principle. Besides I have my sights set way higher."

Darren nodded and appreciated the girl's willingness to be so open and honest. "I know quite a bit about you, Sondra" he told the girl. "About your life and about your racing career so far. A friend of a friend told me about a few of your first local sprint-car races, then Dan Stoltz called me and gnawed my ear off about how to own and manage a race team. When he mentioned you, I was intrigued. As you know I was at your championship race in San Jose and at the dinner. In Canada, I was pleased to see you in the F-Ford. Your weekend proved impressive and I kept tabs on your season from time to time. Your drive here last September showed a lot of maturity. Well, with the possible exception of that aggressive top-of-the-hill crap" he added, laughing to himself. "I also happened to meet Lydia Velstein that weekend and she had quite a bit to say. Tell me something. You ran off and left everyone on that Friday race, and on Saturday, up until the last five or six laps, that was just for show, wasn't it?"

Sondra's shy smile said it all. "After that big crash it got serious" she told Darren. "And I only like winning."

Darren was sold on the kid. "I don't want to get your hopes up" he told her. "And I really have no business telling you this, but Patrero's a bit old-school when it comes to young drivers, especially if they're women drivers. He's gonna run two Lights teams next season. Ordinarily you wouldn't get thirty feet from him and all this but he let me have my way and you got your shot. You didn't let me down today and you impressed the hell out of him and everyone else. If things don't come through with Blue Sea, you hang tight and keep doin' what you're doin' at school. I can't make any promises but I'll do my damnedest to help you get in a Lights car, even if it's not with us." He stood and patted the glossy Toyota roof, telling her that he'd be in touch and to drive safe home.

A pleasant routine developed for Sondra, Doug and Karen during the week, with each looking forward to their evening mealtimes together. School occupied the majority of Sondra's existence but they managed to go see a movie and have dinner every so often. A belated birthday present for Sondra that Doug and Karen had previously arranged involved a day of travel. They wouldn't tell her where they were going or what they'd be doing, but on this crisp Autumn Saturday morning the trio found themselves headed north on Highway 99. Doug was at the wheel of Karen's Mercedes and eventually pulled into the parking lot of a diner on the property of the Lodi municipal airport. As they were each enjoying their tuna-melt sandwiches Doug pointed out the window and got a kick out of watching Sondra's eyes light up when she noticed several skydivers floating majestically to the ground. "Wow" breathed Sondra.

"Wow, indeed!" Karen laughed. Not taking her eyes off the action Sondra wished out loud she could do that, and Doug and Karen looked at each other with large grins. After finishing their lunch, Doug suggested they get a closer look at where all this skyward activity was originating. Sondra, usually so ultra observant, was extremely fascinated by a large hangar-full of people practicing their sky moves or packing their chutes. She didn't notice that Karen had slipped away and paid the fee for the girl to take a tandem jump. The three watched a training video, and when it ended Sondra was quick to make a sarcastic comment. "That was really cool, but ten minutes on how you could die? Edit, people, edit." Sondra, Doug and Karen soon entered a room with all manner of skydiving gear and a man with a video camera mounted on top of his white helmet introduced himself. "Hi, I'm Steve. Let me see here. This harness should fit you" he said pointedly to Sondra." She looked to Doug and Karen, and with an enormous smile she exclaimed, "Really?" The couple simply smiled and nodded.

Sondra's instructor for this high altitude excursion entered the room and was pleased when he experienced the girl's strong handshake. He introduced himself. "I'm Zack. You saw the video, now lets go over some really important rules and procedures." Minutes later, Doug and Karen were waving to their enthusiastic little skyward-bound champion. Sondra took a short bus ride with seven other jumpers and noticed that she and one other guy were the only ones not going solo. She loved the immediate camaraderie and the enthused verbiage from her fellow jumpers.

"Part of me hates this" Karen said to Doug as they watched the bus pull to a stop in front of a white and blue twin engine turbo-prop airplane. "How'd you ever talk me into letting her go skydiving?" Doug grabbed hold of Karen's hand as they looked on, soon watching the two three-bladed propellers of the jumper plane begin to gain speed. "This is one of those determined bucket list things of hers" he told his fiancée. "It's hard to ever get her to talk freely about her dad, or anyone in her family for that matter" he furthered, "but on one of those rare occasions she told me all about how her father would talk about doing this on his fortieth birthday. She's mentioned a few other times as well wanting to do this, once when we saw skydiving in a movie and another time when we both looked up at the same time to see a plane flying overhead. She was so determined and so intense about it. I think it's more for her father and in his honor than it is about her true desire to jump out of a perfectly good airplane."

"Hmm" voiced Karen. "My insightful man" she added, smiling at her betrothed.

Once on board the sleek aircraft, Zack had positioned himself behind Sondra and began strapping himself to her back, all the while giving her instructions. She loved every single second of the experience and it amused her when she and Zack enacted a crouched turtle-walk to the plane's exit once they'd reached 13,000 feet in elevation. As soon as Sondra and Zack leaped from the aircraft she was hit by a 130 mph sudden rush of air that had her struggling to breathe normally. She quickly learned to take short breaths through her nose. After an incredibly exhilarating six seconds of free-fall, which seemed longer because of such fast-paced action, Zack tapped Sondra on the shoulder. This was the prearranged signal of a question whether to remain as they were or use the air with their hands to twirl this way and that. Sondra had a closed mouth ear to ear grin and she nodded her head as best she could. They soon began twisting and turning as cameraman Steve came into view, and with a number of fast counter revolutions Sondra wondered how much her stomach could take. As if on cue they became steadied and the main chute opened, with Sondra thinking it the most peaceful and gentle ride she'd ever experienced. Once on the ground, happier than she could possibly say, she was given a video of her triumphant skydive along with still-photographs and an introductory jump certificate that had a quaint passage: *Oh, I have slipped the surly bonds of earth, and danced the skies on laughter-silvered wings.* Sondra was all smiles and excited energy as they headed for home. "Thank you guys so much for that" she exclaimed. "It was amazing. I know it doesn't look like it but you never feel like you're falling. I flew, really flew. It's a tiny bit like being in my race car on a fast track, but I mean obviously with no engine. Once Zack pulled the cord to the parachute, it was two totally different worlds. Like riding a really gentle Ferris wheel. Man, that was fun."

"Fun for us too, sweetie" said Karen. "I've always loved airports" she added. "Always wanted to learn to fly." Doug got instant goosebumps and glanced over at Karen, smiling and nodding. He too had these desires.

Sondra, riding in the car with her two favorite adults replayed the skydiving action in her head and basked in the moment, though her thoughts were never far from her family. She bit down on her tongue as she could almost hear her father's voice talking at the dinner table of doing the very thing she'd just done.

It wasn't much of a surprise to Sondra that no one from Blue Sea Racing bothered to get in touch with her upon her contract's lapse, but still it did sting a bit. She threw herself into her schoolwork and also began an extremely intensified fitness routine. Even Doug and Karen occasionally got into the act, utilizing their discounted family plan gym membership for two-hour sessions. They also began embarking on three-hour long bicycle rides. For the first time in many years Sondra went to bed happy every night and ceased having as much difficultly falling asleep.

True to his word, Darren Brown gave Sondra another opportunity to drive the #84 Patrero-McDonald's Indy car. The venue for this was Sonoma Raceway, and this time Doug and Karen were both able to go with her. All but two of the IndyCar Series teams were on hand for practice and testing that day. The Patrero pit crew and engineers remembered Sondra well and set the car up in full race trim, unlike before when a qualifying set-up was given to her at Laguna Seca Raceway. Once Sondra was on track and at speed, she no longer cared about Adrian Valderez or the other well-known drivers surrounding her. She utilized her photographic memory of the track and the car, and her new physical conditioning along with her severe competitiveness gave her an impressive edge, by anyone's standard. Engineer John Younge shook his head and alerted his boss and team owner to a computer screen. Hugo Patrero squinted and studied the telemetry numbers, then walked closer to Darren. "This is that skinny little girl?" queried Hugo. Darren nodded. "Adrian technically has a stronger car today" he told his boss. "The kid there's currently third quickest and this is only the second time she's been in an Indy car. Just my opinion, but I'd put her in one of your Lights cars before someone else snatches her up." Hugo didn't necessarily want to hear this. He cringed at the very thought of hiring a teenage girl to drive one of his cars. "Keep her out there and lets see when she starts getting too weak to continue" Patrero snarked. Darren gave a quick shake to his head. "That kid is way tougher than you think" he countered. "You're not gonna want that goin' up against you in the future" he reiterated with a flash of a smile. Doug and Karen were standing within earshot and felt enormous pride.

Sondra's laps in the Patrero Indy car gained the attention of many that day, and by day's end Hugo Patrero reluctantly made up his mind that he'd give the girl a chance at one of the two slots now available on his newly revamped Indy Lights program. However, he didn't make any announcements or avail this decision to Sondra or her dad-manager. Three days later, word of Sondra's recent driving stints managed to get back to Greg Wilente and other members of the Blue Sea Racing organization. Greg had been in North Carolina the day Sondra had been at Sonoma with the Patrero team. He called Sondra as she was sitting at her bedroom desk studying for an applied economics test. He asked her how she was doing and about college but was suspiciously coy, which did not sit well with her. She made an attempt to abruptly end the call, stating that she had a lot of homework. The man then got down to the real reason for reaching out to her, aside from trying to find out about his ex-driver's four-wheeled extra curricular activities. "A friend of mine runs a GT-Two car in the IMSA sports car series" informed Greg. "His second driver just had knee surgery and he asked if I could recommend someone. You interested?"

Sondra was extremely interested but gave only a flat answer. "Yeah."

Greg then filled her in on more of the details. "It's the number fifty-six Greylime Gear Porsche team. They'll be at Lime Rock Park next weekend. You liked that track, as I recall."

"I won there, remember?" she asserted. Greg dismissed the girl's response and proceeded to give her pertinent information on the upcoming event. Moments after the call had ended Doug knocked on her open bedroom door. "Dinner's ready" he informed his daughter. He whispered his next words. "Double whammy tonight. Sautéed mushrooms on the side but avocado in the salad." "Blah" she returned, making a face as she followed him to the dinner table.

Karen enjoyed the occasional "mmm" noises that came from her little family as they consumed the London broil, baked potato and green beans, watching with amusement the care Sondra took picking out the avocado from her salad, the enemy as the girl referred to this particular accompaniment. During the meal Sondra gave a full account of her phone call from Greg. When she mentioned that she would get a little bit of pay but that travel expenses would have to come out of her own pocket, Karen shook her head. "He's such a jerk" she announced of Sondra's former employer. "And a cheap one at that." They all nodded but Sondra dreamed out loud. "Yeah, but I get to drive a tuned Porsche GT-Three for two and a half hours, as fast as it'll go." Karen smiled to herself and briefly crossed her arms when Sondra and Doug launched into full-scale discussion about this particular racing opportunity, instead of eating. She let this go for a while but then set her fork down loudly and cleared her throat dramatically. "All right, you two" she scolded. "That's enough shop-talk at the dinner table. And Sondra, your napkin belongs in your lap." She continued as soon as the girl sheepishly complied. "I think you're both forgetting about a little thing we're doing in Pennsylvania around this time?" she scolded. Doug shook his head as he swallowed. "Oh we haven't forgotten" he countered. "In fact my guys have been workin' on bachelor party plans for months."

"Your guys?" questioned Sondra. "I have guys" said Doug, nodding and grinning like a Cheshire cat as Karen sat back in her chair, contemplating Doug's words of "for months." She was happy. Very happy.

CHAPTER 18

The year-long careful planning of Doug and Karen's nuptials had come as a slow steady stream for Sondra. Focus on her racing and then school were forefront but the idea that the two people she was willing to accept as parents living together without being married had been a subconscious anxiety producer. On the flight to Pennsylvania, Sondra's glance went from cloud formations miles below the right wing of the airliner to Doug and Karen, sporadically chatting about the family and friends who would be attending their wedding. During a pleasant dinner of chicken and dumplings in the McCormick's cozy dining room the conversation diverted, albeit for just minutes, from wedding talk to discussion on Sondra's next day sports car race. Mary couldn't have cared less about auto racing and was quite content with staying home. She was firmly ensconced in wedding mode, as was her daughter. George on the other hand was fascinated by Sondra and her quest to race cars. He leapt at the opportunity to get away from wedding prep for a day of travel and being a race spectator with his soon-to-be son-in-law.

During the long day at the natural-terrain racing venue of Lime Rock Park in Lakeville, Connecticut, Doug and George became much better acquainted. They enjoyed their day as spectators and watching Sondra drive the #56 Greylime Gear Porsche GT to an eventual 3rd Place finish within their class. On the drive back to the McCormicks' home, Sondra went into excited detail of the men and women she'd met from the Greylime Gear team and all about her driving/racing experience that day. They arrived just in time for dinner. Karen and her mother greeted them and headed back to the kitchen to put the finishing touches on the meal. "How can you let that sweet little thing do something so dangerous?" asked Mary. "We don't just let her, mom" said Karen. "This is her chosen career. She's really good at it and she's smart about it too." Karen then eased the conversion to Doug, his friends who would be attending the wedding and Karen's chosen maid of honor, Valerie Hughes. At the breakfast table the next morning, Sondra graciously accepted the idea and invitation of being Doug's co-best man. "You'll have a tux and everything" he told her. This idea had once been lightly suggested but Sondra thought it mostly a joke, and it had never been spoken of since.

"So does this mean I'll also be in charge of finding you booze and strippers for your bachelor party?" inquired the girl with a quick smirk.

"Sondra" scolded Karen, shocked that the girl would say such a thing. Being that this was such a preposterous question and thought however the room quickly filled with laughter. "You nutty girl" said Doug, putting his arm around her.

Though Sondra liked the idea of being included in the wedding and becoming a part of this clan, she couldn't shake the feeling that she was betraying her family. The church wedding ceremony was mostly traditional, and immediately after came a four-course dinner reception in an adjacent building. When a wireless microphone made its way around the room to Sondra felt put on the spot but gave a toast, first covering her anxiety with a quick witticism about "some fine real-estate properties I'm sure you'll all be interested in."

"Nutty girl" Doug called out as the room erupted in laughter.

While Doug and Karen were on their honeymoon in Hawaii, Sondra's week proved challenging. She told herself and a few college classmates that she loved being alone and having her independence, but the condo seemed so cold and quiet without Doug and Karen. At school she was quickly and effortlessly becoming a popular fixture amongst her peers, especially the male students. She never consciously sought popularity nor did she really encourage this but noticed that she was rarely alone for lunch or coffee breaks, and in class was always among the few who engaged in spirited purposeful debate and interesting conversation. She was also glad to find that her professors were inspirational and the subject-matter they taught fascinating. Walking with several students from her sociology class Sondra received a call from Greg Wilente. She waved goodbye to her classmates and went into detail of Doug and Karen's wedding while heading for her truck. She was seated behind the wheel when they got around to why he'd called. "Caught some of the Lime Rock Park IMSA race on TV" he told her. "I hear you were nothin' but professional and a real team player."

"Good" said Sondra, noticing that he didn't make mention of how she'd done in the race. "I worked hard for them and they treated me great" she added, trying not to sound as angry as she'd instantly become. "We started seventeenth in class and worked our way up. I mean third isn't first but they haven't finished higher than ninth all season, so they were pretty happy with the results."

"Been hearin' other things" said Greg in an accusatory, prodding tone, dismissing her sports car success. "Got to drive an Indy car, did you? How do you know Darren Brown?"

"You know how I know Darren" said Sondra. "You let our contract run out without saying so much as a word to me about it" she then asserted. "I won a lot of races and the championship for you, just like I told you I would the day we met. I appreciate you recommending me for the sports car stint but as you'll recall I also told you I had my career sights set on IndyCar and Formula One. Brown offered me the opportunity in the Patrero car and I took it."

Greg took instant offense to what he perceived as an ungrateful tone from the girl. He would have loved to have gone deeper into the subject, perhaps give her a piece of his mind, but his wife and young son were seated on the sofa nearby and Cynthia adored Sondra. "Well keep in mind" he offered, feeling generous and full of himself.], "Darren Brown isn't a car or team owner, so I'm not sure how helpful he can really be for your career. I'll let you get back to your schoolwork but I just wanted to let you know the Greylime guys had nothin' but good things to report. I also wanted to let you know that we're not continuing with our F-Ford program. We've run it for five years straight and we made our final decision the other day to put all our focus and resources elsewhere. So thanks for helping us go out on a high note."

"You're welcome" said Sondra, willing to be charitable. "Thank you for the opportunity" she added. After wishing each other luck and saying their goodbyes Sondra threw her phone on the seat beside her, watching it bounce. She let loose an expletive and pounded the steering wheel with her fist. She didn't want another year in the #12 Formula Ford but this kind of ending didn't feel good to her. It was another loss. Another thing that was being taken from her.

Fortunately for Sondra the week went by in a flash, and when Doug and Karen made their happy return it meant more to her than she would have thought, or would care to admit. Her daily schedule was full, by anyone's standards. She put in six to eight hours a day at school, depending on which set of classes she had, and completed roughly three hours of homework each night. Sondra's day also included a vigorous gym workout. She often left before Doug and Karen got up in the morning and returned home long after the sun had set. The parents applauded their girl's work ethic and how well she was doing but after a while they missed having her around at mealtimes. When Sondra started her Thanksgiving morning by burying her nose in one of her applied economics books, Doug went to collect her from her bedroom. As they reached the kitchen a smiling Karen handed Sondra a knife. "You're on onion and celery duty until further notice, Missy" she informed the girl. The three talked and laughed as they performed their assigned tasks, and after Sondra helped Doug put the turkey on the barbecue they took a five-mile preemptive walk, as Karen put it. When later that night

Sondra snuggled down in her bed she reflected on the day and how it had been even better than the previous year's Thanksgiving. The horrific pain of not having her family or what had been her normal life was still and always at or near the surface, but she was grateful to be part of a loving family with a solid home.

Time seemed to accelerate at an enormous rate for Sondra and college was challenging but successful, peppered with the occasional testing and working with Darren Brown and the Patrero team. On an early December morning Doug, Karen and Sondra drove to Sonoma Raceway. The couple observed, with a bit of concern, the non-verbal stillness of their racing college student during the long drive. Hugo Patrero had initiated vast and swift changes within his two Indy Lights teams and Sondra was being given an opportunity to prove she was worthy of being in the #10 Patrero-McDonald's Indy Lights car for the upcoming season. As she rode in the back seat of Doug's newly acquired vintage silver Acura Integra, her stomach was in knots over how her day would unfold. She hadn't spoken directly with Darren about this test session and wondered if he would be there at all. Phil Wallin was the General Manager for the Patrero Lights program. She'd spoken with him by phone on two occasions within the last three days. He had a thin grainy voice and spoke with an Australian accent. In her mind's eye she pictured him to be old, bald and grizzly. He'd been friendly enough in their conversations but was not a light-hearted jovial person. She thought of him as extremely goal- and business-oriented.

As soon as Doug, Karen and Sondra came to a stop in the vast main parking lot of Sonoma Raceway they were dumbfounded to see a particular young man in a white, orange and red race suit and black baseball cap ride quickly up to them on a shiny red Vespa 50cc scooter. "Ah, jeeze" said Sondra under her breath, exiting the Integra after Karen. Doug's face registered dubious surprise but Karen smiled as the boy rode the scooter toward them. "Hey-ya, teammate" spoke the young rider, extending his hand to Sondra. She hesitated but then extended her hand in greeting as well.

"Brice Crandle" she said. "Of all the gin joints in all the world" she quipped. He laughed at the movie-line reference.

"Small world, huh?" he said with a large smile and a nod.

"Microscopic" she returned, chewing gum. "You remember my parents, Doug and Karen?" she asked him. After pleasantries the two new teammates proceeded to the #10 and #9 pit boxes. Brice formally introduced Sondra to Phil Wallin. The man was nothing like Sondra had pictured. He had short straight blond hair and was a wheelchair-bound paraplegic. He'd been a main fixture of the Australian V8 Supercar series for many years but had suffered a vicious crash in Melbourne, crushing his lower spinal-cord in two places. He and Hugo Patrero had known each other as young teens, racing against one another in amateur sports car events and then lower-devision formula series until Hugo stepped away from driving to concentrate on team ownership. Phil had successfully run the Patrero-McDonald's Toyota-Atlantic division, and when Hugo disengaged from that series to put resources into an Indy Lights program he all but insisted that Phil take the reins.

Sondra took an instant liking to Phil. He had a much different and lively demeanor in person than she'd experienced over the phone and was genuine in his interest of her life story and potential as a driver. The surprises that morning for Sondra didn't end there however. While she, Doug and Karen were being introduced to the other members of the #10 team, a familiar figure soon appeared. Sondra's face registered astonishment as Steven Barnes greeted the group. "Well, well, well" said the man, extending a hand to Doug then to Karen. "Small world, isn't it?" For the second time that day Sondra used the word, microscopic.

"I didn't see you or any Gavins Racing cars during my F Ford season" announced Sondra in a close-to-angry voice. "You know, where I won a lot of races and the championship" she added, her voice pointed, near a growl. He shook her hand, not surprised at her grip, wondering for a fraction of a second if she was going to try and crush his fingers. She didn't. Steven's glance went from Sondra to Doug and back again. "We'll all do some catching up about ancient history a little later" he told her. "But right now why don't we get to it. Your engineers will go over a few things with you, and Patrero should be here shortly." Phil Wallin was sitting nearby and again spoke to Sondra. "We're gonna put you and Brice out there together but I don't want you to engage. You're running separate programs this hour. Get familiar with the car and give us the best feedback you can."

Sondra had secretly hoped that Greg Wilente would be there to see her drive, and drive well. She was getting an unexpected wish on this day to have Steven Barnes eat a little crow and was eager to enact a little I told you so personal victory on Wilente as well. Later that day Sondra got her wish, but being kept extremely busy and completely focused on the matters at hand never got her moment to gloat in person. On the drive home Doug told her that he'd had a very pleasant conversation with Greg, with him mentioning that the upcoming Nascar season and the Blue Sea Racing School were going to be his main focus that year. Sondra again had that feeling of being robbed but said nothing of this to Doug or Karen. Instead she complained that she was hungry and then talked about her new teammate. "He's such an idiot and I don't think he ever stopped talking the entire day" she said of Brice. "And during the afternoon break he comes walking over with a can of Coke, drinking it through a straw. Stupid. And he kept annoying the hell out of me with these really horrible one-liners and puns. I swear I'm gonna have to invest in rolls of duct tape for the year to put over his moronic mouth." Doug was doing seventeen miles an hour over the speed limit and was only half listening to Sondra, needing to concentrate on the road and watching for Highway Patrol. Karen however had caught every word and nuance of Sondra's mini rant. She smiled to herself knowing the tell-tale signs of a girl who has developed an interest in a boy.

Close to ten miles from home Sondra's cell phone rang. Doug and Karen were then subjected to the one-sided conversation. "This is Sondra. Oh hi, Darren. Yeah. Yep. Yeah, you were right. The Lights car is a good fit. I mean it's not as exciting as a full-blown Indy car but the engineers today were sharp and easy to work with, so was the pit crew. Turns out I'd met my Lights crew chief Steven Barnes almost two years ago. He was kinda a negative jerk back then but he and dad talked, then Barnes and I had a decent chat. Patrero never actually came out and said I'd be given the position but he seemed pretty happy with my performance. I think they'd be pretty stupid not to hire me. Thanks for giving me seat-time in the Indy car. I'm pretty sure that set me up big-time to be comfortable in the Lights car today." She listened for several moments as Darren had a number of things to say. Doug and Karen then again heard their girl's voice. "Okay. Yeah, I will. Thanks for calling." Doug glanced back as Sondra was tucking her phone into a small pocket of her backpack.

"What'd he say?" he asked with anticipation.

"I got the job" she said, pumping her fists in the air and grinning wide. "Contract signing's in two weeks. He wants you to call him tomorrow in your capacity as my manager. Lots to work out, I guess."

"Yeah" he agreed, glancing over at his wife with a broad smile. "Lots to work out" he reiterated. "This feels like an official start to those big goals we've talked so much about" he told Sondra. "Let's pick up a pizza and go home and celebrate." "Congratulations, champ" said Karen, matching Sondra and Doug's smile.

Doug stayed up later than usual, watching a four-hour documentary on the Roosevelts. Karen watched the first hour and a half but was having trouble keeping her eyes open. She headed to bed, passing Sondra's room, noticing the light was on and the door slightly ajar. This was not an unusual occurrence. Sondra often studied late into the night. She also seemed to have somewhat of a phobia about being in her room with the door shut, not liking the feeling she was being left out or all alone. Karen had mentioned this to her friend Valerie, who had hypothesized that this was most likely a defense mechanism that Sondra had developed stemming from the loss of her family. "

Hey, kiddo" Karen said softly as she entered the room. Sondra wasn't at her desk. She was sitting on her bed examining a white coffee cup with a one-inch checkerboard pattern stripe around the rim and #1 centered on the face. Karen settled next to the girl.

"This is one of the spoils from when I won my first race" Sondra explained. Karen watched Sondra glance around the room at the trophies on the shelves.

"You know what popped into my head today?" Sondra asked rhetorically. "When we talked the evening before the wedding you said you were getting everything you wanted."

Sondra expelled a loud breath through her nose before continuing. "I want my family back" she said in a tone filled with instant pain and anger. "I mean I know I can't have that but ..."

Karen took the mug out of Sondra's hand, fearing she was about to throw it against the wall. She set the trophy-mug on the desk and came back to sit next to Sondra. "I wish I could give you that" she told the girl.

Sondra cleared her throat and shook her head. "This is coming out all wrong" she told Karen. "What I really wanted to say is that I love you and Doug and that I'm getting what I want, too. I like being here with you guys. I like being at college, and I like that I just got on an Indy Lights team."

"So how'd your chat with Steven Barnes really go today?" asked the mom. "Were you angry and bitter? Put him in his place?"

Sondra again shook her head. "I never got the chance" she said. "He just started explaining things. He said he was going through an ugly divorce at the time and that he wasn't at all happy at Gavins Racing. They weren't treating him well and they weren't letting him run things the way he wanted. Not really an excuse for being a jerk to me but I guess that was his way of apologizing. He's known Phil Wallin for years and just happened to call when they were looking for a new team leader. Barnes said he was surprised but impressed with my F Ford championship, and we talked about our goals for the Lights car and team and how hungry we both are for wins and the championship."

"I'm proud of you" said Karen. "You did so great today and this is a good way to start things off with Steven and your new team." She stood, giving Sondra a kiss on the top of her head. "Sweet dreams, angel."

Sondra tried to get in a little studying but couldn't seem to focus. She went out to sit next to Doug on the couch. They positioned themselves shoulder to shoulder, slumped down with their feet up on the coffee table, something that would have met with stern disapproval from Karen. When the documentary came to an end Doug touched the off button on the remote. "No doubt in my mind that you were gonna get the ride" he told Sondra with a nod of his head. "Karen and I did some serious talking when we were in Hawaii" he informed the girl. "Stoltz and I built up a hell of a business in a surprisingly short period of time. Worth a lot of money. I'm gonna sell off my half and create a legit management group with you as the sole client. Karen's gonna be my partner, and with her marketing strengths we're gonna make our mark in the racing world."

"What about her job at Snap-on?" inquired Sondra. Doug repositioned himself so that he was facing Sondra directly. "Competing at the level you want takes an insane amount of behind-the-scenes detail that needs to be worked out and kept on top of" he stated. "Karen'll still have major ties with Snap-on but she won't be confined to an office. We're going racing as a family. You concentrate on your part and we'll take care of the minutia."

Karen wasn't asleep when Doug crawled into bed. "So how'd the movie end?" she joked. "Did FDR ever become president? And what about the world and the country? Did they survive?"

"Funny, funny girl" laughed Doug. "Sondra came out and watched the last forty-fifty minutes with me" he said in a more serious tone. "I told her about the family plan. I know we were gonna tell her together but I just sensed that she needed to hear it right then. Sounded like she was worrying about how things were gonna work about the licensing and about the three of us, and about her new race car."

"She mention her new teammate?" inquired Karen.

"No. Why?" asked Doug. Karen smiled sweetly.

"That boy has a thing for her and she's not a stupid girl" she told her husband. Doug snorted a breath through his nose and settled in the bed. "Doug?" prompted Karen. He leaned over and kissed her. "I know we need to talk about Sondra and the Crandle kid" said Doug, shaking his head. "But first of all, I don't really want to, and second of all, I don't want to right now." Karen looked up at the ceiling and was relieved when moments later Doug reached over and held her hand. "We'll talk. I promise" he whispered. "Goodnight, my amazing wife" he added.

"Goodnight, my amazing husband" she returned.

Doug and Karen spent three days in Pennsylvania for Christmas but Sondra remained at home, owing to a massive amount of studying, research papers and projects that would be coming due when classes resumed after the winter break. For weeks, George and Mary had been peppering the newlyweds with guilt over not seeing them and their granddaughter at Thanksgiving. The Pennsylvania couple were ecstatic to learn of their daughter and husband's plan to visit for the Christmas holiday but disappointed that Sondra would not be joining them. Doug and Karen were both quite torn, almost afraid to leave Sondra home alone. The girl was deeply entrenched in study-mode however, claiming that a considerable amount of her time would be spent either at the library or at the gym. After dropping Doug and Karen off at the airport Sondra proceeded with her daily routine of studying. She then engaged in a particularly heavy workout at the gym and arrived home physically drained and with a stomach-churning emptiness. The house was still. Too still. She felt guilty for suddenly missing Doug and Karen as much as she did and sat on the couch in a falling-backwards motion with a large stack of mail on her lap. She looked down at the stack of cards, bills, junk-mail and magazines, amazed at how many pieces of mail Karen and Doug received each day. Thumbing through the pile she was surprised to find four envelopes with her name on them. One was a shockingly large bill for detective and legal services rendered to her during the Brenda ordeal. She tossed it angrily on the coffee table and tore into a second envelope addressed to her, with the address label showing the name of an insurance company. She stood as she read and reread the print.

"What?" she called out in instant anger. "Are you kidding me?" she shouted out loud. Sondra was being sued by family members of the monster who'd taken her family from her. They were now trying to recover monies that John Farnsal had worked so diligently on in awarding her damages. She shook with instant white-hot anger and felt on the verge of vomiting. She crumpled the pages and threw the wad on the floor, then stormed outside slamming shut the front door. She began to run, picking up speed as she went around the block, letting out a scream from the bottom of her lungs, not caring who saw or heard her rage.

Back inside the safety of the condo Sondra stuffed the two hideous letters into a kitchen drawer and decided not to think about it until Doug and Karen were back home with her. She returned to the living room couch and opened the other two envelopes with her name and address hand-printed on the front. These were both Christmas cards. One was a generic corporate card. Happy Holidays From The Gang At Patrero-McDonald's Racing. Sondra smiled when she noticed that Darren Brown had signed his name and penned a short line: "See you at the races." The second Christmas card was from Brice Crandle. For reasons she couldn't explain or dare to think of she took it into her bedroom before fully examining the contents. She sat on her bed with her back against her pillow and read the two-page handwritten letter, holding in her right hand two photos he'd included. There were numerous spelling and grammar atrocities but she liked his sense of humor and he wrote some nice things to her. The photos were clearly of him and his family on their Wisconsin wheat farm. She recognized Brice's parents and sister from the F-Ford championship banquet and smiled at the obvious stiff pose they'd made for their Christmas card. She laughed out loud when she examined the second photo. The image was of Brice and a kid his age in an obvious race on lawn tractors. She surmised that this was taken a number of years ago and guessed at the identity of the lawn tractor competitor. She studied both photographs for several minutes before putting them and the letter in her sock drawer, then went out to the living room and proudly displayed both Christmas cards on one of the bookshelves.

At 7:32 p.m. the home phone rang. Sondra answered it, expecting the call to be from Doug or Karen. "Hello" she greeted.

"Uh, hi. Sondra?" said a tentative voice.

"This is Sondra" she confirmed.

"Oh hi, it's Brice ... Crandle" said the caller on the other end of the line. "I hope I'm not interrupting you."

"Oh hey, Brice" said Sondra. "No, not at all. Perfect timing, actually. I just got your Christmas card. Thanks. So is that our F Ford competitor, Wendell Grayson, on the other lawn tractor?"

"Yeah, good eye" said Brice. "Wendell's actually my next-door neighbor, on the farm just to the east of us. His folks own a farm equipment repair business."

"Wow, that's cool" said Sondra.

"So" said Brice. "How's your Christmas vacation going?"

She explained that Doug and Karen were in Pennsylvania and that she had stayed behind to study. Brice jokingly referenced the movie *Home Alone*, which had Sondra rolling her eyes and breathing a laugh. "Well not exactly" she told him. She then made mention of the Indy Lights licensing process and they both agreed that they were looking forward to getting back in their cars for preseason testing. When the call ended Sondra sat back in Doug's lounge chair in the den, not sure what to make of the call. She had vehemently despised the boy in the maroon F Ford car but came to enjoy driving against him, especially when she beat him. The kiss he'd given her at the championship banquet was still a cloud of intrigue, worry and confusion for her, and now they were to be teammates.

There were agonizing moments on the 24th and 25th where Sondra experienced intense anger and bitterness. Her memory-banks spilled forth sights and sounds of precious past family Christmases. She cried, wept and threw childish temper tantrums, wallowing in self-pity. Not being able to focus on her studies she watched TV, flipping around the channels constantly, feeling guilty for watching at all, thinking she was doing something she shouldn't. Doug and Karen arrived home at 11:53 p.m. on the 26th. Due to the late hour of their arrival it had been previously decided that they would take a taxi home from the airport. They were a bit surprised to find Sondra still awake and dressed, and enjoyed how the girl seemed to hang on every word and detail of their trip. They also noted that Sondra was trying her best to appear as if she hadn't gone through emotional torture in their absence but knew otherwise. There were tears that the girl tried to hide as she opened several small Christmas packages from Grandma and Grandpa, and after a bit of gift exchange between Sondra and her now-parents Sondra told of the bill for legal services as well as the letter and intended lawsuit by the Tillman family. With this, the late hour and the emotion of the bit of impromptu Christmas exchange, Sondra broke down in tears. Doug and Karen watched their precious tough as nails daughter collapse under the weight of unthinkable pain and anguish, doing their best to comfort her. She had a fitful night's sleep and at the breakfast table the next morning stated without emotion that she would pay the one bill incurred for legal services for the Brenda debacle without trying to fight it. "That other thing" she growled, referring to the lawsuit initiated by the family of that monster as Sondra referred to him "is another matter." She later wrote to John Farnsal, but less than two weeks later received a communiqué from Leanna that John had suffered a mild stroke. "John's doing fine wrote," Leanna. "He's in no pain and suffered very little debilitating physical impairments, but he's really in no position to help you with future legal matters. He sends his love, as do I, sweetheart. Thank you for your beautiful Christmas card, picture and newsy letter. We treasure them and you greatly. Love, Leanna and John." Sondra took this as yet another heavy blow but forced herself to put the Farnsals out of her mind. It worried Karen and Doug how the girl could bury so many intense emotions seemingly without effort. This made the couple all the more determined to make things right with the lawsuit. Doug called Frank and Sheila Brandon and they gave him solid recommendations and resources. As necessary discussions with Sondra arose on the subject it often resulted with her initiating some fist-pounding on the table or counter-tops as well as some foul language. Doug and Karen let most of the outbursts slide but Karen did lightly admonish Sondra for some of the harsher words. She didn't disagree with the sentiment and had used the words herself on occasion, but had been taught that strong language was unladylike and just fueled more ugliness. It just didn't seem right for these words to come from such a normally sweet creature.

On a bright but bitter-cold January morning Sondra sat at the breakfast table and listened to Doug crunching on a piece of bacon while reading a postcard from a couple who had attended the wedding but had been neglectful in sending out Christmas cards that year. Karen matched Doug's acoustics while chewing on a piece of toast, and after swallowing her last bite of egg Sondra voiced an announcement. "I'm not gonna worry about the lawsuit anymore. I mean they're not gonna see so much as a dime without having to spend a ton of money or by jumping through a trillion hoops. They're a damn sick bunch for going after me, and that's some wickedly bad karma they'll have, but I don't really care about the money. They can have all that crap. I only used it to rent that Bakersfield apartment, and for school and my auto insurance. Everything else comes from what I earned from jobs and racing, and no one can ever take that from me." Doug took a breath and sat back in his chair. At the point in which he'd become Sondra's legal guardian he was entrusted to be the safe-keeper of a large trust-fund that John Farnsal had set up for her. Sondra was to have access to this once she turned 18, but due to her emancipated minor status she'd obtained early control. "I hear you, Sondra" he told the girl, watching her sit angrily, gritting her teeth. "No amount of money can fix this or give you back who and what you lost, but you were awarded that money for a reason. This wasn't set up to torture you. It's supposed to be there to help you all throughout your life and there's no way in hell I'm gonna let that get taken away from you."

"It's nothin' but damn blood money" Sondra growled, pounding her fist on the table. Karen reached over to soothe the girl but Sondra exploded away from the table and rushed to her room. The new Mrs. Trent burst into tears, putting her head in her hands. Doug came around to comfort and soothe his wife, and minutes later Sondra reappeared.

"Sorry" she told them. "Going to the gym. Be back in a while." With tears still streaming down her face Karen began to clear the table and take the dishes to the sink. Doug helped, and when the two were side-by-side he slammed a juice glass down forcefully, producing an alarmingly sharp noise. Luckily it didn't break or crack. Karen turned and flung her arms around her husband. "Let's go back to Hawaii and take Sondra with us" she sobbed. Doug held his bride tightly for several minutes. "Shh" he soothed. "Things will be okay. Our girl's tough as nails."

Sondra arrived home from an intensified workout to find Doug and Karen in different clothes but still in the kitchen. They were organizing lunch and looked on as Sondra tossed her cell phone on the counter. It slid four and seven-eighths-inch on the slippery surface. "I have a three o'clock meeting with Gina Perschwen at Triple A, downtown LA" she informed her now-parents. "Ordinarily I'd want you to go with me but I really need to do this on my own today. I'm gonna hop in the shower, then head out." She didn't give the couple time to respond. Thirty-seven minutes later, on her way out the door, Sondra made a point to give Doug and Karen each a tight embrace and tell the couple she loved them.

It was after 7 p.m. when she arrived back in Fresno. Sondra was full of energy and in a completely different frame of mind than she'd been that morning. Doug and Karen got a kick out of the immense detail their girl went into as she described the trip down and back, plus the meeting she'd had at a main branch of AAA. "They asked me a trillion questions and we worked out a ton of details. They want to meet with you both. Here's Gina's card." Sondra handed the small gold-leaf embossed piece of card-stock to Karen. "There's more details and paperwork to come" she continued. "But they seemed excited about getting into business with me. With us. They'll be my main race sponsor and insurer. I'll do national ads for them and it'll hopefully be a total symbiotic relationship that'll last for a lot of years." Doug and Karen suspected that Sondra had co-opted the word symbiotic from Gina Perschwen, and they both smiled to themselves at their girl's excited energy.

There were a few details of Sondra's LA trip she'd decided to keep to herself. During the meeting with Gina Perschwen and the other AAA lawyers Sondra had floated an idea about something she'd been thinking of for some time, to create a nonprofit organization that would help kids who found themselves in the same orphaned situation as she. Sondra had even come up with a name, Safen-Up. Gina was quite intrigued by the idea and vowed to noodle around with it. Sondra had also inquired about incorporating herself, a business tool she'd learned of at school, coming up with a name for this as well. Sierre High-Speed Inc. Gina and the other lawyers told her this wouldn't be feasible without significant capital, but after going over specifics of her financial situation it seemed more a future possibility. None of this did she mention to Doug or Karen however. It wasn't that she was trying to keep things from them. At this point, Safen-Up and coming up with articles of incorporation were just abstract ideas, plus she never wanted to say or do anything that would worry or hurt them. Sondra also kept to herself what she'd done after leaving the Triple A office. She'd headed over to Santa Monica, an area of familiarity. The first key personal landmark she visited was the house she was supposed to have lived in with the Jenners. She next drove by the rehabilitation hospital where she'd spent hard, almost unbearable days and nights. She made a rude finger gesture toward this large three-story blue-gray building as she motored past, feeling relief when she'd reached the next block. Sondra made a point in not going anywhere near the CPS building, the police station or the hospital where she'd last seen Mrs. Jenner. This decision felt like a victory, as though she was a prize-fighter who had just punched someone and knocked them down and out. Though she didn't generally have violent thoughts she liked the idea of being in a boxing rink and knocking out Judith Tredou and the people she thought had treated her so badly. Sondra proceeded with determination to her next memorable location. It was the building where she had spent important recovery and life-restructuring time albeit brief, with the dearest of human beings, John and Leanna. As she came upon the block of the Misty Ocean Inn and Apartments it came as a shock and intense blow to see that the old yet once majestic building was now boarded up with a chain-link fence all around the property. The heartbreaking sight slapped her hard and began to squeeze breath from her lungs. She pulled over and came to a stop, getting out and walking around to the back of her beloved vehicle. Clutching tightly onto her keys she sat down on the curb and studied the tailgate, with the name Toyota and Tacoma printed in black block lettering. She then eyed the tread on her tires and the position of the exhaust pipe. Staring blankly across the street, not focusing on anything in particular, the full realization of what she'd just done hit her with brutal force. She'd blown right through a four-way stop without thinking or looking. Clearly she was in no condition to be in command of a moving vehicle at this second in time. She looked down at her legs making a bridge over the gutter that had a slow-moving stream of dirty water, with tiny bits of twigs, leaves, cigarette butts and other pieces of trash floating lazily underneath and away from her. She sat there for quite some time, and in a way it seemed to her as if she were studying the most violent of white-water rivers.

Finally feeling a solid grip on reality she drove to the Santa Monica Pier and walked to the farthest end. Alone at the railing with the onshore breeze almost choking her, Sondra was slapped with a wave of major emotion. She closed her eyes tightly, trying to force back tears and pounded her fists angrily on the blue metal railing. Images of her family, the Jenners and all the bad things that had happened to her sliced, pounded and exploded inside her brain and deep within her soul. The past few years of bottled-up emotion came out in convulsive tears, along with screaming and fist pounding.

Knowing better than to get right back in her truck Sondra began walking aimlessly. She passed by many shops that had continuous dozens of people drifting in and out and smelled food, realizing that she hadn't eaten anything substantial since breakfast. By odd coincidence moments later she came upon a fish and chips restaurant she'd been to several times while staying with John and Leanna. Sondra discovered it wasn't fun to eat alone and wolfed down her food before heading back outside, noticing that the gray fog had given way to a light sprinkling rain. She could smell coffee from a café just down the street and, though she'd just spent time sitting in a restaurant, headed toward the aroma. Sondra didn't necessarily love or even like the taste of the bitter and tortured bean but growing up she'd always treasured how it smelled. The fragrance now seemed comforting. Her parents had loved coffee, often savoring a cup or two with the Jenners after a big evening meal as if it were a fine brandy. Doug, for the most part, had basically two beverage favorites, Coke or coffee. She'd even known him to drink hot coffee on those 108 degree days in Bakersfield. She had practically willed herself to enjoy it as much as he in order to be more like him and to appear more grown-up.

Brew Ha Ha was a cheery but fairly small café and Sondra liked that it didn't have the look or feel of a typical coffee establishment. She noticed immediately the total madhouse of packed-in people all talking wildly and demanding various types of caffeinated beverages. For reasons that could take her ten lifetimes to explain, she snapped into action immediately when she noticed there was only one employee, an attractive blond, working at a frantic pace to keep up with the orders. Grabbing a long brown apron with the café's logo in large green print on the front, which was hanging on a wooden peg on the wall at the end of a long counter, Sondra set to work clearing and cleaning tables and doing whatever she could to make everything flow in a seamless, pleasant fashion. It wasn't until there were only two customers left in the place and she was taking off the apron did she get caught by the barista. Sondra watched her lean against the counter with an extremely puzzled look, then ask a question in disbelief. "Did you just do what I think you did?" Catching herself by surprise at thinking so quick on her feet, Sondra pointed to the Help Wanted sign in the window. "You needed my help" she stated. The woman stared at her with an odd expression and asked a second question. "How old are you?" "Seventeen" asserted Sondra. "Uh huh" groaned the woman, not believing her for one second. "More like thirteen or fourteen. You a runaway or something?" Sondra reached into her pocket and threw a handful of laminated cards onto the table she was standing nearest. The woman hesitated for just a second but came around from where she'd been working for the past few hours to take a look at the girl's offerings. The first thing she recognized was Sondra's California driver's license and she studied it closely for the date-of-birth and to see if the article was in fact real. Sondra noticed that the woman had an exaggerated perplexed look as she sifted through the rest of the cards and held up one in particular. "SCCA. Sports Car Club of America" the woman read aloud. "So, Sondra Sierre. You like sports cars?" she guessed. Sondra went into detail about each card and felt a powerful need to give the woman her verbal résumé and a recount of her life the past two years.

The blond woman laughed lightly. What the girl had just related did seem more like the reaction of a thirteen or fourteen year-old. She handed Sondra back the cards not quite knowing what to make of all this but then spoke with a voice that was a mixture of authority and concern. "I'm Shelley, the owner here. Wow you look young, and with all that going on it kind of boggles the mind why you would just come in and do what you did. Are you needing a job or something?"

Sondra shook her head. "I have a job" she said. "Racing."

Shelley eyed the girl, gesturing for her to sit. "Why do I get the feeling that there's something more to the story?"

"I should get going" Sondra told Shelley. "Home to your parents?" inquired Shelley. "Well they're not my biological parents, but yeah" said Sondra. "So you're adopted?" Shelley asked. "Orphaned" whispered Sondra bitterly.

In addition to owning and operating the coffee shop, Shelley Marie Enesbridge was a college student, a psychology major. She'd had several other declared majors but this one had stuck. Throughout her 23 years she'd always been compassionate about the human condition. Staring at the girl now before her she couldn't exactly put a finger on it but there was just something about Sondra that intrigued and resonated with her. "Well you've certainly got moxie, my friend" she announced. "Too bad you're not looking for a job. I'd give it to you in a heartbeat."

"Thanks" said Sondra with a smile that warmed the room. She then suddenly found herself telling this complete stranger her life story. She cried. She used profanity but apologized, pounding her fist on the table a few times, emphasizing certain perceived horrors. Shelley was moved to tears herself and had a hard time resisting the temptation in not holding the girl in her arms to comfort her as if she were a small child who'd taken a bad fall. She didn't, of course. "Oh how awful" said Shelley at Sondra's conclusion of her perceived hard number of years. "I'm so sorry you've had to deal with all that, baby" she added, her voice dripping with emotion. Sondra shrugged, forcing herself to be strong and finding it odd that the woman had just called her baby.

"I don't know why I just told you all that" she told Shelley. "I mean I don't even know you."

"Well sometimes it's best to tell things to a complete stranger, but somehow it doesn't feel like we're such strangers. Perhaps we knew each other in another life." Sondra wasn't so sure she bought into the another life scenario. "I gotta get going" she told the woman, extending her hand. When Shelley experienced the powerful grip she gasped.

"Whoa. Easy there, crusher" said the proprietor. "Women's wrestling night isn't 'til Wednesday."

Sondra's pure laugh and radiant smile won her over and Shelley returned the smile. "So, speedy Guadalupe" prompted Shelley. "Where's home?"

"Oh jeeze," voiced Sondra with a roll of her eyes. "You're a pet-name person. You're not gonna keep calling me that, are you?"

"I like you, Sondra Sierre" laughed Shelley. "Come back any time."

"Thanks" said Sondra. "Fresno" she added. "That's where I live. It's a bit of a drive so I don't know when I'll be back. I used to love this area."

"You used to love this area?" inquired Shelley. "Seems like a trillion lifetimes ago" said Sondra. "But you were happy here?" asked Shelley. "Well I don't know if I was really happy" said Sondra. "But the last little bit wasn't horrible, 'til I was forced to go."

"Who forced you to go?" prodded Shelley.

"Stupid foster system" growled Sondra. "They made me go to that foster home in North Hollywood I mentioned earlier, the Collins House."

"Are you happy now, Sondra?" inquired Shelley.

"Yeah, I guess" said the girl. "Doug and Karen are really great.

They officially adopted me. I even call 'em Mom and Dad instead of Doug and Karen. I feel guilty that they're putting so much time, energy and money into me though. Racing's super expensive and time-consuming. I mean it's my whole life now but it shouldn't have to be their lives."

"Sounds like they really do love you, and I doubt they'd do all this if they didn't truly want to" said Shelley.

"Yeah" breathed Sondra. "I guess so. Thanks."

Shelley gave the girl a warm hug and wrote down her private contact information on the back of one of her business cards. "Call me any time" she told Sondra. "I'd love to hear more about your racing and your life."

Chapter 19

By February 18 Sondra had received her hard card, a laminated FIA/IndyCar professional racing license, specific to the Indy Lights Series. Just over a week later the team of AAA lawyers had convinced a judge to throw out the lawsuit brought on by a particularly unpleasant ambulance chaser-type lawyer who had involved another insurance agency's lawyers on behalf of the Tillman family. It was a complicated and costly affair but one that resulted in a permanent, absolute conclusion. Sondra Sierre, Sondra Sierre-Trent, Mr. and Mrs. Doug and Karen Trent, The Trent Management Group, or the Sierre High-speed Merchandising Co. could never be touched by the Tillman family or by lawyers or agencies they might employ. Nor would they be able to bring successful legal action to the possible future Sierre High-Speed Inc. College for Sondra was challenging but in a way it was more like what she thought high school should have been, with interesting classes and instructors and fellow students who were also there to acquire much knowledge and enjoy the experience. Successfully completing her first term at Fresno State, with exceptional grades, it was gratifying for her in a way she'd never dreamed. There came some guilt however over postponing the next term but the Indy Lights racing season was having its gravitational pull and she rationalized that college would be easily resumed in the Fall.

Darren Brown called Sondra early one evening. She was seated at her desk in her bedroom reading a book that Karen had found at a used bookstore, *Flying on the Ground* by the legendary race car driver Emerson Fittipaldi. Sondra had chosen to use this book as the subject for an assigned paper in her Applied Literature class, one of the required courses in the BA program. Darren spoke to Sondra about her new lead strategist, Steven Barnes, and the overall Indy Lights manager, Phil Wallin. They also discussed the upcoming Indy Lights preseason testing and practices at Homestead Miami Speedway. Sondra asked many questions about what she could expect of the mile and a half oval racetrack and informed him about her readiness. "You seem to be a quick study in pretty much every situation" said Darren. "This is gonna be a lot different than what you were used to in a sprint-car but adaptable in many ways. I have every confidence that you're gonna do good. So here's why I called ... I wanna put you in the eight-four car at some point. Not your typical thing to throw an inexperienced kid into a situation like this, and I don't want to get your hopes up, but like I've told you before you're on a path for big things and I want you tested and practiced for when the time comes for you to step up. I'm takin' a big damn risk and a hell of a lot of heat in putting you in our Indy machine. Don't let me down."

Sondra shook her head even though she knew he couldn't see her. She stared at a black-and-white photo in the opened book before her. It was an image of Emerson Fittipaldi's #6 John Player Special Lotus 72 at Monza, Italy in 1972. This was the race in which he'd clinched the Formula One World championship. "You can count on me" she told Darren as she patted the page and closed the book. "I mean most of me thinks I'm ready to just go straight to IndyCar, but I get it. Experience is everything and I really do like driving the Lights car. What you've done for me is huge and I don't take any of this for granted."

Doug, Karen and Sondra left Sunday morning, February 26, at 7:06 a.m. for the next day's one-day Indy Lights Series test at

Homestead Miami Speedway in Homestead, Florida. Upon arrival they checked into their accommodations, and later going through the speedway's entrance gate Sondra felt anxiety stab at her insides after showing their ID badges and participant passes. The venue didn't have the throngs of humanity that would normally exist during a given race weekend but those who were there scurried around like ants in perpetual motion. The colorful vans and tractor-trailer rigs were parked in neat rows and pit lane was a mass of people and machinery. Sondra's anxiety subsided during the check-in process as Karen easily snapped into her newly created role as partner with her husband in being their daughter's business manager. She quickly delved into establishing the Sierre High-Speed Merchandising Co. Her first order of business at the Florida race venue was to meet with owners and operators of existing marketing endeavors. Doug was constantly amazed at Sondra's focus and professionalism. Her overall maturity level however was put on trial Monday afternoon during the second Indy Lights practice of the day. On Lap 38 Sondra was within a group of five cars. The bright red #77 car of Wes Coley dove underneath her orange and yellow with brown pin-striping #10 car. Coley was carrying far too much speed into Turn 1 and his Right-rear tire began to step-out underneath him. His inexperience had him panicking and applying brakes, which immediately caused the car to spin and hit the #10's left-rear tire. Sondra spun instantly, her displeasure coming out over the radio in the form of profanity-laced shouting. With lightening-quick reflexes she caught the car before it hit the outside retaining wall with any kind of force but the bits of rubber and debris at this high portion of the track gave her no traction. She slid and scraped along the retaining wall as if she were riding on ice for nearly 20 feet. Steven Barnes spoke to his driver over the radio, ordering her to pull to a stop and calm down. The spin and skid had flat-spotted all four of the #10's tires, one of which became completely devoid of air within milliseconds.

After being released from the in-field medical care unit, a mandatory trip that Sondra complained of incessantly, she arrived back at her pit. It was clear that her anger hadn't subsided. "What a little dumb-ass" barked Sondra as she eyed the mechanics and engineers working on her car, replacing suspension pieces on the right-front as well as giving the car a new rear wing. She made a tight fist and jabbed it in the air. "Where the hell's his pit? I'm gonna go flatten that little punk, just like he did to my car." Doug leaped over the pit retaining wall and grabbed the girl by the arm. No one heard the verbal exchange between father and daughter but many watched as the young driver went from an angry fight stance to her normal focused demeanor.

Hugo Patrero, Darren Brown, Phil Wallin and Steven Barnes had witnessed the entire on-track incident between Coley and Sierre. Three laps earlier Sondra had posted the fastest lap-time of the field. The men were impressed and secretly congratulating themselves on giving her the opportunity. The crash and following display of unbridled quick temper was something they'd not expected. As safety crews were rushing to the scene Hugo spoke to his colleagues, shaking his head. "The kid's a natural talent, I'll give you that, but that little girl's a damn immature hot-head. Probably something hormonal." Darren turned and gave his boss a disapproving look at the blatant politically-incorrect sexist remark. In the pits some time later, Hugo watched how Doug had managed to change the young driver's demeanor. "Give her father some kind of official position on the team" he told Wallin and Barnes as they watched Doug's obvious calming effect. "I think I like this guy and maybe he can keep her from starting World War Three out there." Steven and Phil chuckled as they watched Hugo turn and head toward the engineering staff.

At a dinner given by Cooper Tires, the official supplier of tires for the Indy Lights Series, Karen, Doug and Sondra were standing and chatting amongst a group of team members and various sponsor representatives. A 5-foot-6 stocky young man approached. He had short jet-black shiny hair and was wearing a bright red team uniform shirt with gray slacks. He tapped Sondra on the arm. "I'm glad you didn't get hurt" Wes told her. "That was my mistake today. Bad judgment on my part and I'm sorry." He held his hand out but when Sondra hesitated in reciprocating Doug lightly tapped her other arm with the back of his hand. “Thanks” said Sondra, responding to the boy’s gesture at Doug’s prompting. The two Indy Lights drivers shook hands.

“Apology accepted” she told him. “No hard feelings. Racing incident.” Sondra wasn’t telling the truth. She harbored deep ill-feelings about what had happened on the racetrack and the person she held responsible. To her it felt extremely similar to getting bullied at that Bakersfield high school and it had hurt her beloved car. The ordeal with this Coley boy was now firmly filed deep within the recesses of her brain. Not long after Wes had departed the small gathering, another young man entered the fray. “Aw, good” said Steven Barnes as Brice Crandle sidled up next to Sondra. “Our two-star players” Steven announced. “Now if we can just keep this one from making so many R-rated comments over the radio and this one from speeding on pit lane, we’re gonna have us a very good year.” IndyCar regular and popular driver Adrian Valderez was standing nearby and had overheard Steven’s comment. He’d been asked by Hugo Patrero to be a mentor for the two new Indy Lights drivers and was happy to pass along some of his vast knowledge of open-wheel racing, as well as offer advice and tips on stress and racing etiquette. Steven Barnes’ sarcastic jovial wit that he’d aimed at his drivers brought an involuntary smile to Adrian.

Doug found himself oddly in favor of Hugo Patrero. He wasn’t sure why and it did feel odd. The man was a famous-infamous icon in IndyCar racing and Doug had seen signs of his skepticism with regard to Sondra. It was a bit of a surprise when Hugo clearly made a point in singling him out for private conversation but accepted this gladly. The two men had opportunities to chat on more than one occasion, and with familiarity and agreeable conversation there came mutual respect. Hugo officially offered Doug the role as the #10 team’s mechanical logistics technician. Doug was basically going to be in charge of making sure any and all necessary items from the garage were brought to pit lane during practices or during a race. This insured him of being closely involved as a team member as well as one of Sondra’s business managers. He would be kept quite busy as would

Karen in her role taking care of logistical details for Sondra. The Trent racing family picture was complete.

Members of the #10 team and various other astute witnesses soon discovered that Karen Trent was even more of a behavioral enforcer to the young female Patrero-McDonald's Indy Lights driver than her husband. Sondra's periodic quick temper when she thought she'd been wronged or dismissed had been noted from day one, along with her occasional crude language. For the most part, Sondra was viewed as an extremely focused professional, demanding perfection of herself and those around her. She was no queen bee nor one necessarily given to childish temper tantrums. Sondra took her job deadly serious and saw winning as the only option. Doug, along with most of the men on the team, thought her fierce dedication and attention to detail were admirable, and when this at times resulted in less than lady-like verbiage, gestures and actions they found it amusing. Karen did not. Though the one-day Indy Lights test session had ended for Sondra with a mishap, the day overall was deemed a success. Both Patrero-McDonald's Indy Lights teams had run consistently in the Top 6 in all required practice sessions and Sondra demonstrated to Hugo, Phil and Steven that she was up for the challenge.

The Trents were back at the Homestead Speedway track the next day to observe the IndyCar Series teams in action as well as meet with numerous sponsors, promoters and racing dignitaries. That evening, Sondra, Doug and Karen were invited to a dinner given by Firestone Tires, the official tire supplier for the IndyCar Series. Before leaving the motel to attend the festivities Doug sat in a semi-comfortable chair and listened with amusement the arguments Sondra presented to Karen on what she was and was not willing to wear to the event. "Aw geez, Mom," complained Sondra. "This is too girlie. Why can't I just wear my team uniform shirt? I mean we're not going to some fairy princess ball. I'm a professional race car driver. None of the other guys'll be in some lacy, flowery dress-top thing. And these shoes are stupid." This was only the tail-end of the girl's clothing rant and Karen's patience was now threadbare. "Oh, Sondra, stop" said an exasperated mom. "You're not four and you're not wearing tennis shoes or a pair of racing shoes to this dinner. You refused to pack the ones I suggested so I bought you these. They look nice. They're flat-black and pretty much nondescript. And there's no lace or flowers on this top. No one'll even notice it under your black blazer anyway and you'll look like a professional business person. Now stop arguing and get in there and change. And hurry. We're not gonna show up late for this." Sondra stormed off to the bathroom and Karen turned toward her husband, taking a deep breath. "Why are you smiling?" she asked. "Oh nothing" said Doug with a wide grin.

Sondra endured a number of positive reactions to her attire that evening, including from Brice Crandle. He took particular note of his teammate and that she was quite popular, being constantly surrounded by fellow drivers as well as various racing dignitaries. He deemed it quite annoying that Sondra was often flanked by either Karen or Doug, and had to bide his time and watch for an opening. Nearing the end of the evening he finally got his chance to interact with the intriguing young woman. "Ya clean up nice, kid" joked Brice as he came to stand next to Sondra at a table dotted with many cookies, pastries and other enticing desserts. Making a quick fist, Sondra squinted at the boy. "I swear, if one more person tells me how pretty or nice I look, I'll deck 'em." "Oh I wouldn't dare tell you that" he told her. "I mean you're no super-model" he said with a smirk.

"Shut up" she said with a scowl, punching him on his right shoulder. His quick laugh further annoyed her and she grabbed two peanut-butter cookies and set them on a small paper plate. Brice selected a coconut macaroon and a mini chocolate cupcake. "That chicken pasta thing was pretty good, don't ya think?" he asked of their earlier meal.

"Yeah" she responded. "I went back for seconds." Young Crandle turned and spotted one of his engineers and a pit crew member chatting with a statuesque blond and her shorter female friend with curly dark hair. "I wish we could get in another day of track time" he told Sondra. "We were just getting the downforce levels worked out and I was really starting to get into a good rhythm." Sondra nodded, relieved that they could get in a little shop-talk. "Yeah" she agreed.

"One of the Cooper Tires guys, Jerry something, was working with us on real-time specs." Sondra followed Brice's gaze as she took a bite of cookie. "I had some weird gearbox issues this morning" she announced to her teammate. "When I'd shift from fifth to fourth, going into the wind gusts on the backstretch, either nothing would happen or it would go in gear and then pop back over to fifth. I lived with it for a little while, trying to work around it, but then we changed the steering wheel and I never had that problem again. Guess it was just something in the electronics." Brice nodded. He hadn't come across this particular anomaly in his car but was glad for the information exchange. The two stood enjoying their sugary treats in contented silence and proceeded with a bit of people-watching, until Brice's publicist Abby Kennet arrived to escort the young man to an important sponsor contact. Sondra complained to Doug and Karen on the way back to the motel that she wished she didn't have to go to any of the dinners or social engagements. She would have much preferred to just drive her race car and go home. The moment they entered their room however she flung her arms around her now-mom. "What's all this?" asked a surprised Karen. "I like how I looked tonight" said Sondra. "And the shoes aren't stupid. I love you, mom."

Karen used some vacation days and remained in Florida with Doug and Sondra for the next several days. The participants of the Indy Lights series had a myriad of mandatory tasks. There was much paperwork to fill out plus several short classes that included tests on race-day track procedure, participant conduct, general safety protocol and publicity obligations. These consisted of signing stacks of promotional material as well as being photographed in team uniforms and race suits for future promotion. A number of Indy Lights social events were scheduled, one of which was a luncheon that Sondra attended only long enough to grab a 6 inch deli sandwich and make her way to pit lane, as requested. The IndyCar Series had arrived for their on-track test time and as promised Sondra was getting her chance to showcase her talents in the #84 Patrero-McDonald's IndyCar. Her Indy Lights teammate was jealous and irked that he'd not been given the same opportunity but for the most part Brice tried to keep this to himself. Hugo Patrero had taken a liking to the boy from the start – he, too, had been raised on a farm although in Italy. He felt an immediate kinship with Crandle, and at one point during the day's proceedings he'd made aware his future intentions of procuring seat time for Brice in the #84-car.

Sondra's time in the #84 didn't disappoint, and after debriefing with the engineers and Patrero managers, Darren invited Doug and Karen to an early evening cocktail party for sponsors and managers of the IndyCar series. This would leave Sondra to fend for herself for dinner. In their absence, Sondra remained in the motor home that the Patrero organization had rented for her and her parents that weekend. She was glad for the chance to further study the rules and regulations of the IndyCar and Indy Lights Series and have the time to reflect on the long day's events. A knock on the RV door interrupted her concentration. "Oh hey, Brice" greeted Sondra, looking down from her vantage point on a smiling boy holding a large flat box and a 1 gallon bottle of apple juice. "Hi-ya, teammate" he cheered. "Just wanted to know if you and your folks might like to join me for pizza." Sondra gestured for him to climb up the steps and enter her mobile sanctuary. "Pizza sounds great" she told him. "My folks went to some big shindig" she informed the boy. "Be back in a couple of hours, then we're headed for home." Brice set the beverage and food container on the small dinette table as Sondra retrieved two clear plastic cups. He smiled to himself, fully aware of said shindig and knowing that Sondra's parents were in attendance.

The pizza smelled good to Sondra, realizing just how hungry she had become, watching him take a slice and folding it lengthwise in half. She then reached down to retrieve a slice herself from the opposite end. "Good pizza" she thought out loud. "This isn't from any track vendor. Where'd you get it?"

"Oh I have my sources" said Brice with a smirk.

"Hmm" voiced Sondra. "Dubious sources" she announced sarcastically.

"But you like it" said a smug Brice. "I debated a little on the toppings" he added. "But you seem like the Supreme type, so ..."

"Shut up" she laughed, rolling her eyes.

Happy with how things were going, young Crandle altered the conversation. "You're lucky" he told her. Sondra hated the word lucky. Whenever someone would say that to her it felt more as though they were inflicting this upon her. No part of her now-life seemed lucky. It seemed to her that she'd had to fight dearly for where she was and what she currently had. She chewed a bite of pizza and did her best to put the lucky business out of her mind as she listened to Brice tell his tale. "My parents aren't exactly thrilled about my chosen career" he disclosed. "And the only two races my mom's ever come to were the F-Ford race at Elkhart Lake and that last one in California. She's scared to death of watching me drive. I keep trying to tell her how safe it is now and that I'm really good at this." He took a long loud gulp of juice before continuing. "We Crandles are fourth-generation wheat farmers. My dad and both my grandpas were supportive of my racing when it was just a hobby, especially when I won or had any kind of success but I guess I was supposed to have grown out of this nonsense, as my dad calls it, and go into the family farming business. Our operation is pretty interesting and I've actually come up with some pretty cool innovations, if I do say so myself. I always thought I'd study mechanical engineering when I got to college but when I won my first kart race all that went out the window. All I want to do is drive and go further and further. Indy Lights, IndyCar and hopefully Formula One." Sondra nodded enthusiastically as she swallowed. "Yeah, same with me" she said. "I mean my circumstances are different but IndyCar and then Formula One are my ultimate goals."

Brice took a moment to study the girl. He watched as she wiped pizza sauce from her lips with the back of her right hand then pick several topping items off the front of her dark green shirt and pop them into her mouth. He found it cute that she was a bit of a messy eater and he liked her conviction that she'd make it to Formula One, even though it had always been a man's sport. "So your parents obviously support your racing career" he stated. "That's amazing that they're okay with you stopping your school stuff for this" he furthered.

Sondra shrugged her right shoulder then went into detail about her schooling, past and present. "So no high school prom or graduation ceremony?" he asked.

"Hated high school" she told him. "Bet you were class president and homecoming king" she surmised.

Brice took a second slice of pizza. "Well I was a little too busy with farm obligations to be involved in most school extracurriculars" he told her. "But yeah, I was voted homecoming king at my senior prom. The day I graduated, there was a big irrigation levy break so I didn't get to go out with my friends. I was up for over twenty hours, pretty much doin' the job of three men. A lot of that time I was cussing that I didn't get a normal graduation party but my dad was so damn proud of me. Totally made up for it. I hate to disappoint him because I look up to him so much but I'm not a farmer. I'm a race car driver."

Sondra scooped up her second pizza slice. "Nothing in my life turned out normal" she growled. She then forced herself to be cheerful and asked about Brice's racing origins. He was more intrigued with her life but was also eager to inform her of his. "Our old F Ford competitor Wendell Grayson and I basically grew up together. Like brothers, really. His older brother Mathew is a Supercross star."

"Wow" voiced Sondra. "Matty Grayson?" she guessed of the famed motorcycle racer. "I don't know why but I never even thought to put that together" she added.

"Well he got his start on a mini bike" Brice continued. "And when he outgrew it he gave it to Wendell. Let me ride it one day I was over and we got his dad to weld up a frame for a second bike. I was like seven or eight. We rode the wheels off those things and one day his dad took us to a kart race. The both of us were hooked from second one. Did everything I could to earn money for a second-hand chassis and engine. Shocked the hell out of me and pretty much everyone else when I won the first race I entered. From then it was on. Two years later, me and Wen were called The Winning Wisconsin Boys."

"Wen and I" corrected Sondra of Brice's grammatically incorrect sentence. He ignored this and watched Sondra take a gulp of juice. "I only know a little about you and your past" he admitted. "So, um ..." he began to ask.

"No" she growled through gritted teeth, shaking her head. Her powerful instant anger went through him like super-chilled needles. "I don't talk about that" she barked. "You can ask about Doug and Karen. You can ask about my racing history, even my damn bra size, but my family and what happened is off limits."

Brice momentarily fixated on her mention of bra size as he watched the young woman rise to retrieve a roll of paper towels from a cupboard near the sink. "Sorry" he breathed. "Hard subject. Got it." He studied her figure as she had her back to him, standing and ripping the plastic wrapper off the roll. He'd never before seen her in her own casual clothing. She was either in her race suit, a team uniform or special-occasion fancy-dress clothing for banquets, ceremonies or sponsor obligations. He suspected that she tried her best to always do everything possible to appear as if she were simply one of the guys. Her hair was usually tied back or stuffed under her team cap, and her race suit for the most part obscured her feminine features. He now saw her as a quite-attractive woman. There were the usual and alluring curves but as he examined those curves he could now see a lean and powerful athlete. Many conversations, mostly crude, had taken place with fellow race competitors during the Formula Ford season on how such a skinny little girl or tomboy could manage the strength and stamina it took to be successful in a race car. Brice could see it all clearly now. The combination of strength inside and out and her natural feminine elements were a powerful allure and intoxicant to him in this moment. When Sondra again sat across from him she was calm, as if the quick-tempered outburst had never taken place. She also changed the subject, stating that she'd lobbied for him to get time in the #84 Indy car. "Thanks" he said in earnest, feeling a bit in awe of her. "Patrero talked to me about it, too" he admitted. "I'm supposed to get my shot when the team goes for preseason testing in Arizona." By the time he bid her adieu they were more than just simply past enemies or current teammates. They'd forged a solid friendship.

Doug and Karen arrived back at the RV roughly 30 minutes after Brice had departed. Sondra's backpacks and jacket were ready to go, neatly placed inside deep shelving in back of the motorhome driver's seat, and there was the distinct but faint aroma of pizza hanging in the air. The girl was curled up on the couch fast asleep. "Hey, kiddo" said Doug as he gently shook her awake. "You ordered pizza and ate all this by yourself?" inquired Karen. Sondra sat up, rubbing her eyes. "My teammate came by with it" she informed her parents. "He wanted to have dinner with us." "Hardly" said Doug, shaking his head with a bit of a dubious scowl. "Damn Crandle kid came here to see you" he told his daughter. "His manager was at the same dinner we were and that kid knew it."

Sondra shrugged, not quite sure if she should be defensive or matter-of-fact. "No big deal, Dad" she said. "Just pizza and a couple of teammates hangin' out for a bit." The mom was intrigued, not to mention proud and happy of her daughter's impromptu dinner-date. The dad clearly was not. "Well we'll talk about all this later" announced Doug. "Our flight leaves in two hours. You did a damn good job in both cars and people are happy and excited. I'm glad you had dinner, now let's get going."

On a day when Karen had multiple work conferences in Oakland, Doug took Sondra to an early dinner at The Novel Cafe. This was a relatively small eatery in an upscale strip-mall where he'd taken Karen to lunch on their second date, with a dining room that looked like a miniature library. When they'd finished their meal and were enjoying coffee and a scoop of spumoni ice cream Doug made an observation. "You seem happier and much more relaxed about this new race season than before any of the others." Sondra nodded. "It's just different this time" she told him. "I'm a college student and I have a stable everything with you and Karen. And with the Patrero guys I don't have to fight for the respect I deserve. They don't make me feel like I have to prove anything to them. I've had a bunch of really good talks with Wallin and Barnes. It's like they really believe in me and really want me on this team. Hugo Patrero's kind of a piece of work though, if you ask me" she added. "I mean Darren told me that he's thought of as a laid-back, kind Italian but to me he seems the complete opposite. Anyway, this is so much of a better beginning than with Blue Sea Racing and I think Brice is gonna be a decent teammate."

Doug too was looking forward to the racing season, but during the Indy Lights testing in Florida he'd seen how much an interest his daughter had drawn, a percentage of it due to the fact that she was a female driver. The Crandle kid was also a growing concern to Doug. He remembered Brice's awkward behavior around Sondra at the Monterey Formula Ford awards banquet and had read the Christmas card the boy had sent his daughter. Doug also hadn't liked finding that Brice had spent time alone with Sondra in the motorhome that last evening in Florida. The subject of Sondra and intimate relationships with boys was not one he wanted to bring up but he'd always had a powerful sense of protectiveness when it came to this girl. "Hmm" voiced the dad of Sondra's observations. "The Crandle boy" he said in a disapproving tone, watching his daughter make designs in her ice cream with her spoon. "You know, um ... You were fifteen and you'd just been through so much when we first met" he began in earnest, clearing his throat in order to get the girl to cease in her food-play. "I've watched you grow up in a lot of ways. You're now older and with more education, and when you're not being nutty you're a poised and beautiful young woman."

"Dad" cautioned the girl.

"You haven't dated" continued Doug with a quick shake of his head. "In fact boys haven't been any kind of major part of your life."

Sondra looked up from her dessert with an alarmed expression. "This is sounding dangerously close to the start of a birds and bees talk" she complained. "I'll give you a thousand dollars not to go any further."

"Hmm" pondered Doug.

"Dad" complained Sondra. "Really, really ew" she added. "I mean here in public? In front of the books?" she said partially in jest, trying to alleviate the seriousness and discomfort of the topic.

Doug eyed the girl, thinking that perhaps Sondra was not quite as mature as he'd thought. "Well I wasn't about to launch into anything specific or heavy, sitting here in a restaurant" he clarified. "But ignorance isn't bliss when it comes to this subject. I just want you to know you can always come to me or Karen with anything."

Sondra looked down and stabbed at her ice cream with her spoon. She then looked up at her now-dad. "I know" she said in a low thoughtful voice. "I love you for that, and you don't have to worry about me or Crandle. I can take care of myself. I mean he's my idiot teammate, that's all. Besides, he has a girlfriend. Jillian."

In the Tacoma, still in the restaurant parking lot, Doug hesitated in putting the keys in the ignition. "In your sprint-car season I didn't like sending you out on the road like that unchaperoned" he began. "And I felt a little guilty about just sending you off on your F Ford adventure without having any kind of talk with you about boys and dating. It's a relief that you're not some boy-crazy teenage girl, but ..."

"I don't need the birds and the bees talk" said a slightly agitated Sondra, cutting off Doug's intended speech. "I heard it all from girls in the Social Services housing places, and in my high school health class we covered reproduction" she furthered. "Besides, my friend Kari told me a ton of crap. I mean I'm sure she told me some of it because she thought it might be funny to see if she could shock me, but I'm not some naive kid." Fifteen-year-old Sondra was still a naive kid back then and Kari had shocked her, not that Sondra would ever admit to it. Now sitting in the passenger seat of the Tacoma she went from glancing out the side window to staring down at her tightly clasped hands. "I'm not a normal or typical girl" she told Doug. "I can never be after everything was taken away. I can't see ever wanting some big relationship thing. I just don't think it's possible."

"Well it is possible, Sondra" assured the dad, feeling suddenly sad for her. "Don't worry about what's normal or typical" he told her. "Those are just BS relative terms. You're an amazing person and there are so many great possibilities out there for you."

Sondra bit down lightly on her lower lip, contemplating his words. "When I was nine" she began, momentarily squeezing the fingers of her right hand into a tight fist. "I went to a farm equipment show with my dad and my brother Dave. We got a free lunch, a Coke with chili beans and these warm buttery little rolls, then sat on metal bleachers watching a tractor auction as we ate. Dave and Dad started talking about girls instead of tractors or any of the other great machinery we'd seen so far. That seemed so strange to me at first but all of a sudden it was like they were having the most important discussion in the world. I've thought about that on and off for years, always thinking I'd have the same sort of similar discussion one day." She swallowed hard and glanced out the passenger-side window for a few seconds, not focusing on anything in particular. She then stared down at her fidgeting fingers, trying to force away a torrent of emotions.

Doug shook his head and patted the girl's knee. "Sondra, look at me" he requested. She did. "I'm not gonna let you sink" he told her. "I can't change the past and bring back your family but I'm here for you now. Always. Karen too. I didn't bring up this whole subject to bring you pain or to make you uncomfortable. I just want to make sure you're gonna be okay, in any and every situation."

"Kay" nodded Sondra.

Karen arrived home at 10:34 p.m. The condo was warm, a pleasant escape from the below average temperature outside, and there was light from the range-hood over the stove in the kitchen as well as light emanating from the den. Faint audio could be heard from the TV, and after hanging up her coat and purse in the entryway closet Karen went to investigate. She smiled to herself as she came up to the back of the sofa, finding that her husband and daughter had fallen asleep, the girl's cheek propped against Doug's shoulder. Karen put her hand on top of Sondra's head as she bent down to kiss the top of Doug's.

"Yay, you're home safe and sound" squeaked a waking Sondra. Doug tilted his head back until his lips met his wife's. Sondra rolled her eyes through the lovey-dovey-ness and smiled when her now-mom straightened and inquired about their current activity. "What on earth are you two watching?" she asked.

"Well it was a comedy special" defended Sondra.

"Yeah" added Doug as he turned off the A/V system. "I don't know what this is. So how'd it go?" he asked of Karen's day. "Not too much fun" she admitted. "The guy that's taking over my position is a sniveling little sycophant, but I'm officially on to bigger and better things. I'll be solely in charge of the Snap-on Tools sponsorship account. So Sondra, that means if you have any questions or grievances, you come to me." Sondra flashed a smile.

"Well first of all" joked the girl. Karen let out a laugh and shook her head. "Go to bed, you silly goose" she told her daughter.

"Night, Tiger" said Doug.

"Night mom. Night dad" said Sondra, quickly disappearing from sight..

Karen sat next to Doug on the couch so they could continue to talk. "It was that easy?" he asked. "Just changing your position in the company and getting them to go along with what you wanted?"

"No" she said flatly. "I'm taking a big cut in pay and there's a lot of restrictions and red tape to sort out. Lets not talk about that tonight. I'm worn out. So what about your day? And how's our girl?" Doug described further work with Dan Stoltz on finalizing the sale of the sports car business, then transitioned into the dinner he'd had with Sondra. "Our waiter remembered me and remembered you too, just from that one time" he told his wife. "We should go back there more often." "How'd Sondra like it?" Karen asked.

Doug nodded with a quick smile. "She liked it a lot but we got into talking about relationships a bit. There's a hell of a lot of anger and bitterness just under the surface with her."

Karen nodded in agreement. "How deep into the subject did you go?" she asked. "Nothing too intense" said Doug. "We were in a public place after all and she shuts down pretty fast when things get too heavy. We talked a bit more in the truck before heading home though. Uncomfortable subject but I feel pretty good about things. She's not a stupid kid and I suspect what she does know would probably shock the hell out of the both of us." Karen repositioned a small throw-pillow on the couch cushion before speaking. "She may dress and sometimes act like a silly teenage tomboy but she's growing up, in spite of herself" asserted the wife and mother. "She and I've talked a little as well and I think we'll definitely be talking again."

Doug nodded, feeling grateful he had such a perfect partner and was thoughtful as Karen continued speaking of Sondra. "I know you see her as that little girl you basically rescued" said Karen. "But Doug, she's gonna date, she's gonna hold hands, she gonna kiss and she's gonna fall in love."

"Oh god" expressed Doug, briefly putting his hands over his ears. "I'm buying a thousand shotguns and a thousand baseball bats," he joked.

The next morning Doug was off early to collect a project car in Stockton, an old non-running green Fiat Spider. Dan Stoltz had purchased the vehicle sight unseen from a man selling it on Craigslist. The plan was to have it refurbished and then give it to Vanessa for her birthday, this being her favorite sports car. Roughly an hour and twenty minutes after Doug's departure from the condo Karen began making poached eggs on toast for Sondra and herself. "Mm" voiced the girl of the aroma as she came into the kitchen. "Morning, sweetie" greeted Karen. "So I hear you and dad had a nice dinner last evening."

Sondra nodded. "You had a good talk?" prompted Karen, taking a sip of coffee and hoping to get into a dialog about the boys and relationship conversation Sondra had had with Doug. Sondra again gave a simple nod.

"Well" said Karen. "Talking about sex and relationships with your parents is tricky but …"

"Oh, god" voiced Sondra, rolling her eyes. "*Et tu, Brute*? I swear you and dad are sex-obsessed. You can stop with the carpet-bombing. There's no birds, no bees and there's no boys. Jeeze."

"We're not sex-obsessed, you nutty girl" negated Karen, chuckling at Sondra's exaggerated denial. "But we are obsessed with you." Sondra let out a Ts sound and shook her head.

"Well you're gonna have to be obsessed from afar today" she told Karen. "I have that Triple A promotional photo shoot in LA with Gina Perschwen and the gang at ten o'clock." She checked her watch to see how much time she had before needing to get on the road. Karen smiled and nodded. "Think you'll be home for dinner?" she asked her daughter. "I'm planning on making stuffed cabbage" she added as an enticement.

"Oh I'll definitely be home for that" said an enthused Sondra. "Mmm" voiced the girl, thinking of the pending meal. "Could you make extra sauce?" she encouraged. "That was so great last time you made it. I swear I wanna take a bath in that stuff."

"You goofy girl" laughed Karen.

The meeting at the Triple A office and then the promotional photo shoot went off like clockwork for Sondra. Rushing straight home to one of her favorite meals with Doug and Karen was a powerful draw but she'd set up a 1 p.m. meeting with the coffee shop lady as she thought of Shelley Enesbridge. Sondra was unsure why she'd felt drawn to Shelley from that first encounter and they had been in contact a number of times by phone since. She also didn't know why she hadn't talked about Shelley with Doug or Karen. It was if she'd made a monumental discovery and didn't want anyone to take it away from her or suggest that it wasn't worth her time and energy.

Instead of going to the Santa Monica coffee shop Sondra drove to the Malibu address Shelley had given her; the twenty-three year old lived in a white cliffside tri-level Victorian mansion with a red brick circular driveway. Several years prior she had moved from the East Coast to attend UCLA as a psychology major. Shelley gave her guest a brief tour of the first floor, talking almost non-stop. They eventually sat down to elevated grilled cheese sandwiches and tomato bisque in a second-story solarium overlooking the ocean. Sondra spoke of her Indy Lights car and upcoming race season but Shelley was more interested in the personal subject-matter of their last conversation. "So I've been thinking a lot about something you mentioned over the phone the other day" said Shelley. "About your Safen-Up idea to help kids in your similar situation and how people from Three A were interested in possibly helping you with that." She watched with amusement as Sondra put the white cloth serviette carefully in her lap, then wiped her soup-laden lips with the back of her left hand. "I hope you don't think it presumptuous of me" continued the host. "But I made several calls and finally spoke with one Gina Perschwen." Sondra nodded and smiled at hearing the familiar name. She let her sandwich half rest on the lip of the green seashell-shaped soup bowl.

"Shelley, SeaShell" Sondra joked with a chuckle, tapping the food vessel with her finger. She then cleared her throat and spoke in a more serious tone. "I just came from seeing Gina" informed Sondra. "I'm working with her and the lawyer-guys on racing sponsorship stuff. They've been really supportive and great and I've been kind-of blown away that they want to help make a go of a nonprofit. I want the organization to be pretty comprehensive, and I've tentatively been calling it Safen-Up for a little while now."

Shelley nodded, matching Sondra's smile and enthusiasm. "Well as you can clearly guess" she said, gesturing with her hand at the opulence of the room,"I have a bit of wherewithal to hopefully make a difference in several areas. I come from a pretty distinguished family upstate New York. Having a lot of money isn't really who I am or what I want to be all about but it does allow me and my family to open doors and help people." After lunch, Shelley discussed and showed Sondra what she'd come up with so far.

"Wow" said Sondra of the woman's efforts in creating an outline for a potential nonprofit organization. "You put a lot of thought into this." Shelley sat in a tan plush leather swivel-seat office chair with a proud smile. "Well my father and sister are lawyers" she explained to Sondra. "And my mom is in the medical field. This is just some preliminary stuff and they promised to help me with more. With this and what I know about running a business, I think we might have something really exciting to offer. If this is really something you want, I'd like to schedule some time to nail down the details. This kind of stuff really resonates with me. I'll want to talk more with Gina Perschwen and I'd like to meet your parents. Not in a permission-approval sort of way, but you mentioned something about them being your business managers." Sondra nodded, lightly biting her lower lip. "I can't believe you're doing all this for me" she told Shelley. "I mean we hardly even know each other and it's a really involved ton of work."

"I think you're worth the effort" Shelley told Sondra. "Don't you?"

Sondra shrugged and looked at her watch. "It's like a four-hour drive" she announced to her kind host. "Thank you a ton for this and for the great lunch but I should be getting on the road."

Before Sondra left, they began a more personal conversation. "You talked about a lot of things during lunch" began Shelley. "But you didn't seem to want to get into anything too personal."

"I made a hideous fool out of myself the day I met you" said Sondra, with a shrug of her right shoulder. "I don't usually cry and fall apart like that" she furthered.

"You've been through a lot" Shelley offered with a nod of her head. "Expressing raw emotion for the big things is natural and nothing for you to be ashamed. I was honored that you shared that with me and I didn't think you made a fool out of yourself. You hold a lot inside. I can feel it. I can see it."

"I have to" countered Sondra through lightly gritted teeth. "I mean screaming, swearing and throwing things only gets you so far" she added with a nervous laugh.

"Sure" agreed Shelley, quickly understanding that Sondra used humor as a defense mechanism. "But we all need some kind of a pressure relief-valve" she suggested to the girl. "I'm wondering if your racing isn't an extension of your rage and a kind of relief-valve for you. What do you think?" Sondra looked down at her feet for a few seconds. She was wearing a pair of blue racing shoes she'd worn only a few times during her Formula Ford season. "No" she answered Shelley's question in a calm thoughtful voice. "Racing to me is pure. It's like a clean slate every time I get into the cockpit. It's what I love the most and what I'm best at doing. I mean yeah, you can't just shut everything in your life completely out once you put on a helmet but I don't race because of anything."

Shelley watched as Sondra took note of the Grandfather clock's chime. "That's great that you have that" she said to the girl, a pleased smile coming naturally. "So it's more of an art form or skill set to you rather than a release?" she prompted, wanting Sondra to elaborate.

"Yeah" smiled Sondra. "Exactly. I like that."

Shelley then altered the subject. "How is it for you to have your parents, Doug and Karen, now so deeply involved in your art?"

Sondra shrugged her right shoulder. "Great" she told Shelley. "But it's hard not to feel guilty about them changing their entire life-focus just because of me. I mean we're gonna be a great racing family and we're all fully committed and happy about what we're doing but it still feels like I'm getting away with something I shouldn't."

"You have a lot of guilt in your life" stated Shelley. "You feel guilty about the financial settlement you received. You feel guilty about how much time and energy your adoptive parents are giving you, and I can hear it and see it that you feel guilty about you're being here when your family is not. Survivor's guilt" she suggested.

Sondra made a fist inside the pocket of her dark blue fleece sweater upon hearing the term survivor's guilt. She bit down on her tongue before speaking. "People keep telling me how lucky I am to have survived and have all this money. Damn blood money" she growled through tightly clenched teeth. "I should have died with them. It's not fair."

"Oh Sondra" said Shelley, briefly closing her eyes. She let out a loud breath before continuing. "Sometimes the universe works in ways that seem strange and harsh."

"The universe sucks" growled Sondra angrily.

"I'm so sorry, Baby" soothed Shelley. "But we're all here for a reason. It isn't fair but I also don't think it's random. We're here to learn from the hard lessons and even from the ones that seem fun and easy. It's like what you were talking about with your racing earlier at lunch. You have a strategy going in and you pick a line, then unforeseen things happen. If you stop to dwell on the how and the why, and you wallow in self-pity, you don't get far and it's not likely that you'll win the race."

Sondra shrugged but this did resonate with her. She was also impressed that the woman paid such close attention to the things she said.

"So maybe racing is a metaphor for life" Sondra thought out loud. "I mean it doesn't change things or make it better" she added. Shelley didn't respond, hoping Sondra would further her thoughts. She didn't. "I guess this isn't the happiest conversation in the world" stated Sondra, standing and searching in her pocket for her car keys. "But I really like talking to you, SeaShell."

Shelley let out a quick laugh at the nick-name Sondra had just given her.

"I'm sure we'll talk again" she told the girl. "Have a safe drive home and let's set up a meeting with Doug and Karen soon." Before Sondra stepped out the front door, she and Shelley shared a tight embrace.

CHAPTER 20

On a bright but hazy Thursday morning, seven days after a successful second test for the Indy Lights Series, managers Doug and Karen delivered Sondra, suited up and ready to roll, to her assigned #10 pit box at the Homestead, Miami 1.8 mile 14-turn temporary street-course. Sondra was focused and all business for the day's important practices, but after only two initial laps let Steven Barnes and her engineers know what she'd been experiencing out on the track. "I'm getting an ugly push on the exit of most right-hand corners, and there's a strange inconsistent throttle response."

"All right, Sondra" acknowledged Steven. "Lets bring it back in and see what we can do."

"Copy that" said Sondra. "Pitting this lap."

Once in the #10 pit-box, with the engine still running, a three-man engineering team uncowled the engine compartment and also took off the front nose cone/wing assembly. Twelve minutes later Sondra went back out for the entire remainder of the practice session. When she climbed out of the car she had a discussion with Steven Barnes and her engineers about running a slight decrease in tire pressures due to high track temperatures. This would give her more grip especially in the opening laps of the race, important for gaining track position early-on. Issues like ride-height and spring-dampening were also discussed.

Steven was pleased, if not relieved, at how smoothly things seemed to be starting. He sat down next to his driver as Sondra sipped water from a clear plastic bottle watching her pit crew attend to her car. "You were officially fourth fastest" he told the girl. "Even with all the different set-ups and changes we threw at you" he added. "I had a feeling you'd be quick here, straight out of the gate, judging from that first road-course test in Sonoma. You did better than your teammate in this session and I hear he's got quite a bit more pavement experience." Without taking her eyes off the pit action her confidence was evident as she responded. "Well fourth isn't first" she complained. "But I mean if we have even a fraction of the mechanical grip in our first race that we did just now we'll be at the top." She turned and looked him square in the eyes and waited for him to again speak, knowing full well that he was going to either once again apologize for the past or pretend that they never had a brief history. She'd long since let all that go and was only interested in having a great year but certainly wasn't going to let him think she excused his previous behavior. Steven took a sip from his can of Dr. Pepper. He spoke softly. "You and I are now in completely different places than we were a while back" he began. "I know I sure as hell am." She studied him. His macho arrogance of the past had somehow been replaced with warmth and sincerity. She nodded her head with a smile. "I sure as hell am too" she told him. "I'm really confident that the Patrero guys will give us good support. We're gonna have success and some fun, I just know it. I'm glad you're getting to know Doug and Karen. They're really great as parents and they're gonna be equally great managers."

"I like your folks" Steven told Sondra. "They're both sharp as tacks and your dad's a real good guy."

Sondra and her team leader continued to chat for a number of minutes about the upcoming race schedule, touching on the subject of her plans to continue college in the Fall. They were soon joined by Brice Crandle. Steven left the two as Brice sat down next to Sondra and initiated a conversation by asking how she liked her car. Finishing her explanation she noticed he was looking down and fidgeting with his empty soda can. She leaned over and bumped her shoulder against his. He looked up at her smiling.

"Been racing any more lawn tractors?" she asked.

"Not lately" he responded with a bit of a nervous laugh. "So, uh" he began in a tentative manner.

"So, uh" she repeated, annoyed at the boy's obvious hesitation in explaining the young blond woman who'd been close by his side at every opportunity that day.

"You going to that IndyCar dinner tonight?" he asked.

"Only if I'm forced to go" she said, half joking. "Probably a good place for you to take your girlfriend" she added. "Well me and Jillian kinda broke up a while back but neither of us has really moved on" he told Sondra. "Jillian and I" corrected Sondra. Brice gave Sondra a bit of an annoyed look. "Well anyway" he continued. "Sorry I haven't had the chance to introduce you. We've been together for a little over three years now but she's never been too keen on racing. She has family here in Florida so she's basically just here for the day. So, um, you've never mentioned having a boyfriend or is that subject off limits with you too. I mean you're pretty enough and you seem to turn a lot of heads."

"No time" said Sondra with a quick shake of her head, hoping to cut off any further discussion about her looks or her romance interests. "My focus is always a hundred percent on racing" she told the boy. "Well sure" agreed Brice. "That's good for the team and your car but sad for you" he told her as he stood. Sondra made a face at his insolence but he again spoke before she could respond. "And I don't really buy it" he added with a touch of arrogance in his voice. "See ya later." With a furrowed brow Sondra watched him walk away. "Idiot" she said to herself under her breath.

At 11:18 a.m. on a warm but overcast Saturday morning, Sondra was strapped into her car on pit lane with the engine idling. The motor ran smooth but made occasional grainy gurgling sounds, like someone with a light coating of food or liquid passing over their vocal chords as they talked. She revved the engine twice to see if would change anything. It didn't. Moments later the line of cars on pit lane began to roll onto the streets of St. Petersburg for their warmup lap. Sondra had qualified 5th for this event the previous day. When the green flag waved she got a clean start but was shuffled to 6th Place by the third lap. The #9 was able to get around her and Sondra began to use the many practice sessions and her photographic memory of the circuit to push limits. Eight cars broke away from the field of 19 and Sondra stuck to the back of her teammate as they sliced their way slowly forward. This wasn't at all like her previous racing ventures. Not only was this a new and different car configuration for her but the guys in this series were a few years older, with quite a bit more open-wheel pavement experience. The entire field was also incredibly close in skill level. Sondra liked the idea that this would push and challenge her to learn more and at an accelerated rate but the more difficult challenge came from a few drivers who weren't exactly kind or sportsman-like. Once again she found herself the only female driver in the field. Sondra told herself she didn't care but over the past week could feel building resentment from her fellow Indy Lights competitors that they were going to have to share the track and spotlight with a young-looking girl. Three quarters into the race Sondra watched a puff of white smoke as Brice locked up all four tires under heavy braking. A slower car a lap down cut him off going into a quick left-hand turn. Sondra was carrying excessive speed into the corner and didn't have much of a choice. She wasn't about to run into the back of Brice and possibly take them both out of the race, so opted for the only decision that made sense at the time. She turned in harder, the front-end now slightly drifting, nudging the already loose rear tire of the slower car with her right front which resulted in him spinning off and away. With all the commotion, Brice lost concentration briefly and Sondra flashed around him. She called to her crew chief immediately. "I didn't mean to take out the Fifteen. He was slow and in the groove and I had nowhere else to go." Steven responded back to his driver. "That's what we all saw. The Fifteen recovered so let it go and keep your focus. You're lookin' good." Barnes didn't tell her that an immediate warning had come in from Race Control about Sondra's possible race etiquette violation, which was now under review by the race stewards. Eight minutes later Steven got word that no disciplinary action would be taken.

With eleven laps remaining there came a crash involving three cars. This brought out a full-course caution, tightening up the field. Sondra was shown in 3rd Place. After the crashed cars and debris were cleared Steven got on the radio to his driver. "Okay, Sondra. We go green next time by. Keep your tires scrubbed clean and lets get a solid restart." Just over a minute later she did in fact get a tremendous start using the push-to-pass button on her steering wheel, giving the engine a boost of horsepower and flashing by the 2nd Place car going down the front-straight. A number of turns later she out-broke the leader, slicing in front of the #91. In clean air and open racetrack she settled down into full concentration on being smooth as well as bringing down her lap-times. "All right, Sondra" said Steven over the radio. "Lets see some of those smooth-as-silk qualifying laps." The gap did increase between her and the 2nd Place car but in the last three laps she began losing the over 4-second lead that she'd been able to build. Her brakes were fading in much the same manner as her teammate's had in the first practices of the week, and the 4-cylinder motor began to run intermittently rough. She persevered however, with many of her #10 team members holding their breath. The #91 got around her with just under two laps to go. Sondra made several attempts in the remaining moments and couldn't believe it when the orange car locked up his brakes in the same corner as Brice had earlier. She won by 0.382 seconds. Her teammate's outcome hadn't been as lucky, with Brice having a hard time recovering from his earlier incident. He'd soldiered on however and managed to snag 4th Place from Derrick Snybrough on that last lap.

On the cool-down lap it seemed impossible to Sondra that she'd actually won the race. The car was surging and running increasingly rougher, and she'd worked harder than ever before in a race car. She felt completely exhausted. A climbing headache made her feel a bit dizzy, and instead of any kind of victory antics she went straight to her pit. The attention she received for winning was overshadowed by her bit of instant infamy for being apparently the girl who didn't know she'd won. Sondra hated being known for this because she did in fact know she'd won. To her it made it seem like a failure not a victory. After a few words from a man who kept shoving a microphone in her face she posed for the podium photos and quickly hid in between Doug and Karen, making a swift retreat to the motorhome. The inside was well designed for comfort and had clever space-saving innovations. Sondra especially liked all the wood cabinetry because it reminded her of stories she'd read many years ago about people who crossed vast oceans by themselves in sailboats. When the weather would turn vicious they would batten down the hatches and secure the lines, then wait out the storm in their safe little cabins. Sondra actually preferred being in small spaces, which may have accounted for her success in a race car. It was where she felt the most comfortable and at peace. Large rooms made her feel too alone, like she was missing something. Someone. Some important people.

Once inside the motorhome Sondra took a deep breath and lay down dramatically on the floor. Karen sat down on the surprisingly comfortable hide-a-way couch and Doug sat on the floor across from his wife. After a few moments Doug lightly slapped Sondra on the leg. She sat up and took a deep breath. "I put every thing I had into that, all week long. I'm really wiped. My hands hurt. I can barely make a fist." After another deep breath she continued. "Did you hear that guy call me a bitch? It was the guy that I couldn't help tap." She paused but Doug and Karen didn't respond. "Did you see all the TV cameras? Brice told me that they may not broadcast all our races like they do for IndyCar but we at least get some media coverage. Now everyone thinks I'm some stupid idiot girl who's reckless and who couldn't find her way through a door if it hit her in the face. I mean the win was awesome, and I know I deserved it but …" Doug was thinking it but Karen spoke first. "Stop that" she told the girl. "I don't care how tired you are. I won't have you thinking or even saying the words. You're not stupid and you are no idiot girl. No one thinks so. The guy who called you the B word is small-minded, petty and sexist."

"We were there, Sondra" interjected Doug. "Karen and I were standing next to Barnes when you apologized about the incident, and when you mentioned about your brakes and overheating motor. It was obvious to all of us why you came directly to your pit. And lets keep in mind that Race Control called it just a racing incident. No penalties or repercussions. You won and that's what will be remembered. You gotta let this go, kiddo. Don't keep everything bottled up. Your podium interviewer was trying to give you the chance to tell your side of the story but you didn't."

"People like and respect when racers do that" added Karen.

Having his drivers finish 1st and 4th for the season opener was not only satisfying to Steven Barnes but was of utmost importance to him as a team leader and race strategist. He'd felt tremendous pressure to perform well in front of the Patrero-McDonald's car and team owner. Hugo Patrero was a white-haired 64 year-old man with a deep tan and surprisingly few age wrinkles. He was from a small town in southern Italy, and for as many generations as there were motor sports, driving and race-team ownership was the main occupation of the men in the Patrero family. His great-grandfather, grandfather and father had built up quite a reputation, and Hugo himself had had some mild success early on as a driver. It was Hugo's prowess as a car and team owner however that had put him in good standing in the F1 world. With the famous family name and wealth they'd built, Hugo's quest to build the ultimate Formula One team was soon on a rising path. After a few highly successful years of picking the right driver and support, the Patrero name became synonymous with the winner's podium and world championships. Hugo had taken a chance on a promising young driver, Adrian Valderez. Although Adrian had not won a world title in the three years since his employment with Hugo he had a most impressive string of Formula One victories and was one of the most celebrated drivers in Europe. Tiring from the staggering rise in cost to keep an F1 team going, as well as the monotony of his life, he brought Adrian to the US to compete in the Indianapolis 500. He soon-after rediscovered his passion and put together a Champ Car World Series team. Adrian took to US open-wheel racing in dramatic form, and after many wins and three championships, with ChampCar morphing into the IndyCar Series,

Hugo was now considered a legendary motorsports figure. His ego and quest for future greatness propelled him to be receptive of Darren Brown, Keith Hestrovich and Steven Barnes when they pitched the idea that he give new rising hopefuls of the sport a chance in the Indy Lights Series. With a typical macho chauvinistic European response, he was not particularly interested in the Sondra Sierre pick, though he trusted Darren completely as a friend and his IndyCar team's leader. When Steven Barnes was tapped to run an Indy Lights team for Patrero he'd originally suggested Brice Crandle to be his driver choice. Patrero was immediately on-board with that, and Darren's strong influence, bordering on insistence of picking Sondra, had Hugo cautiously agreeing to enter two cars for the season, interested to see how things would go with the boy and girl. After Sondra's win on the streets of St. Petersburg Hugo was willing to give her the benefit of the doubt.

Round 2 of the Indy Lights season took place Sunday morning on the same Miami circuit, ahead of the IndyCar Series season opener. In this event Sondra didn't fare as well as the previous day. There was nothing technically wrong with her car but she qualified a dismal 11th Place. Though she made good passing choices during the race and advanced her position steadily she got no higher than 5th. She felt fuming-mad at the result but did her best not to show it. Her teammate had started 3rd, and after a drama-free race finished in that same position. This new racing adventure produced the least amount of anxiety for Sondra than the previous three. She wouldn't be away from Doug and Karen and they were in a comfortable "home away from home." Sondra also noted that her Indy Lights pit crew members were of a much higher caliber than those of her previous situation and seemed genuinely happy to be working with her. They were educated, professional, and took pride in their jobs. John Briers, a man she'd first met at Laguna Seca the day she drove Adrian Valderez's Indy car, was now assigned double duty. He was Adrian's Lead Engineer and had been asked to oversee the two Lights team engineers, Gary Spouler and Tim Carmine. Sondra was encouraged to get to know Gary and Tim well since communication with them would be of the utmost importance. In order for success, the three needed to work as a seamless team on car set-ups and specific mechanical issues throughout practice and qualifying sessions plus each race. Gary was in his late 40s, a bit overweight, and had thinning gray hair. At first Sondra found him to be a bit stand-offish, as if he were either skeptical of her or perhaps a bit jaded from years of his chosen profession. Tim on the other hand was a muscular light-hearted jovial man of 28. He had blond hair with streaks of dark brown and was an avid gym-goer, which had ingratiated himself to Sondra from their first meeting. Athleticism became a common topic of conversation between Tim, Sondra and Phil Wallin, who had impressive arm and upper-body strength. Sondra liked that Phil made himself available to both her team and Brice's equally, imparting wisdom and strong leadership. She also knew that Darren Brown had his plate full with IndyCar duties as Adrian Valderez's Lead Strategist but it was a relief to her that he was often on hand for advice and good camaraderie.

The Birmingham, Alabama race track of Barber Motorsports Park was a natural-terrain road course Sondra was looking forward to being on, however the weather was something she'd never before experienced, with temperatures in the low 90s and oppressive and intense humidity levels. Like Miami this was scheduled to be another double-header weekend, with two chances to earn valuable championship points. Sondra liked the look of the facility from the start, with its lush green grass and rolling hills. After only three initial practice laps she found her rhythm on the twisty 2.3 mile, 17-turn track, posting the fastest lap-time of the morning, but Saturday morning's Indy Lights race turned sideways for the #10 car on Lap 12. Gearbox issues came on slow but steady. Even with her quick-thinking and smart driving she drifted further back in the field, well off the podium.

The second race of the double-header Indy Lights weekend on Sunday was a one-hundred degree turnaround for Sondra. She started Round 4 from the fifth position and steadily picked her way through the lead cars. With radio silence on her part and fierce determination she was 14.031 seconds in the lead when the checkered flag flew.

She gained high praise during her podium interview and post-race conversations with a number of high-profile IndyCar drivers and dignitaries, but to Sondra it seemed that they were more impressed with her previous day's efforts than her runaway victory. Her teammate, who'd started on Pole, developed engine overheating issues on Lap 14 and was forced to drop out of the race, relegating him to a 19th Place finish. He was bitterly jealous of Sondra's luck and kept his distance from her and her manager-parents throughout the rest of the day.

The next two championship rounds were in Indianapolis, the first on the road course within the famous 2.5 mile Indianapolis Motor Speedway. Sondra had been on this track a year before in the Formula Ford with disappointing results. She looked at this as an opportunity in the Lights car to redeem herself. Going through the first few turns in Friday morning's practice she immediately felt comfortable with the track's layout. The 2.439 mile, 14-turn road course ran in the opposite direction from that of the oval configuration. The concept had seemed strange to her a year ago, but once on track the feel was completely normal.

Sondra started Saturday's race, Round 5, from 3rd on the grid and forced her way into the lead in just under half a lap. There was an immediate bit of controversy about how aggressive she'd been in those opening laps but once out front she pretty much just ran off and left everyone. Brice had qualified 7th but raced his way to 2nd. After the post-race interviews were concluded Sondra secretly despised the fact that Brice seemed to be given far more attention and praise for his efforts than she. In the next day's Indy Lights GP Sondra started Round 6 from Pole but was hampered by handling issues, putting her mid-pack by the first half of the race. A two-car crash brought out a full-course caution and the field tightened up as the cars circled the track under yellow conditions. Sondra used this as a reset advantage and when the field went green began passing cars in attention-grabbing fashion. The last 7 laps were a savage battle between teammates, both drivers receiving a number of warnings from their respective Lead Strategists. Brice out-drug Sondra to the finish line, beating her with the slimmest margin ever recorded in Indy Lights history. Crandle gloated heavily during the podium ceremony and post-race festivities, which did not sit well with Sondra. Even though they'd developed a friendship, and what Sondra had once or twice dared to think of as a possible future boy-girl relationship, memories of her Formula Ford season surfaced on how she'd despised and hated him. She became determined to avoid him as much as possible.

A week of intense and extremely serious Indy Lights testing on the famed Indiana oval came next. Being out on hallowed ground was both exciting and daunting to all Lights participants, especially the rookies. The G loads encountered on this track at the 195 per hour speeds were like none other . After Sondra's first 50 minute practice stint Karen noted black and blue areas on the muscles of Sondra's arms and legs, emphasizing just how physical the high-speed oval was for a driver. Mandatory safety classes were observed for the Indy Lights Series drivers in addition to media and sponsor obligations. In the midst of these, Sondra's teammate managed to weasel himself back into her good graces by being courteous and professional in both the garage and pits as well as during a number of simulated duels on the race track. Brice Liam Crandle had straight light brown hair, a bit on the shaggy side at times, with an All-American-boy look about him. He was an outgoing young man with a mostly positive attitude and outlook on life and had been a popular figure amongst his peers since day-one of grade school, continuing through high school. He enjoyed this level of high favor among his racing contemporaries throughout his burgeoning racing career, recently gaining much hopeful interest with many of the VIPs within the racing business community. Brice began insisting upon his teammates' inclusion when a group of drivers and pit crew members of various teams would invariably gather for quick lunches or a bit of fun and games with a Frisbee or football. These activities with the silly boys as Sondra thought of them were next to last on her list of anticipated activities but she found the camaraderie comforting and was grateful to Brice for convincing her to join in on the fun. In this way Brice was good for Sondra. She tended to be quiet and at times hermit-like, determined to be a serious professional.

Ignition issues kept Sondra from qualifying well for the Indy Lights Freedom 100. The #10 car was late to final Tech Inspection and only minutes away from missing the deadline to make the field at all. Sitting on pit lane, Sondra's motor went silent and remained that way as the first of the 18 cars in the field ahead of her began their qualifying laps. Sondra did eventually manage her qualifying run but posted the slowest time, designating her to start the race from the last position on the grid. Her engineers and mechanics, including Doug, worked through the night to sort out the problems and get the car ready for the big event the next day. Friday morning, Carb Day at the Indianapolis Motor Speedway, brought the largest crowd Sondra had ever encountered as a race participant. This day was about the all-important 90 minute IndyCar practice session, followed by the Indy Lights Freedom 100, a 40 Lap mad dash at just under 200 miles per hour. The day would conclude with the IndyCar Series' Pit Competition, both fun and prestigious for drivers and teams.

Starting the forty-lap, one-hundred mile race from the rear added a level of anxiety for Sondra that she was sure she'd never before felt. It seemed to her that she was on the verge of throwing up at any minute but when the green flag waved for the 19 Indy Lights cars she got a tremendous start, passing five of her competitors on the outside before going into Turn 1. For the next twenty-three laps the #10 car steadily inched forward through the field. With twelve laps remaining Sondra began to wage a more noticeable war. She had cracked the top-5, and after overtaking a white and blue car going into Turn 1 she came upon the back wing of Wes Coley. Sondra followed him for just under two laps, observing that the #77 car seemed to be battling worsening understeer, possibly from tire-wear. Once around him she went after the 3rd Place car, the #9 of Brice Crandle. Brice had spent his time battling within the top 4 cars, leading a total of 9 laps. With the laps now winding down he began to feel a sense of urgency and managed to get around the green-white-orange car of Gene Beasley for 2nd, then drive within feet of the rear wing of the black and turquoise #92 car. Billy Osterouche had led most of the race. He was a second-season Lights driver with the Anditelli Autosports managed team that had come 2nd in the championship the previous year and it was widely known that his main strength was on ovals. Sondra slotted into the 4th Place spot, gaining on Beasley after putting her car where she could be towed along by his momentum. As she got just a few feet from his rear wing, going down the backstretch, she was suddenly met with violent turbulent air. "I can't get around him" she told Steven Barnes over the radio in a panicked, frantic voice. "Brutal aero-wash" she added.

"All right, Sondra" Barnes told his driver. "Try backing off and then regrouping, then try a different line but stay in the groove. Watch that loose stuff up at the top." Sondra didn't respond and at first it didn't appear as if she was following her lead strategist's suggestion. After falling back almost 6 car-lengths into the waiting clutches of Zak Palier she did manage to regroup. She was able to find a good rhythm and again approached Beasley. This time it was with a better line and she was 3 miles an hour faster. With her thumb on the push-to-pass button on her steering wheel she overtook him on the outside just before getting to Turn 1, with a momentum that brought her to the battling Brice Crandle and Billy Osterouche. "Nice move, Sondra" Barnes called out over the radio. "You're P-Three with four to go. Four to go at the line. Position three on the wheel. Position three. You have fifty-two seconds of push to pass. Wind's shifting just a bit. Use your tools." The position three that Barnes had mentioned was a fuel-map setting designed to give Sondra's motor a rich fuel mixture for optimum power, and the tools Steven spoke of were not as advanced as an Indy car but would allow the ability to adjust the car's balance in changing wind and track conditions.

Going into Turn 3 Sondra watched her teammate overtake Osterouche. She had a strong car and was able to stay with the top two, and going down the front-stretch with now three laps remaining she closed in on the #93, using the overtake (push-to-pass) button. To her, the race now became a subconscious return to how she'd approached and raced during her fierce sprint-car battles. Steven Barnes and the #10 team's Spotter Jeff Cauls began talking to their driver almost non-stop over the radio, giving Sondra information on the whereabouts and the time-gaps from cars around her. With two laps to go Sondra pulled out of the slipstream and got around Osterouche before going into Turn 1, but coming out of Turn 3 the #93 got back by. As Jeff Cauls let Sondra know when the passing car had cleared her, Steven began giving his driver a string of information. Sondra had her hands full but moved her thumb on the radio button. "Stay off the radio and let me drive" she ordered. While the white flag waved in the air the #10 began moving closer to the #93, and for most of that last lap they were either side-by-side or swapping positions, allowing Brice Crandle to sprint away in mostly clean air. Osterouche ran wide in Turn 3 and Sondra dove in underneath, nearly running on the grass. Billy made a hard charge after coming out of 4 but the #10 got to the bricks first, by just over a foot.

Sondra was a very tired and dejected race car driver as she climbed out of her car on pit lane at the conclusion. Her manager-parents and the entire 10 team however were ecstatic with their result. Starting the race from dead-last on the grid and then getting a 2rd Place podium finish was something they saw as equally epic as the #10 team's victory. Though Sondra saw this as a colossal failure there were many who had watched in amazement at how the orange-yellow-brown car seemed to slice through the competition with efficiency and make breathtaking passes. In addition, with Karen at the helm of Sondra's social media fan page, it soon became apparent that Sondra's day of heroics was beginning to overshadow her teammate's win and Darren Brown himself insisted Sondra sit by him on the #48 Adrian Valderez pit-box stand the next day to watch the five hundred mile IndyCar race.

During a two week break, Karen spent time with her mother as Mary recovered from a broken ankle. Doug and Sondra traveled with the Patrero-McDonald's IndyCar team to Kentucky, where Adrian Valderez won. Father and daughter then spent time at home before heading to Wisconsin. Rounds 8 and 9 were held at the Elkhart Lake Road America facility where Sondra had crashed in practice in her

Formula Ford. To her this was a welcomed chance to redeem herself on the roughly 4 mile, 14-turn natural-terrain road course. She had put this crash out of her head for the most part, never even referring to it as a crash. To her it was simply hideous luck that resulted in hurting her beloved car and she was glad that any remembrance or dreams of the sights and sounds of the incident hadn't followed her. In addition to a hopeful weekend Sondra was pleased to learn that Darren Brown had talked Hugo Patrero into letting her and Brice get 20 minutes each of seat-time in the #84, Adrian's backup car, during Thursday afternoon's IndyCar unofficial practice. The next day, while Brice was in meetings with several of his sponsors, Darren put Sondra in that same car for the full 50 minutes of the IndyCar mandatory practice. With Hugo Patrero constantly on the radio with her she stayed within the top five the entire session and ended up posting an unofficial 3rd quickest overall. When she later found Brice in the #48 team's assigned garage talking with three of the team members she noted an edgy but supportive reaction to her latest IndyCar driving stint. The last time she'd been given the opportunity and not him it had not been at all pleasant. Unbeknownst to Sondra, he'd since managed to curry favor with Hugo Patrero and the organization's management and was confident about his IndyCar future. Saturday morning for Brice resulted in quite a bit of bitterness and jealously when he learned Sondra would be given the opportunity to drive in Sunday's IndyCar GP.

The Indy Lights race didn't go well for Sondra or her teammate. Sondra had qualified 4th and during the one-lap warmup before the start she began noticing some unusually loud popping noises emanating from her engine on acceleration. She alerted Steven to this but from the laptop telemetry readings engineers Gary and Tim saw nothing technically wrong. Though the #10 car's motor ran without incident during the race there was a lack of top-end horsepower and she finished in 12th. She was upset by the poor result but didn't have time to brood over it or confer much with her team. Karen quickly escorted her daughter/client to the #84 IndyCar pit in preparation for the three rounds of IndyCar qualifying, where in the hazy afternoon sun she made it through Group 1, Round 1 in 5th. She later missed advancing to the Fast 6 by .038 seconds. That early evening she attended an Indy Lights fan meet & greet function that was put on by the IndyCar Series organizers. Karen and Doug had plans as well, dinner at a Mexican restaurant several miles away with two men and their wives. Both gentlemen had been in the sports memorabilia and merchandising industry for many years and Karen, ever on the lookout for people who might impart ideas on launching a merchandising line exclusively centered around Sondra and her racing career, had spoken with them earlier that morning. Karen had already made some headway in setting up the business and was excited about moving it forward, especially with Sondra's burgeoning popularity. Sondra and her teammate went from their meet-and-greet to attending a dinner given by some of the Patrero organization's sponsors. Sondra was relieved that the conversation between them seemed to flow easily, and upon hearing a tablemate speak the words high speed chess match, referring to IndyCar racing on high-speed ovals, Brice revealed that he'd always wanted to learn how to play chess. Sondra had been trying her best to be neat and tidy with her table manners. She carefully wiped her mouth with her napkin and nodded, looking over at the boy seated beside her. "Oh I used to love playing chess" she told Brice. "I can teach you if you want." "Yeah, I want" he said with a smile. Sondra's father had made a chess board in high school and it had been part of the living room furniture ever since she could remember. Kal had taken great pride in teaching his oldest son about the game and Sondra picked up on it quickly just by watching. Dave would absolutely trounce her in the first number of matches but as Sondra's budding fierce competitive edge began to emerge she rarely lost a game. Dave and several of his friends soon became far more interested in fishing than indoor games, and as soon as Haley was up for it Sondra got her turn to trounce her little brother just as Dave had first done to her. The only thing was, Sondra could see the hurt on Haley's face when he couldn't even make more than three moves without getting beaten, so she would prolong the game and would often have a candy bar to split with him afterwards. Her reign as family chess champion had lasted about seven months, when everyone seemed to move on to other interests.

The Indy Lights Round 9 race awarded Sondra some luck when she inherited the runaway lead from Serge Vianessi on Lap 19. His 7.485 second advantage over her disappeared when the Black #31 developed terminal motor issues. Sondra was ecstatic, to say the least, when she hopped out of her car for the winner's circle celebration, though it was short-lived because she was needed once again at the #84 IndyCar pit. Darren was to be her Lead Strategist in the race that afternoon, while Hugo insisted on calling the event for Adrian Valderez in the #48. The Elkhart Lake Road America IndyCar event was marred by many full-course caution periods due to single-car spins or multi-car contact. Darren used his instincts and knowledge plus a bit of racing luck to guide Sondra through many harried situations, and by the halfway mark the #84 was running in the 8th position. By the race's conclusion, after gaining more spots due to pit strategy and a crash involving two of the front-runners, Sondra Sierre was unofficially scored with a 5th Place Finish. Unofficial because according to IndyCar rules and regulations she wasn't old enough to compete in this series nor was she a regular part of the designated field. Her usual no points for second best attitude waned when Hugo gave her hearty congratulations on this accomplishment. She made a point to avoid a very jealous Brice. His weekend hadn't gone as well as he'd planned. He'd grown up miles from the race facility and thought of this weekend as his home-race. A year ago in the Formula Ford his family (minus his grandmother) had all been there to see him to victory. This weekend however it had been quite a letdown for him to learn that the only family member planning to attend was his Aunt Heather, who would be there with her current boyfriend. Brice loved his aunt and was happy she would be on hand but there was limited time for them to spend together. In Saturday's Indy Lights Round 8 he finished a disappointing 4th Place, still dealing with prior clutch issues. In the next day's event he retired on Lap 26 due to transmission complications stemming from those very same clutch issues.

Round 10 for the Indy Lights Series occurred on a 1-mile oval in Newton, Iowa. With Sondra's last victory in Wisconsin she was now 2nd in points for the championship. She was also doing what she wanted and loved. Though reminders that her parents and brothers were not part of her now-life often clobbered her, she was constantly enveloped in the unconditional love and support of Doug and Karen.

The #10 car rose to the top of the speed charts from the start of the first practice of the weekend but it was Brice Crandle who was "the class of the field" during Saturday's race. He won with an impressive 7.104 second lead over Phil Grumenchino and Michael Debexis. Sondra finished the race in a dismal but hard-fought 9th. She and her 10 team struggled with balance and downforce levels, never finding that elusive formula to be able to extract the necessary confidence and speed. Throughout the fast-paced event and the next few days her bristling anger and frustration stabbed the ears of all who were forced to hear her comments and complaints. Doug and Karen chose a mostly empathetic and supportive stance but drew the line with rude behavior or inappropriate language and negativity, not to mention her stubbornness when it came to eating or joining in on social activities.

The next stop on the race schedule was a street-course in Toronto, Canada for Rounds 11 and 12. Cold gray rainy weather matched Sondra's gloomy mood. She'd taken the last race loss extremely hard, relegating her back to 3rd in the championship. To her it felt as if she'd been personally attacked. Doug and Karen also noted an odd phenomena. The young driver's harsh attitude and hyper-fierce determination seemed to spread to the members of her team. Missing were the usual light-hearted jokes or easygoing attitudes. Under the vast tent of the designated Indy Lights garage stalls, engineers Tim and Gary worked at a mostly silent feverish pace, and in the pits Steven Barnes displayed a cold almost angry facial expression. At 9:12 a.m. Sondra sat in her car on pit lane with the engine idling. The light rain turned into a steady downpour and the sporadic wind gusts increased. With headphones, Karen listened to the team communication. There was grave concern that track officials would cancel the first Indy Lights practice session of the weekend, costing the team valuable test time. Sondra was very new to running on street courses and this 1.786 mile, 11-Turn tight bumpy configuration was tricky for even the most seasoned IndyCar veterans. There were both asphalt and concrete patches making for a slippery roadway, even in the dry. There were also fencing and concrete barriers that surrounded the track, standing at the ready to collect and crumple any car with a mechanical problem or a driver who's concentration lapsed, even for a fraction of a second.

On a very wet racing surface Saturday morning, Sondra emerged victorious on the streets of Toronto, finishing an astonishing 17.031 seconds in the lead. As with her Formula Ford experience, her fellow Lights competitors initially had found it hard to take the skinny tomboy seriously. She and her orange-yellow-brown #10 car now had the attention and respect from the majority in the field, including a number of the esteemed IndyCar drivers. This weekend's win also awarded her a 3-point lead in the championship. Her teammate was having a solid 3rd Place day but a slower car spun into him on the slippery surface. Brice limped back to pit lane and received a new front wing/nosecone and continued with a determined drive, finishing in 7th Place.

Rounds 13 and 14 were to take place at the mid-Ohio race facility in Lexington. On a day of glorious sunshine, with stunning blue sky and several bright white puffy clouds, Sondra and Brice sat alone on the top row of bleachers overlooking pit lane. There were shiny and dazzling-colored cars assembling, the Continental Sports Car Challenge vehicles getting ready to go out on track for a 30 minute practice session. Sondra smiled to herself thinking this a perfect moment. Karen had put together a sack lunch for her that morning in their motorhome's kitchenette. Brice had purchased from one of the racetrack's food vendors two sodas along with a burrito for his main lunch and two small bags of potato chips. He watched Sondra carefully pull each item from her small brown paper sack and put them in her lap. His smile was involuntary when he heard her comment on the food choices. "Oh yay" she exclaimed. "Mom makes the best chicken-salad sandwiches, and she cut off the crust. I hate crust on my sandwiches."

"Pretty strong emotion for the outer layer of bread" Brice kidded her. "I'm afraid to ask how you feel about the skin of an apple, or about banana peels." Without taking her eyes off the activity on pit lane Sondra swatted at the boy's shoulder with the back of her left hand. "Hey" announced Brice, with a quick chuckle. The two ate in silence for the next few minutes. "So do you remember Andrew Placer?" Brice asked, watching the various cars out on the track. "From our F-Ford days?" he further inquired. Sondra nodded as she chewed, glancing over at her teammate. "He's in Europe" supplied the boy. "Driving an F-Ford but trying to get onto an F-three team, and he's got an IndyCar deal in the works for next year."

"Wow" said Sondra.

"Yeah" continued Brice. "We got to be pretty good friends during the F-Ford season and we keep in touch pretty regularly. I've been to his parents' place in southern California. Naples. At the back of the house, well it's a total mansion, there's a river, more like a canal, that's basically their backyard. They're all super into boats and sailing. Andrew's dad is a part owner of an America's Cup racing boat. We went to Catalina Island on a nineteen footer when I was there last. The Placers are super rich but really nice. Never make you feel like crap for not having money." Sondra narrowed her eyes at the boy. She hated talking about money but felt the need to make an exception in this case. "You're not exactly on skid-row" she argued. "I mean your family's wheat farm is a pretty substantial operation. Something more than just some small family farm. And it allows you to be doing what you're doing." Brice took a bite of his burrito and studied the girl as she went back to her sandwich. His insides suddenly felt as if they were doing flip-flops over the fact that Sondra had most likely taken the time to go online to look up his family's business. It was this revelation that gave him the courage to divulge something of a more personal nature. "The life of a farmer and the life of a racing driver are so polar opposites" he began. "My choice hasn't been easy on my family and it just basically destroyed things between me and Jillian."

"Jillian and me" corrected Sondra of the boy's grammar.

"Oh sorry, teach" he responded with a sarcastic edge to his voice. "We country folks don't know 'bout such learnin' things." Sondra observed him through narrowed eyes before looking down at the blob of chicken-salad filling that had dropped, bouncing off the middle of her chest and into her lap. She quickly grabbed it and stuffed it into her mouth, then wiped her lips with the back of her hand. Brice scrambled to come up with a sarcastic line about her being a sloppy eater but was mesmerized by her and his brain turned to mush.

"Sorry about Jillian" offered Sondra. "I know you cared a lot about her."

"Is there someone you care about?" asked Brice. "You've never mentioned a boyfriend, past or present and you always get mad when I ask you anything personal."

Sondra shook her head, determined to ignore the last part of what he'd just said. "I liked this guy way back in grade-school" she diffused. "I mean we weren't really boyfriend and girlfriend but we had fun at recess together and we held hands a few times. Just silly kid stuff. I don't have the interest or the time now for all that lovey-dovey crap. I just don't care. I'm one-hundred-percent focused on my racing career and there's no room for anything else." She took a determined large bite of sandwich and chewed with vigor while Brice went from staring at the girl to watching the pit action, feeling sorry for Sondra and guessing that her view on romance and dating had everything to do with losing her family. With the remainder of time they spent together he purposely kept the topic of conversation to cars and racing.

The Mid-Ohio Sports Car Course was 2.258 miles in length and featured eleven turns. Sondra loved the flow of the track and was quick to develop a rhythm that had her in the top three in all practices for this next championship round. Qualifying efforts the next day didn't go as planned. She was on a hot-lap but was forced out onto the grass by a car that had spun and slid back out onto the racing surface. The #10 car sustained a broken front wing, a bent front A-arm and other minor rear-suspension damage. She started

Saturday morning's race from last place on the grid, but due to smart strong driving coupled with an unusual number of crashes further up the field ultimately finished 3rd. Her teammate had been one of the unfortunate crash victims, as was the current series points leader Phil Grumenchino who'd not won many races this season but always seemed to finish in the top 5. Round 14 of the championship the next day was a complete turnaround for the two Patrero-McDonald's Indy Lights teams. During qualifying Sondra got her first Pole Position of the season and in the race she led from flag to flag, stretching her lead to 7.553 seconds. Brice started from the 3rd position and remained there to the end due to questionable blocking by Phil Grumenchino. The two boys got into a fist fight in the pits seconds after the conclusion of the race but no disciplinary action took place over the physical altercation. There were also no penalties assessed for Grumenchino's race tactics, even though Hugo Patrero himself lodged a formal if not animated complaint to IndyCar and Race Control.

With Sondra's Round 14 win she'd clawed her way into the top spot in the championship, something she was far happier to celebrate than turning 18 the next day. She was grateful to spend this particular Monday mostly in travel and alone with Doug and Karen. From her seat in the motorhome, behind her now-parents, Sondra silently brooded about the fact that yet another milestone in her life had to be marked without the mom and dad she'd grown up with or the brothers who always made celebrations such as birthdays so bright. Doug and Karen were determined to spoil their girl rotten and by day's end Sondra went to sleep feeling loved and grateful for the things and people she did have in her life. Since the next four days would be void of mandatory race activities Karen seized the opportunity in orchestrating a visit to Pennsylvania, where George and Mary were happy to get in on a continuation of Sondra's birthday celebration.

Gateway Motorsports Park in Maddison, Illinois was the site for Indy Lights Testing. This was to precede the second-to-last race of the year. The 1.25 mile oval was something Sondra worried herself literally sick over but catching a cold and not feeling her usual self may have contributed to her focus and determination to step up her game, as she put it, in paved oval-track racing. She'd been upset with herself for what she saw as her shortcomings at Indianapolis and now was determined to prove to herself and others that she could be strong on any track. Within the first few practice laps it was obvious that she had a fast car and her team was quick to help in getting the handling dialed in for the first of four full days of on-track testing and important lectures by IndyCar officials. Brice was hoping that there would be the usual hanging-out time with his teammate and felt robbed that the opportunity never seemed to present itself. If Sondra wasn't giving interviews, posing for pictures or signing autographs, Doug and Karen were either next to her or taking her somewhere.

Qualifying for Saturday's race gave Brice his third Pole of the year, with his teammate qualifying 4th. That night at a dinner given by Cooper Tires he seized an opportunity to spend a few minutes alone with Sondra. After a bit of small-talk about the meal that had been served, Sondra congratulated him on his Pole achievement. "Thanks" he smiled, ushering her to a quiet corner of the vast room. "Haven't had time to talk much to you lately."

"With you" she corrected. He ignored the grammar lesson and pulled a small cloth satchel from his sport-coat pocket. "This is a little bit late but, happy birthday" he told her as he presented the gift.

"Thanks" she cheered as she pulled on the strings to open the soft purple bag. "Wow. Thank you" she said as she pulled out a unique bracelet.

"I got it for you a few weeks ago" he admitted. "At Mid-Ohio. The promotion guys at Firestone were giving these out. I guess this is kinda silly but …"

"No" said Sondra with a shake of her head. "Not silly. I wanted one of these. You're awesome." The bracelet was made from recycled tires and there was a short metal clip crimped around the rubber material that featured the tire company's logo embossed into it. Sondra had seen many fellow Indy Lights drivers with them and had intended to pick one up herself. She slipped the band onto her right wrist and flung her arms around Brice, engaging the two in a tight embrace. Young Crandle was in heaven. He didn't want to let her go but was mindful not to prolong the hug revealing his growing feelings for the young woman. He felt her warmth, and though she was a finely toned athlete he enjoyed her feminine softness. He also breathed in the intoxicating scent of her hair. As the two released each other Sondra squinted at him. "Did you just kiss my hair?" she asked.

"No" Brice adamantly denied. "I wouldn't do that. That would be …"

"Weird and creepy?" she said, finishing his sentence.

"Well I would think it would be more like sweet and endearing" he countered.

"Okay" she said in a half whisper, smiling and again flinging her arms around the boy. "We'll go with your thing" she added. This second embrace didn't last as long as the first, both feeling a bit embarrassed for the sudden outburst of affection toward one another. When she pulled away she slugged Brice on the shoulder. It wasn't a hard or painful hit and she observed the same goofy smile on his face as the one she'd witnessed when he'd kissed her at their Formula Ford banquet a year ago.

During Sunday's Indy Lights race Brice's 1.204 second lead came to an abrupt halt when car #49 lost grip and slid into the #9, who was going around him on the outside of the entrance to Turn 1. This resulted in heavy contact with the retaining wall for both cars, shredding wings and collapsing suspension pieces. Matt Facia and Brice Crandle were off-track friends and though the crash and championship implications for Brice were devastating he was quite relieved that neither he nor Matt had been injured. On Lap 31 Sondra inherited the lead from Gary Menard when the #3's engine went sour. After a few minutes in the pits with Menard's mechanics looking over the power-plant, Gary's crew chief ordered him to cut the motor because their day was done. Sondra never liked winning this way. It didn't seem like a fair and square race victory but a win was a win and this meant a healthier lead in the championship going into the final round the following week. She was particularly pleased with the winner's trophy, thinking it resembled the shape of a soup tureen that

Karen and Doug had received as a wedding present.

Watkins Glen, New York was the sight set for the Indy Lights' Rounds 16 and 17, their season finale. Sondra was stoic and focused as usual but there was a new element, extreme anxiety over the ending of her race season. The names and faces she'd come across each and every week, as well as a few new and memorable people she'd encountered along the way would be lost to her by Sunday night. Sondra never spoke of this and tried her best to push it out of her mind. It felt to her like a hard and lonely fall down a dark tunnel, sure she'd never be able to stop or return unscathed. It hurled the unthinkable loss of her family at her with the ugliest of forces. Then there was her teammate. Over the course of six months she'd gone from extreme loathing to tolerating him and just recently she'd begun to view him as a fun and attractive boy. So many times she'd find Brice near or next to her in team meetings, sponsor events and the mandatory pre-race drivers meetings. He'd make observations, ask rhetorical questions and crack jokes that Sondra thought to be moronically nutty. She wouldn't and couldn't admit this to herself but was feeling both emotional and physical pain at the very notion of separation from him. She knew this separation feeling all too well, experiencing it for the first time years ago while lying in a hospital bed and becoming cognizant of the fact that she was alone, without her family. This painful wound never seemed to lessen or heal. Even in her happiest moments now it was always just beneath the surface.

Sondra, in her #10 car, qualified 3rd for the Watkins Glen Indy Lights Grand Prix, and Saturday's event started out quite similar to the last Formula Ford race at Laguna Seca, with Brice and Sondra making quite a few people very nervous about their seemingly vicious attacks on one another. The lead strategists for both teams didn't want to discourage their driver's competitiveness but they did remind them that they were ultimately teammates, with a boss and car-owner who would not be okay with them taking each other out. Deep into the race and going through the bus-stop, a chicane before Turn 5, Sondra was saving fuel and tires, 1.003 seconds behind Crandle when she got tapped hard from a guy missing his breaking point, spinning off track but then bouncing back onto the racing surface. It was a glancing blow into Sondra's right-rear tire, hard enough to send her spinning and severely breaking the A-arm. The driver of the #10 car became irate, shouting obscenities and pounding her fists on the steering wheel. Both Steven Barnes and Phil Wallin emphatically warned her not to get out of the car or have any altercation with Michael Schelds. Penalties for inappropriate racetrack procedures could possibly jeopardize their championship. At the conclusion of the race the #9 car received the checkered flag, just over three seconds in the lead. Brice's post-race enthusiastic and emotional victory celebration rivaled his Indianapolis win, though he did feel bad for his teammate. The next day, with all sorts of momentum on his side, Brice snagged the Pole for the final race of the year, while Sondra was slated to start 5th. When the field went green for the Indy Lights finale, Sondra flashed by the 4th Place car going into the first turn on Lap 1. She then entered into a terrific battle with the #3 and the #28 for the next seven laps. Brazilian-born Manuel Polenzio in the #55 red-white-blue car got around Brice going into Turn 11 on Lap 14, and two laps later Sondra was tucked right to the back of her teammate. She out-broke him going into Turn 1 and got around, setting her sights on the leader. Three laps later Sondra caught the #55 and went around him coming out of the last corner. Crandle took over that second spot two and half laps later, going into Turn 1. These top-three cars broke away from the field, lapping most. The #10 of Sierre, the #9 of Crandle and the #55 of Polenzio dueled and swapped the lead for the next eight laps, but when it counted Sondra was not to be outdone. With 4 laps remaining she took back the lead from her teammate and began to distance the 2nd and 3rd Place cars handily. Darren appeared in the #10 pit and hollered to Steven Barnes. "That kid's just been playing with them the whole time, hasn't she?" The proud Indy Lights lead strategist developed a wicked grin and adjusted his headset mike. He then spoke to his driver, giving Sondra the current lap-time and interval from her to the 2nd Place car.

The podium celebrations for the Indy Lights Series lacked a bit of the luster and large-scale public viewing as the IndyCar series, but on this day Sondra, Brice and Manuel celebrated as if they were high above thousands of fans on a Formula One podium. The two boys hated being beaten by a girl, again, but they'd done well all season long and this race had proved to be some of the most fun driving they'd ever done. Hugo Patrero was on hand for the Lights podium ceremony as well, where the top three race finishers were given their trophies and their due. There was also acknowledgment of the top three finishers in the championship. Sondra took highest honors, followed by Phil Grumenchino and Brice Crandle. The festivities only lasted about 12 minutes, being that the main focus of the day was the IndyCar race, which was about to get underway in roughly an hour and forty minutes. Out of earshot of many, especially race media, Hugo put his arm around Brice and congratulated him on a gallant effort that day and on a damn fine season. Sondra listened in disbelief as the legendary car and team owner offered Brice the IndyCar #48 seat and team position for the next season. Tradition usually had it that when an Indy Lights driver wins the championship and there is a position available on the IndyCar side of a team's organization, that driver gets the spot. Sondra had been counting on this for many months, picturing herself working with Darren Brown and the Patrero IndyCar engineers on all the big important races next season, especially the Indy 500. She stood there feeling devastated and stunned, then mad as hell as she hurried over to the nearby Doug and Karen. They made a hasty retreat to their motorhome.

"Stupid Brice" growled Sondra as she sat on the RV's couch to take off her racing shoes. "And Patrero's such a piece of ..."

"Sondra" scolded Karen, cutting off the girl's intended foul language. "I know you're mad" continued the mom. "And you have every right to be, but whining and swearing about it doesn't change anything. Now go hop in the shower."

When Sondra later emerged from the back of the motorhome and entered the small mobile living room dressed in her team uniform she noted that Karen was nowhere in sight. Doug was seated on the couch reading a book that Sondra had been studying. It contained information on Hot Laps around many race courses, with detailed descriptions of certain factors to watch for on the track as well as lap-times in various classes of cars. “Where’s Mom?” asked Sondra.

“She went to meet Betty-Ann Fernlauo at the administration building to discuss the future promotion of Safen-Up. Your friend Shelley Enesbridge sent us a long text message. She said she’s sorry for being so busy these last two weeks.”

Sondra nodded and shrugged her right shoulder. “I wish we could skip the championship banquet thing tonight and just go home right now” she told Doug.

“Well” he began, hoping to redirect her energy. “You don’t want to miss getting that big trophy and those great big cardboard checks, do you?” Sondra again shrugged and came to rest next to Doug, briefly leaning her head on his shoulder. She was sore and tired and closed her eyes. In the safety and serenity of the RV, next to the person she loved and trusted, she drifted off to sleep. It wasn’t a long nap however. She woke with a start, hearing someone knocking on the door to the motorhome. Doug got up to answer it. “Oh hey, Darren” Doug greeted the man. “Come on in.”

Once inside and seated, Darren spoke in a pleasant but quick manner, glancing at his watch and looking mostly at Sondra. “The GP starts in less than thirty minutes so I need to make this quick” he said. “Congratulations on the championship, Sondra. That was a hell of a drive you just did. Your career so far wouldn’t even make a believable movie.”

Doug smiled with pride as he thought about how Sondra had won four championships in four years, all while finishing high school, growing up so well and starting college. He became concerned however when he glanced over at his daughter. He’d seen this face before. She was clenching her teeth, obviously mad and her deadly serious stare made Darren noticeably uncomfortable. The man recovered quickly however and leaned forward in the chair across from Sondra and Doug. With his arms on his legs and his fingers intertwining, the tone of his voice changed to match Sondra’s intensity. “I know you think you’re getting a raw deal, with Crandle getting the forty-eight seat instead of you” he said with a nod. “I agree" he furthered. "I see great things in your driving and I've tried to do the best I could to help your career. It hasn't been widely known but this is actually my last year with the Patrero-McDonald's team, and it's not just because I disagree with Hugo about the Crandle pick. I've been wanting a change for a little while now. You may have heard a rumor or two floating around that Craig Pines and I are planning on making the move to Holt Racing." Sondra nodded. T.J. Holt was a celebrated driver and team-owner, with four Indianapolis 500 victories as a driver. All throughout Sondra's childhood she and her father had rooted for T.J. while they listened to the 500 on the radio or watched it on TV.

"I can't go into detail just yet" said Darren, glancing at his watch. "But he and I have actually been in talks here and there for the past several years now. He's hungry for change and success and I'm ready for change myself. I think Patrero is too. I've known Hugo for a lot of years. He's been damn good to me and he's really impressed with you Sondra, but here's the thing ... He's unwaveringly old-world when it comes to women in sports, especially auto racing. He's gonna offer you a good chunk of change and another year as lead driver for this Lights team, but he wants to bring Kenneth Overton and Brice Crandle along for their IndyCar efforts. I know that offer should have gone to you, and rightfully so, but this is a brutal sport. Don't get discouraged, Sondra. I'm working on things with you in mind. Gonna be a hard sell with T.J. because he's just as old-school but we've talked about you."

"Wow" said Sondra, feeling a rush. To have such a famous driver and team owner give her any kind of thought was heady stuff indeed.

"You enjoy your championship awards ceremony tonight" said Darren in conclusion, getting to his feet. "And good luck in school. I'll be in touch, you can count on that."

"Thanks, Darren" said Sondra, standing and holding out her hand. "I can assure you, everything you've done for me hasn't gone unnoticed or unappreciated" she told him in earnest.

The evening's Indy Lights championship awards ceremony had Sondra doing her best to adhere to her parents-manager's request of being calm, polite and a gracious winner. She skillfully avoided her teammate as much as possible but at one point Brice found an opportunity to speak with her. Sondra had just come from the restroom and was choosing a bottle of water out of a large ice-filled bowl. "I know you must hate me now" he began. "I didn't lobby for the forty-eight ride, honest" he told her. "And I told Hugo that it should go to you" he added.

"I don't hate you, Brice" said Sondra in a sharp voice that suggested otherwise. She punched him on the shoulder. He knew for sure now that she was mad because the contact was a bit painful, though he tried his best not to show it. "Well, congratulations again on the championship" he told her. She gave a slight nod of acknowledgment. She wanted to tell him off, that she'd beaten him fair and square on the racetrack that day and many others, and that she'd now beaten him in two consecutive championships. Instead she opted for a more civil tact.

"I like your sister, Lauren" she told him. "We had a nice talk about school. That's really great that she and your folks could be here tonight." Brice used this as an opening. "Yeah, my folks being here means a lot" he told her. "Especially now. It's been a tough year for the farm. Bad weather and low wheat prices." He wanted to say more but Sondra hadn't altered her flat stare nor did she offer any kind of sympathy for his family's predicament, as he had pictured.

"Well I wish you and your folks good luck with that" Sondra told the boy. She set the plastic bottle of water on the table and gave a quick wave. "We have a really early flight tomorrow morning" she told him as she began to turn away. Brice stood stunned, with an ever increasing sick feeling in his stomach as he watched Sondra disappear from sight, perhaps from his life.

CHAPTER 21

Several weeks after Sondra had resumed her academic career Shelley Enesbridge paid a visit to the Fresno condo. Sondra's business math lab had run long, and upon returning home she opened the front door to hear the voices of Doug, Karen and Shelley in the kitchen. "SeaShell!" exclaimed the young college student, setting her cell phone and keys on the counter. Doug chuckled lightly upon hearing his daughter's pet name for Shelley, especially since Sondra often denounced pet names. Shelley had arrived just over 40 minutes prior and was happily getting better acquainted with Sondra's parents. She quickly initiated an embrace with her friend, Sondra. "Winning a championship and now back hard at it at college" stated Shelley. Sondra shrugged and developed a shy smile. "I like my classes so far" she told the small group. "Socioeconomics class is gonna be pretty brutal. There'll be lots of quizzes, papers and projects, but nothing I can't handle. I have a business structuring class and a marketing class that are gonna be a lot of work but really interesting, and I think they'll be sort of fun. And I thought my business math class was gonna be a tedious snooze-fest but it's pretty cool and I have really great classmates. Wanna see my big fancy trophy?" she asked Shelley in an abrupt child-like non sequitur. The two women exited the kitchen and headed to Sondra's bedroom.

"Wow, that is fancy" said Shelley of Sondra's copy of the Indy Lights championship trophy. "And you have a mighty impressive collection of other trophies here as well" she added as her eyes drifted upwards to scan the shelves Doug had installed around the room, holding proof that Sondra was a successful race car driver. Shelley sat on the bed and patted the space next to her, indicating an interest in a more meaningful conversation. "I really like Doug and Karen" she announced softly.

"Yeah, they're pretty okay" said Sondra, sitting next to her friend.

"Pretty special people" stated Shelley. "And thank you for letting me use you and the creation of Safen-Up for my master's thesis. Dr. Okursta loved the idea when I pitched it to the master's board but he's been on my case every step of the way with the details. It's been a bear but now I'm glad he pushed me that hard. It was just what I needed, and my parents and sister Caitlin have been so supportive and a lot of help. They even helped me fast-track the licensing process. I'm now a full-fledged doctoral clinician. I can join a practice or start my own."

"Is that why you're here?" asked Sondra. "Because you think I need therapy?"

Shelley did think Sondra could benefit from some form of talk therapy, and with the schooling she'd just been through she'd come to think most could. With the limited time she'd spent in talking with Sondra, Shelley had found the young woman to be an intuitive and highly intelligent seeker of answers but one who also worked within a rigid framework and was determined to figure out the complexities of her life on her own, skillfully avoiding the tremendous darkness and pain that stemmed from losing her family. "One doesn't need therapy" soothed Shelley. "And that's not remotely why I'm here. You've entrusted me with Safen-Up, and what I've created is something that basically has your imprint in all aspects but it's something that you can have as much or as little input into as you want. You'll be able to have oversight and a lot of control but it won't ever detract from your racing."

"So you're gonna do this for real?" asked Sondra. "Safen-Up? A real nonprofit? Not just something for your Masters degree?"

"For real" said Shelley, nodding with sincerity.

Sondra went to her desk. She pulled from a bottom drawer an 8x10 photograph of her in her race suit. "I kinda like this picture" she told her friend. "Doug took this last year and I think it looks like a professional promo shot, but it's not connected to anything that would have copyright issues. Maybe we could use it somehow for …"

"Definitely" nodded Shelley. "Perhaps the Safen-Up masthead." Sondra and Shelley proceeded to talk for close to 20 minutes, mostly about the nonprofit but other topics were touched upon as well, including a number of anecdotes Sondra had about her Indy Lights race season. Shelley picked up on the anger and bitterness the girl harbored for Brice on how things had transpired with driver advancement within the Patrero-McDonald's team.

"He's called and texted me like a billion times" said Sondra. Brice had called once and had sent only two text messages. "I'm back to hating him and I sure as hell have no intention of talking to him or answering any of his moronic messages" she added, making a fist. "Boys are so stupid."

Shelley took a deep breath, surprised and pleased when Sondra followed her lead in the breathing exercise. "Sure" she agreed, leaning to the right to bump Sondra gently with her shoulder. "Boys can be stupid sometimes" she added. "But you worked together as teammates for what, the last seven months? How was that?"

Sondra shrugged her right shoulder before answering. "Well I guess maybe he wasn't stupid all the time" admitted Sondra reluctantly, subconsciously playing with the bracelet on her right wrist that he'd given her. She suddenly wondered why she hadn't taken it off and discarded it.

"Yeah?" prodded Shelley. Again Sondra shrugged her right shoulder. "I mean we had some laughs and some good talks but it seemed like he was always babbling on about someone in his family."

"You used the word babbling" pointed out Shelley. "You didn't like when he spoke of his family?"

Sondra shrugged and looked at her watch. "I'm staying for dinner"

Shelley informed her friend. "You have a cooking mom" she added with a nod. "Karen was telling me earlier that she made a big chicken pot pie from scratch. That sounds delicious. The extent of my mother's cooking when I was growing up was the occasional making of toast or heating up soup. We had chefs and an entire kitchen staff." Sondra pictured in her mind the scene out of a TV movie she'd once watched with her friend Kari in Bakersfield. The filmed sequence took place in an underground kitchen in an elaborate castle in England. There were many maids and kitchen staff working frantically to assemble the main meal of the day for the prominent family that lived upstairs.

"Karen's a great cook" informed Sondra, looking down at her dark blue running shoes. Shelley thought about getting the girl to elaborate on Karen and then inquiring about her biological mother but they were talking about Brice and she didn't want to lose this conversational thread.

"Did you like the stories Brice told about his family?" asked Shelley.

Sondra looked up at a poster on the wall that Doug had given her for her last birthday, a colorful photo of the celebrated late Ayrton Senna at speed in a blue and white Rothmans Honda Formula One car. "I usually tried to stick to topics of cars and racing" she told Shelley of Brice. "We did for the most part but sometimes I got the feeling that he talked about his family on purpose because he wanted me to talk about mine. I mean I had to tell him like a trillion times that was off limits."

"Why off limits?" prompted Shelley. Sondra swallowed hard and loud.

"Because it's my family" said Sondra, sounding as if she were on the verge of tears. "My memories" she growled. "I have to protect them and keep 'em safe." She bit down on her tongue and clenched her fists.

"Sure, I get that" soothed Shelley. "And good for you. But sometimes one can hold on too tight. From the few things you've told me about your parents and your brothers they sound great and worthy of celebrating and even bragging about a little. Do you think maybe it's less about them and more about you being afraid of getting close to Brice?"

Sondra stood and walked over to her desk, pulling open the drawer from which she'd earlier retrieved the photo of herself. She took out a Patrero-McDonald's promotional photo of her and Brice in their race suits, standing in front of their Indy Lights cars. She handed the unframed picture to Shelley and sat back down, watching her friend study the image. "If I use the word adorable" began Shelley.

"Don't be gross" interjected Sondra. Shelley looked at her friend with a knowing smirk. She watched the girl fold her arms and roll her eyes. "So tell me about the hate" Shelley requested of the girl's earlier statement. "Tell me more about this Brice that you hate" she added, tapping on the photo. Sondra shifted her seated position on the bed and fidgeted but eventually detailed the beginnings of her involvement with Brice all the way through to their current status. The act of doing so, with Shelley's occasional observations and comments, seemed to take away much of the anger, fear and resentment of the boy. "I still hate it that he got the IndyCar spot and not me" she concluded. Shelley nodded and offered a further observation. "But it doesn't sound as if he set out to intentionally hurt you or rob you of the position. It sounds like he honestly likes you and respects you. Besides, from what you just described it doesn't sound like this Hugo Patrero is the nicest of employers. Doug and Karen seem to be incredibly confident that you'll find a much better situation."

Sondra shrugged and gave a single nod. "I hope so" she told Shelley with a shy smile. "Lets go see if dinner's ready, and I'll show you a race video that mom shot of me during the Lights GP at Watkins Glen in New York a few weeks ago, where I won."

During the after-dinner viewing of the Watkins Glen race footage Sondra felt almost giddy with contentment as she Doug, Karen and Shelley enjoyed the blueberry cheesecake that Shelley had brought. The doorbell rang out and Sondra was the one to jump up to open the door. "Oh hey, Darren" said an astonished Sondra. "This is a nice unexpected surprise. Come on in." Sondra announced Darren's arrival and introduced the man to Shelley. "This is my great friend

SeaShell" she told him. "And SeaShell, this is Darren Brown. A great friend to our family."

"Shelley Enesbridge" corrected the woman with a quick laugh and a smile, extending her hand. Darren was instantly captivated by Shelley and during their warm handshake he returned her smile, chuckling to himself that Sondra had referred to the beautiful woman before him as SeaShell.

"Loveliest seashell I've ever encountered" he announced.

"Thank you, Mr. Brown" Shelley responded. "I've heard Sondra speak of you many times. Always positive, I can assure you."

"Call me Darren" insisted the still-smiling man. "And Hi Karen. Hi Doug" he added. "Sorry to interrupt and just spring by unannounced but I spent a couple of days with friends in San Francisco and I'm on my way for meetings in LA and San Diego. Thought I'd make a bit of a detour to check in on our little champion hothead here" he said, looking over to Sondra.

"I'm not a hothead" denied Sondra, folding her arms and feigning indignation as the four elders chuckled lightly observing the girl's reaction.

"Well I should get going" announced Shelley. "Oh don't leave on my account" said Darren. "I really do apologize for the interruption." Shelley shook her head. "I was about to head for home anyway" she assured the man.

"Where's home?" Darren inquired. Shelley revealed her destination and Karen stepped forward, instinctively trying to play matchmaker. "Darren" she announced, "perhaps you'd be so kind as to give Miss Enesbridge a lift to the airport."

"Be happy to" he agreed. "But first I have a little bit of race business that I didn't want to do over the phone."

"Well have a seat" invited Karen. Sondra eyed the man as he settled on one end of the living room couch, dubious of his next words. Darren didn't exactly have good news for Sondra, the news he knew she wanted but what he had to say wasn't exactly bad.

"Well like I've told you before" he began, speaking mostly to Sondra. "I'm sorry how things turned out with Patrero but as you may have heard, Pines, Hestrovich and a few other of my longtime crew have joined me in switching organizations."

"I know" said Sondra. "There's been quite an uproar on social media about your switching from one huge-name team to another."

Darren nodded, fully aware and proud of all the attention he was getting. "Well going to Holt Racing is a monumental switch" he continued. "But T.J. and the Holt management group are a better fit for me. There's an energy there that was missing from my situation with Patrero. Holt Racing's been wanting a major change for a while and the driver choices for next year were some pretty intense discussions, I can tell you that. I fought for you, and you were seriously considered. It was between you and three other guys. These are tricky economic times and this is a tough business. A lot of teams are just too afraid to take chances on young inexperienced drivers and T.J. wants to go with experience in a teammate for Delgato this season."

Sondra felt a mixture of emotions. A wave of heavy goosebumps hit her as she thought of the legendary 4-time Indy 500 winner and high-profile team owner T.J. Holt actually giving her serious thought for his team. On the other hand it was upsetting to be so close yet so far away from her IndyCar dream. She was counting on being in this series and had been fantasizing for weeks about driving for T.J. Holt. Darren's news was a devastating blow and she sat frozen, staring intently at Karen's wedding ring as her now-mom's fingers gripped the handle of her coffee cup. Sondra waited, barely able to breathe in anticipation of Darren's next words. "T.J. Holt's a grumpy cantankerous old curmudgeon with views on women in racing that make Hugo Patrero seem like he might be next in line for the new leader of the National Organization For Women" he announced. "But like I said, that's not why he's going with someone else. He is impressed with you, Sondra. A lot of people are. Sometimes it just comes down to money and timing." Darren stood and took a business card out of his shirt pocket, offering it to Sondra. "Every time you get into a race car you manage to do things no one expects. I've been watchin' this for years and so have a hell of a lot of others" he told her.

Sondra took the piece of paper without looking at it and stood, along with the others in the room. "Call this guy" Darren instructed. "It's not IndyCar but he's looking for a driver and he knows all about you."

"Boy" said Shelley, shaking her head and putting an arm around Sondra. "This racing business seems pretty dicey."

"Oh you don't know the half of it" smiled Darren. "I can tell you stories and I'd love to hear some of your stories as well."

Before Shelley left with Darren to the airport she gave Sondra a hug. "I'll call you, soonish" she told the girl. As soon as the front door closed, Sondra crumpled the card Darren had given her and threw it angrily on the gray carpeting. Doug and Karen watched as the girl stormed off to her room and slammed the door shut. Karen started after her but Doug held her back with a gentle but firm touch to her upper arm. "No" he said in a soft deep voice. "Give her a little space." Karen took a deep thoughtful breath and wrapped her arms around her husband.

"Doug?" she whispered.

"It's gonna be okay" he assured her. He gave his wife a soft kiss and picked up the discarded item Sondra had thrown on the floor.

Doug and Karen were over halfway through the viewing of an old James Bond movie when Sondra emerged from her room. She was wearing the blue plaid flannel boy's pajamas Karen had given her for Christmas. The couple parted and encouraged the girl to sit between them on the couch. When the movie ended Doug turned off the entertainment system and Sondra sat on the coffee table facing her now-parents. "I called Greg Wilente" she announced.

"What on earth for?" inquired Karen. "The man's a jerk and they all barely believed in you" she added."

"I know" said Sondra. "I told him about almost getting to drive for T.J. Holt and I wanted to let him know I was shopping around for a future ride. No stone left unturned, as they say."

"So what did ol' Wilente say?" asked Doug.

"Well he congratulated me on my Indy Lights championship, in a round-about sort of way" said Sondra. "And he suggested I look into international teams. Formula Ford or Formula Three." Doug nodded and pulled the card Darren had given her from his left-front jeans pocket. "Like this guy?" he asked Sondra rhetorically. "Bernard Hesmith" he added, reading from the card. "I called the number while you were in your room pouting" he told his daughter. "Didn't get to actually speak with him but his assistant gave me a little info. You interested?" Sondra nodded. She'd either heard or read the name Bernard Hesmith somewhere but in the moment she couldn't quite place him. "Apparently he's a pretty multi-faceted guy" explained Doug of Bernard. "Longtime chassis innovator for Swift. He's been involved in Formula One a few times as a co-owner but his main focus these days is on his two V-Eight Supercar teams. As it happens he's looking for good but below-the-radar test drivers for a new Formula Ford Swift chassis. The operation is based out of Silverstone, England. There'll be plenty of testing but they plan on running the new cars in a few F-Ford championship races. This is an incredible opportunity and it means the chance to get a European racing license." Sondra shifted her position so she wasn't sitting on an uncomfortable stack of magazines. "Formula Ford" she pondered, sounding a bit dejected. "Seems like a step backwards in my career but I'd love to be on that Silverstone track. Would you guys go with me?"

"No" said Doug, surprising Karen. "It's a pretty limited two-week deal. Not much pay. They'll cover your food, lodging and transportation expenses and you might have a little extra left over. I hate the idea of you going so far away but I think this is something to seriously consider."

"I agree" said a reluctant Karen. "As long as it's not gonna interfere with school and will only be for a couple of weeks" she added. Sondra changed the uncomfortable subject of being away from her beloved now-parents to her previous conversation with Greg Wilente. "Greg said that they're planning on auctioning off my old F Ford car in the near future but they're willing to give me dibs on buying it first. We didn't talk price but I told him I wanted it and I'd rent a trailer to come pick it up."

Doug smiled at the prospect but a rather dubious Karen stood and collected the empty coffee cups from around the room. "To what end?" she asked the girl before heading to the kitchen. "And just where are you planning on keeping it?" furthered the mom.

"Oh I think Stoltz would be more than happy to have it in his showroom" said Doug. "Yeah" agreed Sondra, not having thought of this herself. "I mean he made quite a display out of my old sprint-car" she added. "I don't think it's too big a leap to think he wouldn't want my F-Ford car as well." "Sure" said Karen with a quick smile. "It's late. Lets go to bed and we'll talk more about it in the morning."

Sondra accepted the offer from Hesmith Motorsports to be part of an international test team for the Formula Ford Swift chassis. With solid future plans in place she finally resigned to speak with Brice. By the end of an 18 minute phone conversation, where she purposely kept to a mostly scholastic theme and the many racing opportunities available in Europe, they were back on friendly terms. Absent however were the unspoken romantic overtones of previous interactions. She maintained a level of resentment for his new position on the Patrero IndyCar team but her future focus was allowing this feeling to slowly dissipate.

Darren stayed in touch with the Trents from time to time but knew Sondra needed to stay focused on school. On graduation day, a triumphant milestone in Sondra's life, it was a happy surprise for Sondra that he took the time to make a heartfelt congratulatory call. He was in Birmingham, Alabama, at the Barber Motorsports Park track with the newly reorganized Holt Racing team for preseason testing. His call came to Sondra not long after she'd arrived home from a magical graduation dinner with Doug, Karen, Dan and Vanessa Stoltz. She was sitting on her bed feeling full from the meal and completely exhausted from a week-long push of studying for finals. She'd set her cell phone on top of her dresser and it began to make an annoying buzzing noise. Letting it alone at first, she considered simply allowing the call go to voice-mail, but took a deep breath and answered in as energetic way as possible. During the relatively short chat Sondra thanked Darren for the call and cherished his words of how preseason testing was going. She also felt a rush at hearing how he was continuing to plant the seed in convincing the powers that be make her part of Holt Racing's future.

When the call ended she set her phone down next to the bouquet of red geraniums Brice had sent from a local florist as a graduation present. One of the very few times she'd given Brice a glimpse into her past came during the weekend of Indy Lights oval testing in Illinois last August. She and Brice had been walking with several others back to the pits after a team meeting. Kathy Dornman, the logistics coordinator for the #9 team, was wearing a hat in the shape and color of a sunflower. Several comments and a bit of ribbing derived from this and when Sondra was jokingly asked if they were going to see her wear similar headwear in the future Brice took note when she gave a definitive, no. "I mean I don't have a thing against flowers" she had stated. "I used to love the row of red geraniums that were growing all along the side of a barn when I was a kid."

Sondra stood in front of her chest-high dresser and looked at herself in the horizontal mirror above it, clutching the beads on the necklace that her mother had purchased for her years ago. She'd debated in her mind for several days on wearing it on this day, worrying that it might bring her to tears at an inopportune time, but in the end allowed Karen to persuade her to wear it on this auspicious occasion. Sondra's eyes went from the image of herself in the mirror to the geraniums. Shiny teardrops appeared and got thicker and heavier, threatening to carve their way down her cheek. Karen entered the room through the open doorway to say goodnight. She took quick note of the girl's emotional state and stood behind her, wrapping her arms around Sondra and squeezing, with a gentle rocking motion. Little Miss Tough as Nails made a half-hearted attempt at wriggling away but Karen squeezed tighter and planted a gentle kiss on top of the girl's left shoulder. "Happy day and hard day, all in one" stated Karen in a soft whisper. She let go and Sondra turned to face her. She noted that the girl was still wearing the necklace. "Your parents and your brothers would have been so proud of you today" she told her. Sondra was afraid to open her mouth in answer. She'd been going on raw emotion since 3:47 a.m. and was now collapsing inward without being able to stop it. She flung her arms around Karen and held her tight, flooding her now-mom's shoulder with a torrent of steady tears. As if on cue, Doug entered the fray. His arms encircled both women for as much comfort and encouragement as he could administer.

The day before Sondra was to leave for England she decided to prepare her own bon voyage family dinner. Going to the grocery store with nothing but excellent intentions in obtaining ingredients to create a culinary masterpiece she quickly altered the plan, coming upon several items. The first was a bag of salad mix she planned to put in one of Karen's fancy salad bowls as if she'd chopped and created the salad herself. Sondra then spotted a large frozen lasagna, the kind one simply heats and serves, which she would place in a casserole dish as if it had been made from scratch. She also found frozen and sliced garlic bread to thaw and heat in the toaster oven.

Doug had resumed his towing business in this off-season. Walking through the front door of the condo after his long day he gravitated to the audio sounds in the den, smiling to himself when he discovered Sondra intently watching, for the third time, the video of the last Indy 500 that Dan Stoltz had recorded and given her. Without a word he gave his daughter two heavy pats on the top of her head, enjoying her slight giggle as he came around to sit next to her. Karen arrived home close to twenty minutes later. Unlike Doug, she outwardly reacted to the smell of something cooking, then noticed that the dinner table was beautifully set. "Wow" she exclaimed. "What a nice thing to come home to." Doug immediately jumped up, and as they kissed and embraced affectionately Sondra turned off the audio/video system and raced into the kitchen to turn on the toaster-oven. She put the salad, dressing, and Parmesan cheese on the table then collected a pitcher of water from the refrigerator, pouring the cold liquid into wine goblets. She smiled to herself as she retrieved the main dish from the oven while Doug went on and on at how impressive it was that Sondra had gone to so much trouble to cook such a nice meal for them. He then kidded her a bit. "Hey, aren't you supposed to be putting us through some sort of hell with a bunch of teenage angst instead of doing such nice things like this?"

"Yeah" Sondra volleyed. "But I'm saving that to coincide with my mid-life crisis."

Karen wasn't buying any of this for a second, especially since she'd tried to pull off a similar little stunt when she was about Sondra's age to fool her mother when it was her turn to cook dinner. In those days Mary McCormick was a strictly no-nonsense home cook, never using prepackaged foods. While Karen did appreciate coming home to Sondra's sweet gesture she deftly snaked the lasagna packaging out of the trashcan from a cabinet under the sink. She held up the item to her husband and upon spotting the incriminating evidence Doug shook his head. "You nutty girl" he said to Sondra with a coughing laugh. He made a lunge for her and the couple smiled and clung to each other as they watched and listened to Sondra scramble away, laughing and briefly producing a high-pitched squeal.

The dinner-table discussion began as usual, with Doug and Karen recounting their day. Typically Sondra would contribute anecdotes of her own, often getting so carried away that she'd have to be reminded to eat and observe proper table manners. On this occasion however she was unusually serene and mindful of dining etiquette. "You're awfully quiet" observed Karen. Sondra shrugged her right shoulder. "This really is a nice dinner, even if it came from a package" Karen added with a smile. Sondra gave a nod and bit her lower lip. A sudden melancholy drifted into the room.

"It's only two weeks" offered Doug, knowing that Sondra was worrying about going so far away and with an uncertain schedule. "And we'll be right here when you get back" added Karen. "We promise." Sondra was on the verge of tears and now bit down on her tongue. She then took a deep breath. "I know this is so silly" she said. "Especially since it isn't the first time I've gone off by myself for racing, but I kinda feel like I have a tearing sensation at the top of my stomach. I mean I really am excited about going to England and Europe to test and race but I hate the idea of being away from you guys. Guess I'm just being childish and stupid" she added with a shrug of her right shoulder. "No" said Karen, tears welling up in her eyes. "Not childish or stupid. We love you so much. It's practically killing us not to go with you."

Doug nodded. "You're gonna be kept so busy" he told Sondra. "We'd most likely be in the way, and it's time and money that we need to put into future things. If you really need us to go with you, we will, but everything's been so carefully worked out with all the transportation and where you'll be staying." Sondra nodded and forced a smile. She then wiped her lips on the back of her right hand, prompting a customary light scolding from the mom. Karen soon came to mention that a coworker had just seen a new movie about five friends who turned into old-time cattle rustlers because they'd heard an urban legend that one particular Jersey bull had a nose ring of gold and five-million dollars in diamonds carefully embedded into his hooves. With Doug leading the way, the three exploded from the dinner table and scrambled to the car, leaving the food on the table and the radio on while they raced to catch the next showing.

CHAPTER 22

When Sondra arrived at the Silverstone International Raceway for testing in a new Formula Ford car, she met Jake Greniesi, director of operations at Hesmith Motor Sports. Before Sondra's first turn on the famed circuit she was schooled on track rules and procedure along with a myriad of particulars about the car, then introduced to Bryon Chulevista, the Team Principal. "Everyone seems to think the car's pretty unmanageable" said Byron. "So take it easy at first and tell us what you think." After three laps of driving and communication with Byron, Sondra came in for two significant changes less down-force on the left front wing, a gear-stack change and slightly lower tire pressures. She went back out for the remainder of her time and turned some stunning laps that the team had not seen with this car. After climbing out Sondra explained to the engineers what she'd been experiencing. "It gets a little twitchy under really heavy braking and I'd like a bit quicker throttle response but it's a fast car and fun to drive." After a bit more conversation, the team's lead driver Saul Trevor introduced himself to Sondra. He wasn't thrilled with the idea of a young-looking American girl joining the team and sharing driving duties but was polite and extended an invitation for her to join him and his "mates" for a bite. By the end of the first intense week of testing she was seen more as a little sister from the men of the team than a potential dating partner and they developed much respect for her race-craft and mechanical knowledge.

Sondra and the team flew to Hockenhiem, Germany, where she was to compete in the Formula Ford GP. She qualified 3rd for the next day's main event, and on the seventh lap of Sunday's race sliced down in front of the leader going into Elfkurve, a tight but fast right-hand corner. Though the top spot for the remainder of the race was hard-fought she never relinquished the lead, taking the checkered flag 1.302 seconds ahead of Sherman Dooreser, the man who'd won last year's European F-Ford championship. Sondra's teammate Saul Trevor was none too happy that she got the newer equipment, driving the very car they'd been testing. He easily let this go owing to the fact that she would be going back to the states soon and that he'd been given high praise by Jake Greniesi for his third place podium finish. During Sondra's second week there was promise of another race start when the group went to Valencia, Spain. On a mostly clear day she was in between driving stints and took note of a Formula One team at the ready for some scheduled test-time. Several men in team uniforms gave off body language that seemed to discourage her from close observation so she began walking from the garage area to where she knew there were food vendors. She suddenly found herself surrounded by four men in dull yellow and red uniforms. A tall man with a thick yet manicured beard called out her name. "Miss Sierre." Sondra halted and turned to face him. "My name's Bernard Hesmith" said the man. He was about to say more but Sondra cut him off pleasantly.

"Oh cool" she said with an infectious smile. "Nice to finally meet you, and thanks for all those checks you've been signing." This was a bit of silliness since she was working with a contract and a bank transfer. There were no individual checks. The men around her chuckled at the girl's jovial nature. "I'm sure you're aware of my name and our Formula One team" continued Bernard, gesturing to their #68 F1 mobile installation. "Yeah" nodded Sondra. "Jochen Voight finished fifth in points last season. You guys have a bit of ground to make up on the Mercedes and the Ferraris but you made pretty great strides with that last year, even doing better than the Red Bull cars."

How would you like to help us with that?" asked Bernard. Sondra was stunned and studied the faces of the four men to see if this was some kind of joke. She then cautiously agreed. They proceeded to give her a few details and promised to get her in a car the next day.

Sondra was in a daze from what had just transpired as she again started walking toward her destination. Striding along she was looking down at her timing and scoring sheet from her last on-track stint when she bumped into, literally, a young man who'd hurried over to say hello to her. After the abrupt incident she was just about to tell the jerk who'd hit her to watch where he was going. The man in question had stood in her path on purpose and spoke to her in a laughing voice. "Hey, Sondra. Good thing you don't drive the way you walk."

Her scowl turned quickly to a smile as she recognized her old F-Ford rival, Andrew Placer. "Oh shut up" she quipped. "I'll have to see the video replay on that because I'm pretty sure it was you who hit me." The two old competitors laughed and joked for a few moments along the same theme, then Andrew spoke more seriously. "Good seeing you again. Talked to Brice lately?"

"Not really" Sondra told him with a quick shake of her head. "I mean he left a few messages and we spoke for a few minutes before I came over here but I've been really busy with school and stuff. Besides, it kinda ticked me off for a while that he was given the IndyCar ride I think should have gone to me. I'm totally over it now because he's buried in a two-year support-driver, very limited contract. I get to do all this traveling and driving on these amazing famous tracks in cool cars."

"Glad to hear it" said Andrew with a nod of his head. "That you're not really mad at him" he qualified. "Because he's so totally into you. He and I are pretty tight. He talks about you all the time and he really feels bad about how things turned out. He almost walked away from the Patrero deal because of that but his family put a lot of pressure on him to sign because I guess they really need the money for the family farm or something." Andrew's revelation was quite a heavy chunk of information and she gestured ahead. "I have a lot of stuff to do" she told him. This was a total lie. She was basically done for the day and was planning to get a bite to eat and head to her flat. "It was nice seeing you again" she added. Not willing to just leave it at that, Andrew made further inquiries. "So what's your schedule like? I'm actually going to be joining your team for the Formula Ford Swift testing. Maybe we can grab a bite and catch up a little more." Sondra shrugged her shoulders and looked down at her favorite watch, the one that Doug had given her. "I guess" she announced in a tentative voice. "I'll have to check." He didn't walk away and she realized that he wasn't going to take no for an answer.

Jake Graniesi had spotted Sondra talking with the good-looking boy and had been walking toward the two, overhearing the tail-end of the conversation. Jake had met and worked with Placer several years prior. He was happy to have him back on this team and was pleased to see Sondra at ease, talking with the young man. He observed that Andrew seemed to be asking the girl out to dinner. He'd also observed that Sondra never seemed to have much of a social life while she'd been briefly in their employ. "We have all we need for the day" he told the girl. "Go out, go eat, and have a little fun."

Sondra saw Andrew Placer as basically a walking cliché of a Southern California golden boy. Born into a wealthy family and raised in a mansion overlooking the waterways in the town of Naples, he was well educated, confident and extremely smooth in his dealings with the opposite sex. All this was accented by a muscular physique, a boyishly handsome face and short blond wavy hair. She had taken a disliking to him immediately during their Formula Ford season. He, Brice and Wendell Grayson were almost always seen together, and Andrew had a different girl hanging all over him every week. On the racetrack however he'd been a force to reckon with and she'd grown to have some respect for him. Brice had defended his friend on a number of occasions during their Indy Lights season together and she eventually decided that Andrew Placer wasn't the worst guy on the planet.

Sondra's next week in Europe did indeed go by quickly. She was leading a Formula Ford race at Snetterton, UK when the timing belt let loose, shredding the motor and spewing oil and debris everywhere. It was a colossal disappointment, especially since there had been no warning signs of impending mechanical doom, but she was commended for her quick thinking in getting the rupturing machine quickly out of the racing groove and off the track. Her last European F-Ford race came at Mugello, Italy. Sondra took the Hesmith-Swift F-Ford from 19th to 3rd. They'd been struggling with this elusive chassis for weeks and the car was still a nightmare but on Sondra's suggestion, almost insistence, they went with a lighter-weight gearbox. It was tricky and not at all reliable but she knew how to finesse it and not be so aggressive like the other guys on the team. The decrease in weight had made a big difference, and even though she hated not getting the win she was given many accolades for her heroic efforts. Her teammate was spun from another car who missed his braking point and skidded into him but Saul continued the race, with a 9th Place finish. Andrew Placer, driving for Tracer-Vetec, started 5th and won his first race of the highly competitive F-Ford season.

Bernard Hesmith kept his promise to Sondra, putting her in a two-year old Formula One car. On a 68 degree mostly clear day at the Silverstone, England race track she was given intense instruction. With unwaveringly meticulous rules in F1 about testing for individual teams, Hesmith was pushing the limits on this day. Highly engineered and fiercely guarded wing modifications were painstakingly adapted to the #60. The goal was to test their efficiency in hopes of discovering a better design that they could transfer to their current F1 car. These were mostly fractional changes not necessarily visible to the naked eye, but any incremental bit of efficiency in airflow could mean the difference of winning, losing, or finishing a race in the Points. With the car idling, Bernard himself bent down to give Sondra some last instruction. "No expectations" he said to her. "Use your track knowledge to your advantage. This is a once-in-a-lifetime experience. Enjoy."

Less than two full seconds after exiting pit lane and feeling the indescribable force of acceleration, Sondra recognized that she was in so far over her head that it bordered on the absurd. The thing of it was however, nothing was actually going wrong. In fact, while she was having this little mental debate, her body was going through the exact natural proper motions. Bernard and the engineers watched as the highest technological telemetry of all motor sports was showing them that Sondra and the car had quickly become in sync. She was beginning to drive the way the car was meant to be driven. The V-6 fuel-powered engine and the two highly engineered electrical power units were putting out roughly nine hundred horsepower, and Sondra was miraculously keeping all this within their proper and highest efficiency ranges. It was also duly noted that her speed and lap times improved dramatically after her second go-around. Bernard truly hadn't expected her to do this well. In fact he had figured that the power, speed and G-force of the car's capability would scare her senseless or be far too demanding physically for her to make even one complete lap. He'd witnessed many a driver new to an F1 car become so squeamish or afraid of the power that they failed to produce or maintain any sort of the all-important heat in the brakes that it took to operate the vehicle with any sort of confidence. On this day he was seeing that Sondra was the exception.

The journey back to California gave Sondra time to reflect on her days in Europe and the reunion with Doug and Karen was joyous. The trip home from the San Francisco airport was not direct. Sondra's never-ending string of immense detail had her so enthusiastically wrapped up in her many tales of driving experiences as well as the people she'd met and the places she been that it only marginally registered when Doug's alternate route eventually had them driving down Highway 1. When Karen called out a particular road Sondra began to get suspicious. "Why are we going through Santa Barbara?" she inquired. "This is like way out of our way."

"Oh we have a little errand to run" said Karen. "Won't take but a minute and we'll be home before too long."

Sondra said nothing further, beginning to feel the effects of weariness from her long day. To her surprise, they went to an open house on a 16-acre property above Santa Barbara. She wasn't quite sure what to make of this and her anxiety level was high as they toured the home.

"Kinda beautiful there" said Sondra as Doug headed the car homeward. "Probably out-of-reach expensive but beautiful" she added.

"Maybe not so out of reach" countered Doug. "If the three of us went in on it together" he added. "It would be a lifelong commitment and we'd all have to be in total agreement." Sondra took a careful look at their surroundings. "I'm in" she heard herself say. "I mean as long as it won't ever screw up my racing career" she asserted. Doug hadn't really expected this reaction. "Actually" he began. "I think it would end up enhancing it. Your mom and I have been talking about something like this. A place we can stretch and grow. Something sustainable and solid for our future."

For your future" said Karen. "You need roots, kiddo. Can you see a future here Sondra?" Karen didn't give the girl time to answer. "This is absurdly pricey and it's gonna be a lot of work to get it to look how we ultimately want" she continued. "But as a family and three equal investment partners it's really the right place at the right time."

"We lived on a five-acre farm when I was little" Sondra announced. "I mean it was in the Central San Joaquin Valley and there were no rolling hills but this place feels a tiny bit like what I remember, with the wide-open spaces. I'm in if you guys are."

Days later Shelley invited Sondra for an overnight stay at her home in Malibu, mostly to discuss in person the myriad Safen-Up details. Sondra was eager to see her friend and talk about all that had been going on in her life for the past several weeks. Instead of driving, Shelley arranged a chartered jet to the Santa Monica Airport, which Sondra loved equally as much as being greeted at the terminal then getting a ride in Shelley's red Porsche Boxster. She remembered Shelley mentioning the sports car and the woman's complaints that it was in the shop more than on the road. Shelley was amused at Sondra's reaction to the Porsche upon walking up to it in the parking lot. "My father's always trying to give me fancy sports cars" she told Sondra. This was an exaggeration. Her father fancied himself a car guy and would either give or loan certain vehicles to his daughters.

Shelley now had three in her possession. The Boxster, a vintage Lincoln Towncar she'd loved being driven in as a child, and her favorite, a dark blue Mazda Miata, a vehicle she was most comfortable driving around town. "What is it with you car nuts," Shelley asked rhetorically of the Boxster as she made her exit from the airport property. "This is cute-looking but I can't stand the thing because it breaks down and it's stick-shift and I hate that. Seems stupid for a modern car."

"Okay, first of all" began Sondra, appalled at her friend's lack of understanding of all things automotive. "Manual transmission isn't stupid. And secondly, it's not cute. It's a cool machine and this one's a very rare limited edition." Their first destination was the Huntington Beach condo of a woman Shelley had newly hired as an assistant in the Safen-Up organization. Michelle Black had a Masters in child psychology, had taught grade-school and high school, and for years had volunteered for numerous children's charity organizations. This meeting was simply to exchange paperwork and signatures and Shelley was happy to have this opportunity to introduce her to Sondra. Heading southbound, Shelley drove only a short distance from the airport when Sondra pointed out a critical transportation error. "You just missed the freeway on-ramp. Nice going, Thelma."

"Shut up, Louise" said Shelley with a quick laugh and glance at her passenger. Sondra soon gasped and looked on in horror at seeing and hearing her friend miss shifts, grind gears and torture the clutch, though she tried not to be an obvious backseat driver. It was no wonder the car was in need of constant repair. Shelley was not at all a confident driver and on more than one past occasion she'd mentioned to Sondra that she was terrified of freeways. After a few of Sondra's dirty looks and vocal sneers Shelley finally pulled over to let Sondra drive. "Wise move" announced Sondra, with a sarcastic smile.

On a rare perfect Southern California early afternoon, with a gentle and clean onshore breeze and the sky a magnificent blue, Sondra piloted the flashy red sports car, the convertible top decidedly down. Shelley experienced a powerful sweeping motion of goose bumps as the air tousled and whipped the long hair of both women.

She caught sight of how the sun glinted off Sondra's forearm as her powerful muscles flexed and relaxed when executing each gear shift. Shelley nestled back in her seat, briefly closing her eyes. She took a deep breath as she felt the safest and most content she'd ever felt in a car, even though Sondra had doubled back and was now on the loud, fast-paced freeway. Shelley, ever the searcher of the perfect song, had been switching radio stations when Sondra heard a familiar tune. "Oh hold up" called out Sondra. "This is a really cool song. Brice was always watching CMT in his RV and I liked the video to this. It should really be on rock-radio not Country." Shelley was now more interested in Sondra's mention of the boy than the song. "So you never mentioned this before" she began. "That you two hung out, listened to music and watched videos." Sondra glanced over briefly with an annoyed expression. "It wasn't really like that" protested the girl. "Besides, he and the guys were always playing these violent macho video games."

Shelley smiled to herself at this defense and turned to her right to witness a woman in the car next to them brushing her teeth as she drove.

Later that day Shelley took Sondra out to an early dinner at a Malibu seafood restaurant. "Thanks for taking me here" said Sondra. "I like this place. It's fun, and these lobster raviolis are amazing. I ate surprisingly well when I was in England."

"Surprisingly?" inquired Shelley. Sondra carefully blotted her mouth with her serviette before qualifying her statement. "Well I mean you hear so much talk of the bland or gross food in England. Maybe that was true in the past but I didn't see anything gross and everything I had tasted great."

Sondra spoke of various meals, eventually going into great detail about the braised lamb-shank meal she'd had at a restaurant with Andrew Placer. She then abruptly stopped talking. "What?" asked Shelley. "What just happened there, baby?"

Sondra shrugged before explaining. "Well I mean it was a little shocking to hear Andrew go on and on about how much Brice likes me and talks about me" she told Shelley. "Maybe I've been stupidly naive, or maybe I'm just horribly dense."

"Or maybe you've learned to be quick in judging yourself harshly" suggested Shelley. She let that sink in as she took a bite of red snapper. "I don't remember learning that" negated Sondra with a shrug of her right shoulder. She stabbed at the center of a ravioli several times with her fork before looking up at her table mate. "Nothing in my life was ever really harsh when I was growing up" she informed Shelley. "I mean, sure, there were the usual injustices pretty much any kid deals with, like having to do chores when you'd rather be playing or when one sibling gets to do something and you don't. Or someone at school says or does something you think is mean. Sometimes I worry though."

"What do you worry about?" asked Shelley. Sondra bit down on her tongue and briefly looked away, spotting two female patrons overtly flirting with their waiter. "Sondra?" whispered Shelley. Sondra made an incision with the edge of her fork diagonally down the length of her last ravioli before responding. "Do you think going through something so horrifically harsh changes you deep inside? Takes away some of your good?"

"Do you feel changed?" asked Shelley.

"Well I mean I don't think I've changed into some evil monster or anything but I don't think I look at things the same as I used to." "Sure" said Shelley. "That's understandable. You've also grown and matured since you were a child, before the accident. It's natural for one to see the world differently from every age or from any stage in one's life. You've had to go through something that most people don't." Hearing Shelley say the word accident was like getting hit with a blast of super-cooled air. She took a desperate deep breath before speaking. "My friend Kari once suggested to me that she thought I was kinda jaded because of it."

"Perhaps your friend Kari was projecting" suggested Shelley. Sondra nodded. "I kinda miss her" she admitted. "Hope she's doing okay" she added. Shelley sat back in her seat and smiled, wondering about Kari and why Sondra and her friend had completely lost touch. With so much communication technology available this seemed to

Shelley a near impossibility. "That doesn't sound like the thoughts of a jaded person to me" she told Sondra. "So maybe you can get to a place within yourself to see how much easier it might be for you to be less hypercritical and judgmental of you" she added. Sondra shrugged her shoulder but developed a small involuntary smile. She liked what Shelley had said and meant.

Upon returning to Shelley's residence they sat out by the pool, touching on several light topics. After a quick lull in the conversation Sondra stretched and took a loud deep breath. "This is like a perfect spot" she thought out loud. "Beautiful, quiet and protected." Shelley was about to inquire into her friend's use of the word protected but never got the chance. "I might be moving to Santa Barbara" stated Sondra in an abrupt non sequitur. "Well it's certainly beautiful there" offered Shelley. "And a more direct and closer drive to my house" she added with a smile. She took a moment to observe Sondra's facial expression and body language. "Quite a change in your life" stated Shelley. "How is that for you?" Sondra shrugged and bit down on her tongue. Shelley moved to a closer deck chair on the other side and whispered her last question. "How is that for you, Sondra?" "I don't know" said the girl, shaking her head several times. "I mean it's a three bedroom farmhouse out in the rolling hills and Karen's been raving on and on about how much she loves the big spacious kitchen. There's a four-car attached garage and the last room is a separate insulated gym room. There's even a pool out back."

"Wow" smiled Shelley. "Sounds like quite a place." Sondra didn't respond. "So you're not smiling or jumping up and down, excited about it" observed Shelley. Sondra shrugged both shoulders and took a quick breath, thinking about Shelley's observation. "I am excited about it, mostly" defended Sondra. "I mean inside the house it feels like a real home and I kinda picked out what could be my bedroom. In a tiny way it reminded me of my room back home, back when I had my real life. My real home." Shelley put a gentle hand on Sondra's shoulder. "You don't think this could be a real home?" she asked the girl.

"Well it's not set in stone that we'll even get the place" said

Sondra, trying to force herself to be strong. "But I guess it could be. I mean it'll have to be. I'm pretty much forced into it now."

"You see everything being forced upon you?" asked Shelley in a gentle voice. "Yeah" said Sondra through clenched teeth. "I mean intellectually I know we all ultimately make our own choices in life but..." Sondra pounded her fist on her leg and let out an expletive.

"But what?" prodded Shelley. "Well I don't care how damn philosophical one can get or what intellectual BS someone can come up with because it doesn't change the horrible facts. I didn't cause the crash and I sure as hell didn't want to be left behind."

Sondra did her best to wipe away and hide from Shelley tears that were threatening to stream down her face. She cleared her throat and became determined to be strong. "Property in Santa Barbara is mostly for millionaires. I mean it's ridiculously out of reach for most people. The three of us would have to be equal financial partners in order to buy it. I mean I don't really give a crap about the money but the only thing I have in this world that's truly mine now is racing. It's all I want to do, all day, every day."

Sondra could tell that Shelley was about to ask a question so she purposely kept talking. "There was this moment when I was in that F-One car. It was like all of a sudden someone turned on a light switch. I know you don't understand this because you don't even like cars all that much but it was kinda like at first walking along in a cluttered gutter and then you suddenly step up on the smooth clear sidewalk. You can walk easier and go faster. You have a whole new energy. I pushed that car and those tires to edges that even those seasoned big-time engineers couldn't believe. I love that kind of driving. That's my everything, and before you say it or even think it, this is who I am and deep-down who I was. That drunken bastard didn't take that from me. He'll never take that from me."

Shelley reluctantly let Sondra alone with her rage and anguish, deliberately not comforting her with a hug or soothing touch. Two full minutes passed before Shelley spoke. "I love that you're so passionate about your driving" she offered the girl. "But I also hear fear and anger. That perhaps you somehow feel threatened that someone or some thing is trying to take that away from you. What do you think?"

"Well it's a rough male-dominated sport" Sondra said with a shrug of her right shoulder. "I mean even though there have been quite a few women drivers over the years, you still have brutal attitudes and some roadblocks. And, well..."

"Well what?" asked Shelley. Sondra wiped her eyes with the back of her right hand before answering.

"I hate talking about money but the settlement stuff I was awarded from the crash would be my financial share of the Santa Barbara place. I've never wanted to use it for much before but I was actually kinda planning on using it to further my racing career. I mean I have other money but it still feels like a bit of a horrific setback for my career if I use the blood money for the house." Shelley was alarmed that Sondra used the words blood money. She wanted to explore this further but decided to let it go, for the moment. "It's an intense dilemma" said Sondra. "I mean, do I go for the greater good of a family life with Doug and Karen who I really do love, or do I take a stubborn stand and go my own way?"

"Does it need to be an either-or?" asked Shelley. Sondra shrugged. "Depends on them, I guess."

Shelley shook her head. "No, Sondra. "It depends on you. It's your choice. You have a right to be selfish, but Sondra, be selfish for the authentic you. The Sondra with a loving caring family. The Sondra without the horrors of the accident. You can choose peace and happiness and what's best for you." The two women went inside and talked late into the night, and the next morning Shelley noticed a much lighter, brighter energy from Sondra as they enjoyed eggs benedict and discussed Safen-Up in detail.

Chapter 23

Darren Brown invited Sondra to be his guest in the Holt Racing pits for Saturday's IndyCar qualifying at the Long Beach Grand Prix. Her love of being around these high-tech vehicles and the esteemed race teams outweighed her bitterness over not being part of the series for this year. Doug and Karen had work that day and SeaShell was in New York, so Sondra drove down in the Tacoma. Though Darren was extremely busy he made time for Sondra, giving her pertinent detailed IndyCar information and having small but specific tasks for her alongside the engineers, like keeping track of specific fuel numbers. The men on this team were happy to see her and made her feel like an important part of the family.

Brice Crandle was strolling along a line of temporary garages, headed to the Patrero-McDonald's stall when he spotted Sondra inside the Holt Racing enclosure. He halted, did an about-face with his heart leaping into his throat, then used his cell phone to enlist the moral support of his friend. Halfway around the world Andrew Placer had just gone to bed. He had remained in Europe and was now third in the Formula Ford International championship. Brice explained his current Sondra dilemma, with Andrew doing his best to calm down his friend and offer a bit of sage advice. "She's the same cool chick you hung out with all that time last year when you were teammates" he told Brice. "Just be yourself but be cool, and get your butt over there and talk to her. This opportunity just fell in your lap and you don't know when or if you'll have another chance like this again any time soon." Crandle took his friend's advice and summoned the courage to turn around.

Sondra had eaten lunch in the temporary garage with the Holt Racing engineers and was sitting in a lawn chair after finishing her sandwich. She tossed the crumpled-up wrapper into a trashcan about five feet away and looked around proudly to see if her magnificent over-the-head hook-shot had been witnessed by anyone. Her eyes caught sight of Brice heading quickly toward her. She didn't have time to stand so she reached out her hand and greeted him. "Hey Brice. Good to see you again." Without saying a word he accepted her firm grip and pulled the girl up toward him. He hugged her solidly in full consciousness not to squeeze too tight but very aware of how soft and warm she was as well as taking in her always pleasant fragrance.

"Did you just kiss my hair?" Sondra asked, squirming away and punching him lightly on the shoulder. "What? No" he denied. "I wouldn't do that. That would just be …"

"Weird and creepy?" she interjected.

"Well" he countered. "I'd say sweet and endearing but …"

"Okay" she breathed. "We'll go with your thing." They both produced shy smiles but then Sondra remembered Andrew Placer's past words of how Brice felt about her. She felt a few seconds of panic when Brice suggested they go back to his RV so they could talk in peace and quiet but reluctantly agreed.

Once inside the relatively clean motor-coach it was a relief to both that they seemed to fall into what had been their usual rhythm of jokes, conversation and simply enjoying each other's company. Sondra liked that Brice was so enthusiastic about her experience in the F1 car and that he had asked so many questions. Time slipped by quickly and she checked her watch. "We should head to pit lane pretty soon" she suggested. "You have a job to do and Darren's letting me hang with the engineers for qualifying. Oh hey ... I saw Andrew Placer a while back and we had dinner and a nice chat. He was on my F-Ford Swift test team." She laughed and continued. "He still hasn't broken that stupid double apexing habit of his in long fast corners. I watched him do it from behind at Snetterton and I nearly ran myself off the road, laughing so hard." This was a complete exaggeration. While in a race car at speed her acute concentration and determination never lapsed into moments of hilarity. Sondra noticed a slight worried look shoot across Brice's face.

"Yeah, um" he muttered. "We talk all the time" he admitted. "Actually I talked to him like seconds before I ran into you." He looked down briefly at his black racing shoes but then raised his head to study Sondra's face. His next voice was low, with a slightly depressed tone. "So, uh, he told you?"

Sondra nodded, reaching out to touch him briefly on his shoulder. "I like you a lot too, Brice" she told him. "But I love winning in a really well-tuned race car. I'm not sure I'm capable of some lovey-dovey relationship thing. Besides, our worlds are so far apart right now and they probably will be for quite a while."

"Well I'm glad I wasn't just imagining things" he said with an awkward smile. "But I think you're wrong. If you're capable of loving all things racing I'm sure you're capable of loving a person in a relationship. Hopefully me" he added with a nervous laugh. "Our worlds aren't really that far apart. Word around the paddock is that you'll be in an Indy car next season."

"Well, fingers crossed" said Sondra. "It's weird how things work out" she added. "I mean I really thought I wanted the situation you have now but I think there's better opportunities for me."

"I think so too and I'm glad you think that." Sondra gave Brice a light punch on the shoulder but then leaned in and kissed him softly on the cheek. "Drive safe and don't do anything rookie-stupid" she told him with a mischievous grin. "And relax about all this lovey-dovey crap, will you?"

"All right, tough-girl" he said with a nod and a smile. "And you go change that shirt, ya damn sloppy eater." She glanced down to find several smudges of catchup on her bright yellow Yamaha sweatshirt.

At the conclusion of Qualifying, Ryan Delgato had put Holt Racing 4th on the grid for the next day's Long Beach Grand Prix. Sondra had also been keeping secret track of the qualifying efforts of the #48 Patrero-McDonald's Chevy-powered Indy car. Brice missed out on the Fast Six round by .053 seconds but was slated to start Sunday's GP 7th on the grid. She wanted to further chat with him but found herself in a pleasant conversation with Delgato and several Holt Racing team members. T.J. Holt wandered over to offer a few words of warning and encouragement to his driver for the next day's battle. He took note of Sondra and tapped the girl on her shoulder with the back of his hand, gesturing that they move a few feet away from the small assembly. "Hear you put down some hot laps in an F-One car" said the legendary race figure, chewing gum loudly. "And now I suppose you think I'm gonna put you in one of my Indy cars" he added. Sondra smiled. Not at T.J. and not at this particular exchange but at the memory of being in the Hesmith Motorsports race machine. "Something like that" she told the man in bold confidence. "Mostly I'm here at Darren's invitation to be around what I love most but he's put me in an Indy car before and I proved myself. I surprised the hell out of the F-One guys, too, and in all three championships that I've entered I've won, and I will be in another Indy car. I can either drive for you or against you, and I drive to win. Thanks for today" she added, daring to touch the man's shoulder with her fist. "See you 'round." She turned and began walking away but T.J. called after her.

"Tough talk from a little girl" he said in a harsh serious tone.

"Yeah" she countered, struggling to let go the little girl comment. "But I do most of my talking out on a racetrack, and it's big and loud." The man snorted a laugh through his nose as he chewed his gum and watched her disappear.

Sondra began shaking a bit as she continued to walk toward the parking area. She'd managed to get through a dreaded anxiety-producing reunion with Brice and it had gone much better than expected. She'd also figured that Darren would introduce her to T.J. Holt but she certainly hadn't planned on being so bold as to demand that he consider giving her a job in the future. She thought of what her father would think of her meeting him, let alone talking to him in the manner in which she'd just done. She then wondered and worried if she'd overplayed her hand with the legend and worried what T.J. might say to Darren. On the drive home she played the scene over and over in her head, adding other possible scenarios. At home later that evening she purposely kept her exchange with T.J. Holt to herself when telling Doug and Karen all about her Long Beach experience, fearful that her manager-parents would greatly disapprove.

Three days later the Trents were in the midst of a breakfast-table discussion on the immense undertaking of the purchase and move to Santa Barbara. Doug's cell-phone buzzed and he fished it out of his shirt pocket. "This is Doug" he greeted the caller. "Oh, hi, Darren." Sondra sat frozen with fear of what the communiqué might reveal. "No, not at all" continued Doug with his side of the conversation. "Yeah, she did. I think she learns a lot every time she gets the chance to hang with you guys." Now Sondra knew for sure they were talking about her. "Oh really" said Doug with a disapproving tone, responding to what Darren had just disclosed. "Hmm" he voiced, shaking his head and glancing over at Sondra. "I'd like to say that I can't believe what I'm hearing, but I can believe it" said Doug. "Oh yeah? Huh. Okay. Yeah I will, and thanks for calling." Doug set the phone down on the table so gently it aroused the interest and suspicions of both Karen and Sondra.

"So you had words with T.J. Holt, did you?" Doug accused Sondra. "Demanding, arrogant words?" he added.

"Oh dear" complained Karen. Sondra could barely breathe, feeling the eyes of her now-parents drilling into her. Doug shook his head as he spoke. "I don't even know what to say to this" he told the girl. "Apparently in all your schooling you haven't learned the meaning of words like tact, respect and diplomacy."

"Sondra, what on earth did you say to the man?" asked Karen. "And don't just shrug your shoulders at me."

Sondra swallowed hard, trying to remember the exact verbal exchange she'd had with the sports legend. "I didn't say anything bad or impolite" she defended. "I was on purpose but I was respectful."

Doug sat back in his chair and eyed his daughter. There had been many occasions in the past where he'd felt concern and disappointment when hearing about anger-fueled incidences and exchanges the girl had with various individuals. This latest exchange with T.J. Holt, a hopeful prospect in giving Sondra an IndyCar ride, was only different because of the potentially high stakes. "So what are we thinking?" asked Karen. "A carefully worded letter of apology?" she furthered.

"No" said Doug, taking a loud deep breath. "Apparently the kid's insolence impressed the hell out of Mr. Holt."

Sondra smiled and triumphantly bit down on a crunchy piece of bacon. "No" said the dad, shaking his head in disapproval at his favorite brat. "That was nowhere near appropriate and you damn-well know it" he scolded. "And at some point you are gonna apologize to both Darren and T.J. when you see 'em in Texas." Doug paused for dramatic effect and looked across at his wife. "Apparently T.J. himself invited our girl to test in his number Twelve car."

"Really?" asked an instantly excited Sondra, producing an enormous smile. "Where and when? I can't wait. And oh man, the number Twelve, that's totally like my lucky car number. How great is that?"

"Don't get ahead of yourself" chuckled Doug. "Darren didn't say if this'll actually happen."

"But it could" said Sondra. "And I just have a feeling it will." Karen shook her head as she eyed the girl. "Well do you have a feeling you have grape jelly on your sleeve?" scolded the mom. "And don't lick it off. Use your napkin."

Sondra borrowed an enclosed trailer from Dan Stoltz to pick up her old F sports car. In the familiar offices of Blue Sea Racing she found Greg Wilente's wife/receptionist on the phone. Cynthia waved and smiled warmly. Moments later Greg invited Sondra into his office. "Congratulations on last year's strong Nascar finish" Sondra offered the man in a light blue button-down dress shirt with a dark brown tie that had a squiggly diagonal wrinkle toward the bottom. In this moment Sondra thought he looked more like a vacuum cleaner salesman than a race team owner. “Thanks” acknowledged Greg without much emotion. There was an uncomfortable silence before he spoke. “So you want your old car now, do you?” Sondra nodded, remembering how she had hated his condescending game playing. “Well it needs quite a bit of work. It’s been used pretty hard.”

“That’s okay” said Sondra. “I’m pretty good with a wrench. Besides it’ll mainly be used as a display in an auto dealership alongside my old sprint-car.” She spoke briefly of moving to Santa Barbara and her plans for a well-equipped shop.” Greg’s demeanor softened. It had been some time since he’d last seen her in person but he didn’t think Sondra had changed much from that determined 16 year-old girl he’d first encountered in this very office when she’d tested then argued for a driver position on their F-Ford team. “Been hearin’ things about you” he told her. “Mostly good” he added with a bit of a snicker. “I hear you did a real fine job across the pond with the Swift testing and a few F-Ford races. You seemed to have learned a hell of a lot from us here at Blue Sea.”

Sondra didn’t show it but was instantly enraged that Greg seemed to be taking all the credit for her success and neglected to even acknowledge the fact that she’d won last year’s Indy Lights championship.

“So you got to run laps in an old F-One car, huh?” continued Greg. “Yep” she said, leaning back in the chair and taking a quick look at the photos around the room, noticing several framed images of her and her Blue Sea Racing Formula Ford team. “Loved every single second of it” she told Wilente. “I remember sitting in this very chair and telling you I’d be in a Formula One car. During my Indy Lights championship season last year, you know, where I won, Darren Brown pretty much took me under his wing and put me in one of the Patrero Indy cars a few times. Now that he’s with Holt Racing he’s working on getting me in one of their cars as well. IndyCar is my focus, whether it’s driving for T.J. Holt or someone else.”

“You go, girl, as the kids are saying these days” he quipped with a sarcastic laugh.

“The kids aren’t saying that” said Sondra.

Sondra arrived home at 4:26 p.m. and burst through the front door full of energy. "I'm home" she called out in a sing-song tone. "Office, sweetie" answered the mom. Karen was sitting in an ornate navy-blue chair that she'd purchased years ago, thumbing through a catalog with her feet up on a brown leather footstool that had been Doug's grandfather's. Soft piano music was playing from a George Winston CD, a favorite of hers, and the late afternoon sun was making mystical patterns as it shone through the large white mini-blinds. "Dad should be here in about thirty minutes" informed the mom. "So how was your day?"

Sondra went into immense detail as Karen knew her to do, and soon Karen led the way to the kitchen, all the while being pleasantly barraged by Sondra's tales of how she got the F-Ford into the trailer. "I swear it was like thirty guys standing around watching me drag heavy stuff up the ramp and load it inside that dirty, smelly trailer" said Sondra. "They were mostly the students from the racing school there. I mean at first it was great to hear all about the cars they're using now, the new model of the FJR-Fifty. True monocock design modeled after the Formula Three cars, with a turbo-charged in-line Four cylinder Mitsubishi motor with that Hewland FTR five-speed sequential gearing. Supposed to have really good power to weight ratio, too. Even better than before. One of the instructors told me he could get me some seat-time in one, for a fee of course." Karen smiled to herself as she attended to the tasks of preparing a salad. "Thanks for the lunch" she told her mom in a bit of a non sequitur. "I ate in the main grandstands above pit lane. Practically had the place to myself. There was this one other guy though that had the same lunch idea as me and we ended up talking and eating together. He said he's like eighty percent blind. He gets around fine but can't see good enough to have a driver's license. He loves racing though, especially IndyCar and Formula One. I told him a ton of my experiences and he told me all about being a guitar player and recording artist. Not famous or anything. I love that racetrack. It's a magical place."

Karen put the knife down and wrapped her arms around her daughter. "You're magical" she told Sondra. "I love you so much." She gave the girl a kiss just above her right ear and released her but Sondra refused to immediately relinquish her grip. “I can hardly wait to move to the new house” said Sondra in a diminished almost desperate voice. “I love you, mom” she added, meaning this for both the mother she’d known and loved the first thirteen years of her life as well as Karen, who she also loved and was certain had earned the esteemed title of Mom.

CHAPTER 24

The move to Santa Barbara was time-consuming and arduous, spread out over four days. Surprisingly, the sale of the condo had gone quickly and it was a push to get things packed up and transferred to the four-car garage of the new house for temporary storage. Doug and Karen found it both sweet and silly that Sondra named their new residence Casa de Trent. While Karen's main focus was on the cleaning and painting of the interior, Sondra had big ideas for the landscaping around the house and beyond. Doug's towing business was unusually busy but when he had time he floated between helping with both the interior and exterior. On a northerly portion of the property, obscured by the tan rolling hills, Sondra discovered a wooden shack with a corrugated tin roof. It had been used as a utility shed for the feeding and caring of goats, which had been brought to the property for the purpose of brush and weed control during the last three years of inactive use. The goats and contents of the shed were gone but the small enclosure gave Sondra an idea. This would be the site of her own special place. She pictured a grand garage and shop that would double as her future home, walking around the outside of the shed with a smile on her face, thinking of the possibilities. She lost that smile moments later when childhood memories clobbered her, suddenly remembering the red scooter she'd found at a garage sale down the street from her house that summer before the end of her normal life. She wondered why this memory chose to present itself at this particular moment and could see clearly in her mind the two-wheeler and was sure she could smell the fuel and old dirty grease clinging to the filthy machine. She also remembered her backyard and a time before the pool was put in, where she, Dave and Haley had created a large dirt town. It was elaborate, with many roads, parking spaces and make-believe houses and garages. A favorite activity of hers was to back one of her Hot Wheels cars or Tonka trucks into a garage. She would go slowly and make the noise of the engine and transmission with her mouth and throat.

Sondra ran back to the house, fearful of more family memories and how they seemed to always punch and stab at her. She found Karen kneeling on the kitchen counter, lining the cupboards with shelf paper. She hoped the signs of pain, anguish and tears that she'd just suffered through at the loss of her childhood while exploring the goat shed were not visible, though she thought she could feel the vibration from it and hear the ringing of the enormity in her head. "There you are" said Karen, smiling as she turned to face the girl. "Your dad's on his way with the last of our stuff. Tonight's gonna be our first official night here. I think we'll try another of the downtown restaurants for dinner. "You okay?" asked Karen as she hopped down from the counter. She knew instinctively that the girl had been crying. Karen had a developed sensitivity and was quite intuitive when it came to Sondra. This had begun with that first evening she'd spent with Doug and his daughter at the condo, now seemingly a lifetime ago.

"I'm good" said Sondra as she removed her sweater, hoping to avoid any further questions of her well-being. "Why is it so hot in here?"

"Oh" said Karen. "I put the oven on self-clean to sanitize everything. Warmed things right up."

At Mac's Fish and Chips restaurant that evening Sondra went into immense detail about the fish and chips she'd had in England, with Doug and Karen smiling to themselves as they treasured every second of their girl's enthusiastic tales. Toward the end of their meal at the popular Santa Barbara eatery Sondra dragged a chip through a blob of ketchup and made an announcement. "I have some great ideas. Potentially expensive ideas, but great ideas."

"Does one of those ideas involve you not getting tartar sauce on your sleeve?" asked Karen rhetorically.

"Mom" complained Sondra, rolling her eyes. "And use your napkin, sweetie" instructed Karen. "Don't just lick it off like that as though you're some wild animal."

"So tell us about these great expensive ideas" said Doug.

"Dirt-bikes" suggested Sondra. "And maybe a couple of ATVs." Doug nodded but Karen sat back in her chair and shook her head.

"Oh dear" she muttered. As Sondra and Doug launched into a discussion about the acquisition of motorized entertainment vehicles and the possibility of creating a motocross track, Karen felt a mixture of exasperation at her two constant gear-heads and a feeling of extreme love and happiness with her little family. "I found this little shack" informed Sondra, scooping out the remains of a small paper cup of tartar sauce. Doug and Karen had been told of the goat shed by the Realtor but hadn't given it much thought. "I'm gonna tear it down and that's gonna be the site for an amazing garage and machine-shop" continued Sondra. "I mean there's electricity and a water line already there and I could turn it into a real house in the future. I want to put in a paved track, too. I mean we don't have to call it a racetrack but ..."

"Hmm" pondered Doug. "Like a kart track?"

"Yeah" enthused Sondra, smiling wide and lightly bouncing up and down in her seat. "We'll get three or four karts and have our own little raceway" she said with excited eyes. "I mean it'll be really good for my driving and racing skills for reaction times and stuff, so this'll be something super practical as well as super fun."

"Yeah" agreed Doug. "Those One-Twenty-Five cc shifter-karts look like fun and they go pretty good" he added.

"All right, you two" said Karen. "Enough of this. We're concentrating on the house and the yards before any of this little raceway nonsense takes place."

"Nonsense" said Sondra, feigning indignation that such a monumental idea would ever be considered anything but great.

The home's interior was going to be quite an undertaking since it was an as-is sale. Though Doug and Karen delved headlong into all this, they had jobs that took them away from full-time work on the house. The continued daily work on the home's inside and out now fell to Sondra. She did this without question or complaints at first but as days and weeks went by Doug and Karen began to notice subtle changes in the girl's attitude and general behavior. For Sondra, not being in a race car or having a sole focus on her career began to take its toll and enter into her subconscious. She was never outright disrespectful, rude or combative but there were definite changes that her now-parents noted. As a young girl, Sondra had been taught the importance of keeping her room and surroundings neat and tidy. Doug and Karen had often marveled at her fastidious nature, bordering on the obsessive-compulsive when it came to cleanliness and order with her Fresno bedroom. This virtue however was becoming increasingly relaxed. She began to leave her bed unmade and clothes on the floor of her room. Sweaters and shoes would be left wherever she'd taken them off, and several times she'd left her dirty dishes in the sink. On rainy days she'd watch an inordinate amount of mindless TV. She would also complain about the seemingly never-ending house and yard work she was asked to accomplish. Several times Karen had mentioned to Doug that Sondra was starting to act like the quintessential bratty teenager. Doug thought this was funny and perhaps an exaggeration, Karen did not.

Doug left the house just before 8 a.m. to drive down and attend Tracy's Cal State Fullerton college graduation ceremony. He knew her mother, his ex-girlfriend Brenda, was still incarcerated and wouldn't be able to be there and figured none of Tracy's siblings would be in attendance for various reasons. Sondra had childishly refused to go, still harboring much resentment for how Tracy had treated her, and Karen didn't feel her presence was appropriate. Karen had the day off work and was planning on using this day to put the finishing touches on their new home's setup and decoration. Her morning had started early, seeing her husband off and was surprised at the degree of difficulty in getting Sondra out of bed.

"Come on, sweetie" ordered Karen, pulling the bed covers off the girl.

"Mom" complained Sondra. "I'm not getting up at the crack of dawn just to do yard work."

"It's after eight-thirty" corrected Karen. "Not exactly the crack of dawn. Get up and get dressed, and have some breakfast before you go out."

"Aw jeeze" muttered the girl, reluctantly sitting up and swinging her legs over the side of her mattress.

Sondra became downright surly and argumentative, at first ignoring her mom's request to take care of her laundry and pick up a pair of shoes she'd left in the den. She grumbled through these great inconveniences and exited the kitchen, refusing breakfast, a cardinal sin in Karen's book. The work that engaged Sondra on this day, the pulling of five tree stumps with a rented tractor, was hot and dusty. Doug had removed a considerable mountain of brush and other stumps the day before and they had two more full days of use before the machine needed to go back to the rental facility. Sondra had volunteered to pull the rest of the stumps as well as create a terraced surface just beyond the pool area, so Karen could plant a vegetable garden. Once she did get going that morning Sondra was the model of a hardworking farm laborer. She enjoyed working the controls on the faded yellow backhoe as well as the sound and smell of the tractor's diesel engine, remembering her dad on a tractor a number of times.

Sondra had done the terracing first and was wrapping a chain around the fifth pulled tree stump, planning to drag the stump and root-system with the tractor to the large refuse pile when she felt her cell phone buzz. It was clipped to her belt loop and she soon determined the call was from Karen. Lunch was ready. Sondra was tired and annoyed at the interruption but dusted herself off, splashed pool water on her face and sat at her usual seat at the kitchen table.

"No" scolded Karen as she put a towel-covered basket of hot sourdough bread on the table. "Go wash up, change that shirt and lose the hat, please."

"I'm going right back outside" argued Sondra. The mom turned her head back toward the girl and shot her a look of authority. "Jeeze" breathed Sondra, reluctantly getting up to do as she was told. She returned a few minutes later wearing an old T-shirt that Karen had voiced her disapproval of many times, and though the mom didn't say anything about her wardrobe choice she was not exactly happy. The girl was wearing a faded navy-blue garment with small holes and dark stains that refused to come out no matter how many times it went through the wash. Karen brought over a large bowl of shrimp and pasta Alfredo, along with the butter to set near the bread, eyeing her daughter settling back in her chair. "Hat" Karen reminded the girl, figuring this would produce the required outcome. When she came back to the table with small bowls of salad she noticed that Sondra's headwear was still in place. "Sondra, take off your hat, please" she again requested.

"What's the big deal?" argued Sondra in an unusually snotty tone. "It's just you and me here, and I'm going right back outside anyway. God, mom."

"Sondra, we don't wear hats at the table" said Karen, beginning to lose her patience and her temper. "You know that. And don't god mom, me. I'm not gonna tell you again. Take that damn hat off this minute or go to your room." Karen watched in stunned disbelief as her daughter stood with such instant anger and force that her chair came close to falling over backwards. The girl then threw her yellow baseball cap with the Pennzoil logo on the front to the ground as if she were a pitcher with a 90 mile an hour fast-ball. She rushed out of the room, and seconds later Karen heard and felt the girl's bedroom door slam shut. Sitting down at the table and staring at her empty plate, Karen brought her cupped hands to her face and began to cry. She stood and took the kitchen land-line wireless phone outside, settling on a redwood bench facing the pool, watching a bird do his funny little walk around the pool decking and take several jerking pecks at the ripples in the water close to the edge. Karen stared blankly at this scene and tried to comprehend what had just happened with Sondra then dialed the phone number of her parents.

"I don't know what just happened, mom" Karen sobbed after giving a brief description of recent events. "Sondra and I don't ever have fights like this. I … I snapped. I yelled at her and sent her to her room. Oh god. I'm like an evil stepmom."

"No you're not" said George, who'd gotten on the other line as soon as he figured out with whom Mary was talking. "You're the mom" he said. "It's your job to set boundaries." Mary agreed and added to her husband's statement. "You went to all that trouble to make a nice lunch. Good for you for not letting her get away with being such a disrespectful brat." Karen's parents offered further agreement in how their daughter had handled the situation with Sondra. They also offered a number of punishment suggestions, although Karen thought most of them went too far. She loved her mom and dad for their encouragement and strength, and when the call ended went back inside to have a somber lunch. With each bite she seemed to gain strength and energy and pondered the fact that 18 year-old Sondra, a strong and intelligent woman, not only acted as if she were half her age at times but had never seemed to question their parent-child dynamic.

It was a quarter to four in the afternoon when Sondra quietly appeared in the living room. Karen was sitting in one of the new soft red lounge chairs reading the newspaper. "I'm sorry, mom" Sondra said in a tentative and desperate voice. Karen's talk with her parents had bolstered her strength and conviction that she was on the right path with Sondra. She was glad for the apology but wasn't about to just back down and let this go as if nothing had happened. The unspoken agreed-upon rules of their unique relationship had been forged during these past few years and she felt as though she'd been quite fair, but this only worked if lines were not crossed or blurred.

Karen set the paper in her lap and stared at the girl for a few seconds. Sondra had changed into a nice emerald-green plaid top and black slacks. She'd also combed and tied her hair back into a neat ponytail. After a loud breath Karen began a semi-rehearsed speech. "Sondra, I work hard and put a lot of thought into having a nice home and coming up with healthy and good-tasting meals. I sure as hell don't deserve this kind of disrespect."

Sondra was stunned and felt as though she were frozen in place. She figured that she would apologize and that everything would go back to normal. This reaction and attitude from Karen was unexpected and unsettling.

"I know" she moaned, now afraid that she'd crossed too big a line with Karen. "I do respect you and I'm sorry" she added desperately. "I won't wear a hat at the table again. I promise."

"There are rules to everything in life, Sondra" said Karen. "And there sure as hell are rules in this house."

She watched tears begin to stream down the girl's face. "M-sorry" whispered Sondra. Karen took a deep breath and folded the newsprint, setting it on the table next to her. Just as she was not willing to let slide the rules of the house she was also not willing to allow the delicate balance Sondra rode each and every day to teeter into harsh uncertainty. "Okay" she offered her daughter, getting up to put an arm around her. "I accept your apology and I declare this fight over. You must be starved. Lets go get you some of what you missed. It was delicious, by the way, you hot-headed brat."

Karen sat across from her daughter, watching the girl eat her delayed lunch. Several mmm noises from Sondra and some light conversation of how the yard work was going served as a reset between the two. After the meal Sondra changed back into her work clothes and went out to finish what she'd started. Roughly two hours later she'd completed her task and proceeded to load the tractor on the trailer. Doug arrived home, going into the house through the garage/kitchen door. He found Karen seated at the table on the phone with her boss from Snap-on Tools. After giving his wife a kiss on the top of her head he went to find his daughter. "Hey, kiddo" he greeted. Sondra was securing the loading-ramps to the trailer. "Impressive" he acknowledged of the work she'd done. "All finished, I see" he observed.

"Yeah" said Sondra with a proud smile. "Mom said we can get a one-time burn permit for our mountain of yard waste here, and if we can get the tractor back to the rental place early enough tomorrow we won't have to pay for another full day."

Doug hadn't expected Sondra to do as much as she'd done. "Had a couple of interesting phone calls today" he told the girl. Sondra was curious but first wanted to know how his day had gone. "So was the graduation thing good?" she inquired. "Long drive in heavy traffic" he began. "And a lot of sitting around waiting, suffering through speech after speech. But I'm glad I went."

"Well Tracy wasn't my favorite person" said Sondra. "But I'm glad for her accomplishment and I'm glad you went."

"She's gonna be okay I think" said Doug with a nod. "She wants to continue school and pursue criminal justice as a career. She and her boyfriend are getting married soon and his family has been in law-enforcement for generations."

He reached over and tested one of Sondra's tractor tie-downs. Satisfied, he altered the subject. "So I hear a little law and order was instituted around here today. Glad you two worked it out."

"Mom called you?" asked Sondra. Karen had in fact called Doug but at this moment in time he chose not to give the girl an answer. Instead he studied her for a few seconds. Her hair was a tangled mess and she had streaks of dirt on her cheeks.

"Got a call from Darren Brown" he informed his daughter. "I guess T.J. was indeed impressed with whatever you did or said at Long Beach and he wants you to meet him and the team in Texas. Darren said he plans to put you in a car and push you harder than you ever thought possible. If you do better than just survive, you're in for next season." Sondra smiled. "Thank god" she whispered, wrapping an arm around her dad as they made their way to Karen.

CHAPTER 25

Sondra's big day of testing for Holt Racing at the Texas Motor Speedway came on a mostly clear Thursday mid-morning that brought a 3-to-7-mile-an-hour wind out of the north. The humidity was at 16 percent and the ambient air temperature was 74 degrees, with track temperatures roughly 18 degrees higher. Eighteen members of Holt Racing were on hand when Doug and Karen delivered their client to pit lane, where the #21 and the #12 Holt Racing machines sat defiantly throwing off the gleaming sun from their slick shiny surfaces. The quiet morning added to the sizable venue's eerie emptiness, void of spectators and other IndyCar teams. The grandstands gleamed in the morning sun but seemed almost sad without the thousands of fans that would normally accompany them on any given race weekend. Darren, Craig Pines and driver Ryan Delgato greeted Sondra and her parents warmly, but T.J. Holt waited for Sondra to walk over to him. He was standing next to the Holt Racing mobile pit-box stand with his longtime engineers Mieko Ondi and John Briers. "Morning" said Sondra to T.J., with a smile and a nod. She reached out with her right hand in greeting but T.J. pushed on her left shoulder with three pudgy fingers. He smiled when the girl refused to budge, staring at him through narrowed eyes.

"Morning" he returned, smiling as if he'd just beat her at a game of high-card draw. He introduced Sondra to Mieko and glanced at his watch. "We got the track for three hours today" he told the girl. "Use that motorhome over there to suit up." Sondra nodded and glanced over to pit lane as men in Holt Racing uniforms hovered over both cars, performing important last-minute preparations. Less than 20 minutes later Sondra was sitting in the #12 car with the engine idling.

Doug and Karen inserted earplugs and then held hands as they looked on nervously. Darren and right-front tire changer Denny Hulzor leaned into the cockpit and helped Sondra with the strap-in process as Darren gave the girl specific instruction. When the two men backed away, with Darren going to his place on the pit-box stand, Doug felt a wave of relief as Sondra executed several strings of quick engine revs. He knew she wouldn't dare do this if she wasn't comfortable and confident. Seconds later the serene world in which this gathering resided exploded in a deafening scream of the Honda twin-turbo V-6, with a light plume of gray smoke expanding quickly from its origin. The rear tires of the #12 Indy car struggled to gain grip and the back-end slid out to the right then straightened. Sondra immediately had her thumb on the rev-limiter button contained within the steering wheel as the #12 car rolled majestically toward pit-exit. Reaching a white line and orange cone, marking the end of pit lane, Sondra began to accelerate and go through the gears. Her arc through Turn 2 was conservative as she gained speed and confidence. Coming around to the Start/Finish line the engine was at full song and her speed was recorded at 221.846 miles per hour. Doug glanced over at the car's owner. The man was chewing gum in a bit of an exaggerated fashion and was slowly pacing back and forth. T.J. adjusted his headset with his left hand while his right was down at his hip, holding down a button on a small electronic box attached with a cord to speak with the driver of his #12 machine. In this moment T.J. Holt didn't care that Sondra was a girl. He didn't consider her age, size and weight, nor did he even consider her limited professional experience. His sole focus was on watching and listening to his car, hoping for and expecting the very best he and his team could muster on this scheduled four-lap run. T.J. was not a cheerleader. He'd never heaped flowery words of encouragement on his drivers or team members. He expected success and had high standards for near-impossible performance from everyone around him.

Sondra's drama-free opening lap intrigued the famous team owner. His #12 car looked stable as it exited Turn 4 and the speed at the line was an impressive 223.592 miles per hour. Sondra was now in familiar territory. The nerves were gone and she was beginning to use the car to its full potential. She felt understeer as she entered Turn 3. The wind had shifted and there was a bit of tire degradation. With both T.J. and Darren in her ears over the radio she was encouraged to use the car's performance tools. Sondra made an adjustment with the weight-jacker in order to give the car the balance she needed to not only maintain but improve her lap-time. This was duly noted by the Holt Racing engineers, seeing the real-time data from the car's telemetry on their laptop computer screens. Lap 3 awarded the Twelve car's fastest speed, 224.668 miles per hour, but on her final go-around the tire degradation reduced Sondra's lap-time by .003 seconds. As Sondra sped toward the Start/Finish line on her 4th and final lap T.J. took off his headset and patted Darren on the back. "Checkered flag, Sondra" said Darren as the car continued on its fast journey. "Awesome job. We're gonna pit this lap. Pit this lap." The driver repeated the pit instruction and proceeded to reduce her speed. "Easy in" instructed Darren, "pit lane speed is fifty-five. Hit your mark and don't slide the tires." Sondra received help from Denny Hulzor in the unbuckling process after coming to a stop and cutting the engine. She stepped out of the car and removed her helmet and balaclava, revealing a wide grin. "Oh man, oh man, oh man" she enthused. "I love this."

"Well that's pretty obvious" said Denny with a light chuckle. He patted the girl's shoulder and pointed toward Darren and the others.

"So, boss?" said Sondra, smiling and rubbing her hands together as she approached T.J., Darren, Craig, the two engineers and the longtime driver of the #21 car, Ryan Delgato.

"When are we going again?" she asked. "I could run laps in that car all day, everyday. And big ones."

Darren turned his eyes to T.J., intentionally putting the man on the spot. "I can work with that" Delgato interjected. Ryan had been employed as Holt Racing's #1 driver for seven years and patted T.J. on the back before heading over the pit wall to his car, where he was scheduled to run 25 laps with an experimental setup. T.J. watched for several seconds as Sondra clutched at the back of her head, subconsciously trying to hide her long tresses in order to minimize any perceived feminine features. The team owner directed Sondra's attention to Darren. "Grab a headset and pay close attention to this" he told the girl.

Sitting beside Darren on Holt Racing's mobile pit command center, Sondra nodded as he spoke to her while watching the pit action. "You're gonna watch and learn here" he told her, handing her a set of headphones. "Ryan's gonna run two twenty-five lap segments, one with a qualifying setup and one in full race trim. Pay attention to what he tells us about how the car is handling and what the engineers relate back to him. We'll break for lunch and then you'll be out on track with Ryan."

Sondra nodded, feeling instant nerves grabbing her. She knew this was going to be her one chance with this team. Fifty-three minutes from the time Sondra and her parents left for lunch, she and her potential teammate Ryan Delgato were back in their cars turning speeds in the two-twenty-three's. They drove separate programs for the better part of their allotted track time but after pitting each driver for fuel and tires they were encouraged to race each other, and race they did. Ryan showed no mercy to the kid. He'd follow a few car lengths behind for one or two laps, then come up close, intentionally making moves as if he were about to flash around the #12 at any second. He did, and on more than one occasion. In all four race seasons Sondra had learned not to let the other guy rattle her. She could predict and counter any move and she knew how to be the aggressor. This was different. With elevated speed, enormous downforce and the unpredictability of air turbulence, every single second the Indy car was rolling was high-risk, knife-edge intensity.

The smallest changes in track conditions had enormous effect. A light 3-mile-an-hour wind while standing still was hardly noticeable, but at over 200 miles an hour the sensation in the cockpit was more akin to one swinging a sledge hammer at another with quick and blunt force.

An involuntary smile swept briefly across Darren's face as he listened to spotter Craig Pines speak to Sondra over the radio, letting her know the second-by-second whereabouts of the #21 car. Sondra had gone from simply reacting to her car and the track as well as the other car to now taking full ownership. She was constantly using the in-car tools to make subtle handling changes in order to find a cleaner, quicker line around the speedway. While she was in front of Ryan it was obvious she was confident and comfortable, and when tailing the #21 found ways to not only stay right with him but then execute a well thought-out plan of attack. With the white-blue-red #12 car leading by 1.035 seconds Darren's voice filled the driver's ears. "All right, Sondra. You're gonna let Ryan by without any radical moves or giving up momentum."

"I'm faster than he is in Three and Four" she announced.

"Copy that" said Darren. "Start formulating the switch in your head in One. By the time you get to Three and Four he'll be on your gearbox and the pass'll happen naturally on the front-stretch. Don't question it. Don't fight it."

Darren held his breath, not 100 percent sure that Sondra was quite mature enough as a driver for this, but once the pass had happened without drama he smiled to himself and gave a triumphant swing of his fist. He congratulated himself on his instincts that Sondra was indeed something special when it came to driving race cars. "Text-book perfect, kiddo" he told her. "We're gonna pit this lap. Pit this lap. Don't pass your teammate. Do not pass your teammate. Follow the twenty-one car down pit lane. Find your pit and hit your marks. Easy in. Don't slide your tires. Do not slide those tires."

"Copy that" responded Sondra, ecstatic that Darren had used the word teammate in the communication. She could barely contain herself.

"Hire that kid" said Ryan to T.J. over the radio as he was rolling to his pit-box. "I haven't had that much fun since Homestead with Kelarzo last March." T.J. didn't give a vocal response. He watched as both his cars came to a stop in their respective pit-boxes, then developed a bit of a smile as Sondra hopped out of the cockpit with a triumphant skyward fist punch. Doug and Karen had been permitted to be much closer during this session and were allowed to take limited photographs. T.J. observed Mrs. Trent, camera in hand, direct Sondra to hold her helmet at her hip and stand next to the left-front tire of the very car that only moments ago had been traveling at a high rate of speed. As Karen took several photos, T.J. stepped closer. He could see the tell-tale signs of relief on the woman's face as she tried to get her daughter to stand still for the camera. He'd seen that same expression before from a number of wives, mothers, sisters and girlfriends over the course of his career, with them thankful that the perceived danger of their loved one had come to a peaceful end. T.J. studied Sondra for a few seconds. Darren had told him on more than one occasion that the girl was not only an extremely capable young driver but could net the organization some good PR from her life story and race career thus far. T.J. had rarely cared about publicity when he was driving but as a car and team owner he was forced to consider all options that would further his business. Having just witnessed this girl hold her own in a duel with one of the most respected race car drivers in today's IndyCar field had him pondering the possibilities of media-boost versus practical racing success, if they did in fact hire her. In past several years he'd given a number of hopeful drivers an opportunity to test in his cars, searching for a more suitable teammate for Ryan, and as he watched the energetic Sondra begin to interact easily with the members of the #12 team he decided on giving the girl a fair shake. "Quite a kid ya got there" T.J. said to Doug. "Why don't you come out to my ranch later today. The wife's always got somethin' cooking and she usually makes enough to feed an army."

"Wow" said Doug, smiling as he shook the man's hand. "That's incredibly kind. We'd love that." The Trents were booked on a flight back to California in roughly three hours but Doug kept this to himself. If there was any chance that Sondra would be offered a driving position on the Holt Racing team he was willing to switch flights and move mountains in order to make that happen.

While Darren kept Doug and Karen engaged with the rest of the team and procedures, T.J. gave Sondra a tour of his permanent garage and shop at the Texas Motor Speedway. He appreciated that she was a respectful good listener and asked only pertinent technical questions about the cars and equipment, not of his famed career. He eyed the girl as she studied an old Chrysler V-8 motor on a stand in the corner. Sondra could feel him watching her and turned, knowing that this was the right time to plead her case. "I meant what I said to you in Long Beach" she began. "I mean I apologize if you took offense for the way I said it but I meant every word."

"Why do you wanna drive for me?" asked T.J. "Got anything to do with Patrero or Crandle? Or maybe you see Darren as some kind of father-figure and you just wanna follow him now that he's switched race teams." Sondra became instantly enraged at the man's suggested hypothesis and hated the term father-figure, suggesting that her dad, her now-dad and Darren had to compete with one another. With clenched fists she mounted a hard defense. "The sole reason I'm here is because you have an intense attitude and approach to racing that's never changed or diminished since your early days. I know where you basically stand on women drivers but I can't change who I am or how I was born. I don't want to be known as just a female race car driver. I don't follow anyone around. I lead, and I sure as hell would never let some stupid boy get in the way of my career." T.J.'s mentioning of Crandle had not been meant in any other context but as the guy that had taken the IndyCar spot on the Patrero team. He knew nothing of their friendship, close or otherwise. "I want to be known for winning races and championships" continued Sondra. "That's what I do. I win races and championships. I'm not here to embarrass you or your team for hiring a girl driver. I don't want that kind of publicity for myself either. I've known that this is what I'm supposed to be doing ever since I could walk and talk. A lot of people told me that coming to you or any other top IndyCar team owner and asking for a ride would be insanely fruitless but I don't care. This is what I want and I'm gonna fight for it as long and as hard as I can."

At the Holt ranch the Trents were introduced to T.J.'s wife Beverly, a 5-foot-7-inch relatively slender, woman with an outgoing and warm personality. Beverly took to the Trents, especially Sondra, always loving to have the younger generation in her home. Sondra was happy to find that Darren Brown and Craig Pines had also been invited to dinner. T.J. soon suggested that Doug join him out on the patio just outside his den to have a more in-depth chat, while Karen and Beverly retired to the library for further conversation. Darren, Craig and Sondra remained at the dining table, which had Sondra feeling a bit nervous over being separated from her manager-parents. "Looked like you took to speedway driving like a duck to water" said Craig to Sondra. In actuality there had been several on-track moments in the car that afternoon that had frightened her to the core. The wheel-to-wheel high-speed chess match she'd engaged in with Ryan was really nothing her past experience had prepared her for, even though the individual driving components were familiar. She'd driven fast and dueled hard before, but high-speed-asphalt oval racing demands far greater mental and physical strength than one can fathom by simply watching it on TV or from sitting in the grandstands. The highest degrees of concentration and natural lightning-quick reaction times were of utmost importance. In a literal blink of an eye one can go from relatively normal to a potentially life-threatening catastrophic crash. Sondra had loved every second she'd been in the Twelve car that day, more than she had even imagined, but this had also shown her to respect and revere what she loved. She wouldn't or couldn't however let these men or anyone else for that matter know of her fears or anxiety.

"Yeah" said Sondra in answer to Craig's statement. "I do have two oval-track experiences from Indy Lights, and I started on dirt ovals in sprint cars, but it's really apples and oranges kind of different. I loved every second of today. This is what I was born to do. I mean T.J. seems like a tough nut just like I always thought him to be and from what people have told me, but I'm good with that. I mean I don't want to be treated like a girl. I'm a school of hard knocks person and I learn damn quick." Sondra pounded her fist on the table. "Easy, Tiger" said Darren. "You got the gig" he assured her. "You have a damn hell of a lot to learn and you're gonna have pressure like you've never known before, but by the time the beginning of next season rolls around you'll have built up enough seat-time to really bring the heat." Sondra nodded, wanting to ask many questions but for some reason suddenly couldn't get the words to emerge. "I wasn't a bit surprised at how you did in the car today" continued Darren. "I saw that potential two years ago." He then leaned forward with his elbows on the table, looking at Sondra with deadly serious eyes. "You stay focused and do what you do naturally and the rest'll basically take care of itself, but know this ... this is a harsh business and we're lookin' for results. Your contract's gonna be pretty standard but it's also pretty limited."

"I know" said Sondra, nodding and interrupting her new IndyCar boss. "T.J. didn't go into any kind of detail" she admitted. "But he basically let me know the score." Craig produced a two-inch stack of paperwork from his briefcase. It made a loud slapping sound as he half-tossed it on the table in front of their new driver. "A little light reading and signing material for ya" he joked with a slow smile. Darren then began a much more inspirational coach-like talk to Sondra, giving her details of what was to come.

Outside on the second floor patio that looked out over the dark Texas landscape, Doug and T.J. chatted about houses, property, married life and first cars and motorcycles they'd possessed. T.J. took an immediate liking to Doug. He saw the man as an intelligent straight-shooter and a bit of a kindred spirit. There was also a bit of an instant son-in-law vibe that T.J. felt on a subconscious level. By the same token Doug felt at ease with Mr. Holt, something he'd not expected, and he too experienced a subconscious father-son vibe. He waited for just the right moment, when there was a quick lull in the conversation, to tell T.J. what he'd loosely rehearsed in his head. "Sondra's not gonna let you down, T.J." Doug told the racing legend. "I know just looking at her it's hard to imagine her lifting a thirty pound bowling ball above her head let alone being in command of a powerful race car, mixing it up with a bunch of strong seasoned drivers." He had more to say but T.J. basically cut him off by patting him on the shoulder, son-in-law style. "Well" he began. "You may be right about that but I agreed to give her a shot and she's got the right attitude. Besides, there's no denying her stats and I saw what I saw. She very well could have stuffed it in the wall three times today. I've seen my fair share of veteran drivers who didn't have that kind of car control. Been doin' this a lot of years. I know from a hell of a lot of experience what it takes to even have a little bit of success at this. I'm not gonna stand here and blow smoke up your ass, Doug. This is a damn hard business and there are no guarantees that she won't wash out within a year, but I'm a man of my word. I made my choice and I'm behind the kid a hundred percent. And I don't really see her washing out" he added. The two men shook hands and Doug glanced down at his watch.

Now that Sondra had a set future of being employed as an IndyCar Series driver for Holt Racing, with all the necessary sponsorship and finances in place, she felt more at peace with her current life. Casa de Trent was a comfortable and happy place to live with her now-parents and she was excited about her future there. She drained a portion of her main savings account in order to get the construction under way for what she dubbed Sierre-Trent Raceway. Road-graders formed a dirt-track and a kart track was paved with asphalt. She dismantled the goat shack herself and hired a construction company to lay the concrete foundation and erect the steel structure for the new garage and shop. Karen was finessing the permit process for all of this like a politician snaking a controversial bill through the House and the Senate, and Doug was bringing materials to the sight and overseeing the progress.

"So what's on the agenda for the day?" asked Karen as she brought a plate of pancakes stacked seven inches high to the table.

"Found a Yamaha dealership in Goleta" said Doug. "On Hollister Avenue just to the north. Thought I'd take the kid and go check out a few dirt-bikes."

"Really?" said an instantly excited Sondra. "The kid could go for that" she added with a wide smile.

"Well if the kid could put her napkin in her lap I'm sure that would be perfectly fine" said Karen, sitting down and leading by example. Karen wasn't thrilled about the prospect of purchasing or riding dirt-bikes, especially since she was seeing an abundance of money going out, but loved the father-daughter bond the two shared of all things motorized. She also knew that dirt bikes weren't the only alternative vehicles that held Doug and Sondra's interest. There had been much previous mention of ATVs and shifter karts.

As mentioned at the breakfast table, Doug and the kid ventured over to Goleta. Sondra took hold of Doug's hand as they walked through the doors of Santa Barbara Motorsports. This was a subconscious action and felt as normal to her as breathing. When she was young, many a time she'd gone with her father to motorcycle dealerships as well as auto and electrical supply stores and various other industrial businesses. "Mmm" voiced Sondra after breathing in the aroma of the motorcycle showroom. "I love the smell of new tires and engines" she enthused. Doug nodded and smiled as they stepped a few feet inside, staring at the multiple gleaming and dazzling rows of new dirt and street-going two-wheelers. Sondra let go of Doug's hand and walked over to the display of a mannequin in full helmet and riding gear, seated on an orange and white ATV. She then followed her now-dad up and down each eye-catching aisle until she came to a large poster on the wall of nine-time world FIM Moto GP champion, Valentino Rossi. At the ages of nine through twelve Sondra and her father had gone to many AMA road races at Sonoma Raceway and Laguna Seca Raceway. They each had their favorite riders, with one being a local hometown hero. Sondra used to picture herself on a road race bike as her father would read to her articles and stories contained within two different motorcycle magazines he received each month. There were many battles with great men on grand racetracks. In recent years Sondra had read about Valentino Rossi and had seen a few videos of him racing in Europe. Coming to stand next to Doug at the sales counter, Sondra listened to him talk with two employees, Carla Vasquez and Eddie Grisban. She soon learned that Carla was the daughter of the business owner and Eddie, who worked the parts counter during the week but doubled in sales when needed, was a semi-pro motorcycle road racer. He began a separate conversation with Sondra, who told him about being a newly signed driver for Holt Racing. Eddie acted as if he wasn't as impressed as he was and began to openly flirt with her, though Sondra was oblivious. When she spoke about her two race tracks and the plan to purchase shifter karts he motioned with his head. "Oh we got a couple of used ones for sale" said Eddie. "Or we could order some new ones for you."

"Have a couple of used ones" corrected Sondra of his grammar. "You have a couple of used karts" she repeated. "I'm looking for One-Twenty-Five cc shifter-karts, to be specific" she clarified. While Doug and Carla attended to business in the sale of the two YZ 250s as well as ordering a blue ATV for Karen, Eddie invited Sondra through a swinging door that led into the repair and assembly shop. He asked her age and boldly tried to pry into her personal life, mostly with the intention of finding out whether or not she had a boyfriend. Sondra was vague on all counts, immediately spotting the used karts that he'd mentioned. "These two just came in the other day" Eddie informed Sondra. "This one needs a whole new back bumper, and the motor won't even pull through on this one. Here's a box of extras that came with 'em" he added, pointing to a large beat-up and stained cardboard box.

"Kay" said Sondra as she more closely inspected the lot. "Wanna talk it over with your dad first?" he asked. Sondra shot the impertinent boy an angry glance. "I'm eighteen, not twelve" she snarled. "I can buy whatever the hell I want." Eddie wasn't expecting this kind of reaction and followed her back out to the sales floor, intrigued with her apparent feistiness and natural beauty, which refused to be fully disguised under the masculine T-shirt and jeans she wore.

As Doug and Sondra were walking to the Tacoma a black Ford F-150 entered the parking lot pulling a trailer. On top was a red and black three year-old BMW M-3 Coupe. "Nice ride" offered Sondra to the man stepping down from the truck's cab. "Thanks" he said with a smile as Sondra and Doug approached to get a closer look at the trailered vehicle.

"Is that the two-point-eight liter motor?" asked Sondra.

"Yeah" he said, beginning to study the girl. "The engine rebuild is pretty new" he offered, mostly to Doug. "It's got oversized pistons, S-Fifty cams and twenty-four pound injectors. I just installed a new baffled oil pan and I'm running Koni double-adjustable shocks."

"Nice" said Doug, introducing himself and Sondra after noticing the man was wearing the same kind of blue Santa Barbara Motorsports shirt as the two employees inside. Doug smiled at Rob's facial response to Sondra's powerful handshake and felt a sense of pride when Sondra inquired as to what fly-wheel and brakes package the young man was running on the car. From the various advertising stickers and the concealed headlights and tail-lights, not to mention the obvious roll-cage inside, this was clearly a race vehicle. Sondra and Rob soon entered into an enthusiastic discussion about being on several different tracks.

"I'm in an M-Three club there" said Rob when Sondra mentioned Laguna Seca Raceway. "I've taken it to Willow Springs a few times but never been to Sonoma." Sondra told of her current status as well as detailing some of her experiences on all three racetracks. Her exchange with both Rob and Eddie plus the excitement about the new purchases gave her a sense of hope and power.

Sondra drove down to LA for a meeting with Gina Perschwen and several other AAA executives. This was to assure that the insurance company's commitment to her would remain strong and intact for her first contracted season with Holt Racing. She first stopped at Shelley's and the two went to the AAA office together for Shelley to meet with Gina about further Safen-Up details. Sondra loved that she was given another chance to drive Shelley's Porsche and spend a night at her Malibu home. After a fun swim in the pool the two sat under heat-lamps, with Sondra detailing the construction work that was continuing on the garage-shop of Sierre-Trent Raceway. Her phone buzzed, and when she announced the name of the caller Shelley encouraged her to take the call. "So yeah, that was Brice" announced

Sondra after the relatively short chat had ended. "He's in LA visiting our friend and F-Ford competitor Andrew. They're going sailing to Catalina Island tomorrow and Brice asked me if I'd go with him."

"Well what are you waiting for?" said Shelley. "Tell Doug and Karen about the plan and call the boy back."

Thursday was a glorious 77 degree mostly clear morning in Southern California. Sondra drove her Tacoma from Malibu to the San Pedro Marina to meet Brice, Andrew and his fiancé Stephanie at Slip 247. The sailing vessel was an old forty-two foot Westsail that had been given to Andrew by his grandfather on his 14th birthday. The Placers were avid sailors, from generation to generation. "I've never been in anything but a raft or a small wooden rowboat" announced Sondra after greetings were administered. "I've always wanted to go sailing. Arr, matey. Hoist the main sail and pass me the rum or it's the plank for all ye land lubbers" she added in an over-the-top pirate voice. Sondra experienced goosebumps when it was discovered that at some point in their lives they'd all read the same book, The Wydah by Martin W. Sandler, about a famous pirate ship that was sunk off the east American coast. Discussion about the book and modern-day pirates gave way to Sondra inquiring how Andrew had come to get into sailing. As it turned out, the boy had practically grown up on and around boats, and Sondra remembered Brice telling her that Andrew's father was a sixteen-year veteran as an owner/crewman aboard an America's Cup vessel.

Sondra thought it rude and weird how Andrew seemed to suddenly bark out orders, with Brice and Stephanie obeying them without question. Everyone had a job, and as Sondra helped stow covers and all unnecessary gear inside a container mounted to the dock, she was given specific and highly important instruction on the do's and don'ts of being aboard a sailboat. Even though they were basically a small group of young adults going out for fun they treated it with the utmost respect and seriousness, just as one might around a race car. Sondra quickly got into the spirit of the adventure, asking many questions and finding many similarities with sailing and racing. Race cars and sailboats use some of the same basic principles when it comes to dealing with aerodynamics and drag. She was also quick to see how big a role safety plays in a successful sailboat outing. Sondra watched in amusement as her three shipmates clambered around securing items and untying the main sail, all the while explaining to her the use and importance of things like a Jib sheet, a Halyard line, and to always pay close attention that your feet never step on or get tangled in any of the lines. Once out of the harbor, the sails and course set, Andrew, Brice and Sondra engaged in a bit of race car talk as Stephanie disappeared into the cabin. Andrew took off and threw his shirt down after her, then kicked off his sandals. Sondra looked over, wondering if Brice was going to do the same. She was relieved when all he removed was his sweatshirt. A few minutes later Stephanie emerged wearing a white bikini that was particularly striking against her deep tan and the thick multi-colored beach towel she'd wrapped around her neck.

"Come with me, Sondra" she offered. "I'll give you the two-second tour of the cabin and we can have us a little girl-talk." She turned to address Andrew. "Listening to you guys go on and on about tires, brakes and suspensions is giving me a headache." The racers laughed, each thinking they probably could sit there all day and talk about cars and racing. Girl-talk didn't sound too appealing to Sondra. She was perfectly content staying right where she was, especially since both Brice and Andrew had alluded to some big news they had for her, but followed Stephanie down the cabin steps anyway. Stephanie motioned for Sondra to have a seat on one of the small dinette benches.

"Andrew took me out in this very boat on our third date" she told Sondra. "We anchored in the same harbor we're going to today, Avalon. We took the Zodiac ashore and had a really nice dinner. It was a little scary going back home in the dark but Andrew's been all over the world on sailboats with his dad, and in all sorts of different conditions. When we were like halfway home he told me all about this time they were sailing from the Caribbean and ran into some actual modern-day pirates. They had to stand on the deck with guns under flood lamps from the mast until the other boat started heading away. The next day I asked his dad if that was really true, because I wasn't sure Andrew hadn't just told me that to scare me so he could have an excuse to hold me close and be all strong and brave, Mr. big protector. So what about you and Brice?"

Not really knowing how to answer Stephanie's question, Sondra shrugged her shoulders but gave an abbreviate version of their meeting and relationship. The women returned to the deck and Sondra liked what she saw. Brice was at the helm. He had a firm and confident stance and had turned his Patrero-McDonald's baseball cap around backwards. The sleeves of his pure white T-shirt ruffled in the steady breeze and his eyes seemed to sparkle. Stephanie smiled to herself before heading over to where Andrew was napping as she watched Brice position Sondra in front of him, putting her hands on the large wheel then encircling the girl with his chiseled muscular arms as he clearly enjoyed their closeness. He lightly kissed the back of her head and Sondra briefly closed her eyes, developing a involuntary pleased expression. A year ago she most likely would have turned around and slugged him on the shoulder, making a nervous joke to try and cover her embarrassment. At this moment however she felt no embarrassment, only a rare happiness and a feeling of deep warm contentedness. Not only did Brice really care for her but she was now in charge of the boat, and with his gentle encouragements was learning how to keep the sails full while maintaining their compass heading.

There were two more precious moments shared by Brice and Sondra that day. One was while they were all having a deck picnic, anchored in the Avalon harbor. Sondra felt a wave of happiness as Brice cut small pieces of apple with his pocketknife and thoughtfully offered them to her. He told the little group that his grandpa Tom had given that knife to him, with his grandfather recounting the history of the wooden handle and warning about the sharpness of the blade. Sondra laughed knowingly about the sharpness of a pocketknife. She didn't divulge her memory to the group but her dad had once given her a knife that was his dad's. She was ten and Kal too had warned her about the potential dangers, telling her to put the knife in a safe place until she was older. Well of course she put it in a safe place but not until she'd managed to cut herself several times. The ultra-thin lacerations didn't hurt or even produce significant red marks but she was amazed at how such a light touch of her finger could end with those results. The other special moment Sondra and Brice shared was on the way home. Once again they were in basically the same position as before, at the helm. The sun was getting lower in the sky and the temperature dropped significantly. Sondra shivered as she gripped the steering wheel and Brice wrapped his arms around her tightly. She felt instantly warm, safe and happy.

After a day of oceanic fun and adventure the two women watched as Andrew and Brice played the roll of macho he-men. Andrew skillfully motored the boat into position and Brice jumped onto the dock to secure it with thick rope. The boys went straight to the tasks of hosing the salt water off its surfaces and putting all the protective covers over the sails and ornate wood fixtures. Dinner at a nearby pizzeria was agreed upon and as Sondra enjoyed her first slice she made what she thought to be a very bizarre observation. "It feels like I'm still on the boat. Am I swaying or is it just my imagination?" Her friends all laughed, recalling the first time they'd had that same experience. Brice quickly volunteered to hold her steady, with Andrew lightly kicking him under the table. A warning to be cool. Saying goodbye that evening just seemed wrong for this little band of sailors. They'd bonded as a unit and vowed to get together again as soon as possible. During their time in the pizzeria Sondra learned that Brice and Andrew were to be Patrero-McDonald's IndyCar teammates for the upcoming season, with hopes for them both to qualify for the Indianapolis 500.

Though the drive back to Santa Barbara was long, especially with being out to sea all day, Sondra enjoyed the trip, going over in her head each and every moment. It was just after 10 p.m. when she arrived home, loving that Doug and Karen had stayed up waiting for her. "I didn't feel at all seasick" she bragged to her now-parents as they sat with her on the large rust-red couch in the living room. "And I thought for sure that Stephanie was gonna irritate the living crap out of me but she turned out to be really cool. And Brice was a total gentleman. I had so much fun. I love sailing. These big seagulls would swoop down and dive-bomb the water for their lunch. Oh, and I always thought it was just something that TV or movie people made up, but there were real dolphins that porpoised alongside us, just like in the movies. It was awesome."

"So Brice was a total gentleman?" prompted Karen. Sondra let out a quick nervous laugh, instantly embarrassed and worried about what Doug might be thinking, perhaps disapproving of her spending the day with the boy she'd hated and now liked. She shrugged her shoulders and stared down at the assembly of books on the coffee table. "I don't know" she uttered. "He was just, well nice."

Karen smiled and touched Sondra on the knee. "Nice?" she asked the girl. "It must have been way more than just nice, Sondra. Your face is turning all red."

"Na-uh" protested the girl, turning away and trying desperately to keep from grinning ear to ear. "It's probably just from all the sun" she added.

Karen didn't want to pry too hard about the details of Sondra spending the day with Brice, especially in front of Doug. Instead she declared it late and that they all go to bed. Sondra nodded but then spoke in a low thoughtful voice. "Sometimes I have these really horrible nightmares. Like a theme. I'm floating in space and I know I won't ever be able to get back to earth. Another kinda recurring nightmare I have is where I'm drifting out to sea, lost and all alone." She yawned before continuing. "I was out to sea today and I wasn't lost and I wasn't all alone. I even got to steer the boat on the way back home. Brice was right there behind me but it wasn't like I needed his help or anything. For that little bit of time I didn't think about my past and how my life turned out, and I didn't worry over how my future's gonna be. I was just there and I belonged."

"You always belong, Sondra" assured Doug, putting a solid arm around her.

CHAPTER 26

Dan Stoltz helped locate some used but well-maintained shop machinery and on one particular visit he arrived in a large hauler van, bringing with him Sondra's old F-Ford car. "Hate to give 'er up" he confessed to Sondra and Doug as they stared at the race vehicle now sitting majestically inside the Sierre-Trent Raceway garage. "Looked pretty damn nice in my showroom but I guess this is a more appropriate home, for the time being."

"Yeah" agreed Sondra. "It needs some intensive care but I'm looking forward to it."

"I like the floor in here" Dan said of the shop's interior. "With the black and white checkerboard pattern" he added as he looked around the work space. "Thanks" said Sondra, taking full credit for its conception. "I had to practically argue with the flooring guys 'cause they were gonna go with one-inch squares instead of the one-foot squares I told them from the start I wanted."

"This is quite a place" said Dan, moving on from the floor issue as he took further study noticing the two new dirt-bikes along with the two used and two new karts. He smiled to himself when he spotted Doug's old arc-welder and large red rollaway tool chest and silently congratulated himself on his part in helping to secure the several pieces of shop machinery, now placed in thoughtful arrangement.

"Got a line on an old end-mill" he told Sondra and Doug. "Needs some new parts and some cleanup and paint but the guy just wants to get rid of it. It's yours free if you go down to San Diego and get it by next Thursday. Here's all the particulars" he added, handing Doug a piece of paper. "Now then, lets see a little action" he said, gesturing to Sondra and then over to the row of karts.

For the next seventeen minutes Dan and Doug watched Sondra race around a ribbon of asphalt, the new blacktop surface making a striking contrast to the lazy ankle-high light-brown grass with tiny yellow and blue flowers covering the gentle rolling countryside. "So how's the kid these days?" Dan asked his friend as they eyed Sondra at the furthest end of the track.

"Good" answered Doug. "She's quite an enigma. Tough as nails and stubborn as a mule at times but mostly she's the sweetest little thing. Karen and I love her even more each day. This may sound strange but there are moments here and there that it just doesn't seem possible that she's not our biological daughter. I'm really proud of her. She's worked her ass off, especially around here, and maintains the biggest focus on her career of anyone I've ever known. Darren Brown may have gone to the mat for her and opened some big doors but she got that IndyCar ride all on her own, if you ask me. Just watch how she attacks that switchback section over there. It's really something super-special, and that's just her natural base talent. You can't teach that sort of thing. Her new race team and first IndyCar season are gonna be a huge challenge for all of us. I'm not at all worried about her driving but she holds everything in so tight. She still won't really deal with her past but when some things do come out it can be downright alarming."

"What do you mean?" inquired Dan. Doug took a deep breath and waited for Sondra to come by the Start/Finish line so he could start the stopwatch feature on his watch.

"Her family's belongings have been in a storage facility up north" he related to Dan. "I bought two of those big truck shipping containers. You can get old ones for pretty cheap, well, relatively.

I had the contents of the storage unit packed up and put in the containers, then had 'em trucked down. That wasn't cheap either but I'm convinced this is the right thing to do. The containers are sittin' just a little ways from the garage, next to a small storage shed that has some of Karen's and my old stuff. Sondra won't go near those containers and if we even mention it she becomes really moody and angry. We're not sure if we should just let her alone with this or get her to take a look inside. I keep thinking she might find something of her past that can give her at least some peace of mind or some closure of some kind."

"What about this Shelley woman?" inquired Dan. "Karen's told me a little about her and how she's been sort of an unofficial therapist to Sondra."

"I don't know" said Doug. "I'm not quite as optimistic about the therapy angle as Karen. I don't think Shelley actually does like traditional psychotherapy with Sondra but if she can say or do anything to help our girl in that area I'm all for it. I think I'm more interested in encouraging Sondra to develop some appropriate longtime friends."

The two men looked on as Sondra attacked Turn 4, on the ragged edge of losing the back end. Her car-control was uncanny as she caught it and sliced toward the apex, then rocketed to the next turn. "So what about this boy I keep hearing about?" Dan inquired. "The one that was her teammate last year?"

"Oh" groaned Doug. "The Crandle kid" he said shaking his head. "Don't even get me started. I know it's inevitable but I don't think I'm ready for her to have a boyfriend." Dan chuckled at that as Sondra went by in a blink of an eye. "Nessa's said several times that if we could be guaranteed to have a kid like Sondra she might want to start a family" he told Doug, squinting into the late afternoon sun and following the mini low-to-the-ground racer speed around the twisty track with shocking intensity. "I don't know if I'm ready to go through the fatherhood thing again though" added Dan. "Not at my age. Besides, we're looking at some property in Napa. A spread kinda like this would be my baby."

"Napa, huh?" said Doug. "Don't tell Sondra that. She'll want to move in with you just to be near Sonoma Raceway. She loves that place. She once told me that if it were possible she'd live in a tent in the infield." The two men had a good chuckle at that as they continued to monitor the young race car driver for the next number of minutes.

Dan and Vanessa took the Trents out for dinner that evening at Victorina's, an upscale seafood restaurant approximately thirty minutes down the coast. They were a bit early for their reservation and were encouraged to wait in the cocktail lounge until their table was ready. After settling into soft red velvet chairs and ordering drinks, Sondra listened to the conversation within their immediate group as well as bits and pieces of dialog by others around the room. The actual words began to cease to have real meaning for her. A flashback of the evening she'd spent with her family and her godparents at the Tahoe restaurant years ago slapped her hard. She could suddenly smell her mother's perfume and hear her brother Dave's voice. She looked around desperately, biting down hard on her tongue. When Vanessa asked her a question, for the second time, Sondra snapped back to harsh reality, apologizing, then excusing herself to find the Lady's Room. She washed her hands and stared at herself in the mirror. "What am I doing here?" she breathed out loud. Sondra concentrated on her eyes staring back at her, threatening and willing them not to produce tears. It didn't work. Rivulets meandered their way down her cheek but she didn't make a move to wipe them away. Her eyes blurred with moisture as she tried to remember the voices and physical characteristics of each family member. Her father's presence always had a very specific feel. It was as if his arms were wrapped around her at all times, no matter if she was just inches or feet apart from him or if he was at work or nowhere near her current location. Her brother Dave's voice and mannerisms were always of special interest to her. He was the trusted leader of the Sierre kids. Maureen had once referred to her children as The Dave, Sondra and Haley coterie. Dave was eighteen months older than Sondra and she loved that he was far more knowledgeable on the latest social trends, sayings and slang. This occasionally met with parental disapproval, which made Sondra treasure and admire her brother all the more. She also thought that Dave was learning far more interesting concepts and subjects. Her little brother Haley represented a perfect blend of unique individuation and unquestionable solid trust and loyalty. His voice had a bit of a squeak but it was by no means mousy or meek and he often said things that seemed far beyond his years. Sondra's mother was a constant power source for the entire family, guiding, teaching and encouraging. She was a gentle and sweet person who seemed to be able to harness an electric awe-inspiring strength at always the right moment. It was easy for Sondra to see her father's physical and authoritative strengths but her mother's power lay just beneath the surface, and when she on occasion flexed the potency of her life-force Sondra's world would seem to stand momentarily still.

Sondra forced herself to be strong and to act happy during the dinner with Doug, Karen, Dan and Vanessa. She enjoyed her crab cake appetizers, even secretly savoring a light scolding from Karen about eating the first one with her hands instead of using a fork. For dessert the agreeable assembly elected to leave their table and head to the cozy warmth of the small coffee bar located at the other end of the cocktail lounge. Dan suggested to Sondra that she join him in a quick after-dinner walk on the beach before consuming any more food. She accepted without question. On this clear night the moon was unusually bright as she and Dan walked along the shore. She made nervous small talk and went into detail about her recent race car driving stints. Dan waited patiently for the girl to wind things down, and when there came a break he halted and gently grabbed her by the upper arm. "I don't know whether to hug you to bits or throw you in the damn ocean" he told Sondra. He let go and walked closer to the surging water. Sondra raised her eyebrows at his suggestion that he throw her in the water but hurried over to him, childlike. "I'm voting for the hug" she chirped. "It's too cold for swimming." His laugh was labored as he put a thick arm around her. "So how ya doin', honey? Really," he asked. Sondra pushed past the dreaded honey and told of the move to Santa Barbara from her perspective, how she thought it great and the possibilities there exciting. It also reminded her of living on a farm when she was little and she didn't know how much a future she'd have in Santa Barbara because, after all, she was now an adult with big-time career goals. "I can't tell Doug or Karen that though" she said to Dan. "I mean they're so amazing and I only want them to know how happy I am to live here and have them in my life."

Sondra stepped away and reached down to grab a handful of sand. After squeezing it tight she threw it angrily into the wet shiny surf. Dan could only guess what was going through her head. "So I hear you have a couple of big storage sheds full of all your family's stuff" he prompted.

Sondra shrugged her right shoulder. "We have three sheds, actually" she informed him. "Two big metal shipping containers and a smaller light-metal shed that has a trillion boxes and other things of Doug and Karen's that they didn't want to put in the new house." Dan had a quick internal laugh at the girl's tendency to occasionally over-exaggerate. It would be tons of this or billions of that, or her usual go-to, trillions. When describing situations she would often use adjectives such as horrible, hideous, absolutely unbelievable, or catastrophic.

"When Travis was killed" he imparted, his normally booming voice reduced to half as he spoke of the son he'd lost years ago, "we closed the door to his bedroom. Eventually his mother started spending quite a bit of time in there but I just couldn't. That was pretty much the beginning of the end to our marriage, especially when she started to really blame me for teaching him to fly in the first place and being so supportive when he wanted to go into the Army Air Corps."

He watched Sondra look downward and walk in a short circle, her shoes leaving footprints in the wet sand. "Let me give you some advice, honey" he continued. "Don't shut down all your emotions and memories. You end up basically cutting yourself off at the knees with the people closest to you. I can attest to that."

Sondra glanced up and nodded, sensing they were both on the verge of tears. She sniffled away tenacious emotion as she remembered the Honor Wall Dan had created for his military hero son at the Fresno auto dealership. "Your honor wall's still there, isn't it?" she asked, a bit of desperation in her voice.

"Yeah" he assured her. "And it's grown. Every once in a while someone he served with comes by. Some bring snapshots to pin up but they all sign the wall and salute him."

"That's nice" she said, watching the moon vibrate on the bay and suddenly remembering a fifth-grade teacher once reading from a book with that exact phrase, "vibrate on the bay," to her class. "When my family's stuff was delivered, there were some loose pictures" she announced in an uncertain voice. "The mover guys wrapped 'em up and had them in the cab with them. They handed them to Doug and Karen and they suggested we hang them up somewhere because they thought they were touching. I don't know." She looked down and dug her heel into the earth, then kicked at the indentation she'd made. "I do kinda want you to see 'em" she said in a ragged squeaky voice. Dan put a solid arm around her. "I'd like that" he told the girl. "I'm glad you have Doug and Karen in your life, honey. They love you more than you could possibly know. I hope you do choose to put up pictures of your family. It honors who they are."

Sondra nodded and forced herself to be strong. "Nessa and I'll come back soon" he continued. "We're headin' down to LA tonight. Good to see your shop and kart setup. I'm sure that's all beneficial to your racing."

"Yeah" agreed Sondra. "Speaking of beneficial" she said as they began walking back to the restaurant. "I don't know if I've ever thanked you enough for giving me that sprint-car ride. I mean that was tons of great driving experience but I know you ended up shelling out more money than you planned, and ..."

"Don't worry about that, honey" he told her, patting Sondra on the back. "I spent what I needed to and we won. That's what matters. You've thanked me enough, and by the way I didn't lose money on the deal. I don't do things that aren't profitable, and I sold that all off at a handsome profit." Sondra disliked talking about money and profits, especially in regards to racing. For her the harsh realities of finances seemed dark and dirty. She saw racing as something pure and noble. On the journey back to the restaurant with Dan, she breathed deeply as their steps propelled them forward, thoughts and memories pounding in their heads and hearts every bit as hard and as loud as the waves that swooped and crashed down on the smooth sand.

Chapter 27

With this year's IndyCar season looming ever closer, Doug and Sondra flew to Holt Racing headquarters for the official contract signing. The offices and shop for the race organization resided within a large building of an older business park adjacent to the Texas Motor Speedway. At the conclusion of the legal matters the newest Holt Racing driver endured a publicity photo session, a quick interview by a local newspaper reporter, and an hour-long session of signing many promotional photos, cards and various items, like keychains, stickers and hats. Sondra was then weighed and measured for her new race-suit, helmet and gloves. The forming of two carbon-fiber tubs was next. These would be the cockpits and lifesaving safety enclosures, the monocoque, of Sondra's two new race cars for her first IndyCar season. One car would be the designated road car and the other would be set up for ovals. She sat surrounded by expandable foam inside two different molds for approximately an hour in each one, simulating a racing stint. This high-tech, highly specialized gel felt similar to being in a beanbag chair at first before it began to harden. She took this activity deadly serious and loved the careful attention to detail the technicians administered. Upon completion she was awarded several sets of team uniforms and escorted into T.J.'s private office by his longtime assistant Jenny Gelverson.

T.J. offered Sondra a Coke and gestured for her to have a seat. The furniture and room reminded her a bit of John Farnsal's office, comfortable but old, stale and mostly brown. "Thanks" she said, acknowledging T.J.'s offering. "Seven Up's gonna be one of my sponsors but an ice cold Coke on a hot day really hits the spot" she told her new boss.

"Well at the risk of stating the obvious" began T.J., ignoring the girl's beverage comments, "I'm expecting a hell of a lot this next season." Sondra nodded. She was well aware his reputation of demanding big things from those around him. "If I didn't think I could win races or the championship for you" she told him. "I wouldn't be here." T.J. studied the girl as she popped opened the can of soda and took a sip.

"Had quite a little chat with your old Lights boss, Steven Barnes" he informed the girl, leaning back in his chair with the beginnings of a smirk. "Did you really tell Patrero to go jump in a polluted lake?"

"He pissed me off" defended Sondra. "Criticized my driving after I'd won both races at Elkhart Lake. I mean I'm always up for constructive criticism but to give me an undue amount of crap after I worked my ass off, and won? Hell no."

T.J. smiled at that. "Well you're gonna fit in well here" he told Sondra. "You won't be given crap about winning, I can assure you of that. Just don't screw up and keep screwing up. You will catch all sorts of hell for that, and then you'll be gone. According to Barnes, you're not in the habit of screwing up" he continued. "Learnin' the ropes and being successful in IndyCar isn't exactly easy but you give me a hundred percent and I'll back you all the way."

Sondra nodded and took a careful sip of her soda. "Speaking of learning the ropes" continued T.J., taking a sip of his own beverage. "Delgato's a hell of a good driver and a good guy and he's a team player. You learn everything you can from him." Sondra gave two vigorous nods. "He really does seem like a good guy" she said. "And I feel comfortable with him, on and off track." "Well I'm not a man for flowery speeches or pep-talks" he told her, laboring to stand, then offering his hand. "So welcome aboard, Tiger, and give 'em hell."

During a Casa de Trent breakfast of scrambled eggs on toast, with bacon and small bowls of sliced peaches, Karen watched Sondra use a piece of bacon as a makeshift spoon to gather up portions of egg. It occurred to the mom that the girl was possibly doing this to get a rise out her. She chose not to take the bait. "I know you two have been busy with the gym construction" she said, focusing on her husband. "But I don't want you to forget that my parents are coming this weekend, and my friend Val is coming over Friday to check out our little oasis here. It's the only time she'll have for quite some time, and my folks love her." Doug nodded at the news but furrowed his brow as he observed his daughter's questionable table manners. She dragged a piece of toast around in an S shape with her fingers, then popped it into her mouth. Sondra nodded as she chewed. "I had a long talk with SeaShell last night" she announced. "I hope you don't mind but I invited her to come see our new digs. It's not set in stone but she thinks she can come up on Thursday morning. It'll only be a short visit."

"That's fine" said Karen. "It'll be nice to see her again, and my parents' flight gets in that afternoon" added the mom, handing Sondra the momentarily unused fork.

Casa de Trent was bathed in glorious full sunshine and striking blue-sky on the morning the Trents were expecting company. Sondra sat on the front porch, watching for her friend, and when Shelley's red Boxster roared closer and pulled to a stop she was pleasantly surprised to find Darren at the wheel. After a home tour, Doug, Karen, Shelley, Darren and Sondra assembled in the kitchen. Shelley took immediate note of the pictures on one of the walls. "Oh I love this" she exclaimed. "You and your family, Sondra. Ah, adorable" she gushed, gesturing to a 4x6 image of 4-year-old Sondra on her red tricycle. Sondra and her steed were tilted sideways on two wheels looking over her shoulder, her sparkling hazel-green eyes narrowed in fierce concentration. Shelley's attention was then captured by a nearby framed 8x11 photograph. "So what's going on here, in this picture?" she asked. Sondra bit down hard on her tongue, worried emotion would get the better of her. She desperately didn't want Darren to see her cry. "Labor Day" she announced, forcing herself to be strong. "I was ten and we used this picture for that year's Christmas card."

"Such a beautiful family" stated Shelley. Sondra deftly wiped away the beginnings of moisture from her eyes before going into detail. "It was basically a family work weekend. Dave and I helped but mom and dad put in that long bench we're sitting on, and also the brickwork in the back and on the sides. The space had kinda been a no-man's-land after the pool was put in." The room fell eerily silent for just under a minute, waiting for Sondra to continue. "I used to love swimming" she said, her voice on the verge of giving away her overwhelming emotions. "The deep end was only eight and a half feet but I thought it was such a huge accomplishment to go down and touch the drain. Dave made that sound like the greatest thing in the world when we used the pool for the first time." Sondra swallowed hard and clawed with her hand at her thigh, making a tight fist. "I guess I sort of idolized him because he was always doing something great and different. You know, like an older brother or a leader should."

Doug and Karen hadn't had any previous luck in getting Sondra to expound upon the detail of these photographs and they along with Darren and Shelley experienced a bit of an ah-ha moment from the girl's last statement. Sondra was the exact same way in a race car. Someone who was a little different and was a natural leader. Tears formed in Shelley's eyes as Sondra's memory flowed. "Mom bought seven tickets for this big charity barbecue dinner at the park but we got so involved in the bench and brick project that Mr. and Mrs. Jenner, my godparents, volunteered to go pick 'em up." Sondra briefly pointed to the image. "Mrs. Jenner took this picture. They were standing on the other side of the pool and ..." She abruptly stopped talking, her teeth clamped tightly together as she stared intently at the scene. No one spoke or dared move as they allowed the girl time to drink in and process the memory. "If you look close" she said in a forced determined voice, "you can see Haley trying to hide a drumstick. He almost fell in the pool when he ran to the Jenners and they gave him a piece of chicken, even though Dad wanted him to wait 'til we took a picture and then ate our box lunches together." Sondra wiped her eyes quickly, hoping no one would notice. "I had barbecue sauce all over my hand because I'd just wiped Haley's mouth clean for the shot." Karen got another ah-ha moment from that. She wondered to herself if this might be a subconscious reason Sondra often used her hand to wipe her mouth clean during mealtimes, instead of a napkin.

"You're practically covered head to toe in dirt and dried concrete" chuckled Darren as he looked at the image of young Sondra.

"Yeah" she said with a shrug of her shoulder and a forced quick smile. "About a year before, there was a section of front sidewalk that was buckling because of a big Sycamore tree" she explained. "And my dad broke it all up. He removed the pieces and poured a new bit of sidewalk. We all put our handprints in it and wrote our names underneath with a stick. When the city put in all new sidewalks on our block they gave us the option of saving it. Dad got some guys from work to lift it out and move it with a piano dolly to the backyard. Not sure where Dave and Haley were that day but I watched and I even helped by coming up with a fulcrum idea to get it back off the dolly. Dad told the guys about his future plans to use bricks and mortar in order to connect it to the pool decking and an expanded patio. After it was off the dolly we all sat in lawn chairs talking and mom came out with chips, salsa and beer. Dad even gave me a sip. Tasted horrible but I thought it was like a great award or something. I'm sure mom would have had a fit about that and would have been so pissed and absolutely appalled if she could have heard what the guys said later. I mean they told some really raunchy jokes and crude stories. Probably not all that appropriate for me to hear but they all seemed to like me being there with 'em. Anyway, this picture was taken months later, finishing the project. I helped mix quite a bit of concrete."

Tears finally flowed for Sondra but she wiped them away without apologizing. "We were a team, you know?" she stated of her family. Darren's eyes went from the image to Sondra, then back again. He liked how she instinctively thought about teamwork, even at that young an age.

Sondra forced herself to recover and be strong, then altered the subject. "I have more pictures in the den" she said mostly to Darren. He followed her lead, leaving Doug, Karen and a devastated Shelley in the kitchen to further discuss Sondra and her family. Once in the den Darren pointed to a poster-sized photograph of Sondra in her blue Formula Ford at the top of the Corkscrew at Laguna Seca Raceway. They stood side by side staring up at the vibrant image. Darren then glanced around the room noting the shelves that had been in Sondra's Fresno bedroom containing her many trophies now lining the upper walls of this cozy room. He nodded and gestured toward the sliding glass door. "So you gonna show me this garage and kart track you've been bragging about?" Sondra's smile was explosive as she opened the door that led out onto the pool area. Darren followed her through the gate and down the curvy twisty roadway that led to their destination. Once inside the race shop she beamed at Darren's approval and hurried over to fold back the tarp covering her F Ford. "Nice" he said with a smile. She went into detail about what was in store for the Formula Ford car's restoration, then noticed that Darren had moved away and was sitting on one of the YZ 250s. She hurried over to sit on its mate. "Haven't been on a dirt bike in years" said Darren. Sondra smiled as she watched him rock the Yamaha off its stand and wriggle it from side to side, determining that there was plenty of fuel in the tank.

"We've been so busy so Dad and I've only had the chance to ride a couple of times" she informed him, reaching down to turn the fuel petcock to the open position. Darren followed suit, then used the kick-starter to start the engine. They rode together at a leisurely pace until getting to the dirt course, with Sondra hanging back a little and watching the man bob and weave as he sped along. He was a pretty good rider she observed but she smiled at the ridiculousness of this particular spectacle. No helmet or gloves, and he was in a nice dress-shirt and slacks. She raced to catch up with him, enjoying the moment and the freedom of wind in her hair and on her face. They played for just under 20 minutes, ending up back in the garage.

"Fun" said Darren. Sondra nodded. "Wait 'til you get a chance to run the karts" she said with a large smile. "Such a blast" she added. "And good teaching tools. I'm gonna get a road bike, too. A Yamaha YZR M One." Darren turned the fuel petcock to the off position and rocked the dirt bike onto its stand. He looked over at Sondra as she did the same, thinking her claim sounded like a 4 year-old wanting to lasso the moon. "That's a really expensive Moto GP race bike, Sondra" he informed her of the intended purchase.

She hated feeling like she was being scolded or ridiculed. "I wasn't asking your permission" she growled with instant white-hot anger, her narrowed eyes drilling into him.

"All right, calm down" he told her, figuring Doug and Karen would soon be dealing with this particular battle.

Darren walked over to the back of Sondra's old Formula Ford car, studying the greasy uncowled motor. Sondra came to stand next to him, holding her silence. "I think I know why you want all this" he said in a soft but serious tone. "The dirt-bikes, the karts, the shop and everything else. Who knows, maybe it'll help harness some of that rage ya got goin' on."

"I don't have rage" denied Sondra.

"The hell you don't" he said with a sarcastic laugh, pointing to the car before them. "When you kids were at Laguna" he began. "I had a good chat with 'ol Greg Wilente."

"He's an ass" growled Sondra. "And I worked damn hard for them" she furthered. "They gave me so much crap and most times they gave me crap setups and I had to really fight for decent results. But I still won and I got those results" she added through clenched teeth.

"Yeah ya did" Darren championed, giving her a quick smile and nod, contemplating the rage issue. "You're a fighter who doesn't back down" he told her. "I saw that the first time I watched you drive and I've watched you learn a hell of a lot in a short period of time. That fight in you is what won T.J. over, but Sondra ..." He looked around the shop and turned back toward her, putting a heavy hand on her shoulder. "There's a big damn difference between fighting for something and fighting against everything. Your rookie year in IndyCar is gonna be high intensity and high stakes. You can't just get pissed off and drive mad. It's more about control and finesse."

Sondra nodded. "Yeah" she agreed. "T.J. said that exact same thing to me." Darren smiled as he knelt down to have a closer look at the V-Tech motor, feeling good about the exchange and the time he'd chosen to spend with his new driver. "If you have a hard time getting parts for this" he told her, go to T.J. and the guys. I'm sure they'd love to help you with this project."

Sondra beamed. She loved Darren's intensity and had a good feeling about her new race family.

After lunch, Sondra insisted on showing SeaShell the Sierra-Trent Raceway. It wasn't that Shelley was necessarily all that keen on garages and racetracks but this was an opportunity for them to talk in private. Sondra and Shelley enjoyed the walk, with Shelley relating a bit of her past. After Sondra's enthusiastic grand tour of her beloved race shop she guided Shelley to a recently purchased black simulated-leather couch located next to the kitchenette, facing the scene framed by the open large roll-up door. "This is just like Doug's couch in the den and it folds out to a shockingly comfortable bed" informed Sondra. Shelley was both puzzled and shocked to think anyone would sleep on a couch-bed and in a primitive enclosure such as this, but she kept this to herself. "This was going to be my future house but mom gave me an emphatic NO when I brought it up" said Sondra. "I mean she made it pretty clear that a garage is a garage and a house is a house. I think there's a huge possibility that in the future I can have my own house next to my garage here but racing's gonna take up most of my time so who knows if that'll ever happen."

"Do you want it to happen?" asked Shelley.

Sondra didn't immediately answer. She looked around the insides of her coveted special space and shrugged. "I guess I'm okay with how things are right now" she told her friend. "But I mean I can't be like thirty billion years old still living with my..., with Doug and Karen."

Shelley watched the girl shut down. She heard Sondra swallow hard and take a few loud breaths through her nose. "Thank you for earlier, allowing us to know a little bit about your family, when you were young" she said to Sondra, intentionally changing the subject from houses and garages. "I'm so happy for your courage in putting up those pictures."

"You know something really weird?" asked Sondra rhetorically. "From the moment we moved here, more and more I keep seeing major similarities from my early past. I mean there's kind of a feel to this place, just like when I was a kid on the family farm. And then with Doug and Karen, the way they are with each other and the way they are with me. I love it more than anything but it also scares me more than anything."

"It scares you? Say more" encouraged Shelley. "How does it scare you?" she further inquired. Sondra looked down and ran circles with her index finger on her pant-leg before answering Shelley's question. "I just worry that maybe I'm being ten kinds of horrible for loving Doug and Karen and loving all this."

"There's that guilt again" said Shelley. Sondra wasn't expecting this response and looked up at the woman, pleading for answers but Shelley held her silence for the moment.

"You think this is like survivor's guilt or something?" she asked Shelley.

"What do you think?" asked Shelley. Sondra shrugged.

"What does your worry and guilt feel like to you" Shelley prodded. "And what is it doing for you, or against you?" she furthered. Sondra swallowed hard and stood, walking over to lean against the door frame. Shelley got up and came to stand next to her. "What color is that guilt?" she asked in a soft voice.

"Black and blood-red" growled Sondra through gritted teeth.

"What about a shape, a sound, a smell?" asked Shelley.

"I don't know" said Sondra quickly. "Just something dark, ugly and foul." She pounded her right fist on her right thigh and burst into tears.

Shelley wrapped her arms around the girl in a tight embrace. "I don't want to do this anymore, SeaShell" sobbed Sondra.

"Shh" soothed Shelley. "Okay. It's okay." She knew Sondra's limits by now, how far and how much to push in order to get some positive movement in her psyche. There was a definite limit.

Sondra leaned against the workbench at the back of the garage and proceeded to explain future plans for electrical independence with solar energy. She told how she and Doug were researching the equipment needed for the collector panels, the plumbing and wiring plus obtaining large deep-cell batteries for the electrical storage at night and when there was no sun due to weather.

"SeaShell?" she then asked in a sudden non sequitur. "Do you think people ever really get over survivor's guilt?"

"The human spirit is capable of immense resilience and movement" said Shelley with a nod of her head. "Through a willingness to do the conscious work within yourself, and by allowing yourself to open up to others and not hold in so much of that worry, guilt, anger and fear, I think great things are possible. Thank you for being willing to be so open with me."

"I don't know why I am" said Sondra with a shrug of her right shoulder. "I mean it just sort of seems so natural. Like I can tell you anything."

"You can" reinforced Shelley. "Do you ever talk to Doug and Karen about these heavy things?" Shelley asked, already knowing the answer.

"No, not really" confirmed Sondra. "I mean I don't want them to think I'm just some poor little weak girl they have to be careful around. And I don't want them to ever think I don't really love them or that I'm ungrateful for everything they are and do for me. They've basically changed their whole lives to be all about me."

"They know you have a past, Sondra" said Shelley. "And I'm sure they're grateful for anything you share with them. The good stuff, the hard stuff and everything in between. From what I've observed, they love you unconditionally, and like I've told you before their life with you is their conscious choice."

"Will you come to at least some of my races next year?" asked Sondra, not-so subtly changing the subject.

Shelley let out a short involuntary laugh. "Of course I will" she told the girl. "I have big plans for Safen-Up, and with Karen's help in the promotional department the race venues will allow us some big-time exposure. Besides, things with Darren and I are going so great. When we're not together we talk on the phone every day. I can't see us going six months with him working and traveling around without me. My family isn't so thrilled but I'm sure that'll change as soon as they get to know him."

"He's a really good guy" said Sondra.

Darren and Shelley's visit to Casa de Trent had lasted just over three hours but to Sondra it had not been near long enough. Their departure resulted in that all too familiar tearing sensation. She pushed down the intense pain and stubbornly delved knuckle-long into the F-Ford engine tear-down process while Karen and Doug went to the airport to retrieve their next visitors, George and Mary McCormick. Karen wasn't thrilled that her daughter had stayed behind. Later during the home tour she appreciated her parents' inquiry about Sondra's whereabouts, thinking out loud that her mechanical dedication and meticulous attention to detail was relatively harmless and cute. "Not very ladylike for an attractive eighteen year-old girl" stated Mary. "But I suppose this is better than the alternative. At least she's not a wild boy-crazy teenager yoked to her phone and watching nonsense on TV."

During the McCormicks' stay, George enjoyed time with his granddaughter, watching her work at the back of the F-Ford. He spent most of his vacation time however chatting with Doug, helping his son-in-law in the process of making the summer vegetable garden into a winter garden. Karen, as always, enjoyed cooking with her mother, and doing so in this new kitchen filled her with a sense of pride and satisfaction. Mother and daughter reminisced about past baking and cooking endeavors and discussed the many aspects of Santa Barbara living. The two women decidedly did not spend all their time in the kitchen however. Mary was impressed with her daughter's office and getting to see first-hand the business Karen had spoken of in recent past. Time was also spent in the pleasant living room, discussing in detail the house and property. They kibitzed about future home decorating possibilities, remodeling projects, as well as several landscaping ideas. Early the next morning Karen and Mary produced fluffy omelets for breakfast, and soon a shuttle-van arrived to collect the McCormicks. Sondra's previous anxiety over George and Mary's visit now suddenly again turned to that tearing sensation. Instead of racing down to her garage she helped with the kitchen cleanup.

"I'm glad they came out" she announced to Doug and Karen. "They got to see us in our natural habitat."

Karen laughed at that as she stood sink-side, rinsing off plates. "You make it sound as if we're wild animals" she said shaking her head.

"Well" began Sondra. "I guess I'm the wild one and you guys are the domesticated momma and poppa bear." Doug laughed and gave his best impression of a roaring bear. Karen made a snarling noise and splashed water in Sondra's direction. "Okay, okay" giggled the girl. "You're wild too." Doug grabbed her from behind and turned her upside down, making snarling noises as well. "Dad" she complained through giggles. "Jeeze. Help mom, help. I'm being attacked by a wild beast." Karen beamed as she watched Doug spin the girl around and gently set her down. Sondra, still laughing, scrambled a few feet away, folding her arms, desperately trying to feign indignation. "I'll have you know, this is no way to treat a professional IndyCar driver" she announced, trying to keep a straight face. "Hmm" voiced Karen. "Perhaps you should lodge a formal complaint with your management. Maybe there's a wild beast clause in your contract." Sondra rolled her eyes and giggled. "You people" she breathed with a wide smile.

Two hours later Doug and Sondra were busy with the F-Ford when Valerie Hughes arrived at Casa de Trent, apologizing profusely for not being able to be there the previous day, as had been planned. Karen gave her dear friend a detailed tour of the home, with the two ending up in the kitchen sharing prep duties for dinner. "So how was it having your parents here?" asked Valerie.

"Oh my dad absolutely loves Doug" said Karen. "Asks him all sorts of questions and hangs on his every word. It's downright adorable."

"That's so funny" said Valerie with a quick laugh. "Your dad used to hate most of the boys you were interested in, and the day before your wedding he was like a super-strict and stern father."

"Well I am his only daughter" smiled Karen. "Mom's always a fish out of water whenever she's not in her own home or town" continued Karen. "But she was really sweet, and I'm surprised she didn't try and rearrange my kitchen drawers or cabinets. She made a few comments but that was about it. I think she was relieved to see that we live in a nice home and area, and she only made one mildly disapproving comment about Doug and me not wanting to have more children."

Karen smiled as she halted her onion chopping and turned toward her dear friend. "Mom and dad clearly love Sondra though" she told Valerie. "It was so touching to see their interactions these past few days."

"Speaking of Sondra" said Val. "How's she doing? Any more little behavioral flare-ups? Hats at the table? Teenage angst?"

"Well that kid does have her moments" said Karen with a quick chuckle. "She keeps leaving her damn cell phone there on the counter, even though I've asked her time and time again not to, but it looks like the hat at the dinner table incident was a pretty big turning point, for us both. In that moment I really and truly became her mom. It's a tricky balance though. I don't want her to ever think I'm trying to completely replace or erase her mother's existence. In fact Doug and I try, mostly in vain, to get her to open up and talk about her mother and her whole family."

Valerie nodded, taking another close look at the photographs of the Sierres. Karen went back to the culinary task at hand. "I've learned to pick my battles" she told Valerie. "She definitely knows that there's a line not to be crossed and it's actually brought us closer together. I love that girl as if she were my own. She is now, in my eyes. It really is remarkable" she added. "And I guess the situation is weird. After all, Sondra's no child, though she acts like one at times."

"I don't think it's weird" commented Valerie. "The three of you found each other. You've been searching for a true love and having your own family for quite some time. And like I've told you before, Sondra really needs you and Doug to give her structure and life focus."

As Valerie and Karen continued chatting and working in the

kitchen, Doug and Sondra worked away in the shop, pouring over the Formula Ford vehicle, readying the four-cylinder V-Tech motor for when it would be hoisted by chain onto an engine stand. Sondra lightly bit her lower lip as she watched Doug loosen bolts with a ratchet. She loved the metallic clicking sounds these wrenches made, doing important work. Doug looked up, wondering why Sondra had halted her own wrench work. "I must've watched my dad do that like a thousand times" Sondra lamented. Doug nodded, hoping she'd say more. "These ignition wires are pretty fried" Sondra announced, trying to sound strong.

"You worked on engines with your dad?" asked Doug. "Well he worked on 'em. I watched and handed him things" said Sondra. "He never really directly taught me about engines and what he was doing, unless I asked, but he did the same thing you do sometimes. Relate life to mechanical work."

Doug smiled at hearing this. "Yeah" he said. "You can fix a lot of things with the right tools."

CHAPTER 28

On a cold overcast February 9th, Doug and Sondra had a much anticipated triumph with the F-Ford. The engine rebuild had gone smoother than expected, and even though there were planned upgrades to the suspension and brakes, the car was now safe and drivable. Karen rode down to Sierre-Trent Raceway on the ATV, hoping her husband and daughter were at a stopping point for dinner. "Hey, you two" she called out. "It's getting close to dinner-time, don't you think?"

"But Mom" argued Sondra. "We're about to take a test-hop." Karen loved that in this moment Sondra seemed more like a happy carefree child than an eighteen year-old young lady and professional racing driver.

"Well all right" agreed the mom. "But I've been doing office work all day. I'm hungry and I don't feel like cooking, so lets get on with this and go out to eat."

"Mom" again complained Sondra. "You can't rush these things" she informed her. "Here" she said, handing Karen a small digital camera. "You get to be our official documentarian." At first Karen thought the level of seriousness Doug and Sondra were giving to all this seemed a tad silly but the F-Ford was not a child's toy. Sondra made a total of 27 laps. As they later made their way back to the house she talked almost non-stop regarding the work she and Doug had done on the F-Ford, going into great detail about the nuances of the car and track.

Rick & Bella's Bistro had become a restaurant of favor for the Trents. It was a cozy pizzeria featuring light pinkish-red brick walls, with white-oak and green furnishings. Various vine-type plants grew in multiple hanging pots and smooth jazz wafted through the air to color the peaceful eatery. Though there were many specialty pizzas, Sondra's favorite was Bella's Ball. She didn't much care for the name but the crust had unique garlic and basil flavoring and the pie itself went a little heavier on the vegetables than the meats. While first enjoying their salads, Sondra and Doug continued their discussion on the progress of the F-Ford. Karen listened for a bit, occasionally glancing down at her watch, but when a detailed conversation about suspension setups began, this was the last straw for her. "Oh for god's sake, you two" she exclaimed with an exasperated laugh. "Enough with the shop talk. You do realize there are other things going on in the world."

"Mom" complained Sondra. Karen reached over and stroked the back of her daughter's hair.

"Don't worry" she told the girl. "You can go back to all things greasy after dinner. Sondra, don't pick toppings off your pizza with your fingers."

"But it was a mushroom" argued the girl. "Big gross and hideous. Blech" she added with a dramatic shiver.

Oh give it here" said Doug, reaching over with his hand to pick up the discarded item. "I love 'em" he proclaimed.

"Doug" scolded Karen. "Honestly" she added with a shake of her head. "You both have the manners of a billygoat." Talk was sporadic and lighthearted as the Trent family happily consumed the remainder of their pizza but Sondra thought it strange and somewhat annoying that Karen kept glancing at her watch. Growing up, Sondra's favorite dining experiences were the ones where there was no concept of time.

After the satisfying meal the Trents walked in the general

direction of the Mercedes, peering into various storefront windows. They soon came upon Swizzles & Swirls, a small but popular ice cream parlor, and when Karen all but insisted they go inside, Sondra complained. "Mom. It's like a thousand degrees below zero." It was 67. "Who eats ice cream cones in freezing February?" asked the girl.

"You silly goose" chuckled Karen. Doug smiled and put his arm around Sondra as they entered. "Oh I don't know" he said. "I think I could go for some triple fudge crunch." As they stood at the counter perusing their sweet and frozen choices, a young woman who'd been sitting at a table against the wall behind them at the pink, white and purple establishment suddenly sprang from her chair. Sondra heard the commotion and turned to find an unexpected figure rushing toward her. "Kari" she said in voice of disbelief as her friend from Bakersfield wrapped her arms tightly around her.

"Oh Sondra" said Kari. "So good to see you again." The two continued their embrace and produced several high-pitched greetings. Sondra then turned to Doug and Karen, shaking her head. "You knew all along she was here, didn't you?" Their broad smiles said it all. "You look great" said Kari as they reluctantly released one another. "I love your hair" she added, running her fingers down the right-side length. "You used to trim it yourself. It looked okay but you could definitely tell. It has style to it now." She gave Sondra another quick hug and continued. "I never forgot you. You changed my whole life" Kari added with tears in her eyes.

"I never forgot you either" said Sondra, her voice tinged with emotion. "So, um. How, um?" Sondra tried to ask. "Do you live here in Santa Barbara?" she inquired. Kari shook her head. "No but I will be" she told Sondra, her head-shake turning to a nod. "I start UC Santa Barbara next month. I'm going for my teaching credential so I'll be around."

"Wow" marveled Sondra, the two girls again embracing. "Good for you" she told Kari. "I knew you had it in you to go to college and go on to greatness."

"Yeah" said Kari. "You were always trying to encourage me for bigger and better."

Sondra pulled away with a puzzled expression. "How did this happen? And how'd you even find me?" she asked.

"I spotted a guy at my high school wearing a T-shirt with your name and a picture of your race car" said Kari. "It was like the one I used to see you drive but it was bigger with these wing thingies."

Sondra laughed at Kari's description. "Yeah that was my first professional car and race season" she told her long-lost friend.

"Well anyway" Kari continued. "I asked him about it and he said he saw you a year ago and that you were in Indy Lights, whatever that is. He said you were super good and that you had a website. I checked it out but I've been so busy and maybe a little too nervous to try and contact you. I kinda procrastinated but I messaged your management just a few days ago and Doug answered me back. We had a long talk on the phone, with Karen on the line too, and here we are."

"Oh, so you're stalking me now?" joked Sondra.

"Yeah" said Kari. "And you better sleep with one eye open tonight" she added with a laugh.

Sondra proceeded to briefly recount the events in her life since they'd last seen one another. She glossed over many details and purposely left out the bad or hard parts but told of living in Fresno and going to college. She also gave an abridged account of Doug and Karen's wedding and how they'd come to live in Santa Barbara. Kari then told a bit of her story. "My mom went ahead and married that guy and he turned out to be a disgusting looser creep. We lived in this gross old apartment in Stockton. Things were sort of okay at first and mom got a really good job at a bookstore, but Curtis started staying out later and later with his drinking buddies from work. He had a construction business, remember?" Sondra nodded and Kari continued. "Well one day mom just kicked him out. She wouldn't talk about it but I'm pretty sure it was because he was cheating on her and she found out. They hadn't been married for long and mom had it annulled. She wouldn't talk about that either. Those were some pretty sucky times. My real dad came back into the picture for a while. It was pretty cool but he's not really the stick-around type." Sondra nodded, remembering how Kari would talk of him, loving when he was around and in her and Brianna's life especially since he often bought them things and spoiled them, but when he went away and stayed away she was bitter and resentful of him. "Then mom met this new guy" furthered Kari of her past. "He was there at the bookstore one day doing some promotion and a signing of a book he'd written." She smiled and shook her head as she remembered this time in her life. "He called mom at home one day and pretty soon they were talking more and more. Sometimes they would talk on the phone for hours. Sweet I guess but it got annoying. He invited us all up to his place in Oregon for the Fourth of July weekend. First time I'd ever been on an airplane and his house is this big gorgeous two-story Victorian. Seven months later mom and Ben got married. It was a really nice wedding in the backyard. Brianna and I got our own separate bedrooms for the first time, and my last year of high school was so different. Really nice. I guess I kinda settled down."

"Yay" cheered Sondra.

"Ben's a college professor" added Kari. "With big family money, and he totally turned our lives around. And I don't mean just with money. He's totally been like Doug has been for you, with me, my sister and my mom. I told him about you, Sondra. What a great friend you were and how you were always tryin' to get me to study and get better grades. So between my new stepdad and you, that's how I ended up getting into college and wanting to become a teacher."

"I knew you had this in you" said Sondra, wrapping her arms around her dear friend.

The two young women continued to chat, not thinking about time or the fact that they were in an ice cream parlor, but as the to-go orders came ready Karen and Doug stepped closer. Kari took her cue. "I'm heading back home to Oregon early tomorrow morning" she told Sondra, touching her arm. "I came down with my mom and sis to check out housing. Got a two-bedroom apartment with a roommate. I haven't met her yet and the place won't be ready for another two weeks but it's a pretty nice building and close to campus. So, you live far from here?" she inquired.

"Just a little ways out of town, in the hills" said Sondra. "It's a big place and the house is beautiful. We haven't been there all that long but I have a motocross course, a kart track and a really amazing garage and shop."

Kari let out an involuntary laugh. "Oh my god" she exclaimed, wrapping her arms around Sondra for another quick hug. "I see you haven't changed a bit. Still hangin' out in garages."

"Well she does spend a lot of time there" interjected Doug. "But we've house-broken her" he added. "She has a very nice bedroom."

"Dad" complained Sondra. "I mean I'm not a puppy" she added.

"Sure you are, Poodle" laughed Kari, petting the top of her friend's hair.

"Ah jeeze" breathed Sondra, trying to feign indignation but not able to hide how happy she was in the moment. After solid plans were made for Kari to visit Casa de Trent when she was next in town the Trents headed for home. They changed clothes and went for a jog along a westerly portion of the perimeter fence fire-break, then sat in the den enjoying blueberry-caramel ice cream.

After a week and a half of vigorous IndyCar preseason testing and work, Kari arrived at Casa de Trent in the early evening. Sondra had always been in awe of how Kari could make it seem as if a loud party had just commenced the moment she stepped into a room. On this day it thrilled her to no end when her fiery blond friend brought that explosive fun energy into Casa de Trent. "Wow. Cool place" exclaimed Kari, looking all around. They sat in the living room discussing the move to Santa Barbara and the house, then Kari and Sondra began reminiscing about their days in Bakersfield. When Doug received a phone call and left the room Karen took the cue and headed to the kitchen, leaving the girls to talk. Sondra took Kari straight through the kitchen and into the den to show off her trophies and the photos of her racing career thus far. Kari's attention was first captured by a 4-foot-by-6-foot glossy color photo of Sondra in her race suit standing in front of her Hugo Patrero Indy Lights car flanked by a nicely dressed Doug and Karen, with official-looking ID badges and passes hanging from thick red ribbons around their necks.

"Wow, you look happy" said Kari. "Where is this?"

"Watkins Glen, New York" said Sondra. "Happy doesn't even come close" she added, remembering how the car and track had felt that afternoon. "This picture was taken the first day of the race weekend. Last race of the year." explained Sondra.

"Bet you won, didn't you?" guessed Kari.

"Yeah" breathed Sondra, her body suddenly remembering just how sore, hot and exhausted she was after the excitement of winning the race and clinching the championship had subsided. Her eyes remained on the photographic image for a few more seconds, also remembering how it had been when she'd heard of Brice's advancement to the Patrero IndyCar lineup and not her. The instant rage that came to her over the past disappeared however when she again heard Kari's voice.

"Whoa" exclaimed Kari. "These are some impressive trophies." Sondra shrugged, and after pointing out several memorable trophies and plaques she and her long-lost friend settled on the couch.

"So is this what your life's all about?" inquired Kari. "I mean this is pretty darn cool but what about other things? You're so smart and you got all A's in high school. Did you give up on further college? Is this like a for-real job for you now?"

Sondra told of bookending her semesters of college with her racing endeavors and of graduating from Cal State Fresno with a BA while continuing to move forward in her racing career. "I'm glad I got my degree" she concluded. "But racing is the only thing I've ever wanted to do. I mean I remember my brothers and me occasionally being asked what we wanted to be when we grew up." Kari watched Sondra make a tight fist. She instinctively reached over to wrap a soft hand around her dear friend's fingers.

"Dave and Haley" whispered Kari, remembering the few times Sondra would allow conversation about of her family to take place. Sondra pulled her hand away and stood, walking over to one of the enlarged photographs.

"It changed weekly for them" she told Kari of her brothers' career interests. She then spoke in a voice that sounded distant and tortured. "Sometimes daily" she remembered of Dave's aspirations. "But not for me. Not ever."

She bit down on her tongue and stared at the image of herself, kneeling alongside her Formula Ford and holding a plaque that read, #12 Blue Sea Racing. Sondra Sierre. 1st Place. Lime Rock Park. Instead of any race imagery coming to her she remembered one particular summer where Dave had periodically announced his desire to be a baseball player, a pro fisherman, a pro bowler, an important businessman, and a fireman. Haley too had wanted to be a fireman, for about 30 minutes after Dave had mentioned it. Haley had a vast imagination and a quick mind. He often wanted to be whatever figure was being discussed at school or if he'd seen a memorable character on TV or in a movie, and he always wanted to be like his brother or father or the people his parents held in high regard.

On the guise of brushing the hair out of her face, Sondra wiped with her thumb a traitorous tear that had escaped her right eye. She then forced herself to be strong and came back to sit next to Kari. "When we were little I thought one of Dave's career ideas the greatest thing ever" she told Kari. "I mean it seems kinda silly now but he really wanted to be an important person at McDonald's and drive a yellow Toyota pickup." This perhaps was one of the reasons why Sondra coveted the Tacoma that Doug had given her, and she had loved that McDonald's was one of the Patrero team sponsors during her Indy Lights season. "That's sweet" said Kari.

"When Haley was six" continued Sondra, surprised that she could talk about her brothers without falling to pieces, "for a while he wanted to be a native American Indian Chief. He really got into it, the dress, the culture and everything."

Kari smiled at that. "Brianna went though a cowgirl stage" she told Sondra of her younger sister. "Me, I wanted to be an Olympic ice skater when I was about five or six" Kari confessed. Sondra smiled and nodded. "We used to go ice skating for a while" she told her friend. "Before the rink burned down. But for me, cars, motorcycles and racing were always my dream and goal."

Sondra then described in detail her racing career from the time that Kari had left Bakersfield. Kari listened carefully in silence with one exception, when Sondra mentioned driving the sprint-car for Dan

Stoltz. "Oh my god" she exclaimed. "You hated him, and we used to make fun of that fat old chauvinistic creep."

"Well he turned into a pretty decent guy" said Sondra. "He's mellowed since then and has been a good friend to us. He and dad even went into a really successful classic car restoration and sales business for a while."

"Supper's about ready, girls" said Karen, breezing into the room.

"Smells great" said Kari as she and Sondra stood.

"Sondra" directed Karen. "Go brush your hair and change that shirt, like I asked you over an hour ago."

Sondra rolled her eyes but complied. Kari followed Karen into the kitchen and watched the last-minute meal prep activity. "Back in Bakersfield" she supplied, "Sondra rarely dressed up or showed her emotions. She was a tough chick and she always seemed to go to great lengths to avoid talking about her family. My mom used to say that Sondra had a chip on her shoulder the size of Texas and that she was spring-loaded in a pissed-off position. Looks like she's made some big progress in that area."

"Some" said Doug as he came into the room. He'd been on the phone in the office and had overheard Kari's last statement. He put his arm briefly around Kari and directed her attention to the photographs that were in strategic places around the room.

"Whoa" she voiced as Doug moved over to help his wife put several items on the table.

"This is Sondra with her family, isn't it?" asked Kari. "Oh my god I love these pictures. Little Sondra. She's such an amazing person and you can see it even when she was little. I'm so glad she has you guys" she added.

"We're glad she has you" said Karen as she came to stand next to Kari. "And I'm looking forward to getting to know you a whole lot better" she added.

"Me too" nodded Kari just as Sondra bounced back into the room. Kari's laugh was loud as she eyed her friend and took note of what the young lady was wearing. "I remember that" she exclaimed. "You silly nut. It's supposed to be a micro-dress, not some top you wear with jeans."

Kari turned toward Karen and gave further explanation. "I gave Sondra a bunch of my clothes before I left." Karen nodded because she'd seen quite a few of the items before, although never on her daughter. "Oh my god" continued Kari. "She had exactly eight T-shirts, four sweatshirts and six pairs of jeans. Such a tomboy. I was hoping my clothes would give her a clue that she's actually a girl."

Sondra rolled her eyes and folded her arms, trying to feign indignation.

"Kari" announced Karen. "You must come to this house, and often."

After a satisfying dinner, Doug had pressing office work to finish and Karen refused to let the girls help with any kitchen cleanup. Sondra and Kari returned to the den for further conversation.

"Oh my god your mom's such a great cook" gushed Kari.

"Yeah, she's amazing" agreed Sondra. "We get a couple of the food channels on satellite and sometimes we have a lot of fun trying new things. Although, some of the experiments have gone way wrong. I mean, trust me, don't ever try to make peanut brittle in the slowcooker. What a biohazard mess that was, and brutal-hard to get the pot clean."

Kari laughed and gave Sondra a tight embrace before the two settled back down on the couch. "So lets talk boyfriends" suggested Kari. "You're gorgeous and I assume you have one now."

"Well I guess. Kind of" said Sondra with a shrug of her right shoulder. "I don't know. I mean there's this guy. He's a fellow driver. I hated him at first and then we were teammates for a year. That's him standing next to me in that picture in front of our Indy Lights cars."

Kari got up to more closely examine the photo. "Oh my god, he is so cute" she announced.

"You think?" asked Sondra, coming to stand next to her friend.

"Oh yeah" said Kari. "You have good taste. So tell me every little thing."

Sondra again shrugged her right shoulder. "Well I mean I'm not sure there's all that much to tell." She detailed her first encounters with him, then told of getting better acquainted during the next race season. "I think Brice and I have a thing but …"

"Brice?" inquired Kari. "That's an unusual name."

"Yeah, I guess" said Sondra with a shrug. "I mean he's from Wisconsin and his family is into wheat farming."

"Ooh" taunted Kari. "A farm boy."

Sondra ignored Kari's remark and continued. "He's a really nice guy and I'm glad we're good friends, I mean maybe even a little more, but I'm not sure if I'd call him my boyfriend."

"Why not?" asked Kari.

"Well I mean we've kissed a few times and we went on this sailing trip to Catalina with another couple. I got to steer the boat and he held me from behind, and he kissed my neck. I even let him touch my boobs."

"Whoa, that's huge for you" said Kari, briefly leaning her shoulder into Sondra's. "So I go away for like two minutes and you turn into some kind of nautical slut?" joked Kari.

"Nah-uh" voiced Sondra, lightly slapping Kari's shoulder. "And it's more like you were gone for two long years" she added.

"So tell me about the boob touching" prompted Kari.

"Well I mean it wasn't anything weird" said Sondra. "It was while I was at the wheel of the boat and he had his arms around me. It was nice and he was telling me about some of the navigational stuff he'd learned from our friend Andrew. When he moved to point at a particular section of the nav unit his hand brushed across me. I mean it wasn't super blatant or like he did it deliberately. No grabbing or anything like that so I didn't really feel like yelling at him or punching him. He held me a little tighter and his hand just kinda rested there for a few seconds."

From the kitchen, Karen kept telling herself that it was wrong to eavesdrop on her daughter's conversation but she did so anyway, straining to catch every word. When her ears and brain deciphered the boob-touching statements she dropped the metal pot she was washing. A wave of soapy water splashed the front of her blouse and she was relieved that the cooking vessel didn't make a sound as it sank to the bottom of the sink.

"So what about you?" inquired Sondra, trying desperately to turn the attention away from herself.

"Oh, no one really special" lamented Kari. "I was pretty heavy into partying for a while so dating was pretty casual for me." She paused for dramatic effect. "I had a girlfriend for a while." Kari studied her friend's face trying to gauge a reaction but Sondra wasn't all that surprised. In the past Kari was often seen holding hands with her female friends and would occasionally insist on helping Sondra with her wardrobe. She was an energetic force and Sondra felt as though Kari liked to treat her as if she were her own real-life Barbie doll. Changing clothes in front of her made Sondra feel a little uncomfortable and self-conscious, but the oddest part was Kari's constant string of compliments about her figure. Then there was that one cold December night at Sondra's above-the-garage apartment, with Kari smelling of alcohol and cigarettes. After Sondra had successfully wrestled the car keys away, Kari then proceeded to wrap her arms around her and kiss her full on the lips.

"I liked Stacy a whole lot" continued Kari. "But I don't think I ever truly loved her and that's pretty much why we broke up. She wanted a big life-long commitment and I just wasn't ready for that. Besides, I like guys too much."

Kari shifted in her seat and altered the subject. "So just the one guy?" she asked. "Brice?"

"Well it's not like I don't notice guys" defended Sondra. "But I don't really have time for all that. I'm super focused on my racing."

"Well I suppose that's good for your career but sad if you ask me" offered Kari. Sondra shrugged and changed the subject to her upcoming first IndyCar season, telling Kari all about the people involved, including SeaShell and the Safen-Up organization. After raspberry pie and watching the movie Roman Holiday, Karen and Doug went to bed, advising the girls not to stay up too late.

After breakfast the next morning Sondra took her friend via ATV for a quick viewing of her race garage and tracks. The two young women stood together in silence for several minutes, taking in the gentleness of the green and light brown flowing landscape. "Are you happy, Sondra?" asked Kari.

"I guess" said Sondra with a shrug. "I mean I'm getting to do what I'm best at and I know Doug and Karen love me. And this place is pretty awesome."

"But you're not really happy?" prompted Kari.

"I think that word has lost all meaning for me" said Sondra with a nervous laugh and another shrug of her right shoulder. "I mean I'm happy you're back in my life" she told Kari, momentarily biting her tongue to keep her emotions in check. "Don't you ever leave like that again" she breathed.

"I promise" said Kari. "I'm on a four-year plan at college and I really like this area. Besides, now I know where you live. You're stuck with me … forever."

Sondra let out a quick nervous laugh and broke away, forcing herself to be strong. "Wanna go into town with me?" she asked her dearest friend. "I have some errands to run and we can have a nice lunch somewhere."

Sondra gave Kari a limited tour of Santa Barbara and picked up tires and motor oil at the Yamaha dealership. It pleased her that Kari liked and approved of Rob, Eddie and Carla, especially Eddie. The girls returned to Casa de Trent after lunch at a luxury hotel's outside dining patio overlooking the ocean. Back inside Sondra's race garage they continued to talk about life and boys.

"So, Kari?" began Sondra as they settled on the couch. "You didn't really say. Do you have a steady boyfriend or girlfriend that you left behind in Oregon?"

"No one special" said the young blond. "No one to say I love you and mean it for like ever. So you never dated anyone else but Brice?" she abruptly asked.

"Well, no" voiced Sondra, biting her lower lip and giving a quick shake of her head. Kari eyed the girl before again speaking. "Ever hear of that old saying, You gotta kiss a lot of frogs before you find your prince? So you're telling me you never kissed any other frogs?"

"No, and ew" said Sondra with a small nervous laugh. "I guess until Brice I never really cared."

"Sad" offered Kari.

"Well I mean" qualified Sondra. "Like I said yesterday, we've hung out together but never anything traditional, like just the two of us for a romantic dinner or something. Nothing I'd call dating."

"Well I don't know" countered Kari. "When things are right, sometimes just hanging out is dating. Well okay, in my world that means having sex, but ..."

There was a short silence but Sondra's next words came out in a pained squeak. "I'm never really sure what my world is. I mean I try not to think about it."

"I think I can understand" said Kari in a soft voice. "And I'm sorry I didn't get to know your world before you lost your family."

Sondra bit down hard on her tongue and pounded her fist on her right leg. "Sometimes I think it would have just been better if I'd have died with them" she growled bitterly.

"God, Sondra" exclaimed Kari. "What a horrible thing to say. You don't know that. Don't you ever say that again."

Kari began to cry and wrapped her arms around her friend. "I'm so sorry they're not here" she offered Sondra. "But this world you have is pretty great. You're smart, gorgeous, good at what you do for a living and have people who love and care about you." She pulled away and shook Sondra by the shoulders. "Goddamn it, Sondra" she told her. "I love you. Never say that again."

"Kay" said Sondra, getting up and walking over to one of the boxes of motor oil she'd earlier set on the workbench. "Weren't we talking about dating?" she asked, trying to deflect and defuse. Kari wiped the moisture from her eyes and smiled to herself. She'd always known Sondra to change the subject whenever things got too serious or emotional. She leaned against the softness of the sofa's back, happy when minutes later Sondra came to stand just inches from her.

"You know" began Kari. "Eddie's a nice guy. He likes you and he lives not far from you" she told Sondra, trying to make a point. "You've obviously gone to that store and hung out a bunch of times. It's not like you have to suddenly get engaged, and you told me yesterday about some Jeff guy you hung out with at a race track. Those could be considered mini dates, in your world."

"Nah-uh" denied Sondra. "You and I are hanging out" Sondra stated. "Does that mean we're dating?"

"Oh yeah" smiled Kari, her voice dripping with sarcasm. "Come over here and pucker up, baby" she giggled, burying her forehead into Sondra's shoulder. Sondra smiled and spoke with matching giggles. "Get away from me, you nutty girl."

"There you are, Kare-bear" said Kari's mom from the open window of the driver's seat of her blue Honda Odyssey minivan. Sondra first looked over her shoulder at the intrusion and then down at her watch, making a face at hearing the pet name. She couldn't believe that time had passed so quickly and she thought this and the pet-name seemed particularly wrong at this moment in time. Karen had ridden down with Kari's mother and quickly came around from the passenger side of the vehicle as Sara got out to greet Sondra. "Oh it's so nice to see you again, sweetheart" said the woman stepping closer to Sondra as the girls stood. "My, you've certainly grown into a beautiful young lady" Sara gushed. "You're looking happy and well" she added, giving the girl a hug.

"You too, Mrs Wilken" said Sondra. "I mean Wilken-Ballard" she corrected. Sara laughed as she released the girl. "Well I guess the hyphenated name thing is a bit much at times but my husband Ben and I did that for several good reasons."

As Sondra was pondering the reasons, Sara spoke to her daughter. "Sorry to interrupt the fun but we have that meeting with your academic counselor, and Ben and Brianna are moving some of your stuff into your new apartment as we speak. I'm sure they'd like your help with that" she added in a slight scolding tone. "We need to get going."

Kari wrapped her arms around Sondra. "I hate to leave" she whispered. "Wish I could just live here with you." Sondra nodded and squeezed her friend a little tighter. Moments later she and Karen watched the van make a clumsy U-turn and head over the short rise of the topography. Sondra hated this all-too familiar feeling of being left behind but Karen put her arm around her daughter, sensing the need for contact and reassurance. "I'm thinking about making a cherry pie for dessert tonight" she told the girl. "I might be a little more definite about that if I knew I had help in pitting the cherries."

"Kay" said Sondra, trying to mask her emotions. "As long as they're famous cherries to go in one of your famous pies."

"Oh I hear they were blessed by the Pope, or at least a reasonable facsimile" chuckled Karen.

"Nutty" giggled Sondra.

CHAPTER 29

Sondra's first IndyCar season didn't get off to the start she'd wanted or expected. Though she had mentally and physically prepared for being on the temporary street course of St. Petersburg, Florida, for the first Round of the championship Sondra found it to be a frustrating, bumpy track. This was all new territory for her. Different specific rules and regulations, new and powerful equipment, new voices over the radio giving her important information and new pit crew members to get used to and be able to trust. The drivers she would be up against were new to her as well with the exception of Ryan Delgato, Brice Crandle and several others that she'd competed against in the Indy Lights Series. Most of the field were seasoned open-wheel veterans with years of experience. In Sunday's GP Sondra finished a lap down in 17th Place. She was bitter and angry, refusing to do more than give a handful of vague post-race answers to race reporters' questions of how her day and weekend had gone. Roughly an hour after the Holt Racing team post-race meeting, T.J. made a point to speak with Sondra. He found his dejected driver in the Trent's rented motorhome and half asked, half demanded that Doug and Karen let him have a few minutes alone with the kid. Sondra knew better than to think her new boss would come by to console her. When he showed up she mostly expected a stern lecture and warning that she was now on thin ice with him and the team.

"It's not like I made bad mistakes" defended Sondra after she and T.J. had talked for a bit. "But now that I'm replaying stuff in my head I can see how I didn't do enough to dig myself out of the hole we got into."

T.J. nodded. He was glad that Sondra wasn't trying to make excuses or put the blame on anyone else. The fact of the matter was that handling and electronic issues had severely hampered the #12 team's day, and then there was an air-gun mishap with the Right-rear on the second pit stop. It had also been brought up in the team meeting that Darren's choice of putting Sondra on a set of sticker blacks, a new set of the hard-compound primary tire, for the last stint had exacerbated their already bad day. This was something that Darren himself had brought up and taken full responsibility. "Well" began T.J. as he sat across from Sondra on the motorhome's dark gray couch. "In Ryan's first rookie year with me he crashed four cars, went in the wrong pit at Mid-Ohio, stalled the motor on more than one occasion and broke a half-shaft leaving pit lane while we were in Fourth Place during the Kansas race. You're a rookie driver with basically a brand new race team. Learn from your mistakes and learn to overcome those of your team. Rest up for next weekend" he told her as he stood. "Barber's a tough track and I expect both my cars to finish in the points." T.J.'s words hadn't exactly been a pep-talk but she internalized them as somewhat encouraging.

Sondra and Brice never had much of an opportunity to interact throughout the weekend, and with his time in the IndyCar spotlight that Sunday evening due to his first podium finish of the year, 3rd Place, he was constantly surrounded by teammates, fellow drivers and sponsor representatives. During a celebration dinner given by several IndyCar sponsors Sondra forced herself to go over at one point to congratulate him on his efforts. As the two were discussing the complexities of the track Darren Brown entered the fray and ushered his driver away for a quick chat. "You were pretty hard on yourself in the team debrief" he said, "and T.J. let me know that you two talked.

Here's the thing. We lose as a team and we win as a team. Ryan didn't even see the checkers." The #21 car had been struggling in 13th and had tangled with another car in Turn 1, Lap 46, ending his day with front and rear wing damage and a bent front A-arm. "But you went the distance with a far less than perfect car" furthered Darren. "I know you see this as a bitter defeat but the team saw a lot of positives with our weekend. I do too, so take that and move on. We're going to a place I know you like next weekend." He messed up the top of the girl's hair and smirked. He began to step away but then turned. "So you and Brice Crandle are on speaking terms again?" he prompted.

Sondra simply shrugged so Darren redoubled his efforts of pointed personal communication. "You guys got pretty chummy when you were teammates last year."

"Chummy?" said Sondra, not liking how that sounded or where Darren was possibly going with this line of inquiry. "Kind of a creepy word if you ask me" she added, intentionally deflecting concern. "Don't worry" she told her boss. "My chumminess with Brice or anyone else for that matter won't get in the way of my serious focus to win. I know how high the stakes are, I can assure you of that."

"Fair enough" said Darren, feeling good about the purposeful chat with his driver.

Round 2 of the IndyCar championship was at Barber Motorsports Park in Birmingham, Alabama, where Sondra used her knowledge from last year's Indy Lights venture victory. This was a natural-terrain, fast, twisty-road course with significant elevation gain and her Indy car behaved quite differently, understeer in slow corners and oversteer in the fast turns. Her goal was always to be first, be the best, and when Saturday's qualifying only netted her a 4th Place starting position she was momentarily upset with herself. Sondra's team however, this new group/family, felt good about their efforts, especially considering the far more experienced teams and competitors they were up against. Sunday's race-day weather was cool and gray, with intermittent light rain. The first twelve laps of the event were run on rain tires behind the pace car, under yellow-flag conditions. When the field was finally given the green flag there was a three-car crash in Turn 2. As soon as the pits were open Darren had Sondra come in and get off the grooved rain tires and onto a set of used red sidewall soft-compound slick tires. The track was still quite damp in a number of places and this was an enormous gamble, but slippery and quickly changing conditions were well within Sondra's wheelhouse and Darren knew it. When the field went green Sondra was only one of two drivers on slick tires. The Twelve car restarted in 11th Place because of their pit stop but began to make passes and take advantage of the misfortunes of drivers further up in the running order. Later, with 46 laps remaining and a track that was now completely dry, Darren pitted Sondra and put her on a set of sticker black-sidewall Firestone Firehawk tires that would take her to the end of the race. He had executed this same basic strategy the previous weekend and had his reputation on the line. He'd taken heat for this from members of the team as well as people on social media but went on gut instinct that this situation was completely different. This was still a gamble and a bit of an educated guess how the race was unfolding. With 12 laps to go there was a caution for debris in Turn 4. Two cars had come together and resulted in sharp carbon fiber debris on the racing surface. Darren pitted his driver along with most of the field but since only a splash of fuel was needed, not tires, Sondra leapfrogged her way up in the running order. At the conclusion of the race the #12 Holt Racing team came away with their first podium finish of the year. "Well I mean third isn't first" said Sondra as she was interviewed by race reporter Tracy Bueler. "We really need to qualify better but with the set of Firestone Firehawk black tires we took on our second stop it seemed to help my Holt Racing Triple A Twelve car really come alive. I mean on that last stint I wasn't fighting understeer like after the previous stop, and during that last caution we just needed a splash-and-go to take us to the end."

Sondra's stomach was in knots on the morning of their arrival in Long Beach for Round 3 of the championship. This was an iconic race on the IndyCar schedule and when she was younger she and her father had talked about this annual event and its esteemed participants, especially the drivers who'd won there. The four-day race weekend kept Sondra and her #12 team constantly busy. After qualifying a disappointing 11th, Sondra was invited by Andrew Placer's girlfriend, Stephanie, to watch some of the IMSA Sports Car race. The two young women sat together on the temporary metal grandstands with a view of the #42 Ferrari 458 GT pit, watching Andrew's progress in the race. Sondra unwittingly relieved Stephanie's anxiety over Andrew's chosen profession as they chatted.

During Sunday's Long Beach Grand Prix the track became extremely slippery. Sondra's sprint-car background helped even the playing field a little with others who had far more experience, and she began to make steady progress. On lap 53 a purple car made an obvious blocking move, coming close to forcing her into a runoff zone. In the next number of laps it seemed to her as though he was deliberately trying to ruin her race. Coming out of the hairpin of Turn 11 the purple car ran wide and she ducked in underneath, getting past and leading him down Shoreline Drive, her thumb on the push-to-pass overtake button. A number of turns later the purple car made a questionable move on her and she backed off, letting him around. They were coming up on lapped traffic and the situation seemed ripe for an entanglement. Darren was watching all this on a video monitor from the Holt Racing mobile pit command center and nodded, approving his driver's good judgment. Several laps later Sondra couldn't help but briefly smile to herself when lapped traffic put the purple menace in a tight spot. She made her move on him and didn't budge. Their tires touched briefly but she got the position, complaining on the radio to Darren about the driver's behavior. With good pit strategy and fuel consumption, Sondra was now within striking distance of a hard-fought top-ten finish. The #12 team then got an even bigger break. A caution came out for debris on the racetrack. When the pits were open the leaders and most of the others came in for fuel, some taking on tires as well. Darren chose to gamble and keep his driver out. After three laps the race resumed and Sondra got a tremendous re-start, managing to grab 3rd place. As if she were in some horror movie, the purple menace appeared again. He had gone a lap down on that last round of pit stops and when

Sondra began to overtake him he drove her to the dirty side of the racetrack into the marbles, the bits of rubber and debris that had been forming since the start of the race. The back-end of the #12 car broke loose and drifted dangerously close the concrete barrier, eventually leaving a faint black line of rubber from her Left-rear tire. Sondra fell from 3rd to 11th in a blink of an eye. Her screams of displeasure were unprofessional and most definitely unladylike. Darren worked hard at getting her to calm down, and with eight laps remaining she managed to claw her way up to 9th. Although Sondra had come away with her second IndyCar top-ten finish she was beyond irate. On an angry march to her RV she ignored race reporter Tracy Bueler's questions and pushed the woman's microphone-holding hand out of the way with a powerful swing, flashing her a fierce look. Doug and Karen were stunned and embarrassed by their daughter-client's behavior, with Karen chasing after and scolding the young driver as Doug apologized to the reporter.

Sondra's rotten mood-fest continued into the next weekend at the Phoenix International Speedway. In the Friday morning driver's meeting she was singled out for using foul language over the radio. It was reiterated to the group that broadcast media frequently monitored, used and commented on the different team transmissions. As if this wasn't humiliating enough she finally got a clear glimpse of the jerk in the purple #17. It was Gary Slesinger, a 24 year-old IndyCar rookie who had come from the stock-car ASA series. Sondra found out from one of her Holt Racing team members that the guy's father was a wealthy stockmarket company executive who had pretty much bought his son a spot on the Granger-NYSE team. She sat angrily eyeing the little cretin as the morning driver's meeting adjourned. Slesinger and his teammate had the nerve to point and laugh at her and she flipped them off, which earned her a mandatory trip to the trailer of the IndyCar vice president. As he scolded and warned her, she stood there frozen in anger, unable to say anything in defense.

The weekend became a struggle for Sondra and her Twelve team to get the balance of the car sorted out and comfortable enough for her to lay down any kind of decent speeds and lap-times. With the

G-loads of oval-track racing she experienced more than ever the safety harness cutting into her inner thighs, causing distracting immense pain. Her teammate Ryan Delgato proved to be a pillar of help and encouragement in driving the ovals as well as dealing with traffic and air turbulence. Before Saturday's qualifying runs were to begin Sondra sat next to Ryan during an hourlong mandatory IndyCar autograph signing session. Though she was not cognizant of it, this activity with smiling fans and the camaraderie with her teammate made a big difference. She was in far better spirits upon returning to the Holt Racing assigned garage, holding up in triumph the hamburger that had been provided by one of the vendors.

The next morning, Sondra's stomach was an uncomfortable bundle of nerves at the mandatory driver's meeting. She was not only considered a rookie within this esteemed IndyCar field but many of her fellow competitors saw her as a skinny kid who looked about twelve years old, and most found it hard to believe by just looking at her that she had the strength to fully handle a powerful race car. A few however had been on her side from the start. Aside from Brice and Andrew and her teammate Ryan, longtime IndyCar stars Tony Kelarzo, Jordan Deratta and Shane Teluchi had been the first to welcome Sondra into the fold with open arms. These men had gone on record as singing the young driver's praises to media and many others. They too had complaints about Sondra's current nemesis Gary Slesinger and had offered Sondra sage advice on how to deal with him. Tony, Jordan and Shane held Darren Brown and T.J. Holt in the highest regard and figured that if Holt and company chose to work with Sondra she must have some major talents that would be revealed as the year unfolded. Tony Kelarzo was one of the most popular among fans and drivers alike. All his dealings with Sondra on the racetrack thus far had been extremely courteous and respectful. Sondra felt safe around him both on and off the track, and during the drivers meeting he and Shane sat next to her, blocking her from several of the most disagreeable competitors. Later that afternoon she took the support, camaraderie and confidence that Kelarzo, Teluchi and several other drivers, family as she chose to think of them, with her as she went out to qualify for the evening's event. Her car however proved to be an ill-behaved beast that was down on horsepower. The results of her timed laps would have her starting Sunday's race 14th on the grid.

As the sun began its downward slope thirty minutes before Sunday's Phoenix 250, pit reporter Tracy Bueler hesitantly approached the driver of the #12 car. Sondra had been standing and chatting to Holt Racing's tire manager Michael Rathlin. Tracy held up her microphone and cued her cameraman. "So, Sondra. You're starting pretty deep in the field but it looked like you guys found some speed in the earlier warm-up today. How are you feeling about your prospects for tonight?"

Sondra was handed a bottle of 7-UP, strategically placed with the label showing to the camera by manager Karen. The young driver took a quick gulp then shrugged her shoulders and answered in a dejected tone. "Well I mean fourteenth isn't first and nowhere near the front. Track position is huge here but the setup on my Honda-powered Holt Racing-Triple A Twelve car is the best it's been all weekend, so hopefully we can manage a decent finish." Tracy wished Sondra luck, and after the camera was off Sondra got her chance to apologize to the woman for her behavior during their last interview.

The race itself for Sondra and the #12 team proved disappointing, to say the least. She found the Phoenix International Speedway to be a frustrating D-shaped one-mile oval with Turns 1 and 2 being so completely different than 3 and 4. With nineteen-second laps and different degrees of banking in each section of track, including the straights, there was also a five and a half G load to contend with, making it a grueling test for all drivers. Wind and sand were major factors in tire-wear and fuel consumption, and the weather was hot and dry. A little under halfway through the race Sondra was accelerating out of Turn 3 when the engine quit cold. There weren't any warning signs and all the temperature and pressure gauges had been reading in the normal ranges. Luckily she was able to coast down pit lane and Darren had her turn toward the garage area. Nineteen laps later she was back out with a new ignition harness, but for her it had gone from being a race to basically becoming a practice run. As if her day needed to get any worse, Gary Slesinger was back to his old tricks and began to race her absurdly hard. She was immediately on the radio. "What the hell's this idiot's problem? We're not even close to racing for position. The guy's nothin' but a damn menace to everyone out here."

"Calm down, Sondra" warned Darren. "Keep your focus and stay the course."

"Where the hell's Race Control looking?" she shot back. "Get this moron away from me" she added angrily. This sort of thing lasted quite a few laps.

Darren Brown was known for being one of the most even-tempered crew chiefs and race strategists in the business, but after a formal complaint that he'd lodged with Race Control hadn't produced any immediate results he himself yelled angrily at one such track official. Other complaints had come in about car #17. Slesinger was finally given a drive-through penalty for over-aggressive driving. When the #17 car didn't immediately heed the penalty he was then shown the black flag and ordered to come down through pit lane at 65 mph. Sondra didn't think it was punishment enough but Darren got his driver to settle down and focus on giving him smooth laps. At the conclusion of the race Sondra scrambled out of her car and went to Slesinger's pit to find out why he was treating her this way and see if they couldn't find a way to put an end to all this ridiculousness. She was stunned when he reacted as if it was her fault for being in his way on the track. He then did something that made her snap, and snap hard. He called her a stupid little bitch. With every ounce of strength she punched his right shoulder. It came so quick and out of the blue that it was shocking to him and he fell over backwards. She stood over him for a few seconds, still fuming mad and with her fists clenched. She then began to storm off toward her motorhome. The incident would have most likely gone unnoticed and then forgotten but it was too soon after the end of the race and TV cameras had captured the entire scene. Doug's reaction was stunned disbelief and perhaps a bit of pride, but Karen raced after her brat and loudly chastised the girl for her behavior. Cameras caught this as well along with loudly roaring fans in the front grandstands, who'd witnessed the entire incident. Sondra was soon collected by race officials and redirected to the IndyCar vice president's trailer, where she was severely scolded, told she was being put on probation and fined ten thousand dollars for inappropriate and unprofessional conduct. It was seriously discussed that Darren and T.J. pay fines as well but for the moment this was just a possibility. Sondra was made to agree to write out a formal apology to the fans and race teams for her unprofessional behavior, and discussion was had on several other meetings about possible further disciplinary action.

On the walk to the main Holt Racing hauler office Karen continued to scold the girl, warning that their sponsors would not be happy with any of this. Once inside the mobile air-conditioned suite Sondra was sure she was going to receive the yelling of her life from Darren and T.J., but the thing of it was, both men were oddly proud. Darren however did manage to tell his young driver that on no uncertain terms was her behavior to be tolerated in the future. "You may have done what we were all thinking" he said to her. "But don't pull that kind of crap again, you hear me?" T.J. Holt, sitting next to Darren, was known for having an occasional explosive temper all throughout his long career. He'd been in quite a number of different scrapes over the years with drivers and team members who did stupid things he didn't appreciate. The tough Texan now had something in common with his newest driver. He liked that Sondra had a fiery temper and wasn't trying to be America's racing sweetheart. She'd been anything but sweet for weeks. He also liked that she wasn't at all timid about getting in and working alongside the guys in the garage. Sondra loved that her team was what she'd imagined it would have been like in the '50s or '60s. Sure, they now had the latest hi-tech equipment and worked within all the current rules and regulations, but T.J. and Holt Racing in general had a definite old-school approach and feel. If you possessed a skill, you were expected to use it. Sondra may not have had years of mechanical experience but she knew her way around a wrench. She'd always paid close attention to her mechanics, especially the Patrero-McDonald's guys, and had become a talented welder. Doug had taught her well, and since joining Holt Racing she had fabricated quite a number of brackets and racks to hold tools and equipment, not only back in the Texas race shop but for the garages they visited and for the transport trucks as well. T.J. was slowly beginning to come around. Besides, she was doing far better than Ryan and thoughts of an early release from his contract were beginning to float through T.J.'s mind. During the post-race team meeting, T.J., chewing gum like a madman, listened to Darren scold Sondra and then move on to other important topics with the race team. At the conclusion, T.J. labored to stand and put an arm around Sondra. "Well looks like we gotta get our prize fighter here a set of boxing gloves" he roared with a large smile.

"T.J." scolded Karen, her arms tightly folded. "Don't you dare encourage this." She then turned and stormed out of the trailer leaving Sondra and the men feeling as though they'd just been profoundly put in their place.

"Hey-ya, slugger" said a voice from several feet away as Sondra and Doug made their way to their own motorhome. Sondra turned with an instant smile and shook her fist at Brice. Doug put a solid hand on Sondra's back and shook his head as he spoke. "You stay out of trouble while I go try to calm down your mom" he told his daughter. Sondra and Brice walked slowly in the basic direction of his motorhome, seven rows away from Sondra's.

"So Fifth Place, huh?" prompted the girl.

"Yeah" nodded Brice, a bit dejected. "Finished where I started" he explained. "We were just struggling so bad with tire wear."

Sondra nodded. She too had been dealing with the abrasiveness of the sandy track surface. "And the wind gusts going into Three" she contributed. "I mean it just kept getting worse no matter what I did with the tools." Brice nodded and watched Sondra take off her cap to run her fingers through her long hair. He leaned in and kissed her.

"Watch-it, buddy" she said with a bit of a smirk and a wave of her fist. "I've already knocked one guy down today."

They walked hand-in-hand to the multiple rows of motorhomes

within the fenced-off RV Paddock. "I have this great peach iced tea in my trailer" offered Brice.

"Tempting" Sondra told the boy. "But I'll have to take a raincheck. We've a plane to catch. Home for two days and then Texas, and then I'll see you in Indianapolis." Brice wrapped his arms around Sondra and held her tight.

"Did you just kiss my hair?" she asked, pulling away a few inches and eyeing the boy suspiciously.

"What? No" he denied. "I wouldn't do that. That would b e..."

"Weird and creepy?" she interrupted.

"Well I was going to say sweet and endearing" he corrected.

"Kay" she whispered, moving back into his tight embrace. "We'll go with your thing" she added.

The Trents arrived at the Indianapolis Motor Speedway on a cool overcast Wednesday morning. The next week and a half was far from fun and games. The focus was not on the five hundred mile race but the Indy Grand Prix which was to be run on the road-course within the famed oval. Sondra was kept busier than she'd imagined. From the time she woke up in the early morning to the time her head touched her pillow at night there was always someone wanting something from her. The most frustrating part of all this was that she just couldn't stop making every single rookie mistake possible. Rookie Orientation was straightforward enough but during both the open and mandatory practices Sondra went into the wrong pits on her second pit stop. She also managed to run over her own airgun hose making a premature dart out of her pit-box after coming in for fuel and tires during a 35-lap simulated race run. The next day she spun on cold tires in Turn 5, luckily not hitting anyone or any thing. Though the emphasis was on next Sunday's Grand Prix, the Indy 500 coming up in two weeks loomed over her like a concrete cloud. She managed to trip over things and spill all over herself just about every food or beverage item she consumed. Her tardiness in getting to meetings or press interviews because she'd either get momentarily lost or distracted by almost anything, did not go unnoticed, especially by her managers. Holt Racing's two-car effort in the Indy Grand Prix turned into a much better outcome than the first four races of the year. Ryan Delgato got his first win in just over two years and Sondra managed a hard-fought Third Place, seven one-thousandth's of a second behind Shane Teluchi and 1.003 seconds ahead of Brice Crandle. The three podium finishers had much to celebrate but Sondra hated losing. She did her best to act happy about the weekend's accomplishments but secretly dismissed it all, setting her sights high for what had aways been billed as The Greatest Spectacle In Racing.

The following Thursday, Sondra's stomach was in knots the morning of her Rookie Orientation and then Rookie Testing on the famed two and a half mile oval. Aside from the all-important proceedings of the day there were to be media events as well as some sponsor obligations. She was constantly aware of her surroundings and the significance of what she was attempting. Overwhelming pain at not having her father, mother and brothers be a part of this was intertwined with enormous pressure to perform. There were a few welcomed light moments here and there however. When Dan and Vanessa Stoltz arrived at the speedway Sondra enjoyed watching their expression of excitement and astonishment at her popularity and that of Doug and Karen. Sondra and her manager-parents were continuously mobbed by race reporters and fans wanting photos, answers to questions as well as autographs.

Practices on the big 2-1/2-mile oval began without drama for Sondra and both Holt Racing teams. A week and three days before the 500 however disaster struck for the rookie Holt Racing driver. It came on an afternoon where the weather had turned gloomy. The first practice of the day had been canceled because of a quick-moving storm, bringing a torrential downpour. At just after 3 p.m. the weather cleared nicely and an hour later the track was dry enough for teams to go out for a 45-minute practice session. Sondra was seven laps away from making a stop for tires and fuel when the car snapped loose in Turn 4. It was a dramatic-looking crash with fire and pieces of her car exploding in a catastrophic flash. When the car skidded to a stop along the outside Safer Barrier retaining wall there came a fast moving river of oil and fluids gushing from underneath and heading toward the infield. Going against instructed protocol, Sondra hopped out immediately, her white-hot temper clearly visible to all. The force of the impact had literally and figuratively stunned Sondra. The fact that she and her car had come ultra-close to flipping was now beginning to sink in as she leaned against her broken steed, trying to catch her breath. Flame was visible at a reduced intensity so there would be no penalty for extricating herself from the cockpit, though she would be questioned about it at a later time.

Karen and Doug had been watching from Sondra's pit and experienced instant terror upon witnessing the dramatic event. They relaxed somewhat when they observed their hotheaded Sondra kick at the ground while clutching at her lower back with her left hand as she inspected the carnage. She stared at the smoke and little bit of flame emanating from the back end, then went from her car to pound the wall with her right fist as safety crews pulled up behind her. Three men swarmed in, trying to calm her, but she argued with them and put up a bit of a fight. The men basically herded her into the safety vehicle, and roughly thirty minutes later at the in-field care center the doctors approved her physical health status and released her. Sondra and her relieved manager-parents encountered a small sea of reporters and curious fans waiting as the young racer stepped through the doors. She was walking rather strangely because of the soreness in her back, a bit like a penguin on uneven snow, but made an attempt to smile and assure everyone that she was okay. Once back at the Holt Racing garage, Karen couldn't seem to let go of her daughter or stop playing with the girl's hair. Brice Crandle appeared as if out of nowhere and Sondra broke free from her concerned and protective parents. Young Crandle held Sondra's hand tenderly for a moment, inquiring about her condition. Soon a large crowd began to form, with Darren and several Holt Racing team members gathered closest around their shaken driver. Pit Reporter Tracy Bueler made an attempt to get an interview. Sondra wanted to run away and hide. She was embarrassed for her perceived mistake but shrugged her shoulder in answer to Bueler's seemingly intrusive questions.

"Well I mean there was just no warning whatsoever" explained

Sondra. "The Triple-A Holt Racing Honda motor felt solid and I was loving the grip. We were doing everything right. Building speed in slow five mile an hour increments. The car just came around so fast and the wall was there before I could even take my foot off the gas."

After answering a few more questions, then doing a post-crash debrief with her team, Karen and Doug escorted Sondra to the privacy of their RV, disappointing Brice that he was not invited. Sondra slid from the couch to the floor, crying like a young unconsolable child. Doug and Karen were surprised by this but immediately administered comfort for their kid and encouraged her to take a soothing shower. When she emerged, dressed in her Holt Racing team uniform, Karen tried to get the girl to eat a peanut-butter and grape jelly sandwich. Never before had Sondra's confidence been so badly shattered to the core in a race car. She'd had a few crashes and mishaps in the past but this one didn't make a bit of sense to her. The feel and instincts that had always been with her had failed her absolutely on this day. There came several knocks on the motorhome door and Sondra shot up to answer it. She was both embarrassed and pleased to find Brice Crandle, Andrew Placer and Wendell Grayson standing at the short RV steps, there to offer support and make sure their fellow driver was okay. Doug and Karen allowed the boys to enter and soon felt privileged as they listened to the four talk seriously about the crashes they'd all had over the years and how the Indianapolis track had felt in certain places that day. The conversation soon began to ease into much lighter topics and by the time the young men departed Sondra felt far more at peace, enough to eat the sandwich and get in a forty-two minute nap.

It was after 6 p.m. when Sondra wandered unnoticed back to the assigned Holt Racing garage. The radio was playing country-rock and the place appeared to be deserted. Guessing everyone was on a dinner break she knelt down and continued with a job that had obviously been left uncompleted. It was astounding to her that her beloved car was not completely destroyed. As she was tightening a bolt on the right-front suspension assembly her hand slipped off the wrench and her knuckles instantly struck sharp metal. She stood and hopped around, letting out a string of obscenities that very well might have embarrassed Satan. When she began to calm down, alternating from shaking her hand to holding it tight, a shop rag struck her softly in the face. Startled, she looked up to see T.J. Holt kneeling on the ground and leaning out from behind the opposite end of the car, with a look that conveyed extreme annoyance. Sondra watched him chew his gum in assertive fashion. He then spoke in a gruff tone. "When you're finished with your little rain dance there, why don't you get your ass back to work and stop being such a girl."

Knowing he wasn't as angry as he was trying to make out, she bent down to pick up the rag with a slight smile and threw it back at him. He caught it in his left hand as she headed back to continue with the task at hand.

With the exception of the radio, Sondra and T.J. worked in silence for the next few minutes. T.J. soon came around to help Sondra muscle a suspension piece into place and their heads were close as they worked together. Sondra felt a small wave of goose bumps as she noticed T.J. taking a look around beginning to speak in a quiet serious voice. He imparted many secrets about the five hundred mile race and the famous Brickyard, mentioning tactics he'd employed and the experiences he'd had over his long driving career. T.J. then went through his observed inventory of what he saw as her strengths, without mentioning her few young weaknesses. Looking around once again he had one more thing to offer. "If you so much as breathe a word of what I just told you, once the year's done, I'll break your arms and legs in at least ten places." His eyes were steel-blue cold and she knew he wasn't being literal but was deadly serious. She nodded once, returning his intense stare. "Don't you have some fancy PR dinner to go to?" he said in a bit of a growl. Sondra looked at her watch. "Yeah, I hate those things" she complained. Before she could take three steps toward the rollup garage door T.J. swatted her on the arm and gestured her toward a work bench. Picking up a piece of black flexible tubing and a fiber washer that looked burnt and mangled he imparted an explanation.

"Oil line seal failed. Sprayed fluid on the right rear tire." He then grabbed a piece of paper and pointed with his pudgy and grease-stained finger to a wavy line on a graph. "Right there is when it blew." He moved his finger to the next graph line and continued. "The tiniest of a millisecond later, this shows that you not only started lifting off the gas but you took the car out of gear and you had your foot down on the brake. That's monster-rare instincts and it's what kept you from completely destroying the car and putting yourself in the hospital, probably ending your month here. Now go away and make sure you sleep good tonight because now we're behind and we have a hell of a lot of hard work cut out for us tomorrow and the days to come."

The morning and afternoon practices ahead of the great 500 mile race for both Holt Racing teams went smoothly and without incident. Later, Sondra went to sleep happy in the knowledge that she was sixth fastest overall that day and they were finally making strong progress. She woke the next morning feeling as if her Indy experience had changed for the better, becoming more relaxed socially and was often seen together with Brice, Andrew, Stephanie, SeaShell and Wendell Grayson. Though these moments were far and few between, each one of them held significance. Amongst racing peers, Sondra, Brice, Andrew and Wendell soon became known as The Rug-Rats of Indy. They're were seen playing aggressive games of Frisbee and soccer in the infield, and while one was giving a serious TV interview the others would show up and clown around in the background, with Tony Kelarzo and Shane Teluchi getting into the act on occasion. The Rug-Rats were occasionally seen laughing and eating together, and it was duly noted when Doug and Karen would come into the fray to curtail and collect their kids, scolding and reminding them of their important and respective duties.

Sondra didn't think it could ever be possible to feel an inner happiness and peace at Indy, especially on the evening ahead of Qualifying and Bump Day, but after a significant conversation with Shelley it came to her that this was indeed the case. Before she went to bed that evening she and Brice climbed up the ladder on her motor home and sat on the roof with their feet dangling over the side. They had their arms around one another, and even though she gave Brice a few annoyed glances, he occasionally put soft kisses on her neck and cheek as they looked around at the many lights of the darkened speedway.

"It looks so magical and so mysterious all at the same time" observed Sondra in a quiet voice.

"Kinda like Disneyland for race car drivers?" chuckled Brice.

Sondra leaned away and swatted him lightly on the upper arm. "Are you mocking me?" she asked through narrowed eyes. He laughed, quickly shaking his head.

"Nooo" he denied sarcastically. "Well okay, maybe a little" he added.

She tilted her head and stared at him with a slight smile. "I was going to let you draft behind me a time or two during the race, but now? Not so much."

Brice grinned at that and they sat in contented silence, enjoying their view and each other's company. "Glad your parents had that cocktail party to go to tonight" he whispered. Sondra noticed that he was staring intently at the tall unlit scoring tower and followed his gaze, then rested her cheek against his shoulder. "We had a big team meeting yesterday" Brice revealed. "Hugo and Adrian basically told Andrew and me to enjoy our Indy experience but not be pressured with any expectations. I don't think they have any idea of how much I want to win, especially after I DNF'd with motor issues last year."

"I know what you mean" said Sondra. "But if it comes down to you and me …"

Brice nodded once and kissed her softly before again speaking. "Even when I was really young, no matter what I was riding or driving, a tricycle, bicycle, motorcycle, go-kart or car, I was always imagining winning here."

Sondra wrapped the fingers of her right hand in his. "Same with me when I was young" she told him. "I mean I didn't have motorcycles or go-karts but I had those thoughts as well. It may sound funny, but even when I was mowing lawns I always made left-hand turns when I could, and I wondered what it was going to feel like coming out of that turn Four on the last lap in the lead. We lived really close to the elementary school I went to. It seemed like miles of blacktop. There was a big space to play four and six-square. There were basketball courts, and there was a baseball diamond that had a huge running track in the outfield, all outlined with white paint. I use to ride my bike around that track as fast as I possibly could."

Sondra stopped talking suddenly and looked over at Brice, studying his face in the moonlight. The two shared a long tender kiss, with his hands gently cupping her face, then moving downward. She briefly wondered how far he was planning on going but it seemed so natural and innocent, then wildly exciting. She became swept up into a warm, energized fuzziness. When the kiss ended they resumed their study of the magical surroundings and she went back to finishing her story. "That school's track is really where I think I first learned the balance of speed and power, and the concept of apexing correctly. I mean I didn't consciously think about it at the time but I'm sure that's why things came so naturally to me in my first sprint-car race."

Brice smiled at that, examining and playing with her fingers. "Do you get people asking you if you're surprised to be here at such an early stage in your career?" he inquired.

"Yeah" she said, nodding. "That's totally annoying, isn't it? I get that all the time, especially since they think I look younger than I am."

Brice ran his fingers softly across her lips and cheek, then got up offering a helping hand, elated that she took it without question. Once on the ground he held her for just less than a minute.

"Thanks for tonight" she whispered. "So perfect."

"Yeah" he agreed. "Guess we better get some sleep. Tomorrow's go-fast day."

He gave Sondra a quick peck on the cheek and she watched him disappear behind one of the sleek RVs.

Sondra was among the first twelve drivers to make an attempt to qualify, hoping to get the top spot or at least run fast enough to guarantee a start in the annual five hundred mile race. It was pretty much textbook perfect weather for this. Air temperature was 68 degrees and the track was 83, with virtually no wind being detected. The #12 driver climbed into her car with extreme focus. Every procedure had been followed to the T and she left pit lane with the engine momentarily screaming after hearing the words she'd always dreamed of hearing from an Indianapolis Motor Speedway official.

"Okay, Sondra. You have two warmup laps, then give us four fast and safe ones. Good luck."

She was cautious through the first three turns but was building speed and confidence, with both Darren and spotter Craig Pines on the radio with her, reminding her to use the in-car tools and be mindful of "tire-deg" (tire-wear degradation). Sondra crossed the line on her first warm-up lap at a speed of 223.862 mph. The next time by she was clocked at 227.249. When the green flag waved for her four-lap run it was noted that the Twelve car gained a significant jump-up in speed, and during the next four circuits Sondra had only one heart-skipping moment for nervous on-lookers, when she was flat-out, accelerating out of Turn 4. Over the radio, Darren gave Sondra encouragement and kept her appraised of any changing conditions. Craig Pines called out each lap number and T.J. began to have a radio presence as well, giving her a particular bit of advice about a roll-bar adjustment. He referred to her as Tiger. This was the prearranged signal that Sondra and the IndyCar legend had set up for her to push hard. She held incrementally less force on the steering wheel going into Turn 4. This would let the car run just a bit wider through the corner and not scrub off any speed. The wall however, the very wall she'd hit days before, came up quickly just millimeters from contact. In the speed-trap before Turn 3 during the #12 car's final lap Sondra was traveling at 238.359 miles per hour. She took the checkered flag at 236.883, giving her a four-lap average speed of 235.972 mph. She now had the provisional Pole by well over half a second and would hold that position for three of the most glorious and exhilarating hours of her life. While she was pulling into her pits after that crowd-pleasing run, live broadcast cameras went from Sondra to T.J. Holt, then to Doug and Karen. T.J. was visibly moved and speechless when asked how it felt to have an eighteen- year-old female driver put him in the position of being in legitimate contention for a Pole and then go on for a possible Indy 500 win. This two-car organization hadn't been anywhere near this position in six long years and T.J. could only shake his head and chew his gum faster. As Sondra was being helped out of her car she caught a glimpse of Shelley and Darren holding hands, with Darren displaying the same proud "I told you so" grin often seen on Doug's face so many times over the past several years. After climbing over the pit wall she was met with hugs and smiles by Doug and Karen. Her world was momentarily hyper-excited with a bit of contented peace. Karen however was more outwardly nervous than Sondra or her team as they watched other drivers attempt to win that coveted top position.

The Indiana weather the next day (Pole-day/Bump-day) gave every indication that it would be quite warm. At 11:30 a.m. it was 79 degrees, with the track temperature 12 degrees higher. The first qualifying activity of the day was the Fast Nine. Since Sondra the previous day had posted the quickest speed within this group, Indy 500 qualifying rules had her going out last. Readying herself for her Pole run she did her best to keep tabs on the performance of the eight other cars going out one by one to obtain the fastest speed. While she was finally on track, Darren, T.J. and Craig were on the radio to coach her though every inch and corner of the big oval. Sondra felt far more nervous during the two warmup laps but when the green flag flew her concentration was at its sharpest point and she managed to better her 4-lap average speed from Friday. Unlike the previous day she hadn't traveled the fastest. This qualifying run had her slated to start the great race from the outside of Row 1, Third on the grid. To her left, in the 2nd position would be six-year veteran of the event Jorden Deratta whose highest finish had been 3rd. Tony Kelarzo snagged the Pole after his second attempt. The first was waved off due to an increasing Left-front tire vibration. This was Kelarzo's eighth Indy start, having won just two years prior.

For the next 1 hour and 53 minutes Sondra watched with interest as the rest of the cars went out to better their speeds, 9th through 33, or bump their way into the great race of the cars that had made the field the previous day. Brice Crandle wasn't too thrilled with his qualifying effort but starting from the inside of Row 6 in such a long race was nothing to get too down about, especially since he'd been showing race-trim speeds the past two days within the top three. Andrew Placer was just happy to qualify for the race at all and would be starting in the 19th position, with high hopes for some good luck at the end. Wendell Grayson, scheduled to start 25th, was not a regular in the IndyCar Series. An Indy Lights rookie, he was the current points leader in that championship. Wendell was part of the Anditelli Autosports family, and when their IndyCar driver Rich Clemens was injured in his crash at Long Beach, Wendell was invited to take Clemens' seat in the big race. Adrian Valderez was set to start in 6th, directly behind Sondra. This was a bit of a worry to her because she knew his personality and driving style. He most likely would try and nose in underneath, forcing her to run dangerously high into Turn 1. She'd have to back off in order to stay out of the dirty slippery part of the track next to the outside wall. In preparation for the start, Sondra would need to spend much time visualizing a number of moves to counter that attack.

The all-important Carb Day had Sondra both excited and eager to participate in the tradition but it also produced high anxiety. This was the final day of practice in order to get everything right on car setup and strategy. Close attention was made in getting the 18.5-liter fuel cell filled as fast as possible while in the pits, as was finding out exacting fuel mileage numbers while running at speed and in traffic. In addition, one-lap runs were made in order to scuff in the thirteen sets of tires each team was awarded, taking off the slick sheen that came from the manufacturing process. During this period Sondra was constantly warned not to execute fast take-offs or slide the tires while pitting. Importance was also put on being able to execute a clean pit-in from Turn 4 and easily identify one's pit-box. Getting on and off pit lane cleanly normally goes without saying but in this five hundred mile race it would be crucial. In addition, Sondra was made aware of a three-area basic but extremely important checklist. The first area included making sure each component on the car was strong and working properly: engine, brakes, tires, suspension and the aero package. The next area was driver-equipment details like helmet, visor and straps, the fit of Sondra's fire suit, her shoes, gloves, the safety harness and drinks system. The third checklist focus was a bit more personal. Sondra would have to be able to get into battle-mode as well as retain a very fine focus for at least three hours during the race. It was also important to her that every Holt Racing crew member knew how much she appreciated their unwavering dedication. Speaking in person or by phone was time-consuming but she was insistent on this.

As Sondra headed through the garage area after a long day she spotted Lydia Velstein. Lydia was in a rush to complete a comprehensive journalistic piece on Sondra's life and career thus far, which would be published in newspapers and periodicals nationwide in just two day's time, ahead of the Indy 500. After answering what Sondra thought a grueling ton of questions she watched her dash away, then noticed another familiar figure walking toward her.

"Oh good, Sondra" said Steven Barnes as he closed the gap. "I'm glad I caught you today" he said with a smile. "I have something here and I didn't know when or if I was gonna have the chance to give it to you because we're all so busy these days."

Sondra lifted her sunglasses to the top of her head and squinted at him with a puzzling stare. He handed her an envelope, the very one she'd mailed to him three years ago. It contained a handwritten note insisting that she was worth the risk for him to hire for his Formula Ford team. In writing, she'd mentioned the phone conversation they'd had, with her promising that she'd indeed make it in this business. She went on in the letter to mention the one-thousand dollar bet she'd made to him, that she'd be in an Indy car and that she would in fact be running in the 500. "I never forgot that phone conversation we had years ago" said Steven. "Seems incredible that our paths had an opportunity to cross professionally and that you were so damn good in a race car, just like you claimed to be years ago. We had a hell of a year last year. I'm not one to give other people a lot of praise and credit for things, but you and your incredible driving really put me on the map in Indy Lights. We were a damn good team. I'm pretty sure we'd have won the Freedom One-hundred here last year if we'd have had just a little bit better luck in qualifying." He looked away, watching a man push a hand-truck stacked with four tires toward the line of garages. "I don't know why I kept that letter of yours" he told Sondra. "But I'm glad I did. You didn't just make a bet that you'd be here at Indy, you made a promise. You kept your promise and now I'm damn proud to honor the bet."

Steven took a piece of paper from his shirt pocket and handed it to the girl. As she examined the check she listened to his explanation. "Sorry for initially doubting you" he began. "But all I saw and heard was a skinny teenage girl claiming what I thought impossible. Hell, back then I never thought it possible that I'd be in the position I'm in or have an extra grand to honor such a bet. This is more than that, though. I've been hearin' about this Safen-Up organization you helped start. Allow me to honor my debt and make a charitable contribution."

Though Sondra's every movement of each day lately was constantly being photographed or filmed, she was impressed that Steven had remembered the exchange from years ago and that he didn't try to make a bigger or more public deal out of it. She beamed at him and patted him strongly on his shoulder. "Wow" she said in astonishment. "Thanks. I mean I've felt like saying I told you so a bunch of times to you this past year and a half. I'm actually kinda humbled that things really did turn out the way they did. We really did have a damn good Indy Lights team. Everything turns out for a reason, as they say."

Steven smiled and nodded, a short snorting laugh coming out his nose. "We'll make time to get together and talk soon" he told his former driver, holding out his hand. They shook hands, with smiles and mutual admiration.

In the wee hours of the morning on the last Sunday of May, Sondra Sierre-Trent lay curled in a warm sleeping bag and in a slight fetal position. Sunrise was still two hours away from the mid-western city and state of Indianapolis, Indiana, yet at 4:06 a.m. Sondra's eyes popped open. "Indy" she whispered, feeling momentarily sorry for herself that she wasn't still a kid surrounded by her family and everything she'd known. She crawled out of her sleeping bag and looked around at the space-saving enclosure of the RV, remembering that halfway around the world another important motorsports sensation was taking place. After plugging in headphones and powering on the satellite system, Sondra found the live broadcast feed of the Formula One Monaco Grand Prix. Moments before the lights went out on the grid of twenty-two F1 cars, Doug made his way from the sleeping compartment. He unplugged the headphone jack, turned up the volume and sat next to Sondra. Karen slipped into the main motorhome space and began making coffee. She turned with her arms folded and smiled as she shook her head, watching her husband and daughter's intense stare at the video screen full of action.

At 3:19 p.m. in the mid-west United States, Sondra Sierre stunned the world with dramatics and phenomenal driving in the remaining 26 laps of this year's running of the Indianapolis 500. Owing to Darren Brown's cagey pit stop strategy and his driver's uncanny ability to save fuel and go easy on her tires while still maintaining her position within the top 10, Sondra charged from 6th Place to 3rd, where she'd started. Just laps prior to this surge however there was a moment of intrigue mixed with a bit of humor. The #12 car's engineers noted and then alerted Darren to a sudden slight decrease in lap-times. They were also closely monitoring the car's dozens of telemetry readings, especially in light of the fact that the weather on this day was the second warmest Indy 500 in history. Darren spoke to Sondra over the radio. "How we doin' there, Tiger?" Her answer was faint and unintelligible, a bit garbled by the radio transmission at the particular position on the race track. Darren made another communication attempt and this time her words were clear.

"I'm hot" claimed Sondra, her voice crackling over the team radio. The cockpit's temperature sensor relayed a reading of 133 degrees, and with lap after lap of no major drama happening at the front of the field Sondra's always fighter-pilot type instincts were momentarily diminished. A very dangerous thing at over 223 miles an hour.

Sondra's Left-rear tire changer Greg Vessor had just taken a large sip of Gatorade and upon hearing the words I'm hot began laughing, a few drips of the orange liquid escaping from his nose. The entire pit crew soon gained much levity from this, catching the double meaning. The week prior, a so-called "celebutant" had been in the news for often using the adjective hot in a more socially relevant manner rather than describing physical temperature. Darren noted his team's reaction to Sondra's words but kept up his intense race focus. "That you are, Sondra" he acknowledged over the radio. "You were the hottest thing out there, until you decided to pull over into the slow lane and take a nap. Wanna pick up the pace a little? You saved us enough fuel for this segment."

With five laps to go in the great Indianapolis race a majority of spectators were on their feet. Karen momentarily buried her head in her husband's chest as high-speed drama and tension seemed to explode before them. The #12 car made a bizarre-looking dive in the short-chute between Turns 3 and 4. Sondra came out ahead of race leader Tony Kelarzo, who had led on and off that day for a total of 78 laps. She made this tricky pass stick by the momentum of her move as she went toward Turn 1 then boldly sliced through lapped traffic on the backstretch, momentarily putting them between her and Kelarzo. Nervous onlookers saw this as a frightening gamble and Sondra herself had involuntarily held her breath through it, but this was a move that had taken two prior laps to set up and complete. Her race spotter, Craig Pines, had a calm but purposeful voice as he let her know when she'd cleared the slower cars. He then gave her a quick rundown of the next car numbers and positions on the racetrack she would quickly be encountering. The next voice she heard was that of Darren Brown. "All right, Sondra. Two to go at the line. Kelarzo and the two behind are in fuel-save. You're not. Wheel One. Position One. Full rich, full rich. Lets finish this thing. Keep your focus and give me smooth qualifying laps. Smooth and fast. You got this, kid. Cool, calm and collected. Lets bring this thing home."

Sondra crossed the yard of bricks traveling at 231.859 miles per hour, 1.426 seconds ahead of Tony Kelarzo. With Darren uncharacteristically shouting jagged words of excitement, she went into a stunned trance on the cool-down lap. Her mind was oddly blank. In this moment she was just a passenger along for the ride, observing colors and movement as she rolled majestically along the famous oval. She couldn't seem to find her voice, and the only celebratory movement she made within the cockpit was an unconscious thrust of her right fist into the strong wind resistance of her still fast-moving race car. This was a mere dream when she was a little girl and she had now just lived it.

Coming to a stop in the iconic winner's circle, Sondra didn't want to get out of her car. This didn't fully seem real and the noise level was intense. The scene around her was all so chaotic. She had a sudden image of being crushed to death by the sea of humanity that seemed to close in around her. Events unfolded at lightning speed and she gained composure removing her gloves and working on the helmet strap, aware of several hands moving to quickly free her from the communication cord and safety devices. The traditional wreath seemed strange and momentarily cumbersome as it went down over her head and she stood tall in the seat of her beloved #12 car. With a smile that strained her facial muscles she punched high in the air with her right fist. Sondra was then given the customary ice-cold bottle of milk, which she savored with three large gulps, rivulets of the white liquid spilling down her chin. She was grateful to see that Darren and members of her team had come to her side. She handed the esteemed bottle to her lead strategist and hopped down out of her car as Tracy Bueler thrust a microphone toward her.

"Eighteen-year-old Sondra Sierre, the first woman to ever win here" began the broadcast reporter. "You made history and you just drove the race of your life. You won the Indy Five Hundred. What's going through your mind at this moment? And can you take us along for those last laps?"

"Oh man" breathed Sondra. "I mean, wow. This doesn't even seem real or possible. I don't know what to say. I mean I really didn't think we had anything for Kelarzo near the end there. He was just so strong all day but I just saw this opening and I went for it. I can't believe that worked." When Sondra saw Doug and Karen being helped through the crowd she felt tears running down her face. She used the back of her hand to wipe her lips and cheek of the milk residue, a way to also wipe away the moisture from her eyes in a discrete manner. While the new Five Hundred champion received congratulatory hugs from her now-parents, Tracy did her best to prompt Sondra into continuing her Indy story.

"Well Darren Brown and my engineers were rock-solid, and my pit crew gave me incredibly fast and perfect stops all day long" said Sondra of the interviewer's new round of questions. "T.J. and everyone on my Holt Racing Triple A number Twelve team worked so hard all month long. The Honda motor ran strong and we were rock-solid-fast right when we needed it there at the end." This year's victor of the greatest spectacle in racing then gave a thankful mention of her numerous sponsors, intending to give praise to other members of Holt Racing as well, but Tracy cut her off and began to pry a little deeper into the emotion of the moment. Sondra was overwhelmed and had been consciously willing herself not to cry or be overly emotional, but when she spotted T.J. beginning to make his way through the tight crowd around her she felt the unmistakable pain in her tear-ducts. "You've been through a lot in your life, Sondra" continued Tracy. "Surviving a bad car crash at age thirteen and having to go on without your family. What does this race and this moment mean to you?"

Sondra bit down hard on her tongue and deftly wiped her eyes before answering. "Well it means everything" she said, her voice dripping with the highs and lows of her life. "I mean I've wanted this ever since I can possibly remember. We used to either listen to the Five Hundred on the radio or watch it on TV. I mean I don't think there was ever any big discussion about me being a race car driver or winning the Indy Five Hundred but I'd like to think that maybe in some way they just knew I'd make it here. T.J. Holt's name and his race team were a big part of a lot of discussions I had with my dad." Sondra gestured toward Doug and Karen before she continued. "I'm so lucky to now have parents like Doug and Karen. They're my world and they've help guide me through everything. I wouldn't be here without them. They're a billion kinds of amazing." She breathed deeply and smiled as she watched first T.J. then Doug and Karen take their turn at a swig of milk, enjoying with her this special moment. Tracy attempted to further the interview, wanting to get to the first female to win the Indy 500 aspect, but the Holt Racing crew swept up their hero in jubilant fashion and began passing her around as if she were the team trophy.

Numerous photographs, video and much celebration went on late into the night. There were a number of different interviews delving into all aspects of the day and the life of Sondra Sierre. The next day the front page of many newspapers, periodicals and social-media pages showed a photograph of Sondra sitting in her race-winning car, running her fingers through her dark brown tresses with a caption beneath. She's Hot. Four days of a never-ending packed schedule of travel and interviews followed. At the conclusion of the third very long day Sondra fell back onto her hotel-room bed, lightly complaining to Doug and Karen that all she wanted to do was to get back into her car and get ready for the next weekend's race.

Sondra's incredible outcome at Indy was just the catalyst that both she and Holt Racing needed to turn their season around. From that weekend forward neither Sondra nor Ryan finished out of the top ten, and the checkers flew for Sondra on three more occasions. Almost as significant as her win at Indy was her come-from-behind victory in Sonoma. It was a bittersweet homecoming for her to be back at this facility. She was an Indy 500 winner now but there was a bit of painful emptiness being there without her father. The Grand Prix of Sonoma this year had come after a week-long break in the IndyCar schedule. Once at the California facility of speed, the driver of the #12 car fell in love all over again with the hilly narrow twisty 11-turn wine-country racetrack, and on a brilliant picture-perfect Saturday afternoon put her Triple A car on the outside of Row 1, missing the Pole by .013 seconds. On Sunday, after jumping to the lead for the first three laps of the Grand Prix, Sondra fell dramatically off the pace. She was the most frantic and vocal she'd ever been over the radio with Darren and he did his best to calm her down and get her into the pits that very lap. He made an educated guess at the problem and ordered a battery change. As it turned out the battery didn't actually need changing. A pit crew member noted a loose connection, most likely due to heat and vibration, and after troubleshooting and fixing the problem Darren ordered the #12 car be put on the harder compound tires and receive a fuel top-off. With speedy pit-work Sondra was able to remain on the lead lap, though she was now shown in the 21st position. By doing all this, Darren had basically switched them to an alternative pit stop strategy and Sondra, driving mad and highly determined, began to claw her way forward, several times being warned of over-aggressive driving. At just over the halfway point of the 85 lap event Sondra stunned the broadcast announcers, TV viewers as well as many on-site patrons. With pure instinct, rare talent and smart pit strategy she had gone from third to last to 4th Place. On Lap 68 she out-broke Shane Teluchi going into the hairpin of Turn 7 and made a daring pass on the outside of Jorden Deratta in Turn 2, running wide and kicking up a small dust storm. Seven laps later Sondra surpassed the leader Emanual Billings as she showed the nose of her car in a late-braking move going into Turn 7. Billings maintained the lead but now felt the pressure from behind. With laps winding down the front-runners came in for their final stop for fuel and tires, with the exception of Sondra. Being on that alternative pit stop strategy, the #12 was now on old tires, as opposed to most of the field but was able to build a healthy lead from Billings and hold off the hard-chargers in the closing laps. She crossed the line with the checkers waving for her at a briefly held 179.366 miles per hour.

After two more race weekends, her first IndyCar season ended with Sondra and her manager-parents being more wildly popular than they'd thought possible. Though Sondra's goal was always to win she came away feeling proud of finishing 3rd in her first IndyCar Series championship, driving for the famous T.J. Holt.

Chapter 30

Sondra drove to Malibu to visit SeaShell. During lunch she spoke of a book Lydia Velstein was planning on writing about her and her career, questioning out loud whether or not she was worthy of an entire book. Their conversation took them through Sondra's budding relationship with Brice, some memories of her family, Shelley's recent college graduation and a discussion about the newly created nonprofit, Safen-Up. It was just after 5 p.m. when Sondra arrived back in Santa Barbara and was met by her now-parents in the garage as she exited the Tacoma.

"Brice crashed" said Karen. "Pretty hard." Sondra instantly clutched at the bracelet Brice had given her. Her face turned pale, her breathing shallow and erratic. She studied Doug and Karen for further explanation but before they had a chance to say another word she ran passed them and barked out an order. "Get me on the next flight there."

Doug and Karen stood momentarily looking at each other, concerned about the emotional well-being of their daughter. They had a quick discussion on whether or not it wise to just let Sondra go without them. Reluctantly, Doug got on the phone with an airline ticket agent and Karen went to talk with Sondra, finding the girl pulling clothing items from her closet and dresser drawer and frantically stuffing them into a large dark blue backpack.

“I spoke with Andrew ‘bout an hour ago” said Karen. “I guess the accident happened when he was testing in an open-cockpit Le Mans-style sports car at Mid-Ohio.”

“Where on the track?” demanded Sondra, momentarily halting her actions. She knew every inch of that racing surface and wanted to know if Brice was on the fastest sections when the crash had occurred.

“I don’t know that, Sondra” said Karen, becoming alarmed at her daughter’s state of mind. “Andrew wasn’t big on details” furthered the mom. “He did say that Brice just got out of surgery and that he was in serious but stable condition. That’s all he was able to find out. His mom and sister are en route.”

“Why the hell was Brice in a damn sports car?” questioned Sondra. Karen had no real details to offer but tried to convey what she did know of the situation. “Well according to Andrew he was doing some testing in a Patrero car for one of their sports car endurance teams. I have no idea why. I don’t really feel good about you just going like this, sweetie” added Karen. “You’re not three so it’s not your going alone that I mind, but first of all I didn’t realize that you and Brice had become this close, and secondly, your dad and I have commitments, otherwise we’d go with you.”

Sondra didn’t respond, only continued to pack. “Well if you stay more than just a day or two we’ll fly out” said Karen. Sondra nodded and halted all action, looking over at her now-mom. Uncharacteristically she began to cry without trying to stop or hide it. Karen wrapped her arms tightly around her daughter. “He’ll be okay” whispered the mom. “He’s gonna be okay.”

Doug and Karen were quite hesitant to put their girl on a plane, especially Doug. The couple would have much preferred to go with her but had many other previously established obligations. Sondra hadn’t exactly kept her growing relationship with Brice a secret but she was a bit more stingy with the details than she had been in the past. Doug had been watching her grow up for over three and a half intense years and didn’t like even the idea that she was an adult woman in an adult relationship. At home and on many occasions she acted more like a preteen than a grown woman. The fact that Sondra was displaying this amount of raw emotion over the boy had him concerned. On the flight that Sondra deemed the longest flight ever she was able to text back and forth with Kari, Shelley, Darren, as well as Doug and Karen. She also tried to think of where on the mid-Ohio track Brice could have encountered trouble. This was a place very familiar to both her and Brice and they'd previously talked about working on late-braking and early-acceleration in Turns 5 and 6, in their Indy cars.

When Sondra arrived at the medical facility she found Andrew sitting in the stale lobby. As she approached, he tossed the magazine he'd been reading onto the chair beside him and immediately stood. They walked quickly through double doors and down a hallway that seemed to Sondra as if it were collapsing in on her. "He's out of the ICU and they're saying he's in guarded but stable condition" Andrew informed Sondra. "Brice's mom and sister got here a few hours ago. I just convinced them to go to the cafeteria to try and get something to eat. I'll go check on them and you can have a few minutes of privacy with Brice. You probably won't get to stay too long but at least they're being cool about not being super strict about letting non-family see him."

Sondra nodded, afraid of speaking and betraying her feelings. When she entered the darkened room she stared down at Brice. If he hadn't crashed and there weren't all sorts of tubes and wires hooked to him it might have appeared as though he were simply sleeping. She ran her fingers through his thick light-brown hair. She then bent down and growled into his left ear quietly through clenched teeth. "Don't you dare do this to me. You wake the hell up and get your ass out of this bed."

Beginning to straighten up, her voice became much softer but it was by no means any less unstable. "I could ... I think I might love you, you idiot."

Making a desperate exit, Sondra burst through the front lobby doors of the hospital, gasping for breath. She sat down hard on a gray concrete bench and fought to wipe away tears that just wouldn't cease. It was some time later that Andrew found her. As the young man spoke, Sondra couldn't seem to fathom how long she'd been sitting, just outside the main hospital entrance. "Mrs. Crandle and Lauren are in with him again" informed Andrew. "They're waiting to talk to the doctors again" he added. "You look wiped. Let me take you to get something to eat and I'll get you a room at the hotel where we're all staying." Sondra nodded and followed Andrew to the parking garage, feeling dazed. She threw her backpack into the backseat of the bright red Ford Mustang rental car and was only vaguely aware of the short drive to a Chinese restaurant. After ordering, Andrew took a careful sip of hot tea and took a loud breath. "This is my fault" he said. "I pushed Brice into joining me and doing the test." Sondra shook her head. "Not true" argued Sondra. "When do any of us really need pushing to get into a race car?" "Thanks" said Andrew with a quick smile. "I was in the pits when it happened but I've seen the team's crash footage. All I know is that there was a four-car pileup going into Turn One. Yesterday, the afternoon practice got called off because of a thunderstorm and this morning everyone was pretty desperate to go out and get all they can before tomorrow's qualifying. What's your schedule like?" he asked in an abrupt non sequitur. "I won't get a chance to come back to the hospital until dinner-time tomorrow evening" he explained. "My flight leaves at one forty-five tomorrow afternoon" said Sondra. "I mean I could stay longer but I have a meeting that I'm supposed to be in the next day. Besides, mom and dad aren't too thrilled that I just dropped everything to rush to a boy's bedside." Andrew gave a knowing smile as their sweet and sour soup arrived.

Sondra had a restless night's sleep in her hotel room and was at the hospital by 5:02 a.m. Since she wasn't family she was not allowed access to Brice's room during non-visiting hours nor was she privy to any information regarding his current condition. At 7:30 Brice's mother and his sister Lauren spotted Sondra fast asleep in one of the lobby's not-so-comfortable orange cloth chairs. Gwen and her husband Taylor, along with their daughter had met Sondra briefly on two occasions, at the Formula Ford championship banquet and the Indy Lights championship banquet. For roughly the past two years they'd had to endure Brice's countless tales and mentionings of this female race car driver he seemed to be so completely infatuated with, especially the year that they were teammates. Gwen had been to only two of her son's races and had been so terrified to the point that she hadn't wanted to see another. Brice's father and grandfather were consummate and dedicated farmers. Neither wanted much to do with racing, which they saw as frivolous and not much of a real profession. Brice was gifted mechanically and had a natural mind for farming and the family wheat processing business, but racing was his dream, his goal and his passion. Since his recent successes, the Crandles had tolerated his chosen career but were never enthusiastic about it. This bad crash did little to lessen the negative attitudes and now had Gwen in such a state of shock at having her precious boy lying hurt in a hospital bed. It didn't immediately register to her that it was her boy's Sondra who was there and waiting in chairs in the lobby, but Lauren recognized her right off and made a point to inform her mother.

"Hey, sweetheart" said Gwen as she shook Sondra awake. "Have you been here all night? Do your parents know you're here?" Sondra was slow to wake and comprehend where she was, let alone what this woman was asking her. "You came to see my son?" inquired the mom. "Is he okay?" asked Sondra. Gwen sat down in the next chair. "He's sleeping right now but he's out of danger" she told Sondra. "The doctors say he should make a full recovery in time but it won't be easy." Sondra nodded, running her fingers through her tangled and matted hair and trying to straighten her clothing. Gwen was puzzled by Sondra's presence but heartened by it as well. Brice's sister however was annoyed. Lauren had loved her brother's girlfriend Jillian. She didn't understand how Brice could break things off with Jillian for some race car girl. "Were you at the race track yesterday when the crash happened?" inquired Gwen. "No" said Sondra. "I don't know if you remember me but I was your son's teammate a year ago and he, Andrew Placer and I were in the same racing series a year before that and we became friends." "Oh Andrew's a saint of a boy" gushed Gwen, ignoring Sondra's words. "He's been so good to Brice and all of us." "Brice won't be able to talk for a few days" interjected Lauren. "Sorry you came all this way for nothing." This wasn't true but Lauren knew Jillian was to be there later that day and she wanted Sondra to leave. Sondra stood and held out her hand to Brice's mom, conscious not to grip the woman's hand too tight. "Well I just wanted to make sure he's all right" she told Gwen and Lauren. "I should get going." "So you like my son" posed Gwen. "He's sure talked a lot about you" she added. "He's talked a lot about you and your whole family" said Sondra with a nod. She deftly handed Gwen a business card, suddenly feeling like she was intruding. "Here's where you can reach me to let me know how he's doing" she said to Gwen and Lauren. "He has a lot of people who care about him."

Sondra would have preferred to stay at the hospital in hopes that Brice would wake up and they could talk but that just didn't seem to be in the cards. Instead she rented a Ford Focus that appeared heavily used and made her way to the Mid-Ohio race facility. She was glad to be at a race track and that the Patrero team seemed to welcome her, allowing her to observe the action from the pits. When Andrew was not in the car he stuck near her, but when he was on track, which was most of the time, she felt like an outsider and it was mostly a pretty lonely three hours. She kept thinking of her brothers and how the three of them would always stick together in challenging social settings. She missed them terribly.

Doug and Karen picked Sondra up from the Santa Barbara International Airport at 7:17 p.m. "God I feel like I've been away from home and you guys for months" said Sondra as they made their way to the parking structure. Karen grabbed hold of Sondra's hand as Doug put an arm around his daughter. "I'm pretty sure Brice's mom hates me" Sondra announced. "I mean she and his sister seemed kinda cold."

"They were deeply worried about Brice" offered Karen.

"Oh man" said Sondra, shaking her head. "I can't believe I just flew across the country and ended up blurting out I love you to Brice. I mean he was asleep so I guess I didn't make a hideous fool out of myself, but still." Both Doug and Karen were a bit taken aback by Sondra's confession of her strong feelings for the young man but kept their comments and concerns to themselves, for the moment. They took her to Rick &Bella's Bistro for pizza before heading home. That night, while Karen was in the office going over budgets and profit projections for the merchandising business, Sondra found Doug in the den. "I'm sorry" she told her now-dad. Doug pushed down on the mute button of the remote. He'd been watching a political round-table discussion on the current potency of the Food and Drug Administration. "You're sorry about what?" he asked his daughter.

"About Brice" answered Sondra. Doug turned off the A/V system and watched the girl settle on the other end of the couch. "You don't need to be sorry for your feelings about Brice, Sondra" he assured her.

"Well in a way they just snuck up on me" she explained with a shrug of her right shoulder. "I mean I guess I've spent all this time hating him and being annoyed by him, but I don't know. I guess I just got to know him and I don't hate him, and I don't find him so completely annoying anymore. I, uh. Well I..."

"You fell in love with him" interjected Doug.

"I ... I guess" said Sondra. "I mean it seems so weird to say that and I'm not really sure where to go from here. It's not like we even live in the same state, and we're both so busy. And now he's lying hurt in a faraway hospital bed. I mean I do have real feelings for him and I like him better than any other guy I've ever met, or even imagined I'd meet."

Doug scooted over and put his arm around his daughter. "I want you to be happy, Sondra" he told her. "If the Crandle boy is the love of your life, I say good for you for finding someone you care this deeply about."

"You don't really feel that way" argued Sondra, knowing that Doug had never seemed comfortable with even the idea of her liking boys, perhaps especially this boy.

"Well" said Doug. "I was hoping you wouldn't start liking boys until you were at least thirty" he joked.

"Dad" complained Sondra.

"Well" he voiced, with a quick shake of his head. "Karen and I got to know him last year and he seems to be a good kid with a lot of integrity, and if you like him this much that says a lot in his favor. We'll get to know him and his family."

Doug didn't divulge the fact that while Sondra had been in transit to Ohio the previous day he and Karen had called Crandle Farms, leaving a message. They eventually got a return call from Brice's father Taylor, and when he mentioned that the farm was where Brice would be convalescing, a discussion was had on the possibility of them or at least Sondra coming for a visit.

On a lazy Sunday, Sondra convinced Doug and Karen to join her for an hour of late-afternoon karting. She loved that her now-parents were energetic willing participants. She enjoyed being a bit of a driving instructor here and there, giving mostly Karen tips on car control and pointers on proper corner entrance and exit positioning. As they were putting away the diminutive vehicles after their exhilarating track time, the three began a discussion of their upcoming work schedule. Sondra's cell phone was sitting on the covered nose of her Formula Ford and began to ring. The girl answered it, with Doug and Karen quickly deducing that it was Brice. The parents gave a wave and headed up to the house to give their daughter some privacy. "So this is a nice surprise" Sondra told Brice as she sat on a stool at the work bench, facing outward at the track she, Doug and Karen had not long ago exited. "I'm so happy you're feeling good enough to talk on the phone" she told the boy. "So how are you?"

Brice ignored Sondra's comments and query. His voice was at half-strength. His breathing was heavy and he occasionally groaned as he spoke. "I heard you. At the hospital. Every word." Sondra sprang to her feet, coming close to knocking over the stool. She then stood frozen, staring at the back end of her F-Ford, not sure what to say, if anything. She then began to worry that perhaps her visit had somehow created problems between Brice and his family. "I knew it was you right away" continued Brice. "I could smell your perfume."

Sondra's heart sank because she was sure that he was either delusional or thinking of some other girl, perhaps his ex-girlfriend.

In a sad, low breathy voice she informed him otherwise. "I don't wear perfume, Brice."

His groan was quite labored and he had to take breaths and hold it before uttering short strings of words. "They have me on tons of medication. So I can rest without the intense pain. I was pretty knocked out but I knew it was you. Because you always smell like some kind of sweet flower. I guess it's your soap or shampoo."

Sondra's eyes immediately brimmed with happy tears as she closed them, smiling to herself. She was elated to know that he wasn't delusional and that he really was talking about her. "Honeysuckle" she told the boy. "I use this Honeysuckle shampoo, soap and lotion. I've always used that."

There was a long pause and then Brice again spoke. "See? I woke the hell up, Sondra. And I've loved you for quite a while."

This seemed like such different and intense territory for her and she didn't know quite what to say but did manage to whisper a response. "Okay." She walked a number of feet and came to a stop on the Start/Finish line of the kart track. She felt the hazy sunshine on her head and arms.

"You scared me" she told him. "Andrew told me where and how you crashed, and he showed me some video. That was an ugly, tangled-up mess in Turn One and Mintresi's Right-rear tire looked like it hit you in the head." Brice did not want to talk about the crash and he tried to make his voice sound stronger. "I'm getting the hell out of this bed. Going home in two days. Patrero and Andrew are all over the internet to find somebody with techniques to help speed up my recovery. Patrero's been awesome." Brice coughed and groaned. "Ow. Broken ribs. Crap." He had suffered two broken ribs, a collapsed lung and a broken thumb. He'd also sustained a concussion and multiple painful contusions over twenty percent of his body.

A quick involuntary smile swept across Sondra's face. Not of Brice's pain but that he'd used the word crap. She had come to occasionally utilize quite colorful language in the past several years but growing up, the word crap had been the only colorful word that had been tolerated, under the proper circumstances of course. She'd learned to use the word from her father, who tried to always convey that her mother probably wouldn't find it acceptable. Oddly, it had pretty much been the same case with Doug and Karen.

"Sorry you're in so much pain, Brice" she said, thankful that he nor anyone else could see the tears streaming down her face. "I don't really want to hang up but I should probably let you get some rest. I'm sure there's probably a nurse standing over you, and besides, your mom already hates me enough."

Brice denied it but Sondra shrugged. "Well anyway" she told him. "I want you to do everything possible to get better."

Brice had now become completely worn out and was in excruciating pain but there were two other items of importance on his mind. "I hate that I'm gonna miss winter testing and probably the first few IndyCar races" he said of the next race season. "When's your first test in the new car?"

"Two weeks" said Sondra. "Texas Motor Speedway. I promise to drive safe if you promise to get better" she added.

"Okay" he groaned. "It's a deal." He swallowed loudly and Sondra thought she could actually feel his pain. His next words gave her goosebumps: "So I think I might love you too, you idiot." She laughed, a bit embarrassed for what she'd said to him days ago. "Okay, okay" she said smiling wide. "I'll talk to you tomorrow. Bye, bye." Sondra wiped her eyes, closed up shop and jogged up to the safety and comfort of Doug and Karen.

In the weeks and months that followed, Brice and Sondra communicated in one form or another almost every day. He'd been making major strides in recovery and their jokes and topics of interest were natural, as always. Brice did his best in trying to persuade Sondra and her parents to visit during both Thanksgiving and Christmas but Karen's parents took top billing at Thanksgiving and Sondra, as an Indy 500 winner, was a very popular figure with sponsors, radio and TV programs as well as the budding Safen-Up organization's various events all throughout the holidays. The Trents' travel schedule was intensely packed, to say the least, and in early January Sondra again sat for the artist making the image of her that would appear on the coveted Borg-Warner trophy, which held the faces of every Indy 500 winner embodied within the large metallic trophy.

CHAPTER 31

Throughout the off-season Sondra had been kept extremely busy with team meetings, detailed work on getting herself and the new cars ready for next year and then travel for sponsor events. There had also been several all-important IndyCar Series practices, but the beginning of March saw a legitimate nine full days of off-time. Sondra seized this opportunity to again broach the subject with her now-parents for her to visit the recuperating Brice at the Crandle's Wisconsin farm. Doug and Karen had begun taking flying lessons when travel and management duties permitted and were apprehensive about Sondra spending the first three of her much-needed rest days with Brice. They would have preferred to go with her in order to get to know the Crandles better but ultimately chose to use their limited free time for pilot training.

Lauren, Brice's younger sister, was determined not to like Sondra. She and her brother's ex-girlfriend had been like sisters and the entire Crandle family loved Jillian. It was almost as if Sondra was seen as the other woman. Around the halfway point into Brice's Formula Ford season he'd had a serious talk with Jillian about the fact he fully intended to pursue racing as a profession and didn't want children or the farming lifestyle that she was clearly expecting for their future. It was an agonizing decision to end their relationship but he knew it was for the best and just couldn't get this Sondra girl out of his head.

After Sondra landed in a twin turbo-prop commuter plane at the relatively small municipal airport, she found herself sandwiched between Brice and his sister in a gray Nissan sport pickup with an odd purple Z stripe down each side. Beginning the 30-minute journey to the Crandle ranch Brice accelerated quickly enough to make the rear tires chirp. Sondra looked over at him through narrowed eyes. "That's a terrible habit" she told the boy. "Do that in an Indy car and you'll break a half-shaft like this" she said snapping her finger for dramatization.

Not wanting the conversation to be all about cars, Lauren commented on Sondra's footwear. "Love the color of your shoes. Are they comfortable?"

"Yeah" smiled Sondra. "And they're water-proof and fire-proof." She was in her blue racing shoes and liked the fact that, for once, what she chose to wear did not provoke a negative comment. When Brice turned on the radio the conversation switched from clothing to Lauren chiming in on her brother's particular taste in music. She then seemed to come up with an endless string of questions for Sondra about living on the coast of California. By the time they reached their destination Lauren had a completely different take on her brother's choice of girlfriend. She could see why Brice liked her. Sondra wasn't at all like the cold angry girl she and some kids at school had thought her to be, and there was far more to her than race cars. Lauren found her to be smart, sweet and humorous.

At the end of the Crandle's meandering driveway were three enormous Sycamore trees in front of two houses facing each other about a hundred feet apart. The smaller one-bedroom home had pale blue stucco walls with white trim and window-frames. A white picket fence surrounded the structure as well as lush deep green lawns and well-maintained flower gardens. Lauren pointed out that this was the home of their grandparents, on their mother's side. The larger farmhouse was a long white building with green trim and had obviously undergone recent remodeling. A whole new section had been added and the outside walls of this had only a primer coat of paint. There was neatly trimmed lawn all around and a wide brick-paved porch stretched across the front, except the new section. "My dad and I, along with some neighbors that do home construction for a living, built the add-on a year ago" stated Brice proudly.

"Yeah" added Lauren, a bit of sarcasm in her voice. "We needed a whole new room to hold his trophies and his ego."

Brice leaned forward to gave his sister a stern look before informing Sondra of the details. "It's a new kitchen and dining room. Most of my race earnings have gone into the farm. That's basically four years of college expenses right there."

Sondra leaned her shoulder lightly into him and smiled softly as she thought how incredible he was to be this selfless. When Lauren again spoke of her brother it was deeply complimentary. "He pretty much saved our farm. I'm sure he probably told you this already but most of what we do here is grow, harvest and sell wheat. It's our own regional brand." This disclosure by Lauren went a long way for Sondra to fully let go of Brice's taking the Patrero IndyCar spot, though this was more in her subconscious.

After a quick home tour, Brice offered to show Sondra a bit of the farm. "Supper's in twenty minutes" said Brice's mom, Gwen, "so don't go too far."

"I hope you like pot roast, dear" she added, looking directly at their visitor.

"I love pot roast and yours smells amazing" Sondra told Gwen with a smile. With that, Brice escorted Sondra through the French doors leading to the backyard patio and then out the gate toward the buildings that had piqued her interest. Brice grabbed her hand and they started off in a slow run, with his movements strange and jerky. Sondra hated to think how much pain he most likely was experiencing from his injuries and suspected he might be trying to show off for her. "Where are we going?" she asked. Brice didn't answer. "Are we there yet? Are we there yet?" she added in jest as she followed his lead around the maze of buildings, under a barbed wire fence, over a low hill and through a small orchard of almond trees. Brice stopped short all of a sudden and Sondra ran into the back of him. “Oh jeeze” she exclaimed sarcastically. “A little hand signal for pit entrance would have been nice.”

Brice laughed, turned and wrapped his arms around her as tightly as he could without causing pain to his still-sore ribs. The hug between the two wasn’t quick or one of desperation. It was a true meeting of hearts and souls. When they reluctantly separated he took her by the hand and they walked along a narrow dirt road that encircled the lake he’d spoken of on several occasions. “Wow” marveled Sondra. “It’s pretty much exactly as you described. Which one is the island you camp out on?” she asked, pointing with her free hand.

“The one with the peach tree” he answered with a broad smile. “My mom helped Lauren plant that when she was five.” They stopped to admire it from afar for a few seconds.

“That first few minutes in the car with your sister was brutal” said Sondra in a soft voice. Brice pulled her hand to his lips for a kiss but Sondra snapped it away and slapped him lightly on his upper arm. “No mushy stuff” she scolded. “Don’t be gross.”

Brice laughed, pushed her away and continued walking. Sondra let him get a few steps ahead but soon ran happily up beside him, their hands clasping together so naturally that neither one took much notice. It became dramatically noticeable a few minutes later however. Sondra stopped and turned to look at a large bird that had taken off noisily from a clump of thick brush to their right. Brice hadn’t stopped, and when their arms came to the end of their reach Sondra tripped forward. This type of incident had taken place dozens of times with her father. Young Sondra would become so engrossed in whatever her dad was talking about or what they were experiencing that she’d just stop. Sometimes she’d become temporarily distracted, usually by cars, motorcycles or airplanes, but once the misstep had occurred Kal almost always picked his daughter up and carried her, or would set her on his shoulders.

Brice and Sondra approached the apex of the first left-hand corner of the unpaved roadway around the perimeter of the lake as if they were in a race car. It was something so completely automatic and natural. Had anyone else been walking with them they would have found it strangely amusing. Brice let go of Sondra's hand and jumped down the embankment near the water's edge. She followed, and after a few steps they came to a section of bank that was a natural small dirt bench, secluded by the overgrowth of tall weeds. Seated with their shoulders touching, Brice spoke thoughtfully. "The whole family, especially Lauren, liked my ex-girlfriend quite a lot but don't worry, they'll like you far better. Oh, and pot roast is like a test my mom has for new people in any of our lives. She thinks that if you thumb your nose at pot roast you're not someone of substance or down to earth, so you can't completely be trusted. You totally passed, by the way. You do actually like pot roast, don't you?"

Sondra nodded and stared out at the nearest small island. Brice watched her take in the scenery before explaining and setting the record straight about Jillian. "It was by the F Ford summer break that I realized I was more interested in you than Jillian. I broke things off with her the day after I got back home, June second."

"I wasn't exactly happy with how you were racing me at the beginning of our F Ford season, and you seemed so smug and arrogant with this Heather Locklear wannabe hanging all over you. And are you forgetting that I saw her at our first Lights race in Florida? Where you talked about her incessantly?"

Brice smiled at her exaggeration of the conversation he'd had with her about Jillian that day in Florida. "Sorry about all that" he apologized. "Everything worked out in the end though because we're here together. This has always been my favorite spot" he added, tapping the earth next to him. "I've never been here with anyone else. Not even anyone in my family." Sondra gave a nod with a slight smile as she understood his declaration of what she obviously meant to him, even more than his ex-girlfriend.

The young couple sat in blissful silence for only a few moments, though to them it was a lifetime. Sondra's eyes were trained on a large clump of tules across the lake when she next spoke. Her voice came across as if she were seeing a ghost. "Meatloaf." Brice was just about to laugh at this completely absurd non sequitur but he happened to glance over and see a face he'd witnessed numerous times in the past when trying to get her to open up about her family. He breathed out loudly and then whispered, "Meatloaf." She didn't say anything else right away but he was willing to be patient. Sondra swallowed hard, and when she did speak her voice was strained. "The last time we all ate at home together. That's what we had for dinner. My mom made the greatest meatloaf on the planet. Most people think meatloaf is like some pathetic tuna-noodle-surprise casserole thing but my mom's meatloaf was a total gourmet dish. And my dad didn't just make mashed potatoes. He whipped them. It was like an art form. Really amazing."

A single tear meandered down her cheek but Brice knew better than to say or do anything about it. She would have twisted away or slugged him in the arm and told him to leave her alone. It surprised him when she continued speaking about her past. "Haley took some of his green beans and made this goofy face with them in his mashed potatoes" remembered Sondra. "Playing with our food was a pretty big no-no but my dad didn't say anything, and Dave just picked up Haley's fork and put it back in his hand to encourage him to eat, not play. We were all talking about leaving the next day for Tahoe." She flung her arms around Brice and he could feel her lightly convulse with several sobs as she added one more enormous detail. "The morning we left to go back home, my dad and I were sitting alone in front of the fireplace. I told him that I wanted to race cars and he said okay, like it wasn't any kind of surprise at all. He didn't try and talk me out of it or say anything discouraging. He just knew this was gonna be my life."

A few moments of silence passed. Brice now knew why she never wanted to talk about her family. It was just too painful and she was always trying to prove she was tough, not wanting to show vulnerability. Sondra suddenly pulled away from Brice and looked at him quizzically.

"Did you just kiss my hair?"

He studied her face and shook his head. "Nooo" he denied. "I would never do anything like that because, ya know, that would just be ...”

“Weird and creepy?” she interjected.

“Well I was going to say comforting and endearing” he said with a slight smile. Her arms went back around him and she whispered in his ear. “Okay. We’ll go with your thing.” This time as the hug concluded Brice leaned in and kissed her. It was a deep soulful kiss, not sloppy or desperate, and when it ended Sondra understood why he’d had such a goofy grin when he’d kissed her that first time at the Formula Ford championship banquet. She was sure her expression now was similar to his almost two years prior. “I think I like this kissing thing” she announced. “And this one was much better than the first one you stole in Monterey a couple of years ago.”

Brice shook his head in denial. “I didn’t steal it. I gave you that kiss, and you don’t know how many times I’ve wanted to do that again, over and over.”

She looked at him through narrowed eyes. “Don’t be gross” she told the boy. “Why didn’t you?” she found herself suddenly asking. “Kiss me sooner I mean?” she asked in clarification. “I mean I knew you liked me but if you felt that strongly about me, why didn’t you say anything sooner? We spent so much time together as teammates. In a way, it was like we were practically living together. How come you didn’t say anything then?”

“Darren” answered Brice quickly. “Well your dad, too, but Darren totally chewed me out this one night that nobody could find you, or expect you to just be in your motor home. He made it brutally clear that I was to keep my feelings in check or he and Doug would pretty much rip me to shreds.”

Sondra looked down and played with the zipper of her fleece sweater. “Doug wouldn’t have done that” she told him. “I mean he’s a fierce protector. Always has been, even from the very first day I met him.” She lightly bumped her shoulder into Brice before continuing. “He’s been totally on to you liking me” she revealed. “I mean even way before I started thinking you were okay. Whenever you would come up in conversation he never referred to you by your name. It was always, That Crandle boy or Oh, the Crandle kid?"

Brice developed an involuntary smile, liking the bit of bad-boy imagery that came to him. "He does actually like you though" said Sondra. "And Karen's thought you were cool since Monterey."

She shook her head and turned away briefly, suddenly remembering the dinner she'd had with Doug when he'd attempted to broach the birds and the bees topic, and she recalled the emotion-laced phone conversation she'd had with Brice just days after she'd visited him in the hospital.

Brice checked his watch and stood. "Better get headed back" he told her, holding a hand out to Sondra. "Being late for dinner is a big no-no with the Crandles."

She lightly swatted his hand away, determined not to turn into a demure and helpless female just because they'd shared such a huge moment with each other. He didn't seem to mind and as they walked with purpose she spoke of Darren. "I can't believe you took relationship advice from Darren. He's an idiot when it comes to that. SeaShell's about ready to clobber him. I mean he flirts with her like crazy but never says how he really feels about her."

"Well that can't happen with me" claimed Brice proudly. "I'll always make sure you know how much I love you." Sondra swatted him on the arm for his mushiness but he observed that she was grinning from ear to ear.

Sondra was careful not to spill anything on herself during dinner, and enjoyed Brice's father explain more about the farm and its history. When he asked what her birth parents had done for a living, Brice shot him a disapproving stare and quickly apologized to Sondra. She set her fork down with extreme gentleness, paused and then assured Brice that it was okay. She turned to Taylor and tried not to sound emotional as she explained what their jobs had entailed and that they'd both grown up on family dairy farms. "You would have liked my parents and my brothers too." The room became ultra still and Gwen set a soft hand on the girl's shoulder. Sondra looked around the table with a strong expression, as if warning them not to continue with this line of questioning. Just as things started to get back to comfortable, there came several odd rhythmic knocks on the front door. Gwen was up in a flash and soon an excited commotion came bouncing off the walls and into the dining room. "Aunt Heather" exclaimed Brice joyously. Thirty-seven year-old Heather Crandle, younger sister of Brice's father, Taylor, had never been married but adamantly abhorred being called a spinster. She was known in this household as Crazy Aunt Heather, a term of endearment, mostly. She ran an arts and crafts boutique from her home in town and taught a class on painting and illustration two days a week. She'd been at the ancient Aztec ruins in Mexico on a particularly spiritual journey with a small group of friends she often traveled with when news of her nephew's crash reached her.

Coming into the dining room with stories to tell and a bag of slides as well as trinkets for all, Heather was overjoyed to see Brice and that there was a strikingly pretty young woman seated across from where he suddenly sprang, presumably the Sondra creature of which he'd often spoken. Brice and his aunt embraced warmly. She then grabbed both sides of his face as she looked him over and spoke brashly. "Well my little crash-test dummy, looks like you're all here. I thought the object of a race was to go around cars, not let them go through you."

"Or over" blurted Sondra without thinking. Heather melodramatically turned her head and diverted all her attention to the little comedienne. Brice made the introduction and Sondra stood with her hand extended for shaking. Heather was not a shaker of hands. She was a hugger and swished over to Sondra, scooping the girl into her arms. Letting go, she put a heavy hand on the top of the girl's head and waltzed in a complete 360 around her. It seemed such an odd action and Sondra had to concentrate hard to not automatically burst out in hysterics. "Well you certainly weren't exaggerating, oh nephew of mine" announced Heather. "She's nothing short of gorgeous. I've certainly been hearing a great deal about this little cutie." Heather completely disrupted the seating pattern at the dinner table and dominated the conversation. "I simply must sit next to my bumper-car driver of a nephew" she told the group as they were resettling. After much commotion and musical chairs this now put Brice and Sondra next to each other. Taylor loved the way his sister appeared as if out of nowhere and had such a great gift of gab. Heather didn't disappoint on this evening regaling them all with tales of her recent adventure. As she spoke, she would include Brice and Sondra in her animated narrative by speaking directly to them or lightly touching Brice on the arm, with him producing the occasional, Wow or Really?

Not long after Heather departed, Gwen set their guest up on the couch in the family room for the night. Sondra had a hard time falling asleep, being barraged with memories of the many hard nights in Bakersfield. Morning came to her like a dreaded chore and after getting ready for the day she went with Brice's father, Taylor, on his usual morning chores. Gathering eggs from the chicken coop was the first task, though Sondra could have done without the noxious aroma. The next chore was more enjoyable, milking the beloved family cow Strawberry. Brice's Grampa Tom was already in progress with this task as they entered the small milk barn. Taylor dragged over stools for himself and Sondra, and as they watched Tom continue his task the two men began a number of questions to their guest that Sondra didn't feel like the painful prying she'd endured the previous evening at the dinner table. School and farming were the general topic, and the conversation flowed freely. She liked this family. Taylor and Tom were intrigued and impressed with Sondra's ability to speak intelligently of grain and wheat markets and futures as well as many of the mechanical production aspects. She'd done some research and enjoyed learning that wheat was a winter crop for them, unlike so many other kinds of crops grown in California. As the three made their way back to the house with their yield, Brice came out to greet them. He took over the bucket of milk that his grandfather had been carrying and made a blatant observation of Sondra. "You look cute as hell in my jacket but completely ridiculous. It's huge on you." She adjusted her AAA baseball cap and Brice thought her smile brighter than any sunrise he'd ever seen on the farm.

Brice showed Sondra around the buildings they'd not had time to explore the prior evening. She was fascinated with the machinery, but when they entered a two-story wooden barn that had been built seventy-two years ago, Sondra was expecting to see horses or other animals. It was dusty and dark in most places, with the rising sun filtering through every crack it could get through. It smelled of old hay, grain, dirt and leather. The stalls that had once housed animals were now the parking spaces for both work and play vehicles. There were two snowmobiles and two old and dirty ATVs. Several lawn tractors, one of which she recognized from the photo Brice had sent her, were sitting along one wall, and she counted four dirt-bikes of various makes and cubic inch displacements. Brice took the opportunity to inform her that the motorcycles and ATVs weren't all Crandle property and would be part of the main day's activities, a neighborhood picnic the Grayson's put on every spring.

After breakfast Sondra and Brice mounted ATVs and embarked on a tour of the vast farm, then picked up Andrew Placer from the airport. Before going back to the Crandle ranch they visited Aunt Heather. The Craftsman-style building was both her home and a boutique business. She was happy to see Brice, Sondra and Andrew come through her front door, an entrance adorned with many bells. Sondra looked around the colorful room, breathing in the aroma of candles and incense as Heather and Andrew engaged in a high energy greeting. Heather showed her guests to a cozy back patio and went to the kitchen to make up a late-morning snack. Sondra watched Brice and Andrew settle into large faded white high-backed wicker chairs that looked to be fairly old. The two boys joked and pelted each other with twigs that had dropped onto the flower-print cushions from the many trees that were all around. This small patio area felt to Sondra like a room in the woods, secluded and sheltered from the elements. There were several heat lamps, dozens of candles on tall pedestals and numerous wind-chimes. She sat on a large wooden tree stump that had been carved out to make a comfortable natural chair. This was one of the most peaceful patios she'd ever experienced and the many trees and bushes gave off a pleasant, earthy aroma. Heather came out to set a basket of muffins on a table in between Brice and

Andrew, then informed her guests that the tea would soon be ready. Brice tossed Sondra a muffin and watched her face change from one of content to that of slight horror. The baked object she was turning all around in her hands was blueberry and she was remembering that awful day in Santa Monica with the police, then the frightening first uncertain moments in the VW Beetle with John Farnsal. As Brice got up to kneel down beside her, Andrew went to see if he could help Heather in the kitchen. "You okay?" Brice asked Sondra in a soft voice. "What just happened?" Sondra didn't want to get into it at first but he brushed her cheek with his lips and she suddenly realized that she felt safe with him. She could share both the good and tough memories and gave an abbreviated tale of the former incident. It was cut short when Heather and Andrew returned, carrying on with joyous conversation and unfettered laughter. Sondra loved how Brice had helped change the meaning and the bad parts of what a blueberry muffin meant to her. He took it gently out of her hands and began breaking off pieces for himself, handing her some every so often. As Heather spoke of changes she was planning for her house and the store she took note of the natural and sweet motions of the two. When it was time for the trio to leave, Heather wrapped an earth-tone colored scarf around Sondra's neck and told her that she must come back soon, and often.

Andrew's arrival at the Crandle farm was cause for much excitement. He had become Brice's best friend and the plan was to be his driving teammate for the next IndyCar season and several IMSA sports car endurance races. Lauren and her friend Emily both had both had crushes on Andrew over the past two years, but after hearing that he was in a serious relationship Lauren turned her interests to Wendell Grayson, who barely gave her the time of day. The Grayson's annual Spring Fling had grown to be something everyone in the area gladly anticipated. It was basically split into several portions, the first being the early picnic in a vast meadow basically for the older folks and the setting-up for the evening feast. There were tables and chairs arranged under many tents and a number of barbecues smoking away. There was also a designated tent for anyone musically inclined to sit and jam. Sondra marveled at the number of people in early attendance when she arrived at the Grayson's with Andrew and the Crandles, wondering where they'd all come from since this was such a rural area. The food, the gathering of neighbors and the music were indeed the main focus. Brice informed Sondra that within the past several years, starting with the first year Andrew had been invited, a motorized exhibition had become a big draw for the under-fifty crowd. Heather always arrived late to the event. She almost always brought along a small group of her friends with either vegetarian or exotic food dishes. Several of her friends were semi-pro musicians and were most welcome, especially as the day turned into evening. Sondra had worried about fitting in with the many people of this special community but Brice, Andrew and Wendell seemed to sense this and never once fully left her vicinity. The three young men were quite popular with this crowd and were constantly surrounded. As more and more people, mostly male, discovered that Sondra, the Indy 500 winner and the infamous slugger was in attendance, she became equally if not more popular.

Sondra figured she'd enjoy the food and music but was actually surprised at how well she had been received, even with the older generation. As the sun was beginning to get low in the sky and the many friends and family dispersed, she helped with the cleanup. Once back at the Crandle farm she and Brice sat in the barn talking about the day as well as his family and neighbors. Before heading to the house, Brice felt the need to say a little more. They were sitting on an old rear car seat staring at the dirt bikes and ATVs they'd just put away, and Sondra leaned her shoulder into him briefly before she heard him speak in a deep, thoughtful voice. "Weird. In some ways this has seemed like a really great lifetime, getting to hang out with you, but at the same time it seems like you just got here. I really don't want you to go home tomorrow."

Sondra agreed, nodding with her entire upper body. "Yeah" she said. "This has been a pretty whirlwind trip. I'm glad I got to meet everyone, especially your Aunt Heather, and it's cool that I got a glimpse of how you grew up. A little hard for me though, I can't do the same for you."

Her shoulders slumped and she looked down, staring sadly at her shoes. Brice shifted in the seat to face her a bit more. When he tried to put a comforting arm around her she pulled away with shocking raw emotion. It was almost a full minute before he dared speak and his voice was low but loud and clear. "I'm sure there's probably like a thousand perfect things I should or could say. I don't know. I can't go back and change your past and I can only imagine what you go through every day, what you've gone though" he quickly corrected. "But I do know this. I love you and I'm not going anywhere. I'm sorry my crash scared you. You've had two big ones, too, that I know of. At Elkhart Lake and at Indy. Both times I never got to know how you were right away. It was an agonizing eternity. We have dangerous jobs, but see? I crashed and I'm still here. I woke the hell up and got my ass out of that bed. I know our careers might push us apart a little but I'm not going anywhere."

He intended to say more but Sondra suddenly stood and walked a few feet away. Her voice was a bit unstable as she spoke. "Don't push too hard, Brice. I told you I don't know how to do this, the boyfriend-girlfriend thing." He came over to her and they studied each other's faces for a few seconds. "Okay" he whispered softly. "We'll go slow, if that's what you need. I'm in this with you, with everything I have."

Sondra stepped away and squeezed the clutch lever of one of the dirt bikes. When she turned back around Brice was standing close. He held her warmly, noticing that she didn't immediately respond. He then moved his head slowly and they rubbed noses. Sondra remembered her dad telling her at an early age that this was how Eskimos kiss. For the first time during this exchange in the barn there came a slight smile from her. The kiss they next shared was long and a bit exploratory. She broke away feeling light-headed and consumed with feelings and emotions that were foreign to her. She wanted to tell him to slow down but instead they were drawn to each other and she stroked his strong chest a few times until he brought her hand up and planted a soft kiss on her fingers. It seemed as though they suddenly melted into one another. The kisses became more passionate, almost desperate, and she stopped caring that her brain seemed fuzzy. She heard a moan, then realized that it had come from deep within her own throat. She became consumed with tingling and buzzing sensations and the growing excitement never ceased as she felt his strong and deliberate hands exploring and soothing her. As the intensity reluctantly slowed, they each experienced the sensation of floating on gentle clouds. The walk back to the house had their hands and fingers happily dancing and playing together.

That night, Sondra's last at the Crandle farm, she was so caught up in the hugeness of the day, especially what had taken place with Brice in the barn, that she only managed a few short periods of restless sleep. At 5:30 a.m. the next morning Brice made sure he was the only one to take Sondra to the airport. They arrived early enough to sit together in a booth by the window at a small coffee shop across the street from the airport terminal. Brice looked sad and Sondra decided a little shop talk would help. "I have a big to-do list at home next week" she began."Then we're flying out to Texas for a final shake-down of both cars and teams. Delgato's gonna be in the Twenty-One car again but he's planning on retiring from racing at the end of the year."

"Wow" said a surprised Brice. "I didn't think he was that old."
"He's not" said Sondra. "I mean he's in his thirties. I'm sure he has his reasons but I sure as hell plan on doing this 'til I'm at least a hundred." Brice snorted a laugh through his nose. "Wonder what the cars'll be like then" he asked rhetorically. He smiled and enjoyed the moment, watching Sondra lay her hand flat several inches above the table to mimic a flying car. He then eyed her slowly spinning the off-white ceramic coffee cup back and forth with her thumb and middle finger. Everything about Sondra he found intriguing and sweet. The sound of her voice, the precision of her actions, even the clothes she wore and the way she tried to always seem tough. There was a gentle sweetness about her that mixed all throughout her many strengths.

"I hate that you're gonna miss the start of the season" said Sondra. "I mean I wish I could just snap my fingers and make you all better."

"I wish that too" said Brice in a coughing laugh. "But I was told that I shouldn't rush my recovery" he told her. "I'm damn determined to be in a car long before Indy though" he added. "I have about three weeks of intense physical rehab and then I'll be back in the Patrero Forty-eight car for testing. I'm counting on joining the season soon after that but we'll see."

Sondra smiled and nodded. Their waitress came by to top off their coffee and Brice ordered a piece of peach pie to share with Sondra. "So, um" she voiced. "Are, um. Are we like officially boyfriend-girlfriend now?"

Brice smiled, understanding how because of her circumstances she liked and possibly needed to have everything clearly defined. "Yeah" he said, emotional seriousness in his voice. He reached across the table and held her hand for a few seconds. "I know we have busy and separate schedules, and it kills me that we won't be able to be together every minute of every day, but we'll make time for each other. We could even plan mini vacations together." Sondra nodded and took a sip of coffee. She wondered if she dared broach the subject of their growing physical relationship. She didn't. "Patrero's been talking to me more and more about putting together two F-Two teams" said Brice. "I think it might have been Andrew's doing. The guy is a good seed-planter. Anyway, the F-Two Patrero cars'll have Ferrari motors and chassis' with lots of technology straight from F-One, more-so than in previous years."

"Wow" said Sondra, not sure what to make of this since he had just professed that he wanted to spend every minute of every day with her. "Well nothing's set in stone" she heard him say as she glanced out the window. "And I know I should be concentrating on the present" he added. "But I love thinking about a real opportunity to go to Europe and get into one of his F-Two cars and hopefully go on to Formula One."

"Well sure" said Sondra, thinking about how exciting it would be if that basic scenario could happen for her as well. She didn't however like the thought of Brice going far away while she remained in the IndyCar Series, and it gnawed on her that he would be getting to move on to bigger and better things in racing, once again because of

Hugo Patrero. She was glad when the pie arrived and she was able to put all the F1 and F2 possibilities out of her mind. The two chatted a bit more about their upcoming race schedules and about Brice's family, then made the reluctant walk across the street and into the airport lounge. They held hands until it was time for her to board the plane, then held each other in a tight embrace. Brice didn't kiss Sondra goodbye but there was a definite closer bond that now existed between the two. Words defining their relationship didn't need to be spoken, and after the commuter flight's take-off, both Brice and Sondra each experienced a feeling of emptiness. For Sondra however the growing distance was like having her insides ripped to shreds. She hated this all-too-familiar feeling, the unbearable chest- and stomach-crunching sensation that she'd felt on occasion while thinking about and missing her family. It came to her at this moment in an even more intensely sharp cruel way.

Chapter 32

Sondra's second season as an IndyCar driver began far better than her first. The new chassis, engine and aero-kit combination had presented minimal problems for the Holt Racing engineers and mechanics all throughout the off-season and Winter Testing. Many of her fellow competitors as well as others who had come to monitor her overall demeanor saw a noticeable change from that of the last season. She seemed far less intense about everything, more outgoing and engaging. It was speculated that her win at Indianapolis the previous May was reason enough for this change in personality. There were other possibilities to consider. She was a second-season driver who had learned well the pace and procedures of IndyCar's intense schedule. In addition, having the stability of Doug and Karen's impeccable management presence provided her with peace of mind at the racetrack, as did the people consistently in her life. Providing a constant solid base for her as well were the treasured close friendships with Kari and Shelley, and having a defined relationship with Brice brought her both peace of mind and excitement over her future. She had anxiety over the possibility of a more physical relationship with him but conveniently squelched these thoughts, rationalizing they were not around each other often especially the first few races of the season. Brice had worked hard on recovering from his injuries but would indeed be missing the IndyCar season opener and in fact would not even be there with his Patrero team during the weekend.

Saturday afternoon's first round of IndyCar Qualifying on the streets of St. Petersburg was done under a blanket of solid overcast and an oppressive humidity. Holt Racing's Ryan Delgato crashed heavily in Turn 1 during the second round and though he was not physically hurt it was a hard blow. He used this as a sign that he was ready to step away from open-wheel racing sooner rather than later. That evening the 39-year-old had dinner with his longtime boss. Years ago, T.J. had hired the promising 20 year-old driver after watching him win all in one weekend a truck-series race on Friday, a Saturday night sprint-car race, and on Sunday witnessed the boy leading laps in his first Indy 500, driving for a one-car low-budget team. "Been doin' this a long time, T.J." said Ryan as their waiter set in front of them plates of thick-cut prime rib, baked potato and cheddar cheese-covered cauliflower. "You've been damn good to me and I'd never just leave you in the lurch" continued Ryan. "But my whole family's here this weekend. Hated to crash in front of them like that today, but it's not about ego or my pride. I just don't want to ever see that look of terror in my wife or kids' eyes again after I'm released from a racetrack care unit. I won a lot of races for you and we've had some damn good times. Been through thick and thin, over fourteen years. Time to pass the torch to the kid. I have every confidence that Sierre's ready to lead you into a bright future."

T.J. chewed his first bite of beef as he took in what Ryan had just delivered. "You sound like a damn speech writer" Holt said in his usual gruff manner. He did however understand what Ryan was telling him and held up his glass of beer in toast fashion. When the traditional clink occurred T.J. spoke in a low thoughtful voice. "Well we've certainly been through it all" he said to Ryan, nodding his head. "I guess I can understand where you're coming from. We talked about you possibly retiring at the end of this year a while back but I hadn't expected you to walk away after the first weekend."

"Well like I said" reiterated Ryan. "You've been so damn good to me. I'll stick with you to September."

"No" said T.J. with a shake of his head. "I won't put Janie and the kids through that. There's just one thing though. I'd like you to stay on as a coach to the girl, then run Indy with us. The kid's learned a hell of a lot in a short period of time. I'm willing to throw the dice with the little slugger but I want her to have a seasoned coach and she could use a teammate at the big speedway."

Ryan smiled and lifted his glass for a second toast. T.J. Holt was a loyal friend and was good to those who gave him 100% in his race cars.

Sunday's Grand Prix brought cooler temperatures and a large crowd. Though Sondra tried her best to present a relaxed easy-going exterior she was wracked with self-administered stomach-churning internal pressure. Her teammate Ryan, in his intended last IndyCar race, started from second to last and three laps after the green flag was dropped snagged the 17th spot. Sondra on the other hand had started from Fifth on the grid but the first few green-flag turns of the course produced far less favorable results. By Lap 3 she'd fallen back to 11th. "No grip, no grip" she complained to Darren over the radio. "Rears are sliding all over the place and I'm getting bad understeer on the back half of the track."

"Copy that, Sondra" said Lead Strategist Darren. "Our first stop is on Lap twenty-eight" he told her. "Hang in there and we'll make some changes then."

"That's a big ask" said Sondra. "Just do your best" he told his driver. Though there came two separate instances where local yellow flags had to be utilized due to single-car spins or contact between two cars, pit stops for a few in the field began on Lap 26. Sondra came in as scheduled two laps later and service to the #12 included a full turn taken out of the front wing to help settle the rear of the car. Sondra had started the race on the softer compound red sidewall tires and on this stop was put on a new set of the harder compound tires, sticker blacks. The plan was for her to be gentle on this set of tires and save a bit of fuel so they could run eight more laps than the cars further up in the field, thus giving her an all-important track position advantage when the leaders needed to pit. Nearing the end of the race she had led seventeen laps due to this pit strategy and was currently 4th. For their last stop of the day Darren took an educated gamble and pitted his driver early. When Sondra re-entered the race she was on the faster, grippier red-sidewall tires and could go to the end of the race with the fuel she now had on board. The Twelve team then got a lucky break. A Full-course caution came when Emanual Billings was spun in Turn 5 by Stuart Toburst. Billings' car was stalled up against the wall and there was quite a bit of carbon-fiber crash debris in the corner. When the pits were open the leaders came in for either fuel, tires or both. Sondra did not, and when the race resumed she was the leader with nine laps remaining. With Three laps to go the #12 was blocked by a lapped car in Turn 7, allowing Tony Kelarzo to squeeze around and get by them both. Sondra was livid inside her car, pounding on the steering wheel and angrily voicing her displeasure in an expletive-laced tirade. For the next two laps Darren spoke constantly to his driver, getting her to calm down and refocus. To those listening to the #12 car radio transmissions it didn't appear as if Sondra had reduced her rage, but in the last third of the last lap she was within millimeters of Kelarzo's back wing. The checkered flag waved for the white-green-orange #25 car, just .026 seconds ahead of the #12, with its traditional AAA colors of white-blue-red. Sondra came to a stop on pit lane, her fury engulfing her as if one had just thrown gasoline on an already out of control bonfire. She fought to get out of her car and was visibly shaking as she threw her gloves inside the cockpit she'd just vacated. Fighting unsuccessfully with the straps of her helmet she began an angry march toward the pit-stall of the car that had cost her the win. Track security quickly caught up with her and blocked her path. As her muffled diatribe commenced, her outstretched fist was caught by her Left-front tire changer Denny Hulzor. He picked her up and turned her 180 degrees, setting her back down on the ground as if she were a toy soldier with a windup mechanism. She made a beeline to her car and sat on the right front tire as she took off her helmet. As Kelarzo enjoyed the winner's circle celebration, Lydia Velstein, in her new role as IndyCar Pit Reporter, made her way into the growing crowd surrounding Sondra. From Lydia's vantage point in the pits she'd not seen the incident that had made the driver of the Twelve car so mad. "Sondra" she began, speaking into a microphone with a cameraman focusing in on the exchange. "You started today's race up front in Fifth and fell back but then made a great recovery, even leading laps. Can you tell us what happened in those last laps between you and Kelarzo?"

Sondra was fuming. Her eyes were narrowed and intense as she sat gritting her teeth. Karen, in her capacity as manager, handed her client a white towel with the Triple A logo on full display. She also placed a red 2nd Place cap on the girl's head and handed her a sports bottle with the 7-Up label facing the camera. Sondra first threw the towel over her left shoulder and wiped her glistening face with the sleeve of her race suit. She then took a long pull of cool liquid before speaking. "Well my Holt Racing, Triple A number Twelve car had some downforce and grip issues early on but my guys were great in the pits and we had an awesome car at the end." Her explosive rage suddenly came back to life. "The blue flag means for slower cars to move over and not impede the leaders. The Thirty-eight had plenty of time to see it and plenty of room" she snarled. "That was just plain rookie-stupid and that little punk better stay the hell out of my way from now on." Karen was now on damage control. She put a solid hand on her daughter's shoulder and could feel an eminent eruption of venom. Before the girl could spew out language not suitable for live broadcast television she held up her hand, indicating to Lydia that the interview was over. She then non-verbally insisted upon a retreat to the main Holt Racing hauler office. Fans of Sondra's feistiness were pleased and entertained by all this, and when her manager parents were interviewed later that afternoon their fans were satisfied that a proper balance in defense of the situation and the scrutiny of Sondra's attitude was achieved.

After the podium ceremony and a few less volatile interviews with race media, Sondra met with her #12 team to discuss the positives and negatives of their weekend. She again addressed the incident with the slower car, stating that Race Control and IndyCar needed to be more on top of drivers who don't observe the blue flag. She then apologized for not getting the win and for any mistakes she'd made on track that weekend. Engineer John Briers rolled his eyes and threw a wadded-up piece of paper at the girl. "So ya got us a Second Place podium finish in our first race of the year" he stated, shaking his head and beginning to smile. "And all you can do is bitch and moan. God this is gonna to be a long year. For the next three days I don't even want to look at you or hear your voice." He stood and administered three heavy pats on the top of Sondra's head, to Darren and T.J.'s amusement.

Holt Racing's weekend of hard work and then race-day driver drama from Sondra included another element. A career punctuation for Ryan Delgato. On the day of his official retirement he'd had one of the most brilliant drives of his life, going from the back of the field to finishing in Third Place, 7.218 seconds back from the leaders. A celebratory dinner was held that night in his honor at a local steak and seafood restaurant. Sondra endured much ribbing for her post-race temper but the main focus was on the highly regarded Ryan Delgato. During the dessert portion of the elongated meal Sondra received a text message from Brice who'd spent most of the day at a physical rehab facility in Arizona. She excused herself from the table and went to a hallway that led to the restrooms. She called Brice, and after their greetings and her inquiry of his physical condition Brice spoke with a bit of a laugh in his voice. "Your mad-as-hell march of the penguins thing on pit lane got captured by a fan's cell phone and the video was uploaded to YouTube" he told her.

"Yeah, I know" bemoaned Sondra. "My guys have just spent an hour at dinner here giving me every possible amount of crap they could about it. Mom said my social media fan page got tons of comments, mostly in my favor. So are you feeling good enough to be in the race at Barber?" asked Sondra.

"Well" voiced Brice. "My rehab coach and the team docs are saying some positive things but the ugly reality is that I'll be at Barber but not as a driver. I'll be there helping out the team. It's gonna be torture not to be in the car but Patrero wants me to be one-hundred percent when I do get back in."

"Well I hope we get to spend some time together during the weekend" said Sondra.

"I do too" said Brice. "I haven't had the chance to hold or kiss you near enough lately."

"Don't be gross, but yeah" she said, smiling wide. When the call ended Sondra went casually back to the table, receiving subtle but dubious glances from Doug and Karen.

Barber Motorsports Park in Birmingham, Alabama, was the second stop on the IndyCar schedule. In her Formula Ford and then in her Indy Lights car Sondra had been successful on this 17-turn 2.3 mile natural terrain road course, winning in both junior-division open-wheel racing series. She'd felt instantly comfortable with the several high-speed flowing corners, the slower technical turns, and the differences in elevation. Sondra had also heard it said by far more experienced drivers that the track drove like a European Formula One circuit, specifically the Red Bull Ring in Spielberg, Austria. After arrival and check-in at the race venue Sondra had specific race team tasks and several sponsor-related obligations. She later had the opportunity to spend some time with Brice inside one of the Patrero-McDonald's motorhomes. Brice gestured they sit on one of the black leather sofa/hide-a-beds. "I've missed you" he told her as he took her hand in his. Sondra took a glance around the room and nodded. "This is gonna be my home away from home" explained Brice. "I'll be sharing it with one of my engineers."

"So you're cleared, medically?" she asked.

"Pretty much" he nodded. "I'll finally be back in my car when we go to Long Beach" he furthered, not necessarily wanting to chat about his fitness or the physical rehab process that he'd endured over the past number of weeks. He leaned over and put a gentle kiss on Sondra's soft cheek and gestured with his hand around the room. "Pretty mediocre accommodations, compared to some" he offered. "You should see Andrew's RV" he added. It's one of many that the Placer's own. First-class all the way for them. Andrew gets satellite and everything. I hung out with him last evening and a few of us guys watched the replay of the Saint Pete's race."

Sondra rolled her eyes, not wanting to rehash or re-live what she thought of as, a disaster. “Two great moments of that race both vying for top billing” continued Brice. “First was that lightning-quick fakeout move you made to get around Greg Raley. Classic, man. But I think my favorite was your post-race stuff.”

“Ah jeeze” said Sondra, rolling her eyes and shaking her head. She folded her arms and glanced at an open sports bag of clothing on the floor a few feet away before elaborating on the episode. “Darren kept telling me that it was just a racing incident and that I needed to let it go and move on” she told Brice. “I mean I did for the most part but Lydia’s questions right there on pit lane seemed sort of clueless and I guess I just blurted out stuff without really thinking.”

“Well if it makes you feel any better” soothed Brice. “Us guys were all thinking the same as you. What Woodall did was totally rookie-stupid, and Sean is a punk.”

Sondra flashed a smile and shrugged her shoulder. “Wanna know something weird?” she asked Brice, rhetorically.

“Always” he said with a smile, wanting desperately to kiss her. “No one actually scolded or lectured me about my conduct” she said. “I mean the guys had a lot of fun at my expense but no one really came down on me, not even Darren” she elaborated. “I mean dad reminded me that I should always strive to sound calm and professional but mom was totally on my side. I mean you should have heard her at dinner that night. She totally defended me and even got all worked up about it.”

Brice smiled at Sondra’s words. He liked that she called Doug and Karen “mom” and “dad.” To him this meant she was far more grounded than he’d previously hoped, with a sense of family even though Doug and Karen weren’t her biological parents. He didn’t want to think of Sondra as a rudderless ship when it came to the important things in life like a stable solid family. It was hard for him to imagine how it would be if he’d gone through the loss of his family the way Sondra had lost her mom, dad and brothers. This notion scared him, though he would never admit it to himself or anyone else. “Here’s the really bizarre thing” continued Sondra. “The infamous punk Sean Woodall is being considered as my teammate replacement. Ryan officially announced his retirement to the team at that dinner after the GP."

"That is weird" agreed Brice. "About Delgato and Woodall, not the dinner" he clarified.

Three days later, the results of Sondra's racing efforts on Sunday were somewhat similar to that of the previous week. She started Third on the grid but ran the first half of the race between 5th and 8th, then led seventeen laps due to Darren choosing to go onto an alternative two-stop strategy. He was gambling there would be at least one or two more caution periods that would get them to the end of the race without a third stop. She would be on the primary compound tire for the last stint of the race and Brown used his driver's fuel and tire-saving ability to maximum advantage. With just five laps remaining, Sondra was 2.182 seconds ahead of Jorden Deratta. The late-race cautions that Darren had hoped for never came. Deratta closed the gap and took a look to the outside of the #12 in Turn 5. "Rears are going off" Sondra informed her strategist over the radio. She'd run 42 laps on this set of tires.

"Keep your focus" ordered Darren as he eyed the video monitor, watching the rear of the Twelve car twitch coming out of the last turn. On the next lap Deratta's shiny deep blue #2 car out-broke the #12 of Sierre going into Turn 1. With fresher tires he accelerated away, quickly opening a gap of 2.005 seconds ahead of her. Twelve turns later Justin Oliver got around Sondra in much the same manner, in Turn 17. Tony Kelarzo, on new sticker reds and a fast car, caught up to the #12 and began showing her his front wing. With two laps to go, Oliver ran wide in Turn 1 and Sondra flashed by and began closing the gap back up to Deratta. Kelarzo also got around Oliver several corners later and soon pulled to the rear wing of the #12, flashing underneath Sondra in Turn 5 with his sights set on Deratta. The #2 ran wide in Turn 1 and Kelarzo got past him for the lead. Sondra was 1.826 seconds behind Jorden Deratta with tires that were at the end of their life, but she managed to keep the gap the same for the remainder of that lap. On the long back straight she utilized the push-to-pass option, giving her car an extra 5 miles per hour advantage. The leaders were now coming up on lapped traffic, and with speed and timing on her side she was able to take advantage of the situation, unlike the previous week. The two slower cars moved out of the way and Sondra was able to make an easy pass on Deratta. It was a satisfying move but in the end she once again had to settle for a 2nd Place finish. She came to a stop on pit lane. Sondra hated losing and the last thing she wanted to do was talk with race media. She'd gone lap after lap, fighting as hard as she could. Her hands were blistered, with searing pain, and she had a skull-crushing headache. She felt weak, empty and on the verge of throwing up but was determined not to show it. Sondra climbed out of her car and received hugs from her team.

Just days prior, Doug had been appointed the #12 team's Pit crew Manager when longtime employee Grant Auberdale announced he needed to resign to be at his wife's side as she was going through harsh cancer treatments. Though Doug had no formal experience at pit crew management Darren and T.J. had come to know him well and had an instinct that the man would excel in this position. "Damn nice work out there" Doug told Sondra as he hugged her, momentarily picking her up inches off the ground.

"Back at you, Dad" she said, becoming surrounded by the rest of her team. Karen administered a towel around Sondra's neck and handed the girl a bottle of refreshing liquid, then set a red 2nd Place cap atop the girl's head. This bit of fanfare helped to make her aches and pains dissipate. She appeared relaxed and at ease when Lydia Velstein came to ask what she thought of her race. "Well I mean" began Sondra, pulling on the rim of her cap before going into detail about the questions she was asked. "The Holt Racing Triple A Twelve car unloaded pretty good and we found even in that first practice session that we seemed to be better on the harder tire than the reds. Pretty much the opposite of a lot of the other teams. We had pretty decent pace throughout the race and after that second caution we committed to a two-stop strategy." Sondra shrugged her right shoulder and flashed a smile. "At the end my tires were really going off fast and I just couldn't peddle any faster. Our Honda motor was strong and my Holt Racing guys worked so hard. We had a fast car and I just hate it that we didn't get the win for a second week in a row, but it's another good points day and we'll go on from here."

With the interview done and the camera off, Lydia patted Sondra on the shoulder. "Good job" she told the young podium finisher. "Here and out there" Lydia added. "And I want to hear all about the kissing in the museum thing later."

Sondra rolled her eyes and gave Karen and Doug a nervous glance. Early Friday morning Brice and Sondra had toured the enormous motorcycle and automotive museum that was located toward the outside of Turn 7. Sondra had later informed her now-parents all about the museum regaling them with all manner of mechanical and historical detail, purposely not mentioning Brice's name only telling them that she'd gone with some of the guys. Throughout the long weekend Brice and Sondra had managed to spend several significant moments together. The talk was mostly light-hearted but their make-out sessions were what one might consider steamy. Since this was basically all new territory for her she felt a mix of happiness, triumphant glory and that she was maybe doing something she shouldn't.

Newton, Iowa, played host to Round Three of the IndyCar Series championship. The roughly 7/8 of a mile of the Iowa Speedway featured varying degrees of banking and four distinct corners. In her rookie IndyCar year Sondra had come to think of it as more of a left-turn-only road-course. With high G loads and 44 degrees of banking on the backstretch this was a track that produced a sensation of speed unparalleled to other oval tracks. Lap-average speeds reached over 180 miles per hour and the straights almost seemed nonexistent. Sondra had heard that many drivers experience a state of dizziness for some time after running a significant number of laps. She hadn't noticed this phenomenon last year but it was on her mind before getting into the #12 car for the first practice of the weekend. Having her former race teammate Ryan Delgato around each weekend, acting as her personal driving coach, awarded her some comfort. His years of experience and easy-going attitude helped her learn even more detail of the track and some race tactics than that of her previous year. However this season she and Holt Racing were forced to contend with the fact that they no longer had a second car and team with which to collaborate. In her Indy Lights year Sondra and her crew had bounced setup ideas, track knowledge and engineering detail with Brice Crandle and his group. Her first IndyCar season employed this same tactic with Ryan and his team but now that Holt Racing was a one-car team they were arguably at an engineering disadvantage to the two and three-car organizations. It had long been established just how big a role a teammate can play when in the thick of oval pack-racing, especially in gaining the necessary data for a strong qualifying effort. It would be spotlighted for Sondra and her engineers this weekend at the Iowa Speedway. For Holt Racing, much of last year's information in regards to car set-up and track condition was used as a base. The first day of the weekend was grueling but by the end of Friday's final practice the #12 team had developed a strong confidence they had a car capable of producing favorable results. With a two-lap average speed of 185.210 mph, Sondra qualified to start the Iowa Corn 300 from 3rd on the grid. This was to be a night race starting at 4:30 p.m. and was also Brice Crandle's scheduled return to IndyCar.

With above-average temperatures, the Saturday evening field of 23 cars took the green flag. Sondra timed her acceleration perfectly and passed Alex Roliegh on his inside before getting into Turn 3. With low tire pressures at the start, the bumps on the inside of Turns 2 and 3 seemed far more treacherous and she held her breath until getting back to the front-straight. She then set her sights on the cars further up, and eventually the Pole-sitter Shane Teluchi. The orange and black #24 managed a four and a half second gap on the field by Lap 17 and Darren instructed Sondra to hold her current pace and position, maintaining a particular fuel number. He and the Holt Racing engineers had immediately begun to map out an advantageous pit stop strategy. On Lap 118 it was Sondra in the lead, with Teluchi 1.135 seconds behind after a lackluster pit stop by the #24 team. At just over the halfway point in the race Sondra found herself in 3rd, behind Teluchi and a hard-charging Kenny Delmare, who'd started the race 17th on the grid. In dirty air from heavy traffic Sondra, was dealing with a growing understeer problem, due mainly to the quickly dropping track temperatures. A two-car crash occurred in Turn 4, and when the pits were open Sondra came in for fuel, four tires and a full turn of front wing. She went back out onto the track still in 3rd but now had the downforce to put the car almost anywhere she needed.

When the field went green she disposed of Delmare easily on the backstretch. Three and a half laps later she went to the high-side coming out of Turn 4 and sliced down in front of Teluchi going into One. This was a crowd-pleasing move, especially when Shane then made many attempts to regain the lead in the next 28 laps, once overtaking the #12 in roughly the same manner she'd done to him. Eventually however Teluchi fell back to fourth in the running order due to the fact that he'd abused his tires and they'd begun to loose their grip. Sondra on the other hand regained that top spot and began stretching her lead to 5.042 seconds ahead of Patrick Colvin, Kenny Delmare and Shane Teluchi. With every hair-raising pass Sondra made on lapped traffic Karen caught the attention of the IndyCar broadcast media. She was standing to the right of the Holt Racing mobile pit-box command center with an intense focus as she watched her daughter-client pass the white and red #17 of John Mallory to his outside, then slice underneath the black and purple #30 of Phil Grumenchino.

Camera coverage went from the on-track action to Karen turning her head briefly with her eyes shut tight and putting her hands on the top of her head. She removed the headphones that carried the team's radio communication but soon put them back in place continuing to nervously watch the high-speed, high-stakes battle, unconsciously biting down on her thumbnails.

Sondra had gone the entire race without saying more than five words over the radio. She'd acknowledged pit-in instructions and answered fine, yeah or no when asked about how the car was handling at key points in the race. Typically she was not a fan of radio chit-chat during a race. Several times in the past she'd given an irritated order for Darren or her spotter Craig Pines to stay off the radio and let her drive after they'd given strings of advice and warnings during harried competition. This had become a source of comical interest to race media and fans alike.

On this evening, with eight circuits to go in this 300 lap event, Sondra initiated a 182.409 mile per hour conversation. "Vibration in the right-front's gone from nothing to ugly."

"Copy that, Sondra" said Darren. "Seven laps to go at the line. We're good on fuel with five point two six two ahead of Delmare. Teluchi and Crandle are makin' a charge. Open your line. Lets run that high groove and take care of those tires. You got this, kid. Keep your focus." After taking the checkered flag 2.042 seconds ahead of Shane Teluchi and Brice Crandle, Sondra drove around on the cooldown lap close to the outside Safer-barrier wall with her right fist punching at the now considerably slower 82 mile per hour wind. The next time around she pulled to a stop under the flag tower and executed four close-to-perfect donuts, with thick tire smoke drifting into an excited and vocal crowd. Minutes later Lydia Velstein conducted the post-race interview in the winner's circle. "Sondra" began Lydia amongst the jubilation of Holt Racing team members who now surrounded their star driver. "Looking at most of your competitors up and down pit lane after tonight's race they look so exhausted and like the heat got to many of them, and yet with this first win of the season for you, you look like you're ready get back in the car and do it all over again."

"Well I wouldn't go that far" said a smiling Sondra, adjusting the rim of her red 1st Place cap that Karen had placed on her head. She clutched at the back of her hair, bringing thick strands around to rest on her right shoulder before continuing. "I mean this is a tough little bull-ring and those bumps at the apex of Two and Three were pretty tricky, but the Triple A, Holt Racing number Twelve was just on rails tonight. I mean we had some understeer issues here and there and we were kinda hard on the right-front on that last stint, but I can't thank the whole team enough for putting all they had into this. Everyone back at the shop, the Honda engineers and all my guys gave me awesome stops all day long. I mean we've been right there for the first races and now to get this win is huge for us. The proverbial monkey's off our back and we can really go for it. Great momentum going to the next round." Lydia had a few more intended questions but the victorious driver was again swept away in team jubilation with the arrival of Darren, John Briers, Doug and T.J. Holt.

The Long Beach Grand Prix temporary track featured rough and bumpy surfaces with a number of tight blind corners. Metal fences and concrete walls lined the circuit on both sides. There were also groupings of tires that were tied together on the outside of numerous corners to act as "softer" barriers, all creating hazards of driving fast on this 11-turn 1.968 mile street course. The pressure to perform was heightened for Sondra due to the fact that she'd won in Iowa two weeks prior and was now twelve points out of the championship lead. There were other factors entering the long weekend mix as well. The IMSA endurance sports car series would be running that weekend along with the IndyCar and Indy Lights, all putting down different compounds of rubber in different lines on the track's surface, which added to the difficulty in car setups and obtaining optimum speeds and lap-times. In addition, Sondra was both excited and anxious that Shelley would be present for the duration of the week-long event, having planned the first Safen-Up/IndyCar collaboration. Heavy promotion of the nonprofit had been enacted and 32 kids were signed up to attend various scheduled events, including the option for them to watch any of the racing action they might choose. Dan and Vanessa Stoltz would also be on hand Friday through Sunday and Kari Wilken-Ballard, now her legally amended name, had let Sondra know she was planning on going down to southern California with her college roommate.

That evening Sondra attended a Safen-Up dinner and video presentation at a hotel banquet room across town. She had hoped Brice would be her date but the boy was quite popular within his circles stemming from his triumphant return to racing in Iowa. He'd had numerous offers to join his teammates and friends for an evening of merriment, originally thinking Sondra would be by his side. At the Safen-Up event, Sondra sat at a special VIP table at the front with

Doug, Karen, Shelley, Dan and Vanessa. Michelle Black, the woman Shelley had introduced Sondra to before her first IndyCar season, was at an adjacent table. Three Safen-Up coordinators, Margret and Jim (husband and wife) as well as Jean, a tall, slender, gray-haired woman, were also in attendance. These leading foster care field specialists had recently been hired by Shelley.

Friday morning's IndyCar practice was a struggle for Holt Racing. Sondra fought with brake issues, downforce levels and challenging understeer in many corners. She uncharacteristically complained incessantly about every issue over the radio to Darren and her engineers and bullied her way through slower traffic around the track, once forcing the #29 car of Jerome Levoy into a runoff area. Levoy was not pleased and Darren scolded Sondra over the radio that Race Control had issued a severe warning of this kind of behavior for her and the Holt Racing team. Needless to say, she was in quite a foul mood when she exited the car after the 50-minute practice session and had only short dismissive answers to several questions about the car and track conditions during an interview by pit-reporter Tracy Bueler. Karen wisely stepped in and directed her client toward the garage area, fearing Sondra would say something that could be construed as angry or rude.

Shelley took Sondra to lunch at an upscale restaurant in a high-rise building not far from the racing action. The race driver was still in a bit of a mood but welcomed the time with SeaShell. "So we haven't been able to talk much lately" said Shelley as a waiter poured the women each a glass of iced tea.

"Busy, busy, busy" joked Sondra. "That was quite a night, last night" prompted Shelley.

Sondra shrugged but knew Shelley wanted an actual answer. "Yeah" she said with a nod, taking a sip of the refreshing liquid. "It was great to see what was just an idea come to real life. I love you for all that. You're amazing."

"Well I think you're the amazing one" said Shelley. "But I appreciate you saying that. Darren really wanted to be there last night. We had breakfast together this morning and he seemed a little concerned about you."

Sondra shrugged and glanced around the naturally-lit room that had a wall of windows looking out on the marina, with every available slip occupied. "Well he's not at all happy with me after that last practice" she admitted to Shelley. "I mean things didn't exactly go good. We're just off on so many things. Brakes are a nightmare, understeering everywhere, and a bizarre turbo-lag that just came on out of nowhere."

"Well that's a lot" said Shelley with a nod. "And I know how crucial these things are to you and to the team but lets talk girl not car, shall we? That was a lot to absorb last night."

Sondra bit down on her tongue and stared out the window at several seagulls playing in the light breeze. Before starting work that morning she had endured a round of questioning by Doug and Karen, concerned about how she was doing with the previous night's emotions. An hour later she had a phone chat with Brice that didn't go well. He was frustrated with her that she hadn't gone out with him the night before and that they most likely would be too busy with their respective racing endeavors that day to spend any significant time together. With Sondra having a less than smooth practice session later, followed by anxiety over the previous night's Safen-Up event, it was turning into a much harder day than she'd expected. "I hate it that everything I do, or try to do, always ends up with me remembering stuff and how I don't have that anymore" Sondra announced, picking up and setting back down her menu.

"Say more" prodded Shelley.

Sondra shrugged but continued. "Last night was great but it was also a glaring reminder that every damn day is a struggle. And I know we've talked before about filling the void of who and what I lost and getting to a place where the void isn't in control, but it's still a damn void. I mean with my car I can control it or the team can fix it, but with me ..."

"You have control over your life, Sondra" said Shelley. "You have the tools and the ability to fix things. They're there, whether you see them or not. No, you can't magically bring back your family and make everything the way it was but you can build any kind of life you want. You're doing it and you're doing it well. Can you see the advantage to giving yourself some credit for that?"

"Yeah, I guess" said Sondra, only half agreeing. She leaned back and twisted the glass of iced tea on the table with the tips of her fingers. "Sometimes I wish I was completely dumb as a post so I didn't have to think about heavy things."

Shelley laughed and shook her head. "Well I'm of the mind that ignorance is not bliss" she told Sondra. She sat back in her chair and developed a wicked smile. "On the other hand" quipped Shelley. "Let's test your brain power. Two and two equals seven and you love liver, right?"

"No and ew" said Sondra, making a face that led to a quick round of quiet giggles.

A pleasant lunch of lobster pasta salad and good conversation with Shelley sent Sondra returning to the Holt Racing temporary Long Beach Grand Prix garage with a much improved disposition. The mechanics and engineers had been making improvements and in the afternoon's final practice she was relatively happy with the car. At one point, Holt Racing had posted the second fastest lap of the session, and after a debrief with her #12 team she was able to catch up with Brice. He was chatting with members of both the Patrero IMSA team and his #48 IndyCar team. He quickly excused himself and rushed over to Sondra. "Sorry for growling at you this morning" he apologized. "But you can't blame a guy for missing his girl, can you?"

Sondra punched his shoulder and rolled her eyes. "Didn't see you out there" she told him with a smirk of the prior practice session.

"Well" smirked Brice. "That's because I was way ahead of you."

"Idiot" said Sondra with an eye roll and a quick shake of her head. She held out her smart-phone. "So there's video of you just a bit ago" she announced. When Brice had stepped out of the car on pit lane he was interviewed by Tracy Bueler asking him how he was coping with his injuries. He had claimed that once in the car with focus and adrenaline he didn't notice or think about pain or injury.

"Well" confided Brice to Sondra, after the short video ended.

"Sunday's race is gonna be brutal but way worth it to be back in the car." Sondra nodded and gave the boy a kiss.

Dinner that evening would again not see Brice and Sondra together. Young Crandle was at a restaurant with many of the members of his team celebrating the birthday of Stan Groubis, director of operations for Patrero-McDonald's. For Sondra's dining experience Darren had insisted on taking the Trents out to a restaurant he'd discovered a year ago, the last time the IndyCar Series was in Long Beach. "Shell really wanted to join us" he told Doug, Sondra and Karen as they enjoyed freshly made tortilla chips and warm bean dip at a Mexican restaurant known for its authentic Yucatan cuisine.

"She's really found her calling with Safen-Up" offered Karen with a nod.

"Yeah" agreed Darren. "But she keeps wanting to take each and every one of the kids she comes in contact with home with her."

"She's gonna make a great mom" suggested Karen. Darren coughed a nervous laugh. "So you already have us married with kids?" he asked, glancing over at Sondra as she was picking bits of tortilla chips off the front of her shirt and popping them into her mouth. "Are you guys talking about getting married?" Sondra asked.

"A little soon for that, don't you think?" suggested Darren.

"No" said Sondra and Karen in unison.

"So Doug" deflected the man, deliberately trying to change the subject. "Nice job getting that air-gun debacle sorted out."

"Wow, Darren" said Karen with a knowing smile. "That was quite a skillful dodge there. You should be a White House press secretary."

"Wanna help me out here, Doug?" pleaded Darren. "Oh sorry there, Darren" said a smug Mr. Trent with a large grin. "You're on your own with that" he added. "I happen to be a big fan of marriage and kids."

"You're fired" joked Darren.

A waiter arrived at the table with a new bowl of dip and basket of chips. After the young man took the dinner orders Darren watched with a smile as Karen deftly put Sondra's serviette back in the girl's lap. "Shelley and I come from such different backgrounds" Darren announced. "But she's the most drama-free and comfortable woman to be around that I've ever dated."

"I'm pretty sure she feels the same about you" said Sondra, reaching for a chip. "Just don't ever James Dean-it with her. She hates that."

"Thanks" said Darren with a quick laugh. "But I'm not sure I should be taking love advice from a goofy kid with bean dip on her wrist and who usually wants to punch every guy she meets."

Sondra quickly licked her wrist and shrugged.

"Sondra, don't do that" scolded Karen. "Use your napkin, please."

Darren tapped Sondra lightly on the shoulder with the edge of his fist. "How is it that you can be such a neat and tidy driver but with food?"

"You forgot to say fast driver" corrected Sondra.

"Yeah" chuckled Darren. "And a humble little pain in the ass, too."

Sondra folded her arms and feigned indignation. "I can win with the car we have right now" she announced, deliberately changing the subject. "But I think we should go lighter on downforce, and I'm still concerned about that left-front brake." Darren nodded.

"Odd that we were quicker on the blacks this afternoon" Darren said of a particular set of tires. "Tomorrow's qualifying is gonna come down to being on the right tire at the right time."

Sondra and Doug both nodded but Karen sat back in her chair smiling and shaking her head. She would have much preferred continuing to chat with Darren about his romance with Shelley.

On a breezy high-overcast Saturday afternoon Sondra qualified the #12 car 2nd on the grid for Sunday's GP. Her entire day had been extremely busy but as the sun began to set she managed to talk a very reluctant Doug and Karen into letting her go with Brice to meet up with Andrew, Stephanie, Wendell and a number of others at the Queen Mary. Doug was firm with the boy when Brice came to collect his daughter. "You behave yourself around my kid" he ordered. "No drinking, and you go straight there and come straight back. Curfew is ten o'clock, sharp. We clear?"

"We're clear" nodded Brice, knowing full well the seriousness of the man, the father. Karen was more charitable. "You be safe and have a nice evening, sweetheart" she told her daughter.

"Man" said Brice minutes later as he opened the taxi door for Sondra. "Your dad's intense."

"Yeah well" she said, proud that she had such a protective second father. "I wouldn't forget that if I were you."

They spent time in the crowded cocktail lounge on board the Queen Mary, talking with race fans and several fellow drivers. Brice and Sondra later found themselves on the deck overlooking the shoreline. There were other couples with the same idea but none were too close. The night was cool but not cold and the haze from the luminous gauzy fog made the city's lights and shapes seem mysterious. The two race car drivers stood hand in hand, taking in the view.

"I can't believe your strict-as-hell folks actually let you come out with me tonight" said Brice in a soft voice.

"Well so far you haven't done anything to obliterate their trust in you" said Sondra. "Don't, by the way" she told him. "And their daughter wouldn't be okay with that either" she added. She broke free from him and grabbed hold of the railing with both hands, exhaling a deep breath. "They are super protective" she informed him of her now-parents. "But they don't put limits on me. They want me to be happy and have good experiences in life. I'm happy right now, by the way. Thanks for this."

She turned and wrapped her arms around Brice. Their kissing session was interrupted by Sondra pulling away to ask a question. "Did you just kiss my hair?"

"What? No" Brice denied. "I wouldn't do that. That would just be ..."

"Weird and creepy?" interrupted Sondra.

"Well I was thinking sweet and endearing" he asserted.

"Kay" she whispered, pulling him back against her. "We'll go with your thing" she added. The kiss they next shared was every bit as intense and fiery as the motors that powered their race cars.

On a picture-perfect 77-degree Southern California Sunday afternoon, Sondra Sierre snagged the lead away from Tony Kelarzo in

Turn 5, Lap 1 and began stretching the distance. Earlier, during the morning's 25 minute IndyCar Warmup, the Holt Racing engineers and mechanics had made minuscule changes to the #12 car. The understeer and brake issues had been eliminated and Sondra felt good about starting the race on one of the sets of the red sidewall tires that had been used in qualifying. When the green flag waved the tires came up to good temperature and grip within half a lap of competition. Positions for the top eight drivers remained the same until Lap 23, when green-flag pit stops were enacted. Sondra, with her knack of saving fuel and being easy on her tires even while leading went five laps longer than any of the front-runners. After a flawless 7.2 second stop for full fuel and four of the hard-compound black sidewall tires, she came out still in the lead. Her next stop was during a caution period for a two-car entanglement in Turn 1. Darren made an educated gamble and switched to a two-stop strategy. He instructed his pit crew to put on another set of sticker blacks. The gamble was that Sondra could now go all the way to the end of the race while most of the other teams would have to make another stop. This also meant she would be forced to save fuel and take extra good care of her tires. If a caution came out again, the challenging cars would come in for fresh tires and a splash of fuel. This would enable them to run their fastest laps at the end, while the #12 would be in protect and maintain mode. Darren instructed his driver to maintain a particular fuel number after conferring with the engineers. They had calculated the distance to the end of the race and were sure they could make it without pitting a third time. "That's a big ask" responded Sondra, feeling the pressure from the cars behind and going into Turn 8 as she and her lead strategist discussed the situation. The plan that Darren had enacted was suddenly very real to her roughly 20 minutes later and she breathed an expletive as she heard Darren's voice. "Caution's out" he warned. "Caution's out" repeated Darren. "Crash in eleven. Crash in turn eleven."

"So what do we do when the pits are open?" asked Sondra. "Do we come in or am I staying out."

Darren had a hasty conference with the engineers and made the call. "Staying out. We're staying out. Good job on the fuel-saving. How you feelin' on those tires?"

"Okay" she responded, sounding apprehensive and a bit out of breath. "Increasing understeer in the back half of the track."

"Copy that" said Darren, glancing over at a nervous gum-chewing T.J. Holt. He looked up at the video monitor when Sondra again spoke. "With everyone coming in for tires we're gonna be a sitting duck" she announced in a worried voice.

"Keep your focus" Darren reminded her. "You're the leader. If we come in now we'll be seventh or worse with four to go."

Sondra didn't respond. On Lap 81 of the 85-lap race the green flag went back in the air. The #12 got a tremendous restart and Sondra remained the leader for that entire lap. "Rears are going off" she informed her team as she sailed through Turn 7. "Bad understeer in the fast corners."

"Copy that" responded Darren. "Do what you can. Use your tools."

The handling of the #12 car was quickly going south. Less than half a lap later she was passed by Jorden Deratta coming out of Turn 9. In Turn 11 he locked up his right-front tire under heavy braking and Sondra squeezed in underneath and made the pass going onto the long front-straight of Shoreline Drive. Tony Kelarzo took advantage of Deratta's mistake as well and soon was nose-to-tail with the Triple A car. The next lap saw Deratta come back to challenge Kelarzo, allowing Sondra a little breathing room. She felt a sudden *deja vu* familiarity. This scenario was similar to the second race of the year. Spotter Craig Pines called out the time-gap between her and the car behind. "One point three back to Kelarzo and you got some clear track ahead." She watched in her mirrors as Deratta got around the green and orange #25. Half a lap later Kelarzo reclaimed the position and began closing back in on her.

With less than two laps to go Darren leaned back, resigned that they were just no match for Kelarzo and his fresh tires. He put his right hand in front of his nose and mouth as he watched on the video monitor and studied the laptop telemetry showing just how hard Sondra was fighting, never giving up. She had been burning through her Push-To-Pass options and had only one more left while Kelarzo had four. The #25 overtook Sondra accelerating out of Turn 11 but came up on lapped traffic and never had the chance to pull away. On the white-flag lap Sondra executed some world-class driving that was arguably beyond her years. This had many on their feet with voices raised. She managed to get back around Tony coming out of Turn 4 but the #12's front tires were now giving up and the understeer in almost every corner was becoming close to unmanageable. Kelarzo dove underneath in the last corner just as Sondra hit the push-to-pass button. The rear of the white, blue and red Triple-A car fishtailed and slid out to the left, evidenced by massive oversteer in this slowest corner of the track. The left rear tire scraped a thin black line on the white outside retaining wall as Sondra fought to keep the car from slamming into it. The #12 straightened, accelerating at its maximum rate and Sondra stared intently at the LED instrumentation on the steering wheel as she rocketed forward. With heavy braking into Turn 1 she looked up, sure Kelarzo had gotten by her for the win. She then recognized celebratory voices over the radio. Driving at a reduced speed around the outside of the track Sondra looked over at the man in the green and orange car waving at her. She bit down on her tongue to keep the tears in check but soon her vision was hampered by some renegade moisture. She had taken the checkered flag just 0.014 seconds ahead of Tony Kelarzo and this victory had now put her in very rare company with the most prestigious names in racing who also had won on the iconic street-course.

Pit reporter Tony Currington did his best to get an interview with T.J. Holt before Sondra was able to make it around to Victory Lane, but the legendary car and team owner just shook his head and chewed his gum in joy and a bit of disbelief at what had just occurred. Doug and several pit crew members hurried forward as Sondra pulled to a stop. The proud dad patted the top of his daughter's helmet several times as Denny Hulzor reached into the cockpit to help with the unbuckling process.

"Beautiful. Just beautiful, kiddo" hollered Doug with tears glistening in his eyes. Sondra sat still for several seconds, smiling up at him. She then raised the visor on her helmet and began taking off her gloves. "You got me here" she told him, her voice full of emotion. Adrenaline and pure joy took over as she stood tall in the car's seat and punched the air with her fists in celebration while confetti and loud cheers greeted her. IndyCar reporter Lydia Velstein, microphone in hand, watched Sondra jump from the cockpit to the pavement and sink to her knees to kiss the nosecone of her beloved #12 car. The Grand Prix winner then stood with a wide smile as she again triumphantly pumped her fists in the air, facing a cheering crowd.

"Sondra" announced Lydia, hoping to get the post-race interview started. "Congratulations. You've just won the Long Beach Grand Prix and you made history. You're the first woman ever to do this in a senior devision open-wheel series. So what does this mean to you and what's going through your mind right now, and can you take us through those last laps after the restart."

"Oh man" said Sondra, a little out of breath and shaking her head. "I don't even know what to say." Karen moved in to take the helmet and balaclava from Sondra. She then put a red First Place cap on the winner's head and handed her daughter-client a white Triple A towel and a sports bottle with the 7-Up logo facing the camera. "I mean I thought for sure Deratta or Kelarzo were just gonna blow past me with their fresher tires" explained Sondra. "Really gave us a run for our money today, but the Holt Racing Triple A, Seven-Up Twelve car was so strong all day."

As if on cue, Tony Kelarzo edged his way through and gave Sondra a hug that lifted her off the ground several inches. "Who taught this kid to drive like that?" he joked with a wide smile. "Never saw that slide and win job in the hairpin of Eleven before in all my years. Can't believe she didn't find the wall. And look at those tires. They're gone, baby. Just gone."

Sondra beamed as Lydia asked a followup question. "So those last few laps, after Jorden Deratta dropped back, you and Tony really had a great battle going."

"Yeah" nodded Sondra, taking a quick pull from the straw in the sports bottle while Tony disappeared from sight. "We were both really going for it. I mean it's hard to pass around here and this is a place where you really want to win. So much history here. We definitely have a lot of trust and respect in each other as drivers and we know we can push each other hard without winding up in a crumpled mess. I mean several laps earlier I really thought Deratta was gonna have it but he had a lockup in Eleven and we were able to get around. Then Tony was right there and I knew we didn't have anywhere near the rear grip to beat him to the line. This just goes to show you that you should never give up, but wow. Now that I'm looking at the tires, especially that left-front, I kinda can't believe we pulled this off."

"Sondra, what does winning here mean to you?" asked Lydia. "The first female to do so in IndyCar history?" she added.

Sondra shrugged her right shoulder and shook her head. "Well neither the car or the track cares what or who I am. I mean my Holt Racing, Triple A guys were so awesome all weekend long. Everyone put a thousand percent into this and I'm so grateful to be a part of them along with Seven-Up, VisQuest, Bell helmets, Snap-on tools and everyone." She pointed to several patches on her race suit and smiled. "T.J.'s won here three times" she continued. "And Darren's won here a bunch of times as a crew chief with other teams and drivers. Ever since I was really young I dreamed of coming here to watch and then to compete. All my IndyCar and Formula One heroes have won here in the past. Senna, Unser, Andretti, Foyte, Stewart, and so many other greats. This is huge and it's so awesome to get a win for my Safen-Up family. They're amazing kids and they all really motivated me to push hard. They're here at a race track for the first time and the organization is growing and growing. I'm so happy."

The podium ceremony and post-race celebration went on longer than most and was energized by the historic nature and future implications. Sondra may not have cared about being the first woman to win in IndyCar on the streets of Long Beach but the global racing community certainly would take note of it. A celebratory dinner was generously hosted by Snap-on Tools at an Italian restaurant in Huntington Beach. Karen had brought forth the idea to the company she'd spent years working for, and with Sondra's success bringing high visibility to the brand Karen enjoyed a fair bit of celebrity herself with the number of high-powered company executives in attendance. Several IndyCar drivers and their respective team members were invited, along with Brice Crandle, Andrew Placer and his fiancé Stefanie. Wendell Grayson and his date, a young woman he'd met two days prior, were encouraged to attend, and at one point during the evening the old F-Ford classmates found themselves in a subgroup. "So I hear she's giving up on IndyCar and going to Formula Drift" joked Andrew of Sondra's noted last lap of the IndyCar race earlier that day.

"Funny" said Sondra, feigning indignation. "I'm ignoring you now. I'd rather talk to someone who actually won this weekend" she told the boy.

"Ooh, ouch" smiled Andrew. During the IMSA endurance race the previous day, Placer's Ferrari had been terminally damaged in an entanglement with a Porsche in Turn 5, Lap 78, and his Sunday IndyCar efforts only netted him a 17th Place finish.

"So Wendell" said Sondra, turning her attention to young Grayson. "Nice little leisurely drive through the city this morning." He had led the Indy Lights race from flag to flag virtually unchallenged.

"Well I wouldn't exactly call it leisurely" he said with a snorting laugh. "Nearly threw it away three times. But enough about me" he said with a large smile. "That was some awesome driving, Sondra, and 'ol Brice here made some pretty decent moves himself."

Brice had had a rough day, being buried mid-pack most of the race, but in the last fifteen laps he'd been one of many who had ducked into the pits during the last caution period to put on a set of new tires. He then managed to march his way forward to a very respectable 4th Place finish. The three racing friends chatted about Brice's return to IndyCar, ignoring Stefanie and Brooke, but the two women soon began their own alternate conversation about clothes.

Karen arrived on the scene to let Sondra know that they would be heading for home shortly, and minutes later Brice took Sondra's hand in his, suggesting a less crowed space to chat. "I'm staying with

Andrew and Stef for a few days" he told her. "There's plenty of room. You should hang with us."

"Oh" said Sondra" feeling guilty that she was about to disappoint the boy. "Wish I could" she shrugged. "But I have a whole schedule of stuff lined up for tomorrow and the next few days." This wasn't necessarily true. Sondra knew it and Brice suspected as much. He gave her a skeptical look and shrugged. "Well anyway" he continued. "I'm headin' out Wednesday morning for England. Hugo somehow snagged me some test time in a Formula Two car at Silverstone."

Sondra nodded, already aware of this information. "Rains a lot there" she offered. "But you'll like the track. It's fast and ..." Sondra was about to launch into more detail but Brice put gentle fingers on her upper arm and shook his head. "Every second I spent with you this weekend makes me realize how much I hate being away from you."

"Well in one week's time we'll be in Indianapolis" pointed out Sondra. "I mean we'll basically be there the whole month of May, give or take a day or two off for promotional travel."

"We don't get to spend near enough time together if you ask me" said Brice with a shake of his head. Sondra swallowed hard. She felt the same but was unable to put her feelings into words. "Don't really know how to fix that though" she said finally with a shrug. "We have busy careers. So what about Indy?" she wanted to know. "You are gonna be back for the GP? And what about the Five Hundred?" she asked, a hint of anxiety in her voice. "Are you healed up enough for that?"

"Hey" he said, holding her by both shoulders, with the intention of soothing her worries. "I'm only gonna be in England for two days. I'll be back in plenty of time to get ready for the GP, and after today's muscle-pounder I feel totally confident about the Five Hundred. No way in hell am I gonna miss the chance to beat you to the yard of bricks by at least twelve seconds." A smile found Sondra's face as she rolled her eyes and shook her head. She then went into detail of her knowledge of the Silverstone track before Doug and Karen insisted she leave with them.

Sondra and her race family went into the fifth round of the

IndyCar championship with a high degree of confidence after their victory at Long Beach. The Grand Prix of Indianapolis, held on the 12-turn 2.439 mile road course inside the famous two and a half mile oval was a familiar track for Sondra and she had high expectations. When Trents arrived in Indianapolis four days prior to the GP the weather at the track was cold and severe, but on the day of IndyCar Practice 1 it was sunny and in the mid-seventies with low humidity. Not all was sunny and pleasant with Sondra's #12 car however. During the first laps of practice they were plagued by Turbo-boost gremlins and mysterious problems with the ECU (Electronic Control Unit). They were also fighting elusive downforce level issues. Sondra initially referred to her car as the abominable snowplow but her Holt Racing engineers worked hard on each and every problem area, and on Saturday afternoon she qualified on the outside of Row 2, in the 4th position. After a successful showing in England with the F-Two car Brice Crandle did indeed make it back to the states to practice and qualify for the Grand Prix of Indianapolis. He would be starting the race in the 11th position, two spots ahead of Andrew Placer. Over the past several days Brice and Sondra saw each other in person only the briefest of moments due to their heavy work schedules. Neither was thrilled about this but they managed fairly regular contact by electronic communication.

Sunday saw much cooler temperatures with high wispy overcast. The start of the Indianapolis Grand Prix didn't exactly go as planned for Sondra. She was on the radio constantly from Turn 3 to Turn 7. "No grip. No grip. Losing spots. Really bad understeer. Every time I come up on the back of someone the front-end just washes away."

"Copy that, Sondra" said Lead Strategist Darren. "Use your tools and hang in there. We'll pit a few laps earlier in this segment and see what we can do." Sondra had experienced fairly similar handling issues before during her driving career but the pressure to perform and get results felt far more urgent and extreme to her. Corner after corner she concentrated on doing the best she could to change her driving style in order to alleviate the car's anomalies, and after the first round of pit stops she was shown 14th in the running order. The handling was now considerably better and she was beginning to pick up spots. On Lap 53 she ran to the outside of the groove going into Turn 1, and just as she was making the right-hand turn-in she was struck by the blue and green #18 machine of Sunny Verdoux. "Idiot" exclaimed Sondra over the radio as Verdoux's left-rear wheel pounded her side-pod, pinching the #12 into the outside retaining wall. Both cars kept going but Sondra was now missing most of her left-front wing. "That's just plain rookie-stupid" Sondra snarled angrily. "Damn it" she continued. "What the hell was he thinking?"

"All right, Sondra" said Darren, trying his best to get his driver to stay calm and focused. "Caution's out" he told her. "Full-course caution for debris in turn one. When the pits are open we'll take a look and get you a new front wing. How's the car feel?"

"Pretty clobbered" she responded, still white-hot angry over the incident. "Might have a little tow-in damage but it's still drivable." When the race resumed Sondra was shown in the 17th position. At the conclusion of the 85-lap event, car #12 was miraculously running in 6th. When asked about the earlier contact with Verdoux in a post-race interview Sondra began with a simple shrug. "Well I mean he just lost the rear-end going into One. Slammed us pretty hard but in a weird way it ended up forcing us to make changes we wouldn't normally have made. I mean no way was that an ideal situation but we were dealing with a car with so little grip in traffic. The hit knocked the Tow out a fraction and we had to come in for a wing change. We kept working on the car throughout and things eventually felt a little better, and we managed to salvage some decent points today."

Sondra had dinner that evening in the motorhome with Doug and Karen. Her Monday morning began on a bright note when she checked her electronic messages. *Hey there, wounded wing,* wrote Brice. *Sorry we didn't get to hang out last night but my guys took me out to celebrate. I can't believe we pulled off that win. Stay off the wall & I'll see ya soon. Love you, Brice.* Sondra was genuinely happy for Brice but she really was putting everything into this championship and it had cut her deeply that she'd had this run of bad luck.

On a calm and sunny Tuesday morning, Sondra woke up

breathing deeply with a relatively contented smile, knowing that later that day she was to be in her #12 Holt Racing Indy car for the first official practice session on the 2 1/2 mile Indianapolis Motor Speedway 4-turn oval. She would also have her trusty teammate back for the 500, the returning Ryan Delgato in the orange and white #21 car. Sondra's day was non-stop busy with media events, team meetings and two 50-minute on-track practice sessions. After the second practice came a debriefing meeting with both the Twelve and Twenty-one teams. Sondra was a bit worn out and ready for an early night but Brice had other ideas. Earlier in the day he'd gone to Doug, hoping to gain permission to take his daughter to dinner that evening. Doug gave his reluctant consent. Karen on the other hand was far more receptive to the date idea than her husband. "You really like our Sondra" stated Karen after Brice had sought her approval as well.

"Yeah" he said with a nod. "She's not like any girl I've ever met. Even when our careers keep us apart, in a way we're always together. I know that sounds really weird but ..."

"No, I get it" said Karen. "There's a connection there and it can transcend time and space."

"Yeah" agreed young Crandle.

It was 4:39 p.m. when Brice found the object of his desires in the garage area, chatting with IndyCar veterans Shane Teluchi and Greg Raley. Shane noticed the boy on approach and bumped his elbow into Sondra's. "And here comes the boyfriend" Teluchi announced.

"Aw, jeeze" breathed Sondra, rolling her eyes. "You guys be nice" she added.

"Hi guys" greeted Brice. He held up his cell phone. "Anyone up for a tour of the Dallara factory in twenty minutes? Just secured us a guide."

The men chuckled and shook their heads knowing that if they were to join Brice and Sondra they would be impeding on Brice's date plans. "Been there a thousand times" said Greg. "Pretty awesome little tour they got there."

"Yes" agreed Shane. "And you two should go to the Brickyard Grill after. Food's nothing too spectacular but it's fun and close by."

"I got parental consent" bragged Brice with a smile.

"Aw, yes" said Shane. "We heard something about that."

"Rumor has it" offered Greg, "Sondra's father is gonna have spies keeping an eye on you two, so you best keep your hands to yourself, boy" he said to Brice with a chuckle. Sondra scowled and folded her arms momentarily but Shane put his arm around her. "You're so serious all the time" he stated. "Go out and have a little fun with this nice young man."

On a clear and cool Indiana morning, Sondra climbed into her Indy car on pit lane. Karen watched her daughter from several feet away, taking video and still photos as Doug and several pit crew members helped the young driver get strapped in and ready for a mock-qualifying run for the 500. Karen observed the rear wing of the car being mostly flat as opposed to what she'd been used to seeing these past few weeks, and suddenly remembered the crash Sondra had been through at this very speedway a year ago. The V6 twin turbo Honda motor came to life with a loud vicious growl and Karen felt as if her stomach was about to climb into her throat. It was startling, to say the least, when the #12 car soon exploded in sound and began to pull away, with the rear tires momentarily spinning in place and producing thin gray smoke. Karen collected herself and walked a few feet to the left, taking her usual position. From this vantage point she could see the pit-box telemetry from video monitors and had a mostly unobstructed view of the speedway's front-stretch. An involuntary smile swept across her face as she heard her daughter's voice through the headphones that carried the team's audio transmissions.

"Strong tailwind down the backstretch" announced Sondra. "Back end feels way-light going into Three." Karen's eyes and head followed the #12 car from horizon to horizon and her body felt the full experience of a Indy car screaming its way through the famous Indianapolis Motor Speedway's front-stretch valley. The mostly empty grandstands created a haunting echoey howl that added to the intensity of the morning and Karen suddenly became aware that she was crying. She deftly wiped the moisture from her face recognizing this as happy tears as she experienced the distinctive sounds of the

Doppler effect. Sondra's car went from a low volume and pitch on approach, and as the #12 got closer the sound became deafening and the frequency pitch rose sharply. When the car sped away the volume and pitch decreased. The overall sights, sounds and feel were dramatic but all seemed right with Karen's world. The voices over the radio were strong and positive and Sondra's third lap was recorded at 235.892 miles per hour. The fourth and final lap saw a slight decrease in speed due to tire degradation but Sondra and her team would work on this over the next eleven days.

This year's Indy experience was quite different for Sondra. A year ago she was a rookie driver learning to wrangle a powerful Indy car in all situations. At the same time she was trying to find her way with the Holt Racing organization as well as familiarize herself with the IndyCar Series routine. This had all been a daunting task in and of itself but coming to the famous Brickyard for the first time as a full-time IndyCar driver had delivered her a near sensory-overload, especially considering the childhood memories she'd had of this time of year with her father. Each year during the month of May, Sondra and Kal would wrap themselves up in the spectacle of it all. From afar the two would discuss the esteemed event and its drivers and would watch for any subsequent articles in the newspaper or other publications. Sondra and her father had listened to every one of the syndicated radio network broadcasts or watched it on TV together since she could remember. With those past Indy memories haunting her during the entire month of May the previous year, she'd been forced to deal with all her personal demons plus juggle the intense pressure to perform as the newest and youngest member on a high-profile race team, owned by a man who's name was synonymous with the Indy 500. Sondra and her father had rooted for, cheered for, and on occasion sympathized with T.J. Holt when he had been forced up against bad luck. Her victory at the speedway in one of Holt's cars had astounded and captivated the world and it was something still almost incomprehensible to her. Throughout the year there had been a number of Indy 500-winner-specific events and conversations. Posing for what would be the small sculpture of her face, which would be placed on the coveted Borg-Warner trophy, was both exhilarating and overwhelming. When she was presented with the Indy 500 championship ring it had been another enormous event in her life, but getting her own baby Borg, a miniature of the famous trophy, was what made the 500 win an undeniable exclamation point on everything her life had been about, not only from her childhood dreams but the past number of years. This year Sondra had a bit more of a calmness about her, enjoying where she was and with whom, cognizant of each special detail of the month of May.

The month was unfolding in a natural manner, with Sondra's engineers and mechanics executing long hours of meticulous work on the #12 oval-track racer. Sondra was at or near the top of the speed charts in most every practice session but with just under two weeks until the big event, heavy rains and high winds suspended all on-track activity. With predictions and warnings of worse weather on the way, such as possible tornadoes, the Trents used this mandatory forced mini-vacation time to spend a few days at Casa de Trent. Karen secured a last-minute United Airlines flight that would have a 2-1/2 hour layover in Los Angeles. While the Trents later made their way through the airport terminal gate where they would catch a commuter flight to Santa Barbara, Sondra listened to Karen ponder the activities of the next few days. When Karen spoke of perhaps having Doug replace the kitchen sink and faucet with items she'd previously ordered, he chimed in with his opinion on the matter. "Well I'm not gonna get into any major home improvement projects in this short amount of time."

Karen suddenly realized that Sondra had fallen behind. She reached out to Doug's arm and the couple turned to see that their girl had stopped dead in her tracks, with a look of extreme astonishment.

"Uncle Leo?" squeaked Sondra. The expanse of the terminal and the throngs of moving purposeful humanity drowned out her voice so she asserted herself a bit more forcefully when she again addressed a particular figure. "Uncle Leo" she called out, much louder this time. Doug and Karen looked on as a tall pudgy nearly balding man in a dark blue suit turned to see who had called out his name. He dropped his luggage clumsily and fell to his knees, quickly coming to the realization that he was suddenly face to face with his long-lost beloved niece.

"Sondra?" he said in disbelief. "My dear sweet little Sondra" he added, emotion beginning to hit him hard. A stunned girl stood frozen before him, momentarily unable to speak. "Oh" Leo began barely able to speak himself. "I ... I'm … I thought that ... Oh I'm so sorry for what you ... You have no idea. You're here. It's really you." Sondra's breathing came in unsteady fits and she raced into his arms in a flash. "You found me, you found me" she said, smiling with enormous relief at this chance family reunion.

Mr. Leo Banes was not Sondra's biological uncle but the childhood and lifelong friend of Sondra's father, having grown up near Kal. The two had served in the Army at the same period of time and after going through basic training then anti-aircraft training together, Kal was put though firefighter school and sent to an Army-claimed firehouse in Anchorage. Leo, with his interest and aptitude mostly in music, served his military duties in multiple places, performing a wide number of tasks. After his stint in the Army, Leo became a probation officer. Kal and Maureen never openly discussed Uncle Leo's profession with their children, not wanting them to know of such human harshnesses at their early ages. Leo pursued his passion for music in his off-time and became an accomplished and highly respected bagpipe player, having played in the Army band and subsequent Army Reserve band. He later joined a civilian Scottish bagpipe troupe that performed occasionally in many locations within the state, the country and around the world. Throughout Sondra's young childhood she'd known Uncle Leo as simply a cherished family member who would magically come for dinner several times a year, regaling them with fun tales and treasured bagpipe soundscapes. One of Sondra's most memorable times with her uncle came one day when he showed up in a dark green sports car, a Triumph TR-7. Though he only took nine year-old Sondra on a short twenty minute ride, her brain and body cataloged the sound and feel of the vehicle and experience, and she'd watched every aspect of his driving motions.

Leo's visit on this occasion was also marked by something the family gained much fun and hilarity from for years to come. It was observed by all three Sierre children that during dinner he crunched his spaghetti. Dave, Sondra and Haley began whispering among themselves in amazement at this feat but Kal and Maureen soon put a stop to the rudeness.

"All right, kids" said the dad in a scolding voice. "We're trying to talk … And Sondra, your sleeve is not a napkin."

"Haley, dear" said Maureen. "Use your fork" requested the mom. "And Dave, will you pass your uncle the salad, please. There's plenty of food so everyone eat up."

"Mmm, this is great" voiced Leo. "I haven't had such a nice home-cooked meal in quite some time. I don't know what to put in my mouth first so I've been going for a little of each, salad and spaghetti, in each bite."

"Oh" said Dave, understanding the anomaly. "We were just wondering how you could make spaghetti crunch."

"Yeah" added Sondra. "All we saw was that you put a forkful of spaghetti in your mouth, and when you started chewing we couldn't believe that you got it to make loud crunching sounds."

"You silly kids" chuckled Kal.

"Will you do it again, Uncle Leo?" requested his niece.

"Sondra" scolded Maureen with a laugh. "Lets not be rude."

Karen and Doug quickly snapped into protect-mode and took several steps closer. "I'm Doug and this is Karen" asserted Doug. "We're Sondra's legal and adoptive parents." Leo looked up and nodded but before he could say anything in response Sondra pulled away and spoke. "They love me and they take really good care of me" she told her uncle. "We live in Santa Barbara now."

Words and rational thought didn't come easy to her in this moment and she went from glancing at her now-parents to the family member she'd known and loved in her normal life. A curly-haired man in his 40s did a double-take when he recognized the young race car driver. He then proceeded to stumble over a woman's collection of luggage. Sondra, now a master at shutting off her emotions, caught the action out of the corner of her eye and was quick to come to his aid.

"You okay?" she asked the man. He accepted her hand and righted himself.

"You're Sondra Sierre" he proclaimed, shocked at her powerful grip and embarrassed by his clumsiness. "I'm Ken and I'm a big fan" he continued. "Can I get your autograph?"

"Sure" answered Sondra. "And maybe a picture?" added Ken. "I watch as many IndyCar races as I can on TV. Congratulations on your big win at Long Beach. I was there for that one."

"Thanks" said the Holt Racing driver with a wide smile. "That was quite a weekend" she added, now feeling larger than life. An autograph and a picture with Sondra were something Doug and Karen were quite used to at this point. The couple momentarily abandoned the Leo issue to produce a Holt Racing publicity photo and engage the man in simple conversation. A crowd of curious onlookers took shape and before the scene became zoo-like Karen made sure to give Leo their contact information.

"So the kid's livin' her childhood race car dream" Leo marveled, handing Karen one of his cards as well. "Isn't that something" he added. "I remember numerous times her talking about racing cars and winning the Indy Five Hundred."

"She won the Five Hundred last year and we have high hopes for another win later this month" said Karen. Leo was overwhelmed, stunned and seconds later was deeply disappointed when he heard the first boarding call for his flight to Chicago.

Sondra experienced her uncle's departure as a searing white-hot pain, something akin to having one's head and stomach kicked repeatedly with spiked boots. She was deep in thought and memory during the flight as well as the taxi ride home. At Casa de Trent, Sondra raced through the house and out the back, running to her race garage. This alarmed both Doug and Karen but they agreed to give the girl a little space. In less than 20 minutes, however, Karen and Doug jogged down to Sierre-Trent Raceway. "Doug, I don't know about this" said Karen as she looked on nervously, watching the back end of the kart Sondra was driving pitch outward going through Turn 4. “That girl’s been going on raw emotion ever since LA” she told her husband. “She’s in no condition to be out there like this. We need to put a stop to it, immediately. She could really get hurt.”

“Hurt more than she already is?” asked Doug. Sondra’s driving was intense but not necessarily reckless. A small amount of dirt and debris had gathered on the pavement in their absence and unlike any previous time on the track Sondra had skipped taking a leaf-blower to its surface prior to driving on it. The roadway in places acted more like a dirt-track than asphalt, which usually allowed for a considerable amount of grip. “This is her process” Doug reminded his wife. “We need to trust it.”

Karen squeezed her husband’s hand as they watched the girl slide through corner after corner, hard on the accelerator at every opportunity. “Well I can’t watch this anymore” said Karen. “I’m going back to the house.” Sondra continued her process and it was a relief to Doug hearing her cut the motor then head toward him in the garage, coasting to a stop a few feet inside. He decidedly didn’t push the girl on the issues surrounding the airport encounter with Leo Banes and observed her meticulously clean and check over her beloved steed. The two talked about the low tire grip she had just been experiencing and how in the future they might create a better runoff area for the outside of Turn 7.

Karen created a vegetable stir-fry for dinner and the Trents sat down to eat under a cloud of melancholy. “Sondra” said Karen in a light scolding tone as she watched the girl pick up a green bean and begin to chew one end. “Please don’t eat with your fingers.”

“So, um” uttered Sondra, putting the half-eaten morsel back on her plate and swallowing hard. “What happens now?” she asked, a definite note of desperation and worry in her voice. “I mean am I supposed to go live with Uncle Leo now?”

“Do you want to live with your Uncle Leo?” asked Doug. When Sondra hesitated to answer, Karen verbally pounced. “Absolutely not” she announced in an authoritative voice. “You’re our kid and we’re not giving you up without a fight. A very big fight.”

Sondra bit down on her tongue and watched tears begin streaming down her now-mom's cheeks. Doug reached over to hold his wife's hand on top of the table. "Very big fight" he reiterated, looking directly at Sondra.

"Kay" said the girl" feeling more relieved than she was willing to admit. "I'm your kid" she said, her voice desperate and hopeful. Dinner resumed but in place of the earlier sense of heaviness there came a renewed and even stronger sense of family. Sondra flashed a grin as she pushed a carrot further to the edge of her plate with her index finger. She looked over at Karen with mischievous thoughts of openly defying the dinner-table rule of not eating with one's fingers, resisting the temptation to simply pick the item up and pop it into her mouth. Using her fork instead, she stabbed the carrot and bit her lower lip lightly, shrugging her right shoulder as she glanced at her now-parents.

"Such a brat" said Karen, trying to resist a smile. "But you're my brat."

"Our brat" added Doug. After a brief discussion on the next day's probable events, Sondra's mood suddenly changed. A distinct touch of darkness soon returned however as the girl spoke. "Uncle Leo was my dad's Best Man" she announced. "He played the bagpipes at their wedding, and every anniversary he would always be at our house to play for them, us."

She bit down on her tongue and tightly wrapped her fist around her fork. "He was planning on playing for each of us kids' weddings" she added in a tortured voice. She dropped the utensil on the table and stood. "Thank you for dinner" she said politely to Karen. "It was delicious. Gonna take a shower and go to bed." .

Sondra had a 20-minute phone conversation with her uncle and later discussed it with Doug and Karen. "He said he took an early retirement option from his job just over three years ago" said Sondra. "He married the woman he'd been dating, Janet. I remember her. Kinda cold and stuffy. Anyway, he said her five kids got more and more wild with time and that Janet turned super religious and they just grew farther and farther apart. She asked him for a divorce less than a year ago and he moved to Chicago to be closer to the other bagpipe troupe members. He's been doing quite a bit of touring with them."

"He said he's tried a bunch of times to find out the details of the accident but since he's not technically a blood relative he couldn't get much out of anyone. He was told there were no survivors. He didn't know about me. Didn't know to even look. He talked to some of our neighbors but they didn't know anything either, and people who bought the Jenners' house told him they had moved away without a forwarding address."

"He said he's not too computer literate but after he got home tonight had the daughter of one of his bagpipe buddies help him pull up the websites listed on the card you gave him at the airport today. He saw my IndyCar fan-page. He told me that he's amazed and proud of me and that my brothers and parents would be as well."

"He's gonna be in Australia and New Zealand for the next three weeks so he'll miss Indy, but as soon as possible he wants to see me again and wants to come here and see where I live and get to know you guys. He also wants us to visit him at his place in Chicago. Didn't mention anything about me living with him in the future though. Weird, and it kinda hurts a little, but it's also a huge relief. I mean I love him but it would just be too weird. Even if I didn't have you guys, too much time has passed and I have a real career and life now. Besides, I remember my dad saying a trillion times that he's a confirmed bachelor." Sondra studied Doug's face for a few seconds. "He could never be a better second dad than you" she told him.

After a morning of yard-work with Doug, Sondra gladly accepted an invitation from Kari to hang out. At a two-story 16 unit complex she cautiously knocked on the door of Kari's second floor apartment, expecting to find some sort of party atmosphere inside. What she found instead was a warm welcome from Kari into a quiet room. "Roommate's away for a couple of days" explained Kari as she hugged Sondra hello. "I've been sort of goofing off a bit so I'm kinda behind at school, and now I'm having to play a little catch-up" she admitted to Sondra, ushering her dear friend further inside the apartment. Sondra nodded, not at all surprised. On several occasions she'd discussed with Karen and Doug the possibility that Kari move in with them so she wouldn't fall prey to the college party lifestyle and neglect her studies.

"Sorry I can't come out and play" joked Kari.

"Well I won't stay too long" said Sondra.

"Hey" thought Kari. "Wanna order in some food and help me study for a bit?"

"Yeah" said Sondra, smiling as she pulled her cell phone from a top pocket of her thin blue jacket. "What do you want on your pizza?"

For Sondra this couldn't have been a better way to spend the afternoon. She stayed just over two hours, and with her efficiency and natural aptitude helped guide her friend to a more manageable place in her studies. Before leaving she and Kari sat on an old dark-brown cloth couch in the living room. During the twenty-minute chat Kari admitted how hard it was to not fall into her old care-free party habits, and Sondra briefly spoke of her recent race win and future Indy schedule. She told of her time with Brice in Long Beach, with Kari insisting that Sondra give detail of the more romantic and amorous activities. Sondra did this, feeling embarrassed and uncomfortable, but Kari's reaction and comments helped ease much of the guilt she'd felt about her new but limited physical relationship with Brice. As soon as she could, Sondra purposely changed the subject, mentioning the chance encounter with her Uncle Leo.

"What?" exclaimed Kari upon hearing her friend's news of her uncle. "Oh my god, Sondra. You've been here all this time and you're just telling me this now? You rat. So? How was it? I remember you telling me you once tried to find him and that Doug tried too. And I know family stuff's been hard for you, but you must be so super happy about this?"

"I am I guess" said Sondra with a shrug of her right shoulder. "I mean it's great and kinda weird all at the same time" she added.

"What weird?" asked Kari, putting solid but gentle fingers on Sondra's upper arm. "I don't know" said Sondra. "I mean I told him last night that I'd call him this morning but I sort of chickened out. I've actually tried a bunch of times to find him" she admitted. "The wild thing is that I instantly felt five years old when I saw him at the airport yesterday. For just a split second I almost felt normal again, like nothing bad had ever happened or ever could happen."

Sondra told Kari about her beloved uncle who wasn't technically an uncle. She included a few anecdotes and memorable family moments of his visits when she was young, then abruptly stopped talking. Her jaw became fiercely set and she made tight fists. "What just happened?" asked Kari. "Tell me what's going on."

Sondra shook her head and swallowed hard. "This changes everything" she told her friend.

"What does it change, for you?" inquired Kari. Sondra didn't want to keep talking about this but felt a kind of desperation to continue, almost like the telling of her romantic interactions with Brice.

"Well I mean he's someone who knows" Sondra uttered. "He knows my family and he knows how and who I used to be. He doesn't know the current me, what I've gone through and what my life is now."

"You're still Sondra" offered Kari.

Sondra shook her head, disagreeing. "I don't think I'm the same person at all" she told Kari. "And I'm afraid that if I tell him about some of the harsh things he'll look at me differently or not want anything more to do with me."

"Well it's not like you've turned into some kind of monster or serial killer" argued Kari. "You don't drink or smoke and you don't do drugs, and as far as I know you don't rob banks" she added with a quick laugh. "He loved you and your family back then" Kari continued. "And from what you just told me about your phone call with him last night I'd say he loves you just the same now. Probably even more, I would expect. He was a major part of your young life. Sure, you've gone through a lot but I don't think you should put pressure on yourself to tell him about the harshness. If you do though, I'm guessing he won't judge you harshly. It's not like you've really done anything to be super embarrassed about. Not like me. God I've done some really stupid things, and anyway he can't report back to your parents."

Sondra didn't know why but she suddenly felt angry. She wanted to get up and walk out, maybe hit or kick something. She didn't. "It would have been a hell of a lot easier if I'd just died with them" she growled through tightly clenched teeth.

"No" said Kari, bursting into tears. "Damn it, Sondra. Stop saying that. I told you before, you don't know that for sure and it certainly wouldn't have been easy for your uncle or for Doug and Karen, and not for me."

"So I'm just supposed to live for everyone else?" said Sondra in defiance. Kari let loose an expletive. "No, Sondra. You're living for yourself and something that's much bigger."

"Yeah, I guess" diffused Sondra. "Sorry." She checked her watch and stood. "I should get going. Big week next week. Indy time trials." The two shared a tight embrace. "I'll always be around for you, but you have to be around in this world too" said Kari, giving Sondra a kiss on the lips. Sondra pulled away and swatted at her friend's arm. "You nutty girl" she called out to Kari as she started down the stairs with an involuntary smile.

Sondra felt too restless and churned up to simply drive straight home, and minutes after leaving Kari's apartment spotted a sign for Goleta State Beach, deciding that a walk in the sand and the noise of the crashing surf would be the best thing for her in the moment. It turned out to be anything but a soothing experience. The parking lot and the beach before her were deserted save for an elderly gentleman walking south with a small unleashed dog. On her march to the water the sand was uneven and had twigs, bits of shell and other uncomfortable anomalies that seemed to mock her bare feet. The water was cold and there was an equally cold wind. She made a hasty return to the truck, and as she brushed the sand from her feet and put her socks and shoes back on she was struck by the memories of past family beach outings. She remembered how Dave had once claimed to be the new king of body surfing and then so eagerly showed her everything she needed to know in order to enjoy it as much as he. She also recalled how Haley would make it back to the station wagon after their day at the beach with hands and pockets full of shells and other treasures. Kal was far from fond of this practice and there would be a short-lived to-do about making Haley leave it all there, though Haley always did manage to come home with a secret stash. Maureen would be at the ready with large fluffy towels to get her children warm and dry, and even with Kal's light grumbling about how his kids insisted on getting into the car in wet sandy clothes, his steadfast efficiency at readying his family for travel added to the grandness of the beachgoing adventure.

After dinner and some kitchen cleanup, Sondra and Doug began discussing the IndyCar driver's new temporary gym workout routine. An hour later Sondra received another call from her uncle. When the call ended Sondra smiled and sat back against the comfortable fabric of the living room sofa. "I got my Uncle Leo back" she announced to Doug and Karen. "It was a little weird and awkward at first but then it was him. Just him. He has one of the most soothing voices in the world. I mean it's grainy, but a smooth kind of grainy. He wants to get to know you guys and we set things up for him to visit us here next October. IndyCar season'll be over and he'll be through with any major travel 'til after the first of the year. He wants to see our place and have us visit him in Chicago. He said he has a nice split-level condo and a very comfortable routine, and that the food and restaurants there are great. He has a girlfriend, from Brazil. I'm glad he's not all alone, and he said we'd like her."

Sondra took a deep breath, feeling self-conscious for perhaps babbling to cover her emotions. She wanted to cry and scream. Having her Uncle Leo back in her life meant a lot but she wanted him back along with her mom, dad and brothers. Uncle Leo belonged to her other life. He belonged in that childhood home, sitting at the dinner table with the food that her mom had prepared. He belonged to those cherished living room after-dinner chats he'd have with her parents, where she would listen to interesting and important conversations, feeling warm, safe and happy. Sondra wanted back all those great moments where her Uncle Leo would stand in the living room and start to blow air into the plaid cloth-covered resin bag of his bagpipes. As the familiar tunes leaped out and danced in the air he'd begin to walk, with the family marching behind. The grand procession would circle around through the hallway, the dining room and out the French doors to the backyard. Leo would lead them around the pool and back toward the house, but instead of simply returning inside he would proceed down the driveway to the front of the property. Kal would then encourage him to keep going to encircle the block, attracting curious and mostly joyous neighbors. The Jenners, if not already in attendance, would occasionally join in upon hearing the bagpipe medley outside their home, accepting Maureen's invitation/insistence that they follow them home for coffee and dessert.

CHAPTER 33

The magnitude of Indy was a welcomed burden for Sondra. With the Trents' return to Indianapolis she was glad to leave the intenseness of family behind to instead focus entirely on the enormous task at hand. Team meetings, interviews and sponsor obligations were part of a daily routine but to Sondra any and all on-track practice was where she lived. The mechanics and engineers had spent tireless hours massaging the #12 speedster, and at over 230 miles per hour going into Turn Four one week before the Indianapolis 500 she felt an exhilarated hope. Her car was strong and her confidence high.

Brice Crandle, having been out of an Indy car for the first two races of the season, found he had an uphill battle getting up to speed at IMS. A high degree of focus kept him extremely busy, but two days before qualifying he had the opportunity to spend a roughly four hour block of time with Sondra. The two watched close to twenty minutes of Indy Lights practice before going to an early dinner. He had done his homework and found a small family restaurant some thirty miles from the speedway, first obtaining consent from Doug and Karen. "Hope you don't mind" said Brice as he drove them to their destination in one of the Patrero-McDonald's blue Chrysler mini-vans. "But this is one of those places where you don't get too many food choices. Basically chicken or beef. We're having beef."

"Had chicken with another girl earlier, did you?" joked Sondra.

"Oh yeah" smirked Brice sarcastically. "The Smith twins. Great gals."

"Hmm" voiced Sondra. "Funny, funny boy" she said, trying to diminish a giggle.

Once seated in a cozy dimly lit booth, Brice carved off a petal of butter with his knife and spread it on a piece of baguette he'd torn from one end. "I had a really nice talk with Doug the other day" he revealed. "You have a cool dad."

Sondra nodded as she twisted off a piece of bread from the other end and set it onto her plate for buttering. She liked that Doug was a protective skeptic when it came to boys who paid attention to her but she was equally relieved that her now-dad saw the good in Brice. This gave her more and more confidence that her biological father would have liked and approved her choice of boyfriend as well.

"Yeah" Sondra nodded in acknowledgment of Brice's statement of her now-dad. "He told me. So you pretty much had to become a Jack of all trades on the farm. And you took firefighter classes?" she asked. "When did you do that?"

"High school" nodded Brice. "It was a really cool elective my Junior year. My folks were really excited about it, Grampa Tom, too. They knew it could come in handy on the farm and well, anything to distract me from racing."

Sondra and Brice then settled into a conversational rhythm that took them through their entire meal. Cars and racing took a decided back seat as Brice spoke of learning many skills on the Crandle farm. Doug and Karen were discussed, both as individuals and as a couple, being Sondra's now-parents. The dialog soon led them to hobbies that had nothing to do with racing or cars, and when Brice mentioned a strange recurring dream he'd had as a kid, they each recounted numerous memorable dreams and nightmares. Sondra tried to only speak of fun and interesting dreams from her childhood but Brice got her to describe several nightmares she'd had since the Tahoe accident. She resisted at first but then surprised herself at how she could now talk of such things without either exploding into pain-fueled rage or collapsing inward. Discussing issues, dreams and memories with Shelley, as well as occasionally with Doug, Karen and Kari had inadvertently lessened the intenseness.

By the end of the long weekend, where Sondra experienced anxious, interesting and excited moments, another one of her dreams came true. She had been the seventh car to qualify on Sunday's famous Pole Day. Speeds in general were up from last year despite rules and regulation changes aimed at aero-safety and Sondra had spoken alone with T.J. in the garage earlier that morning. The last 500-mile race he'd won at this track was in weather and track conditions similar to this year and he advised her not to abuse her tires in the opening laps but to go big if the car is there. Sondra's first warmup lap was recorded at 234.371. With the least amount of downforce of any of the Fast Nine the #12 car was a frightening squirrelly mess to drive and she was barely able to breathe. Taking the green flag for her 4-lap run at 236.758 gave Holt Racing and their fans nervous hope. The next time by, Sondra had posted the fastest of the day in the speed-trap before Turn 3, 238.215 mph. All this seemed like a never-ending lifetime for Sondra. She'd requested mostly radio silence from her team before getting into the car. Absolute concentration was what she needed. With the exception of a calm-voiced Craig Pines spotting from high above the speedway and letting her know what lap she was on, Sondra got her wish. Throughout this qualifying period Karen had a continuous stream of nerves mixed with excited happiness that her daughter was doing what she loved and was truly in contention for the Pole. Shelley was standing next to Karen with her mouth agape, her eyes wide and her hand holding tightly onto Karen's. As the checkered flag waved, both women felt as if they might collapse from relief. Sondra had driven a total of six laps with her car on the absolute ragged edge of breaking loose and slamming the wall at any second. The advantage of doing this however awarded her a 4-lap average speed of 236.837 mph, giving Holt Racing's Sondra Sierre the highly coveted Indy 500 Pole.

The remainder of the month of May was a blur of activity and seemed to zip by effortlessly. When Sondra wasn't in her car making simulated race runs, testing tire wear and finding out how far they could go on a full fuel load, her schedule was packed with interviews, working in the garage, going to sponsor obligations as well as two different Safen-Up events. Even with all these activities she was able to spend time with her friends. She and Brice only had moments here and there to be alone together but just as it had happened the previous year, Brice and Sondra were often seen with Andrew Placer and Wendell Grayson. Wendell's Indy Lights teammate Myrand Fiora joined them for a number of fun moments, running up and down the bleachers, grabbing a quick bite together and playing Frisbee.

Being a second-season driver and having won the Pole for the famed event gave Sondra a sense of peace she'd not had the previous year. The special sights and sounds that make up an Indy experience were now easier for her to fully enjoy. On race day morning, driver introductions became an electrifying proud and happy moment when her name was called, with a deafening cheer from the crowd. She later loved the spectacle of posing with her fellow competitors and then hearing the *Star-Spangled Banner* being sung by the Indiana High School choir, backed by their marching band. As the driver of the #12 car was being strapped into her car Sondra watched the release of hundreds of balloons. Then came the singing of *Back Home Again In Indiana*, a recording, but she loved that they had this year chosen to honor the late, great Jim Nabors. After the order was given to start engines Sondra was all focus and business. Flexing her fingers and getting as comfortable as possible she kept an eye on the steering wheel telemetry and an ear on how the twin-turbo Honda V6 was idling. She listened to her Lead Strategist as he began final radio checks with the team, including a quick chat with spotter Craig Pines high atop the bleachers on the front-stretch. Sondra suddenly heard a much different vocal tone than any of the usual members of her team: "I'm with you, Sondra."

"I'm with you, too" she called out, holding down the in-car radio button on her steering wheel with her thumb. A wave of goosebumps went though her as she realized that no one on her team had uttered those words nor had they even heard them. She recognized the voice. It was her little brother Haley. Sondra bit down on her tongue and willed herself to concentrate on the task at hand, grateful to once again hear Darren's strong voice in her ears. "All right guys" he began. "We're a united front so lets be strong, smart and safe." Sondra had planned on saying a little something to her team before the race in order to bolster confidence and acknowledge their efforts, but hearing her brother's voice had rattled her and she fought with composure.

"Thanks for everything, guys" she was able to say. "I'll make you proud." She again flexed her fingers and shut the visor on her helmet. Seconds later the pace-car moved forward, leading the field of thirty-three cars onto the famous racing surface. Sondra stared at the back-end of the white Corvette, noticing the flashing lights and then having her eye caught by the thousands of spectators with every color of clothing in the spectrum. She glanced down at her steering wheel to re-check the bright-red LED numbers. All was right and she was now in race-mode with only one thing on her mind. Winning.

With the engine of the #12 at full song, Sondra took the green flag and had the preferred line going into Turn 1. She was able to hold the lead for the entire first lap, with all thirty-three cars getting through the first four corners of the 200 lap event without incident. Satisfied that they had a strong car, the Holt Racing strategy was to go up to three laps as the race leader, if possible, then drift back to third, letting the leaders break the wind resistance allowing her to go immediately into fuel-save mode. Sondra slotted easily behind a hard-charging Greg Raley on Lap 4. Upon Darren's encouragement she then allowed Shane Teluchi and Tony Kelarzo around her without putting up a fight. Seven laps later Sondra found that she was being challenged by Brice Crandle. She thwarted several of his moves but let him go as they went into Turn 3. During the first quarter of the race the lead changed six times, with Sondra up to 2nd on Lap 24. Darren then had her stay within the top five until the first round of green-flag pit stops. There had been no caution periods and no cars that had retired for mechanical reasons. Mid-pack had become the focus of media coverage due to the number of changes for position, with drivers moving forward who had started near the rear of the field. After the first round of green-flag pit stops there began a somewhat steady stream of cautions. The bright-red #99 machine of Billy Voolin spun on cold tires coming out of the pits and slammed into the Turn 1 wall. He was not injured but there were seven laps of caution before the field went back to green in order to remove the car and clean up the debris and fluids left from the impact. The lower caution speeds seemed to amp up the adrenaline and anxiety of a number of drivers and three more cautions for one and two-car incidences occurred within the next 40 laps.

On Lap 127, after the fourth caution had come out for a crash in Turn 4 involving Emanual Billings, Darren spoke to his driver over the radio on the third caution-lap go-around. "All right, Sondra. Pits are gonna be open this next time by. Pit this lap. Pit this lap."

"Copy pit" repeated Sondra. "Increasing understeer, especially after right-side tires wear" she added.

"Copy that, Sondra" said Darren. A plan was formulated to give the #12 a quarter-turn of front wing and an incremental tire-pressure change. Sondra followed the leaders Tony Kelarzo and Brice Crandle down pit lane, looking out for her specific waving lollypop pit-marker sign-board. The #17 car of John Mallory had been behind her in 4th Place. He was carrying far too much speed for pit-in and swung along-side the #12, getting hard on the brakes. The Right-rear tire of his neon-orange car made hard contact with the #12, leaving a black half-moon wheel mark on Sondra's shiny blue left side-pod. The hit from Mallory sent her glancing into the outside concrete pit lane retaining wall. Her lightening-quick reflexes kept the car from heavy impact as well as the motor from stalling. She pounded the steering wheel and vocalized over the radio her displeasure as she limped her way to her pit box. "Idiot. Damn it." she barked.

The #12 car went up on the air-jack and the pit crew first went to work on tires and fuel. From Darren's vantage point he could see the obvious front-wing damage and ordered the nose-cone assembly changed. The always observant team leader could also see that Sondra was holding her left thumb with her right hand. While Sondra's car sat idling in the pits as the work was being done, emotion suddenly got the better of her. She faced straight ahead as tears involuntary flowed inside her closed-visor helmet. The enormity of what had just occurred hit her hard. This year's Indy 500 victory would go to someone else, but it was more than that. This wasn't just a race or points toward a championship, it was a chance to prove to herself and everyone else that her win last year wasn't just a fluke. Most races for her had this component as well but this one she held as being absolutely essential. After the Tahoe crash and losing her family, her only real understanding of life came from success in a race car. This was something she didn't fully know how to explain to herself or anyone else for that matter. She viewed the previous year's victory as at least some sort of compensation for the things she'd had to endure since the age of thirteen. Hundreds of drivers from all over the world dream of being on this famed oval, and to have even a modicum of success in this annual event was like an over-the-top nirvana. Equally, there came the devastating effects of having mishaps and misfortune rip a driver and a team away from the highest of highs.

Before releasing the #12 car, Darren made an inquiry about Sondra's thumb. Her answer was a quick lie. "I'm fine. No problem." Once back out on the track, still under caution, Sondra wove her car back and forth to make sure all was well. "We have issues" she reported back to her team, her voice sounding alarmed and tense. "Steering wheel's off-center and there's a minor vibration in the right-front" she said in elaboration. T.J. had been monitoring the progress of both his cars. He'd installed longtime friend and team member Keith Hestrovich (Keys) to be Ryan Delgato's Lead Strategist. Delgato had steadily drifted backwards during the first portion of the race due to balance issues but after his second stop of the day was making progress. The #21 car was now running in 8th. After the incident in the pits involving his other car, T.J. left Keys' side to join Darren on the #12 pit-box. He sat next to Darren, gritted his teeth and made a face while pounding his right leg with his fist. T.J. then gave Darren a hard look, non-verbally telling the man that he expected them to recover and move forward. "All right, Sondra" spoke Darren over the radio in acknowledgment of Sondra's last communiqué. "Come on back in and we'll give it a look." With the lengthy pit stop she'd just had Sondra was already down six spots in the running order. "I don't want to go a lap down" she said, panic and anger in her voice as she made her way back to her pit stall. The field went green while further close inspection of the #12's Tow-linkage and Front A-arm assembly got underway. To compensate for the incremental tow-in angle incurred by the pit lane debacle, a considerable amount of downforce levels were added to the front wing. Sondra pounded her fist on her upper leg and fought to keep expletives from rocketing out of her mouth. When released, now a full lap down, she stormed out of her pit with Darren's harsh words of not exceeding pit lane speed ringing in her ears. The Holt Racing Twelve car was far from perfect and Sondra was never able to get her lap back, but with smart and determined driving coupled with Darren's bold strategy calls, this years running of the Indy 500 was not all entirely disastrous. There had come increasing numbers of incidences and attrition, and with only a handful of laps remaining Sondra was running 11th one lap down. With two laps to go, Sondra made a desperate-looking move out of Turn 4, slicing to the outside of the dull-green #30 car of Phil Grumenchino. Most of the crowd had their attention on the leaders who were putting up a fierce battle. The move from Sierre to grab the last points-paying position (10th) had many on their feet and shaking their heads as they could have sworn the #12 machine made slight contact with the wall. It hadn't.

Shane Teluchi drank the milk and enjoyed his second career victory of the great race. On pit lane, Sondra and her team gathered next to the bug, oil and rubber-flecked #12 car to lick their wounds and console themselves. An increasing number of track personnel, pit-reporters and camera crews seemed to be tightening around the Holt Racing 12 pit. A man in a blue race suit made his way cautiously toward the AAA team's assembly. Sondra noticed him and gave an inviting wave to John Mallory. It took a few minutes for track security to determine that this was going to be an amicable meeting, and as the driver of car #17 stepped closer he pointed at his shoulder. Sondra smiled and made a slow dramatic punching motion, softly connecting her fist with the man's shoulder. John then gave her a quick hug and profusely apologized for his part in the earlier pit lane incident. As he walked away, answering questions from various race media, Sondra soon became the target of network broadcast media coverage, with Lydia Velstein on hand to conduct the interview with the Holt Racing star driver.

"Sondra, as the Pole-sitter I know this had to be such a disappointing outcome for you" began Lydia. "What did John Mallory say to you, and can you give us your prospective on what happened on pit lane?" A very weary and dejected Sondra shook her head slowly before speaking. "Well I was holding my line and pit lane speed, so I don't really know. The hit just came so out of the blue. I mean John's a good guy and I know he didn't do it on purpose but that was so unnecessary and colossally rookie-stupid. I mean I appreciate his apology but the damage is done. We had a really great Holt Racing Triple A, Seven-Up, Snap-on Tools car today. I don't really know what to say. I feel so bad for my guys. They worked incredibly hard all month and after the thing on pit lane they put everything they had into fixing my car. Gave me a ton of encouragement to go back out and fight as hard as I could. It's, it's just so crushing to sit on Pole and then come away with a result like this, but you know, I'm proud that we all kept our heads down and fought back to salvage as much as we could. This track means so much to me. It's mysterious and magical, and I hope this is my one-time bad-luck mulligan."

She later gave abbreviated versions of how her race day had gone to other media outlets, then had a private discussion with her team about the things that did go right that day. There was a bit of concern over her thumb but she again skillfully deflected this focus, and with her trusted race family she could now be far more openly angry at the John Mallory melee and how Race Control had simply called it a racing incident, without giving him any kind of penalty. Darren let his driver rage on for a few minutes but then praised her for the restraint she'd shown over the radio as well as the post-race interviews.

Before Doug, Karen and Sondra made their exit from the speedway they spent roughly thirty minutes in their motorhome. Brice came by and was permitted to have a few minutes alone with Sondra. "Congratulations on your Third Place finish" she told him. "Thanks" he said with a nod, hoping to discuss more than just the Five Hundred. "Teluchi was just in another stratosphere at the end there, and at twelve laps to go I was being told Kelarzo was light on fuel so I was runnin' really hard to catch him" he explained.

"Yeah, said Sondra, nodding in understanding. "He's hard to pass no matter what, but you had a pretty awesome month of May and you can definitely hold your head up high."

"Thanks" Brice said with a bit of a shy smile. "I hate what happened to you" he added. "And let me be the millionth person to ask how you are."

Sondra wrapped her arms around him. "My thumb hurts like hell" she whispered. "And my ego's smashed pretty hard but I'm okay." She held onto him a little tighter. The two then shared a passionate kiss.

After days of travel, rehashing the 500 and then arriving at the next race venue, the first two practice sessions for Holt Racing at the half-mile Kansas Speedway were difficult at best. The balance of the car never felt comfortable to Sondra, no matter what changes were attempted. Friday morning's practice came close to disaster on Lap 28. As she was being passed by a white and black car just before going into Turn 4 she felt the front-end lose grip, as if a giant hand had reached out and slapped her car sideways. With lightning-quick reflexes she caught the violent wriggle but the right-rear tire lost a bit of traction as well and brushed the wall. She kept forward motion but at a reduced speed. "We're a crash waiting to happen" she told her lead strategist. "Understeering everywhere and then snaps to wild oversteer if anyone chops me off like Voolin just did." There was nothing technically wrong with how the #99 of Billy Voolin had enacted the pass on the #12. Sondra's displeasure over this minor incident at 186.463 miles per hour was not directed at the likable Australian driver. Her frustration was more about not having a car that could get her where she needed to be, in Sunday's winner's circle. Her momentary inability in relaying to her engineers exactly what the car needed was downright irritating to her. Ryan Delgato had been in this situation many times. Acting as team driver coach he offered many words of comfort and advice plus possible solutions to the problems when he and Sondra spoke with the team's engineers.

During Saturday afternoon's qualifying session Sondra put her Holt Racing #12 car on the inside of Row 2. The next day she took over the top spot from Greg Raley on Lap 23 of the Kentucky 300 and led for the next 54 laps. She finished 2nd behind a hard-charging Shane Teluchi, who early-on in the race had switched to an alternate pit strategy that in the end allowed him to run full-rich, while Sondra and the top seven cars were in various stages of fuel-save modes. Sondra was not happy, now 3rd in championship points, but much of the season remained. Before heading away from the speedway she made a point to find Brice. He was inside a Patrero-McDonald's motorhome chatting with three men from his #48 team.

"That was so damn fun racing with you around the halfway point" said Brice, holding her close after he'd suggested the others give the two of them some space.

"Yeah" she said, responding to Brice's comment. "Looked like we had pretty equal cars for a while there" she added.

"Well after that caution for Mallory it just seemed like things changed with the handling and we could never get it back" said Brice.

"Well we were chasing things pretty hard, too" admitted Sondra. "My folks are waiting for me but I wasn't about to just leave without that goodbye kiss you promised me."

Brice smiled as he tenderly took her in his arms. He enjoyed the soft deep moan she made during the kiss but felt a painful emptiness when she exited the vehicle.

Sondra liked the next race venue, the thirteen-turn 2.258 mile Mid-Ohio Sports Car Course of Lexington, Ohio. She did her best to put out of her mind that this was the site of Brice's crash many months ago, and in the morning meeting with her two engineers and Ryan Delgato before Friday's practice session she loved how they described it as a real driver's track. Starting from 4th on the grid in

Sunday's Grand Prix, Sondra slipped around Rich Clemens for the lead on Lap 19. She'd taken mindful care of her red-sidewall tires in the opening laps and was given the go-ahead to run as hard as she could until the first round of pit stops. The entire middle of the race she was on the harder compound tire, and dealing with a bit of oversteer in Turn 4 she toggled between 3rd and 5th Place in the running order. With 23 laps to go, Gary Menard and rookie Elias Pasterelli tangled in the Keyhole (Turn 2) bringing out a Full-course Caution. When the pits were open Darren had his driver come in for their last stop, putting the #12 car on a set of sticker reds. During the past few days of practices it had been determined that Sondra could go 29 laps on a set of reds, the softer faster compound tire, running flat-out before they gave up their traditional grippiness. Race leaders John Oliver, Rich Clemens, Shane Teluchi and Patrick Colvin were on either used reds, sticker blacks or used black sidewall tires. Sitting in 5th place on a brand new set of fast tires Sondra began her assent when the field of cars were again shown the green flag. On the final lap she had a 3.169 second lead over Shane Teluchi when her #12 car crossed underneath the flag-stand, with the checkers waving for her. The victory was made a bit sweeter with Tony Kelarzo's 6th Place finish and Greg Raley finishing 18th. This gave the lead in the championship to Sondra and her Holt Racing team by 3 points.

Riding the high of Mid-Ohio, Sondra went into Detroit's street-course double-header with the best pre-weekend disposition she'd had all year. This track did however offer immense challenges. There were tight fast blind turns, light-rail lines that had temporary patches and several man-hole covers that were hard on tires and suspensions. The track featured a combination of asphalt and concrete surfaces with pot-holes, weather-related cracks and buckles that created hazards especially with the roadway construction compounds used to fill them. Ride-height selection was key so the car would be able to stick to the surface without being adversely effected by the track's anomalies. Drivers up and down the IndyCar field complained of the extreme bumpiness, even more-so than in previous years, and after Friday morning's practice Sondra told Darren, T.J. and her engineers that there were several occasions where her feet had come completely off the pedals. John Briers nodded, having seen the real-time results from the laptop telemetry. He, Sondra and the other engineers immediately began to formulate a plan that was both comfortable for the driver and would give them the speed and handling they needed.

By Saturday morning Holt Racing was cautiously optimistic and Sondra came away with a 3rd Place qualifying position. The afternoon's race however didn't exactly go their way. The sports car endurance series had run their race and offered the Indy cars a slippery track and areas where they'd put down rubber on portions much different to that of the IndyCar Series. Sondra's race setup was a bit ill-prepared for this and she fell back to Seventh in the running order by Lap 5, eventually settling in the 9th position. After several cautions and then a smooth mid-race green-flag pit stop, she found herself in 4th, challenging for 3rd. With four laps to go she got around Rich Clemens, breaking later than he going into Turn 1 but roughly half a lap later he got back around her. She wasn't at all happy with a 4th Place finish but kept this mostly to herself. She was however genuinely happy for the surprise winner Brice Crandle, though she could have done without his later gloating and boasting.

Sondra's Saturday evening was quite different than most. During her race season she either had her meals with her team or alone with Doug and Karen, then would tend to some social-network activities followed by personal phone calls and a light physical workout. On this night however her Uncle Leo would be taking her to dinner, much to Brice's dismay. Intentionally avoiding the subject of the Tahoe accident and Sondra's physical recovery, Leo asked many questions about how she had managed to be in her current position with the famous race team. Her answers came mostly with confidence and joy, though she did chronicle the harshness of being young and female and having to fight to be taken seriously on so many occasions. "Well" said an astonished uncle. "From what I saw and heard today, you seem to have a lot of fans and a lot of respect from the members of your team. And you certainly have a busy schedule. When I've called the last few times I've talked to Karen, eventually. She seems quite a remarkable woman and completely dedicated to you."

Sondra nodded, briefly biting down on her tongue. "Both Karen and Doug are a lot like Mom and Dad" she told Leo before launching into some detail regarding parenting focus and direction as well as some of their similar mannerisms. Sondra then talked about her education process, leaving out the struggles and physical fights she had been in while in high school.

In between bites of pepper-crusted steak, Leo regaled his niece with details about his bagpipe troupe and a bit about the two-story condo he'd recently purchased. By meal's end, Sondra felt like they had been talking and eating for a week.

"We didn't really get into anything too heavy" Sondra later told her now parents. "I mean there was this awkward tension pretty much the whole time and it's not like anything for the future was discussed or decided, like where we go from here. One nice thing though is that I got to have a real grownup meal and a real grownup conversation with him. I mean it was obvious that he feels sorry for me, I was just a kid the last time we ..."

She shrugged and made a quick fist. "Well anyway" she said with a loud breath. "Tonight we were two adults having a nice meal and that felt pretty good."

The next day, Sondra and her team utilized to full advantage what they'd learned the previous day. Holt Racing not only attained the Pole during Sunday morning's qualifying but the #12 car led the race from flag to flag. There were only two caution periods during this Belle Isle event. One for debris on the front-stretch on Lap 12 and a second full-course caution was observed for Phil Grumenchino, who'd spun on cold tires shortly after pitting on Lap 67. The Holt Racing team celebration that night took place in a hotel dining room, with much food, drink, talk and laughter. Doug and Karen enjoyed an evening of popularity almost more than the young race winner and eventually lost sight of their daughter-client. Shelley had arrived during the third round of that morning's IndyCar qualifying, and throughout the celebratory dinner that evening purposely kept an eye out for Sondra. When the girl disappeared she went looking for her friend. "Hiding?" asked Shelley after finding Sondra leaning against an empty corridor wall some distance from the banquet room. Sondra was staring obliquely at the opposite elongated surface and didn't immediately respond to Shelley's inquiry. Shelley stepped closer and she too leaned her back against the pale pink wall. "You won a big important race today" she stated. "And now you're out here instead of inside celebrating. What's going on, baby?"

Sondra shook her head but casually reached over to briefly hold her friend's hand before speaking. "I made mistakes today and I pissed Darren off because I kinda defied orders."

"Darren's not pissed" assured Shelley. "He's proud of you." Shelley took a deep breath and shook her head. "That's not it" she said of Sondra's dark mood. "Why are you upset?"

Sondra bit down on her tongue to keep the tears in check. "He didn't want me" she said. "My Uncle Leo didn't insist or demand that I come live with him. I mean I don't really want to live with him. I love Doug and Karen and where we live."

"But you wanted him to want you to live with him" surmised Shelley. "Your uncle that you've known and loved all your life" she added. In a surprise move, Sondra wrapped her arms tightly around her friend. In this moment Shelley saw Sondra as a fragile small child not the tough tomboy she so often tried to portray or project.

The IndyCar Series had a two-week summer break. The first three days for Doug, Sondra and Karen however involved travel to Texas for pit practice and team meetings at the Holt Racing headquarters. The following weekend was an IndyCar Series mandated test at Pocono International Speedway and three days later another test was held at New York's Watkins Glen International Raceway. The remainder of the racing hiatus was more of a true vacation, which Karen referred to as a stay-cation at Casa de Trent. Sondra was physically and emotionally drained from her efforts thus far in the season and this bit of down-time was exactly what she needed. Though there were many chores to complete inside and out, the first two days at home she was more like the stereotypical lazy teenager on summer vacation. She wasn't rude or disrespectful but had no interest in taking on projects and put no energy into the things Karen or Doug suggested, recreational or otherwise. By day three, Karen had had enough. "Rise and shine" chirped the mom as she shook her daughter awake, just after 7:30 a.m. "It's a glorious day outside and I'm making French toast for breakfast."

"Nnn" groaned Sondra, turning over and burying her face in her pillow. "Come on, now" furthered the mom. "Up and at 'em, sweetie. You've been mopey, dopey and grumpy for days now. We're done with the dwarfs. I want my angel back. Up, up."

"I'm not here" spoke Sondra into the pillowy material. "I ran away with the other dwarfs to join the circus. I'll send you a postcard."

"You goofy girl" laughed Karen as she folded back the covers.

"Mom" complained Sondra, laboring to sit up. "Who eats French toast at the crack of dawn, anyway?" grumped the girl as she brushed the hair away from her face with the back of her right hand.

Karen leaned down and gave Sondra a quick kiss on the top of her head. "You and your crack of dawn" she chuckled. "Sun's been up for hours and you should be too."

After breakfast Sondra helped Doug with pool cleaning and maintenance. The two soon found themselves inside the small pool-house located at the easterly end of the pool, just out and to the right of Sondra's bedroom window. The largest portion of this unpainted redwood structure was a changing room that had a thin wall separating this space from the pool's pumps and filters. Doug and Sondra stood over opposite sides of a white thick-plastic cylindrical diatomaceous-earth filter enclosure, loosening the sixteen bolts around the outside of the top lid with socket wrenches. He glanced up and witnessed Sondra working intensely, with an expression of focused anger. "Talk to me, kiddo" he said, calmly going back to the bolt on which he was working. "The driving and professionalism you've been showing most weekends is at an impressive all-time high" he added. "But I know you. There's been something just a little bit off lately."

It was his guess that this was mostly about her Uncle Leo or perhaps the Crandle boy but he wanted Sondra to open up about it. He watched the girl shrug her right shoulder and wondered if he should press the issue further.

"Well I guess I have been learning some good stuff this season" said Sondra of her driving, without taking her eyes off the project at hand.

"But?" prompted Doug.

"Well I mean" began the girl. There was a long pause as the two continued their task. Sondra then leaned back against the wall and watched her now-dad lift the lid, exposing gray-white sludge surrounding the unit's sides and core. Hanging down from the underside of the lid were the numerous dripping-wet fingers that made up the filter. "I hate to say this or even think it" said Sondra. "But finding Uncle Leo is both great and horrible." Doug nodded with what he thought was at least a good understanding of her dilemma. "I had a talk with SeaShell about it" disclosed Sondra. "On one hand it's like getting stabbed and having someone pound salt into your already painful wounds."

Doug hated that Sondra felt this much pain and had such harsh imagery within her. "On the other hand?" he asked, hoping there was another hand.

"Well" shrugged Sondra. "We both share the horribleness of what and who we lost but we also get to share something that nobody else does. I mean there really were some great times back then. Nobody but us really knows how great. I guess in a way that's kinda cool." She took a deep breath and put the wrench on a small dusty shelf behind her. "I had an interesting phone chat with Kari the other day" she announced. "She was telling me about one of her classes and something her sociology professor had said, that every moment in life is both great and tragic. I mean like right now. You and I just unbolted this filter lid but it's now basically just a memory. It's a moment we can't ever get back."

Doug could feel a heavy wave of sadness radiate from the girl. "But Sondra" he countered. "We possess the power of choice in how we look at things and how we remember the moments. Ten years from now, are you gonna remember this moment as a chore you didn't really want to do, or the green T-shirt I'm wearing with this strange-looking yellow squiggly line going across? Are you gonna see this as a great moment or a bad one? Yeah, your Uncle Leo represents so many moments from your past but you get to choose how you see and remember those. The memories of all the great moments aren't there to torture you."

Sondra coughed a laugh, disguising a wall of emotion before responding. "SeaShell once said that exact same thing to me" she admitted. She swallowed hard and took a deep breath. "I'm trying with all this" she told her now-dad in a loud whisper. "I really am."

"I know that, Sondra" said Doug with a nod. "You're a thousand miles from where you were when I first came to know you, and I'm damn proud of you."

Doug intended to say more, prolonging the conversation in hopes that she would open up about what she'd been thinking and feeling lately but instead Sondra changed the subject as she often did when things got too intense for her. "So … um" began the girl. "You and mom are going for another flying lesson tomorrow? Okay if I have Yamaha-shop Rob and Eddie over for some motocross and karting fun?"

"Yeah" said Doug reluctantly. He knew this most likely would be good for her but he didn't trust Eddie. He considered young Grisban a bit of a ragamuffin and the boy openly flirted with her whenever they'd go to the dealership. "Why don't you have Kari come out as well" he suggested.

"I don't need a chaperone" snapped Sondra with shocking sudden fierceness. "Besides, she's still in Oregon on summer break from school."

Doug stared at Sondra for a few seconds, thinking over her volatile response. "Lets go rinse this sucker out" he offered as he held out the filter, choosing to save this particular battle for another time.

With the limited time Doug and Karen could spend on their passion and ambition of learning to fly, they were not too far along. On a day of mostly clear skies and a relatively steady 3-knot coastal breeze, the couple would be engaged in some ground-school going over many important concepts. They would also be getting some-seat-time in a Cessna 172 with instructor Ron Sabins, learning the ultra-important skill of taxiing a plane on airport property, with proper radio communication to inform other pilots on the ground and immediate airspace of position and intent. That morning Sondra woke up early and jogged down to her garage and race-shop, getting ready for Rob and Eddie's visit later in the day. Karen insisted she come back to the house for breakfast but as soon as the meal was finished and her now-parents had driven out of the garage for their journey to the Santa Ynez airport, Sondra made a hasty retreat back to her Sierre-Trent Raceway facility, leaving the dishes in the kitchen sink and other chores she had promised Karen she'd do. She was surprised to see Rob and Eddie arrive just after 9 a.m. in separate vehicles. Rob was in one of the dealership's blue Ford vans that contained his orange and white Yamaha 250. Eddie drove a soft-top black Jeep Wrangler pulling a trailer, with a thick army-green tarp covering what Sondra figured to be his dirt bike. "Hi guys" she greeted. "Glad you could make it."

"Man" marveled Rob. "This is pretty awesome" he told his host of their surroundings.

"Yeah" agreed Eddie. "Killer place ya got here, Sondra."

"Thanks" she said, internally beaming with pride. She then gestured a retreat inside the race shop. She'd purposely left the cover on her Formula Ford car so that she could make a dramatic reveal. When she pulled the tarp over and off the sleek vehicle, she was pleased with herself for doing so as she watched Rob and Eddie's amazed response. "It's still a work in progress to get it to where I want" she told her company, evidenced by the car being up on jacks with all four wheels removed. "But I won some really good races and the championship in this baby."

"It's looking like an IndyCar championship might be in your future" said Rob of her current racing status as he scrutinized the race car before him.

"Well that's the plan" said Sondra, a bit of a cavalier tone in her voice. Eddie's attention soon left the F-Ford. He looked all around the shop, noticing the welding booth, the machining tools and the overall look of a clean well-stocked garage. From this and the impressive vision of the house and property he was immediately jealous of Sondra's apparent wealth. He and Rob had had many discussions about how "cool" it was that they knew an Indy 500 winner, and some of Eddie's thoughts about Sondra were not all that honorable.

"I can't believe this is the same kart that was basically in pieces at the shop when you bought it a while back" Eddie said to Sondra as he examined one of the four shifter-karts.

She smiled with pride at her handiwork. "They're all in top condition and ready to roll" she announced. "I thought maybe after our motocross fun I might talk you guys into a little pavement time."

The morning turned pleasantly into afternoon for the three motorsports enthusiasts. During the dirt bike fun and games Eddie had insisted on riding one of Sondra's 250s and later, after the completion of many karting laps, Eddie's reasons for the bike choice was revealed. "Brought along something that I'm sure you're gonna like" he told Sondra as they sat on stools in the garage enjoying 7-Up and potato chips. Sondra experienced excited short breaths and goose bumps when Eddie uncovered what was beneath the tarp on the trailer behind his Jeep. "Wow" she voiced as she gazed upon the two Yamaha YZFR-1 superbikes.

"The blue one's mine" announced Eddie. "I'll be makin' payments on this sucker for a while but it's a hell of a bike and it's an investment in my career. I'm goin' for a spot on a superbike Moto-America team with factory support. Couldn't believe my luck when I got the call but I've been pushin' for this my whole life."

"Nice. Good for you" cheered Sondra. "So" she said in a hopeful tone about the yellow superbike that stood alongside its dark blue pal. Rob and Eddie gave each other quick glances and seized full advantage of the moment, the opportunity to enter the pitch they'd discussed the day prior with their boss. There was no need of high-pressure sales tactics however. For Sondra it was love at first sight. The retro throwback yellow-black-white paint scheme had immediately taken her back to the days with her father when they had cheered on their favorite Yamaha factory rider and Sondra's motorcycle road racing hero.

"Well I'm sorry I didn't bring an M-One" said Eddie. "But I didn't figure you'd get sudden plans to give up on IndyCar and switch to Moto GP racing. These YZFR-One babies here are specifically set up for the track but they can easily be changed back to legal street machines."

Sondra folded her arms and nodded her head. "The new cowling and overall look is actually modeled after the M-One" explained Eddie. "What we got here is a nine-hundred ninety-eight cc four cylinder cross-plane crank motor that produces two-hundred brake horsepower. It's got Moto GP-style launch control, two-mode ABS brakes and two-mode dampening suspension." Eddie mentioned a few other specifics but Sondra stood mesmerized by the vision before her and the adventure possibilities of owning and riding such a machine.

"So why is my bike still on your trailer?" she asked, trying to hide a smile. "Less talking, more unloading" she told the boys.

After both bikes were set on stands on the surface of the kart track, Eddie went over some particulars before he and Sondra embarked on their ride. Rob, the older and more responsible one of the three in this moment tried his best to dissuade the on-track excursion before a financial transaction could be completed but Sondra shook her head. "We're good" she assured him, holding out her hand to shake on the deal. Rod gave a reluctant nod to Eddie who finished his soda and proceeded to crush the 7-Up can into his chest. The young man belched crudely and tossed the aluminum item into a cardboard box containing other aluminum cans for recycling. Sondra was used to crude boy behavior and briefly wondered if he was showing off for her.

Road racing class was now in session, with Eddie as the teacher. Sondra sat on the new yellow motorcycle tingling with giddiness but paying close attention as he went into specifics, including a number of personal experiences he'd had on his bike. After engine start-up and a quick discussion on a time-frame and number of laps the two pulled away in unison. They rode in a leisurely pace, with Sondra hollering out two additional questions that had Eddie answering with a nod. Going into the last corner on the second go-around Eddie pointed toward the Start/Finish line, indicating that he planned on running off and leaving her. Sondra nodded and kicked down a gear. Starting down the front straight she tucked in tight and rolled on throttle. The race was on. Rob smiled and put his fingers in his ears as the two bikes screamed past, with the engines turning over 3,400 rpm. He shook his head as he watched Sondra brake late and come inches from Eddie's back tire as they entered the Left-hand 60-degree radius of Turn One. A part of him wanted to be out there with them but he knew he was witnessing something special: an Indy 500 winner pitted against his friend Eddie who he knew was destined for two-wheeled greatness.

Sondra's knowledge of her track allowed her to hold pace with the far-more experienced rider. Her ability to quickly learn and then push anything on wheels to extremes was astronomical and Eddie made a few small mistakes as he came to this realization. He found himself truly baffled at how such a pretty tomboy of a girl who looked as if she weighed less than a hundred pounds, could even keep up with him let alone race him as hard or harder than a significant number of his usual fellow competitors. As the laps continued, their attacks became more pronounced. Sondra and Eddie would practically lean on each other and seemed to take turns in out-braking and out-accelerating one another. Just over 30 minutes of track-time had elapsed when Sondra, with a quarter bike-length lead coming out of Turn 9 the last corner of the track, spotted Karen's dazzling fuchsia T-shirt. The mom was standing ten feet from the edge of the first turn with her hands angrily on her hips. The split-second distraction that Sondra experienced was enough to allow Eddie to squeeze around on the outside and pull past her going toward the Start/Finish line. Sondra took her bike out of gear and revved the motor before cutting it and coasting into the garage. She came to a halt next to Rob and a non-smiling Doug. Eddie continued his tear and after exiting Turn 9 popped a triumphant wheelie. He then set the front tire down and came to a stop alongside Sondra. With his left hand he lifted his helmet's visor. His right hand fist lightly tapped the shoulder of Sondra's race suit. "Damn impressive" he voiced, shaking his head. "I take it you like the bike."

Doug and Karen had arrived back at Casa de Trent from their day of progress in obtaining their flying licenses and certainly had not expected to come home to this particular scene. When they found their daughter was nowhere in the house they guessed that time had gotten away from her and her guests. The parents quickly figured that the three were still engaged in motocross fun and games and as they came walking over the rise of a small hill heard different and powerful engines, stunned to see two dueling riders on road racing motorcycles. Karen was instantly livid and perhaps a bit frightened at the possibility that her Sondra could fall and get seriously injured. Doug felt a twinge of this as well but was filled with an equal amount of pride and excitement at what they were witnessing. After watching the action for a few minutes Karen stormed back to the house while Doug engaged Rob in conversation, gathering information and watching the last bit of on-track action. He was cordial to both young men as they each packed up their gear and loaded their bikes. Doug then observed in concerned silence as Sondra and Rob proceeded with the business transaction.

When Rob and Eddie headed out of sight Doug turned to watch Sondra wipe down her new motorcycle with a micro-fiber towel and a can of polish she'd obtained from a cabinet drawer. "Pure fun and games on the dirt track" announced Sondra, trying to deflect focus away from the new purchase. "And when we drove the karts Rob was an appreciative and attentive student. I think I taught him some good stuff. Eddie's got a true racing killer instinct and we had some really great battles but he has a lot to learn and he's a total stubborn macho-head when it comes to any racing knowledge I had to offer. Reminded me of some of the guys I drove against in sprint-car and F-Ford. He's definitely better on two wheels than four. The whole day was nonstop fun and they managed to eat that entire bag of chips. I mean that was a big bag."

"Sondra" said Doug in a low deadly serious voice. She shook her head and kept her eyes fixed on the task at hand. Doug moved closer and knelt down next to his daughter. She worked in silence for just over a minute then crouched down to wipe the lower parts of the bike, briefly looking over at her now-dad.

"You don't understand what this is. What this means" she told him through gritted teeth and a fierceness in her eyes.

"Try me" ordered Doug, matching her fierceness. She stood and walked over to lean her back against the back shop bench, staring at her newly acquired mechanical friend.

"I'd never want to hurt your feelings" she began. "But this brings my dad back to me. He loved riding and riding fast and we both loved road racing. We talked about it. We read about it and we went to races." Doug took a deep breath. He walked over and put his arm around Sondra and together they eyed the two-wheeled machine as if they were watching a television program.

"Okay" he spoke in a forced whisper. "I can understand that, but Sondra this isn't a toy and this isn't just fun and games. And you did this without any kind of discussion with me and Karen."

"Karen and me" corrected Sondra regarding his grammar. "Don't get smart" scolded Doug. "We're a family. We talk to each other. There are rules we live by and our actions have consequences. I know you're not six but Karen and I cut you all sorts of slack. We let you get away with things most parents would never let their kid get away with."

Sondra stood up straight in sudden anger. She clenched her teeth and wondered what slack she was ever afforded. "This is an incredibly expensive purchase" continued Doug. "And I shouldn't have to remind you that you're an IndyCar driver under contract. If you were to fall and get hurt it could end your career and financially wipe us out. We're all in this together, the three of us. Damn it, Sondra. What the hell were you thinking, and what's your end-game here with this thing anyway?"

Sondra fumed and raged in silence, wanting desperately to get back on the motorcycle and blast away from what she perceived was an unjust scolding. It's my life and my money she bitterly screamed in her head. She looked up at her now-dad after hearing him take another loud deep breath and continue to talk. "I do want you to have everything in life that makes you happy" he told the girl. "And if this brings you even a fractional amount of peace, I'm all for that. But you're so incredibly precious to me. It's my job to keep you as safe as possible. So with that in mind, there are gonna be some rules here."

"Like what?" inquired Sondra, suddenly elated that she was getting away with this.

Well" began Doug. "You're gonna buy a pro race suit with all the kevlar and padding. Gloves, boots and helmet, too. And you know how in scuba diving they say to always swim with a buddy? You're always going to be swimming with a buddy. You hear me? Not one leg over that motorcycle without a riding partner or someone around. Are we clear?"

Sondra nodded.

"No" said Doug. "Are-we-clear?" he reiterated.

"Crystal clear" asserted the girl.

"So I can keep it?" she inquired. He gave a nod but then spoke of the third member of the Trent tribe. "You were already in Karen's dog-house when she noticed that you didn't clean up the kitchen from this morning, like she asked you to do. I don't think I even need to tell you how she feels about this." He then gestured with his head over toward the small kitchen area of the shop. "Wash your hands and comb your hair, then go in and talk with Mom" he told the girl.

I will in just a bit" defied Sondra.

"Now" ordered the dad, with a force behind his voice that let Sondra know she was in the doghouse with him as well.

Sondra found her now-mom in the living room sitting in her favorite chair and reading the newspaper. To Sondra this scenario felt quite similar to the hat at the table incident some time ago. She stood for a few seconds before speaking. "So you're mad?" asked Sondra. Karen didn't react. "I can get out of the deal if I have to" offered Sondra. Karen grasped the edges of the paper a bit tighter and lowered the pages a few inches. "I'm not mad" she claimed as she stared at her daughter. "Now go clean up for dinner" she ordered. A sudden shudder of fear sliced through Sondra. There was no aroma of a pending meal coming from the kitchen and Karen's voice had a harshness to it, with a distinct tone of displeasure and disappointment. Also missing was the use any of the pet names she usually had for her, like sweetie, baby or angel.

"You're mad" said a dejected Sondra as she turned and headed to her room. Sondra emerged from a shower just under 20 minutes later wearing a relatively new green T-shirt and faded bluejeans. A thick black towel was wrapped around her wet head and she found her mom sitting on the tile floor with her back against the hallway wall, two feet from the bathroom door. Sondra slid down next to her, noticing the coldness from the wall's plaster against her back.

"I think maybe I am mad, Sondra" said Karen. "Buying a new motorcycle like you did was such a selfish and childish stunt. It's like sometimes you're nineteen going on four, and next month you're gonna be twenty. I'm sure the cost of that thing was astronomical but more importantly, it's just so damn dangerous. What you do for a living is already dangerous enough but this? A full-on racing motorcycle?" Karen slapped her own right leg, emphasizing her point. She stood. "And I'm disappointed that you didn't talk with me or Doug about this first" she added with a shake of her head. "We're gonna talk more, a lot more" announced the mom. "But I'm hungry and I don't feel like cooking. Go change into the clothes I put out on your bed, and when we get back from dinner you're gonna do those dishes and clean up the kitchen like it's never been cleaned before. And I'm thinking a three-month suspension of your purchasing privileges for anything more than a pack of gum sounds about right. Now go change and be quick about it." Sondra knew better than to argue or make any kind of comment about the situation. She also knew that Karen was only half serious about the financial freeze.

Both Karen and Doug were fully committed to being the best parents to Sondra possible. In theory they would give the girl anything and everything she wanted, however simply letting her say and do anything she felt like wasn't good parenting and it wasn't what was ultimately best for her. A family discussion on Sondra's behavior and maturity began in the living room before going to dinner and continued until they arrived at their current favorite dining spot, Lito's Mexican Restaurant. Sondra was several bites into her large steak and shrimp burrito when Karen's phone began to light up and buzz. She normally never allowed electronics at the dinner table but had been expecting a call from a woman at a clothing manufacturer, hoping to make a deal with them for cross-promotional items: T-shirts, sweatshirts and backpacks that would be advertising for both Safen-Up and for Sondra, the IndyCar driver. The call however did not turn out to be from Shunter Enterprises. "Well hello, Brice" greeted Karen, looking over at a surprised Sondra. The conversation Karen had with young Crandle was relatively short. After putting the phone back in her purse she shook her head as she stared at her daughter. "Sondra, use your fork not your fingers" she scolded before explaining the phone call. "So that was Brice" she began. "He's left you several voice-mail messages. Apparently you turned your phone off."

"Oh" said Sondra. "I ran it out of battery. It's on the charger. I'll call him back when we get home."

"Well that's fine" said the mom. "But he wanted you to know that he arrived in California late last night and is staying with Andrew and Stephanie for a few days before going to visit his folks. They were thinking of driving up the coast, and as you just heard I invited them to stay here."

"I'm glad" said Sondra, nodding with a quick smile. "I think you guys are gonna like getting to know Andrew and Stephanie better" she added. "They're awesome and I can finally show Brice and Andrew my kart and motocross tracks. So" she sheepishly began a new thought, "does this mean I'm not in major trouble anymore?" She had intentionally not mentioned the new Yamaha and held her silence as she listened to her parents have a mostly positive discussion on their pending company, never mentioning their daughter's behavior or possible further consequences for her earlier actions.

CHAPTER 34

On a mostly clear early morning with moderate temperatures, Doug took the Tacoma and headed to Fresno for breakfast and a bit of catching up with Dan Stoltz. Karen made poached eggs on toast for breakfast with Sondra and they discussed a significant grocery shopping session in preparation for their guests Brice, Andrew and Stephanie, who were to arrive that late afternoon. "I don't know why but I feel way more nervous about this than before any of the races I've ever been in" confessed Sondra. "My stomach's in knots."

"Nervous?" inquired the mom. "Because of Brice?" she furthered.

Sondra shrugged and stabbed a piece of egg with her fork. "Well I haven't seen him in like a thousand years" she exaggerated. "I mean okay, it was just last week and we text and email but it's not the same. We'll be hanging out in person, at our house." Scattered throughout a forty-three-minute shopping spree Karen did her best to reassure Sondra, telling the girl that she worries too much. Later, after putting away the food and supplies at home Karen encouraged Sondra to go down and engage in some motorized distraction in order to alleviate some of the nervous energy. "Not the road bike" she warned. "If I hear one sound out of that engine you'll be in so much trouble."

Doug got home just over an hour before the guests were to arrive.

He and Karen graciously greeted Andrew, Stephanie and Brice at the front door. "Cool architecture" offered Andrew. Doug and Karen began a tour of the interior with Brice bringing up the rear and looking for Sondra in every corner of every room they entered. When the small group made their way back into the kitchen after spending several minutes in the den looking at the many photographs and trophies, Brice slipped out the sliding glass door and found his way to Sondra. Though both Doug and Karen did notice the sudden absence of the young man neither outwardly reacted to it, Andrew and Stephanie were an energetic and captivating couple who dominated their attention.

Brice was a bit taken aback by what he was seeing of the house and property. Sondra had described it all to him in varying detail from time to time but he found it to be far more impressive in person. Reaching the tan metal structure of Sierre-Trent Raceway he stepped inside and looked all around the spotlessly clean and well-stocked shop, noticing a flickering blue hue and hearing the unmistakable sounds of a person welding. When it stopped he cautiously stepped around a wall of the welding booth. Sondra had earlier gone on a 23-minute dirt bike ride as Karen had suggested, but while anxiously awaiting Brice's arrival she delved into a fabrication project she and Doug had discussed numerous times. With a wire-welder she was tacking together angle-iron pieces that would make up the framing for a mobile mechanic's workstation for the karts. After one of a dozen small welds she became aware of an audience and flipped up the protective eye shield, looking over her shoulder. "Hey there, Rosie the Riveter" greeted Brice. "Wendell's dad used to put quarter-inch thick gussets in the corners for strength when we were into karting years ago" he offered. "That way you don't have any bracing bars or side walls to get in the way when you're trying to work in a hurry."

Sondra tossed the welding hood and torch on the bench and shucked out of Doug's old heavy leather welding jacket, clearly sizes too big for her. She moved quickly to wrap her arms around the boy for a tight embrace. It wasn't necessarily a romantic hug or gesture, more a meeting of souls and a reunion of their chosen closeness.

"Did you just kiss my hair?" she queried, pulling away a few inches with narrowed eyes.

"No" denied Brice. "I wouldn't do that. That would just be ..."

"Weird and creepy?" she interrupted.

"Well I think it's more like sweet and endearing" countered Brice with a smile and a shake of his head. She flung her arms back around him. "Kay" she whispered. "We'll go with your thing." He desperately wanted to kiss her on the lips but she broke free and slugged his shoulder. He knew this was a likely scenario and gave a toothy grin, taking in her disheveled but alluring look. Though the punch she'd just given him didn't hurt he put his hand over the affected shoulder. "Ouch" he voiced. "I'll never play the violin again."

"Idiot" said Sondra, grinning and shaking her head. She proceeded to show off her shop machinery as well as the four shifter-karts and the two motocross bikes, then bragged about the shop's full bathroom and the space-saving kitchenette.

The F-Ford and the new road bike were both under tarps and Sondra deliberately skipped over these, instead taking Brice by the hand and leading him outside to point out her race tracks. "We're gonna have some fun on these" she claimed.

"This is pretty damn impressive" marveled Brice. "I didn't know you were makin' this kind of money." Sondra was instantly incensed. She hated having her life reduced to money and it took considerable effort on her part not give in to her sudden resentment of his reaction to her world. Instead she led him back inside, pulling a portion of tarp from her Formula Ford. "A ton of hard work's gone into restoring this baby" she announced. Brice carefully pulled the remaining heavy fabric from the race car and haphazardly folded it into a makeshift square. He then set the material on a nearby stool and walked all around the vehicle closely examining every detail. When he came back around he stood next to Sondra. "This is really nice and I'm sorry about the money crack. I didn't mean ..." Sondra shook her head and walked over to the refrigerator to retrieve two cans of 7-Up. Returning, she found Brice settling into the cockpit of her old race car.

"Andrew's gonna flip when he sees this" he said. Sondra set the soda cans on a nearby stool and knelt by Brice and her car as if she were a pit crew member getting ready to attend to a driver before a race or practice.

"You guys came at the right time" she offered. "I've had it running for a little while now and before IndyCar season started I installed all new brakes and a stiffer rear roll-bar, like I used to have. I don't know who changed it to the softer one, or why. Idiots. I'll let you guys drive it if you help me dial in a better set-up." Brice nodded as he glanced down and wrapped his hand around the well-worn gearshift knob. His eyes came back up to study Sondra's face. In this moment she looked younger to him than when he'd seen her last. She wore no makeup, as was typical with her, but was wearing a faded yellow Pennzoil T-shirt with smudges of dirt, grease and who knew what else. Her hair, typically hidden under a baseball cap when at the racetrack, was pulled back into a loose messy ponytail. Most of the women Brice had typically been around within the past year were all extremely well made up and dressed like supermodels, with attitudes to boot. Sondra on the other hand had a natural beauty, though Karen and the many women Sondra came into regular contact with did their best to encourage any number of embellishments.

"Had a couple of days of intense talks with Patrero and Valderez," Brice announced. "In October, Hugo's gonna put Kenneth Overton in my Indy car to be Andrew's teammate and send me and Adrian over to Europe."

"Adrian and me," corrected Sondra. Brice ignored the grammar correction. "The F-Two thing is actually coming together pretty fast" he continued. "I'll first be doing mostly testing and learning the ropes but Hugo said to be patient. With Adrian to run the new team I'll be in the number Sixty-four car full-time next season."

"Wow" said Sondra, loving the excitement of Brice going to Europe and driving those Formula Two cars but feeling a crushing sensation at the idea that Brice was leaving her. Brice extracted himself from the F-Ford car and took several sips of soda. He and Sondra settled on the couch facing the paved track and the scenery beyond.

"So you and Raley seem to be sluggin' it out in points so far this year" said Brice of the championship battle going on between the front-runners Greg Raley and Sondra Sierre.

"Well I mean I'm only three points ahead of Greg, and slugging?" questioned Sondra. "Not sure I really care for that word" she added. Sondra was still being plagued with the word slugger in association with last year's incident in Arizona with Gary Slesinger.

"Oh sorry" said Brice, smiling. "You haven't actually slugged anyone this year."

"Yet" said Sondra, shaking her fist at the boy. Brice smiled even wider.

"Well it looks like Slesinger is basically getting his hat handed to him in Nascar so far this year" he offered Sondra. She nodded and made a quick attempt to straighten her ponytail. Brice took a deep breath and appreciated where he was and with whom. "I'm way too far behind in points to make that up and even have a shot at the championship" he told her. "But I'm goin' for as many wins as I can so I can at least finish my year up strong."

Sondra nodded, figuring that if his strategy worked out he would have good momentum to move forward in his F-2 efforts. She didn't want to think that far ahead however and altered the subject. "There's way more pressure on me to perform than in my first season" she admitted. "And things just seem so hit and miss. It's like sometimes we get things right and other times we're just hanging on with any kind of luck that we don't screw up, that I don't screw up. I mean having Ryan as my driver coach is good because he has so much experience but ..."

"Well you always put an insane amount of pressure on yourself" suggested Brice. "But you have an uncanny knack of managing to put things together and get the results."

Sondra flashed a quick smile. "The weird thing is" she told him, "the harder I have to fight for those results, the more respect T.J. seems to have for me. I mean he's as tough as an old Army boot and it doesn't take much to tick him off, but then there are little moments here and there when it really seems like he's family."

"I'm glad" said Brice, feeling surprised and lucky that Sondra was being so open. "You know" he offered, deciding to move away from the subject of their IndyCar season. "This place is really an amazing off-time retreat."

"Well this isn't all from racing" asserted Sondra, recalling Brice's earlier reference to how much money he now thought she was making. "The three of us, Doug, Karen and I, went in equal shares. My share came from settlement money for what that drunken bastard took from me." She pounded her fist on her leg. "Blood money" she growled through gritted teeth.

"Sorry" said Brice. He was afraid Sondra would do as she'd always done when mention of her past had occurred, wall herself off in a bitter angry silent mood. He'd been loving these past months of getting closer to her and hearing her open up about her inner thoughts and didn't want this to just simply end. "I know that none of this can ever replace or compensate for the family you lost" he told her in an attempt to be of comfort."

"I wish I had a magic wand to bring them back but you do have Doug and Karen and they clearly love you big-time. I'm sure your folks would want you to be loved and safe. Maybe in time you can see this place more like a gift from them and not just something you got with blood-money. Maybe in a way you can see them as part of this." Sondra slowly scanned the horizon, her eyes coming around to rest on the boy's face, that clean-shaven cute as hell face. She punched his shoulder.

"Hey" he said in a coughing laugh. "What the hell was that for?"

"You deserved it" she told him with a smirk. "You're here five minutes and you start some big heavy conversation. What, giving up racing for psychiatry?"

"Shut up" he laughed. "Worst patient ever."

Sondra showed Brice her latest motorized acquisition, the Yamaha YZF-R1. "Holly crap, Sondra" exclaimed the boy, throwing a leg over and grabbing the grips on the handlebars as he examined his limited view of the race bike. "You did it" he cheered, remembering her mentioning several times that she wanted to get a road bike. "Man, look at this thing" he marveled. "Almost as gorgeous as you."

"Stop that" ordered Sondra, swatting at his upper arm and losing the battle of trying not to smile. "You'll learn the track on one of the karts" she deflected, "and then you're gonna love this thing. The torque in every gear is unbelievable. I mean you can pull a ninety mile an hour, fifth-gear wheelie, no problem. And the electronics and suspension technology aren't even from this universe. You can dial in anything you need."

Now, thought Brice, the time was right. He reached over and brought her close with his right arm then kissed her. They melted into each other, their passion growing by leaps and bounds. Before things got too carried away a doorbell chime rang out and they reluctantly parted. "I guess we're being summoned to the house"said Sondra.

After enjoying the lemon-chicken dinner followed by a dessert of purple plum crunch, where Sondra boasted that this was one of Karen's famous meals, it didn't take much for Sondra to convince Andrew and Brice to head down to Sierre-Trent Raceway. "No way" exclaimed Andrew when he spotted Sondra's F-Ford. "So awesome that you have your old car. Wonder if mine is still out there somewhere" he pondered out loud, walking around the room and examining the metal-working machinery, the karts and road bike. As the sun was beginning to set, the three walked the kart track reminiscing about their race beginnings.

Andrew and Stephanie were given the guest bedroom for their short stay at Casa de Trent while Brice was relegated to the foldout sofabed in the den. Before going to sleep Sondra went in to say goodnight to him. The two sat side by side at the foot of the bed. "Moving here wasn't an easy decision for me" she told Brice. "As you know, IndyCar isn't cheap. It's gonna take an insane amount of money and a huge effort for me to break into F-One and be taken seriously."

Brice nodded before responding. "Well" he began, "winning at Indy and what you're doing now is gonna go a long way to get you there. And this place gives you important solid roots" he added.

"But you're gonna go away from yours" she countered.

"In a way, I guess" he agreed. "But I see it as finally finding my wings. I mean I don't want to be a disrespectful jerk, going thousands of miles away from my parents and the farm but as Stephanie put it the other day when she and Andrew picked me up from the airport, it's important that I have my own autonomy. I know the path I'm on is right, even on the days that seem crappy. It's a mental struggle though to think of leaving IndyCar when I've only been in it such a short time, and it's killing me to even think of being so far away from you. But we can make it work. I know we can. You'll be here doing your thing and I'll be there doing mine and we'll see each other every chance we get. I can't pass this F-Two opportunity up because it's everything I've always dreamed of. The cars, the tracks, the food and the languages around the world. I want that and you, the girl of my dreams."

"All right, lets not get mushy" said Sondra with an embarrassed smirk. "But yeah, same for me" she added, standing before giving Brice a kiss goodnight on the cheek.

Karen made sure to be the first one up the next morning, her thoughts on starting the coffee and what the group would eat for breakfast when she entered the kitchen. She was surprised to find a light on and Brice, glass of water in hand, studying the photos on the wall of young Sondra and her family.

"Morning, Brice" she greeted.

"Morning Mrs. Trent" he returned. "These photographs are amazing" he said, turning back to the images. "When I drove against Sondra in the F-Fords and when we were teammates I came to find out just how determined she can be, so precise and incredibly instinctive and brutal-fierce both on and off the track. I sometimes wondered if things were different and she hadn't lost her family, would she still be like that. Now that I'm seeing the pictures of her and her family here I can totally see the intensity and the strength she's obviously always had. You can really see something special about her, about this family."

"Special family, special girl, Brice" said Karen. She patted his shoulder and headed to the refrigerator. Brice sat down on one of the kitchen chairs and watched Karen begin the morning brew. She set a ceramic container of cream and a matching bowl of sugar on the table then sat across from the boy, her intense eyes grabbing his full attention. “Sondra’s the most precious thing in the world to Doug and me” she told him. “The most precious” she added, meaning this as a reminder for him never to say or do anything to hurt their daughter in any way. Karen’s message hit Brice as if he’d been yelled at and forcibly shaken.

He nodded, carefully choosing his next words. “The more I get to know her, the more special she becomes to me. I hate that she’s had to go through so much. I can’t even really imagine what it would be like to lose my whole family. It almost doesn’t seem possible that that family is no longer around” he said, pointing to the Sierre images. “And it sucks that she and I are soon gonna be so far apart.” He then went into detail of his future with the Patrero F-Two team. “In a weird way though” he added of the time and distance he and Sondra were to endure, “we’ll both be doing things that we love. We’ll keep close, I’m sure of it. We haven’t ever really talked about this but I have no interest in anyone else. She’s amazing.”

Karen’s smile was slow in coming. She eyed the boy and let his words settle into her consciousness. She then reached across the table and briefly held his hand. After getting up to pour two cups of coffee, Andrew and Stephanie came through the kitchen door, followed shortly by Sondra and Doug.

At the conclusion of a fun breakfast in a popular downtown eatery the group split up, with Doug and Karen acting as tour guides of the many Santa Barbara sites and shops. Sondra drove Brice in her Tacoma on a bit of site-seeing tour as well. As they headed in the direction of Goleta State Beach, she pointed out several places of interest, emphasizing one in particular. “My friend Kari goes to UC Santa Barbara and lives in one of the apartments over there. You remember her, don’t you? She was at the Queen Mary when we were at Long Beach.”

“Yeah, I remember. You’d mentioned her before, from when you lived in Bakersfield. Wild Kari” said Brice.

Sondra coughed a laugh. “Well I don’t call her that anymore” she told him.

Once at their intended destination they got out and walked hand in hand a few hundred feet on the sandy beach, near but never too close to the surging water. Beginning their loop back they stopped to read in silence words on a brass plaque anchored into a large concrete and rock monument. When Sondra began to walk on, Brice pulled her back toward him, executing a gentle kiss and then positioning her against the structure's cool rough surface. The kiss they shared went from soft and tender to intense, with Brice's hands becoming active and bold. The amorous couple reluctantly pulled apart becoming aware of an approaching loud-talking group. Sondra thought she detected a sheepish grin on Brice's face as they walked hand in hand toward the Tacoma.

"I have some stuff to pick up before we head home" she informed him.

Approaching the Yamaha dealership Sondra scanned the parking lot for Eddie's jeep, relieved that the black Wrangler was nowhere to be seen. While inside, she and Brice were given a bit of celebrity status, Sondra the Indy 500 winner and Brice a fellow IndyCar driver rumored to break into Formula 2. After answering questions, signing a few autographs and loading boxes of motor oil and kart tires in the pickup bed, they headed back to Casa de Trent. Brice reached over to the tuning knob on the radio, switching from an NPR program to a country-rock station. Sondra glanced over at her passenger, mildly perturbed at the boy's boldness. She briefly wondered why this provoked more of a reaction from within her than his initiating the earlier public make-out session. Her eyes and concentration soon however went back to the road ahead. Now with a good solid load on the back tires giving the pickup more stability and balance, she accelerated and began to drive as if she were in a sports car.

"So they all seem pretty nice" said Brice of the employees he'd just met at the bike shop. You had a couple of guys over" he inquired? "And it was one of those guys who sold you the R-One? Eddie Grisban?"

Sondra shrugged her right shoulder, not taking her eyes off the increasingly hilly, twisty road. "Yeah, they're all pretty nice in there" she answered, hoping to dissuade Brice from asking further questions, especially about Eddie. Brice didn't like Sondra's non-answer.

"So you and this Eddie guy ride together?" he asked.

"Once" she corrected. "Rob, one of the guys you just met, he and Eddie came out for a few hours" she informed Brice. "We rode dirt-bikes and took some laps on the kart track. Eddie brought out a couple of the road bikes. One was his and he brought another along just basically for show. I rode it, I liked it, I bought it. No big deal. I mean mom was really pissed when she saw it. So was dad but not quite as much."

"Sounds like you're pretty good friends with Eddie" prompted Brice.

"I'm friends with a lot of people" countered Sondra, a sudden annoyed edge to her voice. "Grisban's now officially in the Superbike Moto-America Series" she informed Brice, who was possibly teetering on precipice of jealousy. Sondra drove along mentally renewing her conviction that she'd always despised this affliction in others. During the Indy Lights season as teammates he had told her about his relationship with Jillian and her ultra-jealously. He once mentioned witnessing an ugly discourse between one of his pit crew members and the man's girlfriend, to which Sondra had simply stated, "I don't do jealousy." Sondra added to the Eddie discussion. "Doin' pretty well. You should check out some Moto-America races and Eddie's website."

Brice was not a dense person. He picked up on Sondra's pointed vocal inflection, and with his own experiences of what jealousy could do to a relationship he knew better than to push further with the Eddie Grisban examination. He was also quite sure of Sondra. She wasn't the lying, cheating, manipulative type. "I know a few guys that follow Superbike and Moto GP pretty intensely" he told Sondra, easing away from any further discourse of Eddie. During the remainder of the drive home they slipped into chatting about road racing and many different European racetracks.

Upon arrival at Casa de Trent Sondra wasn't too surprised to find that the others hadn't yet returned, knowing Karen's penchant for shopping. Sondra pulled into her usual garage stall and proceeded to show Brice her gym. A soft romantic round of necking preceded the two of them sitting on a padded bench and lifting 30-pound free weights. Sondra set her weights on the bench next to her and walked over to the poster of Moto GP star Valentino Rossi, given to her by Doug the previous Christmas. Brice drank in the vision of Sondra, the girl looking at him with those sparkling hazel-green eyes and leaning her back against the wall next to the enlarged image. "I don't have the faintest interest in Eddie Grisban or any other guy, if that's what you were getting at earlier" announced Sondra.

"I know that" said Brice. "And I'm sorry for being weird about it." She nodded and returned to the bench.

Upon Andrew's return the three racers spent time on the dirt-bikes and ATV, then Brice and Andrew took turns in Sondra's Formula Ford. Eight laps into Placer's time in the car Brice waited until their friend was nearing the furthest point on the track to begin a conversation. "Sort of seemed like a nerve was struck with you this morning at breakfast, when Andrew and Stephanie talked about their plans for marriage and kids."

Sondra shrugged, her eyes intently trained on her car. "Andrew's been such an awesome friend" continued Brice. "Since the day we first met. He's so generous, and not just with money. He's done so many amazing things in his life so far. He's raced everything from sailboats to Indy cars and he fits in with the whole business world just as easily. I mean I don't want to sound like a total geek or anything but he really inspires me, and now I'm determined to be more than just a wheat farmer or an also-ran in my driving career. I want this so much more now than I ever did before I met him, and I think it's so awesome that he and Steph are gonna get married and start a family."

Sondra didn't like talking about kids or family and doing so with Brice felt particularly uncomfortable. "Turn nine is really tricky if you don't nail the apex" she told him, hoping to change the subject. "Really easy to lose the back end because it's one of the flattest sections on the track."

Brice got the message loud and clear of Sondra's uneasiness to discuss marriage and children, and it gave him a pang of wonder and worry. He waited for Andrew to blow past them before he continued. “Adrian’s wife is about to have their fourth child, so he might not be around much when the new F-Two team first gets going.” Sondra shrugged and gave a slight so-what gesture with her head as Andrew again approached, the engine whining and then taking furious bites as he sped past. Brice pressed Sondra further. “So you disapprove? Or you just don’t care” he demanded to know. Sondra glanced over at the boy, a sudden annoyed fierceness in her eyes. “Well good for Valderez and his wife” she announced, a definite edge to her voice. “If that’s what they want” she added. “Sure as hell not what I want. I mean it’s different for guys. When I retire from racing I’ll be looking back on a big string of major race wins and championships. No way am I screwin’ that up just because a guy wants me to shoot out a bunch of kids.” Her eyes searched for her car and then came back to a clearly stunned and possibly hurt expression on Brice’s face. Sondra really didn’t feel this harshly about children and wished she hadn’t expressed herself in such a blunt manner. She’d heard the expression, shoot out a bunch of kids, from a male comedian on a TV show and had thought it was a funny-tough thing to say. As she watched Andrew attack Turn 4 she opted for a bit more of a charitable tact with Brice. “I don’t know Adrian all that well and I’ve never really seen him around his kids. I do know Andrew though and I’m sure he’ll make a great dad. I mean Stephanie and Adrian’s wife aren’t race car drivers but ...”

“Well” countered Brice. “Loraine was racing mini-Coopers when she and Adrian met.”

“Wow, that’s cool” said Sondra. “I didn’t know that.”

Brice shrugged his right shoulder and elected to move away from this particular touchy topic.

Roughly 40 minutes later Doug walked down to watch Sondra and her friends race around on the karts, alarmed at the sight. Brice made an abrupt cut in front of Andrew from the outside as they entered Turn 6, running wide in the next corner and dipping the left rear tire in the dirt, creating a wisp of a dust storm. The focused duel between the young men slowed them down just enough for Sondra to attack from behind. She seized her opportunity and dive-bombed to the inside of Andrew, swooping past her competitors but then having to run wide in Turn 8. She lost momentum and the boys freight-trained her in the straight before the next corner. Sondra rallied however, chopping in front of Brice going into Turn 1, then blowing past Andrew before the apex of the second turn. This further escalated the situation. They each took advantage of perceived openings to bully their way into seemingly impossible situations, moving each other over and out of the way with their bumpers and engaging in an all-out savage war of wheels, until Doug put a stop to it. He retrieved and waved the checkered flag that was given to Sondra after she'd won her last amateur midget sprint-car race several years ago. Doug watched the kids make their way back into the shop, laughing in hysterics. "Oh man" said Andrew, holding his side, trying to calm himself. "I haven't had that much fun in a long time." Brice and Sondra agreed but all that came from them was panting and continued laughter. After handing out small bottles of water and pushing the karts to their usual space, Sondra attempted an apology to Doug. "Sorry, Dad. I mean that probably looked way worse than it actually was" she added in defense. After the boys apologized as well, Doug spoke in a calm voice. "I'm not really mad" he told them. "And you're probably right about how it looked from a spectator point of view, but you guys each have a lot on the line this season. You should know better than this, to play that hard and risk possibly getting hurt." Sondra looked away and rolled her eyes, contemplating a more vigorous defense. She quickly decided against it.

After a fun and energetic dinner, Sondra went out to turn on the pool lights, inviting Brice to join her. The two soon sat together on a redwood bench, drenched in the water's shimmering glow. The coastal fog was light and the air temperature was 72 degrees, unusual for 7:28 p.m. "I'm so glad you could be here" said Sondra in a quiet voice. "Your visit couldn't have come at a better time" she furthered.

Brice nodded. "For me, too" he told her. "I'm glad I finally get to see where and how you live."

The two sat in momentary silence, shoulder-to-shoulder, their hands and fingers playing and dancing together. "I really want to kiss you and make out with you" whispered Brice. "But I swear I can feel everyone's eyes drilling into the back of my head."

"Funny" said Sondra, nodding once. "I was just thinking the same thing. I was imagining Doug, Karen, Andrew and Stephanie with their arms folded staring at us from the kitchen window." Sondra looked over at Brice and together they turned quickly toward the house, finding no one at the window. She leaned an inch toward Brice and her eyes closed as the two shared an inspired round of kissing. Later that night, Sondra's sleep was intermittent and fitful. She worried that she and Brice had not talked enough about important things or that something she had said might have somehow damaged a future with him. She then fretted over her professional vocation. She wanted so badly to go to Europe and pursue a Formula One career but loved IndyCar and being a part of T.J. Holt's team, wanting an IndyCar championship with every fiber of her being. Her thoughts and concerns soon drifted to whether or not she was being a good daughter for Doug and Karen.

Andrew, Stephanie and Brice needed to get on the road early the next morning and after heartfelt goodbyes Karen was convinced she could literally feel Sondra's pain and anxiety over the perceived loss. "Help me with the breakfast dishes?" she asked the girl. Sondra said nothing as she followed Karen into the kitchen. "I think that went rather well" announced the mom. "Thank you for sharing your friends with us. I really enjoyed getting to know Stephanie." Karen began rinsing off dishes in the sink and continued speaking of her new-found young friend, Stephanie. "She's incredibly mature for her age. We practically talked nonstop the entire time she was here." Sondra smiled and nodded, bringing over several bowls and a handful of silverware from the table.

Doug was summoned to the Holt Racing headquarters in Texas to work with the pit crew ahead of the next important races. Karen dropped him off at the airport, coming back to a mountain of office work while Sondra spent most of the day down at her race garage. That night, before going to sleep, Karen sat in bed reading a biography about the 16th US president, Abraham Lincoln. She received a phone call from Doug, which lasted just over ten minutes, then returned to her book. Though 40 minutes earlier she and Sondra had said their goodnights, the mom wasn't too surprised to see her daughter appear in the bedroom doorway. Karen slipped the heavy literary volume onto the bedside table and pulled open the portion of blankets and sheets beside her. Sondra scrambled childlike onto the bed and maneuvered herself under the covers. "You silly goose" said Karen with a quick chuckle. "Been a long day" she added. "Lets get some sleep. Night, Angel."

Roughly eight minutes after mother and daughter had settled in for the evening's slumber Sondra repositioned herself. "Mom?" she asked in a quiet tentative voice. "Hm?" responded Karen. She was facing away from Sondra and remained in place, hoping the girl would expel one quick thought and go to sleep.

A full minute elapsed before Sondra's voice again filled the room. "How old were you when you first had sex?" Karen's eyes exploded open and her scramble to sit up was less than graceful. "I, uh. Um. Wow" struggled the mom. "Are, are you and Brice having sex?" she finally managed to ask.

"No" said Sondra in a close-to-angry indignant tone. "You once told me I could come to you with this stuff" reminded the girl. "That's okay" she said in a near-whisper. "Never mind. I mean I don't really care. Night."

Karen sat stunned, trying to wrap her head around what had just transpired. She looked down at Sondra. The girl had turned over and was now facing away from her. "You're right, Sondra" she told her daughter. "I did tell you that, and I meant it." Sondra remained silent and motionless. "So let's talk" said Karen. "Come on. Sit up. Talk to me" she insisted, putting a hand on Sondra's shoulder and lightly shaking the girl. Sondra slowly and reluctantly turned over and sat up, repositioning the pillow behind her. "Wow" expelled Karen, coming to grips with the fact that they were about to have this heavy conversation. "Okay" she began. "Well, um. I was seventeen. A junior in high school. We'd just come back from the Easter break and there was a transfer student from Austin, Texas. Todd. He was in most of my classes. Tall, broad shoulders and blondish-brown thick hair, and had a Southern drawl. Very thick Texan accent. He was pretty much instantly popular with most girls on looks alone but he also had one of those outgoing electric personalities. Shot him to fame with practically the entire school. Didn't hurt that he became a star on the baseball team either. It seemed like everyone, especially the girls, fell all over themselves for him, not just me."

"Oh jeeze" groaned Sondra with a roll of her eyes and a shake of her head.

"At the time" continued Karen, ignoring her daughter's reaction. "I was in this social group. We weren't cheerleaders or like the super popular class royalty but we were a fun small clique and we had our own sizable followers."

Sondra again rolled her eyes and shook her head. "Sounds stupid" she asserted. "I probably would have hated and avoided you all" she told her now-mom.

"Oh I don't know" said Karen, not willing to concede. "It's not like we were snobby mean girls. In fact we were sometimes nicknamed The Debbie Do-Gooders." Karen let out a quick chuckle and shook her head. "We were actually proud of that moniker. We did a lot of good things, like organizing blood drives, food donations for the needy, raising awareness for social injustices, and some fun little events, too. After a while though it got to be a bit of a bore and took up too much of my time. And I got to where I really hated being referred to as a Debbie Do-Gooder. Anyway ..." Karen shrugged her right shoulder and took a deep breath before proceeding. "This one day, I was at my locker and I dropped a couple of my books as I was trying to get that stupid stubborn door to open. Todd rushed to my aid. Got the door open with such ease and he picked up my books, all with this amazing smile and what I thought was the most witty banter. I on the other hand was in such a daze that he would even give me the time of day that I'm sure I sounded like a complete idiot, but it was so thrilling when he suggested we hang out some time." Karen shifted her position a bit and laughed to herself. "Let me tell you, that thrill turned to absolute torture for a whole week before he actually asked me to a movie. And wow, talk about some really catty jealously from a number of girls when they found out."

"I'd have kicked their asses" said Sondra.

Karen glanced over at the girl but chose to ignore the comment. "So what movie'd you see?" Sondra asked, leaning forward to straighten a wrinkle in the bedspread near her right knee. "We didn't" said Karen, shaking her head. "We went to Marty's, this gas station that had a big concession stand. It was thee popular high school hangout spot, where you could eat and socialize. They had a pretty good varied menu, as I recall."

So the place was kinda like Grif's Grill, in Bakersfield?" inquired Sondra.

"Well yeah, I suppose it was like that" nodded the mom. Karen had never actually been to Grif's Grill but she'd heard Doug and Sondra speak of it a number of times. "Todd bought me a Pepsi" recalled Karen. "And we sat at one of the picnic tables with a bunch of others while we were waiting for our food. Not exactly the romantic date I was hoping for but I didn't mind too much. After all, I was out with the prettiest boy in town."

"Oh jeeze" groaned Sondra with a roll of her eyes. Karen flashed a smile before continuing. "We didn't actually stay too long. After we got our burgers and things we headed out to a field on someone's farm a ways out of town. There was this huge bonfire and about thirty kids. Plenty of beer, cowboy hats and baseball caps on pretty much every head, and pickup trucks blaring country-rock."

Sondra sported a furrowed brow while she shook her head in unfavored judgment. "Hard to imagine you out in a field, drinking beer with a bunch of red-necks" she told her now-mom. "Well" Karen offered. "It was a little more than just that. It was a fun social gathering and that was fairly typical for a number of Pennsylvania farm-country teenagers back then. And the few sips of beer I did have were warm and pretty disgusting. I was so relieved and happy when Todd suggested we leave to go for a private drive along the canal banks. We had a really good talk. The conversation was effortless and fun, and I felt like the luckiest girl in the world that he'd chosen me to be out with, instead of all the other girls that were practically desperate to go out with him."

Karen took a quick pause on the narration, long enough to readjust her position in bed and to allow meaningful space between what she'd related and what was to come next. "We drove for a little while and then stopped at this levy, where it dipped a little on the horizon. It was a really pretty little spot. Secluded for the most part, with a row of these majestic Poplar trees on one side. Todd made a sort of big deal out of putting a particular cassette in the player. And don't say, god mom, you're old" she warned her daughter. Karen proceeded quickly before Sondra had time to comment. "He had a bottle of champagne in a little cooler on the floor of the back seat and made a big deal out of opening it so the cork flew out with a dramatic pop, but without spilling much. I was so impressed, then. I'm sure it was probably some really cheap stuff and I certainly didn't know the difference at the time. Anyway, we had a few sips straight out of the bottle. It was fun."

Hmm" voiced Sondra. "A total white-trash James Bond" she said of Todd in a judgmental sarcastic tone.

This comment, too Karen ignored and was grateful that the underage drinking-and-driving issue hadn't become an instant main explosive focus with the girl. "The day had been perfect" continued Karen. "There we were, having a great time, sitting in his car, and he kept telling me how pretty I was and that he didn't want to be there with any other girl. So between his sweet-talk and the champagne, I was just as into going further as he."

"What kind of car?" asked Sondra. Karen stared at the girl for a few seconds in disbelief of the question.

"So not the point" Karen told her. "You nutty girl. A light blue, mid-sixties Mustang with a few dents and rust spots, if you must know."

Sondra wasn't expecting the story to go any further and her brain went immediately to picturing a fun car restoration project scenario with her dad and/or Doug. Karen on the other hand was most definitely not done with the tale. She adjusted the pillow behind her before continuing. As her memory flowed she let out a heavy breath through her nose. Her voice was laced with bits of regret, anger and melancholy. Her face registered deadly seriousness and she purposely kept her eyes upon her daughter. "It was an unromantic, fast-paced frantic struggle in the back seat" she told Sondra. "He was super clumsy with the condom and the whole thing was over so quick. Then he hardly said one word to me on the way home and never talked to me again."

"Man, I'd-a kicked his ass so hard" snarled an instantly mad-as-hell Sondra. "Sondra, you can't just go around wanting to kick everyone's ass, even the ones you're sure are deserving of it" scolded the mom. "It scares me that you can be such an angry hot-head. Have we forgotten just how much trouble your little temper got you into with the Gary Slesinger incident?" she asked rhetorically.

"Too bad there were cameras and a ton of people around" growled Sondra, her instant anger proving Karen's point. "That little bastard got off easy" added the girl.

"Sondra" scolded the mom.

"Sorry" said Sondra in apology. "So what happened with you and Todd?" she asked. Karen reached over and patted her daughter's shoulder, momentarily debating with herself on whether or not to have a further discussion on Sondra's anger issues. "I was devastated for weeks" she instead told her. "Not because of the sex" she added. "But it really hurt that he didn't want anything to do with me afterwards. My cousin Emily and a few really good friends helped me get through it. God, my stomach was in such knots. I was so scared that my parents would somehow find out or that I'd get pregnant, or an STD, even though we used protection. Lucky for me I didn't and was able to move on, eventually dating several other guys that were really nice."

Karen purposely held her silence for well over a minute in order for all this to sink in with Sondra. She adjusted her hair and watched the girl fidget with edge of the sheet. "After Todd" she said, resuming the account. "I didn't have sex with anyone else until I was in a committed relationship with a guy at college." "The one you moved with to California?" asked Sondra. Karen nodded but had no intention at this time of reliving or relating any bit of this part of her history. "So" she prompted her daughter. "Where are we with all this?"

"What do you mean?" asked Sondra. "You know what I mean" said Karen, her voice bordering on stern. "Don't play dumb" she added. "Do I need to make an appointment with the Gyno to discuss birth control with you?"

"God" exclaimed Sondra in a surprised indignant tone. "Gross" added the girl, making a face. Karen let out an involuntary quick laugh.

Well if you find this subject gross" she told her daughter, "you're definitely not ready for sex." Karen watched Sondra shrug her right shoulder and it was obvious that she was deep in thought. "Brice and I've had some make-out sessions that've gone, well, I mean we kept our clothes on and things didn't go beyond touching and kissing, but I think it could have. I'm sure he's had sex before and it's pretty obvious that he wants to with me, bu ..."

"But what?" asked Karen. "I don't know" responded Sondra, executing another shrug of her right shoulder. "Well I mean I do think I want that too but there's just something that holds me back." Sondra pulled a portion of the bed covers off and put her right foot solidly on the floor. "Everything got taken away from me" she growled angrily, her hands making tight fists. She bit down on her tongue to keep the tears at bay. It didn't work. Karen moved over to put her arms around her for comfort, arriving at the realization that virginity and sex were among the few things Sondra did have perceived control over, something that had not been taken from her in that horrible auto accident. At age seventeen, Karen hadn't seen her own virginity as something to lose, more a hurdle to get over in order to become a sophisticated knowledgeable fully-developed woman. Sex with her college boyfriend had been a treasured luxury, and years later, starting from her first intimate encounter with Doug, adjectives like amazing, incredible, mind-blowing or spectacular paled in comparison to anything she'd ever before known. Karen had assumed the mom role with Sondra almost immediately from the start of her relationship with Doug. It had begun for her with that first dinner she'd cooked for the two, where she had casually instructed Sondra on proper table manners. Her parental role with Sondra became more pronounced once she'd moved in with them and it was further strengthened when she and Doug were married. With the move to Santa Barbara there was simply no question. She was a wife and mother, and she assumed that mantle of responsibility with every fiber of her being.

As Karen sat with the softly crying girl, her brain worked overtime, wanting to say the right thing in this important moment. She briefly wondered if telling her this story was of help or if it had created more anxiety or confusion. She watched Sondra abruptly throw off the covers and stand, stamping her right foot. Karen was both relieved and surprised when the girl got back into bed and pulled the covers in place.

"I can only imagine what it's like for you" said the mom. "You didn't get to have that natural growing-up process, where just the everyday life of a young girl pulls you along in the learning and growing process, figuring things out about the world, including dating, sex and a whole lot of other things. You didn't get to have the conversations you would have had with your mom, your dad or your brothers about love and relationships. I'm grateful for every day that I get to be your second mom and I'm honored that you trust me when it comes to having a conversation about such a complex and deeply personal topic like this." "

Kari used to tell me details of her sexual escapades" Sondra told her now-mom. "I mean at first I figured she was just saying all that stuff to see how much she could shock me but in a way it was semi-educational and I think maybe it was a form of therapy for her. I mean she was like the classic teen, ticked off that she didn't have everything she thought she should have and acting-out to get attention. I think her wild tales backfired on me though. It didn't make me want to date or have tons of sex. Pretty much the opposite. I think it pretty much helped me make up my mind that I wasn't gonna have sex until it was the perfect situation. I mean I know life isn't actually perfect and it's not ever like some fairytale. I'm well aware that every girl doesn't grow up to fall in love with a handsome prince then get married and live happily ever-after, but I do think I at least deserve a chance at a realistic version of that."

Karen nodded and smiled sweetly. She loved Sondra's deep strength and insightful intelligence. "Pretty much every day something reminds me that the natural growing-up process was destroyed and taken away from me" Sondra continued. "I mean I don't think I would ever have gone to my dad with questions about sex. Dave and I had a few really good talks about dating though. He told me a little about kissing and making out, and mom and I used to talk about boys I liked and the ones who seemed like they liked me. We even talked a few times about me growing up and getting married someday."

For almost a full minute Karen watched in silence as Sondra once again made tight fists. "I guess I was kind of a late bloomer" Sondra announced. "Mrs. Jenner once told me that my development into womanhood was most likely delayed because of the injuries from the accident." She swallowed hard and loud and pounded her right fist on the bedding beside her. Karen put a gentle hand on the girl's shoulder and Sondra expelled a breath through her nose before she next spoke. "I mean I wasn't a dumb or naive kid. I knew what a period was, but my first one scared the living hell out of me. It came in the middle of the night when I was at that horrible rehabilitation hospital."

Tears began pouring from Sondra's eyes. "God I missed my mom so bad that night" she sobbed. Karen wrapped her arms around the girl and held her tight as Sondra cried through the pain of going through such a significant moment in her life alone, without the mom she'd known, loved and trusted. When the tears began to subside Karen let go and retrieved a box of tissues.

"I'm so sorry, baby" she told Sondra. "I think dating, relationships and sex have an even deeper meaning to you than most people because of what happened."

"Yeah" Sondra agreed with a nod. "I mean I get to say who, when, where, how and why, and I really don't see myself going further than I've already gone 'til I'm married. If I get married. I hope that'll be with Brice but we're both young and have careers that come first right now. We talked a little about that, our careers, and I guess we talked a tiny bit of me not going all the way." She took an enormous deep breath and let the back of her head sink into the pillow.

"I think you're an incredibly intelligent strong young woman" said Karen. "And I hope you'll always feel comfortable in coming to me with absolutely anything. This'll always be just between you and me, I promise that, and I love you with all my heart." She leaned over and kissed her daughter on the left cheek.

I love you too, Mom, said Sondra before they each said their final goodnights.

CHAPTER 35

In preparation for the Texas 600, 600-kilometers, 248-laps race, there were two 50-minute practice sessions on Thursday and Friday. Sondra found the track surface to be far more bumpy and slippery than the last time she'd been there, and during the first handful of laps in the late-morning Friday practice she experienced some grueling understeer going into Turns 3 and 4. When in traffic, the car's handling would become momentarily so unstable that it felt as though she was about to be thrown into the grandstands. As always with Sondra, she tried to live with what she had and alter her driving to make it work, relieved when Darren called her to their pit. Engineers made several adjustments and twelve minutes later she went back out on track. With a better handling car her focus was now centered around downforce levels, fuel consumption and shaving lap times. The second practice session on Friday was run at the same time that Saturday's race would start, 4:30 p.m., and Sondra had been given a qualifying setup to test the car's speed and strength. Seventeen laps in, the wind made an abrupt shift, with five to nine mile an hour gusts. Sondra was lightening-fast adjusting to this and on the front-stretch attempted to go from 5th gear to 4th in order to compensate for the headwind. There was a sudden loss of power. The car twitched and the rear tires locked and broke traction with the racing surface. Traveling at 220.083 miles an hour the sliding #12 car was quickly at the entrance to Turn 4. Sondra fought furiously with the wheel. She knew contact with the outside Safer-barrier wall was inevitable but was determined to minimize the impact by making sure the car went into it at a sideways glance. On instinct she kept her foot on the accelerator, wanting to power through and out of the slide. At the last possible instant she let go of the wheel so as not to snap her wrists when the right-front tire slammed the wall. Carbon-fiber pieces from the right-front wing exploded and sprayed like bullets from a machine gun as the wing made first contact. This was immediately followed by a glaring blow to the car's right side, bomb-like in violence. More carbon-fiber pieces flew in multiple directions and a brilliant orange flame emerged from the sliding, skidding vehicle.

Karen had just watched a bright lime-green car make its way down the front-stretch then looked to her right, expecting to see the #12 car in a 3-car pack heading out of Turn 4 and coming toward the Start/Finish line. Her eyes caught the alarming fiery crash and she instinctually knew that Sondra was the one involved. Karen dropped her clipboard and stood with her mouth slightly agape, feeling as if she'd just been kicked in the stomach. Amber lights attached to the tall outside metal chainlink retaining fence began flashing, indicating that race stewards had enacted a Caution period. When the lights turned from yellow to red Karen strained to hear the team communications in her headphones. "Hey, Tiger" said Darren. "You all right? Sondra, you okay?" There was no answer. Three safety vehicles quickly came to surround the crumpled race car and Karen had an enormous sense of relief watching her daughter get out of the cockpit waving her arms, clearly arguing with members of the safety crew that she did not in fact need their help or the mandatory trip to the infield care unit. When the SUV began moving with Sondra inside, Karen knew the girl had not only lost the argument but would soon be in the capable hands of medical professionals.

Doug and Karen were driven in a golf cart to the med center by Denny Hulzor. Sondra spent less than thirty minutes in the speedway's medical care unit and later sat between Doug and Karen on the couch of their motorhome. Here too Sondra's argument over her not wanting to take the doctor-prescribed Tylenol was lost. "That's enough, Sondra" said Karen, finally ending the discussion. "This isn't some heavy medication" she told the girl. "Your body's been through a shock and this is just a simple pain-reliever. Here, swallow these two tiny tablets with some cranberry juice, and no more arguing." The girl made a sour face but complied. The three sat in silence as Sondra finished the remainder of the juice, letting out a long heavy breath through her nose as she watched her fingers play with the rim of the now-empty shiny blue glass drinking vessel.

"I heard everything" she said in a voice that seemed other-worldly and that suddenly pulled an ominous shroud over the entire smallish space of the motorhome. Both Doug and Karen made guesses that the girl was talking about Darren's words over the radio immediately following the crash, or what the doctors and nurses had said during portions of the examination. Karen took the glass from her daughter, rinsing then setting it upside down on a dish towel next to Doug's red drinking glass and her clear one. Doug gave Sondra's knee a gentle pat and was about to stand when the girl again spoke. "Everything was so happy and peaceful" recounted Sondra. "And then Mom said 'Oh god' and Dad said 'everybody down.' He started to say 'hold on' or something but he never got the chance to finish." As Sondra's memory came spilling out, she tightly clenched her fists. A lightning bolt seemed to go through both Doug and Karen at the same time. They knew in an instant that Sondra wasn't talking about the earlier IndyCar incident. Karen quickly sat back down at Sondra's side, looking over at Doug. "Haley was playing with a puzzle that Dave gave him for Christmas" recounted Sondra. "It was these dark-wood squares attached by twine but they could be moved within the whole thing. There were words on one side, numbers on the other. The trick was to get the wooden pieces lined up so the words made up a phrase, and on the other side was a math equation. I heard it fall in between the seat and the car door just before ..."

Sondra swallowed hard and loud. She bit down on her tongue and began to lightly shiver. Doug repositioned himself so that his arm could encircle the seemingly fragile creature. Karen too put an arm around the girl. "I tried to keep my eyes open" continued Sondra in a diminished, tortured voice. "I wanted to see what was going on but I just couldn't. So loud. Like a bomb blast. I tried to reach for Dave and Haley but I couldn't move my arms. I tried to talk or scream but nothing came out." She began sobbing heavily. "I wanted to hear Mommy's voice but all I heard was this horrible, horrible scraping sound. It went on forever and ever. I thought I could hear Daddy say something but I don't know." Sondra's crying increased to the level that she was now having a hard time catching her breath. Doug and Karen held and soothed their girl as best they could, not wanting to say or do anything that might make the situation worse. For the next eleven minutes Sondra cried with years of hurt backing her up and egging her on without apologies or excuses. In the arms of the two people she now trusted more than anyone on earth she was in an unconditionally safe space, where being vulnerable and fragile held legitimacy. An ocean of tears teamed with coughing out years of pain, anger and anxiety erupted, without judgment or limitations.

The next morning T.J. went to the Trents' RV to assess his driver's mood, attitude and well-being. He sat at the dinette table and dined with Sondra on breakfast burritos that he'd bought from one of the track vendors. "Miguel Sanchez, the guy that owns the concession stand I got the grub from" he began, making a bit of light small talk, "has a really good Mexican restaurant downtown. I've known him for years. We go way back to basically when I was just comin' into the thick of my career. He started in the food business right here at the speedway with a simple hotdog cart."

"This is really good" said Sondra with a nod, after taking a large bite of the thick neatly wrapped culinary item. She wiped her mouth with the back of her right hand.

"So how'ya feelin'?" asked T.J., getting down to business. "Ego's more bruised than I am" said Sondra. "Yeah well, that happens" said the man. "Just makin' sure I'm not gonna have to squeeze into an old race suit and qualify my own car tonight" he added.

"Not a chance" said Sondra with a broad smile. "Although" she furthered, "you trying to get into a suit from twenty years ago, I bet I could sell that picture all over the world and make trillions."

"Shut up and eat your breakfast, smart-ass" he countered, trying not to smile. "And try not getting half of it all over yourself" he added. The two talked as they continued to eat. T.J. informed Sondra that the car hadn't sustained as much significant damage as they'd first thought. It wouldn't be necessary to go to the back-up car. The gearbox snafu that had been the source of the previous day's wreck had been diagnosed and remedied. A unilateral engineering decision had also been made that it was now more practical to go with a bit more of a neutral downforce setup on the car during qualifying than they would have ordinarily had the car not gone through a major rebuild the night before. Sondra argued for a moment with T.J., trying to make the case for being more aggressive on the setup in order to qualify up front, but with years of experience and knowledge on his side he negated his young driver's contentions with a simple shake of his head. "Luckily" he added. "We have fifty minutes of track-time today before we go qualifying. That'll show us where we are and give us time to sort out any issues."

Several hours later, after the scheduled 50-minute practice session in which there were indeed multiple handling issues to sort out, Sondra qualified the #12 car in the 7th position. Though it was a relief to the Holt Racing driver and to the team that her confidence hadn't been shattered by the hard crash, Sondra kept to herself the major disappointment she felt for not doing better in qualifying. She knew track position at the start of any race was key and that her team had expended a tremendous amount of effort, working around the clock in putting together a car that was hopefully capable of the best possible results.

"Man" said Brice when he finally had the chance to be alone with Sondra after a dinner given by a main IndyCar sponsor. She'd been seated at a table in a large room, as usual flanked by Doug and Karen. When people began moving about, young Crandle took the opportunity to escort her through a side door looking out on a mid-sized parking lot. "Your folks or someone on your team is always right there around you like a protective shield or something." He gave a light laugh through his nose but his voice turned serious. "I hate that things have been so damn busy and hectic. It's been killin' me that I haven't been able to be with you and make sure you're okay. Let me be the billionth person to ask how you're doing."

I'm fine" said Sondra simply. "I mean video of it looked worse than it really was. This actually gives me even more of an incentive to drive my ass off and win, so I wouldn't advise getting in my way."

Brice smiled at that, loving her playfulness in light of something that could have been disastrous. "Well I was thinking I'd let you draft off me a little, while I lead you to the checkered flag" he joked.

"Ha" voiced Sondra. He lightly grabbed Sondra by the upper arms and studied her face for a few seconds. "The rehab doc I worked with was a bit of a wannabe shrink" he told her. "But he actually had some really good things to help with getting over the mental trauma of going through my crash."

Sondra shook her head. "I don't need a shrink" she told the boy on no uncertain terms. "Nothing I've ever gone through in a race car even comes close to what I went through when I lost my family" she said in a low growling voice, wriggling out of his clutches. She'd previous thought of discussing with him her memories of the Tahoe crash and that they had been triggered by the recent IndyCar incident, but she didn't want to bring those ugly images or that kind of heaviness into what they had together. Brice looked down at Sondra's tightly clenched right fist. He wrapped his arms around her and they shared a long tight embrace. "I love everything about you" he whispered. Sondra momentarily squeezed her arms around him a little harder. "That still doesn't mean I'll let you beat me to the line tomorrow" she whispered. He chuckled at that. "So you did get a concussion after all" he joked. "But I promise to be kind and not sneer at you from my top step of the podium."

Sondra smiled at that and pulled away, shaking her head. "Gee, your charity is boundless" she quipped. After a bit of increasingly passionate necking they reluctantly went back inside the crowded noisy room.

Hours before The Texas 600, winds decreased significantly from the previous days. The sky was clear and there were slightly lower ambient air temperatures. The weather, as always, was taken into consideration along with the track's configuration, with its twenty-four degree banked corners and five degrees of banking in the straights. The start of the six-hundred kilometer race was fairly uneventful until Lap 31 when Benny Jayden crashed in Turn 4, looking somewhat similar to Sondra's Friday practice crash. Unlike hers however this incident was attributed to tire issues. After the race resumed, the #12 car toggled between 9th and 17th. At just over the halfway mark there had been three other crashes. The soreness Sondra had experienced from Friday's trip to the wall was now becoming unbearable. Her arms felt as though they'd been beaten with sledgehammers and she felt like crying but forced any and all tears away with resolute focus. An unconscious stubbornness took over and Sondra began to drive the race the way she wanted to drive. She didn't disobey Darren's pit instructions and didn't block other drivers or break any IndyCar rules, but if she wanted to remain in front of someone or wanted around a particular car she formed a plan and made it happen. In the end, Sondra finished the race in 4th Place, just over eight seconds behind the 3rd Place car of Shane Teluchi. On the drive away from the speedway Sondra felt as if the air was being vacuumed out of her lungs. Not only was this a disappointing race outcome but she and Brice hadn't had a chance for any further chats or time with one another. Brice and Greg Raley had engaged in an epic battle for the lead in the last 43 laps of the race. The top position changed hands thirty-one times and separation between the two at the checkered flag was mere inches, with the nose of Raley's black and white car getting to the line first. One of the most talked-about drivers that day had been Andrew Placer, who'd come from the 22nd position on the grid to finishing 6th. The two teammates and friends, Placer and Crandle, considered their race outcome significant and went out that evening with many team members to celebrate. Brice invited Sondra to join him by an electronic message but knew she would be in transit with Doug and Karen.

Sondra netted a 6th Place finish in Toronto, Canada, and a week later Round 13 was held at the natural-terrain road course of Watkins Glen, New York. She loved this track and the famous facility. It was also the sight of her Indy Lights race victory two years prior and the sealing of that championship. The raceway visit this year in the IndyCar Series included a surprise reunion with Shelley. Inside the RV, after some small talk and a discussion on Sondra's relationship with Brice, Sondra reluctantly spoke of her crash in Texas. "I guess it triggered some memory stuff" she said reluctantly. "For the first time I remembered all those hideous details of what happened just a little while after we left the Jenner's cabin." Sondra bit down on her tongue, not wanting to continue. "Whenever we went anywhere in the car I always loved to listen to how the car sounded going through the air and how the tires sounded on different surfaces and in all kinds of conditions. Before we left, Dad and Mr. Jenner talked about whether or not we were gonna need snow chains. Dad even mentioned it to mom several times after we got underway. For a bit, I think he was actually looking for a place to pull over and put 'em on because the rain turned icy and it did actually start snowing for a minute or two. It hailed really hard, then rained super-hard. Then everything calmed down." Sondra again bit down on her tongue, clenching and unclenching her fists several times. She was afraid to continue but knew that Shelley really didn't want her to stop and perhaps would be insistent. "Dave and Haley were usually like chatterboxes at first when we'd start out on a long drive" continued Sondra. "The sound of the hail and rain was so intense. I mean nobody said much during that time but when things turned to normal, Mom asked us all to say what part of our vacation we liked the best." Sondra lost her battle with tear production but didn't cry hard, making what she hoped was a discrete attempt to wipe the moisture away. "Mom turned in her seat to look around at all of us. I can still see that smile." Sondra now began crying softly and her voice diminished by half. "She was always making these happy announcements about things that had just happened. Like, What a nice birthday. Or, That was such a great dinner. Or, Wasn't that an exciting movie. Things like that." Sondra glanced down at her lap and swallowed hard before continuing. "When she marveled out loud at what a great winter vacation we'd just had, we all agreed. I was looking down at a little wooden game Haley was playing with when I heard Mom say, Oh god."

For close to four minutes the motorhome was eerily still and quiet. Shelley purposely didn't move or make any verbal prompts and it felt a complete shock to her system when Sondra went from staring in the direction of the sleeping compartment to suddenly turning to look directly at her. "It happened so fast" Sondra said in a low growl. "And there were a thousand insanely loud sounds all at once. Like explosions, crunching and scraping for the longest time." She looked toward the two front seats of the RV. "I'm sure we must have skidded for at least a thousand feet, upside down. I was all hunched over and then I couldn't see anything but I could hear my dad breathing hard and moaning, and then the next thing I knew I was in a weird place with bright lights and people standing over me. At a hospital I guess. The pain was so intense. It was Mrs. Jenner who told me what happened and the next time I woke up I was in a different place. I was alone in a sort of dark room, with things beeping and tubes and wires all over me. That was the worst thing in the world, to be that alone and that scared."

"I'm so sorry, baby" soothed Shelley, deep emotion in her voice. She was in awe of Sondra's strength in being able to remember and describe such horrific events without going to pieces.

"I don't know why I never remembered any of those details before" Sondra told her friend. "And now I can't get those monstrous sounds of the crash out of my head." She sniffled and stood, going to the sink where there was a roll of paper towels standing on end on the counter. After wiping her eyes and face, she took a deep breath and returned to where she'd been sitting.

"That's an awful lot for a thirteen-year-old to go through" said Shelley, putting a gentle hand on the girl's shoulder. "The brain can sometimes work in such deep protective ways" she added. "You've had so much to deal with all these years."

"Yeah" whispered Sondra in reluctant agreement. She cleared her throat and spoke in an assertive voice, as if she were punching back at a perceived bully's physical attack. "My race car makes the greatest sounds" she told her friend. "Even with the crashes or mishaps I've had in any of my cars, I've never heard those unbelievably gruesome sounds I had to hear that day with my family. In my Indy car I'm strapped in tight into a cockpit that's highly engineered to keep me safe." She glanced down at her tight fist and let out a breath though her nose before continuing. "I'm absolutely sure Mom, Dad, Dave and Haley would be glad that I'm doing something where so many people are working intensely hard at keeping me safe. I mean with all the accidents and fatalities on the roadways that go on every day, I think it's damn absurd that none of the car manufacturers give you the option to have even half the safety protection I have in my race car."

Shelley didn't quite feel confident in speaking authoritatively on general automotive safety. Instead she turned the focus to Doug and Karen, how they were committed to offer unconditional love, support and dedication to keeping Sondra safe.

The outcome for Holt Racing at Watkins Glen was less than favorable. The often elusive formula for obtaining as close to a perfect setup as possible for the #12 car seemed consistently just out of reach during the entire weekend. Another major factor for the team, especially for Sondra, was that T.J. would not be on hand. He hadn't been feeling well for weeks and was now resting at home, on doctor's orders. Sondra started the GP from the 16th position on the grid and made some risky bold moves in the opening laps. On Lap 51 there was a caution for debris in Turn 9, the remains of a broken rear wing element from an as yet undetermined car. The carbon-fiber pieces were laying dangerously just off-line. Most of the teams elected to make their second pit stop at this time but Sondra made a case for going off strategy. Darren overruled it. Karen, wearing a pair of headsets, listened to the team radio communications and could immediately tell that Sondra was angered by the decision. This was soon evidenced under green-flag conditions when Sondra made an unusually over-aggressive move on Barry Faustine, forcing the #22 to run wide in Turn 7. The move was immediately under review by the race stewards and though only a warning was given to Holt Racing no penalty was assessed. Sixteen laps later Sondra got her first lucky break of the weekend. Two cars entangled in the Bus-stop chicane. The contact sent Emanuel Billings to the garage and Sunny Verdoux limping back to the pits for a new front wing. These cars had been 2.6 seconds ahead of the #12 car in the running order, and when the green flag again waved five laps later after the crash debris had been removed from the racing surface Sondra was shown in 6th Place. This seemed to energize the Twelve team going forward and at the end of the long day they finished in a respectable 5th Place. Sondra, as usual, secretly took this non-win result as a crushing blow but was becoming much better at disguising it. She attended the post-race debrief with her Holt Racing team, then set out on a mission. Though Sondra was now an extremely popular racing figure and many constantly sought her company, she made her way alone to the #22 team's main hauler with determined tunnel-visioned strides, glad to find Barry Faustine sitting on a scooter next to the elongated vehicle. Barry was chatting with three other men but the talk ended as Sondra approached. "I want to apologize for my behavior in Turn Seven" she announced. "I hate it when guys do that to me. Hope it didn't screw up your race."

"No problem" said Barry, trying to act as though the incident hadn't phased him in the least. "Our race was screwed long before that" he added. "I wasn't even on the lead lap so I guess technically it was your line anyway. I could give you a punch on the shoulder, if that'll make you happy."

"It would not" smiled Sondra. "But we'll see how it goes in Phoenix," the men chuckled as she disappeared from sight. Sondra made a point to congratulate Brice on the race win. It was now close to forty minutes after the race had ended and she found him talking and laughing with a group of seven people. She thought that Brice's reaction to her congratulatory gesture nonchalant, bordering on flippant and rude.

Not long after the race had ended, Karen headed to Pennsylvania to attend the wedding of a family friend. Doug and Sondra made their way to the next race venue in Arizona. After a long travel day, Doug pulled the motorhome into their first scheduled overnight destination, a campground specifically designed for motorhomes, camper-vans and trailers. Though not in a high mountainous location the campground seemed forest-like, with an abundance of trees and shrubbery. Dinner was decidedly camp-esque, and in no time Doug had two steaks cooking on the camp space's provided permanent open grill. "Had an impromptu serious meeting with Darren and Keys before we left the Glen" he informed Sondra, electing not to scold the girl for her continued questionable table manners. "T.J.'s on the mend. The docs won't let him go to Phoenix but he'll be with us in Sonoma. He's gonna be fine."

"You're damn right he's gonna be fine" declared Sondra. "I'll make sure of that." She pounded her fist on the weathered wooden picnic table and chewed in anger.

Doug debated in his head whether to go further into Sondra's worry and anguish over T.J.'s medical condition but chose to change the subject. "I was asked to convince you to sign with Holt Racing for an additional two years" he informed his daughter.

"No" said the girl with a quick shake of her head. "I'm going to Europe" she added.

"No" countered the father and co-business manager. "It's not like you have an F-One ride waiting for you" he furthered. "You don't have any ride over there right now." He chewed and then took a sip of cranberry juice, watching his stubborn, suddenly angry daughter stab a piece of steak that she'd cut at a specific angle. "I'm not sayin' that to be mean or negative or to squelch your dreams and goals" he told the girl, hoping to calm her down and reassure her. "You've worked hard to be where you are" he added. "This here is working and you have a championship that's seriously within reach. Teluchi, Kelarzo and Raley had tough weekends, too" he reminded her. "Worse than ours" he added. "And even though we didn't finish at the top either, we're now second in points with three races to go."

"Yeah but two of 'em are on ovals that aren't exactly my strongest tracks" complained Sondra.

"Wow" said Doug. "Where's all this negative crap coming from?"

Sondra shrugged, staring down at kernels of corn she was maneuvering around the paper plate with a metal fork. "We haven't exactly been consistent lately" she stated. "And I'm somehow making a ton of really stupid mistakes. I guess if I have to be brutally honest I think maybe I've been a little freaked out about T.J. and I hate to admit it but the whole uncertainty of Brice and my F-One goals have been on my mind a lot lately" she confessed.

"Yeah, I know that, kiddo" said Doug. "You're not as complicated as you like to think you are, at least not to me." Sondra rolled her eyes and shrugged her shoulder.

"Well" she pondered. "I mean I do want an IndyCar championship super-bad. I guess two more seasons with Holt Racing is only gonna make me stronger when I do go to Europe. Don't know about Brice though."

"We" corrected Doug. "When we go to Europe." Sondra took a deep breath and smiled.

During Friday's two 50-minute IndyCar practices on the one-mile D-shaped Arizona oval, the speed and lap-times of the #12 ran the gambit from hopeful to worrisome. Holt Racing had been working on literally thousands of details since before the beginning of the season and this weekend took them to task. This track was familiar to Sondra and her team, though nothing was easy. For a second straight week in a row Sondra would have to endure without T.J. but switched her worries and anxieties over her boss to her recent uncertainty about Brice. Her interactions with him lately had been a bit intermittent and less than romantic, especially the last several text messages and phone calls.

Holt Racing's #12 qualified 5th for Saturday night's 200-mile race but in the afternoon pre-race warmup an anomaly with the gearbox showed up each of the two times she pitted. A gearbox change was discussed and then made, but according to IndyCar rules this major mechanical equipment change enacted after qualifying relegated Sondra to start the race from the last row. She hated the idea of this but was secretly glad of the engineering change. Since the crash at the Texas Motor Speedway she wanted and needed full confidence in all mechanical systems. During the mostly caution-free Phoenix 250 event it was obvious that Sondra had a fast car, despite growing understeer as the tires wore during each segment. After a routine pit stop at just over the halfway mark the #12 broke into the top-ten. For the last stop of the day Darren took a strategy gamble and pitted his driver early. The stop was fast and smooth, with a significant turn of downforce added to the front wing, but this was a green-flag stop and the Twelve car came back out on track seven spots further back in the running order when the rest of the field cycled through their pit stops. With twelve laps to go there came a caution for debris on the backstretch. Darren's out-of-sequence pit stop strategy was now getting a workout. The leaders pitted, Sondra did not. Holt Racing had enough fuel to get to the end of the race, and by Sondra staying out on track while the leaders pitted it allowed her to leapfrog a number of cars that had been running higher up in the running order. By the end of the race the #12 finished in 4th. Justin Oliver had led the most laps and won by 2.524 seconds ahead of John Mallory and Shane Teluchi. Owing to Tony Kelarzo's 8th Place finish and Greg Raley finishing in 17th, Sondra remained 2nd in the championship points standings. She was given high praise for her efforts by her family as well as from several members of the race media. Not only had she gone from the back of the field to the front but she'd done this with an ill-handling race car most of the evening. She climbed out of her #12 machine sore from head to toe, though she hid it well. When Karen later noticed that Sondra's hands were badly blistered by how hard she'd been working the steering wheel, she administered first aid to her daughter, putting burn cream on the girl's palms and wrapping them in bandages. Sondra also complained of how the safety harness had cut into her inner thighs during the race, more than usual. "It feels like knife blades have been carving into me the past billion hours."

The IndyCar Series would not be racing the next weekend, which meant a two-week break for race fans and a full one-week break for IndyCar teams before going into the second-to-last race of the season. Sondra had all but insisted on a face-to-face meeting with her team boss and Karen skillfully orchestrated the arrangements. At 12:28 p.m. Sondra arrived at the Holt Ranch in a gray Ford Focus rental car, with Beverly greeting the girl warmly at the front door. “Well this is a lovely turn of events” she told her esteemed guest, giving the girl a hug. “Come on in. Your mom said you wanted a quick meeting with T.J. but I’m hoping you’ll stay the night, or at least stay for lunch.”

“Thanks” said Sondra with a flash of a smile. “Lunch sounds great but I have a four-fifteen flight out to Santa Barbara.”

“Well that’s fine” said Beverly. “Lets go and see if you can’t get the old man to turn off the TV for a minute or two.” Beverly led Sondra through the living room and down a hallway. They entered the den where T.J. was napping in a dimly lit Western-themed wood-paneled room, stretched out on a red leather lounge chair with one of his wife’s colorful quilts draped haphazardly over his large frame. “T.J.” said Beverly as she attempted to gently wake her husband, “You have company.”

The man opened his eyes with a bit of a start, first eyeing his wife then focusing on the young girl in a long-sleeve dark blue T-shirt and faded bluejeans. His stare went back to his wife. “Why the hell do insist on parading people through the house whenever I try to take a damn nap” he grumped. With a wicked smile Sondra peeled back the quilt with dramatic flair, then pulled open the curtain in front of a large sliding glass door. She slid open the clear panel and looked over her shoulder before stepping out onto the patio. “Wake up and meet me out on the deck” she ordered. “We need to talk.”

T.J. and Sondra sat on comfortable wooden Adirondack chairs looking out at the hilly Texan landscape. Neither immediately spoke but after a time Beverly appeared, setting a tray of crackers and two glasses of lemonade on a small wooden table between the two chairs. She then handed her husband two pills wrapped in a paper towel. “Take these” she instructed him. “I’ll be back with sandwiches in just a bit.”

Sondra noted that the very moment Beverley disappeared from sight T.J. deftly stuffed the wrapped medication into his right-front pants pocket and bit down noisily on a crunchy salty wafer. “Yesterday sucked" she said of her last race effort. "I know I should have figured it out better, faster. My whole season has been way more of a struggle than I thought."

"They always are" offered the experienced and celebrated race car driver, staring out at the expanse of his property. "I'm not a shrink" he warned. "Hope you didn't come here for some flowery pep-talk. I told you before, you have control over your life and your career, but if you suddenly have the need to stop and figure things out you'll be doing that on someone else's dime."

Sondra wasn't after a pep-talk and was sure she didn't need advice on how to drive or complete her year. She wasn't offended by T.J.'s gruff words but this didn't exactly help. She took a swallow of juice and fixed her stare on an old spindly oak tree. Minutes of silence erupted, followed by a gentle drift of words from T.J. "Only a real small handful of guys can do what you seem to do" he told the girl. "Trick is to figure out how to do it on a regular basis. It's good that you're hard on yourself. You're further along than you think" he added. "Don't know how such a damn scrawny little girl can drive like you do."

"I'm not scrawny" argued Sondra with a furrowed brow. She took a loud swallow of juice and reached for a cracker. "I have to win" she said through gritted teeth. "I can't explain it. It's not like this is just a job for me. It's. .."

"Yeah" said T.J., softening as he glanced over at his driver. "I get it" he added. "Cards you were dealt. That's the kind of crap that'll take you far when you go to F-One in a couple of years." Sondra stared at her fingers twisting the light-blue opaque glass drinking vessel as it sat on the chair's armrest. She was surprised to hear the F-1 mention from T.J. but was afraid to outwardly react. "Yeah" chuckled the man. "I know all about your dealings with Grekko-Cilli. I have no doubt you'll get there, but you're mine now. You keep your damn head in the game here, on American soil." Sondra sat back in the chair, contented. This was everything she needed, the peace of these particular surroundings and the connection with her boss, hero and friend.

Beverly soon came out with a plate of sandwiches and pickle

wedges, refilled the juice glasses and smiled as she stroked Sondra's hair then kissed her husband and was gone in a flash. "No wonder you're s-damn skinny" said T.J. as he watched Sondra peel the crust off one of the sandwich halves.

"No wonder you're not getting better" countered the girl. "Not following doctors orders or your wife's to take your medicine." T.J. retrieved the wad of paper from his pocket and unwrapped the two small white pills, making a face after swallowing them with a loud gulp of juice. "I'm okay" he assured her. "Not like I'm sick or dying or anything."

Sondra nodded and took a large bite of sandwich then wiped her mouth with the back of her hand. "So you'll be there in Sonoma?" she asked.

"I'll be there" he assured her. "Funny" he added with a quick snorting laugh. "None of my other drivers ever really liked it there and best Ryan ever got was Seventh."

"'Til me" asserted Sondra, knowing the statistics. This wasn't ego or immaturity talking. Her Indy car had become an extension of herself and over the past few years the challenges, exhilaration and many nuances of the Sonoma race track were something she had come to revere as well as cherish. Childhood memories with her father were held there and then all the hard work she'd put in, learning the track and developing a oneness that she'd hoped would give her the edge on her competition.

On the drive home after Doug and Karen had collected Sondra from the Santa Barbara International Airport, they smiled to themselves as their daughter went into detailed description of her time with the Holts. "T.J. and I had lunch outside on the deck, just outside his den" began Sondra. "We had a good talk. I mean I totally gave him hell for not taking better care of himself and then we had a great lunch. Mrs. Holt brought out these amazing crackers. I meant to ask what brand they were and where they came from but I forgot. They had a ton of herbs and grains, and they were almost more like chips than crackers, but definitely baked. I mean it's possible that she made 'em herself. She also made these really great tuna sandwiches. She doesn't buy canned tuna. She gets flash-frozen fillets from Alaska, and after she cooks them she shreds 'em and doctors them up with basically the same stuff you do" she told Karen. "But she added fresh minced tarragon leaf and some other herbs and spices. Really different but really good. And the bread was good too but it had a crust that was like a mile wide."

"Nutty girl" said a smiling Doug.

"Silly goose" chuckled Karen. "You and your aversion to crust" she added.

Sondra flashed a smile and shrugged her right shoulder. "T.J. said some great things" continued the girl. "I mean I'm sure he didn't really mean to give me a ton of compliments but in a round-about sort of way, he did. I'm so glad I went. Oh, and here's the really wild thing ... He knows Arturi Grekko. Met him a ton of years ago."

"Wow" marveled Doug. Karen on the other hand was not interested in discussing the aforementioned Formula One team owner and abruptly changed the subject. "Kari called about an hour ago" informed the mom.

I know" said Sondra. "She left a voicemail message. My phone was in my briefcase in the overhead compartment.

Kari was invited to dinner the next evening. Doug grilled hamburger patties on the poolside barbecue as Karen prepared broccoli, and buttered red potatoes with parsley. After the meal, with strawberries and vanilla ice cream for dessert, Sondra all but insisted on taking her friend down to her home race garage. The two girls got on the ATV that was parked just outside the gate to the pool. Kari wrapped her arms around Sondra and held on tight, laughing and complaining about the pace as Sondra piloted the four-wheeler at break-neck speed toward their destination. "You can't just drive like a normal person, can you?" said Kari. "I swear, you're always in a race."

Inside and to the left of Sierre-Trent Raceway the young women settled on the seats of two of Sondra's karts. Sondra knew there wasn't much of a chance to convince Kari to actually drive the mini racers, and the seating choice was more a subconscious act, but Kari didn't question it or seem to mind. "So" began Kari, "classes, homework and college life keep me pretty busy but I always find time to keep track of all your race stuff. Karen posts a lot of cool things on your official website. The in-car video stuff is incredible. It scares the hell out of me and I'm just sitting in a chair watching it. You really get bumped around, don't you?"

"I guess" said Sondra with a shrug of her shoulder. "I don't really notice that though because I'm concentrating so hard. Most of the drivers are super into putting out stuff on social media" she then told Kari, side-stepping the physical aspect of being in a race car. "I know I'm supposed to be more up on that too but luckily Mom's great with it. It's not that I don't like technology or the social media stuff" she clarified. "I mean I loved when I got my first laptop, but that was mostly for school. And this phone" she added, unclipping it from her belt loop and holding it up as evidence. "I mean it's cool and practically does everything but tie my shoelaces but it can also be a pain in the ass. Racing at this level isn't what most people think. I have a thousand obligations and I'm constantly getting pulled in every direction. This phone practically never stops ringing or buzzing."

"Oh, poor little popular girl" mocked Kari.

Shut up" retorted Sondra with smile and a roll of her eyes. Kari turned the steering wheel of the stationary kart left then right. "Bet you like some of the rings and buzzes from your phone though" she prompted. "Well, yeah" said Sondra. "I'm really glad my Uncle Leo stays in touch with me, and you always seem to call or send me something at the perfect time. Loved the little video you sent of you trying to study, with all the commotion of your roommate and the noisy neighbors in the background."

"Oh yeah" recalled Kari. "But I was thinking more about what you get from Brice."

Sondra smiled at the boy's mention. "Well I mean it's not constant" she said of the communication. "But it's pretty cool, sometimes. He's been kinda a jerk lately. We're competitors and usually support each other in our careers. It's like he's thinking ahead to his new European career already. I mean he's come a long way recovering from his injuries in a short time and he's been making a name for himself."

"What bugs you more?" asked Kari. "Him getting attention for making a name for himself or that he's gonna be going far away soon?"

"I can't wait to get over there on all those amazing tracks" deflected Sondra. "I mean I really love what I'm doing right now." Sondra pounded her fist on the steering wheel and took a deep breath, thinking about Kari's question. Her brain flashed on the many things she and Brice had talked of and experienced together in these past months.

"You okay?" asked Kari. Sondra swallowed hard and shrugged her shoulders.

I hate having to always feel like, wrong place, wrong time" said Sondra, her voice full of emotion.

"What do you mean?" asked Kari.

"I don't know if I can really explain it" said Sondra. "It's like I'm always missing a step. Some things are always just out of reach, you know?"

Kari nodded, trying to comprehend. "I hate that you feel like that" she told Sondra, trying to console her friend.

"I don't when I'm in my race car" asserted Sondra with a shrug. "I mean that's pretty much the only time I feel completely okay. Will you come to Sonoma with me next weekend?" she asked, a noticeable wisp of desperation in her voice.

"Well I have classes on Friday that I can't miss" said Kari. "And Saturday I have this breakfast thing I was invited to by one of my professor's assistants."

"A date?" asked Sondra.

"I wish" said Kari with a nervous chuckle. "He's gorgeous but it's at seven-thirty in the morning and there'll be like ten, fifteen of us students. One of the campus clubs is providing the pancake breakfast and Daniel Briggamer's gonna give a powerpoint presentation. Professor Reigs strongly suggested we not miss it. I'll probably have to take copious notes because I'm sure at least some of the material will be on a test or a quiz."

"Yeah" agreed Sondra, suddenly saddened with the notion that Kari would not be joining her for the Sonoma weekend. Kari reached over and touched her friend's arm. "That's a long drive" she told Sondra. "But I could do it."

This year's Sonoma weekend included an added component. Safen-Up would be holding a two-day event, Saturday and Sunday. Shelley had informed Sondra and Karen that she had intentions of making this bigger and more evolved than the one in Long Beach. Public awareness was a main goal and a total of 24 children had been invited and confirmed to participate throughout the entire weekend. Shelley, with Karen's help, had coordinated with the existing Children's Charities at Sonoma Raceway, and in addition to experiencing the world of racing and learning about how the Safen-Up organization could be of great benefit to them, there would be accommodations for the youngsters at a Sonoma hotel. Several planned non-race-related activities were to be offered as well. Though Sondra had been assured that her participation in the Safen-Up activities would be limited to her time availability and not be responsible for any of the logistics, she felt a heavy weight on her shoulders. The nonprofit had been her idea and she desperately wanted it to be successful, not just as an organization but with any of the kids it might possibly help. She was racked with a sense of guilt over having to split her attention between this and the thing that meant the most to her, winning races and the championship.

With cold tires and on a racing surface that was still damp in areas from the morning fog, Sondra gingerly made her way up and over Turn 2, reporting to Strategist Darren, major understeer. By her third lap, nineteen of the 23-car field were on track. As Sondra was deep in the Carousel of Turn 6 on her 15th lap she again used the radio. "Tire temps are just not coming up to normal and we're understeering like crazy." Less than a minute later she again spoke. "Turn Ten chicane is a nightmare at any kind of speed."

"Copy that, Sondra" responded Darren. "Come on in. Pit this lap. Pit-pit-pit" he added quick succession. Sondra's three main engineers had been monitoring the details from their pit lane laptops. Hearing the radio communication and watching the car on a video monitor, they were able to form a solid plan to counter the anomalies she was dealing with on track. While the Twelve car sat quiet in the pits for just over seven minutes, Karen shielded her daughter-client from the brightness of the emerging sun with an umbrella. A new set of black sidewall slicks were put on, followed by adjustments to the suspension. As the engine was being refired Karen patted her daughter on the shoulder and moved away to stand next to her husband. In less than a minute Sondra was shifting from 4th to 5th gear going through the S's, the fastest section of track. "Much better" she reported to Darren over the radio. "Livable understeer and the grip's coming in so much faster." Sondra stayed out for the remainder of the session with a car that seemed to be getting better lap by lap, and at the conclusion of Practice 1 Holt Racing was officially shown 2nd fastest, behind the Penske-owned car of Shane Teluchi.

Karen and Sondra took one of the Holt Racing golf carts up the hill to a grassy area on the outside of the track, just before Turn 2. Karen did the driving as Sondra sat next to her, studying a team Email message on her phone displaying the timing and scoring spreadsheet from Practice 1 as well as other important Holt Racing perimeters. When the cart stopped Sondra looked up to see the white tent with large blue lettering SAFEN-UP that she'd seen from her car. "Kari" exclaimed Sondra with an instant smile. After an enthusiastic hug Sondra swatted her friend's shoulder. "You ditched school and drove all this way?" she asked, shaking her head. "What about your test and the dream-boat professor guy?"

Kari laughed and shook her head. "It was just a quiz and I took it yesterday" she told Sondra. "And Daniel Briggamer isn't a full professor yet. The breakfast thing got canceled because he had some kind of family emergency. Don't know what, but when I found out I called Karen and she said she'd leave tickets for me at will call. That was the longest drive I've ever done by myself, but goin' up the coast was pretty cool and so is all this" she added, speaking of Shelley and Safen-Up. Sondra nodded and took a quick visual survey of the surroundings. "Yeah" she acknowledged. "This looks great. It's a good view from here. The kids are gonna enjoy this."

"Well that's the idea" said Shelley, moving closer to put an arm briefly around Sondra. "But this isn't all for the kids" she added. "We want to attract donors and contributors with deep pockets this weekend. Today'll be a catered affair for a handful of V.I.P.s plus twelve children and their escorts, and tomorrow and Sunday it'll be extended to as many people as we can attract." Shelley took note of her friend's concerned look. "Building the organization like this is what's going help kids the most" she told Sondra. "And I intend to reach a lot of kids." "Kay" said Sondra. "I trust you."

The Historic Grand Prix cars were now on track and Sondra turned to watch a late-Sixties era navy-blue Ferrari navigate up and over the hill. "That scared me earlier when I saw your car sliding a little in that corner there" said Shelley. "Don't worry, SeaShell" said Sondra with a quick shake of her head. "Car-control is my middle name" she joked. "I mean Turn Two can be tricky because the car gets light at the top and searches for grip. Cold track, cold tires don't help but I'm really good at this."

"And humble, too" said Kari with a quick chuckle. A scooter coming up the path caught the attention of the four women and one man under the Safen-Up tent. Sondra recognized the person at the controls as well as his passenger. "Well, well, well" she said as the scooter came to a stop. "If it isn't the notorious Indy Lights green-oil gang, out stealing scooters and causing trouble."

"You mean celebrated" corrected the passenger as he got off the two-wheeler, greeting Sondra with a handshake and a wide grin.

"Hi Myrand" said Sondra. "Hi Wendell" she greeted the other boy. She then made introductions all around, ending with Kari. "Wendell Grayson is one of the guys I drove against in F-Ford, and he grew up on the farm next to Brice" she informed Kari. "And Myrand Fiora here is now driving for my old Indy Lights strategist, Steven Barnes." Sondra watched and listened for a few moments as Myrand and Kari seemed to develop an immediate rapport. She opted to begin a side conversation with Wendell. "Hung out with Brice for a few minutes this morning" Sondra told young Grayson. "It appears he's ditching us in a few weeks for the European scene."

"Wow" said Wendell, not divulging the fact that he'd heard the rumors and had spoken with Brice himself about this. "Good for him" awarded Wendell. "That's gonna be an amazing opportunity, and maybe the best thing for me. I'm kinda dating his sister now."

"You're kidding" said Sondra. "And kinda?" she added of his last comment.

"Well I saw Lauren and her friends at a little deli shop the last time I was home and we got to talking" he informed Sondra. "After that the two of us hung out together a bunch and stuff between us just sort of happened. When she graduates from junior college she'll be going to school to become a dental surgeon, so we'll both be kind of busy for a bit but we have things pretty planned out to see each other when we can."

Sondra smiled and nodded. She'd had no idea of the budding relationship between Wendell and Lauren, though Brice had told her of his sister's career plans. "So you and Brice could become brothers" she wondered out loud.

"Well Lauren and I just started dating" Wendell explained with a nervous laugh. "Brice doesn't know and I'm pretty afraid to tell him because it's so out of left field. Don't know how he'll react."

"Oh I don't know" said Sondra. "I mean you and Brice are longtime best friends and he loves his sister. I'm sure he'll be good with it."

"Yeah, I hope so" said Wendell with a nod and a smile.

That night, after a dinner at a San Francisco Italian restaurant given by several IndyCar sponsors, Doug and Karen returned Sondra and Kari to the motorhome before going to their Sonoma hotel accommodations.

"No boys" warned Karen.

"And don't stay up late talking" added Doug. "Mom and I'll be back here at six-thirty tomorrow morning" he added. While Sondra and Kari did comply with the earlier parental order they ended up talking until just after 10 p.m. "This is pretty cool" said Kari. "So much different from when I went down to Long Beach. I can see now why you like this kind of life. You guys are a bit like rock stars, traveling to places in a motorhome, going to fancy events at nice restaurants, fans wanting your autograph and everyone wanting to see and talk to you."

"Well I wouldn't go that far" said Sondra with a shrug of her shoulder. "I mean I don't think we quite have rock star status, and this is a ton of serious work with a lot on the line. I mean there's a thousand details to keep track of and every weekend has its own dynamic. Most of the time we live like Gypsies and don't eat in fancy places. And the popularity thing was so weird and hard for me when I started. Still is but now I feel it's more of a responsibility to be like an ambassador for the sport. When I'm in my car though, that's all for me. I only care about winning. I love Thursdays and Fridays at a racetrack because it's all about car setups, and there's not so many people watching your every move. Tomorrow and Sunday here are going to be pretty crowded and I have a really intense schedule. This race draws in a lot of fans. I won't be able to hang out with you much. Qualifying on Pole, or at least at the front is my main focus for tomorrow, and then there's Sunday's race. Lots of pressure."

Kari purposely changed the subject. "You looked gorgeous tonight" she told Sondra. "Turned quite a few heads." Sondra rolled her eyes as Kari continued. "It was fun to watch you interact with your colleagues. Some very cute colleagues" she added. "That Tommy guy?"

"You mean Ekelson?" asked a surprised Sondra. "Oh, gross" she voiced. "He's an idiot, and a rookie." "Well anyway" said Kari with a smile and shake of her head. "Seeing you with Brice and how you were with everyone, it's quite a change from the angry introvert I knew years ago in Bakersfield. Ya clean up nice, kid."

"Nutty" said Sondra with an embarrassed chuckle.

Kari put her hair up into a bun and watched Sondra take off her watch, setting it carefully on a cupboard shelf at the head of the sofa-bed. "I like your SeaShell" she told Sondra. "I had such great talks with her today, about different things. She's pretty incredible."

"Yeah" agreed Sondra, wondering if one or more of those talks were about her. "I don't know what it is about SeaShell" she admitted. "But she's super easy to talk to and she's definitely the one I want to run Safen-Up."

"Yeah" agreed Kari. "We talked quite a bit about that. I so totally want to be a part of this now, in any way I can. I know I have a lot on my plate with school, and Shelley was a huge wealth of knowledge about how to manage college workloads, but I think being involved with Safen-Up fits right in with my major and with my ultimate career goals. Besides, it's a part of you and I like that idea. So what do you think of Myrand Fiora?" she asked in a sudden non sequitur.

"I don't know" said Sondra with quick laugh. "I mean I don't know him that well but he's an up and coming talented driver and a super-nice guy. Smart, too. In the off-season he's going to South Western University, studying mechanical engineering." Kari smiled, proud of her instincts to like the boy on more than just a superficial level. She'd found his name to be unusual and had been instantly attracted to him that morning at the Safen-Up tent. She'd become further intrigued when again encountering the young man at the evening's event dressed in a sport-coat and tie.

Sondra listened to her friend speak of Fiora and several others she'd met that night, with Kari then mentioning school several times as well as how impressed she was with Shelley. "Whatcha thinkin'?" Kari then asked, noticing her friend's silence.

"Nothing. It's stupid" said Sondra with a shrug of her shoulders.

"Bet it isn't stupid or nothing" countered Kari.

"Well" voiced Sondra with a shrug. "I guess I was just feeling sorry for myself and then hating myself for feeling that way. I mean I didn't exactly have a normal college experience, and now I have a boyfriend who's going thousands of miles away. Very un-normal. And I hate always having to wonder what my parents or brothers would say or think about what I'm doing with my life."

"That's a lot of thinkin'" said Kari. "And normal is one of those relative terms."

Relativity?" asked Sondra rhetorically. "We're gonna sit here and discuss relativity?"

"Well I'm relatively sure that you're mocking me" said Kari with a quick laugh. "And I suppose it's getting too late to enter into some big philosophical discussion, but I think every college experience is unique. I'm sure mine's different from my roommate's, and I think deep down you do have an idea of what your parents and brothers would say and think about all this. You're doing what you love and you're good at it. You do have some normalcy with Doug and Karen. Besides, you have me and my never-ending friendship, and that's very normal... Except for this." Kari picked up a scrap of paper, waded it up and threw it at her friend.

"Hey" exclaimed Sondra. "Now that's stupid and way not normal" she giggled.

"Nu uh" giggled Kari. Sondra got up and threw the piece of paper in the trash can under the sink, then leaned against the counter, facing Kari. "I'm really glad you're here" she told her friend. "So you really like Fiora?"

"Well yeah" said Kari. "What's not to like? I'm not sure a true Harlequin Romance novel kind of thing is in our future but who knows. Hey, do race car drivers generally end up making a decent living?"

"Most don't" said Sondra with a shake of her head. "This is a brutal business and kinda a hard life. You really have to have this in your blood and want it with every fiber of your being. It's insanely expensive, too. I mean I couldn't have gotten here on my own. Doug sacrificed pretty much everything for me. I'm sure he'll never admit it but he stopped giving Brenda and her jerk kids everything they asked for, just to make things better for me and help me get into racing. He sold his interest in a really successful business just so I could go racing in the Indy Lights Series and so we could live where we live. And he sold his big fancy tow truck to help me get into IndyCar. Karen just jumped in, too. Quit her job and sacrificed her life's savings so I could go racing at this level. I mean everything from leasing this motorhome to band-aids is a big cost. If I don't win races or place well, we don't make money. Tons of pressure."

Kari took note that Sondra made no mention of the large financial settlement she'd received stemming from the Tahoe accident. She watched Sondra bite down on her tongue and pound her fist on her right thigh. She put a gentle hand on her friend's shoulder. "I'm lucky to have the sponsors I have" claimed Sondra, clearly forcing herself to be strong. "But I hate that I got them mostly because of my story. It's like they're using my family. It disgusts the hell out of me. I mean it's a really weird thing to need the sponsors and be grateful for their financial support to help me do what I do, but I can't help feel like they're just evil users."

Kari wrapped her arms around Sondra for a quick embrace, mindful not to say I'm sorry, which she knew Sondra disliked. "Well anyone who's ever watched you race" she began, "or ever spent a few minutes talking with you, knows that it's more about you than any story. Most people don't know what you live with every day, and those that come to find out may think your perceived triumph over that is remarkable. It may seem like some of them are using you and your family, Sondra, but I think getting the story out there can be inspirational to some."

"Yeah, I guess" said Sondra, knowing Kari was trying to say something of comfort. "Did I tell you I got a postcard from Eddie Grisban?" she asked in an obvious non sequitur.

Kari eyed Sondra with a quick furrowed brow, shaking her head. "No, you didn't" she answered.

"I didn't know you guys got postcard-writing close."

"Well I mean we're not really that close" defended Sondra. "But that time a while back when we rode together we talked about Laguna Seca Raceway. The picture on the postcard he sent was of the Monterey coastline and he wrote a quick thing about being there with the Moto-America guys. This was a few months ago. I mean I do think it's pretty cool that he thought of me" she added with a shrug of her shoulder.

"Sondra" began Kari, her voice and thoughts serious. "I think if you ever got involved with Eddie he'd shred your heart to bits. He's cute and a lot of fun and a pretty cool guy, and not a bad kisser, but I know that type all too well. I've vowed to stay away from that and so should you. I know the long-distance thing with Brice is gonna be hard on you but you're surrounded by like at least fifty guys that would kill to have you even look in their direction."

"Oh jeeze" said an embarrassed Sondra, rolling her eyes.

The coastal fog was again contentious early Saturday morning. It was wet, heavy, bitter-cold and refused to relinquish its grip, thus would be delaying practice laps for IndyCar, Indy Lights, USF2000 and the Historic Grand Prix Series. Sondra, with Kari in tow, joined Wendell Grayson and Myrand Fiora in the opportunity to explore the concession area before Sonoma Raceway officially opened the fan gates. The foursome took note of many food and merchandising booths beginning to set up for the day. Sondra had a quick memory flashback of Tumbleweed Speedway when she and Doug had engaged in similar activity. The memory was cut short by the boys as they made a little fun of her for numerous displays of Sondra Sierre branded products for sale at several locations, including die-cast cars, posters and her Sierre High Speed Inc. clothing line. After breakfast burritos were enjoyed, the group wandered over to the Historic Grand Prix paddock, a large tented area further behind the main grandstands. While Kari was enjoying the attention and camaraderie from Myrand and Wendell, far more than viewing the cars, Sondra was like a star-struck groupie amongst the legendary race vehicles. Wendell orchestrated a photo-op, with Kari and Myrand kneeling in front of the #2 Ferrari 312 T5, originally driven by Gilles Villeneuve. The small group then heard a loud gasp from Sondra and they looked over to watch her go quickly to her knees.

"Hey, guys" she called out, never taking her eyes off the car before her. "Check this out. It's the Lotus Seventy-Two that Emerson Fitipaldi drove. I can't believe it's here. I figured it would be in a museum somewhere."

Sudden unexplainable tears found her cheeks as her knees shuffled on the weather-beaten pavement. She moved around the #20 green with gold pinstriped Lotus 72 E with her mouth slightly agape, remembering a magazine article her dad had once read aloud to her of Emo and the '72, complete with photos. Sondra was far too young at the time to know much about Formula One but she'd instantly fallen in love with the shape and look of the car as well as the description of it and the driver. She'd also loved every page of the book she'd found several years prior, Flying On The Ground, written by Emerson Fitipaldi and journalist Elizabeth Hayward. "Whoa" whispered Wendell as he came to settle on his knees next to Sondra at the rear of the car. "I didn't see this on track yesterday" he stated. "Must-a either come in late yesterday or earlier this morning. Motor's a Cosworth, right?"

"Yeah" confirmed Sondra as Myrand and Kari drifted over to see what was of interest. "Cosworth V-Eight, DFV" she added.

"What's DFV?" asked Myrand.

"Stands for Double Four Valve" informed Sondra. "Four valves per cylinder, and Double because there's eight cylinders" she added.

"Give that lady a cigar" said a voice coming toward them. "Ronnie Peterson loved the Seventy-Two, maybe even more than Fitipaldi" conjectured a pudgy man with short straight gray hair, dressed in a dirty white race suit with red and blue vertical lines. Gary was 68 and had purchased the famous Lotus five years prior. He'd been having it meticulously restored while driving a white mostly unreliable BRM in a number of Historic Grand Prix events the past two years. "They say it was a perfect marriage between man and machine" furthered Gary of his Ronnie Peterson comment. "Wow" said Sondra, remembering her father talking about the legendary Formula One driver Ronnie Peterson and his tragic demise. "So you know about this car?" asked Sondra. She stood and her eyes went from the man who'd joined their early morning fun to the car in question. "A little" said the man. "I'm Gary. I bought the car a few years back. So you're Sondra Sierre. Nice to meet you, young lady." Sondra offered her hand and smiled at his obvious surprise of her grip. After greeting the others Gary again spoke to Sondra. "It's been fun watching your career" he said with a nod. "You're a hell of a driver."

Thanks" said Sondra, wondering if he was actually being sincere.

"So I'm sure you're aware" said Gary. "The schedule's been effected because of the fog this morning. In about twenty minutes they're gonna let us Historic guys out there as basically fog guinea pigs."

Sondra took a quick look around the paddock and noted the number of mechanics and support personnel begin to assemble at most of the other F1 cars. "How'd you like to run a few laps?" inquired Gary.

"Really?" said an astonished Sondra, glancing down at her watch. "I'd love that" she added. "I'll be right back with my helmet and gloves. Don't leave without me." With that, the girl was off in a dead run.

Sondra, slightly out of breath from her trip to the RV paddock and back, stood next to Gary, watching the #20 Lotus as it went through final Tech Inspection. In her absence Gary had made several phone calls, having two conversations with track officials about the last-minute temporary driver switch. Sondra signed her name to the intended track roster and donned her helmet. Gary and his mechanic helped her get strapped in, giving specific instruction as well as warning her of this specialized vehicle's hazards. Gary, John and assistant Brent started the #20 and walked quickly alongside as Sondra made her way into the line of cars, waiting to get the signal to go out for a 25 minute practice session. "We'll be talking to you over the radio from the pit wall" said Gary. "Have fun but be careful. Mind those brakes" he reminded. Sondra gave the thumbs-up in answer, then gunned the motor several times, treasuring its sound and vibration. *I can't believe I'm doing this,* thought Sondra as she was rolling toward Pit Exit. She then rolled on throttle and was in 4th gear before she got to the top of the hill. The tires were cold, the air and track temperature were cool and the asphalt surface still a bit slippery from the fog's moisture. She'd been warned numerous times about the brakes and used the gearbox and engine to reduce her speed going into the right-hander of Turn 2. Sondra gingerly pumped the brakes several times, finding them to be an unpredictable scary mess. They gave uneven minimal response and then grabbed savagely. She purposely ran a wide apex and then cautiously accelerated through Turns 3 and 4. This was a well-known and expensive race car and she was determined not to do anything risky or rookie-stupid.

Accelerating out the Carousel of Turn 6 Sondra developed an involuntary smile. She went up through the gears on the straight before Turn 7 and then executed a longer braking zone than she would have in her Indy car. The brakes going into the hairpin felt a little better and this gave her confidence to rocket away and find out what kind of handling the car was willing to give her on the fast twisty section of Sonoma Raceway. Her second lap was still a bit of a stiff learning curve but she was bonding with the Lotus and gaining confidence by the second. Going through the Esses on her third lap she stopped fretting about the possible fragility of the gearbox, and her exit out of the hairpin of Turn 11 was explosive, beginning to catch the ears and eyes of many. The brakes were now far more manageable and her concentration was on a knife-edge.

Gary, John and Brent looked on with a mixture of concern and excitement. With tires and brakes now up to temperature, and the rpms hitting optimal levels, the #20 seemed to scream in anger and laugh hysterically all at the same time as it crossed the Start/Finish line and make its way once again up the hill, snarling like a ferocious lion as Sondra executed down-shifts going into Turn 2. Gary had planned on giving her constant advice and pertinent information about the Lotus, but watching and listening to his car perform at this high level had rendered him speechless. He'd scared himself quite badly several times in this car during the relatively short time he'd owned it and was amazed and proud of how his prized possession was behaving. Sondra on the other hand was in heaven. Even from inside the cockpit, the sound of the high-rev Ford Cosworth V-8 on acceleration and then the tremendous whine on downshifts was just as exciting a sound to her as she'd come to know through films or historic racing engines she'd been privileged to witness in person over the past few years. Though this was deadly serious business, she was playing and living out some of her most joyous childhood dreams. The throttle response and savage horsepower, in much narrower bandwidths than she was used to, would have resulted in disaster for most unfamiliar drivers, but from that very first roll of acceleration and the proceeding gear changes after coming out of the Pits, Sondra had bonded with the car and had simply become part of the machinery. Pure feel and instinct took over as she found the '72s strengths and weaknesses. Witnesses of this spectacle who cared and were paying close attention took note that the #20 Lotus was the fastest car on track. When Sondra once again approached the flag-stand at the Start/Finish line her eyes and brain registered the white flag being waved. To her left she caught sight of the car's owner Gary, leaning on the concrete Pit retaining wall and holding out a 70's era pit-board sign. He'd only spoken to her twice over the radio and had been showing her messages on this communication board. This time by the sign read, #20 - P1 - L28. Sondra was going from 3rd to 4th gear as she heard Gary's voice cracking over the radio in her ears. "Lap twenty-eight, white flag. Last lap. Beautiful drive, Sondra. You made us all proud" said Gary. She didn't acknowledge the communiqué until she was off the gas and downshifting, nearing the top of the hill. "Thanks for this" she told the extremely generous man. "You have no idea what this meant. Awesome car."

A wall of intense sadness slammed into her that this was her final lap. It didn't seem possible that more than two minutes could have elapsed but she quickly forced herself to snap back to razor-sharp focus. As the checkered flag was waving to signify the end of this practice session she made a gear change and took her left hand off the steering wheel for a victory wave. Sondra proceeded around the course with a smile on her face and after exiting the racing surface was greeted by track stewards, ushering her and the #20 Lotus back toward the Historic Grand Prix paddock.

Sondra soon came to rest in the same spot where this had all started. She cut the motor and began unfastening the safety harnesses, aware of a crowd beginning to form. She desperately didn't want to get out of the car but commenced with the procedure, and as her feet touched the ground after climbing out was met with cheers and clapping. The car's owner and his two-man race crew made their way to Sondra and their car. Gary, a man weighing 186 lbs, gave the girl a hug and was immediately surprised to find himself temporarily lifted off the ground a few inches. Sondra's size, weight difference and obvious strength amazed him and amused many. She thanked the man profusely and stared down at the esteemed vehicle. "Man" she gushed, taking off her helmet and balaclava. Video and photographs captured each moment as Sondra began an assessment of her experience. "You weren't kidding about those brakes" she said, shaking her head. "Yikes. I mean I had to really pay close attention to the temps the whole time. This car is so live every second it's in motion" she announced, grinning ear to ear. "You can't break your concentration or ever relax. Busy, busy, busy, but man, so much fun. Those big rear tires really give you some grip, and the understeer and chassis-roll is way different than my Indy car. And I just couldn't get over that sound and the feel. I mean I love all the advancements in technology I get to work with every day but in a weird sort of way I wish I'd have been racing in this era."

Robust laughter came from the increasing numbers surrounding this moment in automotive history, but all that sound and motion came to an odd halt as Karen made her way through the ensemble. "Sondra Jean Sierre" scolded the manager-mom, hands on hips. This further amused the crowd but Karen's displeasure was unwavering. "What were you thinking?" she asked the girl, rhetorically. "Come with me. Darren and the guys are fuming. You're supposed to be in a team meeting."

Normally, Sondra would have taken this as an unjust attack but her triumph was too great and she just couldn't stop smiling. She gave a quick wave and again thanked Gary for the opportunity he'd given her.

"How much trouble am I in?" asked Sondra as she and her now-mom made their way to the main Holt Racing hauler office.

"Oh, I don't know" said Karen. "Never a dull moment with you, is there? I wish you'd have told me what you were planning on doing before you just went and did it, but then you wouldn't be you, would you? And I'm not really that angry" she relented. "You generated quite a bit of excitement, especially after it was determined it was you in that car."

"Sorry I didn't tell you beforehand" said Sondra. "But it was a once in a lifetime thing and I just couldn't pass it up."

"I know" agreed Karen. "So you had fun?"

"Well I mean it's not like I'm a four-year-old playing on a swing" argued Sondra. Karen reached over and put her hand solidly on her daughter's back. "But yeah" admitted Sondra of Karen's question. "Fun, fun and more fun. I mean it was even more amazing than I ever imagined it might be. Wish my dad could have seen this" added the girl in a surprising admission. Karen was well aware that Sondra usually went out of her way to avoid talking about her parents or family. "Maybe somehow, some way he did see you" she offered the girl.

A number of minutes later Sondra found that Darren wasn't quite as angry as Karen had eluded. Sondra was however scolded, mostly in jest, by her engineering and technical support staff, and roughly 40 minutes later T.J. himself was the one to help the girl get strapped in to the #12 Indy car before the morning warmup. He put a heavy hand on her left shoulder and squeezed. Under the privacy offered by loud IndyCar engines idling on pit lane T.J. leaned closer and spoke low and gruff. "Don't put my car in the fence but go out there and show me what you just learned." Though the differences in car age and technology were vast, the way Sondra had been forced to adapt to the Lotus' tire, suspension and brake anomalies had produced a completely different way of thinking and attacking the course. Now during the IndyCar practice session she could test and play with the different lines, braking zones and acceleration points she'd discovered in the #20 F1 car. Some (most) didn't work at all, which came with emphatic admonishments from Darren, but as the session went on a few revelations came to fruition. "Found something" said Sondra as she was entering the Turn 6 Carousel. "Coming in. Pitting this lap."

"Copy, pit this lap" repeated Darren. Moments later, standing in front of her lead strategist as he sat in his usual seat on the mobile pit command unit, Sondra gave detailed description of the car and track conditions. She then spoke of the things she'd found. This resulted in Darren ordering the pit crew to make a wedge adjustment on a rear wing element and fractional changes in tire camber. Sondra then went back out on track for a two-lap test with four sticker red sidewall slicks, while Darren, T.J. and the engineers kept close tabs on their laptops, finding that Sondra had indeed found something. Going through the S's on the second lap, Darren spoke to his driver. "Good job, kid. Pit this lap. Pit this lap. Hit your mark and don't slide the tires. Do not slide those tires." This set of tires were now scrubbed in and would be used during the next day's race. The remainder of the practice session for the #12 was spent on a set of sticker black sidewall tires as the team watched fuel consumption, tire-wear and lap-times. Sondra had gone from running a 1:17.863 on those opening laps of the morning to hitting an average time of 1:16.315.

At the conclusion of the session, Holt Racing had obtained P1 status and pit reporter Lydia Velstein was on hand to ask about the progress of her day. "Well I mean we unloaded pretty decent" said Sondra. "And we've run a lot of laps here during preseason testing and then the IndyCar test a while back. We have a lot of data on our Holt Racing, Triple A, Snap-on Twelve car from last year and from Delgato's car here last year as well. When the fog finally lifted, the track warmed up fast and we got a glimpse of what race conditions are most likely gonna be, and then what we're hoping to get for qualifying later today." Lydia then asked about Sondra's drive in the F1 machine, alluding to the fact that a few of her fellow drivers were not happy that she might have gained some kind of unfair advantage. Sondra shook her head and set her jaw. "There's no advantage" she asserted. "I mean the cars are like a billion miles apart in age and technology. It's like comparing apples and, well, lava-rock."

In the glorious clear-blue sky Saturday afternoon, Sondra rode high the reluctant praise she'd been given for her morning antics and encountered mostly excited and happy fans during a 40-minute autograph signing session that included a number of Safen-Up kids. Later, during Round One of qualifying, Sondra was in Group Two, where she banked a hot-lap on a set of black sidewall tires. At the end of the session Holt Racing was shown 4th quickest. By the conclusion of Round Two however she posted the fastest time, earning her a spot in the Fast 6 final round of qualifying. On Darren's instruction, Sondra went out early for two laps on a set of used black sidewall tires. They then sat in the pits on a set of sticker reds. The top spot changed hands five times, and with time running down, just under 4 minutes remaining, Darren released the #12. Sondra's first lap of 1:15.932 was soon bested by Shane Teluchi, then Greg Raley. The Holt Racing #12 car circulated the course and came up on a critical point of the track, the timing line behind the broadcast building, with seconds to spare. This allowed her to enact one more try at attaining the top spot. With a mistake-free lap she put down a blistering time of 1:15.503. Pole winner Sondra Sierre had pumped her right fist in the air a number of times during the cooldown lap after the checkered flag was waved at the conclusion of IndyCar qualifying. Over the radio she thanked Darren, T.J., her engineers and her pit crew. Moments later she had an ear-to-ear smile as pit reporter Tony Currington began an interview. Sondra's facial expression diminished however when, once again, she felt she had to go on the defensive for her earlier position that the time in the Lotus had not given her any kind of advantage. As Currington pressed the issue, Karen instinctively put a gentle hand on her daughter/client's back, taming emotion and possibly avoiding some sort of foul-mouthed tirade. Sondra managed to skillfully sidestep the morning issue and refocus the conversation to what had just taken place. Minutes later her edgy disposition turned happy and victorious as she knelt down to put the P1 Pole Award sticker on the outside endplate of the #12's right rear wing.

A summer Sunday in Sonoma, California, never looked better. The weather was spectacular. The cool morning fog had been light and had morphed into a 77 degree full-sunshine no-cloud day. The crowds at the raceway were among the highest ever recorded for a single event and the official program prominently displayed Sondra on the cover, with a picture of the Triple A #12 car flashing by the Sonoma track's Start/Finish line. On page 23 there was a short 3-paragraph article written by Lydia Velstein, with quotes from the then 19 year-old driver about why she loved the track. Sondra had described the area, liking the gentle rolling hills, the fragrant vegetation and how the coastal breezes in this particular part of California had a feel like no other. When speaking of the race facility itself she stated that when she was "a kid" she and her dad had "traipsed around pretty much every inch of the place" Sondra had approved and liked the article

Lydia had written because, in print, the raw emotion she always felt when thinking and speaking of her father, with him no longer in her physical life, was not so pronounced.

At 1:04 p.m. Sondra sat in her race car on pit lane with the engine idling after the 23-car field got the command to start engines. The pressure to perform on this day seemed more intense than many previous races, even considering her two Indy 500 experiences. Normally before a race she would perform a mental checklist and calm herself, seeing in her mind the preferred outcome. This particular moment however had her mind going in at least ten different directions. She was on the verge of panic, not being able to find a point to begin her all-important focus. Sondra suddenly noticed her breathing, pronounced and through her mouth, and began worrying that she couldn't seem to swallow. She stared down at the flashing LED lights on her steering wheel but her brain wouldn't focus on the meaning of the numbers and the handful of colored buttons. It was an enormous relief when Darren's voice came to her over the radio. "All right, Sondra. We're starting on sticker reds. It's a long race so lets be smart, strong and focused. Show me some of that drivin' stuff" he added with a slight chuckle. This last bit of levity managed to do the trick for her. She flashed a smile, shut the visor on her helmet and looked down to make sure she was in First gear, then revved the engine twice and focused straight ahead.

On the warmup lap Sondra followed the pace car weaving back and forth in several places to put heat in the tires and make sure they were scrubbed clean for the start. She also lagged back a few times then made a quick charge, listening to and feeling the powertrain's response. Passing behind the broadcast building she noted that the flashing lights had gone out on the pace car. Rounding Turn 11, she watched the white Toyota sedan veer to the right, off the racing surface. Her eyes then trained on the starter stand, and when the green flag thrust forward and began waving she heard Lead Strategist Darren call out, "Green, green, green." The #12 was the first car to reach the top of Turn 2 and Sondra's mind and body went on autopilot. She was diving into Turn 4 when she again heard Darren's voice. "Big crash going up the hill. Stay on it, stay on it, stay on it. Okay, caution's out. Caution's out. Full-course caution."

"Copy caution" said Sondra as she reduced her speed and glanced in her mirrors. Exiting the Carousel, Turn 6, she listened to Darren explain why IndyCar officials had gone to a full-course caution instead of a local yellow. The Holt Racing strategist hadn't actually seen the details of the crash but was repeating the reports that had immediately come to him.

"Three mid-pack cars got together going through Turn One" Darren told his driver. "The number Nine" (Patrick Colvin) "got loose on cold tires and slid into the Fifty-one" (Trace Vanmuesen). "The Fifty-one spun and somehow flipped the Thirty" (Phil Grumenchino). Darren was being alerted to increasing smoke at the crash-sight but didn't mention this to Sondra. After heavy contact from the #51, Phil Grumenchino's car had slid and bounced off course. His front tires caught the uneven dry grassy terrain with severity, flipping the vehicle upside down and igniting a small grass fire. Grumenchino frantically scrambled out from under and tried in vain to kick dirt onto the flames. The track's safety team was immediately on the scene before the fire got out of control and it was quickly extinguished.

Sondra reached the chicane of Turns 9 and 9A at the same time she noted red flags being displayed. She then heard Darren's voice. "Red flag, Sondra. Red-flag. Race control wants all cars to stop where they are. Stop and cut the motor."

"Copy red-flag stop" she acknowledged. "Engine's off" she furthered. "I see smoke. Everyone okay?"

"Yeah, everyone's fine" said Darren. "Fire's out. Sit tight and I'll let you know when we can refire."

"Copy" said Sondra, wondering what would happen if she couldn't get the engine to start. She lifted the visor on her helmet and blinked her eyes, taking a deep breath as Darren made a further clarification.

"We're being told that when the track goes yellow again you'll pick up the pace car in Turn Eleven. If you can't get refired, they'll come to you. The restart will be single-file, with everyone in the position of the last transponder and timing loop. Lap One will count and so will the next caution laps. No change in pit-strategy."

"Kay" said Sondra. "Car feels good" she added.

Seeing or hearing of a crash during any part of a race had always been upsetting to Sondra but this incident may have been exactly what she needed, a race-start do-over. She knew for sure that her car was strong and now a second chance at calming herself, focusing on the details and visualizing the checkered flag waving with her in the lead. When the 75-lap event resumed it went on to be plagued by six more caution periods, though none of these warranted the red flag. Sondra relinquished her lead only once, for three laps due to her first green-flag pit stop. After reclaiming the top position however she was able to stretch her lead to 5.842 seconds ahead of Greg Raley, followed by Shane Teluchi and Justin Oliver. On Lap 58 Darren watched the #12 car accelerate past and head up the hill. "All right, Sondra" he announced to his driver. "We're gonna pit this next time. Pit this lap. Pit this lap."

"Copy, pit"# answered Sondra as she touched the brake peddle and squeezed the left paddle-shifter a third time, going to a lower gear as she neared her apex of Turn 2. "No changes" she added. She was dealing with increasing understeer but knew it was due to the fact that her tires were coming to the end of their optimal life.

While on the short straight before getting to Turn 7, Darren spoke in his usual calm but serious voice. "Caution's out. Caution's out. Spin in Nine." Sammy Verdoux had lost rear grip in Turn 9 and run off into the dirt, raising a significant cloud of dust. When Race Control determined that the #7 was not able to get the engine re-fired they enacted a full-course caution in order to send a safety vehicle to assist the ailing car. Holt Racing's original plan was to go onto a set of used black sidewall tires for this stop. With the #7 bringing out a full-course caution Darren instinctively knew that most if not all of the field would be pitting for fuel and tires and was sure the top-5 were on a three-stop strategy. They would be going on new red sidewall faster grippier tires and he made a split-second calculated gamble to do the same with the tire change, but his strategy was to have Sondra go the rest of the way on this stop. This was a big gamble due the fact that it was Holt Racing's last set of sticker reds. It was also asking a lot of Sondra to put so many laps on this tire compound and save a significant amount of fuel to the end. Though Sondra didn't have the age or experience of much of the field, she'd taught herself to be among the masters when it came to saving tires and fuel. Darren was now counting on this.

Holt Racing's #12 remained at the top of the running order while setting the pace, an average of seven-tenths slower in this segment than that of the first two. With 14 laps to go Sondra's 4.7 second lead advantage and smooth run to the end came under fire with the last full-course caution of the day. Tony Kelarzo was running in 11th Place and trying desperately to get into the last points-paying position. He attempted a bold pass on the outside of Jerome Levoy in the hairpin of Turn 11, but the bright blue #29 of Levoy got loose and made hard contact with the green-orange-white #25. Kelarzo's car did a jagged 180 degree spin and struck the outside retaining wall, shattering carbon-fiber front and rear wing pieces. Both cars sustained heavy damage, with severely bent front and rear suspension elements. Darren immediately wrestled with whether or not to bring Sondra in when the pits were open but fate made the decision for him. "I might-a run through some debris" announced Sondra. "Eleven's a mess. Bits and pieces of wing everywhere."

"Copy that, Sondra" acknowledged Darren. "When the pits are open we'll come in for tires. You're good on fuel 'til the end so it'll be a quick stop." Sondra didn't respond. She was deep in thought, going over in her head that any semblance of their original two-stop pit-strategy had now gone completely out the window. She also knew that she'd be going on the set of used reds that she'd been on for two laps during the previous day's qualifying. Sondra began to question in her mind whether or not they could go flat-out for fourteen laps. The cars behind her would most likely be going on a set of new reds or sticker blacks. As she circulated behind the pace-car she discussed this fact with Darren, stating that if the guys behind her were on new tires she'd be a sitting duck. The steady strategist did his best to ease her worries, and after a blistering 5.2 second pit stop Sondra went back out as the leader.

The track went green after a total of 4 caution laps. Sondra executed a restart that had many on their feet, and the AAA Holt Racing #12 skated over and through Turn 2 like a hockey puck being fired from a gun. The red-white-blue machine twitched on deceleration and then appeared to swivel and snarl as the tires struggled for grip and the motor savagely clawed a way forward. Spectators witnessed the next number of laps as seemingly frantic and uncertain, but for Sondra this on-purpose no-nonsense intensity showed a glimpse into the core of her existence. Her track knowledge and the race craft she'd learned and developed over the years were now being subconsciously enhanced by her experience in the Lotus '72. As the colorful serpentine of Indy cars made their way around the course, broadcast cameras went to a fleeting shot of the Holt Racing mobile pit command center. Three engineers concentrated their stare on computer screens as Darren's gaze went from the track to a video monitor in front of him. T.J. was taking it all in as well, chewing gum as if he were part of the #12's motor. With five laps to go he observed rookie Thomas Ekelson on a set of new red-sidewall tires get around Shane Teluchi for 2nd Place, beginning to inch toward the leader. Three laps later the #4 caught Sondra and made a pass going around her on the outside of Turn 1. The pass looked near-impossible to most on-lookers. Back when Sondra was learning the course and honing her driving skills in the F-Ford she'd discovered instances where this move was possible. She had since used this tactic a number of times over the past two years and Ekelson had once seen her do this from behind, just after the halfway point of the race. Tony Kelarzo, Shane Teluchi and Greg Raley had enacted this move as well several times over the years, but the first time Thomas had tried it in his Indy Lights car a year ago he'd not been as successful, running off course and into the dirt, ending up with a broken front A-arm in roughly the same spot as Phil Grumenchino's disastrous first-lap IndyCar start.

The #4 rocketed up the hill but was carrying far too much speed into the second corner. He was forced to run wide, which allowed Sondra to slice inside and get back into the lead. With two laps to go

Ekelson bullied his way to the inside of the #12 in Turn 11, forcing Sondra in a choice of either running wide or becoming entangled with the #4's front wing. She wisely backed off and followed him up the hill. A short time later, as the two approached Turn 7 the grandstands on the outside of this hairpin-corner erupted in cheering mayhem by fans when Sondra moved to the inside of the #4 and shot in front, accelerating hard. The #4 began to lose ground to the #12 in the fast S's. Brice Crandle had been making up ground and pulled a move on Ekelson going into Turn 10, nearly brushing the outside retaining wall. He was on those fresh red tires and was making a determined charge. The #48 got around Ekelson and as the two cars fought over 2nd Place this allowed Sondra much-needed breathing room. Darren let his driver know the increasing time-gap between her and Crandle and that Ekelson was desperately trying to find his way around the #48. As the corners swished by, the two boys continued to fight with one another, basically doing what many of the macho guys Sondra had driven against had done. They were abusing their tires and equipment. Ekelson got around Crandle in Turn 11 but Sondra was pulling a gap 0.402 seconds per lap on them. The 2nd and 3rd Place cars were now seeing their tires and brakes beginning to give up but on the last lap in Turn 7 Crandle accelerated past Ekelson. Two corners later, Shane Teluchi got around the #4 for a 3rd Place podium spot.

The winner's circle celebration for Sondra was triumphant but felt unusually emotional. This had been an exhausting weekend, with the day being non-stop busy since she'd opened her eyes that morning. These intense hours had suddenly partnered with a late afternoon change in ambient air temperature, up to 83 degrees, and Sondra had worked hard in the 111 degree cockpit of her race car. Before climbing out of her car she sat with her hands still clutching the steering wheel, looking up at Doug and several team members as they moved in to pat her shoulders and the top of her helmeted head. Sondra was next aware of hands moving around her beginning to unfasten the safety harness and disconnect the communication cable as well as the air circulation and drinks system hoses that went to her helmet. She felt like crying as she suddenly remembered her Indy 500 win, and was momentarily haunted by memory flashes of her father and family. Quickly forcing away intense emotion she rose, standing in the seat of her car and punching her fists triumphantly in the air. With Lydia and Karen on fast approach Sondra made a leapfrog jump to the ground, removed her gloves and helmet and received a hug from manager-mom. Lydia then began the interview. By now most of Sondra's post-race words were rehearsed and standard, with the exception of a few specifics about the race she'd just run. Karen was well versed in winner's-circle procedure but for her it had become somewhat tedious. After witnessing the initial driver interview she would stand close-by as many photos were taken, and would usually end up with an armful to hold and carry. This consisted of Sondra's helmet, balaclava and gloves, towels, a drink bottle and numerous sponsor caps. Roughly 30 minutes of this in the hot sun while trying to maintain a constant smile was something to be endured. She did this gracefully and happily but looked forward to the end of the long day, sitting with her feet up in quiet comfort with her husband and daughter.

The next day, Doug and Karen took the opportunity to engage in another flying lesson. Sondra sat on the front porch, cup of coffee in hand, waiting for Brice's planned arrival at Casa de Trent. After her second cup in just over an hour she was about to give up and go inside, perhaps go down to her race garage. Her phone buzzed and Sondra smiled, taking note of the name and number appearing on the small screen. "Hi Brice" she answered.

"Hey" he greeted. "I'm pullin' onto your road. You up for some company?" he inquired.

"Well that depends" quipped Sondra. "Who did you have in mind?"

"Oh you know" joked Brice. "The King of England, the Prince of Wales, the next Formula Two champion."

"Oh sorry" said Sondra "I was expecting a rock star, a movie star and a Formula One champion."

"Well then I guess I'll just have to turn around and go back" chuckled Brice.

"Yeah, too bad" said Sondra, smiling. "You know maybe some other time" she added.

"Yeah, sure" said Brice, also smiling.

"See ya later then."

When Brice pulled to a stop in front of the last space of the four-car garage, the gym, Sondra raced to the car and got in the passenger seat.

"Twice around the park, driver, and step on it" she told him, losing the battle of not laughing in hysterics. Brice chuckled, shook his head and leaned over to give Sondra a kiss.

"My folks are off flying" she said. "Let's go down to my garage." Without a word, Brice put the BMW M-6 that he'd borrowed from Stephanie into reverse, then headed to the new destination. "So" began Brice after he and Sondra had engaged in an enthused round of necking on the Sierre-Trent Raceway couch. "I'm hoping you'll have some time in your off-season to come visit me across the pond but no matter what, I'll be back in the states for Thanksgiving and Christmas."

Sondra nodded, mulling over in her mind the possibility. She then flung her arms around him and clung on tight, experiencing deep emotion. "I'm not just leaving you, Sondra" he whispered. "Well I am technically leaving" he corrected. "But I'm not leaving you. We have today and most of tomorrow, and we'll find time next week when we're at Vegas."

She pulled away and stood. "Wanna do some riding? she asked him.

"Yeah but not right now" he said. Sondra eyed the boy, then glanced at the borrowed shiny red sports vehicle and back to Brice.

"Shot-gun" she announced. "Then I get a chance at the wheel" she added. Brice had had other things in mind for them to do but was always instantly up for automotive fun and games. The two race drivers took turns putting the M-6 through its paces on Sondra's kart track, then headed to a coastal eatery that Kari had recently recommended.

Doug and Karen arrived home just after 3 p.m., not finding

Sondra in the house. They called her cell number, figuring that the girl was down at her race garage. Needless to say they weren't too pleased to find that Sondra had left her phone on the coffee table in the den. However it was approximately ten minutes until Sondra and Brice came through the front door. "Hi Mom, hi Dad" Sondra called out, hearing them in the kitchen. She led Brice to them. "Look what the cat dragged in" she furthered. After greetings and pleasantries were exchanged, Sondra and Brice went down to ride dirt bikes. Before the kids left the house however Karen made a point in handing Sondra her phone. "Don't leave home without it" she told her daughter in a pointed, half-joke. "We'll call you when dinner's ready.

Following breakfast the next day, Brice and Sondra engaged in some karting, agreeable light conversation and a heightened make-out session. Sondra then showed Brice some of her family items in the loft. This meant a lot to him, knowing how hard it was for her to even speak of her beloved family. His favorite of her treasures were her cherished stuffed animals as well as her and her brother's toy cars, trucks and airplanes and several pieces of her family's living room furniture. Maureen had hand-made each of her children the characters from Winnie The Pooh. Sondra's beloved cloth detailed stuffed animal was Tigger. "I always loved Tigger's voice and his energy" she told Brice. "Dave got Pooh-bear and Haley had Eeyore. Mom made Piglet and Roo as well. They always sat on this bench seat that had mom's sewing fabric underneath."

She turned her head toward Brice in dramatic flare. "Would you by any chance have a jar of honey?" she asked, sporting an uncontrolled smile.

"Silly ol' bear" recited Brice, with an equally large smile. The Trents later treated Brice to a nice lunch at a hotel's beachfront outdoor patio restaurant before Sondra and Brice said their goodbyes in the eatery's parking lot. The young couple held each other tight, kissed one another many times and vowed to sneak in every possible second together they could while at the Las Vegas Motor Speedway.

According to IndyCar rules and the championship points structure, the Indianapolis 500 and the last race of the year counted as double points. Coming into Las Vegas there were four drivers mathematically eligible to win the championship. With Sondra's victory in Sonoma she had amassed the most points thus far, 697. Greg Raley had been 2nd going into Sonoma but his disastrous race outcome relegated him to 3rd, behind Shane Teluchi, 24 points behind Sondra with 673 points. Emanual Billings had a terrific first half of the season but now found himself going into the last round 4th, with 563 points. Billings had the slimmest of all chances for championship victory. In order for him to win he'd have to attain the Pole, win the race and lead the most laps. Sierre, Raley and Teluchi on the other hand had only to finish 20th or better. Fifth in points, 96 behind the cut-off line for a chance at the coveted IndyCar title was Justin Oliver. He'd won several races and Poles throughout the season and was profoundly baffled with his end-of-the-season results.

The Holt Racing Triple A, Snap-on #12 car was a handling nightmare in the first IndyCar practice on Thursday morning. At 221.492 miles per hour, going down the arced front-stretch, Sondra reported to her lead strategist, "We're wrecking-loose" her voice sounding frantic and strained. The term wrecking-loose was one Sondra had heard several times during last Sunday's Nascar race at the Michigan International Speedway that she and Doug had watched on TV. "Massive understeer in One" added Sondra seconds later. "But then it snaps to wicked oversteer. Gusting big wind going into Three. We're gonna be in the wall in two laps." Before Darren had a chance to confer with his engineers and verbally agree with his driver, her complaints became quite evident as he and many on-lookers watched the #12 car display a ruthless twitch and slide up dangerously close to the outside retaining wall in Turn 4. Sondra then had another moment as she was again entering Turn 1. Darren wisely ordered his car to pit lane. The #12 machine was close to 4 miles an hour slower than the Penske #25 of Tony Kelarzo, who'd posted the fastest time in the opening laps of the session. As Sondra exited her car on pit lane she was observed by her team members as shaking and white as a sheet as she took off her gloves, helmet and balaclava. The young driver scrambled over a 3-foot retaining wall to speak with Darren and her engineers. She then sat on top of the concrete wall and watched as team members attended to her car. Karen handed the girl a clear plastic bottle containing cool water, then set a dampened cool towel around her daughter-client's neck. "Your SeaShell is here" said the manager-mom, adjusting the towel. The ambient air temperature at 10:48 a.m. was already at 89 degrees, with track temperatures between 12 to 18 degrees higher. Though Sondra had been on track for only a relatively short period of time she'd worked hard to control a very uncontrollable race car, with a cockpit temperature reading of 114 degrees Fahrenheit. She took constant small sips of the refreshing liquid and nodded, happy to hear that her friend had arrived at the track and was planning on being around all weekend.

Shelley took Sondra to lunch at a mom & pop deli and sub sandwich shop just over three miles from the speedway. "The Sonoma Safen-Up event proved beyond a shadow of a doubt that we're on the right path" announced Shelley. "You have no idea how successful it was and how we're going to be able to build from that."

"That's what mom said" voiced Sondra.

"What do you say?" Shelley asked. Sondra took a deep breath and looked over at a middle-age couple ordering food to-go.

"I don't know" she said. "I mean I feel super guilty that I came up with a basic idea, an idea that means everything to me, and I'm not one-hundred percent immersed in it and I won't ever have the time to put everything I have into it."

"No guilt" offered Shelley. "We've talked about this before. You're doing exactly what you're supposed to be doing."

"Kay" said Sondra, now feeling guilty for needing the reassurance from SeaShell. She looked at her watch and took a sip of lemonade. "My car's such a mess" she lamented. Shelley wasn't there to talk cars or racing and offered a quick positive thought on how Sondra and her team would come up with good solutions for a good outcome, then shifted the conversation.

"Darren and I are getting even more serious."

"Good for you" offered Sondra.

"Thanks" said Shelley. "We've been talking about marriage and children."

Sondra didn't necessarily want to talk about marriage or family. She swallowed hard and bit down on her tongue. "You'd make a great mom" she told Shelley. "And I can see Darren as a dad."

"Thanks" said Shelley with a smile. "The trick has been getting my parents and sister to see Darren as more than just some car guy. I think they're coming around now that Mother and Father have spoken with him a few times by phone. I'm taking him to meet everyone in two weeks."

"Wow" said Sondra, interested but her brain was mostly preoccupied with how things were going with her race car.

Sensing Sondra's anxiety about the future Shelley attempted a positive clarification. "No matter what life brings with Darren, marriage and children, I promise I won't abandon Safen-Up and I won't ever abandon you. You're stuck with me. I'm sorry but that's just the way it is" she added with a quick laugh.

"Kay" said Sondra, flashing a smile. She took another bite of her sandwich and breathed in and out loudly through her nose. "Have you ever had like a feeling you might be doing everything wrong?" she inquired.

"You feel like you're doing everything wrong?" asked Shelley.

"Well" Sondra corrected. "Not everything. I get things right but that's in my car and out on the track. Everything else is an unknown, like a mystery and a hideous struggle."

"I'm sorry you feel that way" said Shelley. "I don't see that" she added. "I see a strong intelligent young woman with a big heart and a great direction." Sondra shrugged, only willing to accept a fraction of what SeaShell had offered.

"Sometimes I get clobbered wondering what my parents would be saying or doing" she said. "What direction they might have been giving me. How do I know I'm doing the right thing in every situation. You know, what they'd want me to do. I hate that I can never know that."

"I think you do know" whispered Shelley. "You know your parents and you know you. That voice in your head that tends to second-guess yourself isn't your mom and dad, and that part of you that gets up every morning and works hard at your dreams and goals is far stronger that any negative or self-doubting voice. I see it, I feel it, and I hear it every time I'm around you."

"Thanks, SeaShell" said Sondra.

Saturday's qualifying session was done under a blistering sun, with an ambient air temperature of 97 degrees, with 8 percent humidity and track temperatures from 115 to 128 degrees. The #12 of Holt Racing was 17th in line to go out for a qualifying run. Sondra was both nervous about how things would go and unhappy that she'd never become completely comfortable with the balance of the car. Adding to her anxiety was that she'd not had much time to herself let alone with Brice due to her popularity, especially in light of the fact that she was possibly poised to win this year's IndyCar championship. There was always someone wanting a word, a picture or an autograph in addition to the many important team meetings and individual discussions. After getting up to speed within the two qualifying warmup laps, Sondra took the green flag to her two-lap timed run at 231.081 miles per hour. Her first recorded lap was a bit quicker, 232.004. On her final go-around, with her hands being extremely busy adjusting the tools in order to make the car more stable and cease to scrub off speed she was clocked at 231.649 miles per hour, giving her a two-lap average of 231.826. This was far from what she and her team would have hoped for and it proved to be a half mile an hour slower than the top three cars that had run prior. Adding insult to injury, by the end of the day there had been seven other cars that had posted faster speeds than the #12. Tony Kelarzo had the Pole, with a speed of 232.785 miles per hour. Starting on the front row next to Kelarzo for Sunday's race was rookie Thomas Ekelson, with a posted speed of 232.764 mph. The always-fast on super-speedways, Jorden Deratta, would be starting 3rd, with a speed of 232.761. Next to Deratta on Row 2 would be Shane Teluchi, with a two-lap average of 232.760 miles per hour. There was a full second drop-off between these top cars and the next nine, Brice leading this group with a time of 231.021. The further one went back in the field, qualifying speeds decreased incrementally.

During the morning IndyCar 50-minute warmup, at the practice session before the Indy Lights would take to the track for their final race of the year, the #12 Triple A, Snap-on machine caught the attention of many. Sondra and her Holt Racing team had managed to find some speed in the car. They'd been throwing everything they had at the setup for the past three days and were in agreement to try some extreme low down-force numbers in order to keep them from riding around mid-pack during the race, where the potential for getting caught up in a big wreck was more likely. Normally they might not have taken such an enormous set-up change risk before a race, especially with this one being of great importance because of championship implications, but T.J., Keys and Darren had been building this team carefully the past two years and wanted the big championship result they were sure could be achieved. They'd taken a big chance on the kid. From time to time there was evidence of Sondra's immaturity as a driver. Her overall professionalism occasionally left much to be desired but more often than not Sondra displayed capabilities in the race car that were far beyond her age and experience level. Her personality and unabashed drive for perfection were inspirational and infectious, and all this had led the Holt Racing organization to hope for and expect big things. The opening laps during the morning practice session, with the #12's lower downforce aero package, gave the Holt Racing car equally reduced aero-drag, allowing for speeds compared to the Pole-sitter and the cars in the top four qualifying positions. The downside for Sondra was that her machine was now far more unstable and harder to drive, especially in traffic. This was made evident close to the end of the practice session. Sondra had just reported the conditions she was dealing with as squirrelly and way live. She was making a pass on the outside of Rich Clemens when the rear of her car began to rotate. Her ultra-quick reflexes caught the spin from getting out of control and slamming the wall but it was a high-speed slide that produced an enormous amount of tire smoke. Sondra did end up against the wall, though no significant damage was done to the car or vulnerable tow-in angles of the right side wheels or wishbone suspension.

While opening ceremonies for the Indy Lights race were getting underway, Sondra sat in a beach chair at the front corner of the assigned Holt Racing garage, biting her left thumbnail, her eyes going from her phone to her mechanics and engineers as they went over every aspect of the high-tech vehicle, double-checking to make sure there were no problems stemming from the earlier on-track incident. Though fans trickled by the front of the garage, talking and taking pictures, she was amazed but glad no one engaged her, until two young men suddenly interrupted her world.

"Now see what I mean" said Andrew Placer, slapping the shoulder of his good friend Brice Crandle. "This girl does everything backwards. You're supposed to do the whole burnout and tire-smoke thing after you win the race, not before you even start."

"Kids nowadays" said Brice, smiling and shaking his head. "Can't teach 'em anything." Sondra rocketed to her feet and held up her clenched fist, trying not to smile and jump for joy. "Why I oughtta … If I had a rock I'd ..." she told the boys, her smile exploding as she lightly punched Andrew on the shoulder. "What are you guys doing here?" she asked. "You're the enemies here in Holt Racing territory and now in dangerous waters" she quipped. "And you" she directed to Brice. "I hear you almost went in the wrong pit box yesterday."

"Almost being the key word" defended a smiling Brice. The two boys had not witnessed Sondra's slide-job earlier but had seen several video replays. Race media had also been making much of this particular incident. Sondra lifted the yellow rope that cordoned off the entrance to the garage from the fans and ducked underneath, joining the boys on the outside. Brice grabbed Sondra and gave her a passionate kiss as Andrew removed his eyewear and glanced at the uncowled #12 car. Brice, with his hands on the girl's shoulders pulled away a few inches and smiled.

"Did you just kiss my hair?" asked Sondra.

"Certainly not" denied Brice. "I wouldn't do that. That would just be ..."

"Weird and creepy?" interjected Sondra.

"Well I'm thinking, sweet and endearing" countered Brice.

"Kay" she said. "We'll go with your thing."

Sondra glanced over at Keys, who did not seem thrilled to have Brice and Andrew staring inside their garage. She wisely gestured to her company that they all make a hasty retreat. The three great friends headed over to a section of the garage area that would allow them a view, although limited, of the racetrack. The Indy Lights cars were now on the move for their parade lap, anticipating the green flag.

"Wendell's really come into his own this last half of the Lights season" Sondra stated of their old F-Ford competitor, Wendell Grayson. "I mean he's too far back in points to be in contention for the championship but there's pretty strong rumors that he'll sign with Anditelli Autosports for next year's IndyCar season." This was news to both Brice and Andrew. As odd fate would have it, Grayson started from Pole and dominated the race, lapping all but two cars, but before the event arrived at the halfway point Karen came up from behind the three race car drivers/fans. She put a solid hand on her daughter's shoulder. "Hi Brice. Hi Andrew" shouted Karen over the scream of racing engines. "Sorry to break up the party but we have work to do. Come on, kiddo" she told Sondra. "Hope you boys can stop by the RV later" she said to Andrew and Brice. Young Crandle kissed Sondra on the cheek. "Have a good race" he told her. "And don't do anything rookie-stupid."

"Not a chance" she told him, walking away with a broad smile. "And back at you both" she added.

Before the main IndyCar event of the day and at the conclusion of the national anthem, Karen watched her husband and Denny Hulzor help Sondra get situated in the #12 car. Doug crouched over on one side of the cockpit, Denny on the other and both yanked hard on the straps of the safety harness. Doug then gave Sondra's helmet, light-blue with black and white accents (Safen-Up colors), two hard pats before taking his place on the other side of the 3-foot high pit lane concrete retaining wall. A relative hush came over the speedway as the fans settled in to watch the action. Karen marveled at the row of shiny specialized vehicles, silent and motionless, and smiled as Shelley came to stand next to her. Seconds later the speedway's PA system once again sounded.

"And now race fans, please join me in welcoming your Grand Marshal for today, Comedian Perry Braselton host of the new TV show *Grab Your Ankles*, for those most famous words in motorsports."

In an exaggerated voice, Perry hollered, "Drivers, start-your-engines."

"All right, Sondra" said Darren over the radio once the Honda Twin turbo-charged V-6 power-plant had come to life and was running at a low grumbling idle. "Make sure you're in fuel-map Three. Keep your patience and stay focused. This is a long race. We got plenty of time to make things happen."

Sondra didn't feel the need to respond, and twenty-two seconds later the field of cars began to move, going through pit lane and out onto the racing surface. Getting to a speed of 85 miles per hour behind the pace car, twenty-three Indy cars followed the shiny red next-year's-model Chevy Camaro. On the backstretch of the second and final warmup lap, Race Control was on the radio to all 23 cars. "Lets straighten it up, guys, into a neat and tidy two by two formation. No lagging behind. No stragglers." Sondra next heard the voice of T.J. on the team radio frequency. "All right, Sondra. LTB."

"OM" she replied. This was a secret code of support and strength the two had devised over the past several months. The letters stood for "Lions, Tigers and Bears. Oh My."

The start to the Las Vegas five hundred mile race was waved off twice. The first attempt was thwarted because the back of the pack was indeed straggling, lagging too far behind and there wasn't consistent two-by-two formation throughout the twelve rows of race cars. The second wave-off was caused by Tony Kelarzo getting hard on the gas too early before the green flag and approximately 30 feet ahead of the Start-Zone, indicated and marked with lines of orange-red paint on the inner and outer retaining walls. After making one more circuit the field was amped up to a degree of electrified chaos by the time they approached the flag-stand but the race was allowed to commence. Sondra, from her 17th grid-start position, dove down low and slipped by two cars before getting to Turn 1. She then utilized the high-line to pick off three more cars in the next three laps, gaining the attention of race commentators and fans alike. By Lap 11 Sondra was running in 8th Place. On Lap 17 however she was fighting an increasingly ill-handling race car in traffic and began losing positions in the turbulent air of fellow competitors. With the #12's low-downforce she was slipping and sliding, burning off the important grip in the tires that would normally allow her to place the car where she needed in order to move further up the field. On Lap 42 Darren called his driver to pit lane for their first scheduled green-flag pit stop. "Copy pit" said Sondra, knowing that the Holt Racing strategy for this stop was to be six laps earlier than most in the field. Decelerating for pit-entrance she spoke, sounding a bit out of breath. "Fighting some ugly understeer."

"Copy, Sondra" acknowledged Darren. "Watch your pit speed and hit your mark" he told her. "We'll give you some front wing."

While the #12 was in the pits and getting service there was a vicious crash in Turn 4. Shane Teluchi, gaining ground and six seconds back of current leader Tony Kelarzo was attempting to go around a slower car. The lime-green #37 of Alan Rhettle got loose in turbulent air and slid up into the yellow and blue #24 of Teluchi, causing both cars to slide, spin and impact the outside retaining wall with catastrophic violence. The timing of where the field was when Sondra came out of the pits and when the caution flag flew was what ultimately put Holt Racing back in the hunt for a possible race victory. As the #12 blended back in with the line of cars on track at the slower Caution pace, Darren spoke to his driver. "All right, Sondra. Caution's out for a crash in Four. The pits are now closed but when they're open all the cars in front of you are gonna come in, so you'll be P-One. You'll stay out and be the leader when we go green. Remember, we pitted early so I'm gonna need you to save us a little fuel on this next segment. If you're challenged hard for the lead, don't put up a major fight. Big picture. Lets stay smart."

"What happened to win, lose or draw" joked Sondra, feeling relatively comfortable now that her first pit stop had been enacted without flaw.

"Well I think we stopped playing poker about an hour ago" joked Darren, completely out of character. He was getting reports that the crash was serious and didn't want his driver to worry or be distracted.

"We're on to Pool now" Darren added.

"Sure" said Sondra, surprised but glad for the light-hearted exchange. "But I got snookered into Blackjack" she continued. "Got some heavy losses here and Benny the Mook is threatening to break my ..."

Sondra ceased with the levity as she and the line of cars came around and drove to the inside of Turn 4's accident site. "Tons of debris" she reported. "And a lot of safety guys all around Teluchi's car" she added in a noticeably alarmed voice.

"Our safety guys are the best in the business" soothed Darren.

"Why are we still under caution?" asked Sondra. "Where the hell's the red flag?" she demanded.

"We're monitoring Race Control, Sondra" said Darren. "I'll give you an update as soon as it comes in. Stay calm, positive and focused."

Four caution laps later the Red Flag was indeed displayed and the field of cars were ordered to immediately stop on the backstretch, before Turn 3. The debris field in and beyond Turn 4 was vast and had various sizes of sharp carbon-fiber and metal pieces strewn about, which could easily cut the tires on any of the previously unaffected cars. In addition, the two damaged race vehicles were leaking transmission and radiator fluid, engine oil and fuel. Where the Safer Barrier outside retaining wall had been impacted there was obvious damage, requiring assessment and possible repairs. For Sondra the wait was a torturous eternity. She desperately wanted to ask questions regarding the crash victims and the cleanup progress but didn't want to seem immature or weak. Inside the cockpit the sun was becoming almost unbearable. She bit down on her tongue a number of times as well as opening and closing the visor on her helmet. She also went from gripping the steering wheel hard to rubbing the tops of her legs with outstretched gloved fingers and scolded herself for not remembering to take sips from her car's drinks system.

"How ya doin', kiddo?" asked Spotter Craig Pines, finally breaking the silence.

"Peachy" said Sondra in a flat voice.

"Hang tight, Tiger" Craig told her. "Lots to clean up. Looks like they're putting down quite a bit of Speedy Dry on track so it'll probably be tricky going through all that when we get going again."

"And when is that?" asked Sondra. "I mean we've been stopped for like a thousand years now" she added.

"Not long now" soothed Pines, though he'd not been given any kind of official word. Sondra began to feel panicky. She fidgeted in her seat and strained to see the progress of the crash aftermath.

"How bad?" she asked in a desperate voice. She'd seen the ambulance spend considerable time at the accident site, then roll away in a seemingly determined direction with lights flashing in an angry sobering manner.

"All right, Sondra" said Darren. "We're getting told that the pace car will lead all cars to pit lane. You'll stop directly behind the pace car, not in your pit. They're estimating about forty minutes to make repairs to the Safer-Barrier wall."

"So it's bad?" asked Sondra, fighting back tears and emotion.

"No word, Sondra" said Darren. "Lets stay positive. I'll let you know when they call to refire engines."

"Kay" she said.

The next voice Sondra heard was that of Craig Pines. "So I never got the chance to ask" he began, purposely further distracting the young driver from the heaviness of what was suspected of the crash. "What's with that new little animal sticker on your helmet today?"

"Leo the lion" answered Sondra. "Kind of an inside joke" she added. "Tell you later."

"Seems fitting" said Craig of the black image near the top of Sondra's helmet. "You're just as ferocious" he told her.

Seventeen long minutes later the #12 car began following the pace car and came to rest on pit lane. After exiting the car Sondra used Karen and several team members as a protective shield when walking quickly toward the Trent motorhome. Once inside, Denny Hulzor and Karen sat on the couch as Sondra took the opportunity to use the restroom. When the girl emerged she took several loud swallows of orange Gatorade, which Karen had thoughtfully retrieved from the RV's hide-a-fridge. Sondra then sat down hard in a nearby swivel chair, her eyes narrowing when she took note of Denny. The man was scrutinizing the small screen on his cell phone as video of the crash was being replayed from a live-stream sports app. "Don't show me that" said Sondra. "I don't want to see or even hear it."

Denny turned off the device and put it in his front pants pocket. "I know it's bad" Sondra added. "But I don't want to talk about it. That was a really good stop you guys gave me" she announced, purposely changing the subject.

"Thanks" said Denny. "Doug is a hell of a great motivator" he offered. "Everyone wants to get in there and do great things. It's amazing that he's relatively new to this. It's like working with a longtime pro."

Sondra took several small sips of the orange liquid and nodded. "I'm almost positive I didn't run over anything so we should be in good shape when we go green" she said. "I mean I don't think we have a car that can win today but top-four absolutely."

"Vice president of IndyCar wants to have a quick chat with all the drivers" announced Karen, after reading a message on her phone.

"You ready to get back to it, Tiger?" asked Denny.

"Yeah" said Sondra. "I just want to get in my car and drive."

The race eventually resumed under a cloud of heaviness and uncertainty. Sondra led for 5 laps, using to her advantage the changes that had been made to the Holt Racing car during the 6.9 second pit stop that had been made before the long caution. She then went into fuel-save mode and drifted back to 7th in the running order. There were four more crashes and caution periods as the race unfolded but Sondra's car seemed to be getting stronger, and she stayed within the top 5. Instead of trying to dial in more front wing for downforce as they'd done the first two stops, Darren had his pit crew go back to the settings on the car they'd utilized during the morning warmup. The #12 car was edgy and a tricky beast to drive but Sondra's adaptation to it enthused many. With 24 laps to go Tony Kelarzo, recovering from a bad pit stop, got around Sondra for 3rd Place. Race leader Justin Oliver was coming up fast behind the gray and orange #77 of Abe Kualing. Kualing, a lap down and traveling much slower, made a nervous counter move to the inside, moving across and in front of Oliver. This cut the air to the #2's front wing causing Oliver's car to break loose and slam the wall hard in Turn 1, then spin to the inside. The #77 overdrove the corner and his car came around on him as well, then hit the wall. Kualing's car skidded and spun downward in the corner's banking, and again struck Oliver's machine which spun the #2 back up into the racing groove. Greg Raley, Tony Kelarzo, Sondra Sierre, Thomas Ekelson, Kenny Delmare and Brice Crandle had been in a tight pack and made it through the sliding wreckage, but three other cars behind were not so lucky in avoiding the melee and it created further disaster for five more drivers. With seven damaged and motionless race cars, plus the large debris field, the race was red-flagged for a second time. Sondra was relieved to see Kualing, Oliver and the other drivers out of their cars and moving on their own, but for the next 26 minutes sat with her car still and quiet, fearful of the unknown condition of her racing family members that were no longer in their cars and on track with her.

The green flag again waved for a diminished field and after nine fairly uneventful laps there came two more relatively quick caution periods. The first was for a brush with the wall in Turn 1, ending Alex Roliegh's day. The other caution was for debris on the backstretch. After several low-speed circuits the race restarted with only eleven laps remaining. Race fans were then treated to high-intensity lead-pack drama. Under that last caution, a fast out-of-sequence pit stop had given Sondra the lead, which she held for just over 3 laps. Rookie driver Thomas Ekelson swooped down low to overtake Sondra and a lap and a half later she managed to reverse the position. Tony Kelarzo had a tremendous restart from the 4th position after a lackluster pit stop during the last caution and rocketed his way forward. With 6 laps to go he dove inside Sondra much like Ekelson had done and went on to catch the #4 of Ekelson a lap and a quarter later, getting around him just before Turn 1. As Kelarzo began to stretch his lead the duel of Ekelson and Sierre brought three other cars close, creating a five-way argument over 2nd Place that was breathtaking to watch. Broadcast cameras caught every inch of the constant position-changing action, including shots of Karen, pacing, biting her thumbnails and periodically clutching at the hair on the top of her head. With five laps remaining in this eventful gut-wrenching event, Sondra got around Ekelson coming out of Turn 4 and set sail for the leader. Ekelson made a charge to go back after Sierre but it soon became apparent that he'd abused his tires and was beginning to fall back into the clutches of three hard-charging cars. Caution came out for yet another incident. Phil Grumenchino had run wide in Turn 4 to avoid a slower car and got up into the marbles, rushing the white and red #30 into the wall. The race was concluded under Caution conditions. "Gallant effort, Sondra" Darren told his driver as the field circulated the speedway at a much reduced pace. "Hell of a drive, kiddo. You made us proud all year long."

"Thanks" said Sondra, barely audible. She wanted to be proud of her accomplishment and acknowledge everyone on her team but couldn't seem to find her voice.

"So what do you say?" Darren inquired. "You're awfully quiet for being our new IndyCar champion."

"You may have lost the battle, Tiger, but you won the war" said T.J.

"Awesome job, Lioness" added Craig Pines. As Sondra drove around on the cooldown lap she wished it were possible to instantly transport herself to her childhood home and bed, with the covers pulled over her. She didn't feel like a champion and she hated losing the race. The hard-fought championship was hers however. This had been a lifelong enormous dream and goal but what she suspected of Shane Teluchi began to gut her insides. As she made her way toward pit lane she was directed by race stewards to remain on track and to stop on the checkerboard start/finish line for the scheduled championship ceremonies. A tractor-trailer rig had pulled a large flatbed stage into position in front of her for the festivities but due to circumstances there would be a rather subdued celebration that evening.

The majority of the Holt Racing team came running toward their driver and soon Darren bent over Sondra, speaking in a soft yet strong and purposeful voice.

"Congratulations" he told his star driver. "And I'm sorry but it's pretty bad. Rhettle's got multiple fractures and Shane still hasn't regained consciousness. He's been airlifted to the hospital downtown."

Sondra lowered her still-helmeted head. "Come on, kid" coaxed Darren. "Positive thoughts. Shane's a tough guy and you won this championship fair and square. Now lets go show 'em all why you're the champ."

Sondra stared at her boss for a few seconds and put her hands over the clasps and straps of her safety harness. When hands from her teammates began the extraction process she made tight fists and hollered, "No. Get away. Give me a minute." She didn't want to leave her protective cocoon. The first sight of Doug and Karen on approach however had her taking off her gloves and motioning that she did in fact want help to get out of her race car.

Tony Kelarzo, in the traditional track's winners circle some distance away accepted the accolades for his race victory in a relatively quiet and subdued celebration. As Sondra, still wearing her helmet, was being hugged and passed from team member to team member she could hear over the track's public address system the interview of the race winner. Tony praised the IndyCar safety team that traveled with the series to each and every track. He thanked his team and the IndyCar fans and gave sincere congratulations to Sondra and her Holt Racing team. He ended his short speech on thoughts of his friend and fellow race driver, Shane Teluchi, wishing him and his family hopes and prayers for a good outcome and a speedy recovery. Before the championship Awards celebration got fully underway, Lydia Velstein interviewed Sondra. It took a bit of prompting but Sondra, with Karen and Doug on either side of their daughter-client, gave into it.

"Sondra" began Lydia. "This certainly isn't how the day and the championship was supposed to end, with big crashes and under a cloud of uncertainty for a fellow driver but you're the new IndyCar champion and the first woman to win an IndyCar championship. What are your thoughts right now?"

Sondra clutched the back of her hair, pulling her long tresses over the right shoulder of her race suit as she formed her thoughts. She adjusted the new special champion's cap on her head before speaking. "Hope Shane's gonna be okay" she said with a shrug. "That's all I'm really thinking about. I mean my Holt Racing, Triple A, Snap-on team was so amazing all year. Each and every one of them put their heart and soul into this and I'm glad and honored to be a part of helping T.J. Holt and everyone get this championship. Wish we could have gotten it under better circumstances but ..." She swallowed hard and bit down on her tongue, determined not to cry. She shot Lydia a hard look, trying to convey a message that this would be a horrible time to mention her birth parents or the Sierre family. It seemed to have worked and Lydia focused more on questions of how it felt to be a young female race driver working for the very well-known T.J. Holt and finding herself this year's IndyCar champion, first-ever woman IndyCar champion. Sondra ignored any mention of female or woman, instead focusing on her boss, the team and the fans.

The awards ceremony went on for close to three hours, with the speedway transitioning from the natural light of day to the bright sobering lights of the evening. Hanging in the unspoken air was the possible fate of a fellow driver. There were many speeches, numerous awards given out as well as acknowledgments of IndyCar sponsors, leaders and investors in the sport. By the conclusion, Sondra felt a kind of numbness and was both physically and emotionally drained. Though there were planned team party celebrations later that night, Shelley orchestrated private jet transportation for Sondra, Doug, and Karen back to Santa Barbara. Sondra wanted to be alone. She childishly envisioned getting back in her Indy car and driving as fast as possible along the extended stretches of highway that she'd driven when she'd gone to and from the Grand Canyon. Before leaving the race track, Sondra and Brice said their goodbyes in the privacy of a Holt Racing motorhome.

"You okay?" asked Brice, touching the girl's shoulder.

"Kinda overwhelmed" admitted a very weary Sondra.

"Yeah, I bet" he said, nodding his head. "I'm not at all surprised that you won the championship, but man, you really worked your ass off for it and you've been through every up and down. The word congratulations seems so lame and inadequate right now but …"

"Thanks" whispered Sondra. She wrapped her arms around the boy and took a loud deep breath through her nose. "He's gone, isn't he?" she asked in a crying breath.

"They're not saying anything official to the public" said Brice of Shane Teluchi's condition. "But yeah. This really sucks. Such a great guy."

Sondra bit down hard on her tongue, pulled away from Brice, deftly wiped her eyes and forced down emotion. "He really did a lot for me" she announced, forcing herself to sound strong. "Gave me a ton of really great advice and I learned so much from being on track with him."

Brice nodded. He too had been given solid advice from the experienced and generous racing driver. "Wish I didn't have to go to England now" said Brice. "Just say the word and I won't get on that plane" he added. Sondra shook her head.

"You go over there and set the F-Two world on fire. This is how it's supposed to be" she told him. In an unusual twist it was Sondra who initiated a powerful kiss.

CHAPTER 36

Just before noon on a 76 degree day that featured blue sky with streaks of white thin clouds, Darren and Shelley made their way to Casa de Trent. Doug ushered the couple into the living room. "Karen should be back any minute now" he informed his guests. "Usually takes her about three hours to go to town and back, with all the shopping and errands she runs" he said of his wife.

"Well we're sorry we didn't give you much of a warning that we were coming" said Shelley. "This was a completely last-minute idea" she added.

"No apology necessary" said Doug. "Glad you're here."

"So where's our little champion?" asked Darren.

"Three guesses" said Doug, smiling and shaking his head. "That nutty girl got up early and couldn't wait to get on one of her karts" he added.

"Well if you don't mind" said Darren, "think I'll go down and check on her lap times."

"How's Sondra doing?" Shelley asked Doug after Darren had given her a quick kiss and proceeded to walk toward the Sierre-Trent Raceway garage and tracks.

"Quiet, stubborn and pretty shut-down" said Doug. "Kar and I know she's not happy about Brice leaving for Europe and is feeling the effects of a long hard season, we all are, but we suspect Teluchi's death really walloped the hell out of her."

"It walloped the hell out of a lot of people" said Shelley. "Including me" she added. "I only met him a handful of times but through Darren I got to know him a little."

Doug gave a sad nod. "Well Darren's known Shane and his wife, Rosalyn, and their two girls for years" he imparted to Shelley. "This is so sad" he added, giving his right thigh a Sondra-esque punch.

"Yes" agreed Shelley. "I understand that you, Karen and Sondra got to know Shane pretty well?"

"Yeah" said Doug. "Such a good guy and he really took a shine to Sondra right from the start. Gave her all sorts of advice and was so nice to Karen and me. It's hard to imagine that someone you get to know and like and really respect is suddenly gone, literally right in front of your eyes. The worst part, though, is that Sondra has to go through this. That kid has worked so damn hard to get to this level in racing and she just reached a huge goal in winning the championship, but it's like she's pretty much just dismissing that as if it were nothing. Breaks my heart."

Doug shook his head and briefly closed his eyes. "You know, Karen and I are really grateful for you" he said in a bit of a non sequitur. "You've made such a difference in our girl's life."

"Well thank you" said Shelley. "That's incredibly kind but I think you and Karen deserve so much more of the credit."

Doug and Shelley continued to talk about Sondra and were soon joined by Karen. Darren meanwhile had made his way down to watch his IndyCar driver speed around her 9-turn circuit. He stood and slowly shook his head as he observed a close-to-chaos angry drive, with the rear of the diminutive vehicle twitching and occasionally breaking tire traction on acceleration out of most of the corners. Had Sondra been displaying this kind of behavior in one of Holt Racing's Indy cars the team leader would have been on the radio immediately with harsh words of warning and criticism. Darren started the stop-watch feature on his wristwatch, not necessarily liking the vision before him. On one hand he was being privileged to a rare display of incredible car control with the relative speeds. On the other, this was pure out-of-control unchecked emotion with what was clear to him a blatant disregard of tire wear, fuel consumption and how hard the engine and drivetrain were being asked to work. He watched for close to 20 minutes, becoming more and more amazed at what he first took as a frantic breathtaking drive. Chills and goosebumps then came over him as he realized that every corner of every lap that Sondra made was a precise carbon copy of the last. She soon flashed by the Start/Finish line punching her right fist in the air then drove around at a reduced pace, stopping and cutting the motor inches from Darren's left foot. He watched the girl take off her gloves and unclasp the straps of her helmet then toss them on the couch before pushing the kart back into its usual position near the other three. From a refrigerated drinking fountain that Darren hadn't seen on his last visit, Sondra filled two paper cups of water, offering one of them to him. "If you came to say how sorry you are for me about Teluchi or ask me how I'm doing I will punch you" Sondra told the man as he took the cup from her.

"Fair enough" said Darren. "You got a weeklong media junket to go on, starting Monday" he informed the new IndyCar champion. "It'll criss-cross the country and I'll be joining you for most of 'em. Karen has the schedule."

"Kay" nodded Sondra. "What about T.J.?" she asked.

"Naw, he hates that crap" said Darren with a bit of a smile.

"So do I" said the girl.

"You're a funny kid" Darren told her. "Going on a bunch of TV and radio shows after winning the IndyCar championship is part of the spoils of war" he added.

"Yeah but I'm sure every talk-show I go on or radio interview I do, they're just gonna ask me about Teluchi" she complained.

"Maybe" said Darren. "But just like you figure out how to control adversities in a race car out on the track, I'm sure you can get an angle on controlling the narrative."

Sondra nodded once and gulped down the water, crumpling the

cup and tossing it into a nearby wastebasket. Darren followed suit.

"Can you stay for lunch?" asked the girl. Darren suspected Sondra might be on the verge of tears. He wanted to give her a hug and tell her how sorry he was for her having to go through the pain of Shane's untimely death but resisted the temptation.

"Yeah" he assured her of the question of a midday meal. "I'm here with Shell" he added, glancing down at his watch. "By the way, your best time today was two tenths off your best the last time I watched you run a kart here. You know why, don't you?" he scolded. Sondra did know why but didn't want to admit it. She gave him a bit of a hard look. "Well anyway" said Darren, abandoning the temptation to lecture Sondra on driving angry or upset. "I do believe this puts us right inside the lunch window. Shell and I talked on the way up about possibly getting in on one of Karen's great meals or we could take you guys out to eat. Speaking of Shelley" he added, pulling a small dark brown envelope from his right-front pocket. "I got her this."

Sondra smiled and nodded her approval as Darren held out a sparkling engagement ring. "I think that's perfect" she voiced. "SeaShell's gonna love it. So?" she asked, interested in knowing when and how he was planning on popping the question.

"Well our media tour ends in New York" said Darren. "And as luck would have it, Shell and her parents invited me to stay with them a day or two. I'm sure a perfect moment'll come up."

"Yeah" said Sondra with a smile. "I'm glad" she added, turning her head and deftly wiping away the beginnings of moisture from her eyes. "Dusty today" she stated.

"Yeah" said Darren with a quick coughing laugh. "What do you say we head to the house and get out of the dust and all that tire smoke you kicked up?"

For six back-to-back days Sondra managed to survive the media tour promoting the IndyCar Series and her first championship. Doug and Karen were surprised and proud of their girl. She was professional, gracious and informative during segments on TV shows, radio interviews and a live Q & A session at a large Detroit auto dealership. Sondra's manager-parents were further pleasantly surprised that their kid went from adamant refusal of dealing with the loss of Shane Teluchi to announcing that she would, after all, contribute to the eulogy that was set for that following Saturday evening. The memorial was to be held in a south Florida hotel banquet hall and included a veritable who's who of the racing world. Shane Teluchi was a well-known and well-liked driver, accomplished in many disciplines. Sondra was the ninth person to speak in front of an emotionally charged crowd, gathered to remember and celebrate the life of Shane Armando Teluchi.

"When I came into the IndyCar family" she began, her voice wavering but getting stronger by the word, "some of you, and you know who you are, gave the newcomer a bit of a hard time and treated me a bit like your kid sister."

There was a quiet rumble of laughter from the crowd. "There were a few" continued Sondra, "and again, you know who you are." This produced much louder chucking and laugher from around the room. "You took that concept to some extremes." She took a deep breath and briefly bit down on her tongue. "I kinda love you for that. Well maybe some not so much" she added quickly to more crowd laughter. "My first IndyCar driver's meeting" she continued, "this guy, Shane, sat down and put his arm around me. I may have scolded him a bit for that."

"You did more than scold him" called out Tony Kelarzo. "You told him to knock it off, called him an ass and threatened to break his arm in ten places."

A spiked roar of laughter came from many fellow drivers in the room. Sondra cracked a smile and shrugged her right shoulder. "Well I'm pretty darn lucky that he turned out to be the kind of guy that didn't take offense" she told the crowd. "And I don't even know how it happened but he soon became a mentor and like an older brother to me. In fact, as most of you know, he was usually pretty light-hearted and somewhat of a practical joker. He did a lot of funny things in the couple of years I've been privileged to know him and call him my friend. He knew one of my sponsors is 7-Up and yet one time he set one of these on my car" she said, holding up a can of Coke for all to see. "I asked him if that was supposed to be funny and he said, no, this is supposed to be funny, and took the can that he'd obviously shaken earlier and opened it. It sprayed everywhere. A hideous mess."

The room erupted into laughter and clapping, and when the levity subsided a bit Sondra fought back tears as she again spoke. "Can't tell you how many times I got the giggles from that and the tons of other stuff he said and did. I'm also really blessed with things I learned from him. He was an amazing driver. On the racetrack I could trust him absolutely and he was a dear and trusted friend off the track as well. Gave me a ton of advice about racing and about life. He loved his two girls and his wife, Rosalyn, so much. Talked about them all the time." Sondra gave two shakes of the soda and held it out. "So here's to you, Shane" she announced in an unsteady voice. When she opened the can a small syrupy eruption commenced and bubbled over her hand. She quickly took a drink and licked off much of liquid from her hand and fingers, rushing to her seat in between Doug and Karen, where the mom had moist towelettes at the ready.

Sondra later stood alone, looking at an enlarged picture of Shane in his Formula One days. "Hell of an instinctive driver" said a man coming to stand next to her. Arturi Grekko had gray curly hair and wore an expensive black and gray suit. He nodded, smiling as he spoke. "Independent and ruthless inside a race car but a kind gentle soul outside. Bit of Senna in him. Congratulations on your championship."

"Thank you" said Sondra, recognizing man from pictures she'd seen of him and now recognizing his voice from a phone call he'd once made to her after she'd won the Indy 500. "Gonna miss the hell out of him but he taught me some good stuff" she told the man. Arturi was a popular figure and was soon swept up into a conversation with several men. Sondra stood, stunned by what had just transpired. She then began her search for Doug and Karen, hoping they would be receptive to a hasty departure.

"Liked your tribute" said Thomas Ekelson, sidling up to her. The young man was almost two feet taller than she and the two had never spoken more than a polite few words to one another. Sondra nodded her head in recognition of the boy's comments and continued in the general direction she'd last seen Doug. "Saw you chatting with Arturi Grekko just now" stated Thomas. "That's pretty cool" he furthered. "I hear the guy doesn't talk with just anybody."

Sondra shrugged, not wanting to go into details or start any kind of long conversation with the boy. It wasn't that she adamantly disliked him but she was near her breaking point and felt a powerful need to get out of this room. "Congratulations on the championship" expressed Ekelson.

"Thanks" said Sondra. "Kinda a cloud hanging over it but I won it fair and square" she asserted.

"Sure did" said Thomas. "And I look forward to taking the crown away from you next year" he told her. "See ya around, Princess" he told her, then turned and disappeared into the crowd. Sondra stood for a moment with her eyes narrowed and her arms crossed, vehemently disliking being called Princess. She wished that Brice hadn't already left for Europe and hoped to tell him the details of the evening as soon as possible.

CHAPTER 37

After a four day, three night Caribbean Island vacation with Doug and Karen, a much-needed change of pace, Sondra could relax and enjoy the holidays as much as she was able, then delve into preparing for the next season. This year Sondra was to have a new teammate, Sean Woodall. They knew each other a little as fellow drivers and were encouraged to spend time at both the Texas race shop and Casa de Trent getting better acquainted. She'd come to genuinely like Sean. He was two years older, had a calm and kind personality and was married with a son and another child on the way. Sondra enjoyed their kart and dirt bike duels. They had different driving styles but she liked that he was aggressive without being reckless and unpredictable as she'd known Brice and Andrew to be when they'd "played" on the kart track.

Sondra, Doug and Karen's snippet of off-season respite from IndyCar included a trip to Chicago to visit Uncle Leo. Though Sondra had some anxiety about being immersed in his world and presence, being that he was a direct line to her old life, there was also a mixture of intrigue and excitement. He shared with them several photo albums containing mostly duplicate images of albums Maureen had put together and kept in a hallway bookshelf. To Sondra's surprise there were photographs she'd never seen of Leo and her dad when they were high school and college age. Following a tour of the three story dwelling, they stepped out onto the back patio just off the kitchen, similar to the shape and size of the one Sondra had known in Fresno. It was bitter cold outside but as she explored the many plants and sculptures she came across a startling discovery, the concrete square that had been in front of the Sierre home, the one with their names and handprints. Sondra went to her knees, brushing away plant branches as well as debris of leaves and dirt, then put her hands in each handprint that had been made years ago in the fresh concrete. "Mom, Dad, Dave, Haley … and me, that's me with you all," she cried out. Though the surface was rough and cold, all she felt was her mom, dad and her brothers' warmth. Karen draped Sondra's coat on the girl as the others knelt down to be of comfort. As Leo began the explanation of how this came to be in his possession and the details of its current resting place, Sondra worked though many emotions.

"Sondra?" he asked. "Do you think you might like to have this with you at Casa de Trent?"

She nodded vigorously. Once back inside the warm condo she went into a bit more detail of the day her dad had dug up the crumbling piece of sidewalk, lifted up in uneven portions by the growth of the large Sycamore tree roots in front of the Sierre's home. Kal had made careful forms out of 2x4 inch pieces of pine and mixed two bags of concrete in the wheelbarrow. After pouring and smoothing the mixture with a metal trowel he got the idea to write the family signature in the new wet concrete. On Maureen's suggestion they added their handprints, like Hollywood celebrities had done at Mann's Chinese Theater.

Before the Trents were to leave the next day, Doug and Karen went for a walk to give Sondra and Leo time to talk. "I kinda don't know what to say" admitted Sondra.

"Same here" Leo agreed. "This is really hard" he added. "I know you have this big life going on now with your racing career and all" he began. "And I don't want to interrupt that but I want you to know that you're always welcome to come live with me here."

“Thanks” said Sondra. “That means a ton.” She wasn’t lying about this. Having Uncle Leo suggest a change of living arrangement and knowing he really did want her in his life meant everything. This gave her an immediate boost of personal strength and confidence. It was a building block she’d not had nor expected him to offer. “I love you for that, Uncle Leo” she told him. “I mean I do have a very busy and established life.” She took a loud deep breath before her next words. “I miss Mom and Dad so horribly bad every minute of every day, but Doug and Karen are so great to me and I love them, too.”

“I’m absolutely certain your mom and dad would approve of where and how you live, Sondra” Leo told the girl with a quick nod.

I hope so” Sondra said in a diminished voice. “Sometimes I envision having Dave and Haley with me when I’m on the dirt bike or one of my karts” she continued. “Maybe it sounds silly or childish but I sometimes have little conversations with them.”

“That’s not silly” said Leo, the beginnings of tears forming in his eyes. “I’ve actually spoken like that to your dad” he confessed to his niece in an unsteady voice. “I’ve asked him many questions over these past several years.” Leo shifted his position and turned a fiction novel he was reading right-side up on the small table next to the chair. “Actually, I um” he began in confession. “A few years back I went to your old house, the one out in the country. I guess I was snatching at straws, looking for answers. As you’ll recall, I told you I didn’t get much out of anyone from your in-town neighbors.”

“You saw our old house?” asked Sondra. “I was pretty young back when we lived there” she told her uncle in an unsteady voice. “But in a way I remember it like it was yesterday. I mean in a weird sort of way I can still see and smell so many of the details.” She stopped herself from relating any further memories for fear she’d become too emotional. She got a sudden recollection of the sweet-smelling air just after her dad would mow the vast front and back lawns around that small two-bedroom home on the five acre piece of farmland. The pole-barn, which was mainly built to house her father’s single-engine airplane, had an array of aromas she remembered fondly, from motor oil to burlap sacks of grain for their three horses. She remembered how the pasture smelled just after it had been irrigated, and the collection of hay that was used to supplement the grass consumption for the five black Angus beef cattle. She also used to marvel at how the new concrete, plaster and paint smelled by the back steps of the newly built house and loved being outside for a considerable time, then coming into the kitchen and breathing in the heavenly aromas of what her mom was cooking. These were her sacred family and childhood memories and she didn't want to let them loose, where they might be examined, judged or tarnished. Leo noted that Sondra quickly moved on to a discussion of the future, making sure he knew beyond a shadow of a doubt that she wanted him to continue to do what he'd done all throughout her young life, with his occasional out-of-the blue spontaneous phone calls and visits. He was happy for this idea, perhaps even a bit relieved.

Sondra looked forward to Thanksgiving with Grandma and Grandpa this year and as always delighted in the aroma of food being prepared. She was not necessarily a fan of football but was enjoying the camaraderie of five men gathered in the living room watching a particular game when her cell phone buzzed. Brice had spent over five months in England and Europe, testing, racing and learning the ropes of becoming a full-time Formula 2 driver for the following season. He was given the opportunity to observe the American holiday with his family and had arrived back in the states just under a week before Thanksgiving. Unfortunately he discovered that his parents and grandparents were sick with the flu and that Lauren was planning on spending Thanksgiving with Wendell Grayson and his family. Aunt Heather invited her nephew to stay with her during his time in the US "Last time I saw you" Heather said to her nephew, "you practically talked my ear off about Sondra. You've been here for a full day and you haven't mentioned her once."

"I know" said Brice. "I don't know what's wrong with me. Isn't absence supposed to make the heart grow stronger?"

"Well something like that" offered Heather, lightly chuckling over the boy's misquote. "But life isn't a fairytale or a movie" she told him.

"Yeah" Brice agreed. "It was torture when I first left to go over there" he confessed. "I was getting this huge break and opportunity and I was so excited about my career. I still totally am but when I left for England, just thinking about how I'd be away from her when we only just started a real romance thing was so hard. I've thought about her, I've dreamed about her, and I couldn't wait to come back to see 'er. I don't know why I'm procrastinating in calling her. I know she's in Pennsylvania right now, with her folks and grandparents. We've tried to stay in touch the best we can. Why don't I just get on a plane and go to her?"

"Well aside from the obvious weather and this being peak holiday travel season" said Heather, the voice of reason, "your life's been on a certain trajectory, an exciting one. You're being exposed to new worlds, new people and cultures, new foods and experiences. Life has a tendency to constantly offer many paths and directions. If you and Sondra are meant to be together, which I think you truly are, it'll happen in time. Be patient and let life unfold ... and call her before you head back to Europe."

Sondra figured it was her Uncle Leo and answered in a cheery voice, "This is Sondra, Happy Thanksgiving."

"This is Brice" chuckled the caller. "Happy Thanksgiving to you, too" he furthered. Though it was 29 degrees outside, Sondra proceeded to the back porch. She listened to Brice explain his situation as she stood staring out at a picturesque winter-scape, their conversation lasting just under twenty minutes. The extreme cold she'd felt during the exchange seemed to disappear after the call had ended. It wasn't that Sondra was any less affected by the temperature but now there was a distracting blanket of questions and confusion. She didn't know quite what to make of the overall conversation and hated not having things in her life crystal clear. She went back inside to the warmth, determined to put Brice and this talk out of her mind.

Three days after returning from the Thanksgiving trip, Doug and Karen walked into the Sierre-Trent Raceway garage mid-morning and were perplexed to see their daughter in a furious struggle with a garden hose. With each nonconformity and its refusal to coil to her exact standards, Sondra grew more impatient and on the verge of a childish temper-tantrum. She suddenly threw down in disgust the portions she held in her hands. “Damn cheap hose” she muttered. “I hate finicky crap like this.”

For several days both Doug and Karen had noticed Sondra’s recent edgy temperament, but since this only appeared sporadically and was never aimed at anyone in particular nothing had been said. “We’re heading out for another flying lesson” said Doug, electing not to inquire about the girl’s state of mind.

“Kay” said Sondra.

“Fly safe, and happy landings” she told them.

“Thanks” smiled Karen. “Here’s your phone” she said, handing the device to Sondra. “You left it on the kitchen counter, again” she scolded. “It buzzed several times and then we got a couple of phone calls on the home line. Kari’s back in town and would love to get together with you, and Thomas Ekelson called.”

“Ekelson” sneered Sondra. “What the hell does he want?”

“Well I’m sure he wants to know why you’re in such great spirits this morning” scolded Karen. “We’re gonna talk about your little mood-fest when we get back” said Doug. “Should be long before dinner. Looks like Eddie Grisban also left you a message. You know you’re more than welcome to come with us today, kiddo” he added. “Maybe you’d like a change of pace and scenery.”

“I’m fine, dad, but thanks for the offer” she said, not necessarily convincing him or Karen that she was in fact fine.

“Well call everyone back” advised the mom. “We’ll be back before you know it.” Karen and Doug took turns giving their daughter a hug before they left for their skyward adventure.

Sondra kicked the hose off to one side of the garage and called Kari, and in less than an hour the two were sitting inside a downtown cafe, chatting about their Thanksgiving experiences. Sondra went into detail about her phone interaction with Brice, while gently swirling the thick paper cup of coffee before her with her right hand, occasionally taking small sips.

“So what do you think?” she asked her friend. “Was that like a Dear John phone call? I mean he basically spelled out the obvious that we're gonna be apart for quite some time and then he tells me to take care and live my life to the fullest. What the hell does that mean? I mean on the face of it, that's kinda sweet but, well, that's like total clichéd nonsense. Something you'd read in a cheesy greeting card."

Kari thought her friend's description was funny but this was no laughing matter. "Sounds to me like he's saying, so long and have a nice life 'cause we'll never see each other again" she told Sondra. "I could be wrong though. I hope I am but let me play devil's advocate for a sec here. Would that be so bad? You've basically had a non-physical long-distance relationship from the start. Maybe being completely free of each other for a while will give you perspective and the opportunity to meet someone else. Someone right here, right now. Who knows, maybe in the future you and Brice will meet up and choose to be together forever."

"Yeah," said Sondra with a shrug of her right shoulder. "Maybe I'm way overthinking this and he just means that he cares about me and wants me to be happy. Stupid boys."

"Yeah," agreed Kari. "Stupid boys" she repeated Sondra's words.

That evening, while Doug was at the barbecue tending to skewers of steak, shrimp, onion and bell-pepper, Sondra helped Karen in the kitchen. She mentioned the phone call she received from Brice on Thanksgiving and that she didn't fully know what this all meant. She then let her now-mom know about Thomas Ekelson's possible visit to Casa de Trent.

"Wow, Sondra" exclaimed Karen. "Way to bury the lead or leads. I figured something was going on with you ever since Thanksgiving. You sure can keep things bottled up."

Karen opened a cupboard and retrieved a large dish. "We'll talk more about this later" she told her daughter, handing the girl the food vessel. "Here, take this platter out to your dad" she instructed. Though there had been no direct words to the effect of breaking ties or ending the relationship, Brice's words on Thanksgiving did mean something to Sondra, that he was signaling a status change. She knew that being thousands of miles apart for a prolonged period of time was not doing their relationship any good but to her, someone who's life had been unfairly distanced from those she loved, it was easy to dismiss any negative ramifications of time and distance that occurred between her and Brice. She'd become proficient at rationalization and compartmentalizing, putting out of her head how the long-distance relationship was for Brice. She knew her feelings for him and felt comfortable with their situation. It was a hard blow to hear him suggest that he was not okay with how things were, especially after his previous words of love and the affectionate way he'd been with her. That night, Sondra had a hard time falling asleep. She tossed and turned, thinking about her family and worrying about her future. She got up finally and turned on the small lamp on her desk, then opened her laptop and wrote Brice an email. She started the electronic communication by telling him of her race status, that in two weeks she'd be back hard at work. IndyCar was allowing the teams leeway with their Winter Testing programs due to the major changes in chassis, engine specs and aero-kit design. Sondra then went on to write about the continued progress of Doug and Karen's flight training. In the second half of her letter she wrote about their relationship, mentioning several significant moments for her and asked him to clarify what he'd meant the last time they'd spoken.

Two days later, Doug and Karen arrived home from a particularly grueling but productive day at the Santa Paula airport in the Cessna 172. While Doug returned a phone call from Keys, Karen went looking for Sondra. The girl was nowhere in the house so she took the ATV parked just outside the gate to the pool and drove down to the Sierre-Trent Raceway garage. "Hey, kiddo" prodded Karen, gently waking the girl. Sondra had fallen asleep on the couch, and as she began to wake she manipulated her cell phone and held it out for Karen to see, a text message. Though Brice didn't write anything rude or awful, he effectively laid out the fact that it wasn't fair to either one of them to continue with how things were. He also indicated a change in his thinking about marriage and children and that he knew having kids wasn't what Sondra wanted. Karen sat on the outward-facing couch with her daughter, looking toward the rolling landscape in the lazy late afternoon, where the golden ankle-high grasses interacted and played with a steady gentle breeze. When Sondra next spoke it seemed as if a loud bomb had just exploded.

"Nothing in my life is ever normal" stated the girl.

"I know, baby" soothed Karen. "You've had a lot of unfairness and outright injustices heaped upon you, with a lot of things pretty outside the norm. Relationships can be tricky even in the best of circumstances" she offered. Sondra expelled a loud breath through her nose and pounded her fist on her upper thigh.

That idiot Brice took up a bunch of my time for two whole years" she growled. "No way am I gonna fall apart over that jackass."

"Good for you" championed Karen. "But I hope you don't just take this one boy and one relationship experience and give up on all boys or future relationship possibilities. You're hurting now but that won't be forever."

"You mean I'm hating now" corrected Sondra, with a signature shrug.

On an unusually warm Saturday morning before the scheduled arrival of Thomas Ekelson to Casa de Trent, Sondra made three phone calls. She chatted with her Uncle Leo, although not about Ekelson. Her next phone conversations were with SeaShell and Kari, and these were specifically about the boy. Nothing too groundbreaking came from either call, but for Sondra it was like getting a stamp of approval. As it worked out, Doug and Karen were getting ready to leave for another day of flight training when Thomas arrived. They gave the young man a tour of the house and chatted with him in the living room for about twenty minutes before directing him down to their daughter's location. Working on brake issues on her Formula Ford, wrench in hand and tightening a nut on the left-front brake assembly, she heard the six-cylinder engine of a passenger car pull near and come to a stop. She finished the task at hand and walked outside, wiping her hands on a red shop towel. "What, no Porsche, Ferrari or Lambo?" she asked. The young man exited the white four-door sedan with a smile, clutching a paper bag in his left hand.

"Funny" he said to the girl. "I don't exactly see a stable full of supercars myself" he added with a broad smile.

"Oh yeah well," retorted Sondra, "I keep all those at my Beverly Hills mansion."

"Well sure" he responded. "You wouldn't want to risk keeping 'em in this rundown neighborhood" he said with a quick laugh. Sondra rolled her eyes, chewed her gum and shook her head at the boy's dubious sarcastic wit. "So how ya doin', Sondra?" he asked, extending his right hand as he stepped closer.

"Not too shabby" she offered as an answer.

After the greeting, Sondra directed Thomas inside her automotive sanctuary. "Wish I'd've brought my helmet and gear" he said, taking a look around the room, noticing the two dirt bikes, the four karts and the superbike. He was impressed with the garage display but purposely said nothing of this, reminding himself to play it cool. "Maybe another time" said Sondra of his driving gear. "This thing goes pretty good" she said, nodding toward the F-Ford. "And I designed both the kart track and the motocross course myself."

"Nice" awarded Thomas. "Here, I brought you something" he said, handing her the paper bag he'd been holding. Sondra accepted the brown sack and looked inside. An immediate smile and a quick laugh came to her as she lifted out a six-pack of Coca Cola. "This is really nice. Thanks" she said of the young man's tribute to Shane Teluchi. "You didn't shake any of these up, did you?" she asked, smiling wide. "No" he said, returning her smile. "Maybe later" he added. The host, trying to act much calmer than she felt, suggested a walk of the kart track. The two proceeded in a similar line on the roadway as they would have had they been in race cars, and it was Thomas who initiated their next verbal exchange. "I like your folks" he announced. "I've talked with your dad several times before but never your mom, other than to say hello and stuff. They always seem super protective of you during race weekends."

"Well they're my managers" defended Sondra. "And Doug's the Twelve team's pit crew manager. Pretty important that they be super attentive and close-by most of the time."

Thomas nodded and followed Sondra's lead as she moved toward the apex of Turn 3. "That's pretty cool that they're taking flying lessons" he said, now walking close beside the young woman. "I read the Lydia Velstein book about you" he informed her. "So why aren't you learning to fly? In the book you mentioned that your dad was a pilot."

Sondra swallowed hard and shrugged. "I don't know" she said, suddenly feeling embarrassed by the publication and that he'd most likely read it to learn things about her. "I can't really explain it" she told him. "I mean flying is a really special thing. It's not a hobby you just dabble in. My dad lived and breathed it, even when he didn't have an airplane. It was something so special to him. Ever since I've known Doug and Karen they've talked about it in the same way my dad used to. I loved flying with my dad but I'm a race car driver. That's my thing."

"It sure as hell is" said Thomas, glancing over at her. "You're a champion" he cheered. "So how's that going? You feel any different?"

Sondra beamed on the inside regarding his accolades and inquiry. She knew she shouldn't compare Ekelson and Brice but Brice had never said things like this or asked how it was for her. He rarely fully acknowledged any of her accomplishments. There was always a detectable bit of rivalry and jealousy even though she knew he did care about her and truly supported her successes. In this moment she saw Thomas as far more mature than Brice. She shrugged her right shoulder before giving Ekelson an answer. "Well I've never been one super comfortable with a ton of attention but I've worked so hard for this for so long. Brutal hard. The same with everyone involved on the team. It feels damn good to get the acknowledgment. I mean I do feel the weight of responsibility. You know, to be a good representative of IndyCar and what the championship means, but it's kinda like graduating from college. There's just a natural boost of confidence that I hadn't expected and can't fully explain."

"More than winning the Indy Five Hundred?" asked Thomas.

"Well there's nothing like winning the Five Hundred" said Sondra. "No comparison" she added. She pointed out that Turn Seven on her kart track was a lot of fun, even if one ran wide and dipped the right-side tires off into the dirt. "Forces you to test yourself on car-control" she told her guest, avoiding further talk of what the championship meant to her. It was indeed a big deal to her but with the passing of Shane Teluchi it felt somehow tainted.

"So what's it really like, driving for the famous T.J. Holt?" asked Thomas. Sondra wasn't about to divulge secrets but was relaxed and enjoying herself. "What you see is what you get" she told the boy. "Brutal demanding" she expounded. "He expects a thousand percent effort and demands results. I mean he didn't want a damn girl driving his race car but when I gave him the results he eventually changed his tune. He knows I'm tough and he knows how and when to push me further. T.J. and Darren together are a formidable duo and I love working my ass off for them. They're hard on all of us but when we deliver, man, it's the best thing ever."

"Yeah" said Thomas. "I can relate. Same with my guys. So your boyfriend's now in F-Two?" he asked in a pensive non sequitur. Sondra didn't want to talk about Brice and she most definitely was not willing to tell Ekelson of recent developments. She shrugged her shoulder and bit down on her tongue before giving a relatively vague answer. "Hugo Patrero took a shine to Brice and he's totally taken him under his wing. I guess he's doin' pretty well, gettin' the hang of things over there in Europe. I mean long-distance relationships aren't the greatest but, well, whatever. I don't really have time for a ton of lovey-dovey crap and I'm signed to Holt Racing for two more seasons, so …"

Thomas didn't know quite what to make of this. It intrigued him to know that she might be available for future dating but there was a definite hard edge to her. The whatever comment was possibly a red-flag as well as the crack about lovey-dovey crap. As with many in the racing world, Ekelson saw Sondra Sierre as a very serious and dedicated driver and a bit of a tough tomboy. Few got to see her in casual street-clothes, where the young woman's feminine charms came through despite her often subconscious attempts to hide them. Thomas liked what he was seeing on this day. Her long dark-brown hair was clipped back in a neat ponytail and she wore form-fitting dark jeans. He thought it both cute and appropriate that she was wearing black racing shoes, but it was her top that enticed him most. She had on a relatively snug black T-shirt that on the front featured the Cooper Tires logo, one of several articles of clothing given to her and her competitors by the Series' official tire supplier during her Indy Lights season. In this day's afternoon sun her chest was far more pronounced than he'd ever before seen, especially since she was usually in a race suit that disguised her figure.

For the next hour and eighteen minutes Sondra and her guest chatted about their early careers as well as Casa de Trent. They also spoke of their college experiences. When in the kitchen lunching on ham sandwiches that Karen had earlier prepared for them, Sondra even found herself letting loose a few childhood anecdotes as Thomas gazed at the photos on the wall. She was hoping they would end up back in the race garage, with her showing him the scrap books she'd mentioned on their track-walk, but the boy's cell-phone rang out in a shrill whistle. It was his sister, requesting his return because she now wanted to borrow their mom's car.

Much to Doug and Karen's disappointment, their daughter only gave short vague answers, with many shrugs of her shoulder, to questions of how her time with Thomas had gone. Not even Kari later that night in a phone conversation with Sondra gained much detailed information. It wasn't that she was deliberately trying to hide the exchanges and overall experience she'd had with the boy. She'd actually been pleasantly surprised at how well the afternoon had gone and how much she'd enjoyed his company. Sondra had been pleased to discover that Thomas was a well-read educated person, able to converse about many different topics. Most important however was that his signature pit and garage-area cocky macho attitude that she'd come to know and detest, along with some of the cutting sarcastic remarks he'd previously hurled at her on occasion, never once made an appearance on this day. She was filled with questions and anxiety over why he'd wanted this visit. Sondra had never before been particularly interested in him, physically or otherwise even though he was considered by many to be attractive. He'd often called her princess, which she hated. She did like the fact that someone other than Brice was interested in her. It gave her a sense that she was somehow getting back at him for dumping her, though she knew this to be petty and possibly immature. She felt guilty and conflicted about the many feelings and questions she had of a possible future involvement with this new guy but as typical with her she conveniently pushed this aside.

CHAPTER 38

The reigning IndyCar champion entered her third season with high hopes and expectations, determined to hone her skills and rack up more wins and hopefully a second championship. The winter months had been kind to Sondra, though her bitterness over how and why the relationship with Brice had ended was quite clear to those who knew her best. She also was contending with the newly reopened scars of losing her family by way of moving the Sierre belongings from the storage containers to the Sierre-Trent Raceway garage, basically dealing with all of her emotions by not dealing with them.

For the last two seasons, T.J. had seen how Sondra and her team almost always rallied against the odds. During Sunday's Indy Grand Prix of St. Petersburg, he monitored the progress of both his cars, visibly disappointed when on Lap 46 Sondra's day came to a hard end. The #12 car had been struggling with what Sondra described to Darren as "ugly understeer" on the slower corners. She then reported the motor was "laying down." Coming out of Turn 6 the electronics shut the motor off and the car came to an abrupt stop. Adding insult to injury, rookie driver James Yoleman clipped the #12 in the right-rear, spinning Sondra into the inside retaining wall. Instead of her signature outrage over bad things happening to her and her car she took the blame and full responsibility during a pit lane interview for ending Yoleman's day. "I mean I just stopped in a really awkward spot and I feel so bad for the Ninety-two team and my guys as well."

She was clearly dejected over the weekend's outcome but made sure to praise her team for all their hard work. By race's end, the #21 Holt Racing machine of Sean Woodall had finished a lap down, in 19th. A somber crew packed up and began the journey to the next venue.

This year's race schedule featured a new track for Sondra and the IndyCar series. It was both challenging and exciting to be on a road-course in Austin, Texas, designed with the international spec requirements for Formula One and other international racing series. Sondra was particularly hopeful about the opportunity to show the world that she was ready to be on the big stage. COTA (Circuit Of The Americas) was a 3.426 mile, 20-turn road course. It was not an easy track to drive and learn, with its blind corners, some being off-camber and a total of 133 feet in elevation gain. By Saturday afternoon Sondra had the Pole. Sunday's race saw well below average temperatures, a determined field and at the halfway mark the #12 was running in 4th Place. Fighting with tire degradation and the precise pressures needed, along with understeer in fast corners and oversteer in the S's, she finished the race in 3rd. Wendell Grayson got his first IndyCar win having started in 7th, and Sondra's teammate Sean scored a solid 5th Place. In a post-race interview with Lydia Velstein, Sondra was calm and thoughtful. However, in the privacy of the Trent motorhome she was bitter about her season thus far and livid that things just didn't click that day. Doug and Karen were a bit taken aback at the young woman's childish temper tantrum as she rehashed the weekend and thrashed about, picking up and throwing down several couch pillows inside the RV.

Rounds 3 and 4 in Alabama and Long Beach respectively also did not go as planned. The #12 and #21 Holt Racing cars finished in the mid teens in both events. Sondra was not a happy person but knew deep down that this was just a slump and bad racing luck. The next Round in the championship was in Indianapolis on the road course.

Sondra got a solid 3rd Place finish in the Grand Prix of Indianapolis, and less than a week later at the conclusion of the first day's official practice laps on the oval, the #12 was shown at the top of the scoring pylon. Over the next two weeks both Holt Racing drivers and teams had their fair share of ups and downs, though unlike the previous year Sondra's month of May was drama-free. Before getting the command to start engines ahead of the annual 500 mile race, Darren stood close by and watched Doug and Denny Hulzor reach inside the cockpit of the #12 car, strapping in their driver and making sure the five-point harness was tight. Sondra's lead strategist developed an involuntary smile as Doug stood and gave the young racer two heavy pats to the top of her helmet before taking his place behind the pit wall. Darren knelt and gripped Sondra's left shoulder as he spoke. "We have a car that can win here today. Be aggressive at the start but don't throw it away. You know how to run here. Lets have some good communication and some damn good luck."

Sondra was indeed aggressive at the start. She gained one position before going into Turn 1, and by the time the field had completed the first of the two-hundred laps she was among five cars that had pulled away from the main pack. The weather on this day had turned nearly perfect, with a mostly steady 3-mile an hour easterly breeze. The moderate humidity that the area had endured for the past few weeks was for the most part non-existent and as opening laps rolled on the overall speed of the IndyCar field climbed. The first caution of the day came on Lap 38 when Alex Roliegh spun on cold tires into the Turn 1 Safer-Barrier retaining wall after exiting pit lane for his first pit stop of the day. When the pits were open all but two cars came in for fuel and tires. Holt Racing's Spotter Craig Pines, with his birds-eye view of the elongated oval, could see that the cleanup process for Roliegh's car would take longer than usual. After he'd relayed this bit of info to Darren and T.J., both strategists made a split-second gamble to leave their cars out circulating under the caution flag for two laps before pitting them for service. This, in theory, would allow Sondra and Sean two laps extra fuel and fresher tires at the end of the second stint in the race, provided there wasn't a crash or caution in between.

Woodall, running in the 14th position, was dealing with significant understeer and extreme tire-wear. He would have preferred to pit with the field but trusted the race logic of four-time Indy 500 winner T.J. Holt. When Woodall did come in for service the #21 car was given two rounds of front-wing, for downforce in order to help the car's handling. In addition, an incremental air-pressure change was given to his right-side tires to help with tire-wear. Sondra on the other hand was happy with her car. On her stop she wanted no changes, other than full fuel and four new tires.

The second major crash of the day occurred on Lap 158. Jerome Levoy began slowing on the backstretch with a right-rear tire going down. As he was entering Turn 4 underneath Trace Vanmuesen the back-end broke loose. His spin collected Vanmuesen and both cars slammed the outside wall and skidded to a halt. When the pits were open the leaders, including Sondra, made their way down pit lane. Because of Holt Racing's earlier pit strategy, Sondra had more fuel on board. While the tires were going on the fuel-fill took less time than her competitors and the #12 was able to jump the three lead cars, giving her the top spot. In clean air when the green-flag dropped, Sondra was able to get a tremendous start. While the cars behind her were scrapping for 2nd Place she pulled away from the field. This proved to all that she had a strong car in both traffic and in clean air. Doug and Karen were constantly in view of broadcast cameras. Though not standing next to each other, their reactions to everything that happened on track was shown to all but it was Karen's response to her daughter taking that top spot that had attracted the attention of the broadcast commentators. She was referred to as one proud happy mama bear when the camera caught her jumping up and down, pumping a right hand in the air that gripped and spilled water from a clear plastic bottle.

The #12 Holt Racing driver held onto the lead for 19 laps until she was told by her lead strategist to back off and save fuel. Greg Raley, in the dark red #10, passed Sondra on the outside just before Turn 1, and three laps later Thomas Ekelson challenged her for the second spot, bringing with him a hard-charging Justin Oliver in the neon-orange

#3. Darren instructed Sondra to maintain a particular fuel number and not go out of her way to defend her position. She was determined not to let Ekelson get too far away and asked her spotter to see if the Three car would work with her on freight-training their way to the back of the #4. Thomas Ekelson, in the white-red Four car had driven his way from the 24th starting position. He led for seven laps until Sierre, Raley and Oliver caught him on the backstretch. In the next eleven laps the lead changed five times between the four cars, with Sondra coming out on top at the line on two occasions. On lap 188 Ekelson was tucked in behind Sierre, who was three-wide going down the front-straight with Greg Raley and Justin Oliver. Raley bullied Sondra out of position but Oliver was the victor in the skirmish. A lap and a half later the #12 and #4 were running One-Two. Darren sat with his hands on his head, watching two computer screens while in constant radio contact with the Twelve team's engineers. This was too soon for Sondra to be burning through this much fuel. Darren put a hand over his mouth as he watched his driver get passed coming out of Turn 4. "Stay in that position" he instructed Sondra. "Were gonna be runnin' on fumes in seven laps. Show me some of that magic fuel-save stuff." Sondra didn't respond, and owing to the fact that the top five cars were on basically the same fuel strategy the laps ticked by without change or drama, until three laps to go. Sondra's car was working better through 3 and 4 than it had all day. She made a solid pass for the lead just feet from the famed yard of bricks and stuffed it into Turn 1. Raley and Oliver began working together, and two and a quarter laps later they both challenged Ekelson in much the same manner as Sierre. Sondra encountered traffic that backed her up to her competition. Ekelson tucked right to the back of Sierre's rear wing coming out of 4, bringing with him Oliver and a hard-charging Raley. Ekelson shot past Sondra, then Raley went side by side with the #12, forcing Sondra to alter her line in order to avoid a slower car. This break in momentum brought Justin Oliver up to challenge Sierre but a half lap later the four cars were either nose-to-tail or side-by-side. Sondra had better straight-line speed going down the backstretch and inched her way solidly in front of Oliver. She pulled down low and went underneath Raley going into Turn 1 then pulled to the back of Ekelson and they dueled through 4 and down the front-stretch. Raley and Oliver dueled side by side but quickly lined up nose to tail, catching the first two cars.

There were not many fans sitting for the last lap. It was clearly anybody's race, and coming out of Turn 3 Sondra was behind Ekelson. An unusually excited Darren called to his driver. "Full rich, full rich. We got the number. Do your thing. Nice and easy. Show me some of that drivin' stuff, kid." Again Sondra didn't respond. The Indianapolis Motor Speedway on the last lap of a five hundred mile race was to most drivers almost like a complete 500 mile race in and of itself. The top four cars each had strengths and weaknesses throughout every inch of the high-speed oval and duels and challenges were non-stop. When the checkered flag waved however the only driver who knew for sure he didn't get the win was Justin Oliver. On the cool-down lap Sondra realized that she was breathing much harder than normal. She couldn't seem to make sense of what was being emphatically drilled into her ears over the radio. She looked to her right as Oliver passed her, pointing and then giving her the thumbs-up gesture. Entering Turn 3 she again heard Darren's voice. "You did it, Sondra. You just won your second Indy Five Hundred" cheered a close-to-tearful Darren.

"Are you sure?" said a stunned and slightly out of breath race car driver.

"So damn proud of you, kid" added Darren. "Lets go drink us some milk."

"Oh yeah" said Sondra, smiling to herself as she digested her current universe. "Thanks all you guys. Awesome team. Awesome car." She took a deep breath and had that familiar dreaded feeling that the race was over and that she'd have to get out of her favorite safe place. "Woo, hoo. Yeah" she hollered.

The attention and commotion Sondra received after a race, especially when she'd won, was often a stomach-churning bit of anxiety and a momentarily frightening ordeal. When she was seven, she'd watched a particular movie on TV that her dad had suggested for family movie night. It was the story of Charles Lindbergh and his famous 1927 first-ever completed solo trans-Atlantic flight from New York to Paris. When his epic journey ended after a night landing at Le Bourget Field in France, he hadn't expected a large boisterous crowd scrambling mob-like in his direction. After such a triumphant solo adventure, this was a harsh invasion of his sacred world. It was terrifying when they came at him and he worried they were going to hurt his airplane. This scene in the movie had an impact on Sondra, and years later starting with her first race victory, she completely identified with how Lindbergh must have felt.

Sondra finally noticed the man who had been trying to initiate an interview. "Oh man" said Sondra. "This just means everything. My number Twelve, Triple A, Snap-on, Holt Racing team and every one of my amazing sponsors have worked so hard all month, and I loved every second out there today. We ran hard and ran clean and we have awesome fans. My managers are my amazing parents and I always want to make them proud, and I wouldn't be the person I am without the mom and dad and my dear brothers who can't be with me every day because of a drunk driver. I drive as hard and as fast as I can for my family and for everyone who can't be here because of horrible things. A lot of this win is for them. Don't drink and drive."

This was the first time in Sondra's racing career that in a post-race interview she'd spoken so openly of the family she'd lost as well as making such a public statement against drinking and driving. The images in her head of her parents and brothers combined with the hugeness of the moment suddenly clobbered her. She tried her best to keep her emotions in check but a torrent of painful tears erupted. She managed to quickly tamp this all down as the broadcast interviewer did his best to extract more details.

It was close to 1 a.m. when the Trents made their way to their luxury two-bedroom hotel suite. Sondra had fallen asleep on the ride there and Doug woke her up. "Hey, kiddo" he gently prodded. "Time for our champion to wake up and go to sleep." Once inside the room Doug and Karen sat on either side of their girl as she removed her shoes.

"We did it" claimed the two-time Indy 500 winner, her voice weak but proud. "It was different this time though" she added. "I know what I said in the winner's circle, and I meant it. I didn't do this so much for my brothers and my folks, like every win in the past. I mean they're always a huge part of me but I pushed hard for the win for me, not just to make them all proud. I did this for me and for us, the Trent family."

When Sondra emerged from her shower, dressed in flannel boy-pajamas, Karen helped dry her hair as they both sat atop Sondra's sleeping bag. "Guess we all better get some sleep" said the mom after she was satisfied the hair was sufficiently dried. "We have four big days of publicity travel ahead of us."

"Blah" complained Sondra. "I'd rather be in my race car." Doug chuckled as he knelt down to give his daughter a quick kiss on her forehead.

"He kissed me" said Sondra in an exhausted breath as she was settling into her soft cocoon.

"Who kissed you?" asked Karen.

"Stupid Tommy" said Sondra. "It was in the winner's circle. I mean it wasn't like it was some horrible weird thing" she admitted. "My guys and I were all hugging it out and celebrating such an amazing race, and ..."

"My guys?" questioned Karen with a quick chuckle. "Oh how I plan on mocking you with that for the next six months" she kidded her daughter.

"Mom" complained Sondra with a shrug and a quick grin. "I mean it was all something so completely in the moment. Really great camaraderie" she added.

"Justin and Greg didn't kiss you too, did they?"asked a prodding and slightly alarmed Doug.

"Just Tommy" said Sondra, shaking her head. "I mean it wasn't like it was some wild passionate lovey-dovey thing" she explained. "It was full on the lips though."

Karen nodded as she pondered the situation. "At the risk of sounding like a therapist," said the mom, "how are you feeling about that?"

"I don't know" said Sondra, "I mean he flirts with me sometimes like in driver's meetings and stuff. And sometimes he sits next to me or if he's sitting behind me he'll sometimes throw little pieces of paper at me. So stupid and childishly high school" she added with a cough of disgust. "But he always says hello to me at every track and then he did make that big effort to come for a visit to Casa de Trent. I don't know."

"He likes you" said Karen. "Hmm" voiced both Sondra and Doug in unison. "It's weird but after Brice just so abruptly cut things off" began Sondra, "I can't really see myself ever wanting to try the relationship crap again. I mean Tommy can be a total ass sometimes. He has these little snarky comments, like two-faced compliments that when you really think about it they're not compliments at all. Could be construed as kinda mean."

The long day and the lateness of the hour convinced Karen that this was not the right time to have an in-depth discussion of Thomas Ekelson's personality traits and whether or not a relationship between the two of them was a good idea, or even possible. She bent down to give her daughter a soft kiss on the girl's forehead. "I don't think the winner's circle congratulatory peck on the lips was anything more than that, Baby" whispered the mom. "He does seem to genuinely like you but don't worry about any of this. You just be yourself and get some good rest. We have a very busy schedule coming up."

After a grueling four days of travel for radio and TV interviews, plus autograph signing sessions at three Honda dealerships and a Safen-Up gathering in New York City, the Trents arrived at the site set for the Duel in Detroit, a temporary Belle Isle city street-course circuit. As Sondra focused on preparing for back-to-back races on Saturday and Sunday she was aware more than ever of a constant crew of race reporters around her, with their cameras busy recording every sight and sound. She'd become used to being in the limelight or as she'd always looked at it, watched, scrutinized and hounded, but winning her second Indy 500 and meeting genuine fans away from the racetrack earlier that week had given her a kind of personal permission to enjoy her celebrity status.

The weekend unfolded without much drama. Sondra managed a 3rd Place finish for Race #1 on Saturday. She and her three cohorts, who'd thrilled the masses at Indy the week prior, seemed to find each other late in the race and began to put on another impressive show. Tony Kelarzo got into the act after the halfway point and the top positions changed constantly. This time however it was Thomas Ekelson who came away with his first win in an Indy car. Though Sondra had given the winner a thumbs-up gesture on the cooldown lap she and her car came to rest in her own pit. She was otherwise occupied with post-race interviews as Thomas enjoyed the spoils of victory. Much to Ekelson's disappointment, Sondra was nowhere in sight to return the congratulatory kiss he'd given her in the Indy winner's circle.

The second race of the double-header weekend on the streets of the famous Michigan metropolis was a chance for a race do-over for Sondra but before the morning warmup session, ahead of the three rounds of qualifying for race #2, trouble was spotted with the Holt Racing #12 car as it was up on the air jack in the temporary assigned garage. Upon engine startup for a series of rev tests, transmission fluid sprayed out from a compromised seal underneath the engine compartment, starting a fire that was quickly extinguished before things got out of hand. Sondra was walking with Karen headed to the driver's meeting when this drama had unfolded. The mechanical staff sent Karen an alert text but Karen, acting as both manager and mom, kept the info to herself. Sondra was already feeling intense pressure and anxiety and this news would only exacerbate the girl's high stress level. The Sunday morning driver's meeting was full of warnings of the street-course's dangers and specific race and practice procedures. Sondra and Karen both took notes then made their way to the pit area, noticing upon arrival the added intensity from the earlier fire incident. Four Holt Racing engineers were hurriedly making adjustments and buttoning up the cowling on the Twelve car as Keys explained the current situation to Sondra. With 23 minutes to go until a 50-minute practice session, the IndyCar Warmup ahead of qualifying, there were several race reporters walking up and down pit lane, tracking down drivers for interviews. Sondra's chat with Lydia Velstein was relatively short, answering questions of how she was dealing with the intense media tour and excitement after her major triumph in Indianapolis. The Holt Racing driver was happy to talk about Indy, then spoke of her experience at this Detroit track a year ago. Last year she hadn't had a teammate to compare notes with as well as bounce set-up and strategy ideas off each other.

The #4 team's pit-box was two spots away, and Thomas Ekelson had walked over close enough to hear Sondra's interview. When Lydia and her cameraman moved away, Karen departed to attend other logistical tasks and Sondra noticed as Ekelson moved closer. "No matter how many interviews I do" she told him with a shrug of her shoulder and a shake of her head, "I always feel like a babbling rookie."

"Oh you're no rookie" said Ekelson. "But yeah" he added. "That was a little babble-y."

She scowled at the boy through narrowed eyes as his smirk became more pronounced.

"So how's our IndyCar princess today?" he asked. Sondra folded her arms tight and shot daggers at him with intense eyes.

"Shut up, Tommy" she retorted. "Don't you have anything better to do than come over here and eavesdrop on my interview?"

"Actually" said Thomas, his smile and stance suddenly seeming disarming to her. "I just came over to tell you about a really good restaurant not far from here. I heard some guys going on and on about it. You like seafood, right?" he asked.

"Yeah" answered Sondra, eyeing the boy and chewing her gum.

"Well if you don't stuff me in the wall in the morning warmup" he continued, "maybe you'd care to join me for dinner?"

"That's, um" voiced Sondra, astounded that he would ask her this. "I'm not dating you, Tommy. You're the enemy. You're a driver on a rival team and besides you annoy the hell out of me."

Tommy chuckled at that and shook his head. "I come in peace", he promised her. "No nefarious deeds, just a couple of people chatting over some good food. So what do you say, friend? I'm not asking you to the prom or to the altar and I promise, no shop talk."

"Well thanks, friend" said Sondra. "But I prefer to do my chatting out on the track."

"Rain check then" said Tommy, undaunted by Sondra's words. Denny Hulzor had come to see himself as a big brother and protector to Sondra. He'd been watching the progress of the mechanics on the Twelve car and took notice when Ekelson had come over to speak with his driver. As with Sondra, in Denny's estimation Ekelson was the enemy who had wandered into Holt Racing's sacred territory. Hulzor had immediately begun walking toward the two as if he were a bouncer at a nightclub. The man's macho approach did not go unnoticed by Thomas.

"Well I'm headed to the garage area" Tommy told Sondra before Denny reached them. "See ya out there" he added, pointing to the racetrack. "We'll have us a nice chat" he chuckled. As Tommy disappeared from sight, Denny put his hand on Sondra's shoulder.

"Yeah" he said under his breath of Ekelson. "Run away, ya little punk."

Sondra smiled and leaned into her friend, her self-proclaimed bodyguard. "Brace yourself" she told Denny. "But I think that little punk just tried to ask me out on a dinner date" "

"Eh" growled Denny with a sneer. "You say yes?" he asked.

"No" answered Sondra. "I mean I was pretty noncommittal, I guess. It was kinda out of the blue and caught me off guard but I told him to basically go stuff himself in the wall."

"Good" responded Hulzor. "Although, and it kills me to say this" he added, "Ekelson's a pretty decent guy. Not bad-looking either I suppose and a few inches taller than that punk Brice you were into."

"Must we mention his name" said Sondra of the person she considered her ex.

Sondra's intense schedule managed to keep her from going to dinner with Thomas Ekelson during the weekend. The weather had turned considerably cooler, with a 30 percent chance of rain. Sondra and her Twelve team took in hand everything they'd learned from the previous day, and after qualifying on Pole she led the Grand Prix from flag to flag.

After coming to a stop in the winner's circle she bounded out of her steed with more jubilant energy than she'd had in weeks, then took the traditional water fountain quick swim. Her teammate Sean had a mistake-free race and netted a solid 6th Place, with Thomas Ekelson running 7.026 seconds ahead for what he saw as a disappointing 5th Place finish. He made an effort to find Sondra before leaving the race facility grounds.

"Congratulations" he said as he approached Sondra walking alone toward her motorhome. "That wasn't easy out there today" he furthered, briefly showing the bandages on the palms of his hands.

"Yeah, you're tellin' me" said Sondra with a nod, also flashing her palms showing that they too had wrapped blisters. "We had all sorts of grip early on" she continued. "But, man, the last fifty laps were slippery, no matter what tire I was on." Tommy nodded and flashed a smile. "So we never got our dinner" he commented. She eyed the boy and shrugged her right shoulder. Undaunted, he continued. "Well there's some really good places to eat where we go in three weeks' time, in Texas" he said, full of confidence. "See you 'round, princess."

Sondra narrowed her eyes and folded her arms as she watched him walk away.

CHAPTER 39

During the IndyCar three week break Sondra, Doug and Karen attended the 18th-century-themed wedding of Shelley Marie Enesbridge and Darren Anthony Brown. The event was a painstakingly planned two-day festival of incredible splendor. The wedding ceremony was held at a nearby church and the elaborate reception took place under large tents in a vast garden on the Enesbridge's 578-acre estate. Returning to Casa de Trent, Doug and Karen had an opportunity to further their flying lessons. Sondra went for a dirt bike ride, then raced around on one of her karts before going to lunch with Kari. The two young women sat in a booth at a small Chinese restaurant, with Kari asking many questions about Shelley and Darren's wedding ceremony and reception. To Sondra it seemed that Kari's interest was more about the wealth of the Enesbridges, their guests, and if any major celebrities had attended. Sondra gave reluctant details, purposely avoiding talk of money and the opulence that had been on display. There had been people of distinction and influence in attendance but these were not the typical entertainment celebrities. Among them were captains of industry, two US senators, high-powered legal and medical minds and a few big names in the racing world. None of these would Kari be aware of so Sondra simply spoke in generalities. "Well it was a really pretty place" began Sondra. "Like something out of a movie. The main house looked like a castle from the outside. I mean all that was missing was a moat and a drawbridge, and inside it seemed to go on and on forever. SeaShell and I had a really nice talk in a room that was inside one of the big turrets. I felt so out of place a few times but everyone I talked to was so nice, and the food was amazing."

Kari watched Sondra pick up and eat a snap pea with her fingers. "You okay?" she asked, noting the sudden angry-determined look on her friend's face.

"Yeah" said Sondra with a shrug of her right shoulder. "I mean I'm really glad I went, and the weekend went better than I thought it would, but it's just that ..."

"What?" questioned Kari.

"Well weddings are full of family and tradition" said Sondra. "I mean I hate to seem like I'm having some kind of self-pity party but it was all just another damn reminder that my family and our traditions are gone. I do really love Doug and Karen and I think of them as family but it just gets to me sometimes."

"I know" soothed Kari. "From time to time I've thought about what kind of wedding I would want" she admitted to Sondra. "When I was really young I pictured an underwater fairy princess wedding."

"Like in a cartoon?" asked Sondra.

"Yeah" giggled Kari. "But a few years later I wanted some kind of beach island wedding, or something like a huge celebrity would have, like maybe on the French Riviera. Lately though, I'm thinking something sweet and simple, like what my mom and Ben had. Pretty church ceremony and lots of family and friends in the backyard."

"Well" said Sondra. "On a gargantuan scale, that's basically the kind of wedding that SeaShell and Darren had."

She shrugged and stabbed a piece of shrimp with her fork as though the small morsel had wronged her. "I don't really picture myself getting married" she told Kari, a bit of a growl in her voice. "I mean I don't think I'm actually marry-able, or ever will be."

"Oh I don't think that's true, that you're not marry-able" argued

Kari. "I can see you married, to the right guy, and with me as your maid of honor. So what's happening with Thomas Ekelson?" she asked in an abrupt non sequitur.

Sondra sat back and chewed, pondering her relationship status with Ekelson. "I don't know" she said, her usual beginning to questions of substance. "I mean I feel like this is weird and different territory."

"What do you mean?" asked Kari.

"Well I was basically a naive kid when I met Brice" said Sondra. "Now I'm a thousand years older, and if I commit to dating Tommy that means I basically have to be in a total mature relationship with him."

"You mean sex?" Kari asked.

"Kari" scolded Sondra, looking around, shocked that her friend would blurt this out in a crowded restaurant. When it appeared that no one had overheard, Sondra continued. "Well I mean I know that it's completely my choice whether or not we have a full physical relationship but I'm pretty certain that he isn't the kind of guy that would be okay with dating someone for any length of time without that, and it has crossed my mind that that's one of the things that sunk things with Brice."

"Oh, I don't know" pondered Kari. She took a sip of iced tea as she was organizing her thoughts. "Maybe you really should date someone that's not a race car driver or even in the racing world" she suggested, taking a quick look around the room. "A guy that lives life at a slower pace and isn't an adrenaline junkie."

"I'm not an adrenaline junkie" denied Sondra. Kari thought otherwise. "I see three guys right now that would probably love to get to know you" she told her friend. Sondra smiled at that. She shrugged her shoulder, trying to get a nonchalant look at the three young men sitting, talking and enjoying their beverages at the other end of the room. She then changed the subject to what Kari was currently studying at school, fearful that Kari would insist on interaction with them. She didn't.

With nine races to go in this year's IndyCar season Sondra was crushed that she didn't do better at Holt Racing's home-track, the Texas Motor Speedway. She loved this track and there was nothing technically wrong with the balance or set-up of the #12 car. It was just that four other cars were consistently turning better throughout the race under the lights of the evening event. A week later at Elkhart Lake, Wisconsin, Sondra was walking to the Holt garage area after a team debrief. Glancing down at her watch she looked up as her ears caught the sound of a small two-stroke engine. Thomas Ekelson was piloting a white scooter and on the seat behind, with arms tightly around him, there was a young blond woman wearing dark blue shorts and an orange-colored bikini top, her high-pitched laugh cutting through all the other sounds. Halting her movements, Sondra scowled at the scene. She wasn't sure what to make of this and stood pondering whether she'd missed an opportunity with Thomas or perhaps had dodged a bullet with what might be a playboy. She did her best to avoid him for the next two days. On the rain-slicked natural-terrain road course of Road America Sunday afternoon, Sondra and her #12 team basically put on a Master Class. She led from flag to flag, never once giving up the lead, even with three pit stops and six full-course cautions. In previous day's interviews Sondra had been a bit pessimistic of how things might go based on her recent race results but on race day, when the pressure was on to perform, she struck like lightning and earth-shaking thunder. The winner's circle celebration went on much longer than usual, with Sondra basking in the glory and relief that she still possessed the ability to fight her way to the top.

Just as she was beginning to look around for her manager-parents she came face to face with Thomas Ekelson. "Congratulations" he told her. "Man, you have amazing car control. That got crazy-slippery out there the last ten or twelve laps."

"I guess" she responded. "Kinda my wheelhouse" she added, looking around for Doug and Karen.

Tommy nodded. "I had a fast car but I just kept losing spots" he told her.

"Well" said Sondra, shrugging her right shoulder. "A fifth place finish is a respectable points day" she said charitably. "I mean it's not first" she added with a pointed sarcastic smirk. "We're heading out in a few" she then told him. "See ya later."

"See ya, princess" he said with what Sondra thought to be an irritating smug expression. She briefly shook her fist at the boy before making a hasty retreat.

During the three-day drive in a newly purchased mobile home that Sondra had named, c, Sondra turned 21 years old. She didn't want to celebrate this birthday. That morning in the motorhome, consuming a breakfast of scrambled eggs, bacon and toast while parked in an RV camp, she insisted that Doug and Karen not make a big deal out of the day. She was draped in melancholy as the Trents continued north, feeling sorry for herself and thinking to herself, Stupid birthday, Stupid Tommy and Stupid Brice. She desperately wanted to be at home and on her kart track.

The IndyCar Canadian Grand Prix and the next three race weekends were nonstop hard work and netted a winless streak for both the #12 and #21 Holt Racing teams. Sondra did her best to put this behind her and minimize her deep disappointment but with just two races remaining her championship hopes were long gone. She and her team instead focused on finishing their season as strong as possible and looked forward to a brighter new one. On the natural terrain road course at the Portland, Oregon, facility Sondra got a hard-fought 3rd Place, and two weeks later came the season finale in Pocono, Pennsylvania. Many months ago, when the year's IndyCar schedule was announced, Sondra was both excited and anxious about ending her season at Pocono's Tricky Triangle racetrack. She felt a swarm of angry butterflies in her stomach as Casa de Trent Un Mobiles motored through the speedway's main entrance gate. It was Wednesday late afternoon and the race venue was devoid of spectators. Arriving constantly however were broadcast crews, vendors, sponsors and race team support trucks and vans. Being the last race of the year Sondra was sure this could possibly be the site of an epic wildcard race weekend. As Doug and Karen dashed off to their important respective tasks she decided to head to the garage area. Thomas Ekelson jogged over to walk beside her. "Just got here ten minutes ago myself" he told her. "Been a hell of a year" he added.

"Yeah" agreed Sondra. "Hard year" she confessed.

"Yeah" he agreed. "And we never got the chance to have that dinner" he added. "I think we should do that soon. I'll be out in California all next week."

"Don't you think your girlfriend would mind?" asked Sondra.

"What girlfriend?" inquired Tommy. Sondra studied the boy through narrowed eyes. "The blond I've seen you with a ton of times" she clarified. "The one that seems to prefer wearing bikini tops instead of shirts."

"You mean my cousin, Michelle?" said Tommy, his proud ego feeling a sudden boost. He was pleased that Sondra had noticed with whom he spent his time. "She and my aunt and uncle live in Minneapolis" he informed Sondra. "Michelle's checking out colleges and she's been hangin' with me a bit."

"Well good for her" said Sondra of the young woman's quest to further her education.

Sondra scanned the immediate horizon, hoping to find Doug, Karen or any one of her Holt Racing team members looking for her. She wanted an excuse to end the conversation and move away from Ekelson, especially since there was now a possibility that he might suggest a specific time and day for the aforementioned date. A part of her did want him to ask her out but she was afraid to admit it, and was even more afraid of the ramifications of a relationship with him. He was relatively tall, with a boyishly handsome face and shaggy blond hair that had streaks of brown. The young man was also strong of muscle and self-confidence. She'd originally convinced herself that she disliked him and what she saw of his type but he was intelligent and had a quick wit. During the afternoon they'd spent together at Casa de Trent she'd found him to be warm and kind. "So what's your schedule gonna be like?" asked Tommy. "I mean after this weekend, of course" he added. Sondra was surprised to find that her brain suddenly flashed on how disappointed she'd felt when on her birthday she'd found that Jeff, the chance encounter at Sonoma Raceway, had told her that he had a girlfriend. She suddenly experienced a momentary panicky feeling that if she didn't play her cards right with Thomas now he wouldn't ask her out and she might never get asked out. Irrational thought but she couldn't seem to make the feeling go away easily.

"Well I mean I'm always pretty busy" she told him. "But my friend Kari told me about this burger place along the coast, south of Santa Barbara. Supposed to be a fun and unique kind of restaurant. You like burgers, right?" she added, thinking of how he'd inquired of her opinion of seafood when he'd asked her on a possible date while they were in Detroit. "I'll give you a call next Thursday" he said with a smile and nod. He patted Sondra's shoulder and was soon out of sight. Instead of her original destination she went in search of her parents-managers, trying her best to put out of mind what it would be like for her to commit to dating Thomas Ekelson.

The pressure each competitor and team member had on their shoulders going into the last race of the year was immense. Sondra took quite a bit of it as it came but her first laps in the Twelve car on the esteemed 3-corner speedway were not fun. The car was a squirrelly mess in traffic and on acceleration out of the corners. Downforce levels were annoyingly off and she detected quite a bit of understeer in all three turns. During Saturday's IndyCar warmup, before qualifying later that afternoon, Sondra and her engineers began checking the boxes of even the tiniest problem areas with the car. They had improved the car's strength and stability and it was now proving fast in both race-trim and with a qualifying setup. By 3:48 p.m. she and her Holt Racing #12 car had captured the Pole, and the next day she led all but 14 laps of the 500 mile event. Her win at Indy and the dominant Pocono victory paying double points, plus a string of top-ten finishes, awarded her 3rd in this year's championship battle. "Well I mean we won the battle today but lost the war" she told pit reporter Lydia Velstein, with a mixture of elation for driving a mistake-free race on a track that lives up to it's name, Tricky. She praised her team and sponsors, then enjoyed the podium ceremonies, secretly angry with herself for losing the championship.

Roughly one and a half weeks after the racing season had ended, Karen was pleasantly surprised when Sondra entered the office to solicit help with clothing options, a few hours ahead of the scheduled 2 p.m. lunch date with Thomas Ekelson. The mom soon found herself happily combing her daughter's hair as Sondra talked nervously about how Kari had advised her on how to "play it." Karen fastened a costume jewelry faux-pearl clip to the top of the girl's ponytail.

"So tell me again" she said to Sondra, working the clasp and then reaching for a can of hairspray. "Why exactly did you suddenly change your mind on dating Thomas?"

"I don't know" said Sondra with a patented shrug of her right shoulder. "I mean I don't think I suddenly changed my mind and I don't know if we're actually gonna start dating. Oh god" she said with a loud breath. "I'm starting to feel sick to my stomach. Maybe this is a stupid idea."

"All right, my little over-thinker" warned Karen. "No negative thoughts. Tom's a nice guy and you like burgers. Besides, it's not like this is the first time you've ever shared a meal with a boy, and even if you decide you're not all that compatible and don't want to date, it's a beautiful day for a nice drive along the coast."

"Kay" said Sondra. "I mean I just wanna feel normal" she furthered. "Like a girl that goes on nice dates with nice guys. I don't know if I'm really thinking that Tommy is my forever guy though. I mean I guess he could turn out to be but I thought that with Brice and see where that got me?"

"Try not to compare other guys to Brice, sweetie" advised Karen. "I had many nice dates with nice guys before I met Doug, and see how that worked out?" She kissed the top of Sondra's head and patted the girl's shoulder.

It was just past 5:30 p.m. when Tommy returned Sondra to Casa de Trent. The sun had inched its way downward and a hint of coastal fog was beginning to form. During the lunch date, Sondra had used as a subject the new bus driver that Holt Racing had recently hired and was tasked in bringing the Trent's RV from Pennsylvania to California. "He cracks me up, too," said Sondra. "He's done a million things and he's been a million places, and man can he cook. Real southern and Cajun spices. He tells the best stories, too. I mean I'm not sure exactly how much of them are true but he's quite entertaining. Super nice. He's pretty much become part of our family now. We just love him."

Tommy pulled to a stop in the Casa de Trent driveway, dropping off his date from the pleasant and agreeable lunch. Sondra pointed to the large shiny silver multi-axle road-going machine she'd spoken of during their meal. Al had parked the motorhome next to the garage just under an hour ago and Karen insisted the man stay for a bite to eat. Sondra and her lunch date remained seated in Tommy's mother's Toyota Corolla and watched for a few minutes as Doug and Al stood in front of the sleek elongated RV, chatting as they waited for the airport shuttle. There was a long orange extension cord running from the permanent dwelling to the one on wheels, making a striking visual in the setting sunlight. Lights could be seen from several windows of the RV and Sondra turned to Tommy. "Well I know I babbled on and on about it today" she said to the young man. "Come on" she encouraged as she opened the passenger door. "Now that we're in the off-season and you're technically not the enemy at the moment, this is your chance to see the inner workings of a Holt Racing driver." Tommy studied the elegant yet functional interior but soon turned his focus on the young woman who had taken a seat on the couch. He was enjoying this prolonged time together and watched Sondra abruptly stand to open a cleverly concealed compartment within a beautiful polished walnut wall. "This is where my helmets, race suits and gear were stored" she informed him. He stood and moved toward her acting as if he was interested in what she'd just showed him but instead wanting to maneuver close enough in case there was a chance for a kiss to occur. Sondra sensed this and stepped around the mini cooking island that separated the living room from the kitchen. She leaned against the sink and watched Tommy move to the island across from her, his eyes talking a mile a minute. With both hands on the island's counter he gave out a quiet coughing chuckle. "I really like you, Sondra" he said in a low throaty whisper. She was hit with a flight-or-fight feeling. She nodded but shrugged her shoulder. "That's nice. I mean I like you too, Tommy" she told him, not knowing what else to say. He could sense her uneasiness and backed off his intended move. "You say that as if you're surprised that you do" he said, turning his head to the right and eyeing the open doorway of the Master bedroom. "I'm not surprised" insisted Sondra. "I just don't want you to get the wrong idea. I'm not looking for a boyfriend."

"Because you're still with Brice Crandle?" he asked. He watched her glance down at her fidgeting hands and knew or at least guessed at the answer, that things were either over between the two or were strained.

To Sondra, Tommy's closed-mouth slight smile was both disarming and annoying. "Well the long-distance relationship thing isn't exactly ideal" she told him, feeling relieved at her confession. "Besides" she continued. "I'm afraid I'm kind of a complex nut. I'm not exactly dating material and my sole focus is always on winning races and championships."

"Yeah, well" voiced Tommy, the beginnings of an argument. "Race car drivers are just naturally wired for complex situations."

"Well with me it's even more complex" she asserted. "I mean I've known Brice since I was sixteen so we've sort of grown up together. Career choice led him far away but I'm not sure things would have worked out long-term even if he hadn't gone to Europe."

"Why do you say that?" asked Tommy. Sondra took a deep breath, not wanting to continue with this conversation. She knew, however, that this talk was inevitable.

"Because he knew I wasn't going to give him what all guys ultimately want" she told Ekelson. "I mean I'm not gonna get into a physical relationship with anyone 'til I'm married, and I have no intention of getting married for a long time, or maybe ever. It's not that I'm a prude about the physical thing. It's just something I won't do. I mean I made a promise to myself and to ..."

Tommy guessed with whom she'd made the promise. He briefly wondered if it had been a verbal promise to Doug and Karen or a mental promise to her deceased biological parents. He also embarked on a quick debate in his head whether or not pursuing a deeper friendship and relationship with her was a good idea, or even possible. "Well like I said earlier" he told her. "I really like you. So we'll hang out once in a while and snag us a little food and some laughs" he said, flashing a smile. "After all, I'm not just some sex-craved Neanderthal. Give me some credit." He gave a quick wave and headed toward the exit. "Bye, Princess" he called out to her as he headed down the steps. Sondra scowled at him and shook her fist.

"Stop that" she told him. "Thanks again for lunch, and don't drive rookie-stupid on the way home" she added.

Sondra and Doug spent weeks putting thought into how best to celebrate Karen's 40th birthday, or as she put it, the dreaded Four-O. They invited Valerie Hughes, Dan and Vanessa Stoltz as well as Karen's parents for a celebratory hotel stay, elegant dining and a cruise on the San Francisco Bay. After the pleasant weekend, Doug, Karen and Sondra jumped right back into IndyCar preseason mode. Four days before the Trents left on their seven-month push to win races and the IndyCar championship, Sondra enjoyed a full day at Casa de Trent with Kari. The next day, Uncle Leo came for an anticipated and scheduled visit. The reunion between Sondra and Leo was heartfelt and joyous but held an unspoken tinge of family sadness.

Leo had been true to his word about shipping the concrete slab containing the Sierre's sidewalk handprints. At first, Sondra considered keeping it on the floor of her bedroom but Doug suggested the fabrication of a metal pan to hold it, with heavy-duty wheel casters in order for her to move the family memory square anywhere she wanted and needed. The morning of Leo's visit, Sondra had rolled it from her bedroom into the den. As day began to slip into evening Sondra and her uncle walked down to the Sierre-Trent Raceway garage. She showed him the loft storage space with the idea that he might want the Sierre's dining-room table and chairs. He did and was moved by the suggestion and gesture.

"Oh" he voiced with emotion. "Your dad made this table in high school." Sondra nodded, knowing the full story. "I remember hearing his mom go on and on about how gifted he was, just after he'd brought it home" continued Leo. "And I loved how your mother treasured it as well. Are you sure you really want to part with it?"

Sondra took a deep breath and nodded. "Yeah" she voiced. "I'm sure. This table needs to be used and enjoyed, not stuck here closed off and all alone. That space off your kitchen" she told her uncle. "Your makeshift office area. With this table it could be a nice little formal dining room. I mean this wood and the red chair-cushions don't really match your living room southwest style but off the kitchen I think it could look nice." Leo nodded and gave his niece an emotional hug. "It's only been fairly recently that I've been able to even look at all this stuff" Sondra told her uncle. "I think most of the furniture we had was purchased before I was born, but when we got something new it seemed like such a special big deal. I used to love mom's desk."

"As I recall" said Leo, nodding his head. "Your dad bought that desk for your mom's birthday two years after they were married."

"Yeah" agreed Sondra. "I mean it looked nice but what was inside, with all those little cubbyholes, always seemed mysterious and special. I'm actually thinking of moving it to my room. I don't know."

Leo again nodded, thinking that his niece was perhaps maturing and better coming to grips with losing her parents and brothers. He felt a twinge of guilt over accepting the family's dining table and chairs but appreciated that Sondra was now surrounding herself with her family's items which no doubt held many precious memories. Sondra's experience of her uncle's departure that evening was a mixture of sadness, relief and pride. She had wanted him to stay for at least a few days but he had a bit of travel to do with his bagpipe troupe. Simply being in his presence on this day however brought on those familiar feelings of her contented past life but the knowledge that she could never get back to this cut her deeply. Though she really would have preferred a more prolonged visit with the man who had always been a significant part of her existence, it felt as if a weight was suddenly lifted off her chest when the taillights of his rental car disappeared from sight. The one thing that did bring at least a bit of comfort was the thought that she'd been a good host that day as she'd seen her parents do on many occasions.

CHAPTER 40

The new IndyCar season began with a third place finish on the streets of St. Petersburg, Florida. This year's field of 24 regular-season IndyCar drivers included Wendell Grayson and Andrew Placer. With their connection to Brice, a significant layer of anxiety was added to the start of Sondra's race season. To make matters even more complex for her was the fact that Thomas Ekelson had purposely let it be known that he was now dating Sondra, IndyCar's most popular driver. She both liked and hated the idea of everyone knowing about the relationship. There had been no formal discussion between the two about their dating status and she wasn't clear in her mind what the relationship was or how things might turn out with him. A sense of worry weighed on her conscious that she might receive negative or prying attention from her fans and fellow competitors. She didn't like having her personal life out in the open and this, along with doing her best to avoid Placer and Grayson, would be difficult at best. However Sondra was determined to delve into her job and surround herself with her Holt Racing family.

Sondra's first victory of the year came on the rain-slicked streets of Long Beach, California, 3rd round of the championship. She'd stayed within the top five throughout the event, obtaining the lead by not pitting with the rest of the field under a seventh full-course caution. During this double-yellow flag period, with only 18 laps remaining in the race, it began to rain harder. Race Control soon deemed it too unsafe to go back to green-flag racing and the remaining laps were run behind the safety car. Several weeks later Sondra was disappointed with a seventh place finish on the Austin, Texas road-course of the Circuit of the Americas (COTA). Her race weekend included several uncomfortable personal off track interactions. At a Thursday-night dinner given by one of the IndyCar Series sponsors, she was returning from the lady's room headed back to her table when Stephanie Placer, cradling her infant daughter in her arms, began walking beside her. "You've been avoiding Andrew" she announced. Sondra didn't respond. "You don't have to" Stephanie assured her friend.

"Kay" said Sondra, the two women halting their steps. "How've you guys been doing?" she asked.

"Really good, thanks" said Stephanie. "Momma and baby don't get out much" she added with a quick chuckle. "But we're gonna be in Indianapolis all month to be with Andrew."

Sondra nodded and was about to offer opinion on how her race season was going but abandoned the thought when she recognized a young woman approaching quickly from the right.

"Hi Sondra" greeted Lauren Crandle. "I was hoping I'd see you tonight or at least sometime this weekend. I have some time off school and Wendell invited me to hang out with him. Steph and the guys and I are sitting over there. Come have dessert with us and watch the big presentation the sponsors are about to give."

"Well thanks" said Sondra. "But my folks and I are actually heading out early."

This was a lie but neither Lauren or Stephanie called her out on it. Lauren burst into tears and threw her arms around Sondra. "My brother's such an idiot" she sobbed, releasing Sondra. "We all think it stinks that he broke up with you. He's changed such a lot since he went to Europe" she added, wiping her eyes.

Sondra didn't want to hear about Brice and her brain began

making quick calculations on how best to extricate herself from the situation. "He's grown a beard" volunteered Lauren. "And he has all sorts of different and weird friends. He even talks a little different. You know you don't have to avoid Wendell" she added in a bit of a non sequitur. "He's totally on your side and he even likes Thomas Ekelson."

Sondra most definitely didn't want to talk about Tommy. She shrugged her shoulder as she began a response. "Well I mean Ekelson's a main competitor so I kinda keep him at arms length, so to speak, but he's a nice enough guy and fun to hang out with when our schedules allow." She was purposely trying to convey that her relationship with Tommy was simply platonic friendship not romantic dating. Lauren and Stephanie suspected otherwise. Sondra enjoyed getting to know Tommy. Their talks, hand holding and light make-out sessions enhanced her race season. One evening after they had dined together at a barbecue restaurant, the two sat in the cab of a Dodge Ram pickup Tommy had borrowed from a friend. During an impromptu make-out session Sondra suddenly pulled away when he boldly reached inside her top from underneath to cup one of her breasts.

"What are you doing?" she scolded. "Right here in a busy parking lot?" she asked.

"Well okay, my pretty prude" he chuckled. "Lets go to my motorhome. My roommate won't be home 'til nine or ten." Sondra pulled further away, leaning hard against the cab's passenger door. She suddenly was taken back to that night in Santa Monica inside John Farnsal's VW. Though the situation was not the same, the feeling of fight or flight was quite similar. Quickly forcing that memory out of her head she looked at Tommy through narrowed eyes. She didn't like being called a prude but what sparked instant anger in her was that his suggestion brought up what had been worrying her for weeks. He'd been consistently becoming bolder, almost demanding in their more intimate moments together. Suggesting they go back to his motorhome was an announcement of his intentions of wanting to go physically further. It ticked her off that months ago he was okay with a limited physical relationship and now was clearly not. While she was curious and intrigued about sex, having many dreams and fantasies about it, there was also the fear element and her previous determination that her ideal relationship and situation would align. She looked at her watch and then into Tommy's eager blue eyes. "I promised my folks I'd be home early" she told him, instantly seeing disappointment.

Sondra started on Pole for the Grand Prix of Indianapolis but finished a disappointing 3rd. Two weeks later on the big oval she started from 16th on the grid and finished the 500 in 3rd Place. The next several months of the championship came with a winless streak for Sondra, though she never finished out of the top ten. Round 15 of 17 on the IndyCar schedule was on the 1.25 mile oval of Gateway Motorsports Park, Madison, Illinois. A year ago Sondra had struggled to find a level of comfort with her car's balance and grip. This year, during Friday afternoon's practice session, things came to an abrupt end for her after the #12 snapped to severe oversteer in Turn 4. Her astonishingly quick reflexes kept her from spinning but she brushed the outside retaining wall hard enough to shatter the right-front wing and do damage to the front and rear suspension. She was beside herself with grief over this, blaming herself for pushing an ill-handling race car too far. She loved this car as if it were a favorite person or pet and to see it hurt in any way was torture for her.

Later that evening it took Doug and Karen almost 20 minutes to convince their brooding daughter to join them for dinner. After a mood-lightening meal the three took a walk outside, starting in the back courtyard of the hotel where they were staying. Thomas Ekelson soon came jogging up to the trio and after pleasantries were exchanged the parents excused themselves, allowing the kids their relative privacy.

"So how'ya feelin'?" Tommy inquired, concerned over Sondra's well-being after her crash that afternoon.

"Like a complete rookie idiot but I mean it wasn't that big a hit. I feel fine and my car's gonna be good as new for tomorrow."

Tommy reached out and pulled her close, kissing her and running his hands down toward her bottom. She ended the kiss and pulled away, taking a quick glance at their surroundings and feeling a bit embarrassed for their public display of affection. Tommy took a deep breath and gestured that they sit on a nearby wooden bench. Once seated he took several seconds to study her. She was dressed as if she were a business woman not a race car driver. "We haven't been able to spend that much time together lately" he announced. "And when we do you pull away, like you did just now. You know, when people date they usually grow closer. So there's either something going on with you that I don't know about or ..."

"There's nothing going on" snapped Sondra, feeling instant anger over what she perceived as some kind of nefarious accusation. "I mean I'm trying to win a championship here" she told the boy. "That eats up a lot of my time."

Tommy shook his head. "No" he argued. "That's not it and you know it."

"I don't know what to say" she told him with a shrug of her shoulder. "I mean I like how things have been between us. Well" she qualified, "you've been a lot more pushy lately with the physical stuff and I don't like that."

He took another deep breath and bent down to retrieve an eight-inch twig that lay beside his left foot, then began breaking it into half-inch pieces, throwing the bits off to his left. "I think you're an amazing person, Sondra" he said in a soft heartfelt voice. "And I've enjoyed the hell out of getting to know you but I'm developing big-time feelings for you and you're, well, you're obviously not developing those for me."

"Just because I won't sleep with you, you think I don't have feelings for you?" accused Sondra through gritted teeth. "I mean I've shared more with you than anyone else and a hell of a lot more than I thought I could ever share with anyone. This isn't fair" she added, pounding her fist on the wood slats of the bench seat beside her right leg.

Tommy eyed Sondra for a moment. She appeared to him in this moment as if she were a small child brooding over not getting her way. “You really think how things are with us is working?” he asked.

“Well obviously you don’t” retorted Sondra. “So okay” she continued. “We’ll go back to being acquaintances and competitors and you can be free to have sex with anything in a skirt.”

“Now look who’s not being fair” scolded Tommy. He blew out a loud breath through his pursed lips and shook his head. “Well” he voiced in acceptance. “You did tell me up front that you weren’t looking for or even interested in love, marriage or children. I guess the more I got to know you and the more time we’ve spent together things changed for me. I don’t want to just do the casual dating thing. I like the idea of things moving forward, finding someone, getting married and starting a family. I’m sorry that you don’t.”

Sondra swallowed hard, not knowing quite what to say. “I’m sorry, too” she uttered after several seconds. She held out her hand and he took it in his. They shook hands like business partners and he leaned in to gently kiss her left cheek. The two then stood and began walking back toward the hotel’s lobby. At the elevators, Sondra patted him on his shoulder. “See you at the races” she told him before he stepped through the open doorway. He was baffled by the exchange that had just taken place. “I like you, Sondra Sierre” he told her. After the elevator doors closed he was glad his hotel suite was two floors above hers and that he was the only passenger on the upward ride. He began thinking to himself, feeling dumbfounded how Sondra could be so seemingly cold and matter-of-fact about ending things and moving on without either emotional dramatics or even making a case why their dating relationship had to end.

Many months prior, Sondra had been apprehensive about jumping into a relationship with Tommy but his upbeat unwavering and encouraging personality was not easy to deny. She did find him attractive and unlike Brice he was able to maintain a much better balance between his racing career and personal life. Brice’s intense focus on career goals had been one of his most attractive qualities to her because she felt exactly the same. This had kept them apart much of the time however and then there was the competitive rivalry that ultimately opened the door for career-advancement jealousy. Brice had taken it personally when Sondra seemed at times to be more successful than he and Sondra had viewed a few of Brice's career elevations as more political than pure hard work and talent. Tommy, by contrast, always seemed to display contentedness, no matter where he finished in a race, practice or qualifying session. The wins and his status as an IndyCar driver were significant to him but he had a natural confidence, which allowed for an easygoing attitude overall. He loved what he did for a living and enjoyed the fans and people within his inner circle. Sondra found herself intrigued and excited by him. He was kind but not a sappy romantic, or so she thought. He could hold up his end of a conversation about any topic but never pitied or tried to fix the things with her past. For the first two months of their relationship her level of comfort with him had risen steadily. Though she had taken sex off the table from the beginning, the more familiar the two became with one another the more amorous and adventurous she'd become. For her, the balance of her life, with racing, family and dating Tommy, was more than just comfortable. It gave her energy and peace of mind. Tommy on the other hand had been ultra-intrigued, attracted and absolutely fascinated by Sondra. Getting to know her, really know her, was like a treasure hunt to him, where he'd come across numerous natural wonders. During the first four months of dating however there became an increasing frustration. The closer they became the more he craved physical intimacy. He respected her but it was becoming unbearable that after all they'd shared she was so adamant about them never going all the way. During a few of their more impassioned moments she had pulled away so abruptly it startled him and he could sense her possible fear and instant anger, perhaps resentment. This was definitely not conducive to romance or passion. "I hate feeling like I'm the girl in this thing with Sondra" he had told his lead engineer one evening while they dined together at a sports bar and restaurant. Jim Golster, or as Tommy often referred to him "Goalster," a man who had become one of his best friends, was a sharp engineer who had helped guide the team to consistently strong race results. He was also an insightful person and had become a true confidant for Tommy. "I'm not really wanting to end things with her"

Tommy had told his friend. "She's pretty awesome."

"Yeah, she is" agreed Jim. "But I know you well, my friend" he continued. "You've been sayin' that this is all light and casual and fun but I suspect you were counting on things leading to a lot more."

"Well I hate to admit that" said Tommy. "But I think you're right. Being offered a four-year contract with this team kinda changes my outlook. I really like that sense of stability, knowing the IndyCar schedule and knowing I have a steady income. I want that consistency in my personal life as well and Sondra, as amazing as she is, most assuredly wants something else. She keeps talking about going to Europe and driving Formula One."

"Yeah, fat chance" said Jim, letting out a chuckling snort. "As if she would ever be let into that highly restrictive male-dominated class. She's a tough girl but I don't know if she's that tough" added Jim. Tommy didn't argue, though he knew Sondra could physically handle a Formula One car. One of the things he'd first liked about her was her lean athletic physique. Oddly enough however this was something he had come to find less appealing with time. Where the girls and women he'd dated in the past had soft curves and not much muscle definition, Sondra had the hard-body that he and many men desired to look at in magazines, movies or TV shows. The fantasy and reality had collided for him in an unexpectedly harsh way the first time they'd seen each other's bodies, with pulled up shirts and unbuttoned and unzipped pants. A mean, lean fighting machine physique was fun and exciting in theory but several times he'd caught himself flashing on the disturbing image that he was making out with a guy. Sondra did have the right curves in the right places, so he'd been able to put this out of his mind for the most part but he sadly had been developing serious doubts that dating her was sustainable.

Sondra found Karen sitting at a small desk in their hotel suite, writing postcards. "Where's Dad?" she asked.

"Keys asked him to come to the garage for a bit" said Karen, eying her daughter. "He'll be back in about an hour" she added. "You okay?"

Sondra shrugged and headed to her room. Karen's mom instincts sounded the alarm and she got up, following the girl. Sitting on the bed she watched Sondra kick out of her shoes and angrily throw her sport-coat on top of one of her backpacks. "Sondra?" prompted the mom.

"I know, I know" said the girl. "I'll hang it up" she promised of the article of clothing. "Well that's good" said Karen. "But that's not what I was ... What's going on, sweetheart? Come sit down and talk to me."

Sondra hung the coat on the back of a chair and turned toward Karen. "Well I struck out again" she said, coming to rest next to her now-mom on the edge of the bed. "Another failed relationship" she added, pulling off a sock and throwing on the floor. "What the hell's wrong with me?" "Nothing's wrong with you" said Karen. "What happened?" she asked the girl. Sondra told of the recent development between her and Tommy without too much detail or emotion. "I mean really, this is a relief" she then added. "I didn't really want to date him in the first place" she tried to convince herself. "I'm better off alone. The spinster champion."

"Oh Sondra" said Karen with a smile and a shake of her head. "You're no spinster. It's getting late. Go brush your teeth and get ready for bed. Busy day tomorrow. We'll talk about all this at a better time."

Sunday's race was rough for Sondra on the Gateway Motorsports Park speedway. She started 11th and three times came close to crashing. The first incident was mostly due to an ill-handling race car during the first stint and the other two near-disasters were from other cars doing what she thought rookie stupid driving. The #12 car got better as the race went on and Sondra finished in 4th Place. Both Holt Racing teams went on to have many ups and downs during the next number of races. The downs were luckily never disastrous and the Twelve car was running at the conclusion of every race. Sondra never finished lower than 8th in these events, and at the Texas Motor Speedway not only won the Pole on that Saturday afternoon but went on to snag the fastest lap of the night race as well as winning by 5.218 seconds. The final round of the IndyCar schedule took place on the road course of Laguna Seca in Monterey, California, where Sondra finished a 2.847 seconds behind Greg Raley. This seemed an odd opposite to her from that of last year, to have lost the battle but won the war. She hated losing, especially the last race of the year on this particular race course; however she and her Holt Racing team had managed to amass 27 more championship points than Greg Raley. The coveted Astor Cup, IndyCar's famed championship trophy, would be going to Sondra and her race family for a second time. Unlike the championship two years prior, which had a cloud hanging over it because of losing Shane Teluchi, she and her team celebrated heartily. She'd won significant races this year and was known as a two-time Indy 500 winner. Along with being associated with the Astor Cup, having been in many photos and videos in its presence, she now had two "Baby Borgs." These miniature versions of the Indy 500 Borg-Warner trophy, with her face likeness, stood proudly on pedestals in the den at Case de Trent.

CHAPTER 41

Sondra refused to even think of the ending of things with Tommy as a breakup and didn't want to concede that this was her second failed relationship. She simply did what she'd done with Brice, compartmentalize and blame Tommy for making a stupid choice. Four days after travel to Texas for Holt Racing's post-season wrapup and talk of when, where and how prep would take place for next year's championship run, Sondra finally had some legitimate and significant time to herself. She'd not seen Kari in some time so a plan was made for the two to spend the day together. During lunch at a particular eatery Kari inquired about Thomas Ekelson.

"Oh" said Sondra. "That's over."

"What?" said a surprised Kari.

"Yeah" said Sondra with a shrug of her right shoulder.

"I'll kill him" said Kari.

Sondra flashed a smile but suddenly felt more tired than she had in a long time. "I don't care" she told Kari in an unconvincing voice. "I mean I wasn't gonna sleep with him. He knew it from the start and I knew it would eventually be a deal-breaker, and it was. I mean Tommy's a good guy. He wasn't a mean jerk about it and basically this is all me. I mean if I'd have just given in to sleeping with him we'd still be together."

"Oh god, Sondra" scolded Kari. "I can't believe what I'm hearing. Are you seriously blaming yourself? He's an ass. What happened to my tough-girl? That son of a bitch tried to pressure you into sex by basically giving you an ultimatum. Don't you dare blame yourself. This isn't you."

Sondra shrugged and picked up the second half of her crab-melt sandwich. Sitting across from Kari she began to feel her old strength come back to her. "I was invited to go over and observe the Grekko-Celli F-One team in action the week after next" she told Kari.

"Well maybe a change of pace and scenery will do you some good" suggested Kari. "But ..." Kari cautioned.

Sondra shook her head, anticipating what Kari was about to say. "I'm not going over there to look for that idiot Brice" she assured her friend. "And don't worry, I'm coming right back. I mean I really want to drive Formula One but I have lots of unfinished business in IndyCar."

Doug and Karen were not thrilled about Sondra going to Europe. Just as with Kari, the thought that Sondra was going over there to seek out Brice did cross their minds. They also reminded the girl that she had sponsor obligations and preseason tasks that required her presence at the Holt Racing Texas headquarters.

"Maybe I should go with her" Karen suggested to her husband.

"Funny" said Doug, "I was thinking the same thing, but she's not a child and we have things to do here, important things."

"I know" conceded Karen. "I'm worried about our kid though, Doug."

"Yeah" he agreed. "She's not been in a good place for a while now."

"She sent every one of her trophies from this year to the Texas headquarters, even her baby Borg" said Karen, beginning to cry. "She may not be a child" she added. "But she's a lost girl and it breaks my heart."

Doug nodded, picked up a small pillow from the bed and tossed it on the floor, expelling a loud breath. He wasn't willing to concede that Sondra couldn't pull herself out of whatever she was going through but as a parent he wanted to swoop in and fix everything for her.

On the way home from a fun lunch with Dan Stoltz, Doug pressed Sondra about her wanting to go to Europe. “Well,” she said, “ever since I won my second Indy 500, Arturi Grekko’s stayed in touch with me. I mean once a month, sometimes twice, he texts me.”

“Hmm” voiced the dad, dubious of an old man thousands of miles away contacting his daughter. “Anything in particular?” he probed.

“Well I mean he knows that I want to be in F-One and he’s one of the very few people who says remotely positive things about that” she said. “He has a four-year plan to completely overhaul his two teams and he’s willing to see if I fit into that. I mean, he thinks my name and reputation could bring good things for the Grekko-Celli organization and shake things up in F-One. He offered to test me in Peter Lieburt’s backup car in two weeks, at an airport that gets used as a temporary racetrack often, not far from Silverstone, England.”

Wow” said Doug, glancing over at the girl. “That’s a pretty big deal” he added, wanting to say more but not wanting to say anything discouraging.

“Nothing’s set in stone” offered Sondra. “I mean, it’s basically an abstract idea at this second in time but if they put the deal together I hope I’ll go with your blessing.”

“You will” said Doug, “just as long as you come back.”

“Yeah” said Sondra, glad to hear that he wanted her to come back home. “I mean I’d only be gone for a few days” she told him. “You’re not getting rid of me that easily” she added in jest.

Oh darn” quipped Doug, sarcastic wit dripping from his vocal chords. “Karen was counting on turning your room into a sewing parlor.” “Nu-uh” voiced Sondra, shaking her head and developing a wide smile.

Arturi Grekko and Ricardo Celli were now three years into co-owning a two-car Formula One organization. The cars both ran factory supported Ferrari power plants and the two drivers, Peter Lieburt and Jules Belterini had recently begun to make their mark in the top-level sport. Peter Lieburt had first come on the scene seven years back, driving for Red Bull Racing. After four years and some sporadic success he signed with one of the two Ferrari teams. Though he'd won a number of races and was twice runner-up in the world championship, he had become disillusioned with team politics and not getting the recognition or lead driver status he thought he deserved. It had not been a hard sell to get him to switch to the Grekko-Celli team, which was rising sharply in attention and acclaim. Jules Belterini, a high-visibility rookie driver who had won the F2 championship in his first year, signed with Grekko-Celli just over a year ago. In two years' time it was planned that he would be taking over as lead driver when Lieburt retired from Formula One. Arturi Grekko was an out-of-the-box businessman and liked the idea of setting the F1 world on its end with even the suggestion that Grekko-Celli would hire the American woman race car driver Sondra Sierre to drive for them.

Stomach-churning anxiety plagued Sondra on her journey to England. She went with Doug and Karen's approval, however, and deemed the two-day whirlwind trip to the Grekko-Celli Formula One headquarters, not far from the Silverstone racetrack, a total success. Doug and Karen enjoyed the girl's enthused detail of her trip, and Sondra did go into considerable detail of transportation, food and the people she'd met. There were a few things however she kept from her now-parents. These she saved for discussion with Kari during lunch at one of their favorite spots, an outdoor patio at a luxury hotel overlooking the Pacific ocean. "Everyone was so nice, totally professional but nice" she told Kari. "I loved their headquarters, super modern but tasteful. I didn't get to meet the drivers but there was an engineer I liked, about our age, Quinten." Kari inquired about his looks and if Sondra was planning on going back anytime soon.

In early November, Sondra went back to Europe as planned and traveled with the Grekko-Celli team to the Formula One race in Valencia, Spain. She was pleased that the engineer Quinten Bierch was present and they developed a natural fun flirty friendship. Nearing the halfway mark of Pre-Practice 3, Sondra volunteered to retrieve a briefcase from the Grekko-Celli temporary headquarters building. After completing her task she was walking back to where she'd seen a food vendor. She hadn't had much to eat that day and was now beginning to feel the effects of hunger. Turning the corner she came face to face, albeit over 30 feet away, with Brice Crandle. He'd acquired lead driver status for the Patrero-FSR F2 team and was currently third in points for this year's tightly contested championship. Sondra stopped short, coming close to turning around and going back to the safety of the Grekko-Celli team. "Well, well, well" hollered Brice, waving his right hand, entering into a light jog as he closed the gap, then stood less than two feet in front of her, noticing her clothing and that even under a Grekko-Celli baseball cap she was wearing her hair was a bit different than in the past. His insides did involuntary flip-flops as he gazed upon the woman before him. "You look well" he said, trying not to sound surprised and flustered. "So you're with Grekko-Celli now?" he asked, trying not to sound as astonished as he was at this moment.

Sondra eyed the boy, with his now-shaggy hair and beard. She chewed her gum for several seconds before speaking. "I was invited to be their guest for the weekend" she said coldly. Brice made a quick eye-dart of their surroundings before his next words. "Your folks come with you?" he asked, a bit afraid of a yes answer.

"I hate you" growled Sondra. Brice felt as if the breath had been punched out of him and he took a half-step back, trying to regain his composure. "I know" he heard himself say. "I love you, too" he added in a hopeful desperate voice. With a furrowed brow and clenched jaw Sondra stared at the boy who now seemed more like a stranger.

"Idiot" she hurled at him. He tried his best to hold back a smile, knowing her temperament so well. "So congratulations on your second Indy 500 and another championship" he offered.

"Thanks" said Sondra as her fiery hazel-green eyes drilled holes into him. He took a loud deep breath and felt his shoulders slump, then glanced at his watch, knowing that he didn't have time for a long-winded reunion, one which now seemed terribly uncomfortable.

"My um ... my dad had a heart attack" he blurted out in an unstable voice.

"Oh Brice, I'm so sorry. Is he okay?" she asked, softening immediately. She reached out to briefly touch his arm. He nodded but the intensity of the moment and the ordeal of almost losing his father suddenly fell on him like a wall of bricks. He tried to appear tough as he cleared his throat and deftly wiped his eyes. Sondra wrapped her arms around him, rediscovering his familiar frame. She pulled away, though Brice was reluctant to let go. "Well, uh" voiced Brice. "He's doin' okay now. It actually happened almost a year ago and it really freaked me out. Still freaks me out" he added. "It was a few weeks after I called you at Thanksgiving. It … it happened just two weeks before Christmas. I was back in England by then, working with the team when I got the call. Dad was in the hospital for five weeks and I flew home a few days before he got out. My folks had to sell the farm. Pretty much everything got dumped on my shoulders, dealing with Realtors, packing up the house and getting it ready to put on the market and then finding a house in town for my folks to move to. A million damn details. All our friends and neighbors pitched in, though, and they were great."

Brice debated in his mind whether disclose a particular bit of detail but went through with it anyway. "The Mickels were super-great" he informed Sondra. "Jillian was a rock" he added. "Really amazing with everything. I ... um... I don't even know how the hell it happened but it was like we were suddenly back together again. Actually, I was so focused on things that I didn't even really think about it at the time."

As Sondra stood listening to all this she was now seeing Brice in a completely different light than she had the last year and a half. He was still strong and heroic, evidenced by how he'd taken time from his job to make sure his parents were taken care of but she also saw him as fragile and seemingly weak when it came to women and relationships. It occurred to her that her relationship with Tommy had taught her a thing or two after all. She felt sorry for Brice having to go through such hard times, and having met Jillian she felt sorry for him that he was repeating his past. "Man" continued Brice. "The whole heart-attack thing really hit me hard. I mean, my dad. My strong as an ox, stubborn as a mule, dad." He sniffled and wiped away the remainder of his previous tears. Sondra didn't know what to say. To her, his dad having any major medical problem was so out of left field and she hadn't thought in her wildest dreams that Brice would ever get back together with his ex-girlfriend. She watched him take another nervous glance at his watch before he continued. "I don't how or why but Jillian just seemed so different than when I'd seen her last. After getting my folks settled into a really nice two-bedroom home in town, not too far from Aunt Heather, I left to come back over here and Jillian pretty much insisted on coming with me."

"Wow" said Sondra, surmising this was the reason he'd so abruptly cut things off with her. "Well good for you guys" she offered, covering her bitterness. "I mean you've had a long history so that totally makes sense."

Brice shook his head. "It did, for a while" he lamented. "We had a lot of fun and things were great but I guess she was just seeing it as a temporary thing, like an extended vacation and that I'd wind things up and go back to the states with her to settle down."

He let out a loud breath through his nose as he shook his head. "I love this" he exclaimed. "Every single part of it" he added, "the race schedule, the routine, the different names for the corners on all these amazing tracks, all the incredible history and culture of every town and country we go to, and the cars. My F-Two machine has more power and technology than IndyCar, and I have quite a few hours of seat-time in an F-One car, too. Man oh man. Hugo's been so great to me, and I'm working with a great bunch of guys. They ribbed me pretty hard at first about being a Yankee farm boy but now we're total mates."

Sondra's smile was involuntary, sharing Brice's enthusiasm for all their sport had to offer as well as his farm-boy comment. She lost her smile slowly as she watched him look down and kick away a small rock with his right foot. "The thing with Jillian ended really bad" he told her. "Yelling, screaming, things being thrown across the room. It was pretty damn awful but the guys on my F-Two team were amazing. They got me through it and as you know, I ended up third in last year's championship. We have tracks coming up that suit me, so I'm really goin' for it."

"Well good for you" awarded Sondra. "Good luck and try not to do anything rookie-stupid" she added. He chuckled at that.

"Well thanks for the advice" he told her. "You know, it was really nice bumping into you."

"You too" she said. "See you around."

They hugged goodbye but missing for both of them was their usual routine. Unlike previous times, Brice didn't kiss Sondra's hair and she didn't jokingly confront him for doing it.

CHAPTER 42

Sondra's next season in IndyCar, her fourth and what she thought of as her last before officially going to Formula One, started out strong. She won the season-opener on the streets of St. Petersburg, got a third-place finish in Alabama and emerged victorious at Barber Motorsports Park. She and her Holt Racing family got a hard-fought fourth in Phoenix, coming from 15th on the grid, and then came back to win a week later on the streets of Long Beach, 0.103 seconds ahead of Kenny Delmare. Indianapolis was a disappointing month for Holt Racing. On the road-course the #12 car was plagued with GCU issues, the Gearbox Control Unit, a sophisticated electronic device that controls and guides the transmission system. Developmental glitches ultimately resulted in a loss of 1st and 4th gears early on in the race. Though Sondra was now a master at dealing with adversities she finished 12th. Two weeks later on the Indianapolis super-speedway a blue and orange car came spinning up into her from the low-side, sending them both into the wall and out of the race. The remainder of the year saw Sondra at least finishing in the points every race, and she managed three impressive wins. Holt Racing's #12 team celebrated victories at the road-course of Mid-Ohio, the short speedway of Gateway, Madison, Illinois, and for the final race in Monterey, California Sondra executed a runaway performance at Laguna Seca Raceway. The talent in IndyCar this year was noticeably steep but even with some bad luck and frustrating mechanical circumstances she emerged 3rd in the championship.

Four days after the season ended, Sondra flew to Texas for an overnight stay at the Holt Ranch. She and T.J. stood in the kitchen snacking on chips and dip that Beverly had made two days prior. "Been doin' this a long time" T.J. told his star driver. "Gonna be doin' this 'til I draw my last breath."

Sondra nodded and wiped her lips with the back of her hand. "I hate to leave this" she said. "I mean I've been so goal-oriented since I can remember and Formula One was always the ultimate mountain to climb. I'm not stupid. I know Arturi and Ricardo are bringing me in for mostly a publicity stunt but I think they do at least know that if they give me a decent car I'll put them on the podium. The top step" she said in a determined adamant voice. "It's a very limited one-year contract" she then admitted. "That's all they would offer. Pissed me off but I took it because this is a damn good shot. No matter what happens, I can go anywhere from there."

She looked over at T.J. hoping that if things didn't go her way in F1 he'd put her back in the #12 car. "I, um" she began tentatively. "I don't want you to think I'm just leaving you. I won't go if you don't want me to."

His next words caught her off guard. "Well," he began. "I appreciate you saying that. I don't want you to go, and quite frankly I'm surprised at myself for even saying or thinking that. Never thought I'd have this much success with some scrawny little girl."

"I'm not scrawny" argued Sondra, her eyes instantly narrowed. "And I'm no little girl" she added.

"Well" smiled T.J., pleased with himself that he'd goaded her in this way. "Here's the thing" he continued. "If you stay here you'll no doubt wonder what might have been. Knowing you, it'll eventually eat away at you and piss you off that you're not getting your shot. So go, and go with my blessing. If you're world champion next year, you stay put over there and keep the fire to 'em. Now having said that" he continued, "I don't doubt you'll be successful and make your mark, and a big one at that, but I think you belong here. There's just somethin' about you and the Indy car. Wouldn't even try to put that into words. Your decision though. You'll always have a ride in the Twelve car and a home at Holt Racing."

"Thanks, T.J." said Sondra. "And gee, thanks so much for making my decision way harder now."

"No problem, kid" smiled the man, putting his arm around the young woman for whom he'd grown to have the utmost respect and fondness.

Over the off-season the Grekko-Celli F1 team underwent changes and much reorganization. Peter Lieburt, the team's celebrated lead driver, had stepped away from Formula One to peruse other racing interests, most notably Formula E. This elevated his younger teammate, Jules Belterini, to lead driver status. Sondra Sierre, the American F1 rookie, would now be slotting into the support teammate position and was immediately schooled over and over on her role at Grekko-Celli. Though the specific words team orders were never bandied about it was made clear that she was to protect her teammate and never intentionally overtake or outshine Belterini on the racetrack. Needless to say, this did not sit well with her. She was quickly finding the politics of being a F1 driver instantly distasteful, though she kept all this to herself. Instead she focused on learning the car, the team and F1 procedure. While Doug remained in the states and in his job with Holt Racing, Karen had gone to Europe with Sondra. As both manager and mom she secured a rental flat in a neighborhood not far from the Grekko-Celli F1 headquarters and quickly put into place a day-to-day management system for Sondra. This included personal assistants and a publicist who would be working closely with Karen through phone calls and electronic communications when she was back in the US.

It had seemed a drawn-out eternity for Sondra but on a mostly clear-sky Sunday morning she was finally and officially placed as a Formula One entrant, qualified 19th out of 24 cars on the grid for the season opener on the street course of Melbourne, Australia.

Saturday's qualifying, or as some referred to it go-fast day, had started early for her and had been one of extreme nerves, anxiety and hard work for both Grekko-Celli teams to qualify well enough to make the field let alone guarantee a good starting position. In the end, Jules Belterini managed to put his car on the second row but his teammate had not fared so well. During the previous two days there had been many gremlins with Sondra's yellow and silver #23 car. Frustrating anomalies plagued the sophisticated electronics and this coincided with numerous handling issues. Within the first twelve minutes of Q1, the first of three rounds of qualifying on Saturday afternoon, Sondra's posted time and speed would allow her to go no further. The rumors along with the printed and broadcast stories that had surrounded Sondra Sierre, the young American female to "try her hand" at Formula One, were ugly and potentially distracting but her focus as always was to put herself and her car in a position to win. A daunting task now, starting so far back in the field.

Race-day Sunday morning, with just under an hour until the start of the Australian Grand Prix, Sondra was seated in the cockpit of her car inside the Grekko-Celli garage. The team of engineers and specialized mechanics had worked around the clock to fix problems that had been identified in the three practices and the previous day's qualifying run, and were now cautiously optimistic. Sondra blinked her eyes several times and massaged them with gloved fingers through the open visor of her bright yellow helmet, then listened to her lead engineer and the team principal as they gave last-minute instruction over the radio. The command was given to begin the engine-start sequence and the complex V6 fuel-powered engine along with it's two assisting electronic power units came to life. Glancing down at the LED indicators on the steering wheel she looked up to see the tire-warming material being taken off her front tires. This was it. Seconds later she was on the move for the first time prior to the start of a Formula One Grand Prix. Sondra took a deep breath easing the car onto pit lane, stopping briefly at the stop/go lights at pit exit, accelerating as she blended onto the racing surface. Every turn and bit of movement on this journey around the circuit was critical. This was the all-important reconnaissance lap. For most teams it was more than just one lap. This fifteen-minute session was where a driver could go out and enact a final check on each component of their car. For Sondra, going through each turn, there were several quick moments where a smile swept across her face and she experienced goosebumps. She'd spent each phase of her life telling anyone and everyone that she was going to race and win in Formula One, and now she'd put herself in position to possibly make that happen.

With less than fifteen minutes to go to race-start, Sondra was stationary at her grid-start marker on the front-stretch in front of the long main packed grandstands. She hated being this far back in the field and not even being able to see the silver Mercedes of Peter Louvalla, the Pole-sitter for the race and a two-time world champion. Next to Louvalla on the front row was the bright-red Ferrari driven by Gregory Shierrez, the current world champion. Sondra thought about the second row. It somehow seemed to her an odd coincidence that her teammate Jules was directly behind Louvalla and that next to Belterini was Brice Crandle, in a white with blue and red pinstriped Williams car. Sondra forced herself to put Brice and the others out of her head and stared at the back of a green and black car ahead of her, with an orange and blue machine next to it at the right. Once again Sondra plus the entire field were on the move for the Formation Lap, a full circuit designed to warm up the tires and brakes before the start of the race. She wove her Grekko-Celli Renault back and forth in several places on the track, enacting acceleration and braking points to further test her car's potency. After coming around and settling back on her grid-start marker she suddenly got an image in her head of her father, mother and brothers, as well as Doug and Karen, standing over her to give her helmet two quick pats. Her head bobbed up and down involuntarily with each imaginary pat and she bit down on her tongue, trying to quickly refocus her mind. Less than two minutes later, her heart rate escalated involuntarily as she concentrated on the light bar that stretched across and above the start/finish line. One by one, the string of five red lights came on, and when they all went dark, her pure instincts took over. She accelerated, darting into holes in the field of cars ahead that came available upon fractions of a second's notice.

Years of hard racing and learning her craft propelled her forward. Her incredible lightning-fast reflexes kept her car clean and safe from the desperate actions of other drivers and she gained a whopping six spots on the opening lap. Though she was praised for it over the radio by Team Principal Leonard Rennigier, Sondra kept her focus on the monumental task at hand. Her racing luck emerged yet again. At the halfway point she'd not only given a careful and consistent performance but there had been a number of cars ahead of her that had suffered tire issues or mechanical failures. She was now in an astonishing sixth place in the Grand Prix. Arturi Grekko and Ricardo Celli were caught on a broadcast camera with premature smiles and nods as they observed both their cars in the top-ten points-paying positions. Both Arturi and Ricardo were energetic and passionate gentlemen; however, the excitable joy they exhibited for their perceived success could and often did turn to visible and vocal outrage when things went wrong. At home and away from the track the two were mostly seen as calm and gentle businessmen but at any given race and in the heat of the battle, with so much time and money invested, they were not the easiest of bosses.

With 24 laps to go Sondra was informed that the #16 RedBull machine of Bradly Chareson, 7.296 seconds ahead of her, was reporting electronic issues and was slowing. Sondra had gone an incredible number of laps on the primary tire and was ordered into the pits for her final stop. "Box now, Sondra. Box, box, box" said Team Principal Rennigier. Within the 2.3-second pit stop, Sondra was put on the super-soft tires, designed for maximum grip. Once back out on the track and up to speed, she was told to push, push, push and that Chareson had just retired. This would have put Sondra solidly in fifth place behind her old teammate-rival-boyfriend Brice Crandle, but coming out of the pits on cold tires she had to give up that fifth place to Stephon Werlere, Brice's Williams teammate. She was told to let him go as Werlere was going to have to pit within the next five or six laps anyway. Race leader Peter Louvalla, with his 10.092 second lead, pitted for super-softs. This handed the lead of the race temporarily to Gregory Shierrez, with Sondra's teammate Jules Belterini just 2.480 seconds behind in 3rd. Brice Crandle, who'd occupied the fourth spot much of the race, had been having what a particular broadcast announcer called "a brilliant day." His last pit stop of the race however turned disastrous with the changing of the left rear tire, trouble getting the wheel-nut to thread. Crandle went from a possible podium finish to coming out of the pits in 11th place. Sondra's teammate Jules completed his last stop of the day without incident and once again occupied the third spot. The top five positions were now altered. Gregory Shierrez in 1st, Peter Louvalla 2nd, Jules Belterini 3rd, Stephon Werlere 4th and Sondra Sierre in 5th. Cameron Trussel, a former World champion and teammate of Peter Louvalla began pressuring Sondra for that 5th spot. With twelve laps remaining Louvalla regained the lead. Shierrez fought hard to stay in that top spot but after getting passed fell into the clutches of Belterini. Two and a half laps later smoke began pouring from the exhaust of Shierrez's Ferrari. He pulled to a stop just before an escape access road. Only one lap had to be observed for a Virtual Safety Car.

Arturi Grekko was beside himself. He paced back and forth and chewed nervously on the rim of his characteristic Fedora. Both his teams had a relative newness and he'd taken an enormous gamble and much ridicule for putting the young American woman in his #23 car. As he watched and listened to the action he was acutely aware of the fact that he and his partner Ricardo had both their cars in the top five of the first race of the year. Peter Louvalla's lead had diminished considerably. The set of tires he'd been put on were clearly not working as well for him as his last set, and while there was concern in the Mercedes camp, Stephon Werlere got around Jules Belterini with only eight laps remaining. Werlere closed the gap quickly to Louvalla and began making attempts to get around him as often as possible. The fierce battle that erupted between the two soon brought the 3rd through 6th Place cars closer. Belterini ran wide in Turn 1 and Sondra flashed inside and then pulled three car lengths ahead of him until she heard her team principal in her ears, suggesting that she let her teammate back by if at all possible. She didn't respond nor did she relinquish the spot. Just over a lap later, Crandle got around Belterini and the two began an epic battle, bringing Trussel into the fray. Brice, in the #15 Williams car, had been able to get around a number of cars, though not always gracefully as he tried to recover from that awful pit stop. He now settled into the 5th spot behind Sondra's teammate, desperate to get around him. Belterini was a savage fighter. As the race tapered the two young men dueled without mercy. Brice made a very questionable move on Jules, banging wheels and forcing him to run off track as Crandle flashed ahead. Belterini complained over the radio, and after reviewing the incident the race stewards determined it an illegal move and made Brice give back the spot or risk a time penalty. On the white-flag last lap of the race the top five cars were within one to two seconds of each other. The race commentators, the fans and members of the front-running teams erupted into a deafening cacophony of mixed reaction to the checkered flag.

Most other drivers would have been ecstatic in overcoming seemingly insurmountable odds starting so far back in the field and getting a 3rd Place podium finish for their first Formula One Grand Prix. Sondra was not. To her it felt more like a degrading personal loss. She blamed herself for the poor qualifying position and was sure that she could have driven a better cleaner race. She did appreciate the hugeness of where she was and the people who had teamed with her for her dreams and goals. She also felt she'd made a solid I told you so punch in recognition of her natural talent and her career path. The reaction of the fans and her team after she'd climbed out of the car also seemed to carry her far from any immediate self-deprecation or feeling the pain of loss for those who couldn't physically be with her on this day. During the mandatory post-race weigh-in process, out of sight of fans, Louvalla and Werlere made quiet snide sexist comments to themselves about Sondra's size, weight and figure. They also made a few other not-so quiet comments about her "rookie dumb-luck." Fortunately for all, especially Louvalla and Werlere, Sondra was otherwise engaged in conversation and didn't hear this particular piece of rude unsportsmanship chatter.

During the podium ceremony, with the post-race interviews

conducted by the legendary Jackie Stewart, the two on the top steps had a bit of a change in attitude when Sondra spoke in answer to Sir Jackie's questions. "Well we had a really good start and some awesome pit stops" began Sondra, after being asked how she thought her race had gone. "I mean we were going pretty good there at the end, catching the leaders four tenth's a lap. The Grekko-Celli Ferrari power-plant pretty much gave me what I asked for. I mean I hate it for my guys that the race was a few laps too short for us and that we didn't qualify further up but for a new team that's just basically getting to know each other we showed major promise." When asked about how she felt about being the first modern-day female driver to make it to Formula One and get to the podium Sondra shook her head and spoke with narrowed eyes. "Well like I've been saying for years, the car and the racetrack don't remotely care who or what I am. I came here to win and that's exactly what I aim to do." There came an electrified roar of cheers from thousands of fans after drinking in Sondra's words. More joyous noise could be heard when Peter and Stephon purposely drenched their podium pal with much of their large bottles of champagne. Sondra got in a few shots of her own, including a quick spray that landed on one of her engineers who was on the stage to take the 3rd Place Constructor's trophy. Karen had returned three days prior, planning to remain with Sondra for the entire season. Doug loved his job at Holt Racing but had made an agonizing decision to resign at the end of the IndyCar season to join his family as Sondra pursued a Formula One career.

The Trents attended an exclusive party for Formula One. In addition to Doug and Karen, Sondra was joined by Quinten. Born in Galveston, he had been employed by Grekko-Celli for three years, straight out of college. Sondra enjoyed getting to know him but their relationship was mostly a close friendship. He would be leaving his job in a week, accepting a position in the US aerospace industry. Sondra couldn't imagine leaving a job involving racing and his leaving felt like another hard loss. She'd invited him to be her date for the night as a way of saying goodbye. An hour into the event Sondra noticed Brice standing roughly thirty feet away within a sub-group. A slender young woman with long red hair was standing with her arm looped through his, rubbing her shoulder shamelessly against him. Sondra bit down on her tongue, feeling instantly angered and disgusted by the display, though she forced herself not to examine the reasons. She was relieved when Quinten tapped her on the shoulder. "Just wanted to say again, you look beautiful and that was an awesome drive today" he said with a smile and a kiss. "That was fun to watch" he added. "It was fun to drive" offered the 3rd Place finisher. "But I mean, third isn't first" she told him. "Ever the high-achieving perfectionist" quipped Quin. Sondra rolled her eyes but smiled at the young man. She gave him a hug. "I wish you all the luck in the world" she told him. "Back at you" said Quinten. "You take good care of yourself and I'll be watching your successes."

She felt as if her insides had been squeezed empty as she watched the young man disappear, needing to get home early. David Hareman, a representative from Canon, Sondra's main car sponsor for the season, began a conversation congratulating her on the day and spoke of future races. Sondra had many other short conversations that evening and at one point found herself standing momentarily alone, twisting the cap off a bottle of Perrier. She took a sip of water as her eyes began a search for Karen. "Gee, we gotta stop meeting like this" said Brice as he suddenly appeared next to her. Sondra turned her head toward him slowly with narrowed eyes. "So who's the guy?" he asked.

Sondra chewed her gum and stared at the boy. "You mean David Hareman, from Canon? One of my sponsors?" she said in pointed question. Brice shook his head. "No, the other guy I saw you with earlier. That your boyfriend now?" He thought he had the right to know.

"Oh hell no" growled Sondra. "You have no right to comment on anybody I hang out with or talk to" she furthered. "You broke up with me in a damn email, you coward. Stay the hell away from me, and go find your redhead. I'm sure she's looking for you." She hurried away before any further exchange with Crandle could take place.

Sondra's Formula One season proved to be tough, but so was she.

Everywhere the series went there were questions, comments and rumors about her driving ability and maturity, which mostly stemmed from the words and actions of her past. Her physical stamina was also of constant interest and scrutiny. This in particular angered her the most but she'd learned over the years to let go chatter of this nature, for the most part, and with every race weekend gained incremental respect. Grekko-Celli struggled with reliability issues with their two cars. The outcome for Jules Belterini was better than his teammate and it was eight races into the season before Sondra again had any measured success. The #23 car had suffered two DNFs, one in China and again in Canada. In Austria, Sondra went multiple laps down while in the pits due to a temporarily elusive electronic issue, and in Hungary she was crashed out of the race before the first turn, getting caught up in a five-car entanglement. At the Suzuka, Japan circuit Sondra made it into Q3, the third and final round of qualifying for the next day's Japanese Grand Prix. In the closing thirty seconds of the session she missed the Pole by mere fractions of a second. Though she took this as a tremendous loss she was praised by her team and race commentators for her efforts. On race day, she was both proud and skeptical to share the front row with Pole-sitter Greggory Shierrez. This particular Ferrari driver was known for driving dirty in order to get out in front at the start of a race. A year prior, Sondra and Doug had watched the Canadian Grand Prix from the comforts of Casa de Trent while the IndyCar series had a two-week break. Shierrez crowded the Pole-sitter Mark Carrafelou into the first turn, knocking wheels and forcing the Mercedes driver to back off or risk running off the track and onto some aggressive curbing.

Sunday's race started better for Sondra than most expected, with Shierrez tucking in behind her and being challenged by Alex Kellerdine and Peter Louvalla. By Lap 4 Sondra had a 3.7 second advantage, and as the laps continued to fall the focus for broadcast media turned mostly to the #21 of Greggory Shierrez and the #7 of Peter Louvalla. They had charged their way to 2nd and 3rd Place and soon began an epic battle, as they had many times, until Lap 32. Louvalla managed to get around Shierrez and held that position for nine laps until his tires began to"fall off" and lose grip. Shierrez's Ferrari had been easier on his first set of tires and he took advantage of the situation and got around the #7. Two laps later, after Louvalla's tires had cooled a bit and regained some of their grip, he and Shierrez began another battle, to Sondra's advantage. Sierre ran unchallenged lap after lap. Her driving was solid and consistent and her first pit stop was quick and flawless allowing her to stretch her lead to 8.583 seconds as the field cycled through their pit stops.

Many exciting skirmishes took place during the 56-lap event but a heartbreaking upset occurred with just nine laps to go. From the start of the race it could have been predicted but the two world champions Louvalla and Shierrez took each other out. Shierrez and Louvalla had a long history of personal and professional disdain for one another. Their rivalry bordered on the extreme and had a Senna/Prost-esque air to it. On this day in Japan, Louvalla had overtaken Shierrez but ran wide in doing so. Shierrez charged back three corners later putting a nose underneath but Peter refused to concede the corner. They touched hard resulting in a vicious high-speed two-car spin and a car-damaging journey into the gravel runoff area. Both Grekko-Celli cars were able to take advantage of the safety-car period and duck into the pits for fresh tires. With a 2.3 second stop Sondra was easily able to maintain the lead. After the safety-car period ended for the extraction of the two crashed cars, the race resumed. Sondra held off a hard-charging Stephon Werlere, Jerome Rowes, Brice Crandle and Milton Verner. Jules Belterini had restarted in eighth and was taking advantage of new super-soft tires. With faster and grippier rubber he made several attempts to overtake Verner before he was able to make the pass stick, and with less than 3-1/2 laps to go, the order behind Sondra had changed in exciting fashion. Rowes and Milton were on much older tires and Werlere, Crandle and Belterini had been able to take advantage. They were now nose-to-tail 2.7 seconds behind the leader. A determined Sondra pushed hard to maintain a healthy gap but was soon warned by her team principal to take care of her brakes as they were now approaching above-normal temperature ranges. She was also given a string of other information and then told the specific time-split between her and Werlere and that he was closing a half -second per lap. Sondra hadn't said much over the radio thus far but her voice was like a bolt of lightning when she responded to that last statement: "Stay off the radio and let me drive."

Werlere had a heavy lockup in Turn 1 and Crandle closed in, ready to pounce. In the next DRS range (Drag Reduction System) Brice opened his back wing and darted out from behind Werlere, sailing past but locking up his brakes as well going into the next corner. Crandle's luck held and he kept the 2nd spot he'd just acquired, running faster lap times than the leader. On the white-flag last lap Brice got within DRS range of Sondra on the back half of the track but never had a chance to use it. Sondra ran her fastest time in the next sector and pulled the gap to 1.841 seconds.

She took the checkered flag hollering, "I told you. I told you. Thank you guys for an awesome car. I knew we could do it."

The Suzuka venue erupted into near mayhem at how the race had unfolded. Sondra and her winning car came to rest behind a first-place marker on pit lane and she scrambled to get unbuckled and extricate herself. She soon stood in the seat and punched the air with her fists, then jumped down to the ground and hurried over to a temporary metal barrier where many members of the #23 team had assembled. The celebration was animated, to say the least. Brice, a two-time winner thus far this season, gave Sondra a hug, and Stephon, also a past multi-winner, patted Sondra on the shoulder before the post-race interview was conducted. A short time later on a stage high above a sea full of spectators Sondra had a sense of *deja vu*. This was her dream, her actual childhood dream. She stood on the top step of the Formula One podium taking in the sights and sounds, a deep calmness and a pleased-with-herself smile on her face.

After the three top finishers received their trophies and drenched each other in champagne she found herself back in the small room adjacent to the podium stage. She and Brice toasted each other with small clear plastic bottles of water, acknowledging that they'd each come from humble beginnings and had worked hard to be where they were, among the best in the world. Sondra began to walk away in order to chat with her Grekko-Celli engineer who had accepted the constructor's trophy for the team, but Brice reached out to touch her arm.

"I'm gonna spend a week with my family while we're on the three-week break" he told her. "I caught sight of your dad the other day" he added, hoping Sondra would elaborate on the parental situation. To his surprise she did.

"T.J. let him out of his obligations so he could be here with Mom and me. We're a racing family," she said simply.

Brice nodded. "So you going to the states as well over the break?" he asked. "To be with your engineer guy, or Ekelson?" he further questioned. "I know you dated him" he added.

Sondra took a long pull on her water bottle and eyed the boy, irritated by his grammar and his questions. Brice took a loud deep breath and shrugged his right shoulder in exhaustion. "You were right" he conceded, remembering how she'd scolded him some time back of his inquiry about Quinten.

"I know I don't have any kind of right to ask" he continued. "I just, um ..." He swallowed hard and glanced down at his shoes. He knew from Andrew Placer and Wendell Grayson all about Sondra's relationship with Thomas and that the two had ended things long before she'd come to Europe.

"So, um," he continued. "Leila's history" he told Sondra of the woman he'd been seeing over the past several months, his heart racing as he looked into Sondra's fierce eyes. "The redhead, as you once referred to her," he clarified.

"Aw, that's too bad" Sondra responded in a sarcastic tone. "I mean I'm sure Bambi, Trixy, Bubbles, whatever, will survive, and Peaches, Muffin or Sugar will fill the void for you soon, no problem."

"Well that's a comforting thought, Peaches" played Brice, a smirk quickly finding his face. "Thank you, Muffin" he furthered. "Congratulations on your first Grand Prix win, Sugar."

A bit taken aback by these words, Sondra watched, mouth slightly agape, as the boy turned and walked away, intending to have a chat with a senior member of his Williams team.

With Brice's words still buzzing in her head Sondra reveled in the energy of her many determined accomplishments. In this moment she felt a powerful sense that a continuous ribbon had finally delivered her to a place where both she and the universe gave full permission for her to be content and happy with her now-life.

ACKNOWLEDGMENTS

Aside from the many men and women who dedicate their lives to racing, famous and not widely known, there are several people who have lent their talent and support to make this book possible:

My dad, Ron, has always been an inspiration to me for his mechanical ability and enthusiasm when it comes to racing.

After reading a few rough draft pages, my mom, Rosemary, not only encouraged me to keep going but volunteered to do the initial edits, which turned out to be a time-consuming commitment.

I greatly appreciate professional editor Linda Holderness for a perfect combination of publishing knowledge, language expertise and encouragement that I was on the right track.

My sister, Amy, a talented mural artist, painted the original artwork on the front cover (child playing with a toy car). The book cover was created by Tatiana Vila.

Craig, my younger brother, kept my enthusiasm high by our discussions of Formula One races and drivers, past and present, and he has much knowledge of car suspension and handling.

ABOUT THE AUTHOR

Geoff Sawyer was born in San Mateo, California, to a linguistically and artistically gifted mother and a mechanically gifted father. Soon after he was born, he was diagnosed by a San Francisco ophthalmologist to have a congenital eye defect, which has become progressively worse over the years, and he is now legally blind.

A caring and astute kindergarten teacher noticed his difficulty seeing the blackboard and soon he was wearing thick glasses. Throughout his childhood, he never considered his eyesight as limiting or a disability, though he did notice some activities were more difficult for him than for his siblings, classmates or friends. Then came the day his sister went to procure her driver's license. Just for fun, he took the written test. After getting 100%, he was asked to recite the eye chart. "What eye chart?" he said, squinting. The DMV clerk suggested he see an eye doctor before asking him to move along.

Geoff's father, Ron, a private pilot licensed to work on aircraft and their engines, also worked on the family cars and did all home repairs and maintenance. From an early age, Geoff loved the sound of engines and the mystique of all things motorized and mechanical. His mom and dad never wanted to tell him his eyesight would limit him, allowing Geoff to work that out for himself and go as far as he could. One afternoon, Ron taught Geoff to drive, just for fun. They went to a large deserted parking lot, and after he killed the motor once or twice going from a standing start to first gear (in a 1975 Toyota Celica GT), it was as if Geoff had natural instincts and had been driving for years. Ron rode motorcycles, and he and Geoff enjoyed a mutual interest in motorcycle racing, especially road-racing. The two also listened to the Indy 500 each year and often discussed Formula One.

After junior college, Geoff went to the Guitar Institute of Technology, a yearlong guitar school at the Musician's Institute in Hollywood. He became an accomplished guitar player while supplementing his income by working in a Sears warehouse and, later, 14 years in a job at the local newspaper that he could perform with limited eyesight. With 20 years of professional music under his belt he moved to

Northern California. On his 40th birthday, he sky-dived.

Recovering from inner ear surgery, he discovered that if he sat still in front of a computer screen, the excruciating pain was not as noticeable. *Ribbons of Asphalt* came from his idea for a movie. Upon completion of the screenplay synopsis, he was compelled to keep going, turning it into a novel. Upon completion of the first rough draft of this story, he allowed a professional IndyCar race driver to read it. His comment was, "I can't believe this guy has never driven a race car." Geoff seems to visualize what it's like to be a championship race car driver.

This is a book of his dreams.

Made in the USA
Columbia, SC
11 February 2023